PENGUIN ENGLISH LIBRARY

HIS NATURAL LIFE

Stephen Murray-Smith teaches at the University of Melbourne. He is the founder and editor of the Australian quarterly, *Overland*.

MARCUS CLARKE

HIS NATURAL LIFE

Edited with an Introduction by
STEPHEN MURRAY-SMITH

PENGUIN BOOKS

Penguin Books Ltd, Harmondsworth, Middlesex, England
Viking Penguin Inc., 40 West 23rd Street, New York, New York 10010, U.S.A.
Penguin Books Australia Ltd, Ringwood, Victoria, Australia
Penguin Books Canada Ltd, 2801 John Street, Markham, Ontario, Canada L3R 1B4
Penguin Books (N.Z.) Ltd, 182–190 Wairau Road, Auckland 10, New Zealand

—

First published 1870
Published in Penguin Books 1970
Reprinted 1980, 1984

—

Introduction and Notes copyright © Stephen Murray-Smith, 1970
All rights reserved

—

Made and printed in Great Britain by
Hazell Watson & Viney Limited,
Member of the BPCC Group,
Aylesbury, Bucks
Set in Linotype Granjon

CONTENTS

CONTENTS

INTRODUCTION

I

His Natural Life is a novel which has refused to die. Written in monthly instalments over a period of more than two years by a young English expatriate in Melbourne – Clarke was only twenty-six when he thankfully threw down his pen – it has seldom been out of print. Forty years after its original publication a poll found it the most popular Australian novel. Today, one hundred years after *His Natural Life* first appeared, the bookshops still sell two 'standard' editions of the shorter version, the one that has been most widely read, while this edition makes Marcus Clarke's classic available for the first time in book form in its complete, original version.

No one has ever pretended that the work, in either of its very different versions, is flawless. Its structural inconsistencies, its occasional reversions to the mid-Victorian type, an involved plot-line which strains credibility at all too many points – these are quickly apparent, and led one of Clarke's most fervid admirers and best critics to write eighty-five years ago that 'there are great touches, but the whole is not great'. Yet Francis Adams went on to point out that Clarke does achieve a success with this novel that we are almost ready to call perfect: 'what it sought to do it has done, that which was planned in it is achieved. The man who did this is safe. It is a masterpiece.'

A work like *His Natural Life*, which despite its deficiencies has won at least a large measure of greatness for itself in the space of a century, is always an interesting literary phenomenon, and presents special critical problems. It is easiest to approach these in the first place through the author himself.

2

Marcus Andrew Hislop Clarke was born on 24 April 1846 in Kensington, London. His mother died while he was still a small child, and he was brought up by his father, a prosperous, eccentric Chancery lawyer, who sent him to the Cholmeley

Grammar School at Highgate, where his contemporaries and friends included Gerard Manley Hopkins. It was Hopkins who discerned in Clarke his labile emotional state, which was later to harden into confirmed bohemianism, and who described him as a 'kaleidoscopic, particoloured, harlequinesque, thaumatropic being'. At this stage Clarke's prospects were happy, and he was looking forward to a career in the diplomatic service and a private fortune of some £70,000, when his father suddenly fell ill and then died.

His father's presumed assets were not visible, and Marcus emerged from his childhood with no more than £800, a good classical education and a precocious familiarity with the fringes of intellectual London, to which he had been introduced by his father's friends. 'All that is certain,' says Clarke's biographer, Brian Elliott, 'is that he was spoilt, conceited and aimless.'

The family was of course embarrassed, and as was almost inevitable at the time the answer was 'the colonies'. Which colony was easily decided, for there was an uncle, James Langton Clarke, already in Victoria, a judge at the provincial centre of Ararat. Marcus landed at Melbourne in June 1863.

'Marvellous Melbourne', it was soon to become known as. Less than thirty years before it had been a bit of savannah land beside an unknown river. Now it boasted a population of 140,000, and was the largest city of the Australian colonies, servicing a wealthy hinterland and already the possessor of sophisticated political and cultural institutions. Clarke in his bumptious way wrote home that he found it all 'quite civilised'. With the help of introductions he picked up a job in a bank and amused himself with ephemeral literary work, soon finding that there was a ready market for his brand of cultured persiflage mingled with sharp observation. But at this time broad acres were at the back of every vigorous young man's mind, and 'the round eternal of the cash-book and the journal' (to quote a later Australian poet) held few attractions. His bank manager dispensed with his services, Clarke tells us, with little ceremony, sweetening his farewell, however, by assuring Clarke that he wore the neatest waistcoats that he, the manager, had ever seen. Clarke was soon on his way up country to learn 'colonial experience'.

Clarke spent more than two years at Swinton and Ledcourt stations, in the Wimmera area of western Victoria, within close reach of a fine mountain range known as the Grampians. Legend tells of his lolling under a gum tree in the heat of the day as he made a running translation of Balzac for the station hands gathered round, but legends were quick to gather around Clarke's name, especially after his early death. He probably did loll, but at the same time he applied himself seriously to the prospect of a career on the land, undertook two lengthy and dangerous outback expeditions in search of opportunities (land was already getting 'tight') and, above all, accumulated a store of bush lore and exact bush observation that expressed in his letters and other writings still stands as memorably evocative of place and mood and response.

'Civilised attire, cigars, claret, and a subscription to the Union Club Balls' played a part in Clarke's retreat to the city; so too did his continuing literary ambitions and the success of some of the sketches he wrote by oil lamp or candle while up country. By the later part of 1867 he was working for the conservatively inclined Melbourne *Argus* as a theatre critic and while it is not clear how long he remained a salaried member of the paper's staff it is certainly true that he had quickly blossomed into one of the journal's most important contributors, specializing in satirical and witty commentaries on the passing scene. In 1868 Clarke (with others) bought the *Colonial Monthly*, where he published his novel *Long Odds*, a work of minor distinction in its time; but he was no administrator and the magazine closed down in the following year. A similar fate met his attempt to launch a comic weekly, *Humbug*. Clarke was then offered the editorship of another monthly, the *Australian Journal*, and occupied the chair with little success for some of the time his new novel, *His Natural Life*, was appearing.

The genesis of *His Natural Life* may be found in Clarke's anxiety to find a theme for a successor to *Long Odds*, and in his uncovering of a mass of records in the Melbourne Public Library on the transportation system. His choice of subject was in many ways a highly appropriate one. A series of writers both in the Australian colonies and in Europe had demonstrated over the past twenty years and more that crime and punishment were topics of perennial popular interest; indeed the first novel published in Australia, Henry Savery's *Quintus Servinton* (1830), had a convict theme, and successors included Charles Row-croft's *The Bushranger of Van Diemen's Land* (1846) and Caroline Leakey's *The Broad Arrow* (1859). Clarke admitted that he was influenced by Charles Reade's *It is Never Too Late to Mend* (1853). None of these was of any significance as litera-ture, but the 1860s had seen the publication of two works which placed the treatment of evil, its punishment and its redemption on an entirely new social and artistic plane: Hugo's *Les Misérables* (1862) and Dostoevsky's *Crime and Punishment* (1866). Clarke was certainly well aware of the former at least. And, as Professor R. G. Howarth has pointed out, the influence of Dumas' *The Count of Monte Cristo* (1844–5) is also strongly apparent.

More narrowly, it was a suitable time for the examination of Australia's convict 'stain'. It was nearly twenty years since transportation to eastern Australia had been abandoned, and although pitiful remnants of the yellow-clad men might still be unearthed here and there by the diligent seeker (and are movingly described by Clarke in his article 'Port Arthur Visited, 1870'); the jingling chains of the road-gangs were no more to be heard in the land. The indignation of a generation before at the very existence of the System had given way to a general feeling that Australian civilization had started afresh after the gold-rushes, that the days of the convict era, politically and socially authoritarian, were irrelevant. Clarke saw, or sensed, that there was nevertheless a nerve there to be touched, and in *His Natural Life* he put in train what may be called the 'posi-tive' interpretation or re-interpretation of the System, emphasiz-ing its injustices, inconsistencies, its negations. It is what people wanted to believe, it was what Clarke himself believed, and in a large measure it was true: certainly this remained the 'received' attitude to the System and its sufferers until the recent qualifications put forward by such historians as Professor C. M. H. Clark, Professor A. L. Shaw and Dr L. L. Robson, whose careful studies of the System have suggested that its victims were not predominantly the innocents and oppressed of legend (a point, indeed, that Clarke does not burke), and that transportation and assignment as a system of punishment was according to the standards of its time and despite its enormities neither unsuccessful nor overwhelmingly inhumane. 'For years it offered what seemed the only alternative to the death penalty,' writes Professor Shaw, 'and although finally abandoned as insufficiently deterrent, it provided an essential means of punishment at a time when the unreformed gaols made long terms of imprisonment virtually impossible.'

Finally, and even more immediately, Clarke's sources lay close to hand. To the documentation of the Public Library he added a personal visit to Tasmania, enabling him not only to visit the decaying settlement at Port Arthur in the south-east but also rapidly to pick up local colour from those whose memories of the old times were, in many cases, only too vivid. Within a few weeks of his return from Tasmania the first instalment of *His Natural Life* appeared in the *Australian Journal*, in March 1870.

Clarke had offered to write the serial for his proprietors for £100, and apparently intended to complete it in twelve months. But the novel became an old man of the sea both to Clarke himself and to the publishers – legend relates that they had to lock Clarke up to get the instalments out of him, and it is clear that the story ran away with its author and that he had a bitter struggle with his own creation. The serial ran until June 1872 in twenty-seven instalments (on one occasion the desperate publishers received no copy at all), and totalled 280,000 words. Readers have to be peculiarly devoted to follow an author over this kind of steeplechase, and the *Australian Journal* is said to have lost circulation during this period.

Clarke married Marian Dunn, an actress, in 1869, and shortly afterwards they started to raise their family of six children. These new responsibilities together with his lack of success as an editor and the uncertain rewards of his literary work moved Clarke to accept a position as secretary to the trustees of the Public Library of Victoria: 'I have sold my birthright of free speech for a mess of official pottage.' However, many latter-day public servants would be grateful for the freedoms granted to, or at any rate taken by, Marcus Clarke during his years at the Library. He remained an active contributor to the periodical press, he worked as a staff journalist in all but name for both metropolitan and country newspapers, he wrote plays and pantomimes – and had them produced – and even engaged in theological disputation with the Bishop of Melbourne, though this last was regarded by his principals as overstepping the bounds of prudence. His cares at the Library do not seem to have borne him down: he used to leave his smoking cigars in the lion's mouth at the Library entrance as a signal to his friends that he was 'in'.

Light-hearted he always took care to appear, but underneath there was plenty of worry and no doubt frequent despair. Although recipient of several incomes his lifelong concern with gentlemanly unconcern bore him down into the hands of the money-lenders, or people he called money-lenders, for he could not accept favours gracefully. He twice went bankrupt, in 1874 and 1881, narrowly averting dismissal from his post. Under the protection of his patron Sir Redmond Barry he had hoped for preferment to the post of Librarian, but even this was dashed. Family problems mounted: 'A well-known Melbourne *littérateur*,' wrote the *Bulletin*, 'has been suffering from ophthalmia, measles and bailiffs. Pretty rough on an eight stone man.' His journalism, often gifted and at its best respected to this day, was now becoming cynical and bitter. Pleurisy seized him at the end of July 1881, and complications ensued. He died in a bare cottage, falling into insensibility with a pencil grasped in his hand. He was thirty-five years old.

3

His Natural Life's initial lack-lustre reception was fortunate for Clarke, for it made his publishers happy to give him permission to negotiate book publication on his own behalf. 'I was glad to get rid of it,' Massina said. Clarke apparently took the property straight to the leading Melbourne bookseller and publisher George Robertson, and received a £25 advance. Already Clarke had been giving some thought to the form of the book; he had solicited the advice of Charles Gavan Duffy, a veteran of Irish, English and colonial political life, who was at this time (1872) a trustee of the Public Library.

Duffy's advice was forthright. He criticized the poor motivation of Rufus Dawes, the leading character, in entering voluntarily on a life-long martyrdom, and he felt the narrative unduly drawn out, especially with the material relating to the Eureka Stockade. In fact Clarke's revision went very much further than this, but possibly Duffy's criticisms started Clarke on the difficult and thorough-going revision which gave us the common and popular version of the novel which is now usually referred to as *For the Term of his Natural Life*, though in fact this longer title (which evades the irony of Clarke's original) was used neither for the original serial nor for the revised publication in book form.

His Natural Life appeared in its revised version and for the first time as a book in 1874, published by George Robertson at Melbourne. In 1875 Richard Bentley published a three-volume edition in London with further, but in this case relatively minor, revisions; it is this Bentley edition from which the subsequent editions of the revised novel have descended. In 1876 *His Natural Life* appeared in the U.S.A. published by Harper, and in the following year a German translation appeared. In 1885 the revised edition was published jointly by Bentley and George Robertson, this being the first edition to bear the longer title. Since then there have been numerous further editions.

The publishing history of the original version, the text of the present book, is however more curious. In September 1881, immediately after Clarke's death, the *Australian Journal* began republication of the original serial, pointing out that the fact that Clarke had seen fit to alter the story for publication in book form 'in no way detracts from the merits of the original as a serial'. We are told that this new serialization materially helped the circulation of the magazine, and it was probably this 'edition' that Henry Lawson read and had in mind when he wrote that the sight of the novel 'in book form, with its mutilated chapters and melodramatic "prologue", exasperates me even now'. Five years later, in 1886, the proprietors of the *Australian Journal* again serialized *His Natural Life*, explaining that whatever the merits of the revision 'a large and strong demand exists for the original version of it'.

Readers desirous of the original version of the story had to wait until 1929 before this was available in book form. Angus Robertson, of Sydney, then published a handsome edition in double columns, edited by Hilary Lofting and containing a number of important reproductions of early scenes mentioned in the text, together with photographs and some of the original illustrations. Advertised as 'unabridged' and 'the first complete edition of *For the Term of His Natural Life* in book form', this version, though an accurate transcription from the original, does omit a lengthy (and, admittedly, heavily padded) description of hurricanes in Book Five. This edition is now extremely rare, though in 1937, in the wake of the Depression, the last four hundred copies of the edition were jobbed off at six shillings (the published price was fifteen).

Despite this, a cheap edition in paperback form, following the same text but further condensing the hurricane sequence, was published in Sydney by New Century Press in 1939. Thus it is thirty years since Australian – or any – readers last had an opportunity to acquire *His Natural Life* essentially as it was written, while, outside the *Australian Journal* itself, the complete original text has never until now been printed.

4

The 'popular' version of *His Natural Life* (to stick to the original title) differs radically from that presented here, though assiduous readers may care to judge whether the revision was 'keen and careful' as one commentator has it, or a 'hack job' as is the view of another.

The two versions differ most in their beginnings and in their endings. The Dickensian flourishes of the original Book One of the serial, which have been both admired and execrated by the book's critics, are in the revision reduced to a mere prologue of a few thousand words. More cogently, the air of mystery which lies over Rufus Dawes's self-immolation on the altar of justice is here dispelled: he is the bastard son of the ill-treated Lady Devine, thrown out of the home when Sir Richard learns of the cuckoo in his nest. Crossing the Heath, Rufus (as he was to become) espies Sir Richard agitatedly returning home, and soon comes across the bloodied body of his real father, Lord Bellasis. As he is kneeling by the nobleman he is seized by the locals, and realizes that to attempt to assert his innocence he would have to re-enter his home, and that this would re-open a scene which would 'bring his mother to open infamy, and send to the gallows the man who had been for twenty years deceived'. We next find Dawes on the *Malabar*.

While the opening of the original version is no doubt open to many criticisms, Brian Elliott finding Clarke here 'nonchalently indifferent to the stalest clichés', at least it has atmosphere and verisimilitude and far less of the laughably fruity melodrama of the revision. Clarke cuts very much more cleanly and convincingly, however, with his new ending. Here, as in the original, Dawes escapes from Norfolk Island with North's connivance, and finds himself with Sylvia ('Dora' in the original) on the threatened *Lady Franklin*. In peril they find recognition and love at last, but they die together entangled in the rigging of the wreck. 'As the sun rose higher the air grew balmy, the ocean placid; and, golden in the rays of the new risen morning, the wreck and its burden floated out to sea.' It is undeniably a poignant, as well as an economical, ending. A story of Randolph Bedford's purports to show Clarke's reluctance to make it thus. Walking early one morning in the gardens of Carlton in Melbourne a friend burst out: 'Marcus, Rufus Dawes must die.' Clarke pleaded for Dawes's life as if he were living: 'I can't kill him, Jim. He's been through the hell of Macquarie Harbor, and Port Arthur. ... His mother is waiting.' But after an hour's argument kill him they did. 'We've killed Rufus Dawes,' they announced on their return to their mates, one scamp responding: 'That's fine! Let's have a drink.'

The core of *His Natural Life* from Dawes's transportation on the *Malabar* to his Norfolk Island experiences remains in general outline unaltered, though there are numerous minor revisions of words and phrases, and some more substantial alterations. Dick Purfoy and Dora's child Dorcas do not appear in the shorter version, the description of Hobart Town in 1830 is omitted, a further depth to North's agony is revealed when he confesses to Dawes that it was he who robbed the body of Lord Bellasis. Coincidence is further strained by the revelation that John Rex was the actual murderer and also the half-brother of Dawes. In all some eighty thousand words were excised from the original story. Not all the pitfalls of the condenser were avoided, for the relationship between Dawes and Frere is not accounted for in the shorter version, being simply mentioned in passing in the text.

When the question was raised of the preparation of an edition of *His Natural Life* as the first Australian contribution to the Penguin English Library we accepted that it would be an edition of the 'standard' version. On reflection, however, we decided to return to the original serial, and to edit and issue that instead. In the first place there was the consideration that both Oxford and Collins have editions of the revised version in print and that it is, as it has long been, readily available to the public. Secondly, the original version, which has not been accessible for many years, has many distinct merits. The fact that it *is* the original version is one point; so is the fact that it contains a large number of passages of documentary, historical and even literary interest that do not appear in the later form. 'Much that is now omitted,' wrote a critic on the Sydney *Bulletin's* illustrious Red Page in 1906, 'is marked with Clarke's own cachet of distinction.'

It is true of course that the narrative meat of the novel, as well as the writing of greatest power and distinction, is encapsulated here between the horny carapaces of the beginning and ending sections. Of the former it can be said that, even if derivative and long drawn out, it is still preferable to the prologue of the revised edition. It is more difficult to defend the original ending of *His Natural Life*. Indeed, the received critical view is that it is indefensible; it 'ends happily and badly' remarked the *Bulletin*, while Dr L. H. Allen, editor of the World's Classics edition of the revised novel, claims that the second version contains 'the only fitting end. Like Romeo and Juliet, Lear and Cordelia, Antony and Cleopatra, these ill-starred lovers must encounter darkness as a bride.'

But must they, or is this a form of literary dogma? Mr J. C. Horner has suggested that the *revised* ending 'was dictated by the accepted fashion of a Victorian novel', and there is certainly a sense in which it may be said that for Dawes *not* to die, but to survive and even to be vindicated in circumstances in which personal tragedy and defeat remain nevertheless ineradicable, is the bolder and the harder *dénouement*. In a significant passage in *His Natural Life* Clarke, through North, talks of Balzac: 'The story ends unsatisfactorily of course. Balzac was too great a master of his realistic art to *finish* his books. In real life the curtain never falls on a comfortably finished drama.' There is perhaps more of Balzac in Clarke's original serial than there is in its polished successor.

The merits and demerits of the original *His Natural Life* are those of Clarke alone, working under great pressure and forging his novel from white-hot metal. The revision is no doubt an admirable piece of sub-editing but, as Brian Elliott has remarked to me, it is a mutilation of the original design. There is also a certain disingenuousness about it, a sense of Clarke's anxiety to lay off – he was perhaps influenced by the mixed reception the serial received. By this time he was anxious for patronage: he asked Trollope, for instance, to push the book for him in England. This is all very understandable, but at least it suggests that more serious regard should be paid than has yet been to Clarke's original intent. The relative virtues of the two versions of *His Natural Life* may be controversial, but they are at least arguable, and both editions should be accessible for argument.

5

Much has changed in literary taste and literary judgement in the past seventy years, but on one issue we may stand with our forefathers: that *His Natural Life* is unambiguously the greatest novel to emerge from the colonial Australia whose last day coincided with the last day of the nineteenth century. (Joseph Furphy's *Such is Life*, though written in the 1890s, was not published until 1903.) Taken alone this could be merely a parochial assessment of little more than antiquarian significance. Today it is more relevant to say that Marcus Clarke's one major work remains alive for two reasons: because within the literature of its own time it was a work of power and originality of vision; and because, like other works we still think of and which still influence us, it transcends its temporal placement and carries its qualities forward into modern life.

What are these qualities? Much time could be spent in minor praise, as much time could be spent in minor criticism. The essential and central point is that Clarke was seized by his material and his own creations to go beyond himself, or certainly beyond the didactic purpose he put forward in his 'Author's Preface' to the revised edition:

I have endeavoured in 'His Natural Life' to set forth the working and results of an English system of transportation carefully considered and carried out under official supervision; and to illustrate in the manner best calculated, as I think, to attract general attention, the inexpediency of again allowing offenders against the law to be herded together in places remote from the wholesome influence of public opinion, and to be submitted to a discipline which must necessarily depend for its just administration upon the personal character and temper of their gaolers.

Whether or not Clarke was consciously aware of it, in *His Natural Life* he succeeds in conveying the dual agony of man: man imprisoned in himself and man imprisoned among men. The novel is *not*, or not only, a novel of the System, though the System provides its ominous and ever-present ambience, and in this foreshadows the nightmare novels (and reportage) of the twentieth century, where man becomes the fly on the fly-paper of the society he has built for himself. It is primarily the story of Rufus Dawes, and though the characterization of Dawes has in the past been depreciated by some critics, who see him as devoid of inner motivation in his actions, today we may see him as both more convincing and more sympathetic than others have done in the past. We are less optimistic about man's free will, for we have not only seen collective madnesses in action, but have come to recognize them as such – and are indeed ourselves members of a world community which wants happiness but is committing political and environmental suicide. Thus in this sense the brutalization of Dawes, his animalization, makes him more like us, even if it made him less like our grandfathers.

And yet, of course, while our ancestors saw evil as occasional and avoidable and we, since Auschwitz, see it as central to the condition of man, yet we also have – since we have no alternative – a greater faith, or at least a greater hope, in the individual's own capacity to negate, to fight back, to contract out, to subvert. Dawes is never broken, though he thinks he is. Certainly he is crippled and disastrously changed, and as I have said, it is one of the virtues of the original version of this story that Clarke, perhaps against his own design, brings this out. But Dawes is that most modern of heroic types, a principled survivor. Dawes does not defeat the System – it defeats him. But, though he comes out bloodied and bowed and a partly broken man, he is still recognizably Dawes. We do not admire him, but we are moved; and in being moved we may think back to the writer who has taken us, with Dawes, through the ghastly shades which with other writers have remained shades, but here have acquired substance. We *know* this did happen, not because of the documentation, but because Dawes in all his perversity, and because of it, is a person who is credible. He lacks the glib eloquence of the Reverend Mr North, indeed he lacks eloquence at all, but he has one of the most successful non-speaking parts in literature.

For Dawes is not a victim of the System. If *His Natural Life* was simply trying to tell us that he was, it would be a novel of no more than documentary interest. What makes Dawes a person and not a *dramatis persona* is his own stiff-necked and stiff-minded incoherence. He brings some, but not all, of his own troubles upon himself, and it is often hard to disentangle the causations. It is the dialectic which runs reciprocally between Dawes and the mess of fate, epitomized by the System, which gives *His Natural Life* much of that character of greatness which it holds. And it is this quality which pardons the ludicrous aspects of the book. In form it is a conventional novel of its time and employs conventional devices, especially in the guise of malevolent coincidences. The accidents and perversions of justice which beset Rufus Dawes are merely the curlicues of presentation demanded by a romantic and gullible age. It is perhaps too much to say that Dawes was 'accident prone', but at least a later generation can recognize psychological nuances here which were subliminal a hundred years ago.

Clarke's perception of interplay is also apparent in the *social* aspects of the novel. 'Bond or free?' – the old challenge, so often heard in the streets after dark – was the phrase which epitomized Australia's first half-century. The society was a surrealist one: the utmost niceties of provincial society on the one hand, but balanced against and penetrated by the cruelties, the fears and the humiliations of a prison camp. No doubt the colonial gentry 'saw' as little as they could and thought about less than they saw, in the immemorial tradition of the slave society – but the nightmare was always there, intruding, threatening discomfort, even annihilation. In one of Price Warung's stories Danny the prisoner teaches a new prayer to the young son of John Price (the prison disciplinarian who is the prototype of Maurice Frere in *His Natural Life*). His father hears the child recite his prayer: it is 'breathed, with a palpable reverence which made the words doubly terrible – "God, p'ease damn John Price"'.

A number of writers, both novelists and historians, have sought to give reality to this situation, to suggest the frangible, tension-ridden nature of social life in the prison colonies. William Gosse Hay with his *The Escape of the Notorious Sir William Heans* and Hal Porter with his *The Tilted Cross* have been particularly successful, but the achievement here of Marcus Clarke should not be forgotten. In *His Natural Life* two worlds and two civilizations co-exist, both artificial and imprisoned, their very separation emphasizing the agonies of their mutual dependence. Across the frontier there are two forms of movement: the physical epitomized by Frere and North, the spiritual epitomized by Dawes and North. All who attempt the perilous steps are warped by it. North himself, of course, particularly. He is the one fully realized character in the book, at any rate in modern terms; the one character whom we truly pity, in whom a diabolical interplay of strength and weakness, weakness and strength, each opposing and feeding on the other, produces a condition we must immediately recognize as our own. North's moral vision, however incomplete in practice, speaks to the human eternal. The deep autobiographical component in Clarke's picture of North has often been noted, yet what has not attracted attention is the same phenomenon in another successful creation, Maurice Frere. The swagger and bluff of this bully, his gentlemanly assumptions and his easy hypocrisy, even the flickers of doubt, which are never overtly stated but which are read into his actions because they reinforce them and make them credible – these too in some degree were part of Clarke's *alter ego,* and account for the sinister success of Frere as an authoritarian type who steps outside the pages of the book. Clarke certainly had melodramatic impulses but the chilling thing about Frere is that, though he could so easily have been made one, he is not the traditional villain at all. He belongs.

To sustain Dawes, North and Frere throughout a work of this length is achievement enough, and may allow us to pardon the cardboard cut-out women (I am afraid one is sometimes tempted to think of poor Mrs Clarke herself), with the exception here of course of that remarkable figure Sarah Purfoy, possessor of a single-minded determination which commands not only respect but belief. An early Mother Courage in a way, she is more than a survivor, though she is that: she is a dominator, in the sense that it is through her that we learn, to paraphrase Marx, that the human will need not follow events, but may change them. Dawes, important though he is, is a character on a metaphysical level – at the end he becomes almost a mythological figure. But we *know* that the Purfoys and Freres lived in the purlieus of the System, partly it is true because we have historical parallels, but mainly because of the efficacy of the portraits themselves.

But, portraiture aside, sheer narrative and descriptive capacity carry *His Natural Life* to a greater extent than is common with works of classic stature, and may in the long run be regarded as the outstanding feature of the book. We no longer have the taste for 'fine prose' that Clarke's Victorian readers had, yet there are many descriptive passages in *His Natural Life* which remain memorable for an imagery which draws its power from observation rather than studied effect:

At the bottom of one of these valleys of water lay the mutineers' boat, looking, with its outspread oars, like some six-legged insect floating in a pool of ink. The great cliff, whose every scar and crag was as distinct as though its huge bulk was but a yard distant, seemed to shoot out from its base towards the struggling insect, a broad, flat straw, that was a strip of dry land. The next instant the rushing water, carrying the six-legged atom with it, creamed up over this strip of beach ...

Clarke was always fascinated by the wildness and the loneliness of the Australian bush and the sea, and few who have stood horrified yet compelled on the edge of a cliff against which the Southern Ocean is beating will fail to respond to Clarke's own response. His account of the Blowhole near Eaglehawk Neck, and of John Rex's terrifying sojourn there, has in Australia achieved legendary stature even among those who have not read the book.

Yet it is not the descriptive highlights which are the most important features of the narrative so much as the passages in which Clarke is sketching for us the process illuminating the minds and actions of his characters. North's guilt-ridden account of his drunkenness, for instance, or the extremely moving passage in which Mooney's murder-suicide is described. Prolix and flowery though Clarke could be, one can forgive him much for Mooney's remark when testing the strip of blanket that was to strangle him: '"I think this will do," said he, pulling it between his hands to test its strength. "I am an old man".' And who will forget Gabbett approaching to axe the sleep-starved Vetch 'on clumsy tiptoe'? Or, for that matter, the doctor who was 'sustained and fortified by the familiar presence of a corpse'? As F. H. Mares has pointed out, 'Clarke's style can be sentimental or melodramatic; he often overwrites, but on the whole has a gloomy power that is answerable to his subject.'

Style and characterization and indignant purpose are all aspects of *His Natural Life*, but the book's success is greater than the sum of its parts. As Francis Adams rightly says, there is here a 'kind of whole artistic impulse', and other critics, faced with the problem of this vast intractable novel, have been forced to the same conclusion: Brian Elliott, for instance, talking of Clarke's 'vast creative compulsion'. More than most English visitors to Australia in the nineteenth century, Clarke was imaginatively stirred by the strangeness of the landscape he found himself in. He wrote of 'vast shadows creeping across the desolate and silent plains', 'the subtle charm of this fantastic land of monstrosities', of 'the language of the barren and the uncouth'. In *His Natural Life* Clarke lifted his apperception of the barbarous and the unnatural from the physical plane to that of misshapen humanity. As he moves into his story it starts working on two levels: that of the conventional plot and narrative, and that of the mephitic vision which gives *His Natural Life* a dark significance and meaning which will always assure it of a place in the evolution of the literature of evil. Not, of course, the minor evil which the poor wretches who people these pages perpetrated, but the greater evil which all men do and which lives after them.

It is Clarke's greatness that he glimpsed this, and has been able to give us a glimpse of it too. And in this hundredth year of his achievement it is well to remember the man as well as his book. If this work were mine to dedicate I would dedicate it to Brian Elliott, Marcus Clarke's sensitive biographer, who has written of him that 'those of us who are acquainted with his life story will always remember him with great kindness and affection as a lover of life, an enemy to everything trite and dull, a witty writer and a brilliant representative of the colonial spirit in Australia'. I should like to think that Clarke would agree with such a dedication.

STEPHEN MURRAY-SMITH

ACKNOWLEDGEMENTS

Among others who have given help and encouragement I should particularly wish to thank Brian Elliott and Adrian Mitchell of the University of Adelaide; Gwen McDowall, George Gellie, Hume Dow and Patrick Singleton of the University of Melbourne; Ian Turner of Monash University; Michael Saclier, Principal Archivist of Tasmania; Michael Roe, of the University of Tasmania; Patricia Reynolds, LaTrobe Librarian, Melbourne; and my own patient editor at Penguin Books, James Cochrane.

NOTE ON FURTHER READING

‑‑‹‑›‑

Those wishing further information on Marcus Clarke, and on *His Natural Life*, may find the following select bibliography of use:

Brian Elliott: *Marcus Clarke*, Oxford University Press, 1958. (A booklet, same title and author but only thirty pages long, was published by O.U.P. at Melbourne in 1969.)

'The Making of a Masterpiece', *Bulletin* (Sydney), 26 September 1906.

Francis W. L. Adams: 'The Prose Work of Marcus Clarke', *Sydney Quarterly Magazine*, Vol. IV, No. 2, June 1887.

Francis Adams: 'Two Australian Writers', *Fortnightly Review*, CCCIX, 1 September 1892. (Reprinted in *The Australians*, London, 1893.)

Ida Leeson: 'The Term of His Natural Life', *All About Books* (Melbourne), 15 September 1930.

Vance Palmer: 'Marcus Clarke and his Critics', *Meanjin Papers* (Melbourne), Vol. 5, No. 1, 1946.

Hamilton Mackinnon (ed.): *The Marcus Clarke Memorial Volume*, Cameron, Laing & Co., Melbourne, 1884.

Desmond Byrne: *Australian Writers*, Richard Bentley and Son, London 1896.

R. G. Howarth: 'Marcus Clarke's *For the Term of His Natural Life*', *Southerly* (Sydney), No. 4, 1954.

L. L. Robson: 'The Historical Basis of *For the Term of His Natural Life*', *Australian Literary Studies*, Vol. 1, No. 2, December 1963.

L. T. Hergenhan: 'The Redemptive Theme in *His Natural Life*', *Australian Literary Studies*, Vol. 2, No. 1, June 1965.

L. T. Hergenhan: 'The Corruption of Rufus Dawes', *Southerly*, No. 3, 1969.

J. C. Horner: 'The Themes of Four Tasmanian Convict Novels', *Papers and Proceedings*, Tasmanian Historical Research Association, Vol. 15, No. 1, June 1967.

Marcus Clarke appended a list of sources for *His Natural Life* to the revised edition of his novel, and it is still printed in copies of that edition.

NOTE ON THE TEXT

◄◄‹―›►

With the exceptions listed below, this edition of *His Natural Life* precisely follows the original serial publication in the *Australian Journal* (Melbourne) between March 1870 and June 1872.

1. Obvious spelling mistakes, including those in proper names, and 'literals' have been corrected, though spellings correct but not normal today have been retained (e.g. 'mizen', 'villany'). Punctuation has been corrected where unavoidable, and in one case (p. 875) some apparently 'accidental' words excised.

2. Where necessary the misnumbering of chapters has been corrected.

3. All ships' names have been placed in italics. The practice in the original varies.

4. The murdered man's name, variously given in the original as 'Lassner' and 'Lassen', is here given throughout as 'Lassner'. On p. 727 the name 'McGawler' has been changed to 'McGrath'.

5. Where 'Mc' and 'M'' are variously used for the same name, we have used 'Mc'.

6. Both square and round brackets seem to have been used interchangeably in the original. Here only round brackets have been used.

7. Corrections made during the course of the original serial have here been incorporated in this text.

8. Editorial notes inserted in the original have been omitted, though their substance is given, where relevant, in the notes appended to this edition (pp. 913 ff). Marcus Clarke's own notes have been retained.

9. Where the original has a form such as 'would'nt', we have changed this to 'wouldn't'.

10. Penguin Books have imposed their house style on the text to the extent of using arabic rather than roman chapter numbers and single rather than double quotation marks.

11. It will be noted that the facsimile title page following is that of the first published edition in book form, i.e. the revised version of *His Natural Life*, and not the version printed here.

HIS NATURAL LIFE

BY

MARCUS CLARKE

Author of OLD TALES OF A YOUNG COUNTRY, HOLIDAY PEAK, &c.

MELBOURNE: GEORGE ROBERTSON
33 AND 35 LITTLE COLLINS STREET WEST
1874

BOOK ONE

MR FRERE'S SUPPER PARTY

On the evening of 3rd of May, 1827, the Bell Inn, High Holborn, was in a bustle.

The night coach, containing His Majesty's mails and a promiscuous assortment of His Majesty's lieges, had just boiled over at the pebble-paved gateway, and the tide of humanity, bearing on its bosom such waifs and strays of parcels, bundles, great-coats, and comforters, as had been spared from the general drift on the sidewalk, was surging into the wide doorway, clamorous for supper and bed.

But the periodical arrival of the night coach was not calculated to put the Bell out of its usual swing. For fifty years and more had that old gateway swallowed up the flotsam and jetsam brought by each high night tide, and shut its double leaves of oak upon them, as though the ancient hostelry was a convenient lock half way down life's river. But, in addition to its nightly provision of chops, steaks, tea, toast, butter, eggs, and strong waters, the Bell had been on this particular night called upon to furnish forth entertainment for some twenty persons, the guests of a young officer in His Majesty's service, who was giving a supper party.

It may seem strange that a dashing young gentleman like Mr Maurice Frere, lieutenant in His Majesty's – Regiment of Foot, and nephew to Sir Richard Devine, the wealthy ship-builder, should choose such an unfashionable hostelry as that of the Bell for his house of entertainment. But Mr Maurice Frere – bowed as to his legs, burly as to his body, red as to his hair, and coarse as to his general bearing – prided himself upon his rigorous attachment to old English customs and old English ways. Though only three-and-twenty, and the son of a Nobody, he was very loud upon the subject of the Old English Gentleman, and despised, or affected to despise, the dandyism of the day. He drove hard, swore hard, and drank hard. He gambled violently; not decorously, as did the fine gentlemen at the West-end of town, but savagely, and with much commination. He fought cocks and watermen. He had thrashed a prize-fighter, after a contest of twenty-two rounds. He drank porter by the gallon, and punch by the bucketful. He was foremost in all those amusements in which the wrenching-off of door-knockers, the maltreating of foot-passengers, and the terrifying of harmless women, formed a pleasing portion. He was about five feet four inches in height, powerfully made, broad-shouldered and square-jawed. His commission had been purchased for him by his uncle, who, having paid his debts twice, had just agreed to do so for the third time, on condition that his hopeful nephew exchanged into a regiment under orders for foreign service.

So on this 3rd of May, 1827, Mr Maurice Frere, having just been gazetted lieutenant in a newly-raised regiment about to sustain the reputation of the British arms in the colony of Van Diemen's Land, had invited a few of his boon companions of the same old English way of thinking as himself to meet him, in a hearty old English fashion, over beef-steaks and punch at the fine old English inn, the Bell.

Those fine old English liquids, punch and porter, would appear to have circulated with fine old English rapidity. The room, long and lofty though it was, smelt of tobacco smoke and spirits in a very fine old English manner, and several gentlemen had fallen asleep with that touching confidence as to the appearance of their back teeth which is a characteristic of the fine old English nature under the influence of strong liquors.

Amid the parenthetical snoring of the slumberers, snatches of the most bald and disjointed chat in the world hung upon the murky atmosphere.

A man with a hare-lip was telling how he cut down a shoemaker at Temple Bar, six years ago, on the occasion of the funeral of Queen Caroline, only as he had told the story on an average of once a week since it happened, it was somewhat familiar to his audience.

Major Clutterbuck, one of the 'old lot,' was drawing a map of the lines of Torres Vedras with spilt liquor and lemon peel for the edification of young Merridew, who had been in Burmah with General Campbell, and thought himself great in strategy.

Hips, the facetious cornet – there is always a facetious cornet at military merry-makings – had just given an imitation of James Wallack as Rolla, and was preparing to sing the 'Battle of the Boyne,' while Haws was amusing the company with an account of some queer spirits he had met at 'a chop-house in Drury kept by a fellow named Oxberry,' the night before. Opinions were getting to be divided pretty fairly on the question of a gambling-house and young Mr Kean as Norval; and as Henry Milltown (who had seen him, or said he had), voted Kean a failure, the gambling-house would have got it.

The host was sitting at the head of the table, doing the honours of the punch-bowl in the finest of fine old English manners.

'Hill, some more punch? Help yourself. There's no bigod non-sense about me. Bryant, you don't drink. Jack, my hero, here's to the old colours! Doctor, fill up! What's the old toast – A bloody war and a sickly season! No, no, by the Lord but we want no more sickness.'

He had been drinking a little more than was good for him – in his fine old English fashion – and the potency of the liquor showed itself in his shaking hand, thick speech, and boisterous gaiety.

'What do you say to a rattle at the bones? Shall we shake our elbows a bit? No, d— it, it's early yet. Nine, ain't it? Shall we knock round town? This may be my last of London for many a long month!'

'Poor old Maurice got to the end of his tether at last!' says a long gentleman in hessian boots. 'It's sad, upon honour.'

'I don't know about that,' returned the other with an oath, 'the old fellow may relent yet.'

'Ay, even at the eleventh hour!' said the man in hessians with an affected snuffle that made the table laugh, for the *parvenu* knight bore a reputation for piety that accorded but ill with the present fine old English humour.

'By George, sir,' broke in a little dark man, 'we shall hail our friend Maurice as heir-at-law, or heir in ancient domain, or heir in gavel kind, or some such thing, if he doesn't drink himself to death in Botany Bay.'

'Oh no,' says Frere, pulling at his cigar with that affectation of extreme sobriety which is a characteristic of a certain stage in the fine old English pastime of intoxication. 'There are two boys in the way. That is to say, one of 'em is at school, and the other is abroad somewhere. He's a bit of a prodigal is my cousin Dick. Like me!' he added with a laugh and an impatient puff of smoke.

'Oh, he's away, is he?' echoed the gentleman in hessians. 'Where?'

'Cursed if I know. I haven't seen the fellow since we were at school together ten years ago. Shouldn't know him, I dare say, if I did see him. When they heard of him last he was in Germany, but where he is now the Deuce only knows.'

'And he won't tell under a pint!' added the facetious cornet.

'Come, gentlemen!' roars a hatchet-faced man with a very red nose and a very tight frock-coat. 'Charge your glasses! I give you the health of our esteemed friend, Maurice Frere, and may he find as many new friends as he leaves old ones!'

There was a volley of exclamations and table-thumpings at this sentiment, and then the tight frock-coat leading off with a 'hip, hip, hip,' a tremendous burst of semi punch-inflexioned cheering broke out, that quite drowned the clatter of the windows as the departing night coach, lamps blazing and horn blowing, dashed out of the court-yard.

The esteemed friend rose a little unsteadily on his legs, and began to return thanks in a fine old English manner.

'That was what he liked. No bigod nonsense about that. It was like beefsteaks and punch, ha, ha, sound and solid – he meant the beefsteaks.' (Hear, hear.) 'A fine old English way of bidding a man good-bye. If it *was* good-bye. It might be, and it mightn't. He had had his fling, he wouldn't deny it.' – (Why should you?) – 'but he was hic proud to say in an Old English Style. He was going away. When, he didn't exactly know. Within a few weeks, he believed. Accidents *would* happen, and –'

Here the waiter, who had glided in unobserved, checked this fine old English flow of oratory by a pluck at the speaker's coat sleeve.

He turned round.

The man handed him a letter.

'Beg your pardon, sir, but it came in charge of the guard. He *was* agoing to take it on, sir, but mentioning as how you was here, I took it, as it's werry immediate.'

In the silence which followed this interruption Mr Maurice Frere read the letter. It was not very long, but his ruddy face grew a shade paler ere he raised it. Without heeding the politely inquiring faces round him, or even apologising for the break in his speech of thanks, he asked,

'Has the mail gone?'

'Just this very moment, sir.'

'Then order me post-horses on. I must go down to Harwich to-night.'

There was no sign of intoxication about him now. His eyes were bright, and his voice steady, while the firmly set lips and the ominous scowl on the low narrow brow betokened that when his own interests were involved he did not allow his fine old English hospitality to stand in the way of them.

'You must pardon me, gentlemen, but I have just received a letter calling me to my uncle's house at once.'

'Is the old man ill?' asked the thin gentleman in hessian boots, with a sympathetic and cat-like grin of mingled condolence and congratulation.

'Yes,' said Frere, 'he is.' And bowing, followed the waiter out.

There was a chorus of wonderment and conjecture among the guests.

'Is the old boy dead?' 'Will he get any money?' 'What was it he said?' and so on. While heaven knows what wild stories of murders, heritages, and sudden deaths were not current instantly in the court-yard of the Bell – for the miserly old shipbuilder and navy contractor, the fabulously wealthy Sir Richard Devine, was known by name at all events to all civilised London.

'So old Salt Junk's dead, is he?' said Sam the ostler, as he savagely tightened a girth with his strong white teeth. 'D— him, I wish I had his money tho'. Come, Tom, up you get! Captain Frere ought to pay yer a guinea a mile to drive him to that old hunk's funeral.'

The chaise dashed round to the heavy doorway, with lamps hardly alight, nearly knocking down two passengers by the up mail, who were standing in the shadow of the archway.

'Out o' the way there!' yelled the postboy. 'Now then, Captain Frere's chaise!'

'Whose?' asked the narrowly escaped passenger of one of the little crowd round the door.

'Captain Frere's,' said the man, bestowing the complimentary brevet that Peace in rags confers upon War in a post-chaise with 'horses on', and then adding, as a sort of *bonne bouche* to his dish of news, 'they say old Devine's dead, and he's his nephew. Lucky beggar, ain't he? My eyes!'

The narrowly escaped passenger's face flushed and faded, and he made a stride into the circle of light round the Bell door, as though to stop the 'lucky beggar' as he passed, but he suddenly checked himself and turned away.

As he did so his eyes met those of Mr Frere, who gave a start and a half smile, as men do when they are about to recognise a friend.

But the gleam of intelligence died out at once, as the light fell upon the gaunt body, long hair, and shabby attire of the momentarily seen figure.

'Curse the fellow,' said Mr Frere, in a hearty old English manner, as the chaise rattled out into the gleaming night, 'I thought I knew him.' And then he fell to speculating on the issue of his journey.

And the strange passenger, after standing still for a moment as if in thought, picked up a little bundle and followed his companion into the shadow of the Bell.

⊷ 2 ⊶

FELLOW TRAVELLERS

THE general room had talked itself to bed on the subject of the sudden termination of Mr Frere's supper party.

The guests, after disposing of the remainder of the punch in right good English fashion, had taken their departure by twos and threes, and the remnants of their feast, in the shape of sticky rings of scarcely dried liquor spillings, and a powerful odour of tobacco smoke, were all that was left of them.

The flotsam and jetsam of humanity cast upon the Bell shore by the coach tide, had got itself stowed away into various holes and corners in the shape of bedrooms, had even – some of it – gone walking off into the chill night, or rattling away in post-chaises, with glory of 'horses on', as Mr Frere had done.

Travelling mercantile humanity had taken in supplies of chops and steaks, and gone candle-lighted to bed. Pleasure-taking humanity, for the most part of the country cousin order, had consumed its tea, and shuddered at its London butter, night-capping itself in vain with double jorums of hot Geneva to drown the noise of the night-tide rolling in on that strange London beach. Professional humanity, in the shape of a weasel-faced attorney returned from a country excursion made on behalf of Somebody's Trustees, had double-locked its door, and desired to be called punctually at eight.

The fat white clock in the general room marked the hour of eleven, and, ticking in a sort of wheezily deprecatory way at two figures seated by the dying fire, seemed to urge that it also was weary, and would like to be double-locked and called punctually at eight likewise.

The men had been eating bread and cheese apparently, for the emptied plates yet stood on the table, in company with a huge loaf of brown bread and a jug of ale. It was evident that the passengers by the up mail were not rich; and it was as evident that one of them at all events was in an ill humour.

Sitting with his brown sinewy hands clasped round one bent knee, and his grey eyes – nearly black in the lamplight – vindictively fixed upon a hot coal in the centre of the fire, he seemed to be lost in moody thought. As the ruddy glow fell upon him there, he looked – for those days and that place – a strange figure enough.

Apparently above the middle height, with loosely hung large-boned limbs, and coarsely corded trousers of some dark thick material falling over strong clumsily made boots, the lower half of him might have belonged to the first English dock labourer passing through Fleet-street. But no English labourer ever owned such a garment as the velveteen coat, half blouse, half hunting-shirt, whose unbuttoned sleeves allowed the coarse fragment of blue-striped duck, such as sailors wear, to break the line between the brown velveteen and the scarcely less brown wrist that it was too short to cover.

The open collar, with the black kerchief knotted carelessly round it, exposed a well-cut neck sinking into a broad chest; but the heavy felt hat, pressed down to the broad black brows, met such a wilderness of dark hair, intermingled with such straggling growth of youthful beard, that it was almost impossible to distinguish aught of the features, save that the nose was large and slightly clubbed at the end.

By the side of his chair was a bundle and a stick, while a short black pipe in dangerous proximity to his elbow showed that in the intensity of his thoughts even smoke had been forgotten.

His companion was as opposite to him in appearance as he well could be. He was a little yellow-haired German, with merry blue eyes, widely opened and frank as those of a child, a big fat bald head, a little squat pulpy figure, dressed from head to foot in well worn black broadcloth of the most ordinary cut, and little fat podgy feet drawn up to the second rail of the wooden chair, and spreading themselves to the blaze with a candour that made no attempt to conceal that the soles of the boots that encased them were in holes. A huge meerschaum pipe depended from his lips, and as he smoked he gently fingered the golden coloured bowl with small child-like fingers.

Beside him on the table stood a black leather case, which, from the thickness of the strap attached to it, would seem to be of some weight, and on the top of this case reposed a black cloth travelling cap with a shiny leather peak.

Removing his pipe for a moment, the little man took a long draught at the brown jug, so long indeed that he seemed to be possessed with serious intentions of burying himself in it bodily and never coming out again, and then gave a sigh of satisfaction so profound that it roused the thinker on the other side of the table.

'Hullo!' said he, staring up at the clock, 'it's late!'

The German shrugged his fat little shoulders.

'Drink!' said he simply, with the air of a man who proposed at once a duty and an amusement. 'Drink!'

The other took off his hat with an impatient air, and threw it on the table.

One could see then that he was a young man of apparently about two and twenty, with strongly marked, but by no means handsome features. The brow was contracted by an apparently habitual frown, and there were wrinkles round the full grey eyes that told tales of hard living and strong passions.

He pushed away the proffered jug with an impatient gesture.

'My good Hans, a man is not a beer-butt!'

Hans let out a deprecatory whiff, and then took another pull at the scorned vessel, as if to show that *he* didn't bear malice at all events.

'You are out of temper,' he said at last. 'What has annoyed you?'

The young man began to pace up and down like a caged beast.

'What?' he cried out at last. 'That is a pretty question to ask. Everything! Here am I, starving, struggling, drudging like a dray-horse – come here, go there, – do this, do that, – when I might be, *should* be, rich and respected.'

The other sighed.

'I cannot help you there,' he said.

Coming close to the table, the young man laid his hand on the black leather case with a sudden, significant gesture.

The little black legs came down from the second rail of the chair like a double flash of black lightning, and the little black arm whipped the leather case off the table with a jerk that made the cheese-plates jump again.

'What do you mean, Mr Reckless-devil?' cried the little man, in German. 'Hands off, if you please! That is neither your property nor mine.'

'Hullo, hullo, hullo!' said a voice behind them. 'No quarrelling here. If you want to quarrel, go outside and quarrel. This is a respectable posting-house, patronised by the nobility and gentry. What do you mean, eh?'

The speaker was the landlord, a fussy round man, with a stomach aggressively protuberant. He was followed by a thin person in a stretched suit of plaid, who, with a very battered hat held at a very long arm's length, advanced apologetically.

The young man turned round with such a savage grin upon

his gaunt features, that the proprietor of the respectable posting-house involuntarily drew back a step.

'Mind your own business!' said he with a sneer that, however pardonable to travelling humanity in a post-chaise with 'horses on,' was insolent enough on the lips of a foreign-looking, brown-handed, bread-and-cheese-eating fellow, in a shabby velvet blouse and corduroy trousers. 'This is a public room, and I've paid for my supper and bed.'

'We were not quarrelling, my good host,' said the German, with much hurried gesticulation, and replacing the leather case on the table. 'It was a shoak – a little shoak of mein friend's.' But even as he spoke the big blue eyes wandered uneasily towards his friend's face, as though they were not quite so sure of his friend's jesting intentions after all.

The young man burst into a laugh almost as unpleasant as his sneer had been.

Of course it was a joke. Ha, ha! and he apologised for his violence; but he had been travelling for the last two days, and was nervous. Would the gentleman do him the pleasure of drinking?

The thin gentleman in the plaid suit would be enraptured. He had, in point of fact, just come in for that purpose with his worthy friend, Mr Mogford, the excellent landlord. It was a cold night – a very cold night, and he would take gin and cloves.

'And what will you take, Pogford?' said the young man. 'Will you take gin and cloves, Pogford, or stick to the home-brewed of your native land? Hans, old fellow, have some more beer, and don't stare like an owl in an ivy-bush. Sit down, gentlemen, sit down; I don't look like the Lord Mayor, but I can pay my way!'

And he slapped his pockets with a defiant gesture.

His merriment was in such ghastly contrast to his recent despondency, and his laugh seemed so forced and unreal, that Hans' blue eyes stared more uneasily than ever, and Hans himself edged his chair nearer the fire, with the air of a man who feels that he will be shortly compelled to take part in an unpleasant conversation.

Mr Mogford looked from one to the other mutely distrustful, and turning round on his heel, went into the front bar.

'Nelly,' said he to the smart young lady who, sitting in state in a glass case beneath a dashing picture of the 'Brighton Mail,' was improving her shining hours by totting up the list of drinkables consumed since nine o'clock that morning, and yawning elegantly during the process, 'who are them two in the coffee-room?'

Mr Mogford – Plain Joe Mogford, as he loved to be called – was the architect of his own fortunes, and having risen to the proprietorship of the Bell from the humble station of boots to the Red Lion in Moorfields, did not disdain to look after his own business, for, as he truthfully remarked, 'his business looked after him.'

Nelly gracefully craned her neck, so as to command a view of the table and fire through the half-opened door, and said, 'Oh – the furriners! Up coach. Numbers 29 and 18. Poor folks, I fancy.'

'Hum,' returned Mr Mogford with a hearty old English manner that would have delighted that gallant officer, Lieutenant Maurice Frere. 'Furriners! Dam furriners! Three glasses of ale and a gin an' cloves. I don't like the looks on 'em. More especial that young party. *He's* a Rampageous one, I'll be bound.'

Miss Nelly, sweetly tossing her head as if to apologise for the existence of all 'young parties' of any nation, clime, or calling, drew the ale with a tender jerk, as though it was solid and she was chopping so many lengths of it off.

'They won't stay beyond morning,' said she, 'for I heard the tall one say that he had very important business in the country.'

Returned to the coffee-room primed with this intelligence, Mr Mogford found matters had changed much for the better.

The thin man in the plaid suit had joined in the conversation with such airiness and volubility that he seemed to have cast quite a spell of cheerfulness over the place. He was a bony person, with mutton-chop whiskers, a sharp eye, knuckly hands, a set of very regular strong yellow teeth – like healthy old ivory – and a broad, blunt, bony chin. His clothes were several sizes too small for him, and were strapped down, and braced up, and tautened out generally to a pitch that made one involuntarily speculate on the strength of his buttons.

He had put his hat on the table, and his handkerchief – a large blue cotton one – in his hat, and with one long yellow hand, spiked as it were with long yellow fingers tipped with strong black nails, was warming his back and discoursing the company.

'Very cold for the time of year! Fires in April, quite a joke. England was getting colder every year. Didn't they think so? Oh, only just landed! Continent quiet at last, eh! Beg pardon, Frenchman? No, German – aha, glorious nation. Long way to travel. Not much baggage? Like the snail, eh – house on his back. Had been himself a traveller. Loved the sea. Sailor? No, not exactly, but give him the wind that blows, the ship that goes, and the lass – aha, *here* was the divine fluid. He would drink to their health.'

All this, said with intense rapidity, and a happy knack of putting questions and jumping at answers, was delivered with a shabby imitation of a fashionable lisp, and a vulgar leer and simper, pointed by an occasional wave of the dirty yellow hand that was unpleasant to contemplate.

The little German seemed half terrified at his volubility, and only replied by nods and broken exclamations of assent, but the young man laughed and applauded, and struck the table and slapped his knees with an extravagant affectation of intense interest.

'It *was* cold for the time of year. He had been in England before – oh, many years ago. Didn't know if he should stop, now he had come. What did they think about the Turkish fleet? and what was the opinion in London on the new Alliance?'

The thin man, with his eyes fixed greedily on the black leather case, couldn't say. Wasn't much in the way of hearing political opinions. 'Yes, he would sit down. Might he move the little case? Oh, no offence. Valuables? Indeed! Dangerous travelling now-a-days. The Bath mail had been robbed only last week. Really the daring of the fellows was astonishing. Oh – don't let him disturb the gentleman – 'pon honour.'

But the little German, with a nervous glance at Plain Joe Mogford, had caught up his cherished black case in a sort of sturdy alarm, and drinking his beer in two gulps, had requested to be shown to his room.

'Number 29, Thomas,' said Mr Mogford, severely, to the summoned waiter; and, with a bow to the company and a whispered good night to his fellow traveller, the little man carried his little black body and his little black case off to bed.

His fellow traveller seemed in no hurry to follow him. He was leaning back in his chair, with a sort of graceless gracefulness, cutting up a long stick of black tobacco with a white-handled clasp-knife, such as sailors carry, and was rocking himself to and fro in a sort of nervous impatience.

The thin man on one side of the table and Mogford on the other watched him with some curiosity.

'Your friend seems an unsociable sort of chap now,' said the thin man, gulping down a mouthful of his gin and cloves as though it was a bullet. 'I should say he hadn't many friends, eh?'

'He's tired,' returned the other, with a laugh, – still working the white-handled knife between his lissome fingers. 'He's travelled a good bit to-day.'

'Ah!' said the thin man, with another gulp. 'Comed across to-day, I suppose?'

'Yes,' returned the other.

'Calais?' asked the thin man, with an offhand air.

'No.'

'Oh – Ostend?'

'Guess again.'

The yellow hand fluttered for a moment in the air, as though to dismiss any intention of guessing at anything, and the hard voice, – which mated so well with the hand that, could it take visible shape, it must of necessity been yellow and bony also, – inquired 'Paris?'

'What should you say to Amsterdam?' said the young man, stowing the knife away, blade point uppermost, in the nook formed by his thumb and forefinger, and rubbing the morsels of tobacco between his brown hands.

'Amsterdam, eh!' said the landlord, staring at the velveteen coat with all his might. 'That's a Rampageous long way, too!'

The thin man shut his yellow teeth up with a snap at the word Amsterdam, and then sat staring at the white-handled knife in the young man's hand, as hard as Plain Joe Mogford had stared at the young man's velveteen coat-sleeve, but with quite a different expression.

'He seems mighty careful of that there black box of his,' says Plain Joe. 'I suppose he brought that from Amsterdam, too?'

'I suppose he did,' said the young man with a frown.

'I suppose it's valuable?' says Plain Joe.

'How the devil should *I* know?' exclaimed the young man, jumping up with a vehemence that seemed altogether unwarranted by so simple a question, and looking from one to the other. 'What's his black box got to do with me? – I beg your pardon,' he interrupted, 'but I am nervous and out of sorts, knocked up and worried. I don't know what I am saying. I think I'll go to bed, and, as I am going off in the morning, perhaps you will allow me to pay you now.'

He pulled out a handful of silver as he spoke, and counted out the sum named by the astonished Joe; and then, taking up one of the regiment of flat candlesticks drawn up in martial array on a table just outside the now empty glass case of the smart young lady, swung his bundle over his shoulder and walked off to bed.

'Here! I say! Hullo!' called out Plain Joe. 'Where are you going? No. 18's your room, third turning on the –'

'All right,' said the other, looking nervously down at him from the top step of the first landing place on the broad staircase. 'I know the room; I've been in it before. Don't trouble yourself, I beg.'

'Well,' says Plain Joe, coming back again to his thin guest, 'he's a Rampageous Rum'un if ever there was one. Been in it afore, eh! Ah, and if I had seen you sooner, my chick, you wouldn't have been in it again, I can tell you!'

The thin man had said never a word during this time. Strangely enough, all his volubility seemed to have left him with the discovery of the little German's starting place; and he was staring at the table and drumming on it with his yellow fingers in a nervously absent way.

Plain Joe roused him unceremoniously.

'Come, Jerry,' said he, 'you clear out. You ain't a credit to the family, you ain't; and I don't want you here more than I can help. How much is it this time?'

Jerry, all his versatility departed, and with a wolfishly selfish leer in his hard eye, said that it was twenty pounds.

'Here's ten, Jerry,' said Plain Joe; 'and that's five more than you deserve. You had your quarter's allowance only last week;

you Rampageous Robber, you know you had, and I can't afford to be always bleeding like this.'

Jerry, with his disreputable face leering from under his disreputable hat, and his disreputable trowsers clinging tighter than ever to his disreputable legs, wagged a yellow forefinger, and murmured something about the claims of brotherhood.

'Brotherhood be blowed!' returned Plain Joe. 'You're a pretty specimen of brotherhood, you are! You're a Rampageous, roaring, fine rip of a brother you are! You're the sort of brother folks advertise for, ain't yer? Here, my blessed brother, take this five quidder, and take yourself off as soon as you like.'

'You won't give your own flesh and blood a night's lodging, Joe?' asked the admirable brother, with all his yellow teeth glistening from ear to ear.

'Flesh and blood be Gormandised!' said Plain Joe, apparently with the conviction that he was uttering a fearful imprecation. 'The last time flesh and blood was in this respectable house, flesh and blood stole a silver cruet stand.'

'Plated, Joe, upon my sacred sivvy!' said Mr Jeremiah Mogford; 'and I lived on it for five weeks, I did, indeed.'

'Well,' returned Plain Joe, with ruthless common sense, 'that ain't no satisfaction to me, is it? No, no; I'm a plain man, and I speak plain English. You've been sponging on me ever since I was as big as three penn'orth of ha'pence, and I suppose you'll go on sponging till the end of time; but as for sleeping in this respectable posting house, you don't, so there's an end of it.'

Seeing that his brother was firm, Jerry forbore to urge the point; and stuffing the note into the pocket of his tightly braced waistcoat, and buttoning his tightly braced coat over it, he took off the seedy hat with a flourish, and paused on the edge of the night to take a last farewell.

'Well, if you won't you won't,' said he, 'and it's no use talking; however, I bear no malice. Gord bless you, Joe – Gord bless you!'

To which fraternal benediction Plain Joe responded by slamming the door, and securing it with a multiplicity of chains and bolts.

'You're my brother, wuss luck,' he ejaculated, with a shake of his practical head; 'but you're a Roaring Rampageous Rum'un, and the farther you sleep from my respectable customers, the better it will be for 'em.'

Mr Jerry, on finding his flow of oratory thus cut short, gazed up at the sky, dark with driving clouds, and then taking two strides into the middle of the wet courtyard, faced about, and shook his yellow fist at the inhospitable door.

As he did so, the noise of a closing window fell on his ear. He looked up instinctively, and caught a glimpse of a retreating head, from which depended an enormous pipe bowl, outlined against the yellow light.

'It's that Amsterdam fellow,' said Jerry to himself, and glided under the shadow of the wall.

His hand fell upon the cold round tube of an iron waterpipe, that ran straight up the wall to the gutter, just above the now darkened window. Instantly on touching it, he seemed to experience the shock of a new train of thought, for, after standing a moment, irresolute, with shaking knees and blanched face, he crouched and clung to it, staring up into the darkness, like some monstrous reptile.

++ *3* ++

AT THE BELL INN

No. 18, having reached that room which he seemed so well able to find, flung his bundle on the little bed, and his hat on his bundle, and then, with the candle in his hand, sat down wearily on a sticky-looking rush-bottomed chair, – that was built on a sort of town-drainage principle, and converged to an uncomfortable point in the centre, – as if in indecision.

'I wonder if I have done right,' said he, 'in coming back? I was happy enough where I was. A quiet, peaceful life, with no great pleasures and no great pains. The love of a simple, innocent girl, and the affection of simple, innocent people, should have been sufficient for me – gambler, idler, profligate as I have been. And yet, at the first glimpse of the old life, the first cut into the old sore, I feel the old agony rising. Wealth, honour, esteem, all the world's glory that money brings, were before me – to be purchased by dishonour and meanness. I refused, but I feel the devilish fever, that I thought had left me for ever, again burning in my veins. How the past returns upon me! The old timber-yard, the cool brown river, the harmless scrapes of my wild boyhood, the serious follies of my ill-spent, ill-cared-for youth.' He rose and paced the chamber. 'Ah well: it is all done with now. I have given back my birthright, denied my birth, and blotted out my name. To-morrow, please God, I will begin a new life – that shall have no stain of the old one on it.'

He had begun to undress, and had already pulled off his blouse and boots, when he paused again.

'Poor old Hans!' he said, 'I won't part from him in this way. It was my fault that we quarrelled. I should have been more mindful of his weak points; less impetuous in speech and action.'

Without stopping to put on his boots, he rapidly traversed the long passage, until he came to his friend's room.

'Are you asleep, Hans?'

No; on the contrary, Hans was wide awake – was sitting by the open window smoking like a limekiln. He rose as the other entered.

'Hans, I am come to ask your pardon for my folly down stairs. I was irritable, and out of spirits. Let us part friends.'

'You have done right to come,' returned the other, smiling all over his face. 'I forgive you. Embrace me!' And emitting a cloud of smoke which rendered him a sort of German Jupiter gone Io-courting, the little fellow fell on his friend's neck (standing on tip-toe to do it), and kissed him in the foreign fashion on both cheeks.

'I shall start before you to-morrow,' said the young man, half-laughing at the vehemence of the salutation.

'Home?' asked Hans, sitting down and probing his pipe-bowl with his little finger.

'Home.'

'Don't tell them where I am. You know. Not a word! Not a syllable! Not a breath!'

'Don't be alarmed.'

'But be careful; women are so quick; a hint, an allusion might set them thinking.'

'You need not fear. No one shall know of your whereabouts from me.'

Hans knocked the ashes out of his pipe-head, and then, sticking the stem into his mouth again, essayed to close the window.

'Well, you are the only person who can tell them,' said he, puffing and blowing in his effort to bring down the sash. 'And – unless – you – Help me with this window!'

'It has jammed at the side. Let me raise it. Confound it, I've left my knife downstairs. There, plague on it, I've cut my hand,' cried the young man suddenly. 'A rusty nail, or something. How it bleeds! All over my shirt, too. Lend me your handkerchief, Hans.'

In great concern the little man tore a blue and white cotton one from his neck, and tied it round the wound.

It was a nasty ragged gash, and bled profusely; but after the first few seconds the young man made light of it.

'It's nothing. A mere scratch. Let me try again.'

But the other pushed him back, and applying himself to the refractory window, with a sudden jerk brought it down rattling.

'Pig of a window!' said he. 'It has no hasp, and will rattle all night.'

'It won't wake *you*, at all events,' said the young man, smiling, as though the subject of Hans' capacity for slumber was an old jest between them. 'You would snore through a tornado. Have you got the money safe?'

The German pointed to his bed-head, from under the pillow at which the end of the black case was protruding.

'Trust me!'

'Well then, good-bye – until we meet again!'

'Until we meet again!' echoed Hans, with another embrace, and they parted.

Going swiftly back to his room, the young man who is the hero of this history crossed the orbit of Mr Mogford, who was taking a tour of the premises in his plain way before going to bed.

'Hullo!' says Mr Mogford. 'Mistaken your room, young man?'

The young man – in the shadow of the doorway – had done nothing of the kind. Had forgotten something, and had gone to fetch it.

To which Mr Mogford, shaking his head at the black patch of

shadow in which the young man might be presumed to be standing, gruntingly remarked that he objected to the practice of Rampaging about his respectable posting-house, and so took himself – a moving shade in the midst of his own brightness – up the passage, and to bed.

To bed went – with a smile begotten of his hope of the new life the morrow was to bring him – the young man himself; and to bed went Hans – with the black case under his head, all unconscious of a yellow face peering in at him in a ghastly manner from the outside of his unhasped window.

⤟ 4 ⤠

'HORSES ON'

WITH persistency of 'horses on,' the post-chaise containing Mr Maurice Frere had rattled, and jumped, and jolted itself into Harwich by eight o'clock in the morning. The quaint old town was barely awake, and, save for some few returning fishermen, or outgoing labourers, Mr Maurice Frere, protruding his bullet head from the side window to take inspection of the weather, saw nobody.

The weather did not look propitious. It had been blowing and raining hard, with that sarcastic comment upon the poetical Spring that our fine old English climate is prone to make – all through the night.

At the various stages – where the 'horses on' were munching or drowsing, unconscious of their doom – sleepy ostlers had cursed the arrival of the late coming post-chaise, which dragged them from their beds to be pelted at by hail, and whipped into wakefulness by the bitter wind.

The postboys – pulling their dripping hats well down on their shining faces, and wriggling their numbed hands as far as might be into their drenched coat-sleeves – set their heads to the storm, with mental speculations as to the whereabouts the fit of rheumatism, which they were rapidly earning, would catch them.

The horses even – poor snorting, mud-bedaubed beasts –

splashed through mire and water, with tails tucked in and ears laid back, acknowledging the force of the easterly wind by divers slippings and stumblings, that once or twice nearly brought chaise, postboys, and passenger to a destructive stand-still.

But Mr Maurice Frere – wrapped in roquelaure of military fashion, and tiled in with such odds and ends of shawls, coats, and travelling rugs as the Bell could hastily produce for him, had pulled up his windows against wind and hail, and, fortified with sundry glasses of brandy and water, had bid the boys 'drive on,' in fine old English disregard of anybody's convenience but his own.

He had slept a little between whiles, and being not unused to sit up at nights, and having, moreover, strong incitements, in the way of wonderment and anxiety, to wakefulness, was tolerably ready to admire such prospect as the morning light could show him. This was not much. The signboards – all shining with the recent rain – creaked in the wind. The streets were wet and muddy, the sky gloomy and threatening. The sea – what could be seen of it – brown, heaving, and angry.

A few boats, with brown sails bellied to their biggest, swooped into the protection of the wooden jetty stairs, and the usual distant crowd of sea-gazing fishermen were propped against the weather-beaten posts, or leaning over the slackened chains that ran round the sides of the weather-beaten pier-head, stared at nothing in particular, after the profound manner of their race.

A big, heavily-laden collier craft, coming in with the fresh breeze, was slowly rising and falling in the horizon, as she worked her way through the cross sea to port, and from a brig with a broom at her masthead, warped alongside the wharf, came the faint noise of a barking dog.

Further to the right, close under the guns of the fort, confusion of masts and yards gave signs of more shipping, and then the rising roofs and gables of the straggling town shut out further prospect by a wilderness of chimney-stacks.

The prospect was melancholy enough. A rainy sea and a leaden sky, blown over and under by a bleak bitter wind, and not component parts of a cheerful landscape, and the post-boys seemed to be desirous of getting out of sight of the narrow strip of wind-ruffled water as quickly as possible.

Dashing down the principal street with such miserable imitation of full gallop as steel and whipcord could get out of the reeking and exhausted horses, the chaise turned sharp round at a right angle into a broad country road fringed by tall trees. This road cut into the highway with a sudden twist, and lost itself at one end with a jerk, in a maze of leaf and branch which on a fine sunny morning would have been pleasant enough to look at, but which, seen through the morning mists, was damp, sodden, and haggard, as though the trees had been sitting up late overnight, and had got caught in a shower coming home. The other end went straggling through a handful of old wooden houses narrowing to the water's edge, and seemed to lose itself under the supporting timbers of a black shed that bore in huge white letters on its nearer side the word 'Devine.'

In that shed, fifty years before, had Richard Devine – now Sir Richard Devine, Knight, millionaire, ship-builder, and naval contractor – built the *Hastings*, sloop of war, for his Majesty King George the Third's Lords of the Admiralty – a building which was the thin end of that wedge that eventually split the mighty oak-block of Admiralty patronage into three-deckers and ships of the line that did good service under Howe, Pellew, Parker, Nelson, and Hood, and exfoliated and ramified itself as it were into huge dockyards at Plymouth, Portsmouth, and Sheerness, and bore buds and flowers of countless barrels of measly pork and maggotty biscuit.

The one sole aim of the sharp-faced, thin-lipped son of honest Dick Devine, the Harwich boat builder, had been to make money. He had cringed and crawled, and flattered and blustered, had licked the dust off great men's shoes, and danced attendance in great men's ante-chambers. Stern moralist and pious church-goer though he was, he had not scrupled to beg favours of great men's mistresses, and to smile familiarly on great men's mistresses' servants. Nothing was too low, nothing too high for him. A shrewd man of business, a thorough master of his trade, troubled with no scruples of honour and burdened with no feelings of delicacy, he made money rapidly, and saved it as he made. The first hint that the public received of his wealth was in 1796, when it leaked out that a Mr Devine, one of the shipwrights to the Government, and a comparatively young man of forty-four or thereabouts, had subscribed five thousand pounds to the Loyalty Loan raised to prosecute the French war. So rich a man must be worth making richer, and by this 'sprat to catch a mackerel' the shrewd patriot obtained more opportunities of fishing in Government waters. In 1805, after doing good, and to him profitable, service at the trial of Lord Melville, the treasurer of the navy, he married the daughter of a Bristol merchant, grown rich by West Indian trade. She brought him a large fortune, but was nearly thirty years his junior, and the marriage was not a happy one. In 1817 his wife died, leaving him three children – two boys and a girl – born at long intervals. At that time, what with lucky speculations in the funds – assisted, it was whispered, by secret intelligence from France during the stormy years of '13, '14, and '15 – and the legitimate profit on his Government contracts, he had accumulated a princely fortune, and might have lived in princely magnificence.

But the Old-man-of-the-sea burden of parsimony and avarice which he had voluntarily taken on his back forty years before could not be shaken off, and the only show he made of his money was to purchase with it a rambling but comfortable country house, standing on a small estate near his native town. To this place he had taken his three children on his wife's death; and, save a trip to London when the First Gentleman in Europe (a somewhat obese and oldish gentleman then) was invested by oath with the power he had so long held in fact, and was pleased to bestow, in commemoration of that event, the honour of knighthood upon several favoured subjects, amongst whom was Mr Richard Devine, he had not come out of his retirement.

His retirement was not a happy one. He was a stern father and a severe master. His servants hated him, and his children were terrified of him. His eldest son, Richard – whom the townspeople remembered as an ill-built, awkward lad, never so happy as when he was rambling in the old boat-yard, or sailing with the fishermen – inherited his father's strong will and imperious manner. Under careful supervision and a just rule, he might have been guided to good, but, left to his own devices outside, and galled by the iron yoke of parental discipline at home, he had fallen into bad company, and become reckless and profligate. After three years of village dissipation, college scrapes, and London riot, he had quarrelled with his father – or his father with him – and gone off, no one knew whither.

Sir Richard, strangely overlooking his second son, Frank – a pale, quiet boy of fourteen, and his daughter Lucy, a child of eight – had sent for Maurice Frere, his wife's nephew – (the abolition of the slave trade had ruined old Frere a few years after his daughter's marriage) – and intimated to him that he would take him under his peculiar care. With shortsighted selfishness, the adopted nephew failed to restrain his coarse extravagance, and the result was as we have seen, that the patience of the uncle gave way, and he coupled the payment of the last batch of his ungrateful nephew's debts with the condition that gave rise to the supper party at the Bell.

✦ 5 ✦

THE END OF HIS JOURNEY

THREE miles of winding country road, flanked at rare intervals on either side by farm-houses, were got over, and before the hedgerows altogether dwindled, and the broad low-lying marshes came in view, the chaise turned off to the left, and passing between two ball-topped gate-posts of stone, dashed up to the door of a grim brick house, surrounded by a gloomy and uncared-for garden.

At the noise of its approach, an old man-servant, in gaudy but faded livery of blue and yellow, opened a sort of wicket at the side of the main entrance, and same down to meet its occupant.

'How is he?' was Mr Frere's first question as he ascended the discoloured steps eagerly.

'He's right enough,' answered the man, proceeding to gather up the rugs and wrappers that had done such good service during the past night. 'More frightened than hurt.'

There was no sympathy in the tone, scarcely respect, but young Frere seemed to look for none.

'I got your letter last evening, at nine o'clock, Jarvis,' he said, 'and set off at once. I thought he was dead.'

Jarvis grinned.

'Ay, I thought I'd bring you down quick,' he returned; 'but it wasn't so bad as I made out. He's getting better every hour.'

'What was the matter?' asked Frere, striding into the wide but dingy entrance-hall, with the air of a man who felt himself at home.

'He got some news that startled him, I think. It was after the night packet came. I took it up as usual; and bime-by I heard the bell ring, and found him all white and shaking in his chair. "Get me to-bed, Jarvis!" he says; and when he gets there he has a fit, and so I wrote to you and sent the letter into Harwich by the old dun pony.'

'Who saw the letter?' asked Frere.

'Nobody. He locked all up in the eskytor afore he rang, I suppose.'

'And he's better?'

'Mending fast,' returned Jarvis with another grin. 'You won't be master o' Mere this turn at any rate.'

The other disregarded the sneer, as if it was one he had often heard and could afford to let pass unnoticed.

'Pay the boys,' he said, producing his purse, 'and bring me something to eat. If he's getting better, he can wait until I have breakfasted.'

Early though it might be for fashionable London, the materials for breakfast were already laid out in a long gloomy room that looked out on to a long gloomy lawn, overshadowed by a gloomy cedar tree that had always a wet patch of black earth beneath its cheerless branches.

With a familiar glance into this apartment, Mr Frere passed up the polished cheerless stairs, and made his way to a room which, from evidence of military chests and blue cases lettered with military superscriptions, would appear to be specially consecrated to his use. Having changed his clothes and washed away the stain and dust of travel, he went down, humming the butt end of the facetious cornet's last night's ballad, – into the breakfast-room.

A thin sickly lad of seventeen, who had evidently outgrown

his strength, was leaning against the mantelpiece, with a book between his fingers.

'How do you do, Cousin Maurice?'

'Hullo Frank! How are you? Buried in a book as usual!' says Frere, with offensive old English heartiness. 'I'm as hungry as a hunter, and as tired as a dog.'

'I was waiting breakfast for you,' returned Frank, a faint flush of annoyance rising in his pale cheek. 'Jarvis told me that you had just arrived.'

'Posted down from town as hard as four horses could bring me,' says Frere, dragging a chair to the table and falling to without further ceremony. 'Raining in torrents and blowing a hurricane. Beastly climate. What's this? – Pie? No, I'll trouble you for some beef. You see we were just having a little party – fine old English style, my boy, none of your dam French thingamies for me – when I got old Jarvis's letter, and so off I came.'

'I think he exaggerated the evil,' replied Frank, with a scarcely perceptible frown of disgust at his cousin's coarseness of tone and action. 'My father's better.'

'So the old blockhead told me just now. A slice of that brawn. But it was just as well. How's Lucy?'

'Very well. She is upstairs with Madame.'

'Oh! Haven't got rid of that old cat yet? – Mustard please. – The only foolish thing my respected uncle ever did to my knowledge was to let that old hag of a Frenchwoman into the house to jabber republicanism to his daughter.'

Frank laughed a little shamefaced laugh.

'She isn't an old hag,' he said, 'and she isn't French. She's German.'

'Well, it's all the same,' says Maurice, in hearty old English obstinacy of ignorance. 'They're all alike. Dam frog-eating set. I wouldn't have one of 'em in *my* doors if *I* had anything to do with it.'

'Ah, but then you haven't, you see,' said the other.

It was said quietly enough, but the crimson spot that burnt on Frank Devine's cheek showed that he felt the tacit injustice of Mr Frere's swaggering presence, and that he bore no good-will to the cuckoo cousin who had come to oust him from his nest.

Frere, eating, drinking, and talking with old English stolidity, barely caught the meaning of the intonation; but he did catch it.

'No, you're right there, Frank old fellow,' he replied with an oath. 'I'm only a poor devil in a marching regiment, that can't call his soul his own. What made the old gentleman ill?' he asked, with a sudden change of manner.

'I don't know,' said Frank, rising and pushing his unemptied plate from him. 'He doesn't tell *me*.'

'I should like to see him if he's better,' says the other, helping himself to more brawn. 'You might tell Jarvis.'

'Oh, I dare say you can see him,' Frank said, ignoring the suggestion about Jarvis altogether. 'He was to get up to-day.' And with that he left the room.

Mr Frere's red head turned to the door as he went.

'Amiable young cub,' he murmured. 'I suppose there's another screw loose. I wonder what's come to the old man! He's hearty enough, but seventy's not the age for fits. I'm glad I came.'

He rose and went to the window, but as he did so the sound of a bell violently rung made him turn round.

'Sir Richard, for a poney!' he said involuntarily. 'I wonder what's up now.'

He had not much time for speculation, for in a couple of minutes the door opened to admit the blue and yellow body of the grinning Jarvis.

'The master wants you!' he said, with the impudent familiarity that seemed his privilege. 'The moment he heard you were here, he rang; and a fine humour he's in too!'

'Didn't expect me, eh, Jarvis?' says Frere, following with a somewhat blank look.

'No,' says Jarvis, pausing at one of the bed room doors with another grin, 'he didn't; and, from what I could make out, he didn't want you either.'

The room was lofty, bare, and cold. A fire burnt on the wide hearthstone, but it too seemed to partake of the general gloom, and smouldered sulkily, not daring to blaze and crackle as it might have done under more cheerful circumstances. A big funereal bed occupied a niche in the wall by the side of the jutting chimney, and in an old-fashioned arm chair at the foot of the bed, with his face turned to the fire, sat Sir Richard Devine.

A gaunt angular man, with hard eyes and lips so closely shut that they almost disappeared. He was wrapped in a long dressing-gown, and sat bolt upright in his chair, fingering a snuff-box. Save from his pallor and apparent disinclination to move, one would not have guessed that he had but just recovered from a severe and sudden illness. His hair was white and thin. His fore-head, over which the skin seemed stretched to painfulness, was marked with one deep wrinkle between the brows, and his hands were knotted at the joints.

'Sit down, nephew,' he said, in a clear cold voice, without a tremor of passion or weakness in it.

Mr Maurice Frere approaching, with a smile of mingled pity and welcome, felt himself checked half way, by the short nod that accompanied and pointed the sentence, and, bowing, paused on the other side of the fireplace.

'What brought you from London, Maurice?'

'I – I – heard that you were ill?'

'So I suppose. But you have heard that often enough before.'

'No – not so – so seriously.'

'Oh, not so seriously. Did you think I was dying?'

'My dear uncle!' says Maurice – all his fine old English man-ner vanishing like hoar-frost under the wintry ken of those unrelenting eyes. 'How could you imagine such a thing?'

'Easily. I am past seventy; and when a man passes seventy he may die at any moment. Did you come to see if I was dead?'

Getting more and more alarmed by the turn the conversation was taking, Mr Frere half rose from his seat.

'I came to *see* you,' he said, with a dogged contraction of the coarse brows. 'Is it so very extraordinary that a nephew should come to see his uncle? Especially,' he added, after a pause, 'when that uncle has been so kind to him as you have been to me.'

'Who told you I was ill?'

'Jarvis.'

'Ah! Did he say that I was very bad?'

'He led me to think so.'

'Jarvis is a fool, and you are another, Maurice,' said the old man, with a curving of his lips, that was a silent snarl. 'I am as well as ever I was.'

'Glad to hear it, sir, 'pon honour!' cries Maurice, forcing him-self into his old English manner again.

'I have had a fainting fit, that was all,' he continued, tapping his snuff-box impatiently. 'One gets such things at my age. What did Jarvis tell you?'

'He merely said that you rang the bell for him, and desired him to help you to bed.'

'Ah! Then you came down post haste to see me – eh?'

'Yes, sir.'

'What did the chaise cost, Maurice? Did you pay the boys liberally? An officer in His Majesty's service should be liberal.'

'I paid them their hire,' returned the other, sulkily. 'I don't *always* waste money.'

Sir Richard lifted his white eyebrows with a satirical leer.

'Don't you? I am very glad to hear it.'

Maurice shifted in his chair.

'You needn't hit a fellow when he's down,' he said, with some display of spirit. 'You've paid my debts for me I know, but what's the good of flinging your favours in my teeth?'

The old shipbuilder laughed softly, as if he rather enjoyed the lad's vexation.

'Maurice, Maurice, you'll never get on in the world if you talk like that. When does your ship sail?'

Maurice, sulkily staring at the fire, said he didn't know. It might be in a week, it might be in a month.

'You'll find Van Diemen's Land a very different place from London,' said Sir Richard, with a cheerily sarcastic air. 'I do not think that your temptations will be so great there. I shall allow you a hundred a year in addition to your pay. You will find it a princely fortune among the convicts and kangaroos.'

'I'm much obliged to you,' says Maurice.

'Are you? Perhaps you are. You don't look so. Now as to another matter. Your cousin Richard.'

Maurice started.

'I heard from him the other day. He has been abroad, as you know, for some time – in Germany – living in what I consider a disreputable way. He wrote to me –' the old man's firm voice shook a little here, and his face changed colour – 'an impertinent offensive letter, asking for money. I replied to him, stating certain conditions on which alone I could – consent to – help him, and those conditions he refused point blank.' He paused. 'Give me some of that barley-water; I am thirsty.' Maurice obeyed eagerly, waiting for what should come next. 'And – and – did me the honour to say that he declined to hold further communication with me.'

Maurice Frere gasped as he heard this intelligence. Selfishly keen to his own interests though he might be, it had never occurred to him that the letter which had stricken down his wealthy uncle, was from that very cousin whom he had always regarded as his peculiar enemy.

Despite Jarvis's prediction, and his uncle's mordant manner, he felt nearer to the heritage he coveted than he had ever done before.

'He doesn't care for Frank,' he thought, 'and I dare say that having provided for Lucy, he'll leave me the lion's share.'

The next words of Sir Richard would seem to confirm his impressions.

'In consequence of this occurrence,' said he, 'I have sent for Quaid to come down and make a fresh will. I expect him to-night. I shall not forget you in it, though you are a spendthrift and a fool; but you will have to go to Van Diemen's Land all the same. When I have said a thing I never retract it. Now, I'm tired. You can go and send Jarvis here.'

Obedient to the order, Maurice rose, and turning at the door, he perceived that despite the air of vigour which his uncle had assumed, the white head had sunk forward, and the hand hung listlessly. 'He's worse than he wants to make out,' said he. 'I hope old Quaid won't be too late.' And then lighting a cigar in the hall, he rang the bell for Jarvis, and strolled out on the melancholy lawn, intent on his own selfish thoughts.

'I wonder what Dick has been doing. I wonder why he don't like Frank. I wonder what made him take to me. *Must* go to Van Diemen's Land, eh? I don't know about that. Your ship might sail before mine, uncle Richard.'

By and bye Lucy, a quiet, old-fashioned child of ten, upon whom the gloom of the house and its surroundings would seem to have fallen, came out to him accompanied by her governess, a fat-faced, mild-eyed woman, with no hint of French vivacity about her to warrant Frere's mistake as to her race.

After a gloomy converse with these two, he lunched, and then inspected the stables – horses there were none – and then smoked again, and tried to get up a cock-fight in the yard, and cursed his fate, and wondered when Quaid would come.

Sir Richard, after sipping more barley water, had been got to bed again, and was dozing, 'a little tired,' he had said, with his conversation, and was likewise waiting for Quaid.

At six o'clock, Quaid arrived.

He was an abrupt man, of hale middle age, with black eyes stuck into a white face, like plums in a pudding.

'Sorry for his delay; respected client; bad roads; dreadful weather. Mr Richard –?'

'No, Mr Frere!'

'Oh! a thousand pardons. Of course, yes. How *was* his respected client?'

His respected client was better, according to Jarvis's account – better, according to the Harwich doctor's account, who had ridden over that afternoon, and had promised to ride over again in the evening. He was asleep just now, but had desired to be awakened the moment Mr Quaid arrived.

Mr Quaid, however, wouldn't hear of it.

'At these moments, rest, sleep, repose, were most necessary. *When* he awoke – not before.'

Consequently dinner was served in the gloomy room, and Mr Quaid, Maurice, and Frank ate it.

Quaid was anecdotic and discursive, Maurice old English and hearty, Frank silent and ill at ease. He loved his father, despite his father's slights, and resented this eating, and drinking, and story-telling. Moreover, he was in ignorance of the cause of his father's illness and of the sudden summoning of Quaid, and attributed the presence of the latter to some hostile influence brought to bear by Maurice.

'Mr Frank seems silent, eh?' asked Quaid when Mr Frank had left – 'uncommunicative, self-contained.'

'Very!' said Maurice.

'Anything like Mr Richard?' says Quaid.

'I don't remember Mr Richard, but I should say not.'

'Ah – just so.'

There was silence for a few moments, and then Maurice, after stretching his legs, fingering his glass, and shifting his chair, could contain himself no longer.

'I suppose you know why Sir Richard sent for you, Mr Quaid?' he asked, coming to the point, when he did come to it, with old English bluntness.

'I have some idea,' returns Quaid, with lawyer-like caution.

'He wants you to make a new will,' says Maurice. 'He has fallen out again with my cousin Dick.'

By a gentle twinkle of the black eyes Mr Quaid implied that he had guessed as much.

'I was talking with him on the subject this afternoon,' Maurice went on, desirous of showing that he did not speak without reason for his speaking, 'and he told me that such was his intention.'

Mr Quaid so far came out of his shell at this as to ask in what way Mr Richard had offended his father.

'That's just what I don't know,' says Frere, leaning forward with a bluff nod. 'It's something he has been doing in Germany, I think.'

Mr Quaid shut up like an oyster immediately, and pouted his lips out to the wineglass, as if he would convey to it an assurance of his profound indifference.

'*In*deed!' said he.

This didn't satisfy Maurice, who, all the afternoon, had been puzzling his brains as to what crime the exiled Richard had committed. Gulping down his glass of wine, he drew his chair a stride nearer to that of the lawyer, and said, in his heartiest manner,

'I suppose you have no idea what it is, Quaid?'

Mr Quaid put down his wineglass, pulled down his waistcoat, and walked over to the fire-place, from which station he turned round, and, viewing his questioner from head to foot, replied,

'Not in the least, Mr Frere.'

In the midst of the awkward silence which this direct rebuff of Mr Frere's curiosity occasioned, there came a ring at the door-bell.

It was the Harwich doctor come to pay his evening visit.

Unwinding himself from his wrappers, he came bowing into the dining-room. A spare, short man, with blue eyes and red nose, and a mouldy smell with him, as though he lived in a graveyard.

'Servant, gentlemen,' he said, bowing. 'How is Sir Richard Devine?'

He rolled out the title as though it tasted well, and stood in the doorway, with his whip in one hand and his hat in the other, bowing.

'Come in, doctor, and have a glass of wine!' says Maurice, in a sudden gush of hospitality. 'You've had a cold ride.'

The doctor – his practice lay chiefly among fishermen, shop-keepers, and the like – sipped at the wine with a profusion of smiles, and rolled it in his mouth as if it tasted almost as well as its owner's title.

'Thank you, sir,' he said; 'and *how* is Sir Richard Devine?'

'Oh, he's asleep, I think,' says Frere. 'We have been expecting his ring every minute. This gentleman is waiting to see him on business.'

As the words were on his lips, the bell abovestairs rang violently.

'Ah!' says Mr Quaid, 'there he is at last.'

But a confusion of noises, unusual and uncalled-for, made them pause and look at each other in sudden alarm.

Then Jarvis's cracked voice was heard calling, and they guessed the worst.

The doctor was in the room first, and when Maurice got there he saw him bending over something hanging heavily against the gaudy blue and yellow livery.

'I thought he was asleep,' says Jarvis, with white lips, 'and when I touched him to wake him, I found he was dead!'

The face was quite calm, but the staring eyes and wide-opened mouth had an astonished look, as if, despite the dead man's boasted readiness to die, Death had come upon him rather suddenly after all.

'Aneurism of the heart,' said the doctor. 'I suspected it long ago. Please go down stairs, gentlemen, you can do no good here.'

He was no longer bashful or ill at ease, but spoke with authority. For he was in his own sphere now, sustained and fortified by the familiar presence of a corpse.

Quaid and Maurice obeyed. The shock stupefied them into silence, but at the threshold of the death chamber their eyes met, and each saw his own thought reflected in the other's face.

Whatever had been Richard Devine's sin against his father, it would go unpunished – at least, by that father's hand. There could be no new will now.

++ 6 ++

WHERE THE KING'S COACH OVERTURNED

IT was seven o'clock in the morning when the young man whose habit of Rampaging had so seriously affected Mr Mogford, descended the broad stairs of the Bell.

Those coaching necessities incident to respectable posting houses had already got the Bell into its usual swing.

In the mild April morning – the rain which had fallen so heavily on Mr Maurice Frere, had but threatened Mr Maurice Frere's chosen supper-house – the old fashioned balustraded court-yard looked cheerful and picturesque, the patch of pavement seen through the double-leaved gateway was sunny and white, and such glimpse of blue sky, flecked with wool-white clouds, as the jealous chimneys of the adjacent houses permitted to be visible, was bright and pure.

The polished taps and glittering glasses of the bar wooed him on the one hand, and the spread cloth of the commercial-room breakfast-table appealed to him on the other.

With his stick over his shoulder, and his bundle on the end of his stick, he paused irresolute. Had there been any one to add persuasion of voice to persuasion of eyesight, he might have proved equal to either fortune but, by one of those odd coincidences upon which so many strange events in our lives turn, the entrance to the inn was for the moment deserted.

Plain Joe Mogford was upstairs, receipting, in his plain way, the bill of a hurriedly breakfasting customer, bound for the momentarily expected coach.

The grooms, stable-boys, and yard-loungers had rushed off in a body to hold consultation over a mysteriously lamed coach-horse.

The waiter was filling the cruet-stands behind his screen, and the smart barmaid, hearing that the facetious cornet of Mr Maurice's acquaintance had been put to bed intoxicated the night before, had profited by the general desolation to slip upstairs and put on a new ribbon.

Thus it happened that the young man came down the stairs, looked round, paused, took another step forward, and finally pressed down his hat, shifted his stick to the hollow of his shoulder, and went out into the street – unseen.

'I can get some breakfast on the road,' he said, 'and the sooner I am away from this place the better.'

The day smoke-cloud had not yet settled, the air was balmy and bright, and all things about him had a wealthy, comfortable look.

Regardless of the glances cast upon his tall, bearded, strange-hatted figure by opening shopkeepers and corner waiters for the coming traffic, he strode on at a quick pace. His new life – as he had planned it – seemed to lay straight before him, and shaking off whatever shadow of the past had weighed upon him in the gloom and darkness of the night, he set out through the bright morning eagerly to meet it.

He seemed to know his road well. Perhaps it was an old acquaintance, as the bedroom at the Bell had been.

Turning to the right into Tottenham Court road, and so away to the left again, past the Mother Red Cap tavern – a great house in those days – he skirted along the rising houses and opening fields, apparently with the intention of getting on to Highgate Hill by a shorter cut than the direct pursuit of the Great North Road would afford him.

Here, as in the more crowded streets, his strange appearance attracted no little attention. Beards and slouch hats were rare in those days, and he wore both. Down about the wharves or riverside, where a strange garb and a bearded chin were no such wondrous rarities, he might have passed unnoticed; on the coach-top even – where travellers of his aspect were frequent enough to make a grin the only toll charged for their dissent from English fashions – he would have been unmolested. But in the quieter and less public streets, through which his journey now lay, the laugh and stare were frequent.

School-boys, going in little knots of three or four to morning school, sniggered and grinned at him. Often a whoop of derision overtook him from some more daring spirits who had turned to gaze, and once a stone flung by some instantly flying urchin, from the cover of a corner, struck the gutter at his feet. An old wooden-legged pensioner, selling tracts out of the battered hulk of an umbrella, asked 'Mussoo' to purchase, with mock politeness that a word of reply would have turned into open abuse. A group of men drinking at the open window of a pot-house, burst out in tipsy roar of old English loyalty as he strode quickly by; and, worse than all, a beggar-woman with a child in her arms, against whom in his preoccupied haste he had pushed somewhat roughly, cursed him with that hearty English outpouring of fluent filth that makes an English beggar's curse so bitter. Stopping in haste to put some conciliatory coin into the creature's hand, he perceived on the opposite side of the way the red and white striped pole of a barber's shop, with the barber himself standing invitingly at the door waiting for a customer.

He could get rid of one source of annoyance at all events; and without hearing the blessings which his unexpected dole had called forth, he left the curtseying woman staring at him with all her bleared eyes, and turned into the barber's.

The barber was a big-bellied, soft-headed person, with a long upper-lip and protruding gooseberry eyes, who fell at once into the popular error.

'Mussoo, want shave?' he asked, rubbing his own double chin with fat forefinger to illustrate his meaning, and smiling like a curdling milk-pan.

Irritated by the persistency of error concerning his nationality which had relentlessly followed him all the morning, the young man lost his temper.

'Yes, you fool,' he said, 'and make haste about it !'

All the milk of human kindness in the barber's cheesy face soured directly.

He glanced at the dusty boots, the velveteen coat, the bundle and the stick, and seemed half inclined to request his intemperate customer to go elsewhere, but a certain air of practised authority in the tone of voice, appealed to his lower-class respect for Power under all conditions, and he only stared.

'Make haste,' said the young man, impatiently throwing himself into a chair, and rejecting with some apparent uneasiness the offer to remove his coat, 'I want to get on.'

'Travelling, sir?' asked the barber, shearing at the youthful beard.

'Yes,' returned the other, 'can't you see I am?'

'From the Continong, I presoom?' ventured the barber with a preliminary flourish of the lather brush.

'Mind your own business!' was the reply, 'and make haste!'

Thus admonished, the barber held his peace vindictively, and shaved with such a will that in a few minutes his customer rose from his seat without a hair on his face.

The change in his appearance took five years off his age.

At the Bell Inn the night before, he had looked nearly thirty; in the barber's little shop, he stood up a young man of two and twenty, square-jawed and firm-lipped it is true, but a young man for all that.

'There,' said the barber, stepping back, resentfully mindful of his late rebuff, '*that's* clean enough. Yer best friend wouldn't know yer now.'

The young man started, and peered into the little glass somewhat nervously.

'Do you think so?' he asked, and then added half to himself, 'I'm glad of that.'

The barber had caught the words, and – still smarting under a sense of unrequited snubbing – plucked up courage to say that 'A young man like him,' – the velveteen blouse metaphorically stuck in his throat, and he couldn't say *gentleman*, 'ought to have plenty of friends.'

The young man, fiercely flashing round from the looking-glass at this, deigned only to demand how much he had to pay.

The barber, malevolently soured in a fresh portion of the cheese, said, 'Twopence, and cheap too!'

The right hand of the young man was bandaged with a blue and white handkerchief, and the effort of thrusting it into his trousers' pocket seemed to re-open an old wound, for it began to bleed.

'Cut your hand?' asked the barber, seeming to notice the bandage for the first time, 'I have some excellent –'

'Don't want it,' returned the other, roughly, 'it's only a scratch. Good morning!' and, seizing his bundle and stick, he clapped his hat on, and was gone.

The barber – every atom of casein in his composition coagulating at the insult – waddled to the door, and glared at the retreating figure of his strange customer.

'You're a surly brute,' he said. 'I shan't forget *you* in a hurry.'

And then, attracted by the noise of wheels, he set himself to watch the progress of a hackney coach, which was ascending the hill beneath him at something very like full gallop.

The young man, unmindful of the bad impression he had left behind him, strode on a little angrily.

'Everything reminds me of my unhappy past,' he said. 'Even that dolt must unconsciously put his finger on a sore spot,' and then, as the recollection of the oleaginous fellow's comic display came upon him, he burst into a laugh.

'What a fool I am!' he said, 'making my own annoyances. I want my breakfast, I suppose.'

By the side of the road nestled a little public-house, whose swing signboard, the *Fox and Crown*, was lettered with an inscription setting forth the stumbling of one of the King's horses, and the consequent overturn of the King's coach at a certain stone opposite the doorway.

Turning in to this tavern, sanctified by the departed presence of overturned Majesty, the young man observed a strange occurrence.

A hackney coach, whose exhausted horses had just topped the hill, had stopped opposite the barber's door, and after a few seconds' excited parley, the barber, all aproned and bare-headed as he was, was seemingly dragged into it, and the vehicle dashed towards the *Fox and Crown*.

'He's going to shave somebody in a great hurry,' thought the young man, as he stepped into the sanded parlour.

A buxom girl bid him welcome with a smile.

'I want something to eat,' he said, placing his stick and bundle on a bench near him.

The noise of galloping horses and grinding wheels suddenly

broke with a crash at the doorway, and the buxom girl, looking away over his shoulder, with a strange terror in her eyes, did not reply.

He turned round in the direction of her glance, and was met – as it seemed to him – by a storm of men, tumbling in upon him with outstretched hands and threatening faces.

'That's him! That's him! There! In the King's name!'

There is a sort of blind Berserk fury of fighting born with some men, which needs but the slightest hint of violence to raise it to its height, and our traveller seemed to be of that number.

Setting his teeth and clenching his hands, he struck two crashing blows to the right and left that knocked two of his assailants spinning to the wall, but in the midst of a shriek from the frightened girl in the bar, the others ran in upon him, and in an instant he was down beneath a heap of struggling figures. For a moment the mass – penned in the narrow passage – heaved and swayed irresolutely, then two snaps as of locking steel, hit the ear, and Mr Mogford's customer of the previous night was dragged to air, handcuffed and helpless.

'What in the devil's name does this mean?' he asked, furiously straining at his bonds.

There were five persons before him. The jarvey, the barber (with a bleeding mouth), two constables, and Mr Mogford himself.

'What does it mean!' cries Plain Joe, wiping the blood and sweat from his face. He had been the first man struck in the short struggle. 'It means Murder, you foreigneering dog, and you know it!'

The prisoner, from whose newly-shaven face all the red fire of fight went suddenly out, leaving it white and ghastly, sank back on the bench.

'Murder!' he echoed. 'Whose murder?'

One of the constables – a purple-cheeked fellow with a raw dewlap of coarsely shaven jowl falling over a ragged collar – burst into a grim laugh.

'Take my advice,' he said, 'and hold your tongue. Wot ever you say may be used against yer, mind that.'

'Why, he's got his handkercher on!' cries Plain Joe, staring in unaffected horror at the prisoner's bleeding steel-locked hands, from which the blue and white handkerchief hung pendant, 'I saw it round his neck last night.'

His handkerchief!

The two words explained all. In an instant the full horror of his position burst upon him, and he understood what had happened.

Hans had been murdered, and he was charged with his murder.

The horrible untruth of the accusation took away his breath, and he could only indignantly gasp, waiting for words that would not come.

'Sarch his pockets, Larkin,' says the constable to his subordinate, 'he's got the swag on him, I expect.'

The look of mingled aversion and interest with which the eight eyes looked at him – as though he was a wild beast – when Larkin approached to do it, assisted, even more than the indignity itself, to give him speech. Springing up with a threatening motion of his manacled hands, and that sort of wild authority which is born of innocence wrongfully accused in his glance, he burst out in indignant expostulation.

'Why do you do this? What proof? What warrant? What authority?'

Plain Joe flung an answer to him in coarse contempt. 'Proof! warrant! Didn't we find your knife sticking in the poor old man's throat? The marks of your bloody hands on your own wainscot? Isn't the old man's handkercher round your wrist, and the old man's blood on your shirt? Warrant! There's warrant enough to hang yer, let alone arrest yer.'

The words fell on him like so many blows, and struck him into silence and submission again. There was warrant enough, certainly.

Nothing in the bundle but a change of linen. Nothing in his pocket but silver and copper, – except a chamois leather bag, tied at the neck by a string, which, on being opened, was found to contain cut and uncut stones, diamonds, rubies, garnets, and the like.

At sight of this, Mr Larkin sniffed like a dog at a rat hole, and a red spot came out on the prisoner's cheek.

The constable peered into it with one sharp eye, and then put it in his pocket.

'*That's* what you killed him for,' he said, slapping it with great relish.

The prisoner said nothing.

As he sat, rose, and turned in obedience to the officer's roughly given orders, all the strange circumstances of the past night, to which this death of his fellow traveller had given importance, rose before him. He remembered in their now significant sequence, the quarrel, the loss of his knife, the cutting of his hand, the borrowing of the handkerchief, the meeting in the passage, the hurried departure, and the unexplained presence on his poverty-stricken person of a bag of jewels. The hideous web of circumstantial evidence, into which he had unwittingly flown, was clear to him, thread by thread. He even comprehended how his strange appearance, and casual meeting with the beggar woman, had given a clue by which he had been tracked, and how his removal of his beard, and conduct at the barber's, could be construed into additional signs of guilt.

Being put into the hackney-coach again – after hasty thumbpieces of bread and cheese, and great draughts of well-earned beer had been consumed by the five – he was rumbled away with, through a mist of staring faces, back to London. All the way the web seemed to narrow, and yet to embrace and bring together all the personages of his little day drama.

Plain Joe, sitting on the box-seat with the jarvey, and lamenting about the injury to his respectable posting-house, was one of them. Mr Larkins, eating barcelona nuts on the opposite seat, was one of them. The constable, sitting beefily beside him, rasping his dewlap on the edge of his uncomfortable collar, was one of them. The fat barber – whose name and address had been taken down by the constable – was another of them; and outside these, concentric circles of attorneys, barristers, witnesses, gaolers, and what not, came closer and closer to him.

With this web – assuming now and then the shape of a big wheel turning round and round the pivot of a bedroom at the Bell – surrounding and enveloping him, he tried to think what was best to be done.

As a stranger advising another man, he would have said,

'Explain the apparent mystery of the gems. Tell who your companion was, and what was his business. Bring friends to prove your affection for him, and your absence of motive for the crime. Shew who you are, and what you have been. Summon your past life and character as a witness in your favour, and crush the evidence of circumstance by the evidence of probability.' But he – sitting there with his new life already begun – knew that he could not do this; that there were reasons why he could *not* explain the business of his dead friend; why he could *not* open up his past life and bring witness to his birth and parentage.

He was there in the clutch of the law, – alone, unarmed, defenceless. He could claim no assistance, save the law in its sneering mercy itself supplied. He had begun a new life, and he could not reanimate the corpse of the old one and make it speak for him.

Be it so. He would take his trial alone, and accept such future as fate had in store for him. He had put his hand to the plough of a changed identity and would not look back.

When the coach had rumbled up to the door of the Bow-street police-office, and he was got into a grim whitewashed room, waiting – as it seemed – for the pleasure of the dewlapped constable, his face had regained its usual colour and his eye his usual confidence.

Two or three copies of Mr Larkin regarded him with some show of interest.

There was to be an inquest to-morrow, it seemed, and he could then be committed, they said, on the coroner's warrant.

'Just keep him snug for the night,' the dewlapped constable said with an easy air. 'What's your name, my man?'

'Rufus Dawes.'

'Trade?'

'Sailor.'

'Rufus Dawes, sailor – on a charge of murder,' repeated his captor, looking at him admiringly, as he might have looked at a neat piece of his own handiwork. 'Take him away.'

⊷ 7 ⊶

THE PUBLIC VERDICT

NEXT to a newly-crowned king, in importance of popular estimation, comes a newly discovered murderer.

That morbid love for the horrible which is the portion of ignorant or ill-balanced minds, renders a great criminal a great hero in the minds of the people. They shudder at his iniquity, but they admire the exceptional position in which his iniquity has placed him. The more ferocious the deed of blood, the more popular the doer of it. Women faint at sight of him. Men fling stones and curses. The crowd round the gallows palpitates with mingled admiration and rage. 'The wretch! The villain! See! Look! He stands firm! He has a bold face! He dies game!' The hideous attraction to the exceptional is the secret why all these Newgate calendars, bloody stories, and sensational plays are so popular. The vulgar soul longs to be astonished, and it is astonished most by a violent departure from that state of existence in which it is itself placed. Othello is all very well; but what story of smothered Desdemona can equal in grim horror the sight of Doll Tearsheet lying in the next room with her throat cut? The reverence of a scholar for a poet is prompted by an appreciation of exceptional genius. The awe with which the house-breaker speaks of Corder, Palmer, or Manning, arises from a terribly keen sense of their exceptional atrocity. The common mind cannot understand how Tennyson or Carlyle have become famous, but it acknowledges at once the claims of Muller or Tropmann.

Gross creatures must have gross pleasures. To attempt to interest the people in the 'Holy Grail' is like offering a pinch of snuff to a mammoth. If you want to convince a drayman that he is in the wrong, you must knock his head against the wall; Locke himself could not convince him by sheer logic. This is why the coarse, the broad, and the strong-savouring are always popular. The people like to be rubbed hard, for their skins are tough. Tennyson, Mill, Disraeli, are not thought about, but every labourer in England has heard of Wellington and Napoleon.

Great generals are always popular, for blood, wounds, and pillage are evidences of their excellence, which cannot be mistaken. A murderer is a General viewed through the small end of the telescope. He is the only man who is a prophet in his own country. Hero worship is natural, and the bricklayer who goes to see a hanging, or buys a 'dying speech' to take home as a relish to his pipe, is only displaying another phase of the feeling which got Mahomet worshipped, Cæsar crowned, and Tom Thumb patronised. The populace is equally kind to giants and dwarfs; it is only intelligent mediocrity that comes so badly off.

The monstrosity of a great crime always interests the people. They like a monstrosity in any shape – Tom Thumb, Ching-Chang, Bearded women, Winking pictures, and Tightrope dancers – but of all these monstrosities, a hideous murder is more admirable than all. The blood and brains, the war of evidence, the pomp of judgment, the sentence, the press room, and the gibbet, are so real, so exciting, so different from cut and dried stage performances. The monstrosity of a Hanged Man is delightful.

This delight took possession of the Bell Inn immediately. If it had only been a respectable posting-house two days before, it was now a place of deep interest to numbers of persons.

Men who had never been in that locality in their lives before, came in furtively and demanded beer, staring about them in an awe-stricken way, as though they expected to see the dead man sitting up in a corner grinning at them while they drank it. Passers by would drop in and converse with Plain Joe, casually referring to 'It,' as if 'It' was a well understood term, and meant only and absolutely the corpse of a murdered man discovered in a second-floor bedroom at nine o'clock on a May morning. Old cronies of Plain Joe were eager to give *their* opinion as to 'how it was done,' and in the dingy parlour behind the bar, the scene of the imaginary struggle and stabbing was enacted over and over again.

The house was for a few days turned upside down. The smart barmaid was besieged with strange attentions. Travellers by the up and down coaches stared at the locked door of No. 29, with shuddering curiosity, and the waiters made small fortunes by illegitimate openings of the fatal chamber. The papers were full of particulars, the handbills and 'cocks,' that were in those days sold by the bushel to servant-girls and cook-maids, were headed with a hurriedly executed woodcut, representing a young man lying on his back with a knife sticking in his breast, and a young woman in a low dress and ringlets running away in horror. Not that there was any young woman in the case, but the picture was a good one, and brought money.

One gentleman, more daring than his fellows, boldly sold 'the last dying speech and confession of the Holborn murderer,' though it wanted nearly a month to the Old Bailey sessions, and the Holborn murderer was lying stolidly in Newgate prison, with the avowed intention of pleading not guilty.

His plea would not be of much use to him it was thought. In public opinion he had been hung ten thousand times over, and was as good as dead and buried already.

The evidence was clear against him. At the inquest, proof after proof came out with damning persistency; and the Press, ever ready to tie a knot for the hangman, had commented upon the case as upon one of proved and satisfactory guilt. Public interest was excited, not by any suspicion of innocence wrongfully accused, but by a certain air of mystery that hung over the persons of the murderer and his victim.

The dead man was a German, named Hans, whom the prisoner Rufus Dawes said he had met on board the vessel which had brought them both from Amsterdam. It had been put about that he was a travelling jeweller, but that was but surmise. His name was all that was known about him, and that but on the authority of the prisoner. That the prisoner could tell more if he liked was generally believed, but he would say nothing.

So the stabbed and mangled body of the poor little German having been duly viewed by the jury, was put away in a comfortable hole in some handy churchyard, and left to decay in peace; and the body of his murderer, handed over to the safe custody of the governor of Newgate by virtue of the coroner's warrant, awaited trial and execution.

No one doubted his guilt. There had been some faint attempt at the inquest to bring in a story of some other person. Some 'friend of the landlord,' the prisoner had said, 'who came in while he was drinking and had spoken with his fellow-traveller;'

but Plain Joe Mogford had soon dispelled that cloud by his bluff honesty.

'The man spoken of was a brother o' his – not much credit to him either – who frequently came to see him, and was well known to the neighbours and to several of the jury.'

'What had this brother seen?'

'Nothing. He could only confirm the evidence already given. He was with Plain Joe when the deceased went up to bed, and Plain Joe had let him out himself.'

'Where was he to be found?'

'Well – that was hard job to say. The last time he was aworking was as servant to a genelman at 'Ornsey, but Plain Joe would guarantee to have him up on the trial, if he was wanted.'

Smug jurymen bowing their intense confidence in Plain Joe's honesty and respectability, the guarantee was accepted. The coroner remarking that Mr Mogford's brother might be able to give some additional proof of the prisoner's guilt; though, from the evidence of the knife, handkerchief, and shirt, there seemed to be none required.

The prisoner shut his teeth close at this, and breathed hard; like a wild animal might do, if he found himself in a trap in which the only visible chink that gave promise of escape had been blocked up. Once or twice indeed, when the surmise and suspicion as to his friendship and relations with the dead man was most unfavourable to him, he had seemed about to speak, but checked himself hastily, and relapsed into gloomy, watchful silence.

When the commit-warrant was made out, and he was rumbled off with to Newgate – to all intents and purposes a doomed man, as he well knew – he said nothing.

'He had no friends, and desired to see no one. But if they would bring him a newspaper with the account of the inquest in it, he would be obliged.'

8

MR QUAID'S OPINION

THE newspaper accounts of the inquest and murder did not differ very much, and the story of the crime was told in pretty much the same way in all of them.

That given by the *Globe*, which was read by Mr Quaid and Maurice Frere on the morning of the 6th, will serve as well as any other to show how ugly things looked from a popular point of view.

MURDER AND ROBBERY AT THE BELL INN, HOLBORN

This morning, at nine o'clock, the inquest was held on the body of the unfortunate German pedler who was found stabbed in his bed at the Bell yesterday.

In a paragraph in our last night's issue we published the current report that the murderer had been secured. We are glad to be able to confirm the intelligence. He was taken at Highgate, endeavouring it is supposed, to make his escape to the North, as he would naturally guess that all the seaports would be closely watched, and was to-day committed to Newgate on the coroner's warrant. He is a tall, strongly-built young man of about two or three and twenty, but of harsh and forbidding appearance. He is a sailor by profession, and gives the name of Rufus Dawes. He is cool and collected in manner, and persists in denying his guilt. He was taken at the door of a barber's shop on Highgate Hill, where he had been removing his beard, and otherwise disguising himself. On being examined, his shirt was found to be stained with blood, and the stock-in-trade of the pedler was secreted on his person.

It appears that the pedler, whose name is stated by the prisoner to be Hans, came, in company with the murderer, to the Bell Inn. He had with him a black box, of which he was very careful, and which was supposed to contain jewellery. Before going to bed, Mr Mogford, the landlord, says that he served them with bread and cheese and beer, and that shortly afterwards he heard sounds as of disputing. On coming in, however (accompanied by his brother), the prisoner became suddenly most friendly, and ordered more liquor for the company. Shortly afterwards, all went to bed. About half an hour afterwards, Mr Mogford, who was making his nightly tour of the premises, met the prisoner in the passage – he thinks, in his shirt and trousers – and, on asking him what he wanted at that hour, was told that he (the prisoner) had forgotten something. He thought nothing of the circumstance at the time, nor of the fact that the prisoner persisted in paying him for his bed before going upstairs, although told that it was not the custom of the house. In the morning neither the prisoner ·nor the deceased appeared, but in the usual business bustle of the hotel, their absence was unnoticed. About nine o'clock, however, Mr Mogford found the body of the deceased lying on the floor in a pool of blood. A white-handled knife, which Mr Mogford had noticed in the possession of the man Dawes the night before, was found near the body, and the wainscot of Dawes' room was smeared with bloody fingermarks. Acting at once upon the suspicions thus aroused, Mr Mogford obtained the assistance of a constable, and proceeded to follow the prisoner, whose strange dress and appearance made him very remarkable. They luckily got upon his track at once, and being confirmed in their course by an old veteran and a beggar-woman, both of whom had seen a man answering exactly to the description of the prisoner, they hastened the pursuit and took the ruffian, after a desperate struggle, at the door of a Mr Prell, a barber, in High-street.

He was at once identified by Mr Mogford, despite the change in his appearance caused by the removal of his beard, and taken to Bow-street, whence he was removed this afternoon to Newgate. He seems to have no remorse for the dreadful deed which has rendered him justly amenable to the laws of his offended country, but preserves a moody silence. As an instance of his indifference, we may mention that his right hand, which, it would seem, he had injured in the struggle with his victim, was bound up with a cotton handkerchief which Mr Mogford remembered to have seen on the neck of the murdered man the night before.

The body of the deceased was found lying on the floor of the bed-chamber, entangled in the bedclothes, and it is presumed that he must have partially recovered from the wounds inflicted on him by his cowardly assailant, and died in the effort to summon assistance.

Plunder is evidently the motive for this brutal crime. A number of cut and uncut jewels – evidently the stock-in-trade of the poor fellow who thus so cruelly met his death – were found upon Rufus Dawes. The black case, however, which was last seen in the possession of the deceased, cannot be found. It is presumed that the prisoner took the first opportunity of ridding himself of so dangerous and conspicuous a witness against him.

He was fully committed to take his trial at the next (June) Old Bailey sessions on a charge of Wilful Murder.

Maurice Frere and Quaid were at breakfast when the paper containing this account arrived.

The gloom of death was on the house. Sir Richard was to be buried in a day or two, and the reading of the will would follow as soon as convenient.

Maurice was upon thorns until he should know his fate, and Quaid – sly, reserved, and abrupt as ever – gave him no sign. Thrown much into each other's company during the last two days, they had grown as familiar as was possible to such opposite natures, and chatted easily enough. Quaid, tired of the dreary house, and eager to get back to Thavies Inn and business, had pleaded his work as an excuse for departure, and was to go that afternoon, to return for the will-reading whenever the time was fixed for it.

Frank, sad and sick at heart, never lingered at table longer than he could help; and when the morning mail arrived, the lawyer and the soldier were alone.

Mr Maurice Frere, coming to the tasteful concoction of the reporter for the *Globe*, first started, then swore, and then handed it to Quaid.

'Why curse it, Quaid!' he said, 'I was supping at the infernal place that very night!'

Quaid ran his eye down the proffered column, and started.

'I – I – I slept there,' he said, a little uneasily, and clutched the paper to read.

'The devil you did! What took *you* there?'

'I had been to see about some law business – a trust estate at Egham,' says the other, munching his toast, and talking with eye still fixed on the paper; 'and calling at the office on the way home in the afternoon, got poor Sir Richard's letter. I saw it was urgent, and so took a bed at the Bell, in order to catch the first coach.'

'Did you see anything of the business, then?' asked Maurice, with that eager curiosity in matters of bloodshed which was part of his fine old English nature.

'No,' returned Quaid. 'I left by the half-past seven coach, and nothing was heard of it at that hour. Ah! I see the *Globe* says that the body wasn't found until nine o'clock.'

'Didn't you hear *anything*, then?' asked Maurice. 'No row in the night? No strugglings or thumpings, you know? One would think that it would be a difficult matter to cut a man's throat without *some* noise.'

'No,' returned Quaid, glancing with the faintest possible hint of disgust at the eager face of his questioner. 'I heard nothing, but –'

He paused abruptly, checking himself with a sudden frown, as though a thought had occurred to him which it was best not to utter.

'But – what?' says Maurice.

Quaid, who had for an instant been gazing into vacancy with a somewhat startled look, brought his black eyes back to the room again, and rose from the table.

'But it seems rather a curious case,' he said, carrying the paper with him to a chair, and referring to it as he spoke. 'What could the man be doing with uncut jewels? And this Dane, Daw, Dawes – what's his name? – is a mysterious sort of fellow. I always suspect a mystery when a prisoner talks too little or too much at the inquest.'

'Mystery!' says Frere, throwing himself back in his chair as impatiently as was consistent with that gravity of manner which is held proper to be assumed in a house of mourning. 'I can see no mystery. It seems to me as plain as a pikestaff. The sailor sees the other one's money, you know, slits his weasand for him in the night, takes the black box and bolts. There's no mystery in *that*, bigod!'

Quaid, rubbing his sharp face thoughtfully, glanced up with a queer twinkle in his black eye.

'If the jury are all of your way of thinking, Mr Frere,' said he,

'I wouldn't give much for Rufus Dawes' chance of seeing the second Tuesday in the month of June.'

'How so?' asked Mr Frere, with a not displeased affectation of ignorance.

'Because they'd hang him, my dear sir,' returned Quaid, grimly.

'By George, sir!' says Maurice, 'it seems to me that they're likely enough to do that as it is! I don't see a chink for the fellow to put a finger through. Do you?'

'I was just thinking,' returned Quaid, 'We lawyers have the reputation of being smart fellows, and many a poor devil in a worse plight than Rufus Dawes has saved his neck by our means.'

'Hullo! hullo!' says Maurice, 'are *you* going to defend him?'

'I was thinking about it. I take quite an interest in the case – it having happened when I was in the house. Besides, from a professional point of view, I consider it offers considerable inducements.'

'Oh I see!' says Mr Frere, laughing with a sort of quiet boistrousness. 'You are thinking of the interests of Purkiss and Quaid.'

'Precisely so, my dear sir. The interests of a firm like ours are always benefitted by being concerned in cases of importance.'

'Well, but hang it!' says the other, in his freest and most offensive old English manner, 'you don't call this thing "a case of importance?" I thought it was the money you were thinking of.'

Mr Quaid, Old Bailey lawyer, and chosen repository of many a bitter secret, was pretty thick-skinned – indeed the dead millionaire above stairs had tested the strength of his mental cuticle pretty frequently – but the bluff insolence of the red-headed heir-expectant made him wince.

'Can't you understand that there are other things worth having in this world besides money, Mr Frere?' he said abruptly. And then changing his tone a little, added, 'Don't you see that the clearer the case seems against a man, the greater the credit of getting him off?'

'Oh!' says the bluff Maurice, still unmoved, 'the more certain it is that a man *has* committed murder, the more a lawyer enjoys saving his life! Damme, that's a queer notion, too!'

The facile Quaid laughed.

'Come, come! That's special pleading, Mr Frere. You push me too hard, upon my word.'

Maurice was flattered at the implied compliment.

'Well, I wish you luck,' he said. 'Save the poor devil's neck from stretching, by all means, if you can.'

'I'll try,' says Quaid, with a smile, pulling out his watch. 'Let's see, the chaise will be here in five minutes! I'll go and see after my traps.'

'You won't forget to come down when the – arrangement – you know!' says Mr Frere, giving his head a backward jerk towards the door.

'You mean the will,' says Quaid, abruptly decisive. 'Oh, dear no! I shall be here.'

'When do you think?' asked Frere. 'It's cursed dull here, you know.'

'I should say about the beginning of next month. There are several little matters to arrange.'

And he made for the door.

'I say,' says Maurice, stopping him, 'what about Dick – my cousin, you know? Oughtn't he to be written to?'

'Nobody knows where to write to him. Perhaps we may find his address among the papers upstairs; but I have sealed them up for the executors, and placed them in Mr Francis' charge.'

'Um!' says Maurice. 'It's a strange thing about him, isn't it?'

'Oh,' says Quaid, looking cheerily askance at him out of his bird-bright eyes, 'you mustn't get dispirited! I have no doubt that the mystery will be very easily explained when he comes back.'

'Oh, dam it, *I*'m not dispirited!' says Frere, with clumsy affectation of intense heartiness.

Mr Quaid laughed.

'I'll be down as soon as possible for the will,' he said, as the sound of the wheels on the gravel warned him to be gone.

'All right! Catch a lawyer being too late!' returned the other, stuffing the cloaks and valise into the vehicle. '*I*'m not anxious about it; not I! But it is rather curious, you know, isn't it?'

Quaid smiled a sharply suave assent. He had a smile like mingled vinegar and oil, the oil uppermost; and as he composed himself on the cushions of the departing chaise, he drew from his pocket the newspaper that had so interested him at breakfast, and applied himself to a careful perusal of its contents.

'Yes,' he said at last, restoring the broadsheet carefully to his breast, 'if my surmise is right, it is *very* curious.'

But whether he was replying to Mr Frere's observations, or to his own thoughts, there was nothing to shew.

9

BOUND TO THE WHEEL

THE big wheel, which had for a pivot the bedroom at the Bell, was turning round and round as swiftly and noiselessly as ever.

Rufus Dawes – sitting in the middle of his web, in his cell at Newgate – was getting somewhat confused with the incessant turning. Nothing stopped it. Whether he sat with forehead gripped in his hands, desperately trying to squeeze some assisting thought out of his hot head, and by force of pressure to catch and bring together into serviceable fire of expedient, the multitude of sparks which his throbbing brain was sending off in all directions, he still saw the remorseless wheel bringing the first of June nearer and nearer to him. If he paced his cell in vain endeavour to still the tumult of his mind by the monotonous beat of his footsteps, he was conscious of it. When he woke in the morning he would for an instant forget it; but scarcely were his eyes open, when the knowledge of its ruthless motion would come upon him with a shock that made him unavailingly try to shrink back again into his heavy slumber. If he started – as he often did – from his pallet in the night, with clammy skin, and bristling hair, pale from the clutches of some hideous dream, he would know that in the dimness and the silence of the prison, it was softly and swiftly turning. He knew that by day and night, through clashing of keys and harsh gratings of doors, through dull noises heard afar off, through rough voices heard close at hand, through the muffled, never-ceasing roar which was the London that encompassed him, the mighty wheel would still turn on. He knew that it would so turn through law-pleadings, and Grand Jury findings of true bills, through hum and buzz of court, through sudden silence and clear spoken sentence, through jangling of fetters and muttering of prayers, until – amid one wild yell of hideous delight – it would be stopped for ever by the 'jar' of the plucking rope.

And yet, borne down and crushed by the weight of this knowledge – happily denied in all its terrible fullness to one less imaginative or less sensitive to mental impressions – he was out-wardly calm and quiet. Self-willed, self-reliant, and desperate with the silent desperation of the gambler who has played his last stake, Rufus Dawes, whatever he might have been in his old life, was determined to meet the fortunes of his new one without complaint.

In that past time of folly and sin, which he had resolved to fling behind him and forget, he had often been in need of steady nerves and a strong will, but never was he in such sore need as now. That past time – flung away now and forgotten – held many a secret, at the telling of which respectability might frown, but it held no such mystery as the one he had vowed to keep locked in his own heart, and to carry to the grave, if need be, with him. That past time might have owned to record of violence and vice, perhaps of crime, but in its blurred and blotted leaves – to be pasted down and obliterated for ever in the future – was no such terrible accusation as that under which he now laboured.

He was in his worst strait now. His effort to escape from the unnamed bondage which would seem to have held him, had brought him to this pass. He had leapt from the sinking ship, only to choke amid the surges. His imagined rock of safety had proved but a quicksand, and the rising tide would swallow him up. He was as the King of Arabian legend, who plunging his head beneath the transforming water, withdrew it but to see glitter in its upward sweep the axe of the executioner. His own act had cut off from him all hope of retreat or assistance. If he was to escape at all, it must be by his own ability, and through his own courage in grappling with the difficulties in his path.

And the remorseless wheel was ever silently turning, bringing his doom nearer and nearer.

It had turned for the best part of a week since his arrest, when it paused for a while.

Mr Quaid – of the firm of Purkiss and Quaid, 5 Thavies Inn, attorneys – was the cause of its stoppage.

That gentleman having gathered into his hands the various red-tape strings, which his answer to the sudden summons of Sir Richard Devine had left hanging loose, had taken upon him-self to look after the interests of the unfriended prisoner.

This was not done from purely benevolent motives; for, as

might have been expected from the confidence reposed in him by the dead ship-builder, Mr Quaid was not a benevolent man.

The firm of Purkiss and Quaid was one of the most noted in all London for sharp practice. Its services could always be purchased, and it took care that they should be worth purchasing. Wealth and influence could always range Purkiss and Quaid on their side. Sin, plated with gold, found in Purkiss and Quaid two admirable and all sufficient reasons why the strong lance of legal justice should harmless break; but found to its cost that, when clothed in rags, Purkiss and Quaid would stand calmly by and permit a pigmy's straw to pierce it. How and from whence it rose to its dubious eminence, no one could exactly tell. In the gloomy depths of Thavies Inn it had taken root and flourished noiselessly, and now all sorts of birds of prey roosted in its branches. Old lawyers with long memories said that the first case which brought Purkiss into notice was his defence of a ship-chandler, prosecuted for some flagrant infamy in connection with maggotty beef. But that was years ago, – when Quaid was only a clerk in the office, not the junior partner.

Purkiss was an old man – nearly as old as Sir Richard Devine – with white hair and grandchildren. His passion was money-making; and though feeble in health, he would sit up day and night, did need arise, in the cause of a wealthy client. He was greedy, callous, and secret. No revelation of guilt – made in a professional capacity – could astonish or disgust him. No protestation of injured innocence – if unaccompanied by a fee – could draw from him more than a half-incredulous bow of helpless sympathy. He would not move a finger, gratis, to save an innocent man from the gallows, but he would give the best endeavours of his keen, unscrupulous intellect, the most treasured fruits of his well-earned and sinister experience, to let loose upon society the most hardened and guilty criminal, who was able to pay for the privilege.

Quaid was a bachelor, abrupt, selfish, and hard, but convivial and humorous. He was, comparatively speaking, a young man, and coming into the business when the business was made, had not gone through so fiercely grinding a mill as his partner. He likewise was unscrupulous; but, though recognising to its fullest extent the great principle of 'doing nothing for nothing,' was in his way generous and open-handed. As long as his generosity caused him no self-denial, he indulged it, and knowing how small acts of charity raise the reputation, had laboured, with some success, to sow a crop of reproductive good deeds among that lower criminal class which frequently sought his assistance. He was proud of his ability and reputation; and his vainer temperament, joined to a certain quality of foresight, made him eagerly seize an opportunity of enhancing the professional character of the firm, by the conduct of cases which were intrinsically almost unremunerative.

It was something of this vanity, mixed, perhaps, with some stronger interest than he as yet cared to own, that prompted him to volunteer his formidable assistance to Rufus Dawes.

'I was in the house,' he said, 'and take an interest in the matter.'

Rufus Dawes, finding the progress of his torturing wheel thus checked for a moment, was dumbfounded.

The lawyer – smiled upon by Governor and Chaplain, saluted respectfully by Gaolers, and mutely recognised with shambling bows by Prisoners – had introduced himself with assurance, but – strange as it may seem – the prisoner felt half inclined to look coldly on him.

He had known from the first that he must have some adviser in the coming trial, and that if he was to escape at all he must not trust his fate to merely official hands; but, though the turnkey – whom the wheel brought to the surface three times a day in the course of its revolutions – had suggested 'P's and Q's' (as the great firm was called in the slang of its vulgarer patrons) as the only lawyers who could benefit him in his present plight, he had not decided what to do. Such eminence of Old Bailey practice would cost money to attain, and he had nothing save the clothes he wore; for the little bag of jewels of which he was so strangely possessed, was held in custody as property that of right belonged to the murdered man. He was told, indeed, that the friends of prisoners of the poorest class had often subscribed to purchase the great men's services, – but then – he had no friends.

When the door opened, then, one morning, and gave to him unasked the very man he had despaired of securing, he felt a little alarmed.

He had a secret to guard, though it might not be one of murder; and the sudden intrusion aroused in him that suspicion which is born of concealment.

'My name is Quaid,' said his visitor, 'of Purkiss and Quaid, and I am going to act for you.'

He looked at him curiously as he spoke, and Rufus Dawes shrunk back.

'I am poor,' he said.

The tone of the sentence, not less than the sentiment it conveyed – a strange one in such a place and at such a time – told the lawyer that he had to deal with no ordinary Jack of the forecastle or vagabond of the wharves.

'Of course you are. I don't want your money. I slept in the house on the night of the murder, and I am interested in the case. Take my services or refuse them, as you please.'

The black eyes scrutinised him from head to foot, and Rufus Dawes hesitated.

'I may not be able to save you after all, but still it is as well to have a chance. It's ill work for a stout young fellow like you to swing at a rope's end.'

The wheel began to turn again, and Rufus Dawes accepted.

Mr Quaid pulled the paper containing the inquest from his pocket, and opened it on his knee.

'If this account is correct, Dawes, I think I see just the ghost of a chance for you. You will plead Not Guilty, of course?'

'Yes.'

'Quite so. In the first place, then, did you really do it or not?'

'Do what?'

'Kill him, of course.'

'No!'

'You may tell me without fear, you know. I have kept confidences quite as strange.'

'So help me God, I didn't!'

Mr Quaid raised his eyebrows a little pettishly.

'It will be much better for you if you tell me all about it,' he said. 'I can see my way much clearer if you tell me all about it.'

The wheel began to turn again, and Rufus Dawes got up with a helpless, angry motion of his hands. Even to this man his guilt seemed clear.

'Good heaven!' he cried, staring at his strangely-engaged attorney, 'are you, too, deceived by the terrible evidence of circumstances? I thought you volunteered to defend me because you thought me innocent!'

The respectable lawyer laughed his sinister laugh.

'No,' he said, 'it was because I thought you Guilty!'

The other stared at him. His brain, dazed with the motion of the whirling wheel, could not appreciate these subtleties of criminal practice.

'However, that is neither here nor there. If you won't tell me now, never mind.'

'But I am innocent!'

Quaid ignored the remark, as one would ignore the fretful denial of an obstinate and silly child, and continued.

'You perhaps will get confidence as you go on. In the meantime, tell me about this German fellow. Who is he? – what is he? I see you were particularly careful to know nothing about him at the inquest. Do you intend to carry out that line of conduct in court?'

Rufus Dawes, striking his hands on his knees impatiently, made no reply.

'It would be far better to prove your friendship with him, and say who he is, and so on. But I suppose you can't do that?'

The prisoner sprang up in an irritable outburst at his enforced examination.

'No, no,' he said; ' I can't, of course, or I would have done so then.'

'Exactly. It would be dangerous, I suppose. Well, now, before we go any further, tell me as much, or as little, as you will.'

Rufus Dawes leaned forward as if to speak, and then checking himself, clasped his face in his hands, and rocked himself to and fro silently.

Quaid – watching him with a careful and yet indifferent curiosity, as a chemist might watch the inanimate metal writhe and twist under the action of a corroding acid – waited quietly for the paroxysm to pass.

In a second or two the swaying ceased, and Rufus Dawes raised his face, colourless, but calm.

'Listen to me, Mr Quaid,' he said. 'You have come here to

help me. I need help sorely enough, God knows. You think me guil¦v of this crime. Perhaps, with such evidence as you have, you cannot do otherwise. But let that pass. You ask me to tell you as much or as little as I please. I am not what I seem to be – as you have guessed – but such as I appear to be, I must remain. Nothing can alter that. I can tell you no more than you know already. I am a sailor. I met the dead man at the inn; we were fellow-travellers. I went away in the morning without being seen. He was murdered in the night, and I was charged with his murder.'

Quaid, surprised at the unexpected manner of the prisoner, had raised his head and was eyeing him with keen curiosity.

'Do you mean to say, man, that you're going to stick to that story?'

Rufus Dawes made an attempt to smile.

'It's the only one I have,' he said.

Quaid patted his foot upon the ground and took a huge pinch of snuff.

'But what about the knife and the jewels?'

'The jewels are my own, but I can't prove that; the knife is mine, but how it came in – where it was found, I don't know. It must have been stolen from me while I was asleep.'

'Tush! And the handkerchief?'

'That was his; he gave it to me to bind up my hand. I cut it – here, see – with the window.'

Quaid jumped up.

'With the window! How? Was it unfastened?'

'Yes. The hasp was broken.'

A triumphant flash crossed the lawyer's sharp face.

'You fool!' he cried – 'tell me all that passed that night, and I'll untwist the rope from your throat yet.'

'I can tell you no more,' replied Rufus Dawes, almost fiercely; 'I went into the other's room to bid him good night, and never saw him again.'

'What! Go into the room of a casual fellow-traveller to bid him "good night" at *that* hour?'

The blood rushed to the prisoner's face.

'Well, he was not a casual acquaintance, if you will have it,' he said; 'but who or what he was, doesn't matter.'

The lawyer was quite elated at this admission.

'Ho! ho!' he said. 'No, of course, he wasn't. You Ass, do you intend to blurt out your guilt in the dock like that?'

The wheel went round again, and Rufus Dawes felt himself going round with it.

'Oh!' he cried, 'save me, if you can! Save me, for God's sake, from this dog's death! But I can tell you no more; I can tell you no more.'

Quaid looked down on him, with a sort of admiration. He had seen many staunch fellows, but few so staunch as this one.

'Well then,' he said, not unkindly, 'if you are determined to keep your relationship with the man a mystery, I won't press you for it; but you must be more careful than this. Now tell me about Mr Mogford's brother.'

'The man who came in? He was tall and thin. I don't remember him well. He was there when I went to bed.'

'You had been in the house before?'

'N—'

'Remember, it is in evidence that you said you had.'

'Yes.'

'And you only went once into this man's room?'

'Only once.'

'Did you hear any noise in the night?'

'No.'

'Think again.'

The prisoner shook his head mournfully.

'No. I was tired out, and I slept heavily.'

'No sound as of an opening window, or –?'

'I see what you mean!' cried Dawes, rapidly. 'You mean that it is possible that some one came in at the unhasped window, and –'

'It is possible,' said Quaid, drily.

'But who could know – about the box – the – oh, heaven! could the landlord's brother have been –?'

He stopped.

Mr Quaid, all his usual calmness returned, was looking at him with a puzzled expression.

'You take a hint quickly,' he said: 'but I wonder it never occurred to you before.'

'What do you mean? I never thought – never suspected –'

'Well,' said Quaid, rising, 'now you can think as much as you like; only don't talk, that's all. I'll see you again by and by.'

The explanation of the crime which the words of the lawyer had suggested, seemed like an inspiration.

He caught Quaid by the sleeve.

'Have him found!' he cried. 'Have him found! Hunt him down, and bring him to justice!'

Quaid stopped him with a frown that was not without a hint of alarm in it.

'Hold your tongue, you fool,' he said, 'or I wash my hands of the whole affair. Hunt him down indeed! Are you mad?'

Rufus Dawes was dumbfounded.

'What do you mean?' he asked, in an astonished whisper, as the clash of keys gave warning of the turnkey's approach. 'Why not? Why keep an innocent man in prison when the real murderer is abroad?'

'Innocent man! Hunt him down!' repeated Quaid, with half-contemptuous pity. 'Upon my word, Mr Dawes, you want to go a little too far.'

And so the strange interview ended, and Rufus Dawes was left to watch the wheel going round and round again.

Quaid, returning – with much jingling of keys and clashing and slapping of bolts – into outer air, seemed much tickled by the prisoner's behaviour.

'A staunch fellow,' he said, that night when dining with Purkiss. 'It is quite a pleasure to defend a fellow like that!'

Old Purkiss brought his white eyebrows down over his claret-coloured cheeks, and shook his experienced head unsympathetically.

'You had better take care, Quaid,' he said. 'It's a ticklish trick, you know, and I don't like the man's eagerness. You have shown him a chance of getting off, and he'll take it, even if he hangs somebody else.'

'Oh, we'll manage it without *that*!' says Quaid, laughing. '*That* would be too good a joke!'

10

PLAIN JOE IS PUT OUT OF HIS WAY

PLAIN JOE MOGFORD, partaking of the increased importance that was attached to his respectable posting-house, began to feel the burden of fame.

So many people came to the Bell, and peered about, and looked into cupboards and round corners, and everywhere where they had no legal or ostensible business to look, that Plain Joe was quite put off his balance.

Upstairs and downstairs, in the yard and stable, he was constantly meeting strange faces, staring at nothing in particular with all their might. So much did this annoy him, that he would seize his hat and rush out, endeavouring, by much perambulation of the streets, to regain his wonted calmness. He began to be a little sulky and short with inquiring visitors, and the smart barmaid (to whom the excitement had brought no less than three eligible proposals) remarked, with candour, that 'she wished to goodness gracious that the trial was over and done with, for Mr M. was worrittin' hisself dreadful.' Moreover, it was considered only correct and proper for Plain Joe to drink with every human creature that could by any possibility frame an excuse for drinking; and, as such excuses were easily made, it followed that Plain Joe drank a good deal more than was good for him. Moreover, he was getting a little uneasy. He had promised, at the coroner's inquest, to produce his brother Jerry as witness, if required, and desirous, in his unsuspecting plainness, of fulfilling his promise, had hunted high and low for him. But in vain. Mr Jeremiah Mogford was not to be found.

He was certainly not in the house of the 'genelman at 'Ornsey.' Indeed, Plain Joe did not look there, being conscious that no such genelman really existed; that the house at 'Ornsey was but a figment of his own inventive brain; but, strange to say, he was not – so it seemed – in any other place. His accustomed haunts were mysteriously visited by Plain Joe at all sorts of mysterious hours, but without success.

Mother Bunch, of the Strawberry Pottle, Short's Gardens, Drury Lane, being asked for Jerry the Lurker, replied, with some asperity, that she hadn't seen him for more than a month, and that if Mr Mogford (in a very rough coat, and hat pulled very much over his eyes) was a friend of his, there was a small account extant, in the liquidation of which friendship might be usefully employed.

Old Cocum, the proprietor of the Cat and Wheel, Wentworth-street, Whitechapel – known as the 'padding-ken' – had not seen the lost sheep for a like period. He was not in Portpool-lane, Fox-court, Chequer-alley, or Rochester-row. Seven Dials had not beheld him, and the Holy Land generally knew him not. Mr Mogford, in his eagerness, getting as far as Long-lane and Old Kent-street, found his inquiries hailed with astonishment. Jerry the Lurker had not been there for months, and the 'deputy' at Cagmag's boarding-house, in Kent-street, told him that he believed that the object of his inquiries had given up the 'monkery' altogether.

Used as he was to his vagabond brother's vagabond ways, Plain Joe was a little alarmed. He had promised to produce him on the trial, and the trial was now close at hand. He did not wish the world to know that the respectable host of the Bell owned so disreputable a relative as Pattering Jerry, the thief, swindler, begging-letter writer, and bird of prey generally. His life had been spent in keeping that knowledge secret, and he knew that if his brother did not appear in his respectable character when wanted, inquiry and consequent exposure of his true position would be inevitable. It was seldom that Jerry had been sunk below the surface for so long a time. He usually was only too easily found, and too ready to thrust himself into his rich brother's money-bestowing presence. The ten pounds he had obtained on the night of the murder must, in the natural course of Jerry's financial existence, have been long since spent, and its recipient greedy for more. Why, then, had he disappeared so mysteriously?

At last, Plain Joe's alarm was brought to a crisis. One afternoon he was coming out of Drummond's banking-house – he had the reputation of being a 'warm man' – when he was met by no less a person than Mr Quaid.

It was some few days after that gentleman's visit to Newgate, but his thoughts were still occupied with his client's interests.

'Hillo!' said he, abruptly stopping Plain Joe. 'Beg your pardon, but your name's Mogford, isn't it?'

Plain Joe started a little nervously at this sudden attack, and said that it was.

'Just so,' returned the lawyer. 'Don't remember me? Slept at the Bell on the night of the 3rd. No. 24. Eight o'clock coach.'

Mr Mogford, made a little more nervous by this fresh apparition of his haunting trouble, said that 'there were so many genelmen –'

'Of course!' says Quaid. 'My name's Quaid – Silas Quaid, of the firm of Purkiss and Quaid, Thavies Inn, and we've got the prisoner's case in our hands.'

Mr Mogford acknowledged the great name – Jerry had often sung its praises – by a bow, and said he was glad to hear it he was sure.

Quaid looked at him with that suspicious air with which he looked at everybody, and then said abruptly,

'I want to see you. Private conversation. Not now; to-night.'

Mr Mogford, yielding to his fate, would be delighted. At his own house, at any hour convenient to Mr Quaid.

'Very good,' says Quaid, nailing him, as it were, with his eye. 'I am going down to Ipswich to-morrow, and shall sleep at the Bell. We can just have a few words in the evening – say nine o'clock. Will that suit?'

Plain Joe, changing colour a little at the unpleasant prospect of having to relate all particulars of the murder over again for the thousandth time, said that it would suit very well.

'That's right,' says Quaid. 'It's about that fellow who was drinking with you in the parlour. That's all. Good morning!'

That was all! Quite enough, too, Joe thought. The sharp partner of the celebrated P's and Q's saw the importance of such a witness's evidence, and doubtlessly intended to throw discredit on his story. If, in cross-examination, Mr Jerry was forced to confess that he was a thief and swindler by profession, the value of his evidence would be materially impaired. And if it was discovered – as Mr Quaid would delight in discovering – that this thief and swindler was own brother to Mr Mogford himself, the cherished respectability of Mr Mogford's posting-house would receive a severe, perhaps a fatal blow.

The thought was not a pleasant one, and Plain Joe felt his face getting hot, and his hand shake, as he thought of the coming interview. Yet the interview must be gone through, and, if necessary, Jerry must be found. Perhaps he had been but temporarily absent from his accustomed haunts, and would be by this time returned, and shaping his disreputable course for the Bell. At the worst, he was probably lying dead drunk in some back room of one of the infamous dens he frequented. A more carefully conducted search could not fail to find him.

As Mr Mogford – debating this question within himself – slowly mingled with the crowd, he felt himself pushed against, and his coat sharply plucked from behind.

Suspicious of pocket-picking, he turned round and beheld – squeezing himself into the angle of the wall – a diminutive and ragged boy, who, with one black little finger laid alongside a miraculously turned-up nose, was winking at him with all his might.

'What is it?' asked Plain Joe, slinking out of the way of the foot-passengers. 'Do you want me?'

'You're the cove as keeps the Bell, ain't yer?' asked the urchin, in a preternaturally hoarse voice. 'Bister Bogford?'

'Yes,' says Plain Joe, guessing at once the nature of the creature's errand. 'Who sent you?'

'The Lurker,' returned the boy. 'I followed yer all the way, and could-d't get a chadce of stopp'd yer. 'Es at Blickses, and wadts to see yer. You'r to cub with be.'

As a credential of his mission, he thrust into Plain Joe's hand a crumpled piece of dirty paper, on which was written – in very pale ink, and with a pen that would appear to have stuck into the paper at every third letter –

Blicks,

  Blue Anchor Yard,

    Rosemary Lane.

Come with the boy.

'Screeved it hisself!' says the boy, dancing a sort of triumphant dance, expressive of mingled ambassadorial delight and appreciation of the Lurker's talents. 'Oh my! Ain't he a lubby 'ud?'

'I carn't come now,' growled Plain Joe, looking down at his respectable person. 'It's broad daylight.'

'What's the odds?' says the boy, stopping in his dance to ask the question, with his eye fixed on Mr Mogford's watch-chain. 'Put that 'ere slag id yer garret, button up yer coat, ad who'll 'urt yer? You'd better cub at wuded,' he added – 'Jerry said it was werry partic'lar.'

Thus urged, Plain Joe put his watch-chain into his fob, pulled his hat over his eyes, and buttoning his coat, followed his strange conductor. 'If I've got to see the lawyer to-night,' he said to himself, 'I may as well see Jerry first, though it's a roaring rum time to go down Whitechapel way.'

'Go on, you young beggar,' he added, aloud, 'and don't keep too close.'

It was a good long way; and the boy, dodging under carriages and whirling round corners, was nearly lost once or twice, and it was as much as Plain Joe, puffing, blowing, and cursing, could do to keep him in view.

What with turning cart-wheels, begging, dodging across the road for no apparent purpose, engaging in Parthian combats with other young gentlemen as ragged and dirty as himself, and taking every advantage of double, turn, and twist, which the most minute acquaintance of every short cut between Drummond's Bank and the Minories afforded him, he completely bewildered Plain Joe, and brought him to Rosemary Lane (by an unexpected dive down a court, whose very existence a casual passer-by would not have suspected) in a state of mingled perspiration and blasphemy awful to contemplate.

'Where *is* the place?' asked Mr Mogford, coming to a standstill beneath a festooned trophy of corduroy breeches which hung from side to side of the narrow way by which they had entered, and looking round him rather nervously. 'Is it much farther?'

'Jest round the corder, Bister Bogford,' says the boy, ogling a woman old enough to be his mother with superb affectation of profligate indifference. 'You'd be there before you cad say Dife!'

To verify his prediction, he cut his ogle short with a hideous grimace, and skipping through the filth and impurity of the street, threaded his way through a crowd of men and women, as filthy and impure as the gutter in which they lived, and turned round a blackened and filthy wall into a narrow court of blackened and filthy houses.

The first glimpse of Blue Anchor Yard was not encouraging. It was narrow, dirty, and pregnant with stenches. The houses nearly met, and seemed here and there to bulge to each other, as if they were drunk and could not stand upright. From some, bricks had fallen. Chimneys were wanting in others. Windows had been replaced with rags, and the rags had themselves rotted away and turned into moist lumps of noisome impurity. The population seemed to be all outside, walking, standing, or sitting on steps. They paused to stare at Plain Joe, with a stare of mingled astonishment and ferocity; and a tangled knot of children – from whom all childhood had been sucked out by the ever-ascending steam of disease and crime – came tumbling through the feculence of the street to yell at his conductor.

The urchin threw a last daring cart-wheel, and coming up standing opposite a house somewhat larger than the others, pointed to it.

'There y' are,' he said, indicating a black board that was nailed over the doorway. 'That's Blickses! Bister Blick, lodgid-'ouse keeper, crocus-covey,[1] and dealer in old Betals. The Lurker's up-stairs, Bister Bogford, and waitid to see yer.'

⊷ 11 ⊷

JERRY THE LURKER

'BLICKSES' was a nondescript place. It might have been a rag and bottle shop, but it wasn't. It might have been a chemist and druggist's, but it wasn't. It might have been a public-house, if it had not so much the appearance of a store for old mousetraps, pokers, battered coal-scuttles, and worn-out frying-pans. The best idea of it can perhaps be gained by imagining that an army of

1. Chemist.

travelling tinkers had taken possession of the upper storey, and having made shipwreck of their pots and kettles on the ground floor, were quarrelling as to whether they should open a chemist's shop or start a public-house.

Blicks himself – in a ragged pair of breeches, a hairy breast, one eye, an offensively dirty shirt, and a halo of brandy and water – welcomed the visitors.

'Right, Gammy!' said this gentleman to Plain Joe's conductor. 'Right! Shew Mr Mogford's friend upstairs, and he'll give yer a token of his esteem, in the shape of coin of the Rellum. Mr Mogford, I'm proud to know yer. Any friend of my friend Jerry I'm proud to know. Hic – I'm proud to know –'

Gammy, remarking only that the 'Guvedor was od the booze,' pushed past him, ran up the dirty stairs, and plunging through a dark passage, with Plain Joe at his heels, knocked at a door at the end of it.

'Who's that?' asked a voice.

'It's be – Gabby! 'Ere's Bister Bogford!'

There was a sound as of some one jumping from off a bed, and then two bolts were withdrawn, and the door opened.

The lost brother of Mr Mogford appeared – with the tightly-strapped trousers falling, for lack of braces, about his heels – and stretching out a lean, lank arm, dragged him into the chamber.

'It's you, Joe, is it, at last?' he cried, in tones husky with brandy. 'Come in here! Come in, I want to speak to you.'

Gammy, lurking round the corner of the stair-head, saw Plain Joe shrink back for a moment, terrified at the red eyes, rumpled head, and shaking, bird's-claw hand of the occupant of the evil-smelling den, and then disappear into the chamber, the door of which was slammed behind him.

'S'epb be, but that's a rub go too!' he ejaculated. 'That's a rub way to welcub a gedtlebud!' and stretching himself along the grimy, uneven floor, he set himself to listen.

He did not hear much. There was a sound as though Mr Mogford had been violently plumped into a chair, and a gurgling noise as though the Lurker was lubricating his hard voice with liquor. Then came a rapid sentence or two, delivered in an undertone, and then a startled oath and a heavy bang of Mr Mogford's fist upon the ricketty table.

Excited by this sign of important disclosures, Gammy rose to his naked feet, and fixed his eye at the keyhole.

Although it was broad daylight outside, the gloom and darkness of the place – intensified by the overhanging presence of the adjacent buildings – had rendered candlelight necessary, and a flaring, sputtering tallow dip, stuck into a battered iron candlestick, flung fantastic shadows into every corner of the poverty-stricken apartment. The room was large, but so filled with lumbering chests, worm eaten boxes, and dingy shelves heaped with nondescript rubbish of all kinds, that but little space was left for a deal table, and a heavy old-fashioned bedstead – as worm-eaten and rotten as the rest of the furniture. A bottle, pipe, and a screw of tobacco were on the table. Mr Mogford was sitting on the only chair, and the Lurker, in his shirt, and stockinged feet, was standing over him, holding him by the shoulder.

'I must have money!' he said. 'Money! As much as you can give me; more than you can give me. Money, Joe, money, do you hear?'

Joe raised his face – no longer rubicund and respectable, but white and ghastly. His eyes – protruding from their sockets – seemed to search round the room for some outlet of escape, and then fell before the greedy gaze of his companion.

'What can I do?' he said, in a terrified voice. 'I have no money. It has been hard enough to keep up an appearance as it is. Times is bad, and don't seem likely to get better.'

'Stow that gaff!' cried Jerry, in a savage whisper, shaking the helpless mass before him until the fat paunch quivered again. 'That won't go down with me! I *must* have money. My heart! Do you think I'm going to rot in this den like a rat in a hole?'

'How much?' asked the other, in a faint voice.

'How much! Ah, that's the chat! As much as you can afford, my Flesh and Blood; as much as the respectable Joseph can screw out of his customers. How much shall we say? How much for fraternal affection, eh?'

'Hush!' says the other, wiping his white face with his handkerchief. 'What's that? There's some one at the door?'

Quick as lightning, Gammy flung his legs over the stairhead, and dived into a recess of the passage. It was well that he did so, for in another instant the door was flung open, and Jerry, stretching his vulture neck out of his soiled and ragged shirt, peered out over the broken bannisters.

'Is that you, Blick?' he asked, flourishing the grease-dropping candle above him, and trembling in every limb. 'Gammy! Gammy! You whelp of Satan, if you've been listening, I'll send you to the gallows before your time!'

'What is it?' says Gammy, affecting to be awakened from a profound slumber on the bottom storey. 'Was you a calling *be*, Bister Jerry?'

'No,' says Jerry, with a sigh of relief at the false alarm. 'It's all right. Stop there, and shew the gentleman out.'

And retiring to his den again, the door was locked as before.

'Well!' says Gammy, 'blow be! Blow be but that's a rubbier go than t'other! What's he wadtig buddy for? and what the cribes does he bead by "fraterdal affectiod?" It is subthig he's got to sell, I wodder?'

But he was too frightened at the Lurker's wrath to creep to his old post again, and was fain to content his curiosity by an ineffectual attempt to extract a meaning out of the indistinguishable murmur that came from the room above.

At length the door opened, and Mr Mogford came out.

'Send it to-night,' he heard Jerry's hard voice say. 'Send it by the boy – he's safe enough – and I'll get down the river by some barge or another, and so over to France.'

The other seemed to hesitate.

'Not to-night,' he said. 'I have something to do, and I won't trust the boy. I'll bring it to-morrow. That'll be time enough – nobody suspects anything yet.'

'To-morrow!' cries Jerry, in tipsy wrath. 'To-morrow! Here's brotherly love! And I eating my blessed heart in this ken! Why, curse –'

'It's no use,' returned Plain Joe, with a sort of stolid desperation. 'You *must* stop 'ere till to-night, so that's all about it. I can't do more than I can do, if I was to be hung to-morrow.'

'Hush!' says the other, with that sudden change of manner that belongs to half-intoxicated men – 'Don't talk of hanging – don't; it makes my blood chill. Have it your own way, and manage how you like. I'll wait.'

And then he raised his voice.

'Here, Gammy, you young pudding-snammer, show this gentleman home, and tell that old villain to send me up some brandy. I'm as dry as a limekiln.'

Gammy responding with imperturbable snuffle, Mr Mogford reached the bottom of the stairs.

He was very pale, and the hand he laid on the filthy bannister shook a little, but otherwise he had recovered his equanimity.

'Has he been drinking much?' he asked of the one-eyed Blick, who was lounging as usual in the doorway.

'Like H—!' was that gentleman's pithy reply.

'He talks a good deal when he's drunk,' said Mr Mogford, 'but you mustn't pay attention to what he says.'

'By Blank!' says Blick, with another terrible blasphemy, 'it doesn't matter what he says here. He can (hic) say what he blank pleases here. No blank blank in this blank ken cares a blank what any blank says.'

'Now then!' roars Jerry over the stairs, '*where's* that brandy?' and Plain Joe, turning round as he escaped from the noisome hovel, caught a glimpse of the Lurker looking down at him, candle in hand, from the landing-place – much to Plain Joe's excited fancy, as the strange visitor to No. 18 had looked down upon him from the staircase of the Bell, on the night of the 3rd of May.

⤙ *12* ⤚

MR SILAS QUAID AS A MAN OF FEELING

Six hours later, Mr Quaid, seated in a snug private room – he never grudged his luxuries when other people paid for them – was informed by a bland waiter that Mr Mogford was ready to see him whenever it suited his convenience.

'Ask Mr Mogford to come up,' said Quaid, and putting down his glass, he stood up, with his back to the empty fire-place, and stretched out his arms, as though to prepare for a struggle.

If the pale, undersized attorney had been a fisherman, and the Brussels carpet of the private room a rushing stream, you would have said that he had just hooked a very big and powerful fish, and was about to 'play' him with all the skill at his command.

'Sit down, Mr Mogford; pray, sit down! May I offer you a glass of wine? No! Oh, but I insist!'

Mr Mogford had changed his clothes since his return, and was brilliant with respectability; but the contagious rascality of Blue Anchor Yard seemed somehow to have clung to him. Although his voice was steady, and his protuberant stomach heaved calmly beneath his best black satin waistcoat, his big fat hands twitched impulsively, and his restless eyes glanced nervously into the dark corners of the room.

'No, thank you,' he said, pushing away the proffered decanter; 'I would rather not, sir.'

Quaid looked at him again with those ever-suspicious eyes. A landlord refuse his own liquor! Something must have happened.

'What's the matter, Mr Mogford? You look quite out of sorts!'

Mr Mogford sat down stolidly, as though he had made up his mind to endure this sort of questioning, and was prepared with his replies.

'I am a little queerish. This business has upset me, sir.'

'Don't wonder at it. It's a dreadful thing to happen in a hotel.'

'It is, sir. And in a respectable posting-house like this, which I've grow'd, as it were, into, sir, it's werry hard.'

'I am afraid it will injure the reputation of your house.'

'I am afraid it will, sir.'

'Though, of course, it is no fault of yours.'

'Of course, not, sir.'

'Accidents will happen, Mr Mogford.'

'They will, sir.'

' "In the best regulated families," as the saying is.'

'True, sir.'

'Most of us have a skeleton in our closets, Mr Mogford.'

'S-s-ir!'

'And,' said Quaid, fixing his bright eyes upon the strangely alarmed Joe, 'your brother is the one in yours.'

Plain Joe, his stolidity running, like Acres' courage, from his finger-ends, gave a nervous glance at the door.

'W-w-what do you mean, Mr Quaid?'

'I mean,' says Quaid, admiring his ring-finger with a careless air, 'that Mr Jeremiah, better known as Jerry the Lurker, is a relative who does not add to your respectability. Take a glass of wine, Mr Mogford.'

Plain Joe grew red and pale by turns, and then, with that instinct of stolid Plainness, which stood him instead of more acute perception, met his adversary half way.

'I don't know how you come to know it, Mr Quaid,' he said; 'but I suppose genelmen of your purfession knows all them things. Jerry the Lurker *is* a brother of mine, and a rampageous bad brother he is too.'

'Yes,' returned Quaid, half-angry, half-pleased, at the adroit way in which his attack had been met. 'You're right. He is.'

'But I can't help it, Mr Quaid; it ain't my fault! I'm a respectable plain man, as have kept this house respectable for nine year and more, and if I have a roaring rip of a brother, it ain't my fault.'

'Not at all. But it's your misfortune; and misfortunes are often as bad as faults, Mr Mogford.'

'So they are,' says Plain Joe.

'It is a great misfortune to have fellows always hanging about the house – as I know *he* does; always sponging on you – as I know *he* does; always writing begging-letters, and contriving dangerous impostures – as I know *he* does; always filching plate and money and watches – as I know *he* does. It is a great misfortune to know that at any moment this fellow may be arrested, and convicted, and bring disgrace upon your hard-earned respectability. Take a glass of wine, Mr Mogford. You look quite ill to-night.'

Plain Joe didn't refuse this time, but poured out a glass and drank it.

'You must always feel uneasy at his conduct, Mr Mogford – it has been calculated to make any relative feel uneasy I am sure; but at a time like this, I am afraid it must come very hard upon you.'

Plain Joe, moistening his dry lips with his tongue, intimated that it was very hard.

'This is a very respectable house indeed – very respectable,' Mr

Quaid continued, 'and you are a most respectable man, Mr Mogford. Dear, dear, it's a great pity.'

'What's a great pity, sir?' inquired Joe, with a start.

'Why, Mr Mogford, I'm sadly afraid that they will have this brother of yours up on the trial.'

Joe gulped down an exclamation of relief.

'So I am afraid, too, sir. The crowner, he said it was necessary too, sir.'

'Well, have you got him, then?' asked Quaid, eagerly. 'Is he ready to come?'

'I haven't seen him yet, sir,' says Joe, with a careless air, 'but I've been so worritted with this business, that I haven't had time rightly to look for him.'

The drooping lids of the lawyer's eyes hid whatever sentiment those sharp orbs might have conveyed, but the lawyer's mouth relaxed, as if he had just got his fish into shallow water, and was sure of him.

'Well,' said he, 'you haven't much time to lose, and it seems quite necessary that he should be found. I am sorry for you, Mr Mogford, but I am afraid that it is imperatively necessary that he should be found.'

'Well, sir,' says Joe, 'for the matter of that, he didn't see no more, nor so much as I did. He went away as soon as the young man went to bed.'

'You saw him go?'

'I locked him out, sir.'

'Oh, you locked him out; and I suppose he couldn't have got in again after that?'

'No, sir,' returned Plain Joe, with a shudder. 'How should he?'

'There was no way, I presume?'

'How could there be, with the doors all double locked and bolted?'

Mr Quaid, biting the end of his square forefinger, appeared lost in thought.

'Um. That's true enough. But you see that it is not exactly that. He might be able to give some more details of the conversation.'

'But that would be all *against* the prisoner,' said Mr Mogford.

Plain Joe wiped his bald head with his handkerchief, as if to conceal his face.

'It's a dreadful thing for me, sir,' he said.

'Of course, it is,' returned Mr Quaid, 'but I can't help it, you know. If they put Master Jerry in the box, I must have him cross-examined, and then it will all come out.'

Plain Joe heaved a sigh like a furnace-blast, and wiped his face again.

'Do you think that they're bound to put him in the box, sir?' he asked.

'I should say that they are,' returned the other. 'I am sure I had just as soon they didn't; but, then, you see, it's not in my hands, and if he *does* come, I am bound to do my best for my client. Help yourself to the wine, Mr Mogford – help yourself to the wine.'

A cloud seemed to pass from Plain Joe's brow. Disregarding the invitation of Quaid, he rose, as if to finish the conversation.

'I'm sure I'm much obliged to you for your kindness, sir. It's a terrible thing for me. But I am a plain, honest man, sir, and I must do my dooty I suppose. If my rip of a brother *can* be found, sir, I'll bring him up at the trial. But if he can't – and you know his ways, sir, as well as I do – why I can't do more.'

'Of course not,' returned Quaid. 'You will then have relieved yourself from all responsibility. I am sure I shall be heartily glad if you can get out of the scrape.'

'Thank you, sir,' says Plain Joe at the door.

'And, Mogford,' says Quaid, turning round, with his face in shadow to say it, 'speaking in a friendly way – if I were you, when you *do* find the unhappy fellow, I should send him away. Pack him off somewhere – out of the country, you know, where he can do you no injury by his bad habits. You owe it to yourself, Mr Mogford, you do indeed. By the way, I have my old room I suppose, and you won't forget that I go by the first coach.'

Mr Mogford, seemingly frightened again at this suggestion of the disposal of Jerry, mumbled some inaudible reply, and withdrew.

Quaid, sighing with satisfaction, betook himself to the remainder of the port wine.

'The deuce!' he cried, with the ever-recurring contraction of his suspicious brows. 'He must have been more frightened than I thought. He's drunk nearly half the bottle. Poor devil! Well, I suppose he *was* frightened. However, I think I have disposed of Jerry.'

Had he known, perhaps, of the interview at Blicks', he would have considered him disposed of already, and saved his trouble.

But even Old Bailey lawyers are not omniscient.

✦ 13 ✦

THE READING OF THE WILL

DESPITE the May sunshine – one might almost call it June sunshine, for it wanted but three days of it – the melancholy house in which Sir Richard Devine had died looked as melancholy as ever.

With grim brick front, and windows staring with all the blindness of down-drawn blinds, the place seemed to have absorbed the spirit of the late owner, and to have become miserly and selfish, like him.

The sun, beaming so brightly outside, served but to make the gloomy rooms more gloomy by contrast, and Mr Quaid, coming into the gloomy dining-room the morning after his arrival, felt the cold heavy air strike him, as though he had entered a tomb.

There were not many people present. The dead millionaire had few relatives. His own connections had long since died out; or, if one or two of them were here and there scattered up and down the world, they were too poor and obscure to have a place at such a gathering as this. He had quarrelled – in some unreasoning bitterness of misanthropical feeling – with his wife's kinsfolk, and, save Maurice, had held communication with none of them for years past. Friends he had none.

In the long, dark chamber, streaked here and there by arrows of dusty light from the crevices of the closely-drawn blinds, Mr Quaid found but six persons.

Maurice, Frank, Lucy, the Belgian governess, Jarvis (waiting grimly), and a tall gentleman with severely black hair and brows.

This last was a Mr Gibb, a retired stock-broker of some means, and one of the knight's executors.

Quaid, bowing gravely, advanced down the room towards a table, the further end of which had been laid out for his reception, and was conspicuously resplendent with a decanter and glasses.

'Good morning, Mr Quaid,' said Mr Gibb, with some asperity of manner.

He was to the full as hard and business-like as the friend who had selected him as his executor; but retirement from speculation had led him to more courtly society, and he was a little annoyed at the odd fancy that had made Sir Richard Devine place his law business in the hands of so notorious an Old Bailey attorney as Mr Quaid.

Quaid, however, self-reliant and composed, had taken Mr Gibb's measure at the last night's dinner-table, and returned his salute with silent composure.

Lucy, dressed with that quaint primness which was considered child-like at that period, stood beside her governess's chair, and seemed to divide her attention between her governess's knitting needles and her brother's face. Outwardly she looked a little scared. Inwardly she was repeating the answers to some geographical catechism which she was to repeat when the 'will was over.' Frank was sitting in an easy chair to the right of the table, and patted his foot and perused the carpet uneasily. His sickly cheeks were flushed, and his large eyes brilliant. He knew well how much his future happiness was locked up in that black deed-box of Mr Quaid's. The governess knitted placidly – her motherly German bosom rising and falling with healthy regularity, and her deep brown eyes steadily fixed upon the ever clacking needles. Maurice was red, but quiet, and half sitting half lounging upon the sofa behind his cousin, affected an old English coolness which he did not feel. Jarvis, like a skeleton in a new suit of black, stood silently in the shadow, with his eyes fixed on Mr Maurice Frere.

There was a hardness about the whole proceeding that matched well with the reputed cheerlessness of the miser's life. One could have almost imagined him present, everything wore such a business-like air. Indeed, had it not been for the table with the glasses, and a certain suffocating smell of crape that seemed to pervade the place, Mr Quaid might have fancied himself coming into the shipbuilder's office to receive instructions for the issuing of writs and takings of actions at law.

Looking round the room ere he took his seat at the table, an odd fancy arose in his mind as to the likeness of the assemblage to black crows perched upon a carcase.

'Now, Mr Quaid,' croaked Mr Gibb, with dignity. 'We are quite ready. You may begin.'

Quaid bowed, and opening a single sheet of parchment, on which the engrossed matter looked extremely small, began to read.

The momentous will was dated the 9th of March, 1823, and was short enough.

An annuity of twenty pounds a year was bequeathed to Jarvis. Legacies of five thousand pounds each were left to Lucy and Frank, and every farthing of the rest of the property was left unconditionally to the testator's 'dear son Richard.'

There was a dead silence as Mr Quaid folded up the document.

Frank was too astonished to speak. Mr Gibb would seem to have some shrewd guess at the intention of the testator, and Maurice Frere had braced himself to meet the worst that might happen.

But in a second or two the silence was broken.

'Is that all?' asked Maurice Frere, staggering under the tremendous blow that had at once bereft him of fortune and condemned him to exile.

'Yes,' said Quaid, pursing his lips to repress a smile at the questioner's disappointment, 'that's all.'

'Have you any idea,' asked Mr Gibb, feeding his nose carefully with snuff – as though that organ was a good sort of creature, that merited consolation, but was apt to be wasteful – 'have you any idea what is the amount of the late Sir Richard's property?'

'I should say,' returned Quaid, 'that, taking the real and personal estate together, and reckoning all invested moneys at their present value, there is a quarter of a million.'

Maurice gasped.

A quarter of a million! And he had missed it by a quarter of an hour! A quarter of a million, and not even his promised hundred a year secured to him out of it!

He ground his teeth together in preparation for a curse, but caught the annuitied Jarvis's cold eye fixed satirically on him, and checked himself by suddenly rising.

'But where is Richard?' he asked.

'Yes,' says Frank, 'where is my brother, Mr Quaid?'

Quaid shook his head.

'I don't know,' he replied. 'He was somewhere in Germany when his father heard from him last, I believe.'

'Ah!' cried Maurice, remembering the story of his uncle's seizure. 'There was a letter on the day of Sir Richard's illness.'

Quaid unlocked the box in which the dead man's papers had been placed by his orders, and pushed it across to Mr Gibb.

'All letters that he received about that time, sir,' he said, 'are here, I know.'

Mr Gibb plunged his hand into the box, and drew out some dozen open letters, which he glanced at in silence.

'No,' he said: 'these are all on mere business matters.'

There were others, however, that had arrived after his death, and were, of course, unopened. The first of these was disposed of, then the second, but at the third – a coarse, thick sheet, folded and sealed – the business-like Gibb paused, with an exclamation of astonishment, and then handed it to Quaid.

The lawyer read it out.

Sir I have accepted your proposal, and will go. I have taken my passage on board the 'Hydaspes.' By the time you receive this I shall be on my way to Calcutta.

For the future, our lives shall lie as far apart as you can wish them, and I trust in my new life to blot out the knowledge that I am

Your unhappy son,
RICHARD DEVINE.

There was a general exclamation of astonishment.

'Is there a postmark?' says Frank.

'London. Nothing more.'

'London!' cries Maurice, with frowning brows. 'And the date? Is there a date?'

'Yes. The 3rd of May.'

Mr Gibb took another pinch of snuff.

'The 3rd of May. The *Hydaspes* sailed on the 5th. A friend of mine went in her.'

Quaid did not reply. He was looking at the writing – viewing the bold sloping letters now from one side, now from the other, as if he wished to impress their character upon his memory.

'Then he has sailed!' said Maurice.

'It is very unfortunate,' said Quaid, putting down the letter. 'Very unfortunate but I am afraid he *has* sailed.'

A light hand on his sleeve interrupted him. It was the governess.

'I suppose that Miss Lucy and I may retire now, sir?' she said, in a quiet, even voice. 'There is nothing more?'

'No, there is nothing more,' said Quaid. And as the tall, fair woman, followed by Jarvis and the child, swept gravely to the door, he looked after her not unadmiringly.

Maurice began to pace the room, and Frank hurriedly poured out and drank a glass of water; Mr Gibb took more snuff. The position of executor was likely to be embarrassing, and he did not half like it.

'Barham, of Barham and Levick's Bank, is my co-trustee,' he said, referring to the clause in the will. 'I had better write to him as to future proceedings. I suppose that we shall have to find Mr Richard?'

'It will be necessary to look for him,' says Quaid, drily.

'We can't overtake the ship, of course,' says the impetuous Frank. 'She will be nearly thirty days out by this time.'

'And, after all, perhaps he didn't go in her!' says Maurice.

The words slipped from his lips. They were natural enough, but it seemed as though he had not intended to say them, for, meeting Quaid's ever suspicious eye, he grew confused.

'He might have gone under a feigned name, or fifty things might have happened,' cries Frank. 'We must go to the shipping-offices and write to the agents in Calcutta. Perhaps we may hear something about him from some of his German friends, or at the place where he stopped in London. Poor Richard!'

Maurice stopped walking up and down, and flung himself into a chair.

'There will be a lot of advertising and trouble, I expect,' said Mr Gibb, grimly; 'but, of course, we must do our best.'

'If I can be of any assistance?' began Quaid.

'Thank you, sir,' returned Gibb, shutting his snuff-box with an angry snap, and replacing the papers in the tin box, 'but I have my own solicitors.'

The lawyer bowed with just a hint of natural annoyance at the rebuff visible in his manner, and went to the door.

The annuitied Jarvis was in the passage, bearing himself with all the dignity of a man of property.

'Can you get me some conveyance to the town?' asked Quaid.

'There ain't nothing but the old dun pony!' was the reply.

'How far is it?'

'About fower mile.'

'You lie, you rascal!' cried Maurice Frere, who, moved by some sudden sulky impulse, had followed the lawyer out; 'it's barely three. Curse you! What do you mean by lying, eh?'

It seemed that the pent-up rage within him must spend itself on something, and Jarvis was the nearest object.

The gaunt old fellow grinned his provoking grin.

'That's harsh language, Mr Maurice,' he said 'but I can forgive you. It's enough to make a gentleman swear, sir, isn't it,' he added, turning to Quaid, 'to just get his grip o' half a million, and then lose every shill'n' of it?'

The turgid veins of Mr Frere's forehead swelled with rage.

'You insolent dog!' he said, with a stride that made Jarvis skip back in comical terror, 'hold your tongue, or, old as you are, I shall be tempted to lay my whip over your shoulders.'

'Come,' said Quaid, feeling a little out of place, 'if it's only three miles, I can walk, and send for my portmanteau.'

'Are you going?' asked Maurice.

'Yes. There is not much inducement to stop; besides, they try our friend Dawes on Friday, and I defend him.'

'I'll walk with you a bit,' says Maurice. 'The air of this place is suffocating.'

And they went out.

'I say,' says Maurice, when they got clear of the house, 'that Will rather startled me.'

'Yes,' returned the other, 'I dare say it did. Sir Richard never intended it to be acted on. I believe, if he had lived, he would have left *you* the bulk of the property.'

'That's d—d poor consolation now though!' says Frere, with

a return of his coarse old English bluntness. 'I wonder what the deuce has become of Dick.'

'Sailed for India, I expect,' returned Quaid, carelessly. 'They'll find him easily enough. A quarter of a million of money makes a noise.'

'But suppose they don't find him?'

'If satisfactory proof of his death – without heirs – is obtained, your cousin and the young lady divide the property between them. If he leaves any children, of course it all goes to them.'

'Well,' says Maurice, with an affectation of carelessness, 'of course I'm glad that the poor fellow's come so well off; but I wish I wasn't obliged to go to the colonies.'

'Ah!' returned Quaid, as if he had forgotten Mr Frere's approaching exodus. 'You'll have to go now, I suppose?'

'The 15th of next month,' says Maurice, with a sigh. 'We are to go in the *Malabar*, with convicts, I believe. Hard luck, isn't it?'

'It is; but it can't be helped, Mr Frere. It might be harder. How would you like to stand in my client's shoes?'

'Dawes? Egod, not at all,' replied Maurice, forcing a laugh. 'I'm better off than that!'

Quaid smiled.

'You are indeed,' he said.

Maurice was silent until they reached the angle of the road where they proposed to part.

'Do you think you'll get him off?' he asked, looking up suddenly.

'Who? Dawes? I hope so.'

'Well,' says Maurice, 'you'll have a hard job of it, in my opinion. The trial will last a day or two, I suppose? I'm coming up to town, and I may drop in and see how you are getting on.'

'Do,' says Quaid, and they parted.

AT THE OLD BAILEY

IT was not long before Mr Maurice Frere fulfilled his threat. If he had felt like an interloper in the gloomy Essex house, when his uncle was alive, the feeling returned upon him with redoubled vigour now that his uncle was dead and he himself cut off from his expected inheritance. His hearty old English manner found but few admirers among the inmates of the grim mansion, and conscious that his cousins looked upon him with a dislike almost triumphant in its unconcealment, he had resolved to betake himself – now that his staying could effect no useful object – to the more congenial society of his London friends. The *Malabar* was to sail early in the month, and he had many preparations to make.

'I shall likely not see you again,' he said, as he shook hands at the door. 'But if I can find out anything about Richard, Mr Gibb, I will write.'

In course of his necessary pilgrimages to docks and shipping offices, he did make shift to find out about the *Hydaspes*. She had sailed from Gravesend on the 5th of May, as the businesslike Gibb had remembered. Her owners would be delighted to do anything they could. There was no name like Richard Devine on the passenger-list, but it was unlikely that the gentleman would give his own name. Their agents at Calcutta, however, would furnish all information. In the meantime they would recommend an advertisement.

Maurice transmitting this intelligence to Mr Gibb, received a reply to the effect that advertisements were unpleasant things, and not to be used but in extremity, and that for the present Mr Gibb would confine himself to enquiries. So it came about that when the death and the will were talked of, it was generally understood that the heir was travelling abroad somewhere, and would speedily return.

The first anger of disappointment over, Maurice Frere seemed to meet his altered fate cheerfully enough. After all, he had youth, health, and a good position. The exile to the colonies was the bitterest drop in his cup; and could he have afforded it, he would have purchased an exchange; but he had no money. From henceforth he must live on his pay – as many a better man, he was forced to confess, had done before him. The prospect was not so brilliant a one as he had pictured to himself, but after all it might have been worse. And with this fine old English maxim he endeavoured to console himself.

With not unnatural desire to hear all about the crime, in which both he and Quaid had seemed to possess a sort of vested interest, he had put up at the Bell, and had obtained all particulars from Mr Mogford's own lips.

Pressure of shipping-agent, and other business had prevented his attendance at court on the first day of the trial, but at dinner that night he had announced his intention of dropping in to hear the verdict.

'I am curious to see how old Quaid'll work it,' he had said to Plain Joe; and Plain Joe – looking a little broken after his worry in court, Maurice thought – had promised to do his best to secure a seat for him.

The big wheel, silently but ceaselessly turning, had opened the Old Bailey sessions on the 1st of June, with rather a substantial bill of fare. In addition to the Holborn murder, were some half dozen capital cases concerning the stealing of horses, the burglarious entry of houses, the forging of bills of exchange, and the uttering of spurious coin – all offences which the fine old English law of 1827 punished with Death. Moreover, another sensational crime had come to light – a series of frauds and forgeries by a Quaker, – and this new sweetmeat had almost taken the taste of Rufus Dawes out of the public mouth. The people – fickle even in their capacity for being horrified – were inclined to desert the prosaic sailor for the more romantic Quaker – who would also be hung by the neck if found guilty. Sailors had been hung in plenty; but the gibbeting of a member of the Society of Friends would be something new.

The Court, however, was crowded, and the performance went on with great smoothness. The shoplifters, burglars, and pocket-pickers were rapidly disposed of. It seemed as though the big wheel, turning round and round, met with little checks now and then, in the shape of human lives pushed into its machinery, and that it snapped them off with a scarcely perceptible shock, and continued its course.

A succession of white, wet faces kept popping up behind the spikes of the dock and being pulled down again, and a variety of human creatures made a variety of attempts to say why the sentence of the law should not be passed upon them, and why (why, in the name of fine old English practice) they should not be hung by the necks until they were dead.

So rapidly, indeed, did the wheel turn, that by three o'clock in the afternoon, it had got Rufus Dawes behind the spikes, listening, through the hot shimmering atmosphere, to Mr Solicitor-General proving, and fitting, and piecing, and twisting the evidence into a neat rope wherewith to suspend him from the gallows on Monday morning next.

He had pleaded Not Guilty, and Quaid had given him some hope; but as each successive witness but made his guilt seem blacker than before, he began to lose courage.

The counsel secured for him by Quaid did his best in cross-examination, but to little effect.

Plain Joe's account of the meeting in the passage, the account of Mr Prell – magnificently pomatumed and verbose – of his behaviour in the shaving shop, and Mr Larkin's account of the finding of the jewels, remained unshaken.

Then were produced three terrible witnesses – the bloody shirt, the bloody handkerchief, and the knife; and a sigh of mingled horror and delight passed over the Court. He had done It with *that*, and those brown stains, but barely visible, were Blood. Delightful sensation!

At this juncture, Quaid handed him up a piece of paper.

Will you tell me who the murdered man was, and what you knew about him – *now*?

Rufus Dawes hesitated a moment. The flash of the white paper going up to him had brought the eyes away from the table to his face, and he knew that all the Court, as it were, waited for what he would do. But his hesitation was not for long. Borrowing a pencil from the turnkey next him, he wrote a refusal in a firm, upright hand.

Quaid read the note with a sort of impatient frown of disappointment, and then looked up and nodded. This made a whisper pass over the sea of heads again. The prisoner had written a note to his attorney!

The clothes were sworn to, and the knife also; Mr Mogford saying that he had seen it in the prisoner's hand the night before, and had found it on the floor close to the murdered man.

This closed the case for the Crown, and the Court adjourning until the morrow, the big wheel began to go on again.

As the prisoner was being removed, Quaid leant over to him and was understood to whisper, 'Deliver your defence to-morrow exactly as you repeated it to me. I will get the facts out of Mogford.' To which the prisoner, in a sort of bewildered way, responded aloud, that he could not understand why the facts had not been got out of Mogford before.

The spectators, however, hearing nothing of this, imagined that the lawyer had told his client that all chance of escape was gone; and it was currently reported that evening in town that the murderer had confessed, and would change his plea.

Mr Mogford had heard this report, and had told it to Mr Frere.

'I always said so,' replied the gentleman, with an oath. 'It was all bosh – old Quaid's talking. There isn't a loophole for him.'

Mr Mogford, his hands trembling a little with the excitement of the day, said that he did not think there was either, and yet he was a fine young man, too.

'Eh! Curse it, Mogford, *you're* not going to stand up for the villain, are you? And the murder committed in your own house!'

Plain Joe hurriedly disclaimed any such intention; and indeed, appeared pitiably out of spirits at the suggestion.

'Oh, *he* didn't defend him! Defend him? Indeed no, not he!'

To which Frere said that he hoped not either, and that he would come in to hear him sentenced.

Mr Mogford shuddered visibly at this – fat men are usually kind-hearted – and began to bemoan himself about his respectable posting-house.

He grieved a good deal about the injury to his respectability, although Jerry had *not* been found; and, in consequence of Mr Quaid's silence, his absence had been scarcely commented on.

The big wheel turning round again, brought the prisoner into the court next day, and Mr Mogford into the witness-box.

Now began a new phase of the case.

Plain Joe – forced by questioning – had said something about his brother, who was also present in the room with the prisoner and himself; and the prisoner's counsel, catching at this, had demanded that his brother should be produced.

Mr Mogford, with a startled glance at the immovable face of Quaid, had stammered and stuttered, and avowed at last that he had looked for him and could not find him.

With some crossing of legal weapons as to the right to pursue the subject, it was at last elicited, to the fresh-delight of sensation-loving spectators, that Mr Mogford's brother was not quite as respectable as Mr Mogford himself; that he was in fact a vaga-bond and a thief; that he was known as Jerry the Lurker, and had been mixed up in several most disreputable matters of criminal import.

It was further elicited, that though this brother had been locked out by Mr Mogford himself on the night of the murder, yet the window of the murdered man's chamber had been found to be unhasped, and that there was a water-pipe running to it from the ground, up which water-pipe it was quite possible to climb.

Plain Joe, nervously wiping his forehead as this fact was clearly proved, began, as it were, to lose that halo of respectability which surrounded him, and to appear to sensation-loving spectators as the brother of a thief and possible murderer; and Mr Frere, forcing his way into the hot court at a late hour of the afternoon, found to his surprise that a slight reaction in favour of the prisoner had set in, despite the damning evidence of the knife and hand-kerchief. As he got himself settled, there was a hum and buzz. An ineffectual attempt had been made by the Crown to procure an adjournment of the case, for the purpose of obtaining this strangely-missing witness, and the prisoner was about to address the court.

In a low voice that gradually gained in power, he began to speak.

'Gentlemen – That I am innocent of this crime God knows, but that – with the evidence now before the court – I shall be held so by you I can scarcely dare to hope. My name is Rufus Dawes. I am a sailor. I came from Amsterdam with the deceased, and we slept together in the Bell Inn. He told me his name was Hans Lassner. It has been stated that we had a quarrel – we had..A few foolish words about a foolish matter; and when I went to bed I called in at the deceased's room to make him amends for my rudeness. He was smoking at the window; and asking me to put it down for him, I tried to do so, and cut my hand. He gave me his handkerchief – that one there – to bind it up with.'

He paused here to look at Quaid, but Quaid would not look up at him.

'There was nobody in the downstairs room when we first went there. But by-and-by Mr Mogford, the landlord, and a thin man came in. This man is stated to be Mr Mogford's brother. I could swear to him if I saw him. I paid for some more drink for these two, and in a few minutes Hans Lassner went up to bed. We chatted for some minutes longer, both Mr Mogford and his brother asking where I came from, and what were the contents of a little black valise that Lassner carried.

'I left them talking, and went to bed. When I was trying to close the window for Lassner, I missed my knife, and thought I had left it on the table downstairs. I went away in the morning without seeing anybody. I had paid my bill the night before. I went towards Highgate; I had business in that direction. My beard and appearance attracted attention, and I went into a barber's to get myself shaved – a natural enough action, but which has been perverted into a sign of guilt. I had only just left the barber's, and gone into an inn for some breakfast, when I was arrested. The jewels found on me are my own.'

There was a hum of incredulity at this, and Quaid frowned.

'Gentlemen, the evidence against me is strong, I admit. I have but the consciousness of my own innocence to support me. You will naturally inquire, "If he did not commit the murder, who did?" And to that question I can but reply by a supposition.

'Gentlemen, I stand here accused of a terrible and bloody murder. My life is in your hands, and if you decide against me, I have but a few hours to live. I believe that you will do your duty, but with the weight of evidence against me I can scarcely dare hope that that duty will be justice. I would not – believe me, gentlemen, I would not – attempt to gain my own freedom by accusing an innocent man; but, knowing as I do my own innocence, I have a firm conviction in my own mind that I also know who is guilty.'

Here he paused again, and Mr Mogford, catching his eye, grew ghastly pale.

'Gentlemen, the person who was drinking with me and my murdered friend, on the night of the 3rd of May, has been described to you as Mr Mogford's brother – but he has been also described to you as a thief and a profligate. He was present during the conversation between the deceased and myself. He heard that "the black valise" contained valuables. Here, gentlemen, is a motive as strong as that which is presumed to have prompted me. Mr Mogford states that he let his brother – the thief and profligate – out by the front door. But, gentlemen, what *evidence* is there that he did so? Might not the man have remained in the house until morning, and thus have had full opportunity to commit a silent secret murder upon one of the inmates of the hotel? But Mr Mogford says that he is positive that he did not so remain, and I will assume that Mr Mogford's account is correct. But, gentlemen, what evidence have we that he did not re-enter the house? It has been shewn that the window of the room of the murdered man was unhasped, and an iron pipe running directly to it, access was easy enough. The missing brother of the landlord, gentlemen – the thief and prodigal – understood that one of the lodgers in the house, a stranger without friends, was possessed of jewels – of valuables. He himself was poor; had come, by the landlord's own account, to ask for money that very night. He knew this rich stranger's room. The window was unfastened, the iron spout within easy reach, the night gloomy and dark. What was to prevent him from climbing the pipe, entering the window, and robbing the sleeping inmate? Nay, it is almost a natural sequence of his poverty and recklessness that he should – urged by opportunity and need – attempt and complete the robbery.'

The prisoner paused for while, and again looked at Quaid, but Quaid persistently refused to look up at him.

'If we can assume this – and I assume it with a profound conviction that the assumption is correct – the true story of the crime will be apparent. What is more likely, gentlemen, than that during the process of rifling the valise, the deceased awoke, and calling for help was silenced for ever?

'Much has been made of the discovery of my knife in the chamber. It is a terrible witness against me, I admit. Knowing my innocence, as I do, I can only account for its discovery by the supposition that the knife was left below stairs, or that I dropped it during my brief visit to my friend's room. I will not – even with the shadow of the gibbet upon me – hazard the horrible thought that the murderer *stole* the weapon for the express purpose of casting suspicion on an innocent man.'

Plain Joe, down in the court, wiped his white face again, and Maurice Frere began to listen with increased attention. 'The fellah was speaking devilish well,' he said to a sallow lawyer next him. Amid the heavy silence which had come upon the place, the prisoner went on:

'Frequent mention has been made of a valise – a black case belonging to the dead man, and which was supposed to contain jewels. Where is that case? It has disappeared. It has not been found. It has not been traced to me. No attempt – as far as I am aware – has been made to find it. It has been *supposed* that having killed my friend, and left the accusing knife on the floor, I tied his handkerchief round my hand, and taking the box containing his jewellery, walked quietly away with it. That is the *supposition* of the Crown. Is it not a monstrous one? Is it not, at all events, less probable than the one I have suggested?

'Gentlemen, I have but little more to say. I have already said more than I had intended. I am placed in a terrible position – a position from which I pray heaven may preserve you. An innocent man, friendless and alone in this huge city, I am accused of the murder of the only creature with whom I had interchanged words of friendship. The accusation is supported by that terrible evidence of circumstance which has been often found fallacious – when too late. Gentlemen, I know little of the intricacies of the law. It may be that in setting before you this plain statement, not only have I failed to take advantage of such slight chinks and crannies in that wall of evidence which has been so carefully built around me, but that I have also damaged my own cause and prejudiced the court against me. Perhaps so. The law of

England, gentlemen – while it entrusts the prosecution of an unhappy prisoner to the keenest intellects it can command, forbids him the advantage of another's eloquence. The gentleman who has undertaken the profitless office of my counsel is prohibited from addressing you. I alone am permitted to speak. Alone, I – a prisoner, racked with anxiety, tortured with suspense, and unskilled in legal technicalities. I alone am permitted to attack with my bare hands that wall of evidence which the practised workmen of the Crown have built between me and liberty.

'I have, I am told, "a counsel in the Judge who tries me," and I am content to leave my case in the hands of his lordship; but, gentlemen, my *life* is in your hands, and I would ask you to pause before you send to the scaffold an innocent man, convicted on purely circumstantial evidence.'

He ceased, and a buzz of surprise ran round. He could be no sailor, that was evident. Quaid turned, as if re-released from an enforced quietness, and began to talk to the lawyer next him. Maurice felt the excitement of the moment, and began to have some feeble notion of the feelings of the prisoner himself, as, holding the spikes hard, he glared at the judge.

Then came the charge to the jury. Temperate, concise, and logical; and, as Quaid said, in favour of the prisoner. The disappearance of Mr Mogford's brother was not without its effect evidently.

The jury retiring, the prisoner was removed, and the court buzzed again. 'They could agree' – 'They could not.' 'They would be locked up all night.' 'They were coming out in five minutes.' 'It was a good speech.' 'He had put the rope round his own neck,' and so on.

Quaid, nervously watching the half-seen door of the jury-box, felt himself getting as excited as Frere. As for Plain Joe, he had gone out 'to get a drop o' brandy.'

It was not long before they returned, and Rufus Dawes was put to the bar again.

'By God!' says Quaid, drawing a conclusion from his sinister experience, 'It's against us. Do you see the fellows? *They won't look at the dock.*'

He was right.

'How say you, gentlemen?'

'Guilty, my Lord!'

Plain Joe had caught a rumour of it, and coming in again, heard the grave tones pronouncing judgment.

'... to be hung by the neck until you are dead, and your body to be afterwards dissected and anatomised, and may the Lord have mercy on your soul.'

The wheel had brought it round at last. It was all over. Drawing himself to his full height, Rufus Dawes bowed to the Court, and then – without a look at Quaid – turned to descend the steps he should never mount again. As he did so, the mirror, which in those days hung over the dock, flashed its light into his face, and Maurice Frere, rising in the Court, saw the eyes that had met his in the inn yard on the night of his supper party.

For an instant the condemned man stood irresolute, as if about to speak, and then clenching his hands, he went slowly down, and the dark entrance to the prison swallowed him up. As he disappeared, a sigh of relief broke from the crowd. It had seemed as if his presence had been a weight on all their hearts.

✦ 25 ✦

FOR HIS NATURAL LIFE

ON the fatal Monday morning – Hanging Monday, as it was called in those fine old times – the streets around Newgate were crowded.

The popular pantomime – licensed by the Lord Chamberlain, and under the patronage of the nobility and gentry – was about to commence.

All through the long June night the crowd had begun to gather, and the first faint blue streak of dawn beheld them ranged and eager for the show. Giltspur-street was packed close with people. The Old Bailey was a sea of heads. The open windows of taverns and night-houses were filled with lounging parties of men and women. Such places were the 'boxes' of this truly English stage.

The roofs of adjacent buildings bristled with figures, and beneath the gallows a compact mass of human flesh swayed to and fro. From out this sweating, heaving, malodorous collection of bodies – each with two eyes eager to see the Hanged Men, and two ears agape to catch the fine notes of their dying agony – arose a medley of shrieks and laughter, prayers, oaths, and curses. The crowd was fighting, smoking, pocket-picking, making love. Boys fought for a good place, and women – drabs of the kennel side by side with honest wives of honest working-men – clung to their lovers' sides, or quieted their frightened children by holding them at arm's-height to view the gibbet. All the misery and desperation of the town seemed to have turned out to enjoy the sight of beings more miserable and desperate than itself. It was a hideous jumbling together of night and day – fashion and famine, wealth and poverty. Fashion and wealth, smoking and jesting from its tavern windows, looked down in piteous contempt upon those strange beasts of night – the thieves and vagabonds. And the thieves and vagabonds, smoking and jesting, with bare elbows and empty bellies, would look up at the tavern windows, ferociously thinking what short work they could make of the drunken gentility in broadcloth, and tainted beauty in velvet, could it but get them for five minutes alone in one of these little streets that lay within a stone's throw of the gallows.

It was a popular holiday, a people's dramatic entertainment, a national spectacle. Monday morning at the Old Bailey meant in those days all sorts of things. It meant Mechanics' Institutes, Free Libraries, cheap music, and technical education. The Gallows was the Minister of Public Instruction, and he instructed his pupils sometimes at the rate of a dozen a morning.

In the midst of the confused bass murmur that, rising up, hung like a cloud of sound over the multitude, the bell of St Sepulchre's – like a sharp falsetto note flung high into air – chimed the hour of eight. It was the prompter's bell. The audience shook itself into silence, and during the grim pause before the Door was opened, the Minister of Public Instruction, with one gaunt arm grotesquely akimbo, seemed to address the people.

One! Two! Three! Four! Five! Six! Seve—!

What! Where was the seventh? They had been promised seven. Shame to so disappoint honest men of their rights. And by the storm of hoots and hisses, one would have thought that they had bought the seventh man, body and soul, and had been robbed of him. Reprieve! Who said reprieve? Why should he be reprieved. Had they not come to see seven deaths, and should they be fobbed off with but six? Where were the people's rights? Where was Rufus Dawes, the condemned murderer? Let him be brought out and hung, or all vagabondage – yelling itself hoarse amid confused reports of sudden suicide, pardon, and escape – would know the reason why.

Whereat Justice, feeling its nerves a little shaken, made haste to get the first couple swung off; and Vagabondage, getting the shivering souls of a stealer from a dwelling-house and a coiner of a bad shilling thrown to it, gave a great 'Ah!' of delight, and subsided into growlings, half-appeased.

This outside. Inside, the seventh man, snatched from death, as it were, was leaning against the wall in the condemned yard, faint with the suddenness of his reprieve. The waters of death had gone over his head, and taken his breath. He had been the last, it would seem, to have his irons removed, and the warrant that gave him back to life arriving before the operation was completed, they had left him half unfettered. He had pressed his hands over his ears to shut out the roaring of the crowd; but hearing dimly each 'Oh!' as it burst forth, he shuddered, and as he shuddered, the irons clanked together.

Quaid was there, and a turnkey, and the messenger that had brought the reprieve. The strict justice of the sentence had been a little questioned. It was rumoured that the jury – for all their quick finding – had at first been divided in opinion. The prisoner's defence had made a sensation, and Quaid, hearing that the judge himself had expressed himself doubtful as to the prisoner's guilt, had moved hard for a commutation of the death sentence, and, with an amount of trouble known only to himself, had got it.

'Come, Dawes!' he said, touching him on the shoulder, 'cheer up, man! You are not to die after all.'

Rufus Dawes withdrew his hands from his face.

'I was ready to die!' he said. 'I had done with this world; why did you bring me back to it again?'

Quaid stared.

'Nonsense,' he said. 'I was determined to pull you through, and I've done it, though you are the most obstinate dog I ever met. I suppose,' he added, with his head on one side, and a sort of grim smile on his face, 'you won't tell me who this German fellow was, even now?'

The reprieved prisoner made an impatient stride forward – a stride that was checked midway by the weight of the jangling irons.

'I will tell you nothing more,' he cried. 'You torture me! Your kindness kills me. Even this' – he pointed to the paper in the turnkey's hand – 'is cruelty. "Transported for the term of his natural life." Is that mercy? "His natural life!" Do you know what that means? And I innocent – innocent. Before God, innocent!'

The turnkey grinned at this, and the lawyer frowned.

'You fool,' he said, the claw coming out beneath the velvet, 'I wish I'd left you alone.'

'You might have saved me!' cried Dawes, with the terrible agony of a strong man choking his voice. 'You guessed at the real murderer. It was the landlord's brother. Why did you not have him arrested, and let me go free – not mock me with this death-in-life?'

'Why!' cried Quaid, in a savage whisper, forcing the other back into the shadow of the cells, 'I will tell you why. I slept there that night. I was in the next room to the murdered man, and being awoke by the closing of the house door, I saw Jerry come out, and, after some minutes, climb up the pipe to the chamber.'

'You saw him!'

'Yes, and I saw him merely *look in the window, and then come down and run off*. I thought he had but been baulked in a robbery, but now I know what he must have seen.'

'What?'

'*The Murder*, you hypocritical villain! Now will you understand why – though, to serve myself, I took the rope from off your neck – I refused to lend myself to your infamous designs upon an innocent man. I have saved *you* – go, and repent!'

Rufus Dawes, horrified and appalled, shut his blood-shot eyes aghast for a moment, and then beat the air with his hands, in vain attempts to speak.

'By Heaven, you wrong me!' he gasped out at last. 'I – will tell you the real –' but the attorney had gone – there was no one but his jailer.

The grim walls of the jail rose all around him, and the tones of the iron death-bell smote heavily on his ear. Such sights and sounds were to be his portion henceforth. For him no more the green fields, the brown river, the pure air of heaven. He was parted from the honour of man, the love of woman, the sweet prattle of children. No more for him the glorious burden of humanity. The law had lightened him of it. He was henceforth no longer a man, with hopes, aspirations, ambitions. Between him and the world was a great gulf fixed; a gulf from whence arose curses and cries and the clank of chains and the inarticulate moanings of agonies too great to be uttered. 'His natural life!' He saw it before him – hopeless, infamous, bestial. The convict ship, the chain, the prison, the deadly hatreds that mutilate and murder, the foul friendships that corrupt and destroy. The hideousness of his doom fell like a weight upon his brain. For one wild instant the thought of escape flashed upon him. He took one step forward, and fell senseless to the pavement, – plucked downwards by the fetters at his feet.

BOOK TWO

++ 2 ++

THE PRISON SHIP

It was the breathful stillness of a tropical afternoon. The air was hot and heavy, the sky brazen and cloudless, and the shadow of the *Malabar* lay alone on the surface of the great glittering sea.

The sun – who rose a blazing ball every morning on the left hand to move slowly through the unbearable blue, until he sank fiery red in mingling glories of sky and ocean on the right hand – had just got low enough to peep beneath the awning that covered the poop-deck and awaken a young man who had been dozing on a coil of rope.

'Hang it!' said he, rising and stretching himself, with the weary sigh of a man who has nothing to do, 'I must have been asleep,' and then holding by a stay, he turned about and looked down the ship.

Save the man at the wheel and the guard at the quarter-railing, he was alone on the deck. A few birds flew round about the vessel, and seemed to pass under her stern windows only to appear again at her bows. A lazy albatross, with the white water flashing from his wings, rose with a dabbling sound to leeward, and in the place where he had been glided the hideous fin of a silently-swimming shark. The seams of the well-scrubbed deck were sticky with melted pitch, and the brass plate of the compass case sparkled in the sun like a jewel. There was no breeze, and as the clumsy ship rolled and lurched on the heaving sea, her idle sails flapped against her masts with a regularly recurring noise, and her bowsprit would seem to rise higher with the water's swell, and then dip again with a jerk that made each rope tremble and tauten. On the forecastle, some half dozen soldiers, in all varieties of undress, were playing at cards, smoking, or watching the fishing-lines hanging over the catheads.

So far the appearance of the vessel differed in nowise from that of an ordinary transport. But in the waist a curious sight presented itself. It was as though one had built a cattle-pen there. At the foot of the foremast, and at the quarter-deck, a strong barricade, loop-holed and furnished with doors for ingress and egress, ran across the deck from bulwark to bulwark. Outside this cattle-pen an armed sentry stood on guard; inside, standing, sitting, or walking monotonously, within range of the shining barrels in the arm chest on the poop, were some sixty men and boys, dressed in uniform grey.

The men and boys were prisoners of the Crown, and the cattle-pen was their exercising ground. Their prison was down the main hatchway, on the 'tween decks, and the barricade, continued down, made its side walls.

It was the fag end of the two hours' exercise graciously permitted each afternoon by His Majesty to prisoners of the Crown, and the prisoners of the Crown were enjoying themselves.

It was not, perhaps, so pleasant as under the awning on the poop-deck, but that sacred shade was only for such great men as the captain and his officers, Surgeon Pine, Lieutenant Maurice Frere, and that greatest constellation of all, Captain Vickers and his lady-wife.

That the convict leaning against the bulwarks would like to have been able to get rid of his enemy the sun for a moment was probable enough. His companions sitting on the combings of the mainhatch, or crouched in careless fashion on the shady side of the barricade, were laughing and talking, with a sort of blasphemous and obscene merriment hideous to contemplate; but he, with cap pulled over his brows, and hands thrust into the pockets of his coarse grey garments, appeared to keep aloof from their dismal joviality.

The sun poured his hottest rays on to his head unheeded, and though every cranny and seam in the deck sweltered hot pitch under the fierce heat, he stood there, motionless and morose, staring at the sleepy sea. He had stood thus, in one place or another, ever since the groaning vessel had escaped from the rollers of the Bay of Biscay, and the miserable hundred and eighty creatures among whom he was classed had been freed from their irons, and allowed to snuff fresh air twice a day.

The low-browed, coarse-featured ruffians grouped about the deck cast many a leer of silent contempt at the solitary figure, but their remarks were confined to gestures only. There are degrees in crime, and a convicted murderer, who had but escaped the gallows to toil his life in irons, was a man of mark. The hideous notoriety that had seized upon Rufus Dawes the day after his committal to Newgate, and had accompanied him to the very foot of the scaffold, had followed him from the prison to the hulks, and was with him now on board the convict ship, forty days' sail from England, becalmed on the Atlantic Ocean.

It was customary on board these floating prisons to keep each man's crime a secret from his fellows, so that if he chose, and the caprice of his jailors allowed him, he could lead a new life in his adopted home, without being taunted with his former misdeeds. But, like other excellent devices, the expedient was but a nominal one, and few out of the doomed hundred and eighty but knew the offence their companions had committed. The more guilty boasted of their superiority in vice; the petty criminals loudly swore that their guilt was blacker than it appeared. Moreover, a deed so bloodthirsty and a respite so unexpected had invested the name of Rufus Dawes with a grim distinction, which his superior mental abilities, no less than his savage temper and powerful frame, combined to support. He was respected and admired. The vilest of all the vile horde penned between decks, if they laughed at his 'fine airs' behind his back, cringed and submitted when they met him face to face – for in a convict ship the greatest villain is the greatest hero, and the only nobility acknowledged by that hideous commonwealth is that Order of the Halter which is conferred by the hand of the hangman.

When first he realised his sentence to the full, he felt as if the agony of his doom would kill him. Cut off from hope and surrounded with mystery, he felt estranged alike from Heaven and his kind. The lawyer's sudden revelation had confused him. It clearly could not have been Joe Mogford's brother who committed the crime for which he was condemned; and if it was not he, who could it be? He thought over it until he grew mad with thinking, and could have dashed his head against the walls of his prison in despair at his ignorance. Quaid had not returned, and though he tried to communicate with him from the hulks, the prompt sailing of the transport had baulked his endeavours, and, transferred with the last batch of prisoners to the *Malabar*, lying off Woolwich, with the newly-raised company, he had left England on the 15th of June, barely a fortnight after his trial.

At first he was sullen and despairing; now he was sullen and desperate. Where all were convicts, no one could shame him by his freedom. The officers and soldiers looked on him as one of the herd, a trifle more villainous than his companions; and the herd recognised in him a man of repute, a hero, a leader, and king of men. There was a strange fascination about this homage. He loathed it, and yet liked it. He had resolved, by good conduct, to gain such temporary liberty as might be achieved. He was a man; he had a long life before him; he could keep his thoughts to himself, stifle his agonies, look forward to the future, and work out his freedom. In the meantime, he confessed, it was something to reign, even in Hell.

The young man on the poop caught sight of the tall figure leaning against the bulwarks, and it gave him an excuse to break the monotony of his employment.

'Here you!' he called out, with an oath, 'get out of the gangway!'

Rufus Dawes was not in the gangway – was, in fact, a good two feet from it, leaning against the shrouds of the main mast; but at the sound of Lieutenant Frere's voice he started, and went obediently towards the hatchway.

'Touch your hat, you dog!' cries Frere, coming to the quarter railing. 'Touch your damned hat! Do you hear?'

Rufus Dawes touched his cap, saluting in half military fashion.

'I'll make some of you fellows smart, if you don't have a care,' went on the angry Frere, half to himself and half aloud. 'Insolent blackguards!'

And then the noise of the sentry, on the quarter deck below him, grounding arms, turned the current of his thoughts.

A thin, tall, soldier-like man, with a cold blue eye, and prim features, came out of the cuddy below, handing out a fair-haired, affected, mincing lady, of middle age.

Captain Vickers, of Mr Frere's new regiment, was bringing his lady on deck to get an appetite for dinner.

Mrs Vickers was forty-two (she owned to thirty-three), and had been a garrison *belle* for eleven weary years before she hooked prim John Vickers. The marriage was not a happy one. Vickers found his wife extravagant, vain, and snappish, and she found him harsh, disenchanted, and commonplace. A daughter, born some two years after marriage, was the only link that bound the ill-assorted pair. Vickers idolised little Dora, and when the recommendation of a long sea voyage for his failing health induced him to exchange into the —th, he insisted upon bringing the child with him, despite Mrs Vickers's reiterated objections on the score of educational difficulties.

'He could educate her himself, if need be,' he said; 'and she should not stop at home.'

So Mrs Vickers, after a hard struggle, gave up the point and her dreams of Bath together, and followed her husband with the best grace she could muster.

Once fairly out to sea, she seemed reconciled to her fate, and employed the intervals between scolding her daughter and her maid in fascinating the handsome young Lieutenant Maurice Frere.

Fascination was an integral portion of Julia Vickers' nature; admiration was all she lived for; and even in a convict ship, with her husband at her elbow, she must flirt, or perish of mental inanition. There was no harm in the creature. She was simply a vain, middle-aged woman, and Frere took her attentions for what they were worth. Moreover, her good feeling towards him was useful, for reasons which will shortly appear.

Running down the ladder, cap in hand, he offered her his assistance.

'Thank you, Mr Frere. These horrid ladders! I really – he, he – quite tremble at them. Hot! Yes, dear me, most oppressive. John, the camp stool. Pray, Mr Frere – oh, *thank* you! Dora! Dora! John, have you my smelling salts? Still a calm, I suppose? These dreadful calms!'

This semi-fashionable slip-slop, within twenty yards of the wild beasts' den, on the other side of the barricade, sounded strange; but Mr Frere thought nothing of it. Familiarity destroys terror, and the incurable flirt fluttered her muslins, and played off her second-rate graces, under the noses of the grinning convicts, with as much complacency as if she had been in a Chatham ballroom. Indeed, if there had been nobody else near, it is not unlikely that she would have disdainfully fascinated the 'tween-decks, and made eyes at the most presentable of the convicts themselves.

Vickers, with a bow to Frere, saw his wife up the ladder, and then turned for his daughter.

She was a delicate-looking child of six years old, with blue eyes and bright hair. Though indulged by her father, and spoiled by her mother, the natural sweetness of her disposition saved her from being disagreeable, and the effects of her education as yet only showed themselves in a thousand imperious prettinesses, which made her the darling of the ship. Little Miss Dora was privileged to go anywhere and do anything, and even convictism shut its foul mouth in her presence.

Running to her father's side, the child chattered with all the volubility of flattered self-esteem, and, running hither and thither, asked questions, invented answers, laughed, sang, gambolled, peered into the compass-case, felt in the pockets of the man at the helm, put her tiny hand into the big one of the officer of the watch, even ran down on to the quarter-deck and pulled the coat-tails of the sentry on duty.

At last, tired of running about, she took a little striped leather ball from the bosom of her frock, and calling to her father, threw it up to him as he stood on the poop. He returned it, and shouting with laughter, and clapping her hands between each throw, the child kept up the game.

The convicts – whose slice of fresh air was nearly eaten – turned with eagerness to watch this new source of amusement. Innocent laughter and childish prattle were strange to them. Some smiled and nodded with interest in the varying fortunes of the game. One young lad could hardly restrain himself from applauding. It was as though, out of the sultry heat which brooded over the ship, a cool breeze had suddenly arisen.

In the midst of this mirth, the officer of the watch, glancing round the fast crimsoning horizon, paused abruptly, and shading his eyes with his hand, looked out intently to the westward.

Frere, who found Mrs Vickers's conversation a little tiresome, and had been glancing from time to time at the companion, as though in expectation of someone appearing, noticed the action.

'What is it, Mr Best?'

'I don't know exactly. It looks to me like a cloud of smoke.'
And taking the glass, he swept the horizon.

'Let me see,' says Frere; and he looked also.

On the extreme horizon, just to the left of the sinking sun, rested, or seemed to rest, a tiny black cloud. The gold and crimson, splashed all about the sky, had overflowed around it, and rendered a clear view almost impossible.

'I can't quite make it out,' says Frere, handing back the telescope. 'We can see as soon as the sun goes down a little.'

Then Mrs Vickers must, of course, look also, and was prettily affected about the focus of the glass, applying herself to that instrument with much girlish giggling, and finally declaring, after shutting one eye with her fair hand, that 'positively she could see nothing but sky, and believed that wicked Mr Frere was doing it on purpose.'

In the midst of this, Captain Blunt appeared, and, taking the glass from his officer, looked through it long and carefully. Then the mizentop was appealed to, and declared that he could see nothing; and at last the sun, going down with a jerk, as though it had slipped through a slit in the sea, the black spot was swallowed up in the gathering haze, and was seen no more.

As the sun sank, the relief guard came up the aft hatchway, and the relieved guard prepared to superintend the descent of the convicts. At this moment Dora missed her ball, which, taking advantage of a sudden lurch of the vessel, hopped over the barricade, and rolled to the feet of Rufus Dawes, who was still leaning, apparently lost in thought, against the side.

The bright colour rolling across the white deck caught his eye, and stooping mechanically, he picked it up, and stepped forward to return it.

The door of the barricade was open, and the sentry – a young soldier, occupied in staring at the relief guard – did not notice the prisoner pass through it. In another instant he was on the sacred quarter-deck.

Heated with the game, her cheeks aglow, her eyes sparkling, her golden hair afloat, Dora turned to leap after her recovered treasure, but even as she turned, from under the shadow of the cuddy glided a rounded white arm and shapely hand that, catching the child by the sash, drew her back.

The next moment the young man in grey had placed the toy in her hand.

Maurice Frere, descending the poop-ladder had not witnessed this little incident; and arriving on the deck, saw only the unexplained presence of the convict uniform.

'Thank you,' said a voice, as Rufus Dawes stooped before the pouting Dora.

The convict raised his eyes and saw a young girl of eighteen or nineteen years of age, tall and well developed, who, dressed in a loose-sleeved robe of some white material, was standing in the doorway. She had black hair, coiled around a narrow and flat head, a small foot, white skin, well-shaped hands, and large brown eyes, and as she smiled at him, her scarlet lips showed her white even teeth.

He knew her at once. She was Sarah Purfoy, the captain's wife's maid, but he never had been so close to her before; and it seemed to him as though he was in the presence of some strange tropical flower, which exhaled a heavy and intoxicating perfume.

For an instant the two looked at each other, and then Rufus Dawes felt his collar seized from behind, and he was flung with a shock upon the deck.

Leaping to his feet, his first impulse was to rush upon his assailant, but he saw the ready cutlass of the sentry gleam, and he checked himself with an effort, for his assailant was Mr Maurice Frere.

'What the devil do you do here?' asked that gentleman, with a succession of oaths. 'You lazy skulking hound, what brings you here? If I catch you putting your foot on the quarter-deck again, I'll give you a week in irons!'

Rufus Dawes, pale with rage and mortification, opened his mouth to justify himself, but allowed the words to die on his lips. What was the use?

'Go down below, and remember what I've told you,' cried Frere; and comprehending at once what had occurred, he made a mental minute of the name of the defaulting sentry.

The convict, wiping the blood from his face, turned on his heel without a word, and went back through the strong oak door into his den again.

Frere leant forward and took the girl's shapely hand with an

easy gesture, but she drew it away, with a flash of her black eyes.
'You coward!' she said.

The stolid sergeant close beside them heard it, and his eye twinkled. Frere bit his thick lips with mortification, and followed the girl into the cuddy; but, taking the astonished Dora by the hand, she glided into her mistress's cabin with a scornful laugh, and shut the door behind her.

⤙ 2 ⤚

SARAH PURFOY

CONVICTISM having been safely got under hatches, and put to bed in its government allowance of sixteen inches of space per man, cut a little short by exigencies of ship-board, the cuddy was wont to pass some not unpleasant evenings.

Mrs Vickers was poetical and owned a guitar, and was also musical, and sang to it. Captain Blunt was a jovial, coarse fellow, and Surgeon Pine had a mania for story-telling, while if Vickers was sometimes dull, Frere was always hearty.

Moreover, the table was well served, and what with dinner and tobacco and whist, and music and brandy-and-water, the sultry evenings passed away with a rapidity of which the wild beasts 'tween decks, cooped by sixes in berths of five feet three inches, had no conception.

On this particular evening, however, the cuddy was dull. Dinner fell flat, and conversation languished.

'No signs of a breeze, Mr Best?' asked Blunt, as the first officer came in and took his seat.

'None, sir.'

'Curse the weather,' says Blunt, in an undertone.

'These – he, he – awful calms,' says Mrs Vickers.

'More than a week, isn't it?' asked meek Wilkins, the 'religious instructor.'

'Thirteen days,' growled Blunt.

'I remember, off the Coromandel Coast,' put in cheerful Pine, 'when we had the plague in the *Rattlesnake* –'

'Captain Vickers, another glass of wine?' cries Blunt, hastening to cut the anecdote short.

'Thank you, no more. I have a headache.'

'Headache – um – don't wonder at it, going down among those fellows.'

'It is my duty, doctor. By the King's Regulations –'

'Oh, of course.'

'But it *is* very close!' says Wilkins, with a sort of apologetic air.

'Infamous the way they crowd these ships,' cries Pine. 'Here we have over two hundred souls on board, and not boat room for half of 'em. By Jove, sir, when I was in the *Bombyx*, in the Persian Gulf –'

'Two hundred souls! You must exaggerate, Mr Pine,' says Vickers. 'By the King's Regulations –'

'Not I, my dear sir. One hundred and eighty convicts, fifty soldiers, thirty in ship's crew, all told, and – how many? – one, two, three – seven in the cuddy. How many do you make that?'

'By Jove, you're right, Pine, old boy!' says Frere.

'We *are* just a little crowded this time,' says Blunt.

'It is very wrong,' says Vickers, pompously. 'Very wrong. By the King's Regulations –'

'D—n the King's Regulations!' growled Pine, in Frere's ear. 'Let's go up on deck and have a smoke.'

Frere glanced at Mrs Vickers with upraised brows.

'Hang the woman,' says the ungallant Pine. 'She'll sit here all night. Petticoats are always in the way aboard ship. God bless my soul, when I was cruising with old Tophamper in the Mediter—'

'But there would surely be no danger, Captain Blunt!' cries Mrs Vickers, shaking her curls at him.

'Not a bit, marm,' says tender-hearted Blunt. 'Don't you be alarmed.'

'I'm – he, he! – a dreadful coward!' says the lady.

'All women are,' returned poor Blunt, thinking he was smoothing matters.

'Not *all*,' says gentle Wilkins, hastening to the rescue.

'P'raps not,' says Blunt, suddenly perceiving the slough into which he had fallen. 'Some of 'em have more sense than others.

There's that maid o' yours, marm, *she* ain't one to faint at a mouse, I'll be bound. I never seed black eyes like that wench's but their owner was a tartar, and I've seen a good many rum 'uns in my day –'

At which interesting recollection, he suddenly became aware of outraged sensibility, expressed by the elevation of the lady's nose and, growing purple with honest confusion, changed his chuckle into a cough.

'When I was in the *Formosa*, in the South Seas,' says Pine, taking advantage of the sudden silence to fire off an appropriate anecdote, 'I remember a brown girl – egad, the women used to come up the side like peeled shrimps; not a rag, ma'am, I give you my honour –'

'*Excuse* me, Captain Blunt,' says Mrs Vickers, rising, all the virtue of Chatham flashing in her eyes, 'but I will retire.'

'Lieutenant Frere,' says Vickers, in the awkward pause that followed the rustling of the lady's retiring skirts, 'another glass of wine?'

'No more for me, sir,' says Frere, suppressing a laugh; 'I'm for a smoke.'

And at the signal, the party rose.

'Ecod, Pine,' says Blunt, as the two were left alone together, 'you and I are always putting our foot into it!'

'Women are always in the way aboard ship,' reiterated Pine, who was reasonably savage at having all his stories snapped off at the handle.

'Oh! doctor, you don't mean that, I know,' said a rich soft voice at his elbow.

It was Sarah Purfoy emerging from her cabin.

'Here *is* the wench!' cries Blunt. 'We were talking of your eyes, my dear.'

'Well, they'll bear talking about, captain, won't they?' asked she, turning them full upon him.

'By the Lord, they will!' says Blunt, smacking his hand on the table. 'They're the finest eyes I've seen in my life, and they've got the reddest lips under 'em that –'

'Let me pass, Captain Blunt, if you please. Thank you, doctor.'

And before the admiring commander could prevent her, she swept out of the cuddy.

'She's a fine piece of goods, eh?' asked Blunt, watching her. 'A spice o' the devil in her, too.'

Old Pine took a huge pinch of snuff.

'Devil!' he said. 'I tell you what it is, Blunt, I don't know where Vickers picked her up, but I'd rather trust my life with the worst of those ruffians 'tween decks than in *her* keeping, if I'd done her an injury.'

Hearty Blunt laughed.

'I don't believe she'd think much of sticking a knife into a man, either!' he said.

'Not she. I remember when I was in the *Caliban* –'

'Just so, but I must go on deck, doctor.'

And Blunt hastened away.

Pine – accustomed to be cut short – followed him more slowly.

'I don't pretend to know much about women,' he said to himself, 'but that girl's got a story of her own, or I'm much mistaken. What brings her on board this ship as ladies' maid is more than I can fathom.'

And as, sticking his pipe between his teeth, he walked down the now deserted deck to the main hatchway, and turned to watch the white figure gliding up and down the poop-deck, he saw it joined by another and a darker one, he muttered, 'She's after no good, I'll swear.'

At that moment his arm was touched by a soldier in undress uniform, who had come up out of the hatchway.

'What is it?'

The man drew himself up and saluted.

'If you please, doctor, one of the prisoners is taken sick, and as the dinner's over, and he's pretty bad, I vintured to disturb your honour.'

'You ass!' says gruff Pine – who, like most gruff men, had a good heart under his rough shell – 'why didn't you tell me before?' and knocking the ashes out of his barely-lighted pipe, he stopped that implement with a twist of paper and followed his summoner down the hatchway.

In the meantime the woman who was the object of the grim old fellow's suspicions was enjoying the comparative coolness of the night air.

Her mistress and her mistress's daughter had not yet come out of their cabin, and the men had not yet finished their evening's tobacco.

The awning had been removed, the stars were shining in the moonless sky, the poop guard had shifted itself to the quarter-deck, and Miss Sarah Purfoy was walking up and down the deserted poop, in close *tête-à-tête* with no less a person than Captain Blunt himself. She had passed and repassed him twice silently, and at the third turn, the big fellow, peering into the twilight ahead somewhat uneasily, seemed to obey the glitter of her great eyes, and joined her.

'You weren't put out, my wench,' he asked, 'at what I said to you below?'

She affected surprise.

'What do you mean?'

'Why, at my – at what I – at my rudeness, there! For I was a bit rude, I admit.'

'I? O dear, no. You were not rude.'

'Glad you think so!' returned Phineas Blunt, a little ashamed of what looked like a confession of weakness on his part.

'You *would* have been – if I had let you.'

'How do you know?'

'I saw it in your face. Do you think a woman can't see in a man's face when he's going to insult her?'

'Insult you, hey! Upon my word!'

'Yes, insult me. You're old enough to be my father, Captain Blunt, but you've no right to kiss me, unless I ask you.'

'Haw haw!' laughed Blunt. 'I like that. Ask me! Egad I wish you would, you black-eyed minx!'

'So would other people, I have no doubt.'

'That soldier-officer, for instance. Hey, Miss Modesty? I've seen him looking at you as though he'd like to try.'

The girl flashed at him with a quick side glance.

'You mean Lieutenant Frere, I suppose. Are you jealous of him?'

'Jealous! Why, damme, the lad was only breeched the other day. Jealous!'

'I think you are – and you've no need to be. He is a stupid booby, though he is Lieutenant Frere.'

'So he is. You're right there, by the Lord.'

Sarah Purfoy laughed a low full-toned laugh, that made middle-aged Blunt feel his pulse take a jump forward, and send the blood tingling down to his fingers' ends.

'Captain Blunt,' said she, 'you're going to do a very silly thing.'

He came close to her and tried to take her hand.

'What?'

She answered by another question.

'How old are you?'

'Fifty-two, if you must know.'

'Oh! And you are going to fall in love with a girl of nineteen.'

'Who is that?'

'Myself!' she said, giving him her hand and smiling at him with her rich red lips.

The mizen hid them from the man at the wheel, and the twilight of tropical stars held the main-deck.

Blunt felt the healthy breath of this strange woman warm on his cheek, her eyes seemed to wax and wane, and the hard, small hand he held burnt like fire.

'I believe you're right,' he cried. 'I *am* half in love with you already.'

She gazed at him with a half-contemptuous, half-voluptuous sinking of her heavily-fringed eyelids, and withdrew her hand.

'Then don't get to the other half, or you'll regret it.'

'Shall I?' asked Blunt. 'That's my affair. Come, you little vixen, give me that kiss you said I was going to ask you for below,' and he caught her in his arms.

In an instant she had twisted herself free, and confronted him with flashing eyes.

'You dare!' she cried. 'Kiss me by force! Pooh! you make love like a school-boy. If you can make me like you, I'll kiss you as often as you will. If you can't, keep your distance, please.'

Blunt did not know whether to laugh or be angry at this rebuff. He was conscious that he was in rather a ridiculous position, and so he decided to laugh.

'You're a spitfire, too,' said he. 'What must I do to make you like me?'

She made him a curtsey.

'That is your affair,' she said; and as the head of Mr Frere appeared above the companion, Blunt walked aft, feeling considerably bewildered, and yet not displeased.

'She's a fine girl, by jingo,' he said, cocking his cap, 'and I'm hanged if she ain't sweet upon me.'

And then the old fellow began to whistle softly to himself as he paraded the deck, and to glance towards the man who had taken his place with no friendly eyes. But a sort of shame held him as yet, and he kept aloof.

Maurice Frere's greeting was short enough.

'Well, Sarah,' he said, – 'have you got out of your temper?' She frowned.

'What did you strike the man for? He did you no harm.'

'He was out of his place. What business had he to come aft? One must keep these wretches down, my girl.'

'Or they will be too much for you, eh? Do you think one man could capture a ship, Mr Maurice?'

'No, but one hundred might.'

'Nonsense! What could they do against the soldiers? There are fifty soldiers.'

'So there are, but –'

'But what?'

'Well, never mind. It's against the rules, and I won't have it.'

' "Not according to the King's Regulations," as Captain Vickers would say.'

Frere laughed at her imitation of his pompous captain.

'You are a strange girl; I can't make you out. Come,' and he took her hand, 'tell me what you are really.'

'Will you promise not to tell?'

'Of course.'

'Upon your word?'

'Upon my word.'

'Well, then – but you'll tell?'

'Not I. Come, go on.'

'Lady's maid in the family of a gentleman going abroad.'

'Sarah, can't you be serious?'

'I am serious. That was the advertisement I answered.'

'But I mean, what you have been. You were not a lady's maid all your life?'

She pulled her shawl closer round her and shivered.

'People are not born ladies' maids, I suppose?'

'Well, who are you, then? Have you no friends? What have you been?'

She looked up into the young man's face – a little less harsh at that moment than it was wont to be – and creeping closer to him, whispered,

'Do you love me, Maurice?'

He raised one of the little hands that rested on the taffrail, and, under cover of the darkness, kissed it.

'You know I do,' he said. 'You may be a lady's maid or what you like, but you are the loveliest woman I ever met.'

She smiled at his vehemence.

'Then, if you love me, what does it matter?'

'If *you* loved me, you would tell me,' said he, with a quickness which surprised himself.

'But I have nothing to tell, and I don't love you – yet.'

He let fall her hand with an impatient gesture, and at that moment, Blunt – who could restrain himself no longer – came up.

'Fine night, Mr Frere!'

'Yes, fine enough.'

'No signs of a breeze yet, though.'

'No, not yet.'

'One seems to hear the ocean *breathe*,' said Sarah Purfoy.

The observation was a strange one from the lips of a lady's maid, and though neither Blunt nor Frere were poetically inclined, they stared a little at it.

Just then, from out of the violet haze that hung over the horizon, a strange glow of light seemed to break.

'Hallo!' cries Frere, 'did you see that?'

All had seen it, but they looked for its repetition in vain.

Blunt rubbed his eyes.

'I saw it,' he said, 'distinctly. A flash of light.'

And they strained their eyes to pierce through the obscurity.

'Best saw something like it before dinner. There must be thunder in the air.'

Just then Pine joined them hastily.

'What are you all staring at? A light? A flash?'

'The sea has strange mysteries,' says Sarah Purfoy, leaning her chin on her hand, and speaking but half aloud.

'Strange mysteries! Stuff! A flash of summer lightning, or some phosphorescent gleam.'

'No! Look!'

At that instant a thin streak of light seemed to shoot up and then to sink again.

Blunt seized his glass.

'It's a ship signalling,' he said.

But all was dark again, and a prolonged survey resulted only in a shake of the head.

Pine pulled his sleeve.

'What should she signal for?' he said. 'Never mind that girl's mysteries; but come here. I want to speak to you.'

With a last look at the dark distance and the woman who was still staring into it, Blunt, muttering an exclamation of impatience, followed the doctor across the deck.

❖ 3 ❖

THE MONOTONY BREAKS

'WELL, what is it?' said he.

'We've got the fever aboard!'

The weatherbeaten face grew pale, and he drew Pine closer to him.

'Good God! Do you mean it, Pine?'

Pine shook his grizzled head sorrowfully.

'It's this cursed calm that's done it; though I expected it all along with the ship crammed as she is. When I was in the *Hecuba* –'

'Who is it?'

Pine laughed a half pitying, half angry laugh.

'A convict, of course. Who else should it be? They are reeking like bullocks at Smithfield down there. A hundred and eighty men penned into a place fifty feet long, with the air like an oven – what could you expect?'

Poor Blunt stamped his foot.

'It isn't my fault,' he cried. 'The soldiers are berthed aft. If the Government will overload these ships, I can't help it.'

'The Government! Ah! who's the Government? The Government don't sleep, sixty men a-side, in a cabin only six feet high. The Government don't get typhus fever in the tropics, does it?'

'No – but –'

'But what does the Government care, then?'

Blunt wiped his hot forehead.

'Who is it that's down?'

'No. 97 berth; ten on the lower tier. John Rex he calls himself.'

'Are you sure it's the fever?'

'As sure as I can be yet. Head like a fire ball, and tongue like a strip of leather. Gad, don't I know it?' and Pine grinned mournfully. 'I've got him moved into the hospital. Hospital! It is a hospital! As dark as a wolf's mouth. I've seen dog-kennels I liked better.'

'Have you told anyone?'

'No, and don't mean to until the next man goes. It *may* be nothing after all. Oh, if there was only a breeze!'

And he looked up at the silent, heavy heavens.

'There!' cried Blunt, suddenly – 'there! I saw it again. Look, look!'

There was no mistaking it this time, and a simultaneous exclamation burst from all on deck. From out the gloom which hung over the horizon shot up a column of flame, that lighted up the night for an instant, and then sunk, leaving something that looked like a dull red spark upon the water.

'It's a ship on fire!' cried Frere.

They looked again, and even incredulous Pine was forced to confess the truth of the supposition.

The tiny spark still burned, and immediately over it there grew out of the darkness a crimson spot, that hung like a lurid star in the air.

The soldiers and sailors on the forecastle had seen it also, and in a moment the whole vessel was astir.

Mrs Vickers, with little Dora clinging to her dress, came up to view the new sensation; and at sight of her mistress, the modest maid withdrew discreetly from Frere's side.

Not that there was much need to do so; no one heeded her. Blunt had already forgotten her presence, and Frere himself was in earnest conversation with Vickers.

'Take a boat!' said that gentleman. 'Certainly, my dear Frere, by all means. That is to say, if the captain does not object, and it is not contrary to the King's Regulations –'

'Captain, you'll lower a boat, eh? We may save some of the poor devils,' cries Frere, his old English heartiness of body reviving at the prospect of excitement.

Blunt was superintending the burning of a blue light.

'Boat!' he said. 'Why, she's twelve miles off and more, and there's not a breath o' wind!'

'But we can't let 'em roast like chestnuts!' cried the other, as the glow in the sky broadened and became more intense.

'What is the good of a boat?' said Pine. 'The long-boat only holds thirty men, and that's a big ship yonder.'

'Well, take two boats – three boats! By heaven, you'll never let 'em burn alive without stirring a finger to save them!'

'They've got their own boats,' says Blunt, whose coolness was in strong contrast to the young officer's impetuosity; 'and if the fire gains, they'll take to 'em, you may depend. In the meanwhile, we'll show 'em that there's some one near 'em.'

And as he spoke, the blue light flared hissing into the night.

'There, they'll see that, I expect!' he said, as the ghastly flame rose extinguishing the stars for a moment, only to let them appear again brighter in a darker heaven.

'Mr Best – lower and man the quarter-boats! Mr Frere – you can go in one, if you like, and take a volunteer or two from those grey-jackets of yours amidships. I shall want as many hands as I can spare to man the long-boat and cutter, in case we want 'em. Steady there, lads! Easy!' and as the first eight men who could reach the deck parted to the larboard and starboard quarter-boats, Frere ran down on the main-deck.

Mrs Vickers, of course, was in the way, and gave a genteel scream as Blunt rudely pushed past her with a scarce-muttered apology; but her maid was standing, erect and motionless, by the quarter-railing, and as the captain paused for a moment to look round him, he saw her dark eyes fixed on him not unadmiringly.

He was, as he said, over fifty-two, and burly and grey-haired, but he blushed like a girl under her admiring gaze. Nevertheless, he said only, 'That wench is a trump!' and swore a little.

Meanwhile Maurice Frere had passed the sentry and leapt down into the 'tween-decks. At his nod, the prison door was thrown open. The air was hot. And that strange, horrible odour which is peculiar to closely-packed human bodies seemed to fill the place. It was like coming into a full stable.

He ran his eye down the double tier of bunks which lined the side of the ship, and stopped at the one opposite him.

There seemed to have been some disturbance there lately, for instead of the six pair of feet which should have protruded therefrom, the gleam of the bull's-eye showed but four.

'What's the matter here, sentry?' he asked.

'Prisoner ill, sir. Doctor sent him to hospital.'

'But there are two.'

The other came from behind the break of the berths. It was Rufus Dawes. He held by the side as he came, and saluted.

'I felt sick, sir, and was trying to get the scuttle open.'

The heads were all raised along the silent line, and eyes and ears were eager to see and listen. The double tier of bunks looked terribly like a row of wild beast cages at that moment.

Maurice Frere burst into a rage and stamped his foot.

'Sick! What are you sick about, you malingering dog? I'll give you something to sweat the sickness out of you! You're a sailor, I know. Stand a one side here!'

Rufus Dawes, wondering, obeyed. He seemed heavy and dejected, and passed his hand across his forehead, as though he would rub away a pain there.

'Which of you fellows can handle an oar?' Frere went on. 'There, curse you, I don't want fifty! Three'll do. Come on now, make haste!'

The heavy door clashed again, and in another instant the four 'volunteers' were on deck.

The crimson glow was turning yellow now, and spreading over the sky.

'Two in each boat!' cries Blunt. 'I'll burn a blue-light every hour for you, Mr Best; and take care they don't swamp you Lower away, lads!'

As the second prisoner took the oar of Frere's boat, he uttered a sort of groan and fell forward, recovering himself instantly.

Sarah Purfoy, leaning over the side, saw the occurrence.

'What is the matter with that man?' she said. 'Is he ill?'

Pine was next to her, and hearing looked.

'It's that big fellow in No. 10,' he cried. 'Here, Frere!'

But Frere heard him not. He was intent on the beacon that gleamed ever brighter in the distance.

'Give way, my lads!' he shouted. And amid a cheer from the ship, the two boats shot out of the bright circle of the blue light, and seemed to disappear into the darkness.

Sarah Purfoy turned to Pine for an explanation, but he shook off her hand, and turned sharply away.

'It's no use making a fuss now,' he said. 'Besides, I may be wrong. I'll wait.'

For a moment the girl paused, as if in doubt; and then, ere his retreating figure turned to retrace its steps, she cast a quick glance around, and slipping down the ladder, made her way to the 'tween decks.

The iron-studded oak barricade that, loopholed for musketry, and perforated with plated trapdoor for sterner needs, separated soldiers from prisoners, was close to her left hand, and the sentry at its padlocked door looked at her inquiringly.

She laid her little hand on his big rough one – a sentry is but mortal – and opened her brown eyes at him.

'The hospital,' she said. 'The doctor sent me,' and before he could answer, her white figure vanished down the hatch, and passed round the bulkhead, behind which lay the sick man.

⊷ 4 ⊶

THE HOSPITAL

THE hospital was nothing more nor less than a partitioned portion of the lower deck, filched from the space allotted to the soldiers. It ran fore and aft, coming close to the stern windows, and was, in fact, a sort of artificial stern cabin. At a pinch, it might have held a dozen men.

Though not so hot as in the prison, the atmosphere of the lower deck was close and unhealthy, and the girl, pausing to listen to the subdued hum of conversation coming from the soldiers' berths, felt herself turn strangely sick and giddy. She drew herself up, however, and held out her hand to a man who came rapidly across the misshapen shadows thrown by the sulkily swinging lantern to meet her. It was the young soldier who had been that day sentry at the convict gangway.

'Well, miss,' he said, 'I am here, yer see, waiting for yer.'

'You are a good boy, Miles; but don't you think I'm worth waiting for?'

Miles grinned from ear to ear.

'Indeed you be,' said he.

Sarah Purfoy frowned and then smiled.

'Come here, Miles; I've got something for you.'

Miles came forward, grinning harder.

The girl produced a small object from the pocket of her dress. If Mrs Vickers had seen it, she would probably have been angry, for it was nothing less than the captain's brandy-flask.

'Drink, bumpkin,' said she, 'drink. It's the same as they have upstairs, so it won't hurt you.'

The fellow needed no pressing. He took off half the contents of the bottle at a gulp, and then fetching a long breath, stood staring at her.

'That's prime!'

'Is it? I daresay it is.' She had been looking at him with unaffected disgust as he drank. 'Brandy is all you men understand.'

Miles – still sucking in his breath – came a pace closer.

'Not it,' said he, with a twinkle in his little pig's eyes. 'I understand something else, miss, I can tell yer.'

'What is that, Miles?' asked she, glancing anxiously at the hospital door, and concealing the flask again.

'That you're a — handsome gal!'

The tone of the sentence seemed to awaken her, and remind her, as it were, of some forgotten errand.

She laughed as loudly and merrily as she dared, and laid her hand on the speaker's arm.

The boy – for he was but a boy, one of those many ill-reared country louts who leave the plough-tail for the musket, and, for a shilling a day, experience all the 'pomp and circumstance of glorious war' – reddened to the roots of his closely cropped hair.

'Have you only just found that out? No, that's quite close enough. You're only a common soldier, Miles, and you mustn't make love to me.'

'Not make love to yer!' says Miles. 'What did you tell me to meet yer here for then?'

She laughed again.

'What a practical animal you are! Suppose I had something to say to you?'

Miles devoured her with his eyes.

'It's hard to marry a soldier,' he said, with a recruit's proud intonation of the word; 'but yer might do worse, miss, and I'll work for yer like a slave, I will.'

She looked at him with curiosity and pleasure. It seemed as if – though her time was evidently precious – she could not resist the temptation of listening to her own praises.

'I know you're above me, Miss Sarah. You're a lady, but I love yer, I do, and you drives me wild with yer tricks.'

'Do I?'

'Do yer? Yes, yer do. What did yer come an' make up to me for, and then go sweetheartin' with them others?'

'What others?'

'Why, the cuddy folk – the skipper, and the parson, and that – Frere. I see yer walkin' the deck wi' un o' nights. Dom 'un, I'd put a bullet through his curly head as soon as look at 'un.'

Sarah Purfoy came closer.

'Would you, Miles?'

'Ay, by — would I, the — tyrant!'

'Hush! Miles dear – they'll hear you.'

Her face was all aglow, and her expanded nostrils seemed to throb. Beautiful as the face was, it had a tigerish look about it at that instant.

Encouraged by the epithet, Miles put his arms round her slim waist, just as Blunt had done, but she did not resent it so abruptly. Miles had promised more.

'Hush!' she whispered, with admirably-acted surprise – 'I

heard a noise!' and as the soldier started back, she smoothed her dress complacently.

'There is no one!' cried he.

'Isn't there? My mistake then. Now come here, Miles.'

Miles obeyed.

'Who is in the hospital?'

'I dunno.'

'Well, I want to go in.'

Miles scratched his head, and grinned.

'Yer carn't.'

'Why not? You've let me in before.'

'Against the doctor's orders. He gave me speshul orders to let no one in but himself.'

'Nonsense.'

'It ain't nonsense. There was a convic' brought in tonight, and nobody's to go near him.'

'A convict!' She grew more interested. 'What's the matter with him?'

'Dunno. But he's to be kep' quiet until old Pine comes down.'

She became authoritative.

'Come, Miles, let me go in.'

Discipline seemed to triumph over affection, and Miles grew rigid.

'I can't, Miss.'

'But *why*? I have been there before. I've seen *you* there.'

'So yer have,' said Miles, 'and that was when yer made me love yer.'

'Well, let me in.'

'Don't ask me, miss. It's against orders, and –'

'Against orders! Why you were blustering about shooting people just now.'

The badgered Miles grew angry.

'Was I? Bluster or no bluster, you don't go in.'

She turned away.

'Oh, very well. If this is all the thanks I get for wasting my time down here, I shall go on deck again.'

Miles became uneasy.

'There are plenty of agreeable people there.'

Miles took a step after her.

'Mr Frere will let me go in I dare say, if I ask him.'

Miles swore under his breath.

'Dom Mr Frere! Go in if yer like,' he said, 'I won't stop yer, but remember what I'm doing of.'

She turned again at the foot of the ladder, and came quickly back.

'That's a good lad. I knew you would not refuse me,' and smiling at the poor lout she was befooling, she passed into the cabin.

There was no lantern, and from the partially-blocked stern windows came only a dim vaporous light.

The dull ripple of the water as the ship rocked on the slow swell of the sea made a melancholy sound, and the sick man's heavy breathing seemed to fill the air.

The slight noise made by the opening door seemed to rouse him, for he rose on his elbow and began to mutter.

Sarah Purfoy paused in the doorway to listen, but she could make nothing of the low, uneasy murmuring. Raising her arm, conspicuous by its white sleeve in the gloom, she beckoned Miles.

'The lantern,' she whispered – 'bring me the lantern!'

He unhooked it from the rope where it swung, and brought it towards her.

At that moment the man in the bunk sat up erect, and twisted himself towards the light.

'Sarah!' he cried, in shrill, sharp tones. 'Sarah!' and swooped with a lean arm through the dusk, as though to seize her.

The girl leapt out of the cabin like a panther, struck the lantern out of her lover's hand, and was back at the bunkhead in a moment.

The convict was a young man of about four-and-twenty. His hands – clutched convulsively now on the blankets – were small and well-shaped, and the unshaven chin bristled with promise of a strong beard. His wild black eyes glared with all the fire of delirium, and as he gasped for breath, the sweat stood in beads on his sallow forehead.

The aspect of the man was sufficiently ghastly, and Miles, drawing back with an oath, did not wonder at the terror which had seized Mrs Vickers' maid.

With open mouth and agonised face, she stood in the centre

of the cabin, lantern in hand, like one turned to stone, gazing at the man on the bed.

'Ecod, he be a sight!' says Miles, at length. 'Come away, miss, and shut the door. He's ravin' I tell yer.'

The sound of his voice recalled her.

She dropped the lantern, and rushed to the bed.

'You fool; he's choking, can't you see? Water! give me water!'

And wreathing her arms around the man's head, she pulled it down on to her bosom, rocking it there, half savagely, to and fro.

Awed into obedience by her voice, Miles dipped a pannikin into a small unheaded puncheon, cleated in the corner of the cabin, and gave it her and, without thanking him, she placed it to the sick prisoner's lips. He drank greedily, and closed his eyes with a grateful sigh.

Just then the quick ears of Miles heard the jingle of arms.

'Here's the doctor coming, miss!' he cried. 'I hear the sentry saluting. Come away! Quick!'

She seized the lantern, and, opening the horn slide, extinguished it.

'Say it went out,' she said, in a fierce whisper, 'and hold your tongue. Leave me to manage.'

She bent over the convict as if to arrange his pillow, and then glided out of the cabin, just as Pine descended the hatchway.

'Hallo!' cried he, stumbling, as he missed his footing, 'where's the light?'

'Here, sir,' says Miles, fumbling with the lantern. 'It's all right, sir. It went out, sir.'

'Went out! What did you let it go out for, you blockhead!' growled the unsuspecting Pine. 'Just like you boobies! What is the use of a light if it "goes out," eh?'

And as he groped his way, with outstretched arms, in the darkness, Sarah Purfoy slipped past him unnoticed, and gained the upper deck.

HOW SOCIETY MADE ITS CRIMINALS
FORTY YEARS AGO

IN the prison of the 'tween decks reigned a darkness pregnant with murmurs. The sentry at the entrance to the hatchway was supposed to 'prevent the prisoners from making a noise,' but he put a very liberal interpretation upon the clause, and as long as the prisoners refrained from shouting, yelling and fighting – eccentricities in which they sometimes indulged – he did not disturb them. This course of conduct was dictated by prudence, no less than by convenience, for one sentry was but little over so many; and the convicts, if pressed too hard, would raise a sort of bestial boo-hoo, in which all voices were confounded, and which, while it made noise enough and to spare, utterly precluded all notion of individual punishment. One could not flog a hundred and eighty men, and it was impossible to distinguish any particular offender. So, in virtue of this last appeal, convictism had established a tacit right to converse in whispers, and to move about inside its oaken cage.

To one coming in from the upper air, the place would have seemed in pitchy darkness; but the convict eye, accustomed to the sinister twilight, was enabled to discern surrounding objects with tolerable distinctness. The prison was about fifty feet long and fifty feet wide, and ran the full height of the 'tween decks, viz., about five feet ten inches high. The barricade was loopholed here and there, and the planks were in some places wide enough to admit a musket barrel. On the aft side, next the soldiers' berths, was a trap door, like the stoke hole of a furnace. At first sight, this appeared to be contrived for the humane purpose of ventilation, but a second glance dispelled this weak conclusion. The opening was just large enough to admit the muzzle of a small howitzer, secured on the deck below. In case of a mutiny, the soldiers could sweep the prison from end to end with grape shot. Such fresh air as there was, filtered through those loop-holes, and came in somewhat larger quantity through a wind-sail passed into the prison from the hatchway. But the wind-sail, being necessarily but at one end of the place, the air it brought was pretty well absorbed by the twenty or thirty lucky fellows near it, and the other hundred and fifty did not come so well off. The scuttles were open certainly, but as the row of bunks had been built against them, the air *they* brought was the peculiar property of such men as occupied the berths into which they penetrated. These berths were twenty-eight in number, each containing six men. They ran in a double tier round three sides of the prison, twenty at each side, and eight affixed to that portion of the forward barricade opposite the door. Each berth was presumed to be five feet six inches square, but the necessities of stowage had deprived them of six inches, and even under that pressure, twelve men were compelled to sleep on the deck. Pine did not exaggerate when he spoke of the custom of overcrowding convict ships; and as he was entitled to half a guinea for every man he delivered safely in Hobart Town, he had some reason to complain.

When Frere had come down, an hour before, the prisoners were all snugly between their blankets. They were not so now; though, at the first clink of the bolts, they would be back again in their old positions, to all appearances sound asleep. As the eye became accustomed to the foetid duskiness of the prison, a strange picture presented itself. Groups of men, in all imaginable attitudes, were lying, standing, sitting, or pacing up and down. It was the scene on the poop deck over again, only, here being no fear of restraining keepers, the wild beasts were a little more free in their movements. It is impossible to convey, in words, any idea of the hideous phantasmagoria of shifting limbs and faces which moved through the evil smelling twilight of this terrible prison-house. Callot might have drawn it, Dante might have suggested it, but a minute attempt to describe its horrors would but disgust. There are depths in humanity which one cannot explore, as there are mephitic caverns into which one dare not penetrate.

Old men, young men, and boys, stalwart burglars and highway robbers, side by side with wizened pickpockets or cunning-featured area-sneaks. The forger occupied the same berth with the body-snatcher. The man of education learned strange secrets of house-breakers' craft, and the vulgar ruffian of St Giles took lessons in self-control from the keener intellect of the professional

swindler. The fraudulent clerk and the flash 'cracksman' interchanged experiences. The smuggler's stories of lucky ventures
and successful runs were capped by the footpad's reminiscences
of foggy nights and stolen watches. The poacher, grimly thinking of his sick wife and orphaned children, would start as the
night-house ruffian clapped him on the shoulder and bade him,
with a curse, to take good heart, and 'be a man'. The fast shop-
boy, whose love of fine company and high living had brought
him to this pass, had shaken off the first shame that was on him,
and listened eagerly to the narratives of successful vice that fell
so glibly from the lips of his older companions. To be transported seemed no such uncommon fate. The old fellows laughed,
and wagged their grey heads with all the glee of past experience,
and listening youth longed for the time when it might do likewise. Society was the common foe, and magistrates, jailers, and
parsons, the natural prey of all noteworthy mankind. Only fools
were honest, only cowards kissed the rod, and refused to meditate revenge on that world of respectability which had wronged
them. Each new comer was one more recruit to the ranks of
Ruffianism, and not a man penned in that reeking den of infamy
but became a sworn hater of law, order and 'free men'. What he
might have been before mattered not. He was now a prisoner,
and – thrust into a suffocating barracoon, herded with the foulest
of mankind; with all imaginable depths of blasphemy and in-
decency sounded hourly in his sight and hearing – he lost his
self-respect, and became what his jailers took him to be – a wild
beast to be locked under bolts and bars, lest he should break out
and tear them.

The conversation ran upon the sudden departure of the four.
What could they want with them at that hour?

'I tell you there's something up on deck,' says one to the group
nearest him. 'Don't you hear all that rumbling and rolling?'

'What did they lower boats for? I heard the dip o' the oars.'

'Don't know, mate. P'raps a burial job,' hazarded a short,
stout fellow, as a sort of happy suggestion.

'One of those — in the parlour!' said another; and a laugh
followed the speech.

'No such luck. You won't hang your gib for them yet awhile.
More like the skipper agone fishin'.'

'The skipper don't go fishin', yer fool,' says another. 'What should he do fishin'? – 'special in the middle o' the night.'

'That 'ud be like old Dovery, eh?' says another, alluding to an old grey-headed fellow, who – a returned convict – was again under sentence for body-snatching.

'Ay,' put in a young man, who had the reputation of being the smartest 'crow'[1] in London – ' "fishers of men," as the parson says.'

The snuffling imitation of a methodist preacher was good, and there was another laugh.

Just then a miserable little Cockney pickpocket, feeling his way to the door, fell into the party.

A volley of oaths and kicks received him.

'I beg your pardon, gen'lmen,' cries the miserable wretch, 'but I want h'air.'

'Go to the barber's and buy a wig, then;' says the Crow, elated at the success of his last sally.

'Oh, sir, my back!'

'Shut up, you – charley-pitcher[2] – shut up!'

One of the men in the bunks struck up the fag end of a song.

> Oh, we shall caper a heel and toe-ing
> A Newgate hornpipe[3] some fine day,
> With the girls their ogles throwing,
> And old Cotton[4] humming his pray.

'Stow that — gaff!'

> And the fogle-hunters[5] doing
> Their morning fake in the prigging lay!

'Shut your mouth, you fool! You didn't even get seven penn'orth for tops[6] singing!'

'How der you know, culver-head?' cried out a shrill voice. 'You'll maybe wear a horse's nightcap[7] yet.'

1. *Crow* – The look-out man of a burglars' gang.
2. *Charley-Pitcher* – Low gambler.
3. *To dance a Newgate hornpipe* – to be hung.
4. *Old Cotton* – The ordinary of Newgate.
5. *Fogle-hunters* – Stealers of pocket handkerchiefs.
6. *Tops* – Dying speeches.
7. *Horse's nightcap* – A halter.

'Get up!' groaned someone in the darkness. 'Oh, Lord, I'm smothering! Here, sentry!'

A dozen knuckles were at the speaker's throat in an instant.

'You call out, will yer! Lie still, yer — cat-in-the-pan,[1] or I'll make yer?'

'Vater!' cried the little cockney. 'Give us a drop o' vater, for mercy's sake. I haven't moist'ned my chaffer[2] this blessed day.'

'Half a gallon a day, bo', and no more,' says a sailor next him.

'Yes, what have yer done with yer half gallon, eh?' asked the Crow, derisively.

'Some one stole it,' said the sufferer.

'He's been and blued[3] it,' squealed the singer in the bunk. 'Been an' blued it to buy a Sunday veskit with! Oh, ain't he a vicked young man?'

And the speaker hid his head under the blankets, in humorous affectation of modesty.

All this time the miserable little cockney — he was a tailor by trade — had been grovelling under the feet of the Crow and his companions.

'Let me h'up, gents,' he implored — 'let me h'up. I feel as if I should die — I do.'

'Let the gentleman up,' says the humorist in the bunk. 'Don't yer see his kerridge is avaitin' to take him to Hopera?'

The conversation had got a little loud, and from the topmost bunk on the near side, a bullet head protruded.

'Ain't a cove to get no sleep?' cried a gruff voice. 'My blood, if I have to turn out, I'll knock some of your empty heads together.'

It seemed that the speaker was a man of mark, for the noise ceased instantly; and, in the lull which ensued, a shrill scream broke from the wretched tailor.

'Help! they're killing me! Ah-h-h!'

'Wot the —'s the matter?' roared the silencer of the riot, jumping from his berth, and scattering the Crow and his companions right and left. 'Let him be, carn't yer?'

'H'air!' cried the poor devil — 'h'air; I'm fainting!'

1. *Cat-in-the-pan* — sneak, traitor.
2. *Moisten your chaffer* — Wet your mouth.
3. *Blue* — To pawn.

Just then there came another groan from the man in the opposite bunk.

'Well I'm —!' said the giant, as he held the gasping tailor by the collar and glared round him. 'Here's a pretty go! All the blessed chickens ha' got the croup!'

The groaning of the man in the bunk redoubled.

'Pass the word to the sentry,' says someone more humane than the rest. 'The —'s sick!'

'Ah,' says the humorist, 'pass him out; it'll be one the less. We'd rather have his room than his company.'

'Sentry, here's a man sick.'

But the sentry knew his duty better than to reply. He was a young soldier, but he had been well informed of the artfulness of convict stratagems and, moreover, Captain Vickers had carefully apprised him 'that by the King's Regulations, he was forbidden to reply to any question or communication addressed to him by a convict, but, in the event of being addressed, was to call the non-commissioned officer on duty.' Now, though he was within easy hailing distance of the guard on the quarter-deck, he felt a natural disinclination to disturb those gentlemen merely for the sake of a sick convict, and knowing that, in a few minutes, the third relief would come on duty, he decided to wait until then.

In the meantime the tailor grew worse, and began to moan dismally.

'Here! 'ullo!' called out his supporter, in dismay. 'Hold up 'ere! Wot's wrong with yer? Blarst yer, don't come the drops 'ere. Pass him down, some of yer,' and the wretch was hustled down the line to the doorway.

'Vater!' he whispered, beating feebly with his hand on the thick oak. 'Get us a drink, master, for Gord's sake!'

But the prudent sentry answered never a word, until the ship's bell warned him of the approach of the relief guard; and then honest old Pine coming with anxious face to inquire after his charge, received the intelligence that there was another prisoner sick. He had the door unlocked and the tailor outside in an instant. One look at the flushed, anxious face was enough.

'Who's that moaning in there?' he asked.

It was the man who had tried to call for the sentry an hour

back, and Pine had him out also, convictism beginning to wonder a little.

'Take 'em both aft to the hospital,' he said; 'and Jenkins – if there are any more men taken sick, let them pass the word for me at once. I shall be on deck.'

The guard stared in each other's faces, a little alarmedly, but said nothing, thinking more of the burning ship, which now flamed furiously across the placid water, than of peril nearer home; but as Pine went up the hatchway he met Blunt.

'Well?' said he.

'Two more down,' says Pine. 'I must tell 'em tomorrow.'

Blunt nodded towards the volume of lurid smoke that rolled up out of the glow – 'Suppose there is a shipload of those poor devils? I can't refuse to take 'em in.'

'No,' says Pine, gloomily, 'I suppose you can't. If they come, I must stow 'em somewhere. We'll have to run for the Cape with the first breeze, that is all I can see for it,' and he turned away to watch the burning vessel.

⤙ 6 ⤚

THE FATE OF THE *HYDASPES*

THE two boats made straight for the red column that uprose like a gigantic torch over the silent sea.

As Blunt had said, the burning ship lay a good twelve miles from the *Malabar*, and the pull was a long and a weary one. Once fairly away from the protecting sides of the vessel that had borne them thus far on their dismal journey, they seemed to have come into a new atmosphere. The immensity of the ocean over which they slowly moved revealed itself for the first time. On board the prison ship, surrounded with all the memories if not with the comforts of the shore they had quitted, they had not realised how far they were from that civilisation which had given them birth. The well-lighted, well-furnished cuddy, the homely mirth of the forecastle, the setting of sentries and the changing of guards, even the gloom and terror of the closely-locked prison, combined to make the voyagers feel a sort of security against the unknown dangers of the sea. That defiance of nature which is born of contact with humanity, had hitherto sustained them, and they felt that, though alone on the vast expanse of waters, they were in companionship with others of their kind, and that the perils one man had passed might be successfully dared by another. But now – with one ship growing smaller behind them, and the other, containing they knew not what horror of human agony and human helplessness, lying a burning wreck in the black distance ahead of them – they began to feel their own littleness. The *Malabar*, that huge sea-monster, in whose capacious belly so many human creatures lived and hoped and suffered, had dwindled to a walnut-shell, and yet beside her bulk how infinitely small had their own frail cock-boat appeared as they shot out from under her towering stern! *Then* the black hull rising above them, had seemed a tower of strength, built to defy the utmost violence of wind and wave, *now* it was but a slip of wood floating – as it seemed by sufferance – on an unknown depth of black, fathomless water. The blue-light, which at its first flashing over the ocean had made the very stars pale their lustre, and lighted up with ghastly radiance the enormous vault of heaven, was now but a bright point, brilliant and distinct it is true, but which by its very brilliance dwarfed the ship itself into insignificance. The *Malabar* seemed to lie on the water like a glow-worm on a floating leaf, and the glare of the signal-fire made no more impression on the darkness than would the candle of a solitary miner on the abyss of a coal-pit.

And yet the *Malabar* held two hundred creatures like themselves!

The water over which the boats glided was black and smooth, rising into huge foamless billows, the more terrible because they were silent. When the sea hisses, it seems to speak, and speech breaks the spell of terror; when it is inert, heaving silently, it is dumb, and seems to brood over mischief. The ocean in a calm is like a sulky giant; one dreads on what plan it may be meditating. Moreover, an angry sea looks less vast in extent than a calm one. Its mounting waves bring the horizon nearer, and one does not see how for many leagues the pitiless billows repeat themselves. To appreciate the vastness of the ocean one must see it when it sleeps.

The great sky uprose from this silent sea, without a cloud. The stars seemed to hang low in its expanse, burning in a sort of violet mist of lower ether. The heavens were emptied of sound, and each dip of the oars seemed to be re-echoed in space by a succession of subtle harmonies. As the blades struck the dark water, it flashed fire, and the tracks of the boats resembled two sea-snakes writhing with silent undulations through a lake of quicksilver.

It had been a sort of race hitherto, and the rowers, with set teeth and compressed lips, had pulled stroke for stroke. At last the foremost boat came to a sudden pause. Best gave a cheery shout and passed her, steering straight into the broad track of crimson that already reeked on the sea ahead.

'What is it?' he cried.

But he heard only a smothered curse from Frere, and then his consort pulled hard to overtake him.

It was, in fact, nothing of consequence, – only a prisoner 'giving in.'

'Damn it!' says Frere, 'what's the matter with you? Oh, you, is it? – Dawes! Of course, Dawes. I never expected anything better from such a skulking hound. Come, this sort of nonsense won't do with me. It isn't as nice as lolloping about the hatch-ways, I dare say, but you'll have to go on, my fine fellow.'

'He seems sick, sir,' says compassionate bow.

'Sick! Not he. Shamming. Come give way, now! Put your backs into it!' and the convict having picked up his oar, the boat shot forward again.

But for all Mr Frere's urging, he could not recover the way he had lost, and Best was the first to run in under the black cloud that hung over the crimsoned water.

At his signal, the second boat came alongside.

'Keep wide,' he says. 'If there are many fellows yet aboard, they'll swamp us; and I think there must be, as we haven't met the boats,' and then raising his voice, as the exhausted crew lay on their oars, he hailed the burning ship.

No reply.

'Do you see anyone?' says Frere.

'No.'

'Hail 'em again.'

Still no answer.

'I can't make it out.'

'If they had left her, we should have met them.'

'Let's pull round her.'

She was a huge, clumsily-built ship, with great breadth of beam, and a lofty poop-deck. Strangely enough, though they had but so lately seen the fire, she was a perfect wreck, and appeared to be completely deserted. The chief hold of the fire was amidships, and the lower deck was one mass of flame. Here and there were great charred rifts and gaps in her sides, and the red-hot fire glowed through these as through the bars of a grate. The mainmast had fallen on the starboard side, and trailed a blackened wreck in the water, causing the unwieldly vessel to lean over heavily. The fire roared like a cataract, and huge volumes of flame-flecked smoke poured up out of the hold and rolled away in a low-lying black cloud over the sea.

As Frere's boat pulled slowly round under her stern, he hailed the deck again and again.

Still there was no answer, and though the flood of light that dyed the water blood-red, struck out every rope and spar distinct and clear, his straining eyes could see no living soul aboard. As they came nearer, they could distinguish the gilded letters of her name.

'What is it?' cried Frere, his voice almost drowned amid the roar of the flames. 'Can you see?'

Rufus Dawes, impelled, it would seem, by some strong impulse of curiosity, stood erect in the bow, and shaded his eyes with his hand. Suddenly he uttered a cry.

'Well – can't you speak? What is it?'

'The *Hydaspes*!'

Frere gasped.

The *Hydaspes*! The ship in which Richard Devine had sailed! The ship for which his cousin in England might now look in vain! The *Hydaspes* which – something he had heard at the agents during his hurried enquiries flashed across him.

'Back water, men! Round with her! Pull for your lives!'

Best's boat glided alongside.

'Can you see her name?'

Frere, white with terror, shouted a reply.

'The *Hydaspes*! I know her. She is bound for Calcutta, and she has five tons of powder aboard.'

There was no need for more words. The single sentence explained the whole mystery of her desertion. The crew had taken to the boats on the first alarm, and had left their death-fraught vessel to her fate. They were miles off by this time, and, unluckily for themselves perhaps, had steered away from the side where the shelter lay.

The boats tore through the water. Eager as they had been to come, they were more eager to depart. The flames had even now reached the poop; in a few minutes it would be too late.

For ten minutes or more not a word was spoken. With straining arms and labouring chests, the rowers tugged at the oars, their eyes fixed on the lurid mass before them. Frere and Best, with their faces turned back to the terror they fled from, urged the men to greater efforts. Already the flames had lapped the flag, already the outlines of the stern carvings began to blur with fire.

Another moment and all would be over. Ah! it had come at last!

There was a dull rumbling sound; the burning ship parted in sunder; a pillar of fire, flecked with black masses that were beams and planks, rose up out of the ocean; there was a terrific crash, as though sea and sky were coming together; and then a mighty mountain of water rose, advanced, caught, and passed them, and they were alone – deafened, stunned, and breathless, in a sudden horror of thickest darkness, and a silence like that of the tomb.

The splashing of the falling fragments awoke them from their stupor, and then the blue light of the *Malabar* struck out a bright pathway across the sea, and they knew that they were safe.

SARAH PURFOY MAKES A PROMISE

THOSE on board the convict ship had seen the explosion, and guessed at its cause. There could be but one explanation of such a catastrophe.

'Pray God the boats haven't reached her,' said Blunt, under his breath. 'Another blue-light, Mr Joyce. We mustn't let 'em lose sight of us.'

It was past midnight, and the stars seemed to burn dimly in the moonless heaven, while the sea was as black as ink. The straining eyesight lost itself hopelessly in the soft mist that had spread itself over the surface of the ocean. The fate of the boats could but be conjectured.

'We can do nothing until daylight,' said Pine.

'I wonder if they have saved any of 'em,' said Blunt. 'If they lay off and had the good luck to escape, they might, mebbe, pick up a few poor souls.'

Old Pine grunted, 'More likely to swamp the boats. If they *have* saved any, Blunt, we must run for the Cape. I won't take the responsibility of keeping a straight course if we crowd the ship any more.'

'They'll quarantine us, for God knows how long,' grumbled Blunt.

'Better quarantine us than bury us. However, *I* don't want to do it.'

'See how we get on in the morning,' said the other.

'I say, Pine,' said Blunt, after a pause, during which he seemed to have been lost in thought, 'did you see that girl?'

'What girl?' asked Pine, emerging from the calculation of square inches.

'Sarah.'

'No. What about her?'

'By George, she's got the pluck of the deuce. I saw her during all the bustle. Not a move out of her. As cool as I was, by Jove, and her mistress whining like a spaniel-puppy.'

'Ah!' said Pine. 'Yes – I dare say she's got pluck enough.'

'By God,' cries old Blunt, in a sudden burst of enthusiasm, 'but she's a fine wench!'

'You seem rather taken with her, Blunt.'

'*I?* Not I. I'm too old for that sort o' thing. But she's got an eye in her head – eh, Pine?'

'Two,' returned Pine, grimly, 'and sharp 'uns, both of 'em.'

Blunt chuckled. 'I don't know that she is as sharp as she *looks*, you know,' he said, and nudged the doctor in the ribs.

Pine stared at him, and then laughed. Morality was not the fashion on board prison ships, and the two old sinners understood each other. After a pause, Pine shook his head.

'All right,' he said. 'Please yourself, my son, but *I* don't like the looks of her.'

Blunt brushed up his grey curls with his broad, brown hand. 'God bless you, *I'm* no chicken, old man,' he said, and began to whistle softly.

He was a stanch, honest, sailorlike fellow, but he had quite made up his mind that the handsome lady's maid was in love with him, and projected such end to her love as he had learned to consider usual in such cases. Conscious of his years, the conquest tickled his fancy, and though he would have been mightily ashamed had a *younger* man heard of it – in its present stage – he could not resist the temptation of telling Pine. Pine, however, said nothing more, and then the two men paced the deck, waiting for the dawn.

It came at last. The sky lightened, the mist melted away, and then a long, low, far-off streak of pale yellow light floated on the eastern horizon. By and by, the water sparkled, and the sea changed colour, turning from black to yellow, and from yellow to lucid green. The man at the masthead hailed the deck. The boats were in sight, and Blunt and Pine looked in each other's faces, each wondering what had been the thoughts of the other during the long dark night. The news spread rapidly, and as the boats leapt slowly towards them, the bright water flashing from the labouring oars, a crowd of spectators hanging over the bulwarks cheered and waved their hats.

'Not a soul!' cried Blunt, as he withdrew his glass. 'No one but themselves. Well, I'm glad they're safe anyway.'

The boats drew alongside, and in a few seconds Frere was upon deck.

'Well, Mr Frere?'

'No use,' cried Frere, shivering. 'We only just had time to get away. The nearest thing in the world, sir.' His eyes were sparkling, however, and there was a strange look of triumph in his face.

'Didn't you see anyone?'

'Not a soul. They must have taken to the boats.'

'Then they can't be far off,' cried Blunt, sweeping the horizon. 'They must have pulled all the way, for there hasn't been enough wind to fill a hollow tooth with.'

'Perhaps they pulled in the wrong direction,' said Frere. 'They had a good four hours' start on us, you know.'

Then Best came up and told the story, to a crowd of eager listeners. The sailors having hoisted and secured the boats, were hurried off to the forecastle, there to eat, and relate *their* experience, between mouthfuls, and the four convicts were taken in charge and locked below again.

It would almost appear that Mr Frere's rough remedy had proved effectual, for Rufus Dawes ascended the ladder with a firm step, and, affecting to busy himself for a moment in the gangway, he heard the sailor who pulled stroke in the boat say, 'We saw her name as plain as the nose on your face – the *Hydaspes* – and not a soul saved – not a — soul, mate,' and a smile of triumph – very like that worn by Mr Frere, overspread his face.

Pine, who, remembering the scene the night before, had been looking at him with some interest, turned away in disgust. 'The brute!' he muttered. 'Malingering, I suppose, – and to grin at the death of those poor devils! Now then, prisoners, what are you waiting for? Get below with you!' and he walked aft to hear all particulars.

'Lucky you went, Mr Frere,' Vickers was saying. 'Very lucky. If you had not been there, no one would have known about it. I think that the practice of permitting passenger ships to carry powder is a most reprehensible one.'

'I remember when I was in the *Saraband* –'

'How did you happen to know, Mr Frere?'

'Well, it's a strange accident rather,' says Frere. 'I had occasion to make inquiries about the vessel before I left, and I heard about the powder at the agents. Rum coincidence, isn't it?'

'I should say almost a special interposition of Divine Providence,' said little Wilkins, who had hurried on deck in a most unclerical *deshabille*.

' 'Um,' said Frere.

'Providence or no Providence, it's a thundering good thing!' cries Blunt, by way of smoothing any little difference of opinion that might exist between sword and gown. 'If you hadn't been with the boats, they'd have been blown to shivers!'

'Yes,' says Frere, 'you're right there.'

'And you saw no one?' asked Vickers.

'Not a soul. They must have come to grief somehow, or they would have seen the blue-lights, and made for us.'

'Hang me,' says good-natured Blunt, 'but if we were to get a capful of wind now, I'd drop down and look about for 'em.'

Maurice Frere scowled. 'It's no use looking *now*,' he said. 'It's too late now.'

Blunt laughed.

'And this is the man that was so jolly eager to start off last night! Never say die, Mr Frere – though I thought the pull would take it out of you.'

'Oh, I'm all right,' says Frere, hastily. 'But I don't see the good – there's nobody – it's, in fact –'

Vickers came to the rescue of the reputation of the service.

'Mr Frere speaks from motives of prudence,' said he. 'He thinks that we should but waste time in a search which would be ineffectual.'

'That's it,' said Frere, relieved.

'If there was a breeze, I'd go,' said Blunt.

But not a ripple disturbed the oily surface of the ocean, and the thin serpentine streak that was all that remained of the midnight fire, hung motionless in the waste of sky – already growing brazen, as if in anticipation of the coming heat.

'You had better go and turn in, Frere,' said Pine, gruffly. 'It's no use whistling for a wind *here* all day.'

Frere laughed – in his heartiest old English manner. 'I think I will,' he said. 'I'm dog tired and as sleepy as an owl,' and he descended the poop-ladder.

Pine took a couple of turns up and down the deck, and then catching Blunt's eye, stopped in front of Vickers.

'You may think it is a hard thing to say, Captain Vickers, but it's just as well if we don't find these poor devils. We have quite enough on our hands as it is.'

'What do you mean, Mr Pine?' says Vickers, his humane feelings getting the better of his pomposity. 'You would not surely leave the unhappy men to their fate?'

'Perhaps,' returned the grim old fellow, 'they would not thank us for taking 'em aboard.'

'I don't understand you.'

'The fever has broken out.'

Vickers raised his brows. He had no experience of such things; and, though the intelligence was startling, the crowded condition of the prison rendered it easy to be understood, and he apprehended no danger to himself.

'It is a great misfortune, but, of course, you will take such steps –'

'It is only in the prison as *yet*,' says Pine, with a grim emphasis on the word; 'but there is no saying how long it may stop there. I have got three men down as it is.'

'Well, sir, all authority in the matter is in your hands. Any suggestions you make, I will, of course, do my best to carry out.'

'Thank ye. I must have more room in the hospital to begin with. The soldiers must lie a little closer.'

'I will see what can be done.'

'And you had better keep your wife and the little girl as much on deck as possible.'

Vickers turned pale at the mention of his child.

'Good heaven! do you think there is any danger?'

'There is, of course, danger to all of us; but with care we may escape it. There's that maid, too. Tell her to keep to herself a little more. She has a knack of roaming about the ship I don't like. Infection is easily spread, and children always sicken sooner than grown up people.'

Vickers pressed his lips together. This grim old man, with his harsh, dissonant voice, and hideous practicality, seemed like a bird of ill omen.

Blunt, hitherto silently listening, put in a word for the defence of the absent woman.

'The wench is right enough, Pine,' said he. 'What's the matter with her?'

'Yes, *she's* all right, I've no doubt. She's less likely to take it than any of us. You can see her vitality in her face – as many lives as a cat. But she'd bring infection quicker than anybody.'

'I'll – I'll go at once,' cried poor Vickers, turning round.

The woman of whom they were speaking met him at the ladder. Her face was paler than usual, and dark circles round her eyes seemed to give evidence of a sleepless night. She opened her red lips to speak, and then, seeing Vickers, stopped abruptly.

'Well, what is it?'

She looked from one to the other.

'I came for Dr Pine.'

Vickers, with the quick intelligence of affection, guessed her errand.

'Some one is ill?'

'Miss Dora, sir. It is nothing much, I think. A little feverish and hot, and my mistress –'

Vickers was down the ladder in an instant with scared face.

Pine caught the girl's round firm arm.

'Where have you been?'

'I?'

'Were you on the lower deck last night?'

'No.'

'I caught you there once, remember – with a soldier.'

Two great flakes of red came out in her white cheeks, and she shot an indignant glance at Blunt.

'Come, Pine, let the wench alone!'

'Were you with the child last night?' went on Pine, without turning his head.

'No; I have not been in the cabin since dinner yesterday. Mrs Vickers only called me in just now. Let go my arm, sir, you hurt me.'

Pine loosed his hold as if satisfied at the reply.

'I beg your pardon,' he said, gruffly. 'I did not mean to hurt you. But the fever has broken out in the prison, and I think the child has caught it. You must be careful where you go.'

And then, with an anxious face, he went in pursuit of Vickers. Sarah Purfoy stood motionless for an instant, as though in deadly terror. Her lips parted, and her eyes glittered, and she made a movement as though she would retrace her steps.

'Poor soul!' thought honest Blunt, 'how she feels for the child! D— that lubberly surgeon, he's hurt her!'

'Never mind, my lass,' he said, aloud. It was broad daylight, and he had not as much courage in love-making as at night. 'Don't be afraid. I've been in ships with fever before now.'

Awaking, as it were, at the sound of his voice, she came closer to him.

'But ship fever! I have heard of it. Men have died like rotten sheep in crowded vessels like this.'

'Tush! Not they. Don't be frightened; Miss Dora won't die, nor will you neither.' He took her hand. 'It may knock off a few dozen prisoners or so. They are pretty close packed down there –'

She drew her hand away, and then, as if remembering herself, gave it him again.

'What is the matter?'

'Nothing – a pain. I did not sleep last night.'

'There, there; you are upset, I dare say. Go and lie down.'

She was staring away past him over the sea, as if in thought. So intently did she look that he involuntarily turned his head, and the action recalled her to herself. She brought her fine straight brows together for a moment, and then raised them with the action of a thinker who has decided on his course of conduct.

'I have a toothache,' said she, putting her hand to her face.

'Take some laudanum,' says Blunt, with dim recollections of his mother's treatment of such ailments. 'Old Pine'll give you some.'

To his great astonishment, she burst into tears.

'I don't lul-like Doctor Pine. He hurt my arm.'

'Did he? The brute! There – there! Don't cry, my dear. Curse it, don't cry!'

She dashed away the bright drops, and raised her face with a rainy smile of trusting affection.

'I'm very silly; but, pray, don't notice it, Phin – Captain Blunt.

I am so lonely here. So far from home and – and he *did* hurt my poor arm. Look!'

She bared that shapely member as she spoke, and sure enough there were three red marks on the white and shining flesh.

'The ruffian!' cried Blunt, with another oath. 'It's too bad.'

And, with a hasty look round him, the infatuated fellow kissed the bruise.

'I'll get the laudanum for you,' he said. 'You shan't ask that bear for it. Come into my cabin.'

Blunt's cabin was in the starboard side of the ship, just under the poop awning, and possessed three windows – one looking out over the side, and two upon deck. The corresponding cabin on the other side was occupied by Mr Maurice Frere.

Blunt pushed to the door, and took down a small medicine chest, cleated above the hooks where hung his signal-pictured telescope.

'Here,' said he, opening it. 'I've carried this little box for years, but it ain't often I want to use it, thank God. Now, then, put some o' this into your mouth, and hold it there.'

'Good gracious, Captain Blunt, you'll poison me! Give me the bottle; I'll help myself.'

'Don't take too much,' says Blunt. 'It's dangerous stuff, you know.'

'You need not fear. I've used it before.'

The door was shut, and as she put the bottle in her pocket, the amorous captain caught her arms.

'What do you say? Come, I think I deserve a kiss for that.'

Her tears were all dry long ago, and had only given increased colour to her face. Sarah never wept long enough to make herself distasteful. She raised her dark eyes to his for a moment, with a saucy smile, and then, without a blush or affectation of a modesty which it was evident she did not feel, she kissed him on the mouth.

'There!' said she, 'that must do for you now. I will give you another when I bring the bottle back.'

Her meaning was, Blunt thought, unmistakeable. He caught her and kissed her again.

'When will you bring it back? To-night?'

'Perhaps,' said she, disengaging herself from his embrace, and nodding at him from the door.

Blunt followed her with his eyes, and then gave a smirk to a little looking-glass that hung between the windows. It was evident that he was contented with himself.

In the meantime, Sarah Purfoy, gliding to her cabin, met Pine, looking very grave.

'How is Miss Dora, sir?'

'Miss Dora has caught the fever. How did she catch it?'

'Sir! How do I –'

'The fever broke out in the prison. Have you been speaking to any of the men?'

'No, Doctor Pine, I have not.'

Pine knitted his brows. After all, perhaps, he did her wrong. He himself, or Frere, or even the child's father, might have been the unconscious medium by which the infection had been conveyed.

Suddenly she seemed to remember something.

'Yesterday, sir, do you not recollect? The barricade was open, and one of the men picked up her ball and gave it her.'

'When was that?'

'When they were changing guard, sir. It was a tall young man. Mr Frere struck him. The man who went in the boat. Oh, goodness, I remember now – the man who was sick –'

'What, Dawes!'

'I don't know his name.'

Just then a soldier appeared.

'One of the men, sir. They are calling for you.'

And with an ominous jerk of the head, he left her.

She gained her cabin. It was next to that of her mistress, and she could hear the sick child feebly moaning. Her eyes filled with tears – real ones this time.

'Poor little thing,' she said, 'I hope she won't die.'

And then she threw herself on her bed, and buried her hot head in the pillow. The intelligence of the fever would appear to have terrified her – to have startled her almost beyond terror. It was as though the news had disarranged some carefully considered plan of hers, and that being near the accomplishment of some cherished scheme long kept in view, the sudden and un-expected presence of disease had falsified her carefully-made cal-culations, and cast an almost insurmountable obstacle in her path.

'She die! and through me? How did I know that he had the fever? Perhaps I have taken it myself – I feel sick and ill. If he dies! Ah, God, why would I wish to live then?' She turned over on the bed, as if in pain, and then started to a sitting position, as if stung by a sudden thought. 'Perhaps *they* might be taken! The fever spreads quickly, and if so, all this plotting will have been useless. It must be done at once. It will – ah – never do to break down *now*,' and taking the phial from her pocket, she held it up, to see how much it contained. It was three parts full. 'Enough for both,' she said, between her set teeth. The action of holding up the bottle reminded her of amorous Blunt, and she smiled. 'A strange way to show affection for a man,' she said to herself, 'and yet *he* doesn't care, and I suppose I shouldn't by this time. I'll go through with it, and, if the worst comes to the worst, I can fall back on Maurice.' She loosened the cork of the phial, so that it would come out with as little noise as possible, and then placed it carefully in her bosom. 'I will get a little sleep if I can,' she said, and lay down. 'They have got the note, and it shall be done to-night.'

⊷ 8 ⊶

TYPHUS FEVER

Rufus Dawes had stretched himself in his bunk, and had done his best to sleep. But though he was tired and sore, and his head felt like lead, he could not but keep broad awake. The long pull through the pure air, if it had tired him, had revived him, and he felt stronger and reinvigorated; but for all that, the fatal sick-ness that was on him maintained its hold, and his pulse beat thickly, and his brain throbbed with unnatural heat. Lying in his narrow space – in the semi-darkness – he tossed, and rolled, and tumbled, and closed his eyes in vain – he could not sleep. His utmost efforts but induced a sort of oppressive stagnation of his thoughts, through which he heard the voices of his fellow con-victs.

It was fortunate for his comfort, perhaps, that the man who had been chosen to accompany him was of a talkative turn, for the prisoners insisted upon hearing the story of the explosion a dozen times over, and he himself had been roused to give the name of the vessel with his own lips. Had it not been for the quasi respect in which he was held, it is possible that he might have been com-pelled to give his version, and to join in the animated discussion which took place upon the possibility of the crew being saved. As it was, however, he was left in peace, and lay unnoticed, trying to sleep.

The detachment of fifty being on deck – airing – the prison was not quite so hot as at night, and many of the convicts made up for their lack of rest by snatching a sort of dog-sleep in the bared bunks. The four 'volunteers' were allowed to 'take it out'.

As yet there had been no alarm of fever. The three seizures had excited some little comment, however, and had it not been for the counter excitement of the burning ship, it is possible that Pine's precaution would have been thrown away. The old hands – who had been through the passage before – suspected, but said noth-ing, save among themselves. It was likely that the weak and sickly would go first, and that there would be more room for them. In the meantime, as one of their number observed 'what was the good of making a — fuss?'

Three of these old hands were conversing together just behind the partition of Dawes' bunk. As we have said, the berths were five feet square, and each contained six men. No. 10, that occu-pied by Dawes, was situated in the corner made by the joining of the starboard and centre lines, and behind it was a slight recess, as it were, in which the scuttle was fixed. His 'mates' were at present but three in number, for John Rex and the Cockney tailor had been removed to the hospital. The three that remained were the three that were now deep in conversation in the shelter of the recess. Of these, the giant – who had the previous night asserted his authority in the prison – seemed to be the chief. His name was Gabbett. He was a returned convict, who was now on his way to undergo a second sentence for burglary. The other two were a man known as 'the Moocher,' and Jemmy Vetch, the 'Crow.' They were talking in whispers, but Rufus Dawes, lying with his head close to the partition, was enabled to catch much of what they said.

At first the conversation turned on the catastrophe of the burning ship and the likelihood of saving the crew. From this it grew to anecdote of wreck and adventure, and at last Gabbett said something which made the listener start, from his indifferent efforts to slumber, into sudden broad wakefulness.

It was the mention of his own name, coupled with that of the woman he had met on the quarter-deck, that roused him.

'I saw her speakin' to Dawes yesterday,' said the giant, with an oath. 'We don't want no more than we've got. I ain't goin' to risk my neck for Rex's woman's fancies, and so I'll tell her.'

'It was something about the kid,' says the Crow. 'I don't believe she ever saw him before. Besides, she's nuts on Jack, and ain't likely to pick up with another man.'

'I don't know that. She usen't to be so — particular.'

'Come,' says the other, in a tone of expostulation, 'the girl's a trump, and you've no right to doubt her now.'

'— her! If I thort she was agoin' to throw us over, I'd cut her throat as soon as look at her!' says Gabbett, savagely.

'Jack ud have a word in that,' put in the Moocher; 'and he's a curious cove to quarrel with. He'd down your applecart,[1] old man, if he heard yer talk of his gal in that way.'

'He, be —!' returned the giant. 'He's all the savey, I know; but I'd take ten such philliping screevers[2] as he. I'm a touch above his bend[3]!'

'There don't ride rusty, my ingenious clifter,'[4] said the Crow, who prided himself on his acquaintance with slang terms, and used them as a garnish to his speech. 'What's the use of bringing

---

1. *Down his apple-cart* – to do him an injury.

2. *Philliping screevers* – A 'philliper' is a man who acts as 'stall' or 'crow' to pickpockets, and to 'screeve' is to write. Mr Gabbett probably means to express that his friend would do better as a 'thinker' than as a 'worker'.

3. *Above his bend* – out of his power – 'one too many for him.'

4. *Clifter* – thief.

dissension into this happy family? Sarah's a bit of a "brim," but what's that? She's fair and square enough, I'll go bail.'

'There's too much carneying with that — lieutenant,' says the obstinate Gabbett. 'I know her sort. If she takes a fancy to a man, she'd throw over her own father. By G—, if I thort she'd chaunt the play,[1] I'd –'

'There, there!' cried the other, seemingly fearful lest the giant's gruff voice should be heard, 'stash it! The girl's right enough. Look at the way she got you out of the nose-bag in that Chelsea business. You'd have been taking an autumnal tour[2] long ago but for her, my intelligent super-screwer,[3] you know you would.'

This recollection seemed to appease Mr Gabbett, who, with a terrific adjuration of the infernal powers, admitted the truth of the statement.

'What was that about?' asked the Moocher.

'It was about a crib near St Mark's. Jack he was diving up there then on the quiet. He'd had a good swim[4] out o' some screeving fakement just before, but he was getting low. The bloke had gone away to the country, and there was no one in the place but an old 'ooman. So we thort the next 'ouse was empty, and the Lurker and me got inter it with betties,[5] and we had young Gammy down below watchin'. We forced the trap, and got down under the roof, but we found an under-trap, that was fastened inside. We was flummoxed just as near as nine-pence, when a bright hidear strikes Jerry. "I'll git a numbrella," says he. "Wot for?" says I. "Never mind," says he, "I'll git one." Down he goes, mate, into the back drain,[6] and over the wall. There was a charley handy, but Jerry slips past him, an' seein' an old 'ooman goin' by, he tipped her two bob for a cotton water choker, an' back he comes to me ag'in. "Now my kinchin," ses he, "cut a hole in them laths," ses he; and w'en I'd done it, he shoves the mush[7] thro' and hopens it. "Now," ses he, "rip

1. *Chaunt the play* – inform.
2. *An autumnal tour* – to be hung. An elegance of expression derived from 'the fall of the leaf'.
3. *Super screwer* – one who steals watches.
4. *A good swim* – a good run of luck.
5. *Betties* – skeleton-keys   6. *Back drain* – back yard.
7. *Mush* – an umbrella abbreviated from 'mushroom'.

away, Mat and chance the — ducks!" And, in course, all the plaster was caught in the water-choker. He was a lummy[1] 'un was Jerry!'

'So he was, my wido!' says the Crow approvingly. 'So he was, my accomplished ken cracker!'

'Well, we gets in and looks round us. My heart! we'd come to the right shop, I tell yer! Clocks and tickers, and fawneys,[2] and lots o' rum coins and things. In a booro in the second floor, I found nigh a hundred pounds in notes, and Jerry forced a hormoloo cabiny with his jilt,[3] and got nearly fifty guineas in gold. Just as we were bagging the swag – everythink nice and tidy – I hears Gammy's whistle, and then some one opens the house door. I dubs the jigger,[4] and slips to the back-jump.[5] A water-pipe ran down inter the yard, and out I goes, Jerry arter me. Jest as we gets clear on the ground I sees a light, and some one fires. Missed us both though, and I made for the door, the key was in the inside and out we comes, chock onter the — charley. He grabbed me by the collar, but I gave him a white-chapel one-er that knocked him all ways for Sunday, and away we goes!'

'Did yer bring the swag?'

'Hold on a bit. No. We gets down to Old Blicks's, and lies by. The swag was too big for us, and we jest ad nothin' but what we carried. I'd shoved the notes in the pocket o' my kicksies, and so we 'ad a deal with Old Blick for 'em. They was most of 'em twenty-pounders, but Blick, the old –, wouldn't give more nor sixteen quid a-piece. He passed some of 'em away to a Hamburg Jew, but he said he was afeard to run 'em all out. The job made a noise, as you may suppose, for it turned out that the bloke was a hepiskewer of somethin' –'

'Connyskewer you mean, old cupboard head,' corrected the Crow, with dignity, 'but proceed.'

'Wot – wot ever you please to call him, and the crib we'd cracked was his — collection. I'd dropt my goss[6] in the yard when the old man collared me, and they spotted it. I was nailed, but Jack got Sarah to stall on to the old cove with some yarn

1. *Lummy* – clever
2. *Fawneys* – rings.
3. *Jilt* – a small crow-bar.
4. *Dub the jigger* – shut the door.
5. *Back-jump* – back window.
6. *Goss* – hat.

about my being her brother – her brother ! – and she got round him, so that he refused to 'dentify me, and I got off, though I was — near fulled[1] as it was.'

This story, interspersed with oaths and slang as it was, had an intense interest for Rufus Dawes. In the first place, it hinted at some conspiracy afloat. In the second place, it revealed to him that Jerry the Lurker – the man for whose crime he believed himself to be innocently suffering, was the friend and associate of burglars and midnight robbers. If he had known this at his trial, he might have made another point in his favour. He had hitherto – in his agony and sullen gloom – held aloof from the scoundrels that surrounded him, and repelled their hideous advances of friendship. He now saw his error. The mystery that surrounded him was born of the night in which these men moved; to find a clue to it he must descend into that abysmal darkness. He was free to do so. He knew that whatever name he had once possessed was blotted out, that whatever shred of his old life had clung to him hitherto, was shrivelled in the fire that consumed the *Hydaspes*. The secret, for the preservation of which Richard Devine had voluntarily flung away his name, and risked a terrible and disgraceful death, would be now for ever safe; for Richard Devine was dead – lost at sea with the crew of the ill-fated vessel in which his friends believed him – all unwitting of his fortune – to have sailed. The proof was positive. His own handwriting attested that he had gone, and Maurice Frere himself would write the news of his fate. Richard Devine was dead, and the secret of his life in Germany would die with him. Rufus Dawes alone should live. Rufus Dawes – the convicted felon, the murderer of the 3rd of May – should live to learn the true story of that night, to dive beneath the surface of that noisome ditch into which the law had plunged him, and from its black depths to pluck up the mystery of that murder; should live to claim his freedom, and work out his vengeance; or, rendered powerful by the terrible experience of the prison-sheds, to seize both, in defence of jail or jailer.

With his head swimming, and his brain on fire, he eagerly listened for more. It seemed as if the fever which burnt in his veins had consumed the grosser part of his sense, and given him

1. *Fulled* – to be 'fully' committed for trial.

increased power of hearing. He was conscious that he was ill. His bones ached, his hands burned, his head throbbed, but he could hear distinctly, and, he thought, reason on what he heard profoundly.

'By Crimes, but that's good!' said the Moocher; 'as good as a play. Haw, haw! Where did Jack pick her up?'

'I don't know,' returned Mr Gabbett. 'It ain't no affair o' mine where a cove gets his blowen – is it?'

'Certainly not,' affirmed the Crow. 'Nobody would consult *you* when he went to walk the barber,[1] you jolly old dunk-horn!'[2]

'Come,' says the giant, his small eyes sparkling beneath his shaggy brows, 'that's enuff of it! You can ease that clatter as soon as you like, Jemmy Vetch. I didn't come here to stand your slang. Blarst me!'

'No, my lively drummer,[3] you didn't. But there – no offence, mate. We'll have all Dover-court[4] here if we wag our clappers in this style.'

'Well, stow yer gaff, then,' grumbled Mr Gabbett, 'and let's have no more chaff. If we're for bizness, let's come to bizness.'

'What are we to do now?' asked the Moocher. 'Jack's on the sick list, and the gal won't stir a'thout him.'

'Ay,' returned Gabbett, 'that's it.'

'My dear friends,' said the Crow – 'my keyind and keristian friends, it is to be regretted that when natur' gave you such tremendously thick skulls, she didn't put something inside of 'em –'

'Now then –,' ejaculated Gabbett, '*wot* did I say?'

'Calm your h'agitated feelin's, my virtuous gonof.[5] I wasn't born in a bird-cage, and brought up by hand on parched peas, I can assure you. No, I am a man, sir, take me for all –'

'Will you drop it?' growled Gabbett, seizing the other's arm. 'Come to bizness, yer blethering jackass, carn't yer?'

'Well, then,' says the Crow, suddenly dropping into common-

1. *Walk the barber* – make love.
2. *Dunk-horn* – a term of contempt.
3. *Drummer* – a fighting man.
4. *All Dover-court* – all talkers and no listeners.
5. *Gonof* – a loutish, stupid person. Mr Vetch uses it in its – to his friend – most insulting sense – that of an amateur burglar.

place, 'I say that now's the time. Jack's in the 'orspital; what of that? That don't make it no better for him, does it? Not a bit of it; and if he drops his knife and fork, why then, it's my opinion that the gal won't stir a peg. It's on *his* account, not our's, that she's been manoovering, ain't it?'

'Well!' says Mr Gabbett, with the air of one who was but partly convinced, 'I s'pose it is.'

'All the more reason of getting it off quick. Another thing, when the boys know there's fever aboard, you'll see the rumpus there'll be. They'll be ready enough to join us then. Once get the snapper chest,[1] and we're right as ninepenn'orth o' bad hapence.'

Rufus Dawes redoubled his attention. There was a plot to seize the ship!

The giant scratched his thick head.

'But we can't stir without *her*,' he said. 'She's got to stall off the sentry and give us the orfice.'[2]

The Crow's sallow features lighted up with a cunning smile.

'Dear old caper merchant![3] Hear him talk!' said he, 'as if he had the wisdom of Solomon in all his glory! Look here!'

And he produced a dirty scrap of paper, over which his companions eagerly bent their heads.

'Where did yer get that?'

'Yesterday afternoon Sarah was standing on the poop throwing bits o' toke[4] to the gulls, and I saw her a looking at me very hard. At last she came down as near the barricade as she dared, and throwed crumbs and such like up in the air over the side.'

'Ah!' said Mr Gabbett, as if he understood all about it.

'Ah! What's "ah," my gravel grinder. What do you know about it?' returned the Crow, crumpling up the paper, as if in high-minded indignation at the interruption.

Receiving no reply to the interrogation, and apparently remembering that time was precious, he resumed:

'Some o' these bits dropped on the deck beside me, but I was up to trap and took no notice. By-and-by a pretty big lump,

1. *Snapper chest* – arm-chest.
2. *Give the office* – give the signal.
3. *Caper merchant* – dancing master. The Crow speaks tropically. Thieves who enter houses by the window are called 'dancers.'
4. *Toke* – bread.

doughed up round, fell close to my foot, and, watching a favourable opportunity, I pouched it. Inside was this bit o' rag-bag.'

'Ah!' said Mr Gabbett again, 'that's more like. Read it out, Jemmy.'

The writing, though feminine in character, was bold and distinct. Sarah had evidently been mindful of the education of her friends, and had desired to give them as little trouble as possible.

All is right. Watch me when I come up to-morrow evening at three bells If I drop my handkerchief, get to work at the time agreed on. The sentry will be safe.

Rufus Dawes, though his eyelids would scarcely keep open, and a terrible lassitude seemed to paralyse his limbs, eagerly drank in the whispered sentence. Sarah Purfoy was in league with the convicts – was herself the wife or mistress of one of them. She had come on board armed with a plot for his release, and this plot was about to be put in execution. He had heard of the atrocities perpetrated by successful mutineers. Story after story of such nature had often made the prison resound with horrible mirth. He knew the characters of the three ruffians who, separated from him by but two inches of planking, jested and laughed over their plans of freedom and vengeance. Though he conversed but little with his companions, these men were his berth mates, and he could not but know how *they* would proceed to wreak their vengeance on their jailors.

True that the Head of this formidable Chimera – John Rex, the forger – was absent, but the two Hands, or rather claws – the burglar and the prison-breaker – were present, and the slimly-made, effeminate Crow, if he had not the brains of his master, yet made up for his flaccid muscles and nerveless frame by a cat-like cunning, and a spirit of devilish volatility that nothing could subdue. With such a powerful ally outside as the mock maid servant would appear to be, the chance of success was enormously increased. There were one hundred and eighty con-

victs and but fifty soldiers. If the first rush proved successful –
and the precautions taken by Sarah Purfoy rendered success possible – the vessel was theirs. Rufus Dawes thought of the little
bright-haired child who had run so confidingly to meet him, and
shuddered.

'There!' said the Crow, with a sneering laugh, 'what do you
think of that? Does the girl look like nosing us now?'

'No, by G—!' says the giant, stretching his great arms with a
grin of delight. 'That's right, that is. That's more like bizness.'

'England, home, and beauty!' said Vetch, with a mock-heroic
air, that seemed strangely out of tune with the subject under
discussion. 'You'd like to go home again, wouldn't you, old
man?'

Gabbett turned on him fiercely, his low forehead wrinkled into
a frown of ferocious recollection.

'*You!*' he said – 'You think the chain's — fine sport, don't yer?
But I've been there, my young chicken, and I *knows what it
means.*'

There was silence for a minute or two. The giant seemed
plunged in gloomy abstraction, and Vetch and the Moocher
interchanged a significant glance. Gabbett had been ten years at
Macquarie Harbour, and he had memories that he did not con-
fide to his companions. When he indulged in one of these fits of
recollection, his friends found it best to leave him to himself.

Rufus Dawes did not understand the sudden silence. With all
his senses stretched to the utmost to listen, the cessation of the
whispered colloquy affected him strangely. Old artillerymen
have said that, after being at work for days in the trenches,
accustomed to the continued roar of the guns, a sudden cessation
of firing will cause them intense pain. Something of this feeling
was experienced by Rufus Dawes. His faculties of hearing and
thinking – both at their highest pitch – seemed to break down.
It was as though some prop had been knocked from under him.
No longer stimulated by outward sounds, his senses appeared to
fail him. He felt the blood rush into his eyes and ears. He made
a violent effort to retain his consciousness, but with a faint cry
which he could not repress, he fell back, striking his head
against the edge of the bunk.

The noise roused the burglar in an instant. There was someone in the berth! The three looked into each other's eyes, in guilty alarm, and then Gabbett dashed round the partition.

'It's Dawes!' said the Moocher. 'We had forgotten him!'

'He'll join us, mate – he'll join us!' cried Vetch, fearful of bloodshed.

Gabbett uttered a hideous oath, and flinging himself on to the prostrate figure, dragged it, head foremost, to the floor.

The sudden vertigo had saved Rufus Dawes's life. The robber twisted one brawny arm in his shirt, and pressing the knuckles down, prepared to deliver a blow that should for ever silence the listener, when Vetch caught his arm.

'He's been asleep,' he cried. 'Don't hit him! See, he's not awake yet.'

A crowd gathered round. The giant relaxed his grip, but the convict gave only a deep groan, and allowed his head to fall on his shoulder.

'You've killed him!' cried some one.

Gabbett took another look at the purpling face and bedewed forehead, and then sprang erect, rubbing at his right hand, as though he would rub off something sticking there.

'He's got the fever!' he roared, with a terror-stricken grimace.

'The what?' asked twenty voices.

'The fever, you grinning fools!' cried Gabbett. 'The — Typhus is aboard, and he's the fourth man down!'

The circle of beast-like faces, stretched forward to 'see the fight,' widened at this. It was as though a bombshell had fallen into the group. Rufus Dawes lay on the deck, motionless, breathing heavily. The savage circle glared at his prostrate body. The alarm ran round, and all the prison crowded down to stare at him. All at once he uttered a groan, and turning, propped his body on his two rigid arms, and made an effort to speak. But no sound issued from his convulsed jaws.

'He's done,' said the Moocher, brutally. 'He didn't hear nuffin, I'll pound it.'

Gabbett, recovered from his first terror, scowled savagely. 'If I thort he had,' he growled, 'I'd choke his bag, once and for all.'

'Tush!' said Vetch. 'Be quiet, you bloodthirsty old rampsman. We don't want to be scragged before our time.'

The noise of the heavy bolts shooting back broke the spell. The first detachment were coming down from 'exercise.' The door was flung back, and the bayonets of the guard gleamed in a ray of sunshine that shot down the hatchway. This glimpse of sunlight – sparkling at the entrance of the foetid and stifling prison – seemed a sort of mockery of their miseries. It was as though Heaven laughed at them. By one of those horrible and strange impulses which animate crowds, the mass, turning from the sick man, leapt towards the doorway. The interior of the prison flashed white with suddenly-turned faces. The gloom scintillated, as it were, with rapidly-moving hands. 'Air! air! Give us air!'

'That's it!' said the Crow to his companions. 'I thought the news would rouse 'em.'

Gabbett – all the savage in his blood stirred by the sight of flashing eyes and wrathful faces – would have thrown himself forward with the rest, but Vetch plucked him back.

'It'll be over in a moment,' he said. 'It's only a fit they've got.'

He spoke truly. Through the uproar was heard the rattle of iron on iron, as the guard 'stood to their arms,' and the wedge of grey cloth broke and melted, in sudden terror of the levelled muskets.

There was an instant's pause, and then old Pine walked unmolested down the prison, and knelt by the body of Rufus Dawes.

The sight of the familiar figure, so calmly performing its familiar duty, restored all that submission to recognised authority that strict discipline begets. The convicts slunk away into their berths, or officiously ran to help 'the doctor,' with affectation of intense obedience. The prison was like a schoolroom into which the master had suddenly returned.

'Stand back, my lads! Take him up, two of you, and carry him to the door. The poor fellow won't hurt you.'

His orders were obeyed, and the old man, waiting until his patient was safely received outside, raised his hand to command attention.

'I see you know what I have to tell you. The fever has broken out. That man has got it. It is absurd to suppose that no one else will be seized. I might catch it myself. You are much crowded down here, I know; but, my lads, I can't help that; I didn't make the ship, you know.'

' 'Ear, 'ear!'

'It is a dreadful thing, but you must keep orderly and quiet and bear it like men. You know what the discipline is, and it is not in my power to alter it. I shall do my best for your comfort, and I look to you to help me.'

And holding his gray head very erect indeed, the brave old fellow passed straight down the line without looking to the right or left.

He had said just enough, and he reached the door amid a chorus of ' 'Ear, 'ear!' 'Bravo!' 'True for you, docther!' and so on. But when he got fairly outside, he breathed more freely. He had performed a ticklish task, and he knew it.

' 'Ark at 'em,' growled the Moocher, from his corner, 'a cheerin' at the — noos!'

'Wait a bit,' said the acuter intelligence of Jemmy Vetch. 'Give 'em time. There'll be three or four more down afore night, and *then* we'll see!'

⊸ 9 ⊶

THE STORY OF TWO BIRDS OF PREY

THE reader of the foregoing pages has doubtless asked himself, 'Who is Sarah Purfoy?' This question we will proceed to answer.

In the year 1825, two years before the date at which our story opens, there lived, at St Heliers, Jersey, a watchmaker, named Urbain Purfoy. He was a hard-working man, and had amassed a little money – sufficient to give his granddaughter an education considered in those days to be above the common. At fifteen, the girl – tall, well grown, and somewhat too well developed for her age – could play a little, sing a little, and flirt a good deal. She had read much of such romances as she could beg or borrow, and had a high opinion of her own accomplishments. In the little circle in which she moved, there was no one to appreciate these talents, and she longed for some larger sphere of action. Her life was passed in attending to casual customers, walking on the cliffs, dreaming of the future, tinkling out melodies on the cracked harpsichord in the back parlour, and devouring her beloved novels. Sometimes she would watch her grandfather at his work, and even soil her dainty fingers with file and oil; but he was not an amusing companion, and she languished for society.

At sixteen, she was rather an empty-headed, silly girl, with big brown eyes, and too redundant bust. She had a bad opinion of her own sex, and an immense reverence for the other – if it was young and handsome. The neighbours said that she was too high and mighty for her rank in life. Her grandfather said she was a 'beauty,' and like her poor dear mother. She herself thought rather meanly of her personal attractions, and rather highly of her mental ones. She had found in an old book a history of Madame de Maintenon, and wondered why there were no such kings in Jersey as Louis XIV. She was brimful of vitality, with strong passions, and little religious sentiment. She had not much respect for moral courage, for she did not understand it; but she was a profound admirer of personal prowess. Her distaste for the humdrum life she was leading found expression in a rebellion against social usages. She courted notoriety by eccentricities of dress, and was never so happy as when she was misunderstood. She was the sort of girl of whom women say – 'It is a pity that she has no mother;' and men, 'It is a pity she does not get a husband;' and who say to themselves, 'When shall I have a lover?'

There was no lack of beings of this latter class among the officers quartered in Fort Royal and Fort Henry; but the female population of the island was free and numerous, and in the embarrassment of riches, Sarah was overlooked. Though she adored the soldiery, her first lover was a civilian. Walking one day on the cliff, she met a young man. He was tall, well-looking, and well-dressed. His name was Lemoine, he was the son of a tolerably wealthy resident of the island, and had come down from London to recruit his health and see his friends. Sarah was struck by his appearance, and looked back at him. He had been struck by hers, and looked back also. He followed her, and spoke to her – some inconsequential remark about the wind or the weather, but she thought his voice divine. They got into conversation – about scenery, lonely walks, and the dulness of St

Heliers. 'Did she often walk there?' 'Sometimes.' 'Would she be there to-morrow?' 'She might.' Mr Lemoine lifted his hat and went back to dinner, rather pleased with himself. Sarah let down her back hair at the glass that night, and compared herself with Madame de Maintenon. After all, Louis XIV was a mean-looking man.

They met the next day, and the day after that. Lemoine was not a gentleman, but he had lived among gentlemen, and had caught something of their manner. He was clever also, and sympathised with Sarah's admiration for the widow of M. Scarron. He said that after all, virtue was a mere name, and that when people were powerful and rich, the world respected them more than if they had been honest and poor. Sarah agreed with this. Her grandfather was honest and poor, and yet nobody respected him – at least, not with such respect as she cared to acknowledge. In addition to his talent for argument, Lemoine was handsome and had money, – he showed her quite a handful of bank-notes one day. He told her of London, and the great ladies there, and hinting that *they* were not always virtuous, drew himself up with a moody air, as though *he* had been unhappily the cause of their fatal lapse into wickedness. Sarah did not wonder at this in the least. Had she been a great lady, she would have done the same. She began to coquet with this terrible fellow, and to hint to him that she had too much knowledge of the world to set a fictitious value upon virtue. He mistook her artfulness for innocence, and thought he had made a conquest. Moreover, the girl was pretty, and decidedly passionate. When dressed properly, she would look rather well. Only one obstacle stood in the way of their loves – the dashing profligate was poor. He had been living in London above his means, and his father was not inclined to increase his allowance. The luxury of a mistress all to himself was out of the question.

He suggested that Sarah should allow him to visit her, but Sarah refused. She liked him better than anybody else she had seen, but there were two sides to every bargain. Madame de Maintenon went to Paris, Sarah Purfoy must go to London. In point of fact, the girl – tired of her dull life, sensual, ill-trained, vain, and conscious of her own abilities – had made up her mind to shine in the world. She would be a 'great lady' in the capital, and Lemoine was the Louis XIV who was to take her there. In vain her lover sighed and swore. Unless he would promise to take her away with him, Diana was not more chaste. The more virtuous she grew, the more vicious did Lemoine feel. His desire to possess her increased in proportionate ratio to her resistance, and at last he borrowed a hundred pounds from his father's confidential clerk (the Lemoines were merchants by profession), and acceded to her wishes. There was no love on either side – vanity was the mainspring of the whole transaction. Lemoine did not like to be beaten; Sarah sold herself for a passage to England and an introduction into the 'great world.'

This turned out to be a second floor in a second-rate street – a lodging suited to Lemoine's purse. He promised to take a house for her in a day or two, and a carriage. They went to the theatres, and Sarah was delighted, and to the quieter of the casinos, in order that she might see the fashionable and witty world. On the occasion of their first visit, a woman swore at her, and she begged to be taken home again, and Lemoine got very drunk, which was not, she thought, what Louis XIV would have done under the circumstances. He, however, explained that the wine one got at those places was not of the best, and all women who lost their virtue were not necessarily intellectual in consequence. The next time the girl went she listened, and began to divine that society was not quite as in the days of the Montespan and the Maintenon. Moreover, she saw men there who seemed to her to be superior in many ways to her hero of St Heliers. One of these, attracted by her girlish appearance, paid her some attention, – at which Lemoine was jealous. Her new admirer was a marquis, and she was struck with pleasing wonderment at finding marquises so like other men.

This sort of life went on for a month or so, and as the hundred pounds decreased, Lemoine began to regret his purchase. Sarah was getting stupid. She didn't weep and ask to be sent home again, but she did not seem to be happy. She was tired also. Lemoine's friends were wont to come to his rooms and play cards. One of these friends was a young man of about twenty, who was 'living on his means,' and did not spare them. His name, he said, was Leopold Craven, and he was distinctly connected with a noble family. He was fond of cards, however, though he did not play high, and in two sittings won the balance of Lemoine's hundred pounds. This decided Sarah in a course of action which she had been long meditating. She wrote a pretty farewell note to Lemoine, and went off with the marquis.

The marquis, however, was an intolerably stupid marquis, and a very bad-tempered one. He was fond of Sarah after a fashion, and gave her plenty of money, which she spent freely. She had her own house, and was beginning to enjoy life. She had never loved anybody, and she was very ambitious. With these qualities, she should have succeeded in the life she had chosen for herself, but she had one defect. A phrenologist would have said that her head was both too flat at the top and too broad at the base. She was of too social a turn, and her temperament was too ardent. The marquis, though he did not cultivate fidelity himself, had a high appreciation of that virtue in the other sex, and one day Sarah received a small sum of money – he was a careful marquis – and her dismissal. Her social disposition had made her many friends, and she found no difficulty in compensating herself for her loss of place. She was obliged to come down in the social scale, however. Her next lover was only a wealthy commoner.

We need not particularise her life at this epoch. Suffice it to say that her senses so often got the better of her judgment that she was compelled to change her residence too frequently for comfort; and in twelve months from her first meeting with Lemoine, had discovered the melancholy fact that vice is not always conducive to happiness, and is not as well rewarded as it might be even in this world. Sated, and disappointed, with jaded body and corrupted mind, she was tired of her life, and longed to escape from its wearying dissipations. At this juncture, she fell in love.

The expression, used towards such a creature, may sound strange, but it is literally true. Sarah Purfoy, the cast-off mistress of a dozen different people, fell in love. The object of her affections was no other than the Mr Leopold Craven who had so pleasantly rooked her old flame, Lemoine. Craven was tall, well made, and with an insinuating address. His features were too strongly marked for beauty, and when he smiled he showed two buck teeth. His eyes were the best part of his face, and, like his hair, they were jet black. He had broad shoulders, sinewy limbs, and small hands and feet. His head was round, and apparently well-shaped, but bulged a little over the ears, which were singularly small, and lay close to his head. He had been away on the continent, he said, and was apparently as wealthy as ever. He was attracted by her appearance, heard her story, and took a house for her at Pimlico, where she lived with him as Mrs Craven.

With this man, barely four years older than herself, Sarah at seventeen fell violently in love. This was the more strange, as, though fond of her, he would tolerate no caprices, and was cursed with an ungovernable temper, which found vent in curses, and even blows. He seemed to have no profession or business, and though he owned a good address and cultivated refined tastes, he was even less a gentleman than Lemoine. Yet Sarah, attracted apparently by one of those strange sympathies which constitute the romance of such women's lives, was devoted to him. Touched by her affection, and rating her intelligence and unscrupulousness at their true value, he told her who he was. He was a swindler, a forger, and a thief, and his name was John Rex. When she heard this, she experienced a sort of sinister delight. He told her of his plots, his tricks, his escapes, his villanies; and seeing how for years this young man had preyed upon the world which had disowned her, her heart went out to him. 'I am glad you found me,' she said. 'Two heads are better than one. We will work together.'

John Rex, known among his intimate associates as Dandy Jack, was the son of a butler in a nobleman's family and a tradesman's daughter. His father had accumulated an independence, and retiring from service, took a small house in the suburbs of London, and endeavoured to bring up his son a gentleman. John Rex was sent to as good a school as could be procured for him, and at sixteen was given, by the interest of his father's old master, a clerkship in an old-established banking-house. Rex senior was accustomed to talk largely of 'gentlemen,' and 'high society,' and his son imbibed a great desire to shine in aristocratic circles. He was a clever lad, without much principle, would lie unblushingly, and steal deliberately, if he thought he could do so with impunity. He was cautious, acquisitive, imaginative, self-conceited, and destructive. He had strong perceptive faculties, and much invention and versatility, but his 'moral sense' was almost entirely wanting. He found that his fellow clerks were not of that 'gentlemanly' stamp that his father thought so admirable, and, therefore, despised them. He thought he should like to go into the army, for he was athletic, and rejoiced in feats of muscular strength. To be tied all day to a desk was beyond endurance. But his father told him to 'wait and see what came of it'. He did so, and in the meantime kept late hours, got into bad company, and forged the name of a customer to the bank – a plebeian cheesemonger, named Brown – to a cheque for twenty pounds. The fraud was a clumsy one, and was detected in twenty-four hours. Forgeries by clerks, unfortunately, however easily detected, are not considered to add to the attractions of a banking-house; the old-established firm deciding not to prosecute, contented themselves with dismissing Mr John Rex from their service. His father, properly indignant – indeed, the poor old man's heart was nearly broken, 'gentlemen' so seldom forged in those days – was at first for turning him out of doors, but by the entreaties of his wife, was at last induced to place the promising boy in a draper's shop in the City Road. This employment was not a congenial one – the City Road was so very far east – and John Rex planned to leave it. His companions flattered him, and his mother's kindness allowing him to dress better than they could afford, they called him 'Gentleman Jack.' In order to keep up this title to gentility, he frequented billiard-rooms and night-houses. Here he met stray 'gentlemen' enjoying themselves, and having a quick eye and tolerable assurance, he at once copied their manners and sought their acquaintance. He lived at home, and had his salary – about thirty shillings a week – for pocket money. Though he displayed considerable skill with the cue, and not unfrequently won, for him, considerable sums, his expenses averaged more than his income; and having borrowed all he could, he found himself again in difficulties. His narrow escape, however, had taught him a lesson, and he resolved to confess all to his indulgent father and be more economical for the future. Just then one of those 'lucky chances' which blight so many lives occurred.

The 'shopwalker' – a most distinguished-looking man – died,

and Messrs Baffaty & Co. made the gentlemanly Rex act as his substitute for a few days. Shop-walkers have privileges not accorded to other folks, and on the evening of the third day Mr Rex went home with a bundle of lace in his pocket. Unfortunately, he owed more than the worth of this petty theft, and was compelled to steal again. This time he was detected. One of his fellow shopmen caught him in the very act of concealing a roll of silk, ready for future abstraction, and, to his astonishment, cried 'Halves!' Rex pretended to be virtuously indignant, but soon saw that such pretence was useless; his companion was too wily to be fooled with such affectation of innocence. 'I saw you take it,' said he, 'and if you won't share, I'll tell old Baffaty.' This argument was irresistible, and they shared. Having become good friends, the self-made partner lent Rex a helping hand in the disposal of the booty, and introduced him to a purchaser. The purchaser violated all rules of romance by being – not a Jew, but a very good Christian. He kept a second-hand clothes warehouse in the City Road, and was supposed to have branch establishments all over London. He was very dirty, and very drunken, and in his drunken fits would disappear for weeks together into some one of his numerous shops or houses, but he was a shrewd man of business, and never 'talked.' He had risen by his own exertions from a 'marine store,' and his name was Blicks.

Mr Blicks, being sober, purchased the stolen goods for about a third of their value, and seemed struck by Mr Rex's appearance. 'I thort you was a swell mobsman,' said he. This from Blicks was a high compliment. Encouraged by their success, Rex and his companion took a few more articles of value, and, like the proverbial 'love of money,' their fondness for Messrs Baffaty's silks increased in proportion to the increase of the silks themselves. John Rex paid off his debts, and began to feel himself quite a 'gentleman' again. Just as he arrived at this pleasing state of mind, the plebeian Baffaty discovered the robbery. Not having heard about the bank business, he did not suspect Rex – he was such a gentlemanly young man – but having had his eye for some time upon Rex's partner, who was vulgar, and squinted, he sent for him. Rex's partner stoutly denied the accusation, and old Baffaty, who was a man of merciful tendencies, and could

well afford to lose fifty pounds, gave him until the next morning
to confess, and state where the goods had gone, – hinting at the
persuasive powers of a constable at the end of that time. The
shopman, with tears in his innocent eyes, came in a hurry to
Rex, and informed him that all was lost. He did not want to
confess, because he must implicate his friend Rex, but if he did
not confess, he would be given in charge.

Flight was impossible, for neither had money. In this dilemma
John Rex first showed that ability for rapid consideration, decision, and action, which afterwards made him so distinguished.
He remembered Blicks's compliment, and burned to deserve it.
If he must retreat, he would despoil the enemy. He was defeated, but his defeat should be a Corunna. His exodus should
be like that of the Israelites – he would spoil the Egyptians.
Baffaty should be robbed wholesale. His partner was a little
awed by the magnitude of such a scheme, but promised obedience. The shopwalker was allowed half an hour in the middle of
the day for lunch. John Rex took advantage of this half hour to
hire a cab and drive to Blicks's. That worthy man received him
cordially, for he saw in his eye that he was bent upon great
deeds. John Rex rapidly unfolded his plan of operations. The
warehouse doors fastened with a spring. He would remain behind after they were locked, and open them at a given signal. A
light cart or cab could be stationed in the lane at the back, three
men could fill it with valuables in as many hours. Did Blicks
know of three such men? Blicks's one eye glistened. He thought
he did know. At half-past eleven they should be there. Was that
all? No. Mr John Rex was not going to 'put up' such a splendid
thing for nothing. The booty was worth at least £5000 if it was
worth a shilling – he must have £100 cash when the cart stopped
at Blicks's door. Blicks at first refused point blank. Let there be a
division, but he'd not buy a pig in a poke. Rex was firm, however; it was his only chance, and at last got a promise of £80.
That night the glorious achievement known as 'The Great Silk
Robbery' took place, and two days afterwards, John Rex and his
partner, dining comfortably at Birmingham, read an account of
the transaction – not in the least like it – in a London paper.

Justice was less prompt in those days than she is now, and
Messrs Sims and Perkin were not disturbed. Perhaps, this was in

some measure owing to the fact that Mr Sims' father – otherwise old John Rex – went blubbering to Baffaty and paid him £3000 (two-thirds of his saved fortune) begging him to allow the matter to drop. Baffaty, as we have said, was charitable, and went as near to compounding a felony as he dared. John Rex had now fairly broken with dull respectability, and began to realise his father's wishes. He was, after his fashion, a 'gentleman.' As long as the £80 lasted, he lived in something like luxury, and by the time it was spent, he had established himself in his profession. This profession was a lucrative one. It was that of a swindler. Gifted with a handsome person, facile manner, and ready wit, he had added to these natural advantages some skill at billiards, some knowledge of gambler's legerdemain, and the useful consciousness that he must prey or be preyed on. As long as he had money, he could enjoy life, and defy detection. As soon as money failed, he would be at the mercy of the laws he had outraged. Gold was at once the talisman by which he enjoyed, and the weapon by which he fought the world, and his sole object was to obtain it. John Rex was no common swindler; his natural as well as his acquired abilities saved him from vulgar errors. He saw that to successfully swindle mankind, one must not aim at comparative, but superlative ingenuity. He who is contented with being only cleverer than the majority must infallibly be outwitted at last, and to be once outwitted is – for a swindler – to be ruined. He laid himself out to combat the law, and he saw that he could only do so with the law's own weapons. What is the strength of the law? Union. What is the weakness of the law's opponents? Distrust. In the drama of crime there is one character that never varies – the 'informer'.

Examining, moreover, into the history of detected crime, John Rex discovered one thing. At the bottom of all these robberies, deceptions, and swindles was some lucky fellow who profited by the folly of his confederates. This gave him an idea. Suppose he could not only make use of his own talents to rob mankind, but utilise those of others also? Crime runs through infinite grades. He proposed to himself to be at the top; but why should he despise those good fellows beneath him. His speciality was swindling, billiard-playing, card-playing, borrowing money, obtaining goods, never risking more than two or three *coups* in a

year. But others plundered houses, stole bracelets, watches, diamonds, made as much in a night as he did in six months – only
their occupation was more dangerous. Now came the question –
why more dangerous? Because these men were mere clods, bold
enough and clever enough in their own rude way, but no match
for the law, with its Argus eyes and its Briarean hands. They
did the rougher business well enough; they broke locks, and burst
doors, and 'neddied' constables, but in the finer arts of plan,
attack, and escape, they were sadly deficient. Good. These men
should be the hands; he would be the head. He would plan the
robberies; they should execute them. In crime, large interest
means bad security. It is neck or nothing. One failure outbalances
fifty successes, for one failure means annihilation. Failure is
brought about, in nine cases out of ten, by haste; but unless one
can afford to wait and plan, haste in robbery is imperative. John
Rex determined to obviate this difficulty. He would watch for
days and weeks, make all secure, provide against every contin-
gency, secure a retreat even, when to think of defeat seemed
ludicrous: and then, when all was ready, he would give the
signal, and let the attack be made. But there was another evil to
be guarded against – the 'informer.' Why do thieves betray each
other? From self-interest, or fear. He would make it worth their
while to remain true. He would institute a sort of Freemasonry
of Crime, which, while it succoured the poor, and assisted the
deserving, should bitterly punish the traitor. He would set apart
a certain portion of his gains as a fund for feeing lawyers, and
procuring comforts for prisoners. He would, in fact, focus the
scattered rays of criminal ability, and oppose to the organisation
of the law the organisation of crime. The notion was a grand
one, but John Rex left out one item in his calculations – human
nature. Criminals, differing from lunatics only in degree (for no
habitual criminal ever owned a well-balanced brain) assimilate to
them in this – that they are incapable of acting persistently in
concert. Such an organisation as John Rex proposed to himself
was impossible.

But though he could not achieve quite all he wished, he did
much towards it. Working through many channels, and never
omitting to assist a fellow-worker when in distress, he, in a few
years, became the head of a sort of terrible society of ruffians.

Mixing with fast clerks and unsuspecting middle class profligates, he found out particulars of houses ill guarded, and shops but insecurely fastened, and 'put up' Blicks's ready ruffians to the more dangerous work. In his various disguises, and under his many *aliases*, he found his way into those upper circles of 'fast' society, where animals turn into birds, and where a wolf becomes a rook, and a lamb a pigeon. Rich spendthrifts who affected male society asked him to their houses, and Mr James Crofton, Mr Anthony Croftonbury, Captain James Crofton, and Mr Leopold Craven, were names remembered, sometimes with pleasure, oftener with regret, by many a broken man of fortune. He had one quality which, to a man of his profession, was invaluable – he was cautious, and master of himself. Having made a success, wrung commission from Blicks, rooked a gambling ninny like Lemoine, or secured an assortment of jewellery sent down to his 'wife' in Gloucestershire, he would disappear for a time. He liked comfort, and revelled in the sense of security and respectability.

Thus he had lived for three years when he met Sarah Purfoy, and thus he purposed to live for many more. With this woman as a coadjutor, he thought he could defy the law. She was the net spread to catch his 'pigeons;' she was the well-dressed lady who ordered goods in London for her husband at Canterbury, and *paid* half the price down, 'which was all this letter authorised her to do,' and, where a less beautiful or clever woman might have failed, she succeeded. Of what service she was in averting detection, Mr Gabbett has already told.

John Rex saw fortune before him, and believed that, with common prudence, he might carry on his lucrative employment of 'gentleman' until he chose to relinquish it. Alas! for human weakness. He one day did a foolish thing, and the law he had so successfully defied got him in the simplest way imaginable.

Under the names of Mr and Mrs Skinner, John Rex and Sarah Purfoy were living in quiet lodgings in the neighbourhood of Bloomsbury. Their landlady was a respectable poor woman, and had a son who was a constable. This son was given to talking, and, coming into supper one night, told his mother that on the following evening an attack was to be made on a gang of coiners in the Old Street Road. The mother, dreaming all sorts of horrors during the night, came the next day to Mrs Skinner in the parlour, and, under a pledge of profound secrecy, told her of the dreadful expedition in which her son was engaged. John Rex was out, and when he returned, at eight o'clock, Sarah told him what she had heard.

Now, 4 Bank-place, Old Street Road, was the residence of a man named Green, who had for some time carried on the lucrative but dangerous trade of 'counterfeiting.' This man was one of the most daring of that army of ruffians whose treasure chest and master of the mint was Blicks, and his liberty was valuable. John Rex, hastily eating his dinner, ruminated on the intelligence, and thought it would be but wise to warn Green of his danger. Not that he cared much for Green personally, but it was bad policy to miss doing a good turn to a comrade, and, moreover, Green captured, might wag his tongue too freely. But how to do it? If he went to Blicks, it might be too late; he would go himself. The acute intelligence of his female companion saw the danger of this course.

'If you are taken,' said she, 'you will be thought one of them.'

But Rex had been drinking somewhat freely that afternoon, and would not listen to reason. Opposition only made him worse, and so Sarah brought him a slouch hat and rough coat, and away he went. By the time the hackney coach set him down at the corner of the street, reflection had brought prudence, and he confessed that he was doing a silly thing. But to go back would be to admit that he was in the wrong, and he was not yet cool enough for that. Sarah would laugh at him, and he disliked to be laughed at. So it happened, strangely enough, that it was, after all, the thought of a woman that influenced him to his fate. He looked at a clock in a chemist's shop; it was just eleven. If he was to be of service, he had best make haste, and he hurried on. The house consisted of two rooms, one above the other. All was quiet, and the street door was ajar. He ran up stairs.

Now, at a quarter to eleven this had happened. Three constables – of whom the landlady's son was one – came into the court. One was left at the entrance to secure a retreat, and the other two rapped at Mr Green's door. There was no answer, and Larkin, the head constable, broke open the door with a blow of a sledge hammer. Hearing the noise, Green attempted to run down stairs, but seeing the two officers, ran back, and tried to enter a room at the head of the staircase. Larkin seized him by a leathern apron he wore, and dragged him back. Two more men appeared, but the staircase was narrow, and only one man could pass at a time. Green got Larkin's finger in his mouth, and bit it to the bone, and one of the men jumped clean over the struggling pair into the arms of the second constable. This officer, notwithstanding he received the coiner's knee in his stomach, and was dashed violently against the wall, stuck to his man, and handcuffed him.

In the meantime the third ruffian came out of the room with a saucepan, and beat Larkin on the head with it to make him let go his hold. Larkin twisted Green round, however, and jammed him against the staircase window, making shift to give his new assailant a blow on the arm with the hammer, which disabled him. Notwithstanding this, the fellow turned back into the room, got out through the roof, ran along the tiles, and jumped twenty-five feet on to the top of a wooden shed. He was much injured, but his friends picked him up and carried him away, and he was not taken. The second constable tried to get at Green over his chief's head, but the staircase window gave way, and both men fell into the court, Green underneath, and there Larkin secured him. The two prisoners were brought upstairs, and it was found that the window of a third room was open, and that two of the five men they had expected to find had escaped that way.

The moulds had been broken, and the battery flung out of window, but a quart pot in a corner was full of counterfeit sixpences. The whole affair occupied about ten minutes, and an ominous five minutes' silence ensued while Larkin examined the room. During that five minutes they heard a peculiar whistle, and then some one ran upstairs and opened the door.

'By God!' cries Green, unable to restrain himself, 'it's the Dandy!'

Rex saw his mistake in an instant. Whipping off his hat, he flung it at the candle, and then turning round, jumped the flight of stairs, and made for the door. But the landlady's son had seen him enter, and the door was shut. He was trapped.

On the road to the police office he had arranged his plans. He was taken in direct communication with the gang, and Green had recognised him. It would be useless to plead ignorance and innocence. He would say nothing. There was nothing against him, and he might escape. To give his name and address as a proof of his good character would be to injure, if not to ruin, his hopes of further swindling enterprise. Mr Skinner's character should not be injured. He gave his own name. When Sarah heard of the calamity, she could not repress a feeling of exultation in the fulfilment of her prediction – she loved the scoundrel with the love of a tigress – and then set to work to help him. She collected together all her money and jewels, paid Mrs Skinner's rent, went to see him, and arranged his defence. Blicks was hopeful, but Green – who came very near hanging – admitted that the man was an associate of his, and the Recorder being in a severe mood, transported him for seven years.

When Sarah Purfoy heard this she was like a madwoman, and vowed that she would follow him. She was going as passenger, an immigrant, anything, when she saw Mrs Vickers's advertisement for a 'lady's maid,' and answered it. Fate chanced that Rex was shipped in the *Malabar*, and Sarah discovering this before the vessel had been a week at sea, conceived the bold project of inciting a mutiny for the rescue of her lover. His part was to organise the conspiracy between decks; hers to gain over the soldiers, and dispose of the captain.

Such were the two dangerous wretches of whom the convicts had spoken.

⊷ 10 ⊷

A DANGEROUS CRISIS

It was late in the afternoon when Sarah Purfoy awoke from her uneasy slumber. She had been dreaming of the deed she was about to do, and was flushed and feverish; but mindful of the consequences that hung upon the success or failure of the enterprise, she rallied herself, and bathing her face and hands, ascended, with as calm an air as she could assume, to the poopdeck.

Nothing was changed. The sentries' arms glittered in the same pitiless sunshine, the ship rolled and creaked on the swell of the same dreamy sea, and the prison cage on the lower deck was crowded with the same cheerless figures, disposed in the same attitudes as before. Even Mr Maurice Frere, recovered from his midnight fatigues, was lounging on the same coil of rope, in precisely the same position.

Yet the eye of an acute observer would have detected some difference beneath this outward varnish of similarity. The man at the wheel looked round the horizon more eagerly, and spit into the swirling, unwholesome-looking water with a more dejected air than of yore. The fishing-lines still hung dangling over the catheads, but nobody touched them. The soldiers and sailors on the forecastle, collected in knots, seemed to have no heart even to smoke, but gloomily stared at each other. Vickers was in the cuddy, writing; Blunt was in his cabin, and Pine, with two carpenters at work under him, was improvising increased hospital accommodation. The noise of mallet and hammer echoed in the soldiers' berth ominously, the workmen might have been making a coffin. The prison was strangely silent, with something of that lowering silence which precedes a thunderstorm, and the convicts on deck, no longer told stories, or laughed at obscene jests, but sat together, moodily patient, as if waiting for something. Three more men – two prisoners and a soldier – had succumbed since Rufus Dawes had been removed to the hospital; and though as yet there had been no complaint or symptom of panic the face of each man, soldier, sailor, or prisoner, wore an expectant look, as though wondering whose turn it would be next. On the ship – rolling like a wounded creature, ceaselessly from side to side, on the opaque profundity of that stagnant ocean – a horrible shadow had fallen. The *Malabar* seemed to be enveloped in an electric cloud, whose sullen gloom a chance spark would flash into a blaze that should consume her.

The woman who held in her hands the two ends of the chain that would produce this spark, paused, came up vpon deck, and, after a glance round her, leant against the poop-railing and looked down into the barricade. As we have said, the prisoners were in knots of four and five, and to one group in particular her glance was directed. Three men, leaning carelessly against the bulwarks, watched her every motion. Our readers need not be told that these three men were Gabbett, the Moocher, and Jemmy Vetch.

'There she is, right enough,' growled Mr Gabbett, as if in continuation of a previous remark. 'Flash as ever, and looking this way, too.'

'I don't see no wipe,' said the Moocher.

'Patience is a virtue, most noble knuckler!' says the Crow, with an affectation of carelessness that he did not feel. 'Give the young woman time.'

'Blowed if I'm going to wait no longer,' says the giant, licking his coarse blue lips. ' 'Ere we've been bluffed off day arter day, and kep' dancin' round the Dandy's wench like a parcel o' — dogs. The fever's aboard, and we've got all ready. What's the use o' waitin'? Orfice, or no orfice, I'm for bizness at once, blarst me!'

'There, look at that,' he added with an oath, as the figure of Maurice Frere appeared side by side with that of the waiting-maid, and the two turned away up the deck together.

'It's all right, you confounded muddlehead!' cried the Crow, losing patience with his perverse and stupid companion. 'How can she give us the office with that cove at her elbow?'

Gabbett's only reply to this question was a ferocious grunt, and a sudden elevation of his clenched fist, which caused Mr Vetch to retreat precipitately. The giant did not follow; and Mr Vetch, folding his arms, and assuming an attitude of easy contempt, directed his attention to Sarah Purfoy. She seemed an object of general attraction, for at the same moment a young soldier ran up the ladder to the forecastle, and eagerly bent his gaze in her direction.

Maurice Frere had come behind her and touched her on the shoulder. Since their conversation the previous evening, he had made up his mind to be fooled no longer. The girl was evidently playing with him, and he would show her that so distinguished a *roué* and profligate was not to be trifled with.

'Well, Sarah!'

'Well, Mr Frere,' dropping her hand, and turning round with a smile.

'How well you are looking to-day! Positively lovely!'

'You have told me that so often,' says she, with a pout. 'Have you nothing else to say?'

'Except that I love you.' This in most impassioned manner.

'That is no news. I know you do.'

'Curse it, Sarah, what is a fellow to do?' His profligacy was failing him rapidly. 'What is the use of playing fast and loose with a fellow this way?'

'A "fellow" should be able to take care of himself, Mr Frere. I didn't ask you to fall in love with me, did I? If you don't please me, it is not your fault, perhaps.'

'What do you mean?'

'You soldiers have so many things to think of – your guards and sentries, and visits and things. You have no time to spare for a poor woman like me.'

'Spare!' cries Frere, in amazement. 'Why, damme, you won't let a fellow spare! I'd spare fast enough, if that was all.'

She cast her eyes down to the deck, and a modest flush rose in her cheeks.

'I have so much to do,' she said, in a half whisper. 'There are so many eyes upon me, I cannot stir without being seen.'

She raised her head as she spoke, and to give effect to her words, looked round the deck. Her glance crossed that of the young soldier on the forecastle, and though the distance was too great for her to distinguish his features, she guessed who he was. Miles was jealous.

Frere, smiling with delight at her change of manner, came close to her, and whispered in her ear.

She affected to start, and took the opportunity of exchanging a mute signal with the Crow.

'I will come at eight o'clock,' said she, with modestly averted face.

'They relieve guard at eight.'

She withdrew the hand he had clasped beneath her light shawl, and tossed her head.

'Very well, then, attend to your guard; *I* don't care.'

'But Sarah, consider –'

'As if a woman in love *ever* considers!' said she, turning upon him a burning glance, that might have melted a more icy man than he.

She loved him then. What a fool he would be to refuse. To get her to come was the first object; how to make duty fit with pleasure would be considered afterwards. Besides, the guard could relieve itself for once without his supervision.

'Very well, at eight then, dearest.'

'Hush!' said she. 'Here comes that stupid captain.'

And as Frere left her, she turned, and, with her eyes fixed on the barricade, dropped the handkerchief she held in her hand over the poop railing. It fell directly at the feet of the amorous captain, and with a quick upward glance, that worthy fellow picked it up, and brought it up to her.

'Oh, *thank* you, Captain Blunt,' she said, and her eyes spoke more than her tongue.

'Did you take the laudanum?' says Blunt, with a twinkle in his eye.

'Some of it,' said she. 'And I will bring you back the bottle to-night, if you like.'

'When?' he asked, glancing towards Frere, who purposely turned his back, with that awkward affectation of indifference which such men assume when caught in the act of love-making.

'Half-past seven,' said she. 'Leave your door ajar.'

And then, with an almost imperceptible motion of her head, made Blunt leave her.

He walked aft, humming cheerily, and saluted Frere with a slap on the back. The two men laughed, each at his own thoughts, but their laughter only seemed to make the surrounding gloom seem gloomier than before.

Sarah Purfoy, casting her eyes toward the barricade, observed a change in the position of the three men. They were together once more, and the Crow, having taken off his prison cap, held it at arm's length with one hand, while he wiped his brow with the other. Her signal had been observed.

In the meanwhile, Rufus Dawes had been removed to the hospital, and was lying flat on his back staring at the deck above him, trying to think of something that he had to say.

When the sudden faintness, which was the prelude to his sickness, had overpowered him, he remembered being torn out of his bunk by fierce hands – remembered some vision of a circle of savage faces, and the presence of some danger that menaced him.

He remembered that, while lying on his blankets struggling with the fever that was on him, he had overheard some strange conversation, that was of vital importance to himself and to the ship, but of the purport of that conversation he had not the least idea. In vain he strove to remember – in vain his will, struggling with his delirium, brought back snatches and echoes of sense, which slipped from him again as fast as caught. He was oppressed with the weight of half-collected thought. He knew that a terrible danger menaced him; that could he but force his brain to reason connectedly for ten consecutive minutes, he could give such information as would avert that danger and save the ship. But, lying with hot head, parched lips, and enfeebled body, he was as one ridden by a nightmare – he could not move hand or foot.

The place where he lay was but dimly lighted. The ingenuity of Pine had constructed a sort of canvas blind over the port, to prevent the sun striking into the cabin, and this blind absorbed much of the light. He could but just see the deck above his head, and distinguish the outlines of three other berths, apparently similar to his own. The only sounds that broke the silence were the gurgling of the water below him, and the *tap tap*, *tap tap*, of Pine's hammers at work upon the new partition. By-and-by the noise of these hammers ceased, and then the sick man could hear gasps and moans, and mutterings – the signs that his companions yet lived.

All at once a voice called out, 'Jerry! Jerry Mogford!' and Rufus Dawes felt his scalp bristle.

Here was another man who knew the murderer of his dead friend. Surely he had heard some one mention his name before, or did he dream it?

'Jerry, it's no use, I tell you. All the money in the world can't alter it. Come, be a man!'

The voice was low and hoarse, and subsided into babblings. Presently it rose again.

'Of course they're worth two hundred pounds; but, my good sir, two hundred pounds to a man in my position is not worth the getting. Why, I've *given* two hundred pounds for a freak of my girl Sarah! Is it right, eh, Jezebel? She's a good girl, though, as girls go. Mrs Lionel Crofton, of the Crofts, Sevenoaks, Kent – Sevenoaks, Kent – Seven –'

A gleam of light broke in on the darkness which wrapped Rufus Dawes' tortured brain. The man was John Rex, his berth mate. With an effort, he spoke.

'Rex!'

'Yes, yes, I'm coming; don't be in a hurry. The sentry's safe, and the howitzer is but five paces from the door. A rush upon deck, lads, and she's ours! That is, mine. Mine and my wife's, Mrs Lionel Crofton, of Seven Crofts – Sarah Purfoy, ladies' maid and nurse – Marchioness of Milltown, and Duchess of Damnation.'

This last sentence contained the clue to the labyrinth in which Rufus Dawes' bewildered intellects were wandering. 'Sarah Purfoy!' He remembered now each detail of the conversation he had so strangely overheard, and how imperative it was that he should, without delay, reveal the plot that threatened the ship. How that plot was to be carried out, he did not pause to consider; he was conscious that he was hanging as it were, over the brink of delirium, and that unless he made himself understood before his senses utterly deserted him, all was lost.

He made an attempt to rise, but found that his fever-thralled limbs refused to obey the impulse of his will. He made an effort to speak, but his tongue clove to the roof of his mouth, and his jaws stuck together. He could not raise a finger nor utter a sound. The boards over his head appeared to wave like a shaken sheet, and the cabin whirled round, while the patch of light at his feet bobbed up and down like the reflection from a wavering candle. He closed his eyes with a terrible sigh of despair, and resigned himself to his fate.

At that instant the sound of hammering ceased, and the door opened. It was six o'clock, and Pine had come to have a last look at his patients before dinner. It seemed that there was somebody with him, for a kind, though somewhat pompous, voice remarked upon the scantiness of accommodation, and the 'necessity – the absolute necessity' – of complying with the King's Regulations.

Honest Vickers, agonised for the safety of his child, would not abate a jot of his duty, and had come to visit the sick men, though aware that such a visit would necessitate his isolation from the cabin where his child lay. Mrs Vickers – weeping and bewailing herself coquettishly at garrison parties – had often said that 'poor dear John was *such* a disciplinarian – quite a *slave* to the service.'

'Here they are,' said Pine; 'six of 'em. This fellow' – going to the side of Rex – 'is the worst. If he had not a constitution like a horse, I don't think he could live out the night.'

'Three eighteen seven six,' muttered Rex; 'dot and carry one. Is that an occupation for a gentleman? No, sir; fools were made for wise men to live upon. The law of might is the law of right, isn't it, my Sarah, who shalt lie in Abraham's bosom?'

'A dangerous fellow,' says Pine, with the light upraised. 'A very dangerous fellow – that is, he *was*. This is the place, you see – a regular rat-hole; but what can one do?'

'What did he say?' asked Vickers, regarding the convict with some curiosity.

'Oh, some gibberish. Sounded like a text of scripture. You'd be surprised how pious some of these fellows are when they're sick. The "devil a monk," you know. Have they been pretty quiet, sentry?'

Rufus Dawes felt the sweat break out into beads on his forehead. They suspected nothing. They were going away. He *must* warn them. And with a violent effort in his agony, he turned over in the bunk and thrust out his hand from the blankets.

'Hullo! what's this?' cried Pine, bringing the lantern to bear upon it. 'Lie down, my man. Eh! – water, is it? There, steady with it now,' and he lifted a pannikin to the blackened, froth-fringed lips.

The cool draught moistened his parched gullet, and the convict made a last effort to speak.

'Sarah Purfoy – I heard – to-night – in the prison – MUTINY!'

The last word, almost shrieked out, in the sufferer's desperate efforts to articulate, struck the wandering senses of John Rex.

'Hush!' he cried. 'Is that you, Jemmy? Sarah's right. Wait till she gives the word.'

'He's raving,' said Vickers.

Pine caught him by the shoulder.

'What do you say, my man? A mutiny of the prisoners?'

With his mouth agape and his hands clenched, Rufus Dawes, incapable of further speech, made a last effort to nod assent, but his head fell upon his breast; the next moment, the flickering light, the gloomy prison, the eager face of the doctor and the astonished one of Vickers, vanished from before his straining eyes. He saw the two men stare at each other, in mingled incredulity and alarm, and then he was floating down the cool brown river of his boyhood, on his way – in company with Sarah Purfoy and Mr Quaid – to raise a mutiny in that big ship, the *Bell*, that lay on the stocks in his father's dockyard.

↤ 22 ↦

WOMAN'S WEAPONS

An hour later, any curious person looking through the window of Captain Blunt's cabin would have seen an unusual sight.

That gallant commander was lying on the bed-place with a glass of rum and water in his hand, and the handsome waiting maid of Mrs Vickers seated on a low stool by his side. At a first glance it was perceptible that the captain was very drunk.

His grey hair was matted all ways about his reddened face, and he was winking and blinking like an owl in the sunshine. He had drunk a larger quantity of wine than usual at dinner, in sheer delight at the approaching assignation, and having got out the bottle for a quiet 'settler' just as the victim of his fascinations glided through the carefully adjusted door, he had been persuaded to keep on drinking.

'Cuc-come Sarah,' he hiccuped. 'It's all very fine, my lass, but you needn't be so – hic – proud, you know. Marriage is all my eye, girl. What's good marriage? Marriage be jigger'd! I'm a plain sailor – plain s'lor, Srr'h. Ph'n'as Bub-blunt, commander of the *Mal-Mal-Malabar*. Wors' 'sh good talkin?'

Sarah allowed a laugh to escape her, and artfully protruded an ankle at the same time. The amorous Phineas lurched over and made shift to take her hand.

'You lovsh me, and I – hic – lovsh you, Sarah. And a preshus tight little craft you – hic – are. Giv'sh – kiss, Sarah.'

Sarah got up and went to the door.

'Wotsh this? Goin'! That be dam, Sarah, don't go,' and he rolled erect, and with the grog swaying fearfully in one hand, made at her.

The ship's bell struck seven. Now or never was the time. Blunt caught her round the waist with one arm, and hiccupping with love and rum approached to take the kiss he coveted. She seized the moment, and surrendering herself to his embrace, drew from her pocket the laudanum bottle, and passing her hand over his shoulder poured half the contents into the glass.

'Think I'm – hic – drunk, do yer? Nunnot I, my wench.'

'You will be if you drink much more. Come, finish that and be quiet, or I'll go away.'

But she threw a provocation into her glance as she spoke, which belied her words, and which penetrated even the sodden intellect of poor Blunt. Balancing himself on his heels for a moment, and holding by the moulding of the cabin, he stared at her with a fatuous smile of drunken admiration, and then looking at the glass in his hand, he hiccupped with much solemnity thrice, and then, as though struck with a sudden sense of duty unfulfilled, he suddenly swallowed the contents. The effect was almost instantaneous. He dropped the tumbler, lurched towards the door, and then making a half turn in accordance with the motion of the vessel, fell into his bunk, and snored like a grampus.

Sarah Purfoy watched him for a few minutes, and then blowing out the light, stepped out of the cabin, closing the door behind her. The same dusky gloom that had held the deck on the previous night enveloped all forward of the mainmast. A lantern swung in the forecastle, and moved with the motion of the ship. The light at the prison door threw up a glow through the open hatch, and in the cuddy at her right hand burned the usual row of oil-lamps. She looked mechanically for Vickers, who was usually there at that hour, but the cuddy was empty. So much the better, and drawing her dark cloak around her, she tapped at Frere's door. As she did so, a strange pain shot through her temples, and her knees trembled. With a strong effort she dispelled the dizziness that was about to overpower her, and held herself erect. It would never do to break down now.

The door opened, and Maurice Frere drew her inside.

'So you have come?' said he, unloosing her shawl with too officious hands.

'You see I have. But oh if I should be seen!'

'Seen! Nonsense! Who is to see you? Come, and sit down.'

'Captain Vickers, Doctor Pine, anybody?'

'Not they. Besides, they've gone off down to Pine's cabin suite dinner. They're all right.'

Gone off to Pine's cabin! The intelligence struck her with vague dismay. What was the cause of such an unusual proceeding? Surely they did not suspect?

'What do they want there?' she asked.

Maurice Frere was not in the humour to argue questions of probability.

'Who knows? I don't. Damn them!' he added, with old English heartiness, 'What does it matter to us? We don't want them, do we, Sarah?'

And, slipping off the envious cloak, he pulled her on to his knee.

This one was a more ardent wooer than the other.

'Don't be so rough,' she said, writhing in his arms. 'I don't like rough lovers.'

'Ho, ho! Then you've *had* lovers, eh? I'm not the first man whose knee you've sat upon, eh?' he asked, with a sort of coarse jealousy.

She seemed to be listening for something, and did not reply. Her whole nervous system was wound up to the highest pitch of excitement. The success of the plot depended on the issue of the next five minutes.

'What are you staring at? Look at me, can't you? What eyes you have! And what hair!'

The touch of his hands about her neck awoke her to the consciousness of her duty. She flung her supple arms about him, and kissed him close. The contact of his lips awoke all the slumbering fire within her, and, slipping from his knees, she tore with rapid fingers the ribbon that bound her hair, and laughing a low laugh, shook its rippling masses to her waist.

'Dearest!' she cried, with her large black eyes dilating beneath their languid lashes, 'I love you! Do you hear me, Maurice? I love you?'

Solus cum solá non orabunt Pater Noster, and the young man seized this impassioned, palpitating, abandoned woman in his arms, and stilled her murmuring, moist lips with kisses.

At that instant the report of a musket-shot broke the silence. The mutiny had begun.

The sound awoke the soldier to a sense of his duty. He sprang to his feet, and disentwining the arms that clung about his neck, made for the door. It was the decisive moment. She hung upon him with all her weight. Her long hair swept across his face, her warm breath was on his cheek, her torn dress exposed her round smooth shoulder. He was intoxicated, maddened, conquered, when suddenly the rich colour died away from her lips, leaving them an ashen grey colour. Her eyes closed in agony, and loosing her hold, she staggered to her feet, and pressing her hands upon her bosom, uttered a sharp cry of pain.

The fever which had been on her for two days, and which by a strong exercise of will she had struggled against, encouraged by the violent excitation of her senses, had attacked her at this supreme moment. Deathly pale and sick, she reeled to the side of the cabin.

There was another shot, and a violent clashing of arms, and Frere, leaving the miserable woman to her fate, leapt out of the cabin.

➼ 12 ➻

EIGHT BELLS

AT seven o'clock that evening there was a commotion in the prison. The news of the fever had awoke in the convicts all that love of liberty which had but slumbered during the monotony of the earlier portion of the voyage. Now that death menaced them, they longed fiercely for that chance of escape which seemed permitted to freemen. 'Let us get out!' they cried to themselves, 'we are locked up here to die like sheep.' Gloomy faces and desponding looks met the gaze of each, and sometimes across this gloom shot a fierce glance that lighted up its blackness, as a lightning-flash renders luridly luminous the indigo dulness of a thunder-cloud. By and by, each man, speaking to his particular friend, seemed to discover that something was to be done. There was a conspiracy afloat. In some inexplicable way, it had become understood that they were to be released from their shambles, and that some amongst them had been plotting their freedom. The 'tween-decks held its foul breath in a sort of wondering anxiety, afraid to breathe its suspicions. The influence of this predominant idea showed itself by a strange shifting of atoms. The mass of villany, ignorance, and innocence began to be animated with something like a uniform movement. Natural affinities came together, and like allied itself to like, falling, noiseless, into harmony, as the pieces of glass and coloured beads in a kaleidoscope assume mathematical forms. By seven o'clock it was found that the prison was divided into three parties – the desperate, the timid, and the cautious. These three parties had arranged themselves in natural sequence. The mutineers, headed by Messrs Gabbett, Vetch, and the Moocher, were next the door; the timid – boys, old men, innocent poor wretches condemned on circumstantial evidence, or rustics condemned to be turned into thieves for pulling a turnip – were at the further end, huddling together in alarm; and the prudent – that is to say, all the rest, ready to fight or fly, advance or retreat, assist the authorities or their companions, as the fortune of the day might direct – occupied the middle space. The mutineers proper numbered, perhaps, some thirty men, and of these thirty only half a dozen knew what was really about to be done.

The ship's bell strikes the half hour, and as the cries of the three sentries passing the word to the quarter-deck die away, Gabbett, who has been leaning with his back against the door, nudges Jemmy Vetch.

'Now, Jemmy,' says he, in a whisper, 'Tell 'em!'

The whisper being heard by those nearest the giant, a silence begins, which gradually spreads like a ripple over the whole surface, reaching even the bunks at the further end.

'Gentlemen,' says Mr Vetch, politely sarcastic in his own hang-dog fashion, 'myself and my friends here are going to take the ship for you. Those who like to join us had better speak at

once, for in about half an hour they will not have the h'opportunity.'

He pauses, and looks round with such an impertinently
confident air, that three waverers in the party amid-ships slip
nearer to hear him.

'You needn't be afraid,' Mr Vetch continues, 'we have
arranged it all for you. There are friends waiting for us outside,
and the door will be open directly. All we want, gentlemen,
is your vote and interest – I mean your –'

'Gaffing agin!' interrupts the giant, angrily. 'Come to business, carn't yer? Tell 'em they may like it or lump it, but we
mean to have the ship, and them as refuses to join us, we mean
to chuck overboard. That's about the plain English of it!'

This practical way of putting it produces a sensation, and
the conservative party at the further end begin to look in each
other's faces with some alarm. A grim murmur runs round,
and somebody near Mr Gabbett laughs a laugh of mingled
ferocity and amusement, that is not reassuring to timid people.

'What about the sogers?' asks a voice from out the cautious
ranks.

'D—n the sojers!' cries the Moocher, as though moved by
a sudden inspiration. 'They can but shoot yer, and that's as
good as dyin' of typhus anyway!'

The right chord had been struck now, and with a sort of
stifled roar, the prison admitted the truth of the sentiment.

'Go on, old man!' cries Jemmy Vetch to the giant, rubbing
his thin hands with eldritch glee. 'They're all right!' and then
his quick ears catching the jingle of arms, he adds, 'Stand by
now for the door – one rush'll do it.'

It was eight o'clock, and the relief guard was coming from
the after-deck. The crowd of prisoners round the door held
their breath to listen.

'It's all planned,' says Gabbett, in a low growl. 'W'en the
door h'opens, we rush. The sentry's bin bribed not to fire, and
we're in among the guard afore they know where they are.
Drag 'em back into the prison, and then grab the h'arm rack,
and it's all over.'

'They're very quiet about it,' says the Crow, suspiciously.
'I hope it's all right.'

'Stand from the door, Miles,' says Pine's voice outside, in its usual calm accents.

The Crow was relieved. The tone was an ordinary one, and Miles was the soldier whom Sarah Purfoy had bribed not to fire. All had gone well.

The keys clashed and turned, and the bravest of the prudent party, who had been turning in his mind the notion of risking his brains for a pardon, and by rushing forward at the right moment alarming the guard, checked the cry that was in his throat as he saw the men round the door draw back a little for their rush, and caught a glimpse of the giant's bristling scalp and bared gums.

'NOW!' cries Jemmy Vetch, as the iron-plated oak swung back, and with the guttural snarl of a charging wild-boar, Gabbett hurled himself out of the prison.

The red line of light which glowed for an instant through the doorway was blotted out by a mass of figures. All the prison surged forward, and before the eye could wink, five, ten, twenty, of the most desperate were outside. It was as though a sea, breaking against a stone wall, had found some breach through which to pour its waters. The contagion of battle spread. Caution was forgotten, and those at the back, seeing Jemmy Vetch raised up as it were on the crest of that human billow that reared its black outline against an indistinct perspective of struggling figures, responded to his grin of encouragement by rushing furiously forward.

Suddenly a horrible roar like that of a trapped wild beast was heard. The rushing torrent was stemmed, and choked in the doorway, and then from out the lantern glow into which the giant had rushed, a flash broke forth, followed almost instantaneously by a groan, as the sentry fell back shot through the breast. The mass in the doorway hung irresolute, and then by sheer weight of pressure from behind burst forwards, and as it so burst, the heavy door crashed into its jambs, and the bolts were shot into their places.

All this took place by one of those simultaneous movements which are so rapid in execution, so tedious to describe in detail. At one instant the prison door had opened, at the next it had closed. The picture which had presented itself to the eyes of the convicts was as momentary as are those of the thaumato-scope. The period of time that had elapsed between the opening and the shutting of the door could have been marked by the musket-shot.

The report of another shot, and then a noise of confused cries, mingled with the clashing of arms, informed the imprisoned men that the ship had been alarmed. How would it go with their friends on deck? Would they succeed in overcoming the guards, or would they be beaten back? They would soon know; and in the hot dusk, straining their eyes to see each other, they waited for the issue. Suddenly the noises ceased, and a strange rumbling sound fell upon the ears of the listeners.

↠ 13 ↠

THE OTHER SIDE OF THE DOOR

WHEN Pine and Vickers left the bedside of Rufus Dawes, they were undecided how to act. Vickers was for at once calling the guard and announcing to the prisoners that the plot – whatever it might be – had been discovered, but Pine, accustomed to convict ships, had overruled this decision.

'You don't know these fellows as well as I do,' said he. 'In the first place, there may be no mutiny at all. The whole thing is, perhaps, some absurdity of that fellow Dawes – a murderer, my dear sir, a most bloodthirsty fellow – and should we once put the notion of attacking us into the prisoners' heads, there is no telling what they might do. I remember when I was with old —'

'But the man seemed positive,' said the other, hastening to cut the coming story short. 'He mentioned my wife's maid, too !'

'Suppose he did? – and, begad, I daresay he's right – I never liked the look of the girl, – to tell them that we have found them out this time won't prevent 'em trying it again. We don't know what their scheme is either. If it *is* a mutiny, half the ship's company may be in it. No, Captain Vickers, allow me, as surgeon-superintendent, to settle our course of action. You are aware that –'

'– That, by the King's Regulations, you are invested with full powers,' interrupted Vickers, mindful of discipline in any extremity. 'Of course, I merely suggested –'

'Well,' says Pine, 'look here. We tell these scoundrels that their design, whatever it may be, is known. Very good. They will profess complete ignorance, and try again on the next opportunity, when, perhaps, we may *not* know anything about it. At all events, we are completely ignorant of the nature of the plot and the names of the ringleaders. Let us double the sentries, and quietly get the men under arms. Let Miss Sarah do what she pleases, and *when* the mutiny breaks out, nip it in the bud; clap all the villains we get in irons, and hand them over to the authorities in Hobart Town. I am not a cruel man, sir, but we have got a cargo of wild beasts aboard, and we must be careful.'

'But surely, Mr Pine, have you considered the probable loss of life? I – really – some more humane course. Prevention, you know –'

Pine turned round upon him with that grim practicality which was a part of his nature.

'Have *you* considered the safety of the ship, Captain Vickers? You know, or have heard of, the sort of things that take place in these mutinies. Have you considered what will befall those half dozen women in the soldiers' berths? Have you thought of the fate of your own wife and child?'

Poor Vickers shuddered.

'Have it your way, Mr Pine; you know best perhaps. But don't risk more lives than you can help.'

'Be easy, sir,' says old Pine; 'I am acting for the best; upon my soul I am. You don't know what convicts are, or rather what the law has made 'em – *yet* –'

'Poor wretches!' says Vickers, who, like many martinets, was as tender-hearted as a child. 'Kindness might do much for them. After all, they are our fellow-creatures.'

'Yes,' returned the other, 'they are. But if you use that argument to them when they have taken the vessel, it won't avail you much. Let me manage, sir; and, for God's sake, say nothing to anybody. Our lives may hang upon a word.'

Vickers promised, and kept his promise so far as to chat cheerily with Blunt and Frere at dinner, only writing a brief note to his wife to tell her that, whatever she heard, she was not to stir from her cabin until he came to her, and he knew that, with all his wife's folly, she would obey unhesitatingly when he couched an order in such terms.

According to the usual custom on board convict ships, the guards relieved each other every two hours, and at six p.m. the poop guard was removed to the quarter-deck, and the arms which, in the day time, were disposed on the top of the arm-chest, were placed in an arm-rack constructed on the quarter-deck for that purpose. Trusting nothing to Frere – who indeed, by Pine's advice, was, as we have seen, kept in ignorance of the whole matter – Vickers ordered all the men, save those who had been on guard during the day, to be under arms in the barrack, and forbade communication with the upper deck, placing as sentry at the barrack door his own servant, an old soldier, on whose fidelity he could thoroughly rely. He then doubled the guards, took the keys of the prison himself from the non-commissioned officer whose duty it was to keep them, and saw that the howitzer on the lower deck was loaded with grape. Pine and he then took their station at the main hatchway, determined to watch until morning.

Between six o'clock and seven o'clock nothing had happened; but Vickers going, at a quarter to eight, to see if the relief guard were ready, found his servant in dispute with one of the soldiers.

'He wants to go upon deck, your honour, though I towld him your honour's strict orders.'

At sight of Vickers, the soldier fell back quickly, and muttered something about fresh air.

Pine eyed him curiously, and recognised him as the stupid fellow who had dropped the lantern at the hospital door the previous night, and whom he had once found *tête-à-tête* with the suspected Sarah Purfoy on the lower deck. It suddenly struck him that this fellow might in some way be connected with the mutineers. Perhaps, indeed, his attempt to get upon deck was made for the purpose of warning his sweetheart that her plot had been discovered.

Such, indeed, was Miles's intention. In his blind passion for the infamous woman who had made him love her, he had promised not to fire upon the prisoners. When the door was opened, as usual, for the last inspection at eight o'clock, he was to permit Pine to be seized without giving the alarm, and it was thought that, the sentry once passed, the guard could be easily overpowered, and, armed with the captured firelocks, the convicts would have little difficulty in making themselves masters of the ship. His reward, of course, was to be the person of Sarah Purfoy. By doubling of the guard, and the unusual orders given by Vickers, the poor, lustful booby knew that some knowledge of the intended mutiny had come to his officer's ears; but believing himself unsuspected, and true in his coarse affection for the woman who had ensnared him, he had thought to get to her in time to warn her of the failure of the plot.

Pine whispered to Vickers to say nothing, and Miles fell in sulkily. The prison door was reached, the guard relieved, and the sentry posted. Casting one sharp glance around to see that all his men were in their places, Pine gave the usual order to stand from the door, and then Vickers unlocked it with his own hands, and, drawing the bolts, slipped on one side.

⟵ 14 ⟶

THE MUTINY

What had passed in the prison we already knew. Outside, this took place.

The stream of men pouring out of the darkness into the sudden glare of the lanterns, rushed bewilderedly across the deck. Miles, true to his promise, did not fire, but the next instant Vickers had snatched the firelock from his hand, and, leaping into the stream, turned about and fired down towards the prison. The attack was more sudden than he had expected, but he did not lose his presence of mind. The shot would serve a double purpose. It would warn the men in the barrack, and perhaps check the rush by stopping up the doorway with a corpse. Beaten back, struggling, and indignant, amid the storm of hideous faces, his humanity vanished, and he aimed deliberately at the head of Mr James Vetch. As we have seen, however, the shot missed its mark, and killed the unhappy Miles. Mr Vetch was reserved for a more terrible fate.

Gabbett and his companions had by this time reached the foot of the companion ladder, to encounter there the cutlasses of the doubled guard gleaming redly in the glow of the lanterns. A glance up the hatchway showed the giant that the arms he had planned to seize were defended by ten firelocks, while, drawn up behind the opened doors of the partition that ran abaft the mizenmast, the remainder of the detachment stood to their arms. Even his dull intellect could not but comprehend that the desperate project had failed, and that he had been betrayed. With that roar of despair which had penetrated into the prison, he turned to fight his way back, just in time to see the crowd in the gangway recoil from the flash of the musket fired by Vickers. The next instant, Pine and the two soldiers hurled themselves against the door, and, taking advantage of the momentary cessation of the press, shot the bolts, and secured the prison. The mutineers were caught in a trap.

The narrow space between the barracks and the barricade was choked with struggling figures. Some twenty convicts, and half as many soldiers, struck and stabbed at each other in the press. There was barely elbow-room, and the attacked and attackers fought almost without knowing whom they struck. Gabbett tore a cutlass from a soldier, shook his huge head, and calling on the Moocher to follow, bounded up the ladder, desperately determined to brave the fire of the watch. The Moocher, close at the giant's heels, flung himself upon the nearest soldier, and grasping his wrist, struggled for the cutlass. A brawny, bull-necked fellow next to him dashed his clenched fist in the soldier's face, and the man, maddened by the blow, let go the cutlass, and drawing his pistol, shot his new assailant through the head. It was the sound of this second shot that had aroused Maurice Frere.

As the young lieutenant sprang out upon the deck, he saw

by the position of the guard that others had been more mindful of the safety of the ship than he. There was, however, no time for explanations, for as he reached the hatchway, he was met by the ascending giant, who uttered a hideous oath at the sight of this unexpected adversary, and too close to strike him, locked him in his arms, and the two men went down together. The guard on the quarter-deck dared not fire at the two bodies that, twined about each other, rolled across the deck, and, for a moment, Mr Frere's fine old English existence hung upon the slenderest thread imaginable.

The Moocher, spattered with the blood and brains of his unfortunate comrade, had already set his foot upon the lowest step of the ladder, when the cutlass was dashed from his hand by a blow from a clubbed firelock, and he was dragged roughly backwards. As he fell upon the deck, he saw the Crow spring out of the mass of prisoners that had been, an instant before, struggling with the guard, and, gaining the cleared space at the bottom of the ladder, hold up his hands, as though to shield himself from a blow. The confusion had become suddenly stilled, and upon the group before the barricade had fallen that mysterious silence which so perplexed the inmates of the prison.

They were not perplexed for long. The two soldiers who, with the assistance of Pine, had forced-to the door of the prison, rapidly unbolted that trap door in the barricade (of which mention has been made in a previous chapter), and, at a signal from Vickers, three men ran the loaded howitzer from its sinister shelter near the break of the barrack berths, and training the deadly muzzle to a level with the opening in the barricade, stood ready to fire.

'Surrender!' cried Vickers, in a voice from which all 'humanity' had vanished. 'Surrender, and give up your ringleaders, or I'll blow you to pieces!'

There was no hint of a tremor in his voice, and though he stood, with Pine by his side, at the very mouth of the levelled cannon, the mutineers guessed, with that acuteness which imminent danger brings to the most stolid of brains, that, did they hesitate an instant, he would keep his word. There was an awful moment of silence, broken only by a skurrying noise in the prison, as though a family of rats, disturbed at a flour cask, were scampering to the ship's side for shelter.

This skurrying noise was made by the convicts rushing to their berths to escape the threatened shower of grape, and to the twenty desperadoes cowering before the muzzle of the howitzer it spoke more eloquently than words. The charm was broken; their comrades would refuse to join them.

The position of affairs at this crisis was a strange one. From the opened trap door came a sort of subdued murmur, like that which lies within the bowels of a sea-shell, but, in the oblong block of darkness which it framed, nothing was visible. The trap door might have been a window looking into a tunnel. On each side of this horrible window, almost pushed before it by the pressure of one upon the other, stood Pine, Vickers, and the guard. In front of this little group lay the corpse of the miserable boy whom Sarah Purfoy had led to ruin; and forced close upon, yet shrinking back from, the trampled and bloody mass, crouched, in mingled terror and rage, the twenty mutineers. Behind the mutineers, withdrawn from the patch of light thrown by the open hatchway, the mouth of the howitzer threatened destruction; and behind the howitzer, backed up by an array of brown musket barrels, sullenly glowed the tiny fire of the burning match in the hand of Vickers's trusty servant. To fire the howitzer meant certain death, not only to the mutineers, but to Pine, Vickers, and the nine soldiers. Yet, as we have said, the twenty knew that, at a motion of the captain's hand, the iron-faced automaton who held the match would lower it to the touch-hole.

The entrapped men looked up the hatchway but to see that the guard had already closed in upon it, and that some of the ship's crew — with that carelessness of danger characteristic of sailors — were peering down upon them. Escape was clearly hopeless.

'One minute!' cried Vickers, confident that one second would be enough – 'one minute to go quietly, or –'

'Surrender, mates, for God's sake!' shrieked some unknown wretch from out of the darkness of the prison. 'Do you want to be the death of us!'

Jemmy Vetch feeling, by that curious sympathy which nervous natures possess, that his comrades wished him to act as spokesman, raised his shrill tones.

'We surrender,' he said. 'It's no use getting our — brains blown out.'

And raising his hands, he obeyed the motion of Vickers's finger, and led the way towards the barrack.

'Bring the irons forward, there!' shouted Pine, hastening from his perilous position; and almost before the last man had filed past the still smoking match, the clink of hammers announced that Crow had resumed those fetters which had been knocked off his dainty limbs a month previously in the Bay of Biscay.

In another moment, the trap door was closed, the howitzer rumbled back to its cleatings, and the prison breathed again.

In the meantime, a scene almost as exciting had taken place on the upper deck. Gabbett, furious with that blind fury which the consciousness of failure brings to such brute-like natures, had seized Frere by the throat, determined to put an end to at least one of his enemies. But desperate though he was, and with all the advantage of weight and strength upon his side, he found the young lieutenant a more formidable adversary than he had anticipated.

Maurice Frere was no coward. Brutal and selfish though he might be, his bitterest enemies had never accused him of anything like lack of physical courage. Indeed, he had been – in the fine old English days that were gone – celebrated for the display of very opposite qualities. He rejoiced in the pride of his muscular strength, and, in many a tavern brawl and midnight riot of his own provoking, had proved the fallacy of the proverb which teaches that a bully is *always* a coward. Like most men of his temperament and nationality, he showed but little dash and daring in assault. Though he could fence and box with more than ordinary skill – and in his day young men learned to fence and box, as they now learn to play cricket or pull an oar – he was noted less for the excellence of his attack, than for the perseverance and pluck of his defence. He was one of those 'English' who, according to Napoleon – a tolerable judge in such matters – 'never know when they are beaten.'

He had the tenacity of a bulldog, – once let him get his teeth in his adversary, and he would hold on till he died. In point of fact, he was, as far as personal vigour went, a Gabbett with a college education; and in a personal encounter between two men of equal courage, science tells more than strength. In the struggle, however, that was now taking place, science seemed to be of little value. To the inexperienced eye, it would appear that the frenzied giant, gripping the throat of the man who had fallen beneath him, must rise from the struggle an easy victor. Brute force was all that was needed, – there was neither room nor time for the display of any cunning offence.

But knowledge, though it cannot give strength, gives coolness. Taken by surprise as he was, Maurice Frere did not lose his presence of mind. The convict was so close upon him, that there was no time to strike; but as he was forced backwards, he succeeded in crooking his knee round the thigh of his assailant, and thrust one hand into his collar. Over and over they rolled, the bewildered guard not daring to fire, until the ship's side brought them up with a violent jerk, and Frere realised that Gabbett was below him. Pressing with all the might of his muscles, he strove to resist the leverage which the giant was applying to turn him over, but he might as well have pushed against a stone wall. With his eyes protruding, and every sinew strained to its uttermost, he was slowly forced round, and he felt Gabbett releasing his grasp, in order to draw back and aim at him an effectual blow. Disengaging his left hand, he suddenly allowed himself to sink, and then drawing up his right knee, struck Gabbett beneath the jaw, and as the huge head was forced backwards by the blow, dashed his fist into the brawny throat. The giant reeled backwards, and falling on his hands and knees, was in an instant surrounded by sailors.

Now began and ended, in less time than it takes to write it, one of those Homeric struggles of one man against a dozen, which are none the less heroic because the Ajax is a convict, and the Trojans merely ordinary sailors. Shaking his assailants to the deck as easily as a wild boar shakes off the dogs which clamber upon his bristly sides, the convict sprang to his feet, and whirling the heavy cutlass round his head, kept the circle

at bay. Four times did the soldiers round the hatchway raise
their muskets, and four times did the fear of wounding
the men who had flung themselves upon the enraged giant
compel them to restrain their fire. Gabbett, his stubbly hair
on end, his bloodshot eyes glaring with fury, his great hand
opening and shutting in air, as though it gasped for something
to seize, turned himself about from side to side, now here, now
there, bellowing like a wounded bull. His coarse shirt, rent
from shoulder to flank, exposed the play of his huge muscles.
He was bleeding from a cut on his forehead, and the blood,
trickling down his face, mingled with the foam on his lips and
dropped sluggishly on to his hairy breast. Each time that a
man came within reach of the swinging cutlass, he received a
fresh accession of rage, and his form seemed to dilate and expand with passion. Viewed through the thunderous gloom of
a tropical night, the aspect of this monster, surrounded by
assailants who dare not approach him, brought to mind those
hideously-grotesque pictures of the combats of evil spirits, drawn
by the fantastic pencil of Goya. At one moment bunched with
clinging adversaries – his arms, legs, and shoulders, a hanging
mass of human bodies – at the next, free, desperate, alone in
the midst of his foes, with his hideous countenance contorted
with hate and rage, the giant seemed less a man than a demon,
or one of those monstrous and savage apes that haunt the solitudes of the African forests. Spurning the mob of sailors who
had rushed in at him, he strode towards his risen adversary,
and aimed at him one final blow that should put an end to his
tyranny for ever. Some dim notion that Sarah Purfoy had betrayed him, and that the handsome soldier was the cause of
such betrayal, had taken possession of his mind; and his rage
had concentrated itself upon Maurice Frere. Despite his natural
courage, the aspect of the ruffian was so appalling, that Frere,
seeing the backward sweep of the cutlass, absolutely closed
his eyes with terror, and surrendered himself to his fate. Had
the blow fallen, it must have smashed his skull like a cocoa-
nut; but it did not fall.

As Gabbett balanced himself for the blow, the ship, which
had been rocking gently on a dull and silent sea, suddenly
careened to leeward, and the convict was thrown violently to

the deck, the cutlass flying from his hand. Ere he could rise, he was pinioned by twenty hands.

Authority was triumphant almost instantaneously on the upper and lower decks. The mutiny was over.

⊷ 15 ⊶

DISCOVERIES AND CONFESSIONS

THE shock was felt all through the vessel, and Pine, who had been watching the ironing of the last of the mutineers at once divined its cause.

'Thank God!' he cried, 'there's a breeze at last!' and as the overpowered Gabbett, bruised, bleeding, and bound, was dragged down the hatchway, he rushed upon deck, to find the *Malabar* plunging through the whitening water under the influence of a five-knot breeze from the N.W.

'Reef topsails!' cries Best from the quarter-deck; and in the midst of the confusion, Maurice Frere briefly recapitulated what had taken place, taking care, however, to pass over his own dereliction of duty as rapidly as possible.

Pine knit his brows. 'Do you think that she was in the plot?' he asked.

'Not she!' says Frere — eager to avert inquiry. 'How should she be? Plot! She's sickening of fever, or I'm much mistaken.'

Sure enough, on opening the door of the cabin, Sarah Purfoy was discovered lying where she had fallen, a quarter of an hour before. The clashing of cutlasses and the firing of muskets had not roused her.

'We must make a sick-bay somewhere,' says Pine, looking at the lithe figure, with no kindly glance; 'though I don't think she's likely to be very bad. Confound her — I believe that she's the cause of all this. I'll find out, too, before many hours are over; for I've told those fellows, that unless they confess all about it to-morrow morning, I'll get them six dozen a-piece the day after we anchor in Hobart Town. I've a great mind to do it before we get there. Take her head, Frere, and we'll get her out of this before Vickers comes up. What a fool you are to be sure. I knew what it would be with women aboard ship. I wonder Mrs V. hasn't been out before now. There – steady past the door. Why, man, one would think you had never had your arm round a girl's waist before! Pooh! don't look so scared – I won't tell. Make haste, now, before that little parson comes. Parsons are regular old women to chatter,' and thus muttering, Pine assisted to carry Mrs Vickers's maid into her cabin.

'By George, but she's a fine girl!' he said, viewing the inanimate body with the professional eye of a surgeon. 'I don't wonder at you making a fool of yourself. Chances are, you've caught the fever, though this breeze will help to blow it out of us, please God. That old jackass, Blunt, too! – he ought to be ashamed of himself, at his age!'

'What do you mean?' asked Frere, hastily, as he heard a step approach. 'What has Blunt to say about her?'

'Oh, I don't know,' returned Pine. 'He was smitten too, that's all. Like a good many more, in fact.'

'A good many more!' repeated the other, with a pretence of carelessness.

'Yes!' laughed Pine. 'Why, man, she was making eyes at every man in the ship! I caught her kissing a soldier once.'

Maurice Frere felt his cheek grow hot. He, the experienced profligate, had been taken in, deceived, perhaps laughed at. All the time he had flattered himself that he was fascinating the black-eyed maid, the black-eyed maid had been twisting him round her finger, and perhaps imitating his love-making for the gratification of her soldier-lover. It was not a pleasant thought; and yet, strange to say, the idea of Sarah's treachery did not make him dislike her. There is a sort of love – if love it can be called – which thrives under ill-treatment. Nevertheless, he cursed her with some appearance of disgust.

Vickers met them at the door.

'Pine, Blunt has the fever. Mr Best found him in his cabin groaning. Come and look at him.'

The commander of the *Malabar* was lying on his bunk in that betwisted condition into which men who sleep in their clothes contrive to get themselves. The doctor shook him, bent down over him, and then loosened his collar.

'He's not sick,' he said; 'he's drunk! Blunt! Wake up! Blunt!'

But the mass refused to move.

'Hallo!' says Pine, catching sight of the broken tumbler, 'what's this? Smells queer. Rum? No, can't be rum. Eh! By God, he's been hocussed!'

'Nonsense!'

'I see it,' slapping his thigh. 'It's that infernal woman! She's drugged him, and meant to do the same for –' Frere gave him an imploring look – 'for anybody else who would be fool enough to let her do it. Dawes was right, sir. She's in it; I'll swear she's in it.'

'What! my wife's maid? Nonsense!' says Vickers.

'Nonsense!' echoed Frere.

'It's no nonsense. That soldier who was shot – what's his name – Miles, he – but, however, it doesn't matter now. It's all over now.'

'The men will confess before morning,' says Vickers, 'and we'll see.'

And he went off to his wife's cabin.

His wife opened the door for him. She had been sitting by the child's bedside, listening to the firing, and waiting for her husband's return, without a murmur. Flirt, fribble, and shrew, as she was, Julia Vickers had often displayed, in times of emergency, that wonderful courage which women of her nature often possess, to the astonishment of everybody. Though she would yawn over any book above the level of a genteel love story, attempt to fascinate, with ludicrous assumption of girlishness, boys young enough to be her sons, shudder at a frog, and scream at a spider, she could sit throughout a quarter of an hour of such suspense as she had just undergone, with as much courage as if she had been the strongest-minded woman that ever denied her sex.

'Is it all over?' she asked.

'Yes, thank God!' said Vickers, pausing on the threshold. 'All is safe now, though we all had a narrow escape, I believe. How's Dora?'

The child was lying on the bed with her fair hair scattered over the pillow, and her tiny hands moving restlessly to and fro.

'A little better, I think, though she has been talking a good deal.'

The red lips parted, and the bright blue eyes, brighter than ever, stared vacantly around. The sound of her father's voice seemed to have roused her, for she began to speak a little prayer:

'God bless papa and mamma, and God bless all on board this ship. God bless me and make me a good girl, for Jesus Christ's sake, our Lord. Amen.'

The sound of the unconscious child's simple prayer had something awesome in it, and John Vickers, who, not ten minutes before, would have sealed his own death warrant unhesitatingly to preserve the safety of the ship, felt his eyes fill with unwonted tears. The contrast was curious. From out the midst of that desolate ocean – in a fever-smitten prison on ship, miles from land, surrounded by ruffians, thieves, murderers, infamous women, and self-brutalised men, – the baby voice of an innocent child called confidently on Heaven.

Two hours afterwards – as the *Malabar*, escaped from the peril which had menaced her, plunged cheerily through the rippling water – the mutineers, by their spokesman, Mr James Vetch, confessed.

'They were very sorry, and hoped that their breach of discipline would be forgiven. It was the fear of the typhus which had driven them to it. They had no accomplices either in the prison or outside of it, but they felt it but right to say that the man who had planned the mutiny was Rufus Dawes.'

The Crow had guessed from whom the information which had led to the failure of the plot had been derived, and this was his characteristic revenge.

A LETTER AND A PARAGRAPH

FROM Lieutenant Maurice Frere to his cousin, Frank Devine, of The Mere, Essex:

Military Barracks, Hobart Town, Van Diemen's Land,
5th December, 1827

MY DEAR FRANK, I arrived here safely in the 'Malabar', after a long Passage. The letter you wrote me from Mere I got all safely; the Agents sent it down to Deptford. I have left a brown Trunk at Bowley's; if you will get it I shall be Obliged. You can keep it if you like, as there is nothing in it I Want. We have had quite an Adventurous Passage. We were becalmed on the Line, and a Mutiny broak out among the convicts. Fortunately we discovered it in time, and put it Down. I had a tuzzle with a Scoundrel who very nearly got the best of me, but I showed him O'Shaughnessy's trick, and put him on his Back. There were 20 of the Villains concerned in it, and the Ringleader is that man Dawes, whose Trial was so much talked about before we Sailed. The Doctor and Vickers overheard him Blabbing it when he was down with Fever, and took precaushuns accordingly. He and five moar were kept in Irons all the rest of the Voyage, and are now at Macquarie Harbour, a Penal Settlement on the West Coast. The men call it Hell-upon-Earth, but I have not been there. We had the Fever very Bad; moar than 50 Prisoners died, and Pine, the Doctor, said that if we had not got a Breeze we should have come worse Off. Strangely enuff, the First men down recovered. Vickers had a Wife on board, but I didn't like her, and a pretty little Child, who was very nearly dying of the Fever. The first officer died, and so did the Chaplain, and Mrs Vickers's Made was nearly dead too. The Captain was Drunk on the night of the Mutiny, and Vickers says he'll get Broak. There was a Board of Enquiry when we landed, and they tried to bring the Vickers Wife's Made into it, but there was no Proof against her, though they said she was the wife of one of the Convicts. Old Vickers got the Fever, and so did she; but when she got well she Nursed him and the Little Girl, and he wont here a Word against her. She is still living with them, and I see her often. She is a very good-looking Woman.

Now, my dear Frank, I want to tell you about the 'Hydaspis.' As you will see in the Paper, I have no doubt, we came Across her when we were Becalmed. She was on Fire, and I and Best (who'se Dead) rowed out to her, only in time to see her Blow up. All on board must have been Drowned, for we did not see a Soul. If they took to the Boats, they were probably lost, as it came on a Squall two days afterwards. So you see that poor Dick must be Dead now, and there can be no use Advertising any moar. You will come in to all the Propperty, and I wish you Joy.

This is not a very Cheerful place. There is nothing to Do. They tried to get up A Races at Sandy Point, but they were not much Good. The Convicts here are great Brutes. They are worked like bullocks, and are always Quareling and Fighting. The other Day, Two of them got out of the Gaol by digging a Passage through the Brick wall of the Cook-house. We caught them about three Miles out. I expect I shall be sent Down to a Settlement shortly, to look after the Prisoners. A very stupid Life, but I think I can keep them in Order. It's a Word and a Blow with me.

The Blacks are troublesome. They came to Break-o'-Day Plains last Week, and killed Four men; but we sent a Party out after them, and Shot several. Hobart Town is a beastly Place, though the Climate is fine. I wish I was back in England, but I suppose it's no good Wishing. Tell old Quaid, if you see him, about his Pet Prisoner, Rufus Dawes. The old Fellow always thought himself Sharp.

I have to go on Duty now, so must Conclude. With Love to Lucy.

Your affectnt. Cousin,

MAURICE FRERE.

P.S. There is no Doubt about poor Dick.

Extract from the *Hobart Town Courier* of the 10th November, 1827:

The examination of the Prisoners who were concerned in the attempt upon the 'Malabar' was concluded on Tuesday last. The four ring leaders, Dawes, Gabbett, Vetch, and Sanders, were condemned to death; but we understand that, by the clemency of his Excellency the Governor, their sentence has been commuted to six years at the penal settlement of Macquarie Harbour.

BOOK THREE

THE TOPOGRAPHY OF VAN DIEMEN'S LAND

THE south-east coast of Van Diemen's Land, from the solitary Mewstone to the basaltic cliffs of Tasman's Head, from Tasman's Head to Cape Pillar, and from Cape Pillar to the rugged grandeur of Pirates' Bay, resembles a biscuit at which rats have been nibbling. Eaten away by the continual action of that ocean which, pouring round by east and west, has divided the peninsula from the mainland, and done for Van Diemen's Land what it has done for the Isle of Wight, the shore line is broken and ragged.

Viewed upon the map, the fantastic fragments of island and promontory which lie scattered between the South-West Cape and the greater Swan Port, are like the curious forms assumed by melted lead spilt into water. If the supposition was not too extravagant, one might imagine that when the Australian continent was fused, a careless giant upset the crucible, and spilt Van Diemen's Land in the ocean. The coast navigation is as dangerous as that of the Mediterranean. Passing from Cape Bougainville to the east of Maria Island, and between the numerous rocks and shoals that lie beneath the triple height of the Three Thumbs, the mariner is suddenly checked by Tasman's Peninsula, hanging, like a huge double-dropped earring, from the mainland. Getting round under the Pillar rock, through Storm Bay to Storing Island, we sight the Italy of this miniature Adriatic. Between Hobart Town and Sorell, Pittwater and the Derwent, a strangely-shaped point of land – the Italian boot with its toe bent upwards – projects into the bay, and separated from this projection by a narrow channel, dotted with rocks, the long length of Bruny Island makes, between its western side and the cliffs of Mount Royal, the dangerous passage known as D'Entrecastreaux Channel. At the southern entrance of D'Entrecastreaux Channel, a line of sunken rocks, known by the generic name of the Actaeon reef, attests that Bruny head was once joined with the shores of Recherche Bay; while, from the South Cape to the jaws of Macquarie Harbour, the white water caused by sunken reefs, or jagged peaks of single rocks abruptly rising in the midst of the sea, warns the mariner off shore.

It would seem as though Nature, jealous of the beauties of her silver Derwent, had made the approach to it as dangerous as possible; but once through the archipelago of D'Entrecastreaux Channel, or the less dangerous eastern passage of Storm Bay, the voyage up the river is delightful. From the sentinel solitude of the Iron Pot to the smiling banks of New Norfolk, the river winds in a succession of reaches, narrowing to a deep channel cleft between rugged and towering cliffs. A line drawn due north from the source of the Derwent would strike another river winding out from the northern part of the island, as the Derwent winds out from the south. The force of the waves, expended, perhaps, in undermining the isthmus which, two thousand years ago, probably connected Van Diemen's Land with the continent, has been here less violent. The rounding currents of the Southern Ocean, meeting at the mouth of the Tamar, have rushed upwards over the isthmus they have devoured, and pouring against the south coast of Victoria, have excavated there that inland sea called Hobson's Bay. If the waves have gnawed the south coast of Van Diemen's Land, they have bitten a mouthful out of the south coast of Victoria. Hobson's Bay is like a millpool, having an area of 900 square miles, with a race between the Heads two miles across.

About a hundred and seventy miles to the south of the Heads lies Van Diemen's Land, fertile, fair, and rich, rained upon by the genial showers from the clouds which, attracted by the Frenchman's Cap, Wyld's Crag, or the lofty peaks of the Wellington and Dromedary range, pour down upon the sheltered valleys their fertilising streams. No parching hot wind – the scavenger, if the torment of the continent – blows upon her crops and corn. The cool south breeze ripples gently the blue waters of the Derwent, and fans the curtains of the open windows of the city which nestles in the broad shadow of Mount Wellington. The hot wind, born amid the burning sand of the interior of the vast Australian continent, sweeps over the scorched and cracking plains, to lick up their streams and wither the herbage in its path, until it meet the waters of the great south bay; but in its passage across the straits it becomes reft of its fire, and sinks, exhausted with its journey, at the feet of the terraced slopes of Launceston.

The climate of Van Diemen's Land is one of the loveliest in the world. Launceston is warm, sheltered, and moist; and Hobart Town, protected by Bruny Island and its archipelago of D'Entrecastreaux Channel and Storm Bay from the violence of the southern breakers, preserves the mean temperature of Lisbon; while the district between these two towns spreads in a succession of beautiful valleys, through which glide clear and sparkling streams. But on the western coast, from the steeple-rocks of Cape Grim to the scrub-encircled barrenness of Sandy Cape and the frowning entrance to Macquarie Harbour, the nature of the country entirely changes. Along that iron-bound shore, from Pyramid Island and the forest-backed solitude of Rocky Point, to the great Ram Head and the straggling harbour of Port Davey, all is bleak and cheerless. Upon that dreary beach the rollers of the southern sea complete their circle of the globe, and the storm that has devastated the Cape, and united in its eastern course with the icy blasts that sweep northward from the unknown terrors of the southern pole, crashes unchecked upon the Huon pine forests, and lashes with rain the grim front of Mount Direction. Furious gales and sudden tempests affright the natives of the coast. Navigation is dangerous, and the entrance to the 'Hell's Gates' of Macquarie Harbour — at the time of which we are writing (1830), in the height of its ill-fame as a convict settlement — only to be attempted in calm weather. The sea-line is marked with wrecks. The sunken rocks are dismally named after the vessels they have destroyed. The air is chill and moist, the soil prolific but in prickly undergrowth and noxious weeds, while the fetid exhalations from swamp and fen cling close to the humid, spongy ground. All around breathes desolation; and on the face of nature is stamped a perpetual frown. The shipwrecked sailor, crawling painfully to the summit of the basalt cliffs, or the ironed convict, dragging his tree-trunk to the edge of some beetling *plateau,* looks down upon a sea of fog, through which rise mountain tops like islands; or sees through the biting sleet but a desert of scrub and crag rolling to the feet of Heemskirk and Zeehan – couched like two sentinel lions keeping watch over the seaboard.

⟶ *2* ⟵

HOBART TOWN IN 1830

ENTERING, then, by the D'Entrecastreaux Channel, forty miles long, from one to three in breadth, the vessel bound for Hobart Town in 1830 leaves the fifty miles length of Bruny Island on the right, and passing Birch Bay – the station of the Government sawpits – runs in under Mulgrave Battery, and casts anchor in Sullivan's Cove. Bordering on the water is the cottage of the chaplain, and overlooking it, in protecting juxtaposition, are the Military Barracks. Four miles behind the little town, Mount Wellington rears its 4000 feet of purple grandeur; and in front of it the broad bright river sweeps majestically to the sea. A stream, taking its rise at the foot of the mountain, runs through the centre of the town. The ground around the city is hilly, and the houses, placed at that time for the most part on small allotments of land, allow glimpses of the prospect to appear between them; while in front of the harbour lies Government House, with its gardens sloping to the water's edge.

Landing in Hobart Town in 1830, at a jetty, on what was once Hunter's Island, but which was then connected by a long stone causeway with the mainland, we should find opposite to us, on the right hand, a range of seven houses, belonging to the Leith-Australian Company. Before us, would be the Town rivulet, and behind it, on a promontory called Macquarie Point, we could discern the lumber-yard where the Government employed its convict labour. On this Point the troops were reviewed on field-days, and the town boys played cricket on the summer evenings.

Let us imagine ourselves forty years younger, and walk through the town.

Turning to our right, we find ourselves in Macquarie-street, with St David's Church rising against a background of blue hills. This church has been built about ten years, and has just been 'completely repaired' with stucco, and the ungainly interior remodelled into private pews. A good organ has been erected since 1832. Service is performed in this building four times on Sundays, the morning service, at nine, being for the benefit of those prisoners who are in private service with families in the town, or who hold the indulgence of a ticket-of-leave. Walking up the street, the first building on our left is the Commissariat offices and Treasury, where two sentries keep guard. Two doors from this building is Government House, the residence of Lieu-tenant-Governor Arthur, the offices of the private secretary, and the offices of the Town Adjutant and Barrack Master – all under one roof, surrounded by gardens, and guarded by a sentry at each wing. Next comes the Supreme Court House, then the Female House of Correction, and then at the corner of Murray-street, the Gaol. Three sentries are on guard here, and, rising above the wall, grimly significant, are the black painted beams of the scaffold. Turning past the Court-House, towards the lately-built wharf, we enter Davey-street, in which is the entrance to the Military Barracks, and which is given over, as it were, to the military interest – six houses in succession being occupied by officers. Passing through the market-place into Campbell-street, we observe two more sentries over the prisoners' barracks there, and turning down Brisbane-street, we get into Elizabeth-street, and so back to the jetty again.

The street nomenclature, though it carries now but little significance, was in those days suggestive enough. Macquarie-street was named after Governor Macquarie, and Elizabeth and Campbell-streets after the maiden names of his wife; Murray-street was named in honour of Colonel Murray of the 73rd, Molle-street after Colonel Molle, and Antill-street after Major Antill of the 48th, while Collins-street, the first street built in the settlement, was so called by Colonel Collins himself.

Let us take a glance at the social condition of the city at this period of its history.

Six years before, Colonel Arthur, late Governor of Honduras, had arrived at a most critical moment. The late Governor,

Colonel Sorell, was a man of genial temperament, but little strength of character. He was, moreover, profligate in his private life, and, encouraged by his example, his officers openly violated all rules of social decency. It was common for an officer to keep a female convict as his mistress. Not only would compliance purchase comforts, but strange stories were afloat concerning the persecution of such women who dared to choose their own lovers. To put down this profligacy was the first care of Arthur, and in enforcing a severe attention to etiquette and outward respectability, he perhaps erred on the side of virtue. Honest, brave, and high-minded, he was also penurious and cold, and the ostentatious good humour of the colonists dashed itself in vain against his polite indifference. This lack of sympathy between governor and governed, added to a certain intolerance of a system of petty pilfering that was carried on in certain branches of the public service, induced a feeling of dislike to Arthur, which ultimately culminated in bitter and violent party abuse, and a petition for his removal from his office. In this contest the press was variously engaged, and the governor went the length of forcibly shutting the mouth of one editor who bayed too loudly. The Government journal was taken from Mr Melville and given to Dr Ross – a man of talent and acquirements – who not unnaturally devoted his best energies to praising his patron.

Arthur was, however, by position, no less than by sympathy, at the head of a powerful body of adherents. The military force in the island was large. In 1830, there were ten captains, eighteen subalterns, one hundred and seven non-commissioned officers, and nearly eight hundred rank and file. At the head of the two first-named classes the governor would naturally place himself, and official society held its own against all attacks. In opposition to this official society was that of the free settlers and the ticket-of-leave men. These last were more numerous than one would be apt to think. On the 2nd of November, 1829, thirty-eight free pardons and fifty-six conditional pardons appeared on the books, and the number of persons holding tickets of leave, on the 26th September of the same year, was seven hundred and forty-five.

The system of convict treatment prevailing at that time was

as follows: — Any colonist requiring a servant could apply for
a convict, and upon complying with certain formalities, the
convict, unless there was something 'against' him, was 'assigned'
to service. The master was compelled to clothe his man in a
complete suit of slop clothing, price twenty-one shillings, issued
from the ordnance store, and to furnish him, in addition, with
three pair of stock-keeper's boots, four shirts, and one cap or hat a
year. He was also to give him the use of a bed, two blankets and
a rug. Female convicts were allowed one cotton gown, two bed-
gowns, three shifts, two flannel petticoats, two stuff petticoats,
three pairs of shoes, three calico caps, three pairs of stockings,
two neckerchiefs, three check aprons, and a bonnet, the whole of
a value 'not to exceed £7'; and no female convict was allowed
to be out after dusk unless accompanied by her master or mistress. An assigned servant was allowed also a weekly ration of
10½ lbs. of meat, 10½ lbs. of flour, 7 oz. of sugar, 3½ oz. of
soap, and 2 oz. of salt. The convicts were divided into seven
classes, according to their conduct; the seventh consisting of men
sentenced to Macquarie Harbour — the *ultima thule* of penal
settlement. A convict could get a memorial written for him at the
Colonial Secretary's office, at a payment of 14d. per page, but he
was not allowed to 'write articles in the newspapers' under pain
of being sent to a penal settlement. He was not permitted to
own stock, or to be paid in liquor, and was to keep his servitude steadily in view. A Government order, dated January 11,
1828, says: 'Convicts attempting to pass as free men are
banished to Macquarie Harbour.' A standing reward of £2 per
head was paid for all escaped convicts of ordinary character.
Notorious villains were valued at £50 and £100 a-piece. On the
31st of October, 1832, the total number of convicts in the island
amounted to 11,042 — 182 being at Macquarie Harbour, 240 at
the new settlement of Port Arthur, 46 in gaol, and 543 working
in chain-gangs; making a total of 921 undergoing the additional
punishment assigned by law those prisoners who had committed
offences in the colony. The balance of this terrible sum is made
up of such items as these: 6396 'assigned' to settlers, 1160
tickets-of-leave, 155 acting as constables, 60 missing, 12 executed,
204 absconded and at large. The ticket-of-leave system established in 1823 had been considerably modified. Tickets were

first cancelled in 1827, and in 1829 were granted only on condition of good conduct. By a ticket-of-leave, a prisoner was
exempt from compulsory labour; and an 'emancipist' was per-·
mitted to live at large within the colony. A man who was transported for seven years must have resided four in the colony
before he could obtain a ticket-of-leave; for fourteen, six; for
life, eight. Emancipations were usually granted to fourteen
years' men at the end of two-thirds of their sentence, to 'lifers'
at the end of twelve years; but one act of insubordination or
violence forfeited all chance of such indulgence. All property of
which a convict might be possessed at the time of his arrival in
the colony was taken from him and deposited in a savings bank,
and he was permitted to add to it any moneys he might earn by
his own exertions. When a man was re-convicted of an offence
which placed him in the seventh class, or the 'irreclaimables,' he
was socially dead, and his property passed to the Government.
These seven classes were established in 1826, when the new
prisoners' barracks at Hobart Town were finished. The first
class were allowed to sleep out of barracks, and work for themselves on Saturday; the second had only the last-named indulgence; the third were only allowed Saturday afternoon; the
fourth were 'refractory and disorderly characters – to work in
irons; the fifth were 'men of the most degraded and incorrigible
character – to be worked in irons, and kept entirely separate
from the other prisoners;' while the sixth were the refuse of
this refuse – the murderers, bandits, and villains, whom neither
chain nor lash could tame – and were shipped to Port Arthur,
'Hell's Gates', or Maria Island. In 1830, Port Arthur was only
in process of formation, and Macquarie Harbour held 400
prisoners.

As may be guessed – save where some exceptional case had
stamped the offender as dangerous, or some private hatred had
operated unfavourably towards him – the sixth-class prisoner
was generally an old offender, who, not content with breaking
the law in England, must break it again in the Antipodes. The
punishment for a transported felon was re-transportation – that
is to say, a man sentenced to seven years for theft in London
would repeat the offence in Hobart Town, and be sentenced to
seven more. Thus ludicrous complications arose. Men have been

under three 'life sentences.' As an instance of a convict career which terminated at Hell's Gates, we may take that of James Williams, whose history is given in an almanack published at Hobart Town in 1833. This fellow was transported, at the age of nineteen, for pocket-picking, and sentenced, in the year 1822, to seven years' transportation. He arrived in Hobart Town in 1823, was assigned, and, in 1824, was sentenced to an additional seven years. Placed in a chain gang, he was 'insolent,' and received twenty-five lashes. The week after his punishment he refused to work, and received twenty-five more. Before three months had elapsed, he suffered fifty lashes for 'insubordination.' In two months' time he effected his escape, was re-captured, sentenced to one hundred lashes, and loaded with the heaviest irons permitted by the convict regulations. Being at work on the roads, he was detected plundering a fellow-convict, and received another one hundred lashes. He next stole half a fig of tobacco and received fifty more. In 1829 he was punished with increased hard labour and received twenty-five lashes and a third sentence of seven years (his former ones being unexpired). In 1831 he was capitally convicted for being illegally at large, and was sent to Macquarie Harbour for three years. At that dismal place he joined in a plot to seize a boat, was discovered, and saved his life by betraying his associates. They were hung, and he was condemned to 'life in irons.' He remained at Macquarie Harbour until the settlement was transferred to Port Arthur, and died at that place, in 1849, at the age of forty-five, having passed twenty years in irons, and received during his life-time more than two thousand lashes.

The earlier portion of the reign of Arthur was disturbed by the exploits of desperate men, escaped from the penal stations. From Macquarie Harbour and Maria Island (founded in 1825) a number of ruffians, reckless of life and rejoicing in blood-shed, had succeeded in escaping, to lurk in the bush and forest of the ranges. It was not always necessary to commit crimes in order to be imprisoned at Hell's Gates. The military officers and the Government had unlimited power, and sentences were often passed by partial or vindictive magistrates, which, recorded in the office of the superintendent, gave a false character of desperation to many poor fellows who were more stupid

than vicious. The discipline at the place was so severe, and the
life so terrible, that prisoners would risk all to escape from it.
In one year, of eighty-five deaths there, only thirty were from
natural causes; of the remainder, twenty-seven were drowned,
eight killed accidentally, three shot by the soldiers, and twelve
murdered by their comrades. In 1822, one hundred and sixty-
nine men out of one hundred and eighty-two were punished to
the extent of two thousand lashes. During the ten years of its
existence, one hundred and twelve men escaped, out of whom
sixty-two were found – dead. The prisoners killed themselves
to avoid living any longer, and if so fortunate as to penetrate
the desert of scrub, heath, and swamp which lay between their
prison and the settled districts, preferred death to recapture. A
band of wretches of this description kept, in 1824, the whole
island at bay. Headed by the notorious Brady, a gang of
prisoners seized a boat, got out of the harbour, and landed, nine
days afterwards, on the eastern coast of the Derwent. Seizing
upon arms and horses, they successfully defied all attempts to
capture them. They surrounded farm buildings, drove off cattle,
and shot, burned, and robbed in all directions. Grown bold by
success, and led by their savage and daring captain, they actually
took possession of Sorell Gaol, at Pittwater, twenty-five miles
from Hobart Town, and bound the gaolers. On April 14th,
1825, a reward of twenty-five guineas was offered for Brady, or
M'Cabe, his lieutenant, with fifty acres of land to the chief
constable of the district where they might be taken. In a few
months the reward was doubled, and a pardon and a free passage to England offered to any convict who should deliver up
the gang. At last M'Cabe was captured, but refused to betray
his leader. All attempts to take Brady failed. 'Sometimes,' says
Mr Bonwick, 'as many as twenty-five horsemen were seen following his standard,' and more than a hundred armed
criminals were at large in the country. Defeated in an attempt
to seize the *Glory*, a vessel lying in the Tamar, in order to
escape from the colony, they attacked the Launceston Gaol and
the house of Mr Dry, the father of the late Sir Richard Dry.
Several persons were wounded and two killed in this daring
assault, and the Governor determined to crush the bandits at
all hazards. A sort of campaign was commenced. His Excellency

himself took the field, and bands of settlers and field police scoured the country in all directions. A reward of three hundred guineas, or three hundred acres of land, was set upon the heads of twelve of the most desperate of the bushrangers, and as many as thirty were hung in one morning. Wearied out and deserted by his confederates, Brady was taken, after two years' freedom, and hung at Launceston, in 1826. With him died the terror that had so long hung over the settlers.

Arthur now established a new system. In 1827, he divided the whole country into districts, and placed each division under the care of a stipendiary magistrate. At that time Spanish dollars were more plentiful in the colony than English shillings, and the practice of having a rate of money different from the nominal value of the coin prevailed. Arthur, by a Government order made in 1826, directed that dollars should be taken and issued at 4s. 4d., and Calcutta rupees at 2s. 1d. At that time wheat was sold at 5s. a bushel, flour at 20s. a cwt., and fine bread at 4d. a loaf. Beef and mutton averaged 5d. a lb., and rum was 12s. a gallon. It was strictly forbidden to sell spirits to convicts, or even to give them intoxicating liquor, as payment for their labour. Any person retailing drink without a license was fined £50, and a fine of £25 was imposed upon any publican who was detected in supplying a prisoner with drink, but, as might be expected, punishment was easily and often evaded.

In 1829, the colony took a jump forward, and the seat of government having, two years before, been finally fixed at Hobart Town, public works of importance were undertaken. An aqueduct for supplying the town with pure water was undertaken, and the present bridge across the Derwent commenced. This bridge – now known as Bridgewater – was still in progress in 1830, and large numbers of prisoners were employed upon it. Only two years before, the great attack upon the blacks – known as the Black War – had taken place, but by 1830, the once dreaded natives, reduced to 600 souls, were objects of pity, rather than terror, and the expedition against them was remembered almost as a matter of history, so rapidly had the colony progessed in civilisation and importance.

In 1830, Van Diemen's Land boasted five newspapers – the

Hobart Town Gazette, the *Colonial Times*, the *Tasmanian Review*, the *Hobart Town Courier*, and the *Launceston Advertiser*. The Bank of Van Diemen's Land had been established seven years, the Derwent Bank three, the Cornwall Bank two, and Commercial Bank one. The Derwent Whaling Club was offering a prize of eight dollars to the first person who should give information of a whale being in the river. The population of the island, including prisoners, was computed at 20,500 persons, of whom only 700 had been born during the past year. Out of 15,000,000 acres, only 30,000 were under cultivation, and the amount of coin in circulation amounted to £25,000 throughout the whole island. There was no theatre, and the only thing approaching amusement that had as yet taken place was a lecture on Astronomy, at the new Mechanics' Institute. Convict road-gangs were hard at work at what is now known as the Hobart Town Road. One party was employed in constructing a gaol – the ruins of which are yet standing – for the gang at work at the Derwent bridge. Another, consisting of seventy convicts, was cutting a line from New Norfolk to the Lower Clyde, at a place called 'Deep Gully,' and was 'guarded by an officer and a party of soldiers, night and day.' A third gang was at work at Oatlands, where a 'barrack for thirty soldiers and an excellent stone inn' had just been built. The 'Dutch farm' of Colonel Arthur, at the Black Snake, had just been completed, and the extent of fencing – almost 600 miles – throughout the country is characterised by Dr Ross as 'almost incredible.' Among the notable buildings round the city were the residence of Mr Murray and the saw-mill of Messrs Macintosh and Degraves. Mr Geo. M. Stephen was clerk of the Supreme Court, and lived in Macquarie-street; and the old 'Guard House' was on the opposite side the way, at the corner of Elizabeth-street. The streets were not lighted at night until 1832. There were but 64 houses in Macquarie-street, 43 in Campbell-street, and 97 in Elizabeth-street; and the whole adult free population of the city numbered 1400 to 1900 male persons.

Of the social condition of the people at this time it is impossible to speak without astonishment. According to the recorded testimony of the minority of respectable persons – Government officials, military officers, and free settlers – it was but a few

degrees better than that which had prevailed during Sorell's
government. The profligacy of some of the richer settlers was
notorious. Drunkenness was a prevailing vice. Even children
were to be seen in the streets intoxicated. On Sundays, men and
women might be observed standing round the public-house
doors, waiting for the expiration of the hours of public worship,
in order to 'continue their carousing.' Religious duties, as might
be expected, were but little heeded. 'The duty of a pastor in
Hobart Town,' says Dr Ross, writing in 1831, 'is indeed most
arduous. He is placed, as it were, in the very gorge of sin, in
the midst of the general receptacle for the worst characters in
the world, and if necessity compelled to take the "bull by the
horns", to grapple at the very gates of hell, if he would rescue
a soul from the headlong ruin to which he is hurrying. ... Even
the commonest holiday, the least cause for rejoicing that occurs
throughout the year, is invariably attended with the most
humiliating scenes of drunkenness.'

As for the condition of the prisoner population, that, indeed,
is indescribable. Backhouse, the Quaker missionary, who, four
years later, travelled through the island, refers constantly to the
scenes of drunkenness and riot which he witnessed among the
assigned servants and road gangs. Notwithstanding the severe
punishment which sly grog selling met with, it was carried on
to a large extent. Men and women were intoxicated together,
and a bottle of brandy was considered to be cheaply bought at
the price of twenty lashes. In the Factory – a female prison – the
vilest abuses were committed, while the infamies current, as
matters of course, in chain gangs and penal settlements were of
too horrible a nature to be more than hinted at here. All that
the vilest and most bestial of human creatures could invent and
practice was invented and practised there without restraint and
without shame. Seventeen years later even, under improved discipline and closer supervision, the condition of the prisoners was
such as to draw from the Bishop of Tasmania a pamphlet,
which terrified the Home Government. A chaplain, writing of
the prisoners' barracks in Hobart Town, says: – 'Twelve hundred men are congregated there like beasts, and every kind of
villany and wickedness that imagination can invent is planned
and carried on.' The hours of labour were from six to nine,

and ten to three in summer, and from eight to one without intermission in winter; and, says the chaplain – 'The hours from five till eight are generally occupied by the men in dancing, singing songs, etc., and a passer-by may frequently hear their loud and filthy talking.' When we remember that this is written of the principal gaol in the capital of the island, where the worst criminals were not confined, we can arrive at some standard by which to measure the state of the penal settlements themselves, – the lowest depths in this dreadful deep of sin and misery.

Such a spectacle does the Hobart Town of 1830 present to the thinker, who – seeing, in 1870, its lovely gardens, its winding rivers, its richness of field and fallow, partaking, perhaps, of the hospitality of its educated and wealthy inhabitants, and sharing the comfort of domestic circles graced by beautiful and refined women – looks back to the 'old days,' before the curse of convictism was taken off the land.

++ 3 ++

THE SOLITARY OF 'HELL'S GATES'

'HELL'S Gates' is formed by a rocky point, which runs abruptly northward, almost touching, on its eastern side, a projecting arm of land which guards the entrance to King's River. In the middle of the gates is a natural bolt – that is to say, an island which, lying on a sandy bar in the very jaws of the current, creates a sort of double whirlpool, impossible to pass in the roughest weather. Once through the Gates, the convict, chained on the deck of the inward-bound vessel, sees in front of him the bald cone of the Frenchman's Cap, piercing the moist air at a height of five thousand feet; while, gloomed by overhanging rocks, and shadowed by gigantic forests, the black sides of the basin narrow to the mouth of the Gordon. The turbulent stream is the colour of indigo, and, being fed by numerous rivulets, that ooze through masses of decaying vegetable matter, is of so poisonous a nature that it is not only undrinkable, but absolutely kills the fish that in stormy weather are driven in from the sea. As may be imagined, the furious storms which beat upon this exposed coast create a strong surf line. After a few days of north-west wind, the waters of the Gordon will be found salt for twelve miles up from the bar. The river itself is navigable for thirty or forty miles, and though deep, is never more than one hundred yards wide. The head-quarters of the settlement were placed on an island not far from its mouth, called Sarah Island.

Though now the whole place is desolate, and a few rotting posts and logs alone remain as mute witnesses of scenes of agony never to be revived, in the year 1830 the buildings were numerous and extensive. On Phillip's Island, on the north side of the harbour, was a small farm, where vegetables were grown for the use of the officers of the establishment; and, on Sarah Island, were sawpits, forges, dockyards, gaol, guard-house, barracks, and jetty. The military force numbers about sixty men, who, with convict-warders and constables, take charge of more than three hundred and fifty prisoners. These miserable wretches, deprived of every hope, are employed in the most degrading labour. No beast of burden is allowed on the settlement; all the pulling and dragging is done by human beings. About one hundred 'good-conduct' men are allowed the lighter toil of dragging timber to the wharf, to assist in shipbuilding; but the rest are made to cut down the enormous trees that fringe the mainland, and to carry them on their shoulders to the water's edge.

The denseness of the scrub and bush renders it necessary that a 'roadway,' perhaps a quarter of a mile in length, be first constructed, and the trunks of trees, stripped of their branches, are rolled together in this roadway, until a 'slide' is made, down which the heavier logs can be shunted towards the harbour. The timber thus obtained is made into rafts, and floated to the sheds, or arranged for transportation to Hobart Town. The convicts are lodged, on Sarah Island, in barracks flanked by a two-storied prison, whose 'cells' are the terror of the most hardened. Each morning, they receive their breakfast of porridge, water and salt, and then row, under the protection of their guard, to the woodcutting stations, where they work, without food, until night. The launching and hewing of the timber compels them to work up to their waists in water. Many of them are heavily ironed. The current is strong against their homeward pull, and the 'supper' is often delayed three or four hours. When they die, they are buried on a little plot of ground, called Halliday's Island (from the name of the first man buried there), and a plank stuck into the earth, and carved with the initials of the deceased, is all the monument vouchsafed him.

Sarah Island, situated at the south-east corner of the harbour, is long and low. The commandant's house was situated in the centre, having the chaplain's house and barracks between it and the gaol. The hospital was on the west shore, and in a line with it lay the two penitentiaries. Lines of lofty palisades ran round the settlement, giving it the appearance of a fortified town. These palisades were for the purpose of warding off the terrific blasts of wind, which, shrieking through the long and narrow bay as through the keyhole of a door, had in former times torn off roofs and levelled boat-sheds. The little town was set, as it were, in defiance of Nature, at the very extreme of civilisation, and its inhabitants maintained a perpetual war with the winds and waves.

But the gaol of Sarah Island was not the only prison in this desolate region.

Some little distance from the mainland is a rock, over the west side of which the waves dash in rough weather. On the evening of the 3rd December, 1833, as the sun was sinking behind the tree-tops on the left side of the harbour, the figure of a man appeared on the top of this rock. He was clad in the coarse garb of a convict, and wore round his ankles two iron rings, between which ran a short and heavy chain. In the middle of this chain a leather strap was attached, which, splitting in the form of a T, buckled round his waist, and pulled the chain high enough to prevent him stumbling over it as he walked. His head was bare, and his coarse blue-striped shirt, open at the throat, displayed an embrowned and muscular neck. Emerging from out a sort of cell, or den, contrived by nature or art in the side of the cliff, he threw on a scanty fire, which burned between two hollowed rocks, a small log of pine wood, and then returning to his cave, brought from it an iron pot, which would seem to contain water, he scooped with his hard and callous hands a resting place for it in the ashes, and placed it on the embers. It was evident that the cave was at once his storehouse and larder; it seemed that the two hollowed rocks were his kitchen.

Having thus made preparation for supper, he ascended a pathway which led to the highest point of the rock. His fetters compelled him to take short steps, and as he walked, he winced as though the iron bit him. Indeed, a second glance showed that a handkerchief or strip of cloth had been twisted round his left ankle, as though the circlet had chafed a sore there. Painfully and slowly, he gained his destination, and flinging himself on the ground, gazed around him. The afternoon had been stormy, and the rays of the setting sun shone redly on the turbid and rushing waters of the bay. On the right lay Sarah Island; on the left the bleak shore of the opposite coast, and the tall peak of the Frenchman's Cap; while the recent storm hung sullenly over the barren hills to the eastward. Below him, on the left, appeared the only sign of life. A brig, under close-reefed sails, was being towed up the harbour by two convict-manned boats.

The sight of this brig seemed to rouse in the mind of the solitary of the rock a strain of reflection, for sinking his chin upon his hand, he fixed his eyes on the incoming vessel and immersed himself in moody thought. More than an hour had passed, yet he did not stir. The ship anchored, the boat detached itself from her sides, the sun sank, and the bay was plunged in gloom. Lights began to twinkle along the shore of the settlement. The little fire died, and the water in the iron pot grew cold; yet the watcher on the rock did not stir. With his eyes staring into the gloom, and his gaze fixed steadily on the vessel, he lay along the barren cliff of his lonely prison, as motionless as the rock on which he had stretched himself.

What was this man?

A SOCIAL EVENING

In the house of Major Vickers, Commandant of Macquarie Harbour, there was, on the evening of December 3rd, 1833, unusual gaiety.

Lieutenant Maurice Frere, late in command of Maria Island, had come down with news from head-quarters. The *Ladybird,* Government schooner, visited the settlement on ordinary occasions twice a year, and such visits were looked forward to with no little eagerness by the settlers. To the convicts, the arrival of the *Ladybird* meant the arrival of new faces, intelligence of old comrades, news of how the world, from which they were exiled, was progressing. When the *Ladybird* arrived, the chained and toil-worn felons felt that they were yet human, that the horizon of their universe was not bounded by the gloomy forests that surrounded their prison, but that there was a world beyond, where men, like themselves, smoked, and drank, and laughed, and rested, and were Free. When the *Ladybird* arrived, they heard such news as interested them – that is to say, not mere foolish accounts of wars or ship arrivals, or city gossip, but matters appertaining to themselves – how Tom was with the road gangs, Dick on a ticket of leave, Harry taken to the bush, and Jack hung at the Hobart Town Gaol. Such items of intelligence were the only news they cared to hear, and the new comers were well posted up in such matters. To the convicts, the *Ladybird* was town talk, theatre, stock quotations, and latest telegrams. She was their newspaper and post-office, the one excitement of their dreary existence, the one link between their own misery and the happiness of their fellow-creatures. To the Commandant and the 'free men,' this messenger from the outer life was scarcely less welcome. There was not a man on the island who did not feel his heart grow heavier when her white sails disappeared behind the shoulder of the hill.

It would appear that some business of more than ordinary importance had procured for Major Vickers the honour of his guest, for, in the Commandant's little household gathering, Maurice Frere was decidedly the lion of the party.

He was sitting by the empty fire-place, with one leg carelessly thrown over the other, entertaining the company with his usual indifferent air. The six years that had passed since his departure from England had given him a sturdier frame and a fuller face. His hair seemed coarser, his face redder, and his eye more hard, but in demeanour he was but little changed. Sobered he might be, and his voice had acquired that decisive, insured tone that a voice accustomed to be exercised only in accents of command invariably acquires, but his bad qualities were as prominent as ever. His five years' residence at Maria Island had increased that brutality of thought and overbearing confidence in his own importance for which he had been always remarkable, but it had also given him an assured air of authority, which covered the more unpleasant features of his character. He was detested by the prisoners – as he had said, 'it was a word and a blow with him' – but, among his superiors, he passed for an officer, honest and painstaking, though somewhat bluff and severe.

'Well, Mrs Vickers,' he said, as he took a cup of tea from the hands of that lady, 'I suppose you won't be sorry to get away from this place, eh? Trouble you for the toast, Vickers!'

'No, indeed,' says poor Mrs Vickers, with the old girlishness shadowed by six years; 'I shall be only too glad. A dreadful place! John's duties, however, are imperative. But the wind! My dear Mr Frere, you've no idea of it. I wanted to send Dora to Hobart Town, but John would not let her go.'

'By the way, how is Miss Dora?' asked Frere, with that patronising air men of his stamp adopt when they speak of children.

'Not very well, I'm sorry to say,' returned Vickers. 'You see, it's lonely for her here. There are no children of her own age, with the exception of the pilot's little girl, and she cannot associate with *her*. But I did not like to leave her behind, and have endeavoured to teach her myself.'

'Hum! There was a – ha — governess, or something, was there not?' said Frere, staring into his tea cup. 'That maid, you know – what was her name?'

'Miss Purfoy,' said Mrs Vickers, a little gravely. 'Yes, poor thing! A sad story, Mr Frere.'

Frere's eye twinkled.

'Indeed! I left, you know, shortly after the trial of the mutineers, and never heard the full particulars.'

Nevertheless he spoke not as one who desired information, but who was, the rather, curious as to what answer would be given him.

'A sad story!' repeated Mrs Vickers. 'She was the wife of that wretched man, Rex, and came out as my maid in order to be near him. She never would tell me her history, poor thing, though all through the dreadful accusations made by that horrid doctor – I *always* disliked that man – I begged her almost on my knees. You know how she nursed Dora and poor John. Really a most superior creature. I think she must have been a governess.'

Mr Frere raised his eyebrows abruptly, as though he would say, 'Governess! Of course. Happy suggestion. Wonder it never occurred to me before.'

'However, her conduct was most exemplary – really *most* exemplary – and during the six months we were in Hobart Town she taught little Dora a great deal. Of course she could not help her wretched husband, you know. Could she?'

'Certainly not!' said Frere heartily. 'I heard something about him too. Got into some scrape, did he not? Half a cup, please!'

'Miss Purfoy, or Mrs Rex, as she really was, though I don't suppose Rex is her real name either – sugar *and* milk, I think you said – came into a little legacy from an old aunt in England.'

Mr Frere gave a little bluff nod, meaning thereby, 'Old aunt! Exactly. Just what might have been expected.'

'And left my service. She took a little cottage on the New Town road, and Rex was assigned to her as her servant.'

'I see. The old dodge!' says Frere, flushing a little. 'Well?'

'Well, the wretched man tried to escape, and she helped him. He was to get to Launceston, and so on board a vessel to Sydney; but they took the unhappy creature, and he was sent down here. She was only fined, but it ruined her.'

'Ruined her!'

'Well, you see, only a few people knew of her relationship to Rex, and she was rather respected. Of course, when it became known, what with that dreadful trial and the horrible assertions of Doctor Pine – you will not believe me, I know, there was something about that man *I never* liked – she was quite left alone. She wanted me to bring her down here to teach Dora; but John thought that it was only to be near her husband, and wouldn't allow it.'

'Of course it was,' said Vickers, rising. 'Frere, if you'd like to smoke, we'll go on the verandah. She will never be satisfied until she gets that scoundrel free.'

'He's a bad lot, then?' says Frere, opening the glass window, and leading the way to the verandah. 'You will excuse my roughness, Mrs Vickers, but I have become quite a slave to my pipe. Ha, ha, it's wife and child to me!'

'Oh, a very bad lot;' returned Vickers, 'quiet and silent, but ready for any villany. I count him one of the worst men we have. With the exception of one or two more, I think he is the worst.'

'Why don't you flog 'em?' says Frere, lighting his pipe in the gloom. 'By George, sir, I cut the hides of my fellows if they show any nonsense!'

'Well,' says Vickers, 'I don't care about too much cat myself. Barton, who was here before me, flogged tremendously, but I don't think it did any good. They tried to kill him several times. You remember those twelve fellows who were hung? No! Ah, of course you were away.'

'What do you do with 'em?'

'Oh, flog the worst you know; but I don't flog more than a man a week as a rule, and never more than fifty lashes. They're getting quieter now. Then we iron, and dumb-cells, and maroon them.'

'How?'

'Give them solitary confinement on Grummet Island. When a man gets very bad, we clap him into a boat with a week's provisions, and pull him over to Grummet. There are cells cut in the rock, you see, and the fellow pulls up his commissariat after him, and lives there by himself for a month or so. It tames them wonderfully.'

'Does it?' said Frere. 'By Jove, it's a capital notion. I wish I had a place of that sort at Maria.'

'I've a fellow there now,' says Vickers. 'Dawes. You remember him, of course – the ringleader of the mutiny in the *Malabar*. A dreadful ruffian. He was most violent the first year I was here. Barton used to flog a good deal, and Dawes had a childish dread of the cat. When I came, in – when was it? – in '29, he'd made a sort of petition to be sent back to the settlement. Said that he was innocent, and that the accusation against him was false.'

'The old dodge,' says Frere again. 'A match? Thanks.'

'Of course, I couldn't let him go, but I took him out of the chain-gang and put him on the *Osprey*. You saw her in the dock as you came in. He worked for some time very well – he seemed to know all about ship's carpentry – and then tried to bolt again.'

'The old trick. Ha! ha! don't I know it?' says Mr Frere emitting a streak of smoke in the air, expressive of supernatural wisdom.

'Well, we caught him, and gave him fifty. Then he was sent to the chain-gang cutting timber. Then we put him into the boats, but he quarrelled with the coxswain, and then we took him back to the timber-rafts. About six weeks ago he made another attempt – together with Gabbett, the man who nearly killed you – but his leg was chafed by the irons, and we took him. Gabbett and three more, however, got away.'

'Haven't you found 'em?' asked Frere, puffing at his pipe.

'No. But they'll come to the same fate as the rest, I suppose. No man ever escaped from Macquarie Harbour.'

Frere laughed his rough laugh, – the remnant of his fine old English manner.

'By the Lord,' said he, 'it will be rather hard for 'em if they don't come back before the end of the month, eh?'

'Oh,' says Vickers, 'they're sure to come – if they can come at all: but once lost in the scrub, a man hasn't much chance for his life.'

It was remarkable how the atmosphere of the place had absorbed, as it were, the excess of Vickers's humanity. His six years' residence had brought him to a condition of hardheartedness which would have more than satisfied old Pine.

'When do you think you will be ready to move?' asked Frere.

'As soon as you wish. I don't want to stop a moment longer than I can help. It is a terrible life this.'

'Do you think so?' asked his companion, in unaffected surprise. '*I* like it. It's dull certainly. When I first went to Maria I was dreadfully bored, but one soon gets used to it. There is a sort of satisfaction to me, by George, in keeping the scoundrels in order. I like to see the fellows' eyes glint at you as you walk past 'em. 'Gad, they'd tear me to pieces if they dared, some of 'em!' and he laughed grimly, as though the hate he inspired was a thing to be proud of.

'How shall we go?' asked Vickers, referring to apparently some former conversation. 'Have you got any instructions?'

'No,' says Frere. 'It's all left to you. Get 'em up the best way you can, Arthur said, and pack 'em off to the new peninsula. He thinks you too far off here, by George! He wants to have you within hail.'

'It's a dangerous thing taking so many at once,' suggested Vickers.

'Not a bit. Batten 'em down and keep the sentries awake, and they won't do any harm. The *Cyprus* affair has sickened 'em, you may depend; they won't try any more games of that sort.'

'But Mrs Vickers and the child?'

'I've thought of that. You take the *Ladybird* with the prisoners, and leave me to bring up Mrs Vickers in the *Osprey*.'

'We might do that. Indeed, it's the best way, I think. I don't like the notion of having Dora among those wretches, and yet I don't like to leave her.'

'Well,' says Frere, confident of his own ability to accomplish anything he might undertake. '*I'll* take the *Ladybird*, and *you* the *Osprey*. Bring up Mrs Vickers yourself.'

'No, no,' said Vickers, with a touch of his old pomposity, 'that won't do. By the King's Regulations –'

'All right,' interjected Frere, 'you needn't quote 'em. "The officer commanding is obliged to place himself in charge" – all right, my dear sir. I've no objection in life.'

'It was Dora that I was thinking of,' said Vickers.

'Well, then,' cries the other, as the door of the room inside opened, and a white figure came through into the broad verandah. 'Here she is! Ask her yourself. Well, Miss Dora, will you come and shake hands with an old friend?'

The bright-haired child of the *Malabar* had become a bright-haired girl of twelve years old; and as she stood in her simple white dress in the glow of the lamplight, even the unaesthetic mind of Mr Frere was struck by her extreme beauty. Her bright blue eyes were as bright and blue as ever. Her little figure was as upright and as supple as a willow rod; and her innocent, delicate face was framed in a nimbus of that fine golden hair – dry and electrical, each separate thread shining with a lustre of its own – with which the dreaming painters of the middle ages endowed and glorified their angels.

'Come and give me a kiss, Miss Dora!' cries Frere. 'You haven't forgotten me, have you?'

But the child, resting one hand on her father's knee, surveyed Mr Frere from head to foot with the charming impertinence of childhood, and then shaking her lovely hair, inquired – 'Who is he, papa?'

'Mr Frere, darling. Don't you remember Mr Frere, who used to play ball with you on board the ship, and who was so kind to you when you were getting well? For shame, Dora!'

There was in the chiding accents such an undertone of tenderness, that the reproof fell harmless.

'I remember you,' said Dora, tossing her head; 'but you were nicer then than you are now. I don't like you at all.'

'You don't remember me,' said Frere, a little disconcerted, and affecting to be intensely at his ease. 'I am sure you don't. What is my name?'

'Lieutenant Frere. You knocked down a prisoner who picked up my ball. I don't like you.'

'You're a forward young lady, upon my word!' says Frere, with a great laugh. 'Ha! ha! so I did, begad, I recollect now. What a memory you've got.'

'He's here now, isn't he, papa?' went on Dora, regardless of interruption. 'Rufus Dawes is his name, and he's always in trouble. Poor fellow, I'm sorry for him. Danny says he's queer in his mind.'

'And who's Danny?' asked Frere, with another laugh.

'The cook,' says Vickers. 'An old man I took out of hospital. Dora, you talk too much with the prisoners. I have forbidden you once or twice before.'

'But Danny is not a prisoner, papa – he's a cook,' says Dora, nothing abashed, 'and he's a clever man. He told me all about London, where the Lord Mayor rides in a glass coach, and all the work is done by free men. He says you never hear chains there. I should like to see London, papa!'

'So would Mr Danny, I have no doubt,' said Frere.

'No – he didn't say that. But he wants to see his old mother, he says. Fancy Danny's mother! What an ugly old woman she must be. He says he'll see her in Heaven. Will he, papa?'

'I hope so, my dear.'

'Papa!'

'Yes.'

'Will Danny wear his yellow jacket in Heaven, or go as a free man?'

Frere burst into a roar at this.

'You're an impertinent man, sir,' cries Dora, her bright eyes flashing. 'How dare you laugh at me? If I was papa, I'd give you half an hour at the triangles. *Oh,* you impertinent man!' and, crimson with rage, the spoilt little beauty ran out of the room.

Vickers looked grave, but Frere was constrained to get up to laugh at his ease.

'Good! 'Pon honour, that's good! The little vixen! – half an hour at the triangles! Ha-ha! ha, ha, ha!'

'She is a strange child,' says Vickers, 'and talks strangely for her age, but you mustn't mind her. She is neither girl nor woman, you see, and her education has been neglected. Moreover, this gloomy place, and its associations – what can you expect from a child bred in a convict settlement?'

'My dear sir,' says the other, 'she's delightful! Her innocence of the world is amazing!'

'She must have three or four years at a good finishing school at Sydney. Please God, I'll give them to her when we go back, – or send her to England, if I can. She is a good-hearted girl, but she wants polishing sadly, I'm afraid.'

Just then some one came up the garden path and saluted.

'What is it, Troke?'

'Prisoner given himself up, sir.'

'Which of them?'

'Gabbett. He came back to-night.'

'Alone?'

'Yes, sir. The rest have died – he says.'

'What's that?' asked Frere, suddenly interested.

'The bolter I was telling you about – Gabbett. He's returned.'

'How long has he been out?'

'Nigh six weeks, sir,' said the constable, touching his cap.

''Gad, he's had a narrow squeak for it, I'll be bound. I should like to see him.'

'He's down at the sheds,' said the ready Troke – a 'good conduct' burglar. 'You can see him at once, gentlemen, if you like.'

'What do you say, Vickers?'

'Oh, by all means.'

⊷ 5 ⊶

THE BOLTER

It was not far to the sheds, and after a few minutes' walk through the wooden palisades, they reached a long stone building, two stories high, from which issued a sort of horrible growling, pierced with shrilly screamed songs. At the sound of the musket butts clashing on the pine-wood flagging, the noises ceased, and a silence more sinister than sound fell on the place.

Passing between two rows of warders, the two officers reached a sort of ante-room to the gaol, containing a pine-log stretcher, on which a mass of something was lying. On a roughly-made stool, by the side of this stretcher, sat a man, in the grey dress (worn as a contrast to the yellow livery) of 'good conduct' prisoners. This man held between his knees a basin containing gruel, and was apparently endeavouring to feed the mass on the pine logs.

'Come, bo'!' he said, cheerily, 'open yer jaws and lem'me shove something into yer belly. Yer nigh clemmed,[1] or ought to be.'

'Won't he eat, Steve?' asked Vickers.

And at the sound of the Commandant's voice, Steve arose.

'Dunno what's wrong wi' 'un, sir,' he said, jerking up a finger to his forehead, 'He seems jest muggy-pated. I can't do nothing wi' 'un.'

'Gabbett!'

The intelligent Troke, considerately alive to the wishes of his superior officers, dragged the mass into a sitting posture, and woke it.

Gabbett – for it was he – passed one great hand over his face, and leaning exactly in the position in which Troke placed him, scowled, bewildered at his visitors.

'Well, Gabbett,' says Vickers, 'you've come back again, you see. When will you learn sense, eh? Where are your mates?'

The giant did not reply.

'Do you hear me? Where are your mates?'

'Where are your mates?' repeated Troke.

'Dead,' says Gabbett.

'All three of them?'

'Ay.'

'And how did *you* get back?'

Gabbett, in eloquent silence, held out a bleeding foot.

'We found him on the point, sir,' says Troke, jauntily explaining, 'and brought him across in the boat. He had a basin of gruel, but he didn't seem hungry.'

'Are you hungry?'

'Yes.'

'Why don't you eat your gruel?'

Gabbett curled his great lips.

'I have eaten it. Ain't yer got nuffin better nor that to flog a man on? Ugh! yer mean lot! Wot's it to be this time, Major? Fifty?'

And laughing, he rolled down again on the logs.

'A nice specimen!' said Vickers, with a hopeless smile. 'What *can* one do with such a fellow?'

1. *Clemmed* – starved; a north country word.

'I'd flog his soul out of his body,' says Frere, 'if he spoke to *me* like that!'

Troke and the others, hearing the statement, conceived an instant respect for the new comer. He looked as if he would keep his word.

The giant raised his great head and looked at the speaker, but without recognising him. He saw only a strange face – a visitor perhaps.

'You may flog, and welcome, master,' said he, 'if you'll give me a fig o' tibbacky.'

Frere laughed. The brutal indifference of the rejoinder suited his humour, and, with a glance at Vickers, he took a small piece of cavendish from the pocket of his pea-jacket, and gave to the recaptured convict. Gabbett snatched it like a cur snatches at a bone, and thrust it whole into his mouth.

'How many mates had he?' asked Maurice, watching the champing jaws as one would watch a strange animal, and asking the question as though a 'mate' was something that a convict was born with – like a mole, for instance.

'Three, sir,'

'Three, eh? Well, give him thirty lashes, Vickers.'

'And if I ha' had three more,' growled Gabbett, mumbling at his tobacco, 'you wouldn't ha' had the chance.'

'What does he say?'

But Troke had not heard, and the 'good-conduct' man, shrinking, as it seemed, slightly from the prisoner, said he had not heard either. The wretch himself, chewing hard at his tobacco, had relapsed into his restless silence again, and was as though he had never spoken.

As he sat there gloomily chewing, he was a spectacle to shudder at. Not so much on account of his natural hideousness, increased a thousand fold by the horrible appearance of the tattered and filthy rags which barely covered him. Not so much on account of his unshaven jaws, his torn and bleeding feet, his haggard cheeks, and his huge and wasted frame. Not only because in looking at the animal, as he crouched, with one foot curled round the other, and one hairy arm pendant between his knees, he was so horribly unhuman that one shuddered to think that tender women and fair children must of necessity confess to fellowship of kind with such a monster. But chiefly because, in his slavering mouth, his slowly grinding jaws, his restless fingers, and his bloodshot, wandering eyes, there seemed to live a hint of some terror more awful than the terror of starvation – a memory of a tragedy played out in the gloomy depths of that forest which had vomited him forth again – and the shadow of this unknown horror thus clinging to him, repelled and disgusted, as though he bore with him the reek of the shambles.

'Come,' said Vickers, 'let us go back. I shall have to flog him again, I suppose. Oh, this place! No wonder they call it Hell's Gates.'

'You are too soft-hearted, my dear sir,' says Frere, half-way up the palisaded path. 'We must treat brutes like brutes.'

Major Vickers, inured as he was to such sentiments, sighed. 'It is not for me to find fault with the system,' he said, scorning, in his mute reverence for 'discipline', to utter all what he thought. 'But I have sometimes wondered if kindness would not succeed better than the chain and the cat.'

'Your old ideas!' laughed his companion. 'Remember, they nearly cost us our lives on the *Malabar*. No, no. *I*'ve seen something of convicts – though to be sure, my fellows were not so bad as yours – and there's only one way with 'em. Keep 'em down, sir. Make 'em *feel* what they are. They're there to work, sir. If they won't work, flog 'em until they will. If they work well – why a taste of the cat now and then keeps 'em in mind of what they may expect if they get lazy.'

They had reached the verandah now, and the rising moon shone softly on the bay beneath them, and touched with her white light the summit of the Grummet Rock.

'That is the general opinion, I know,' returned Vickers. 'But consider the life they lead. Good God!' he added, with sudden vehemence, as Frere paused to look at the bay, 'I'm not a cruel man, and never, I believe, inflicted an unmerited punishment, but since I've been here ten prisoners have drowned themselves from yonder rock, rather than live on in their misery. Only three weeks ago, two men, with a wood-cutting party in the hills, having had some words with the overseer, shook hands with the gang, and then, hand in hand, flung themselves over the cliff. It's horrible to think of!'

'They shouldn't get sent here,' says practical Frere. 'They knew what they had to expect. Serve 'em right!'

'But imagine an innocent man condemned to this place!'

'I can't,' said Frere, with a laugh. 'Innocent man, be hanged! They're all innocent if you'd believe their own stories. Hallo! what's that red light there?'

'Dawes's fire on Grummet Rock,' says Vickers, going in, 'the man I told you about. Come in and have some brandy and water, and we'll shut the door on the place.'

⊷ 6 ⊶

MISS DORA

'WELL,' says Frere, as they went in, 'you'll be out of it soon. You can get all ready to start by the end of the month, and I'll bring on Mrs Vickers afterwards.'

'What is that you say about me?' asked the sprightly Mrs Vickers from within. 'You wicked man, leaving me alone all this time!'

'Mr Frere has kindly offered to bring you and Dora after us in the *Osprey*. I shall, of course, have to take the *Ladybird*.'

'You are most kind, Mr Frere, really you are,' says Mrs Vickers, with a recollection of her flirtation with a certain young lieutenant, six years back, tinging her cheeks. 'It is really most considerate of you. Won't that be nice, Dora, to go with Mr Frere and mamma to Hobart Town?'

'Please, Mr Frere,' says Dora, coming from out a corner of the room, 'I am very sorry for what I said just now. Will you please forgive me?'

She asked the question in such a prim, old-fashioned way, standing in front of him, with her golden locks streaming over her shoulders, and her hands clasped on her black silk apron (Julia Vickers had her own notions about dressing her daughter), that Frere was again inclined to laugh.

'Of course I'll forgive you, my dear,' he said. 'You didn't mean it, I know.'

'Oh, but *I did* mean it, and that's why I'm sorry. I am a very naughty girl sometimes, though you wouldn't think so' (this with a charming consciousness of her own beauty), 'especially with Roman History. I don't think the Romans were half as brave as the Carthaginians. Do you, Mr Frere?'

Maurice, somewhat staggered by this question, could only ask, 'Why not?'

'Well, I don't like them half as well myself,' says Dora, with feminine disdain of reasons. 'They always had so many soldiers, though the others *were* so cruel when they conquered.'

'Were they?' says Frere.

'Were they! Goodness gracious, yes! Didn't they cut poor Regulus's eyelids off, and roll him down hill in a barrel full of nails? What do you call that, I should like to know?'

Mr Frere, shaking his red head with vast assumption of classical learning, could not but admit that *that* was not kind on the part of the Carthaginians.

'You are a great scholar, Miss Dora,' he remarked, with a consciousness that this self-possessed girl was rapidly taking him out of his depth. 'Are you fond of reading?'

'Very.'

'And what books do you read?'

'Oh, lots! "Paul and Virginia," and "Paradise Lost", and "Shakespeare's Plays", and "Robinson Crusoe", and "Blair's Sermons", and "The Tasmanian Almanack", and "The Book of Beauty", and "Amadis of Gaul." '

'A somewhat miscellaneous collection, I fear,' said Mrs Vickers, with a sickly smile – *she*, like Festus, cared for none of these things – 'but our little library is necessarily limited, and I am not a great reader. John, my dear, Mr Frere would like another glass of brandy and water. Oh, don't apologise; I am a soldier's wife, you know. Dora, my love, say good night to Mr Frere, and retire.'

'Good night, Miss Dora. Will you give me a kiss?'

'No!'

'Dora, don't be rude!'

'I'm not rude,' cries Dora, indignant at the way in which

her literary confidence had been received. '*He's* rude! I won't kiss you. *Kiss* you indeed! My goodness gracious!'

'Won't you, you little beauty!' cried Frere, suddenly leaning forward and putting his arm round the child. 'Then I must kiss you!'

To his astonishment, Miss Dora, finding herself thus seized and kissed, despite herself, flushed scarlet, and lifting up her tiny fist, struck him on the cheek with all her force.

The blow was so sudden, and the momentary pain so sharp, that Maurice nearly slipped into his fine old English coarseness and rapped out an oath. Luckily he caught Mrs Vickers' eye, and refrained.

'Oh, you naughty girl! My dear Mr Frere! There, go to bed instantly, miss.'

'My *dear* Dora!' cries Vickers, in tones of grave reproof.

But Frere laughed, and then catching both the child's hands in one of his own, kissed her again and again, despite her struggles.

'There!' he said, with a sort of petty triumph in his tone. 'You got nothing by *that,* you see.'

Vickers rose, with annoyance plainly visible on his face, to draw the child away; and as he did so, she, gasping for breath, and sobbing with rage, wrenched her wrist free, and, in a storm of childish passion, struck her tormentor again and again.

'Man!' she cried, with flaming eyes, 'let me go! I hate you! I hate you! I hate you!'

'I am very sorry for this, Frere,' said Vickers, when the door was closed again. 'I hope she did not hurt you?'

'Not she! I like her spirit. Ha, ha! That's the way with women all the world over. Nothing like showing them that they've got a master.'

But as he spoke, he felt in his own breast that he had not done a very heroic action.

The expression of annyance on Vickers' face looked as if he was much of the same opinion, but he hastened to turn the conversation, and, amid recollections of old days, and speculations as to future prospects, the little incident seemed forgotten.

But when, an hour later, Mr Frere traversed the passage

that led to his bedroom, he found himself confronted by a little figure wrapped in a shawl. It was his childish enemy.

'I've waited for you, Mr Frere,' said she, 'to beg pardon again. I ought not to have struck you; I am a wicked girl. Don't say no, because I am; and if I don't grow better, I shall never go to Heaven.'

Thus addressing him, the child produced a piece of paper, folded like a letter, from beneath the shawl, and handed it to him.

'What's this?' he asked, bewilderedly. 'Go back to bed, my dear; you'll catch cold.'

'It's a written apology; and I shan't catch cold, because I've got my stockings on. If you don't accept it,' she added, with an arching of the brows, 'it is not my fault. I have struck you, but I apologize. Being a woman, I can't offer you satisfaction in the usual way.'

Mr Frere stifled the impulse to roar with laughter, and made his courteous adversary a low bow.

'I accept your apology, Miss Dora,' said he.

'Then,' returned Miss Dora, in a lofty manner, 'there is nothing more to be said, and I have the honour to bid you good night, sir.'

And drawing the shawl around her with immense dignity, the little maiden marched down the passage as calmly as though she had been Amadis of Gaul himself.

Frere, gaining his room choking with laughter, opened the folded paper by the light of the tallow candle, and read, in a quaint, childish hand –

SIR, – I have struck you. I apologise in writing,
Your humbel servant to command,
DORA VICKERS.

'I wonder what book she took that out of?' he said. ' 'Pon my word, she must be a little cracked. Gad, it's a queer life for a child in this place, and no mistake.'

7

A LEAP IN THE DARK

Two or three mornings after the arrival of the *Ladybird*, the solitary prisoner of the Grummet Rock noticed mysterious movements along the shore of the island settlement.

The prison boats, that had put off every morning at sunrise to the foot of the timbered ranges on the other side of the harbour, ceased to make their appearance for some days. The building of a sort of pier, or breakwater, running from the western point of the settlement, was discontinued; and all hands appeared to be occupied with the newly-built *Osprey*, that was lying on the slips. Parties of soldiers, also, daily left the *Ladybird*, and assisted at the mysterious work in progress. Rufus Dawes, walking his little round each day, in vain wondered what this unusual commotion portended. Unfortunately, no one came near him to enlighten his ignorance.

About a fortnight after this – that is to say, about the 15th of December – he observed another curious fact. All the boats on the island put off one morning to the opposite side of the harbour; and, in the course of the day, he saw a great smoke along the side of the hills. The next day the same mystery was repeated; and on the fourth day the boats returned, towing behind them something that had the appearance of a huge raft. This raft, made fast to the side of the *Ladybird*, proved by-and-by to be composed of planks, beams and joists, all of which were duly hoisted up and stowed in the hold of the brig.

This set Rufus Dawes thinking. Could it possibly be that the timber-cutting was to be abandoned, and that the Government had hit upon some other method of utilizing its convict labour? He had hewn timber and built boats, and tanned hides and made shoes. Was it possible that some new trade was to be initiated? Before he had settled this point to his satisfaction, he was startled by another boat expedition. Three boats' crews went down the bay, and returned, after a day's absence, with an addition to their number, in the shape of four strangers and a quantity of stores and farming implements. Rufus Dawes, catching sight of these last, came to the conclusion that the boats had been to Philip Island, where the 'garden' had been established, and taken off the gardeners and garden produce.

Rufus Dawes decided that the *Ladybird* had brought a new Commandant – his eyes, trained by his half-savage life, had already distinguished Mr Maurice Frere – and that these mysteries were 'improvements' under the new rule. When he arrived at this point of reasoning, he was led to make another conjecture, which, assuming his first to have been correct, would have followed as a natural sequence. Lieutenant Maurice Frere would be a more severe Commandant than Major Vickers. Now, severity had already attained its height as far as he was concerned, and so the unhappy man took a final resolution. He would kill himself.

Before we exclaim against the seeming sin of such a resolution, let us endeavour to set before us what this miserable man must have suffered during the past six years.

We have some dim notion of what life on a convict ship means; and we have seen through what a furnace Rufus Dawes had already passed before he set foot on the barren shore of Hell's Gates. But to appreciate in its intensity the agony he had suffered since that time, we must multiply the infamy of the 'tween decks of the *Malabar* an hundred fold. In that prison was at least some ray of light. All were not abominable; all were not utterly lost to shame and manhood. Stifling though the prison, infamous the companionship, terrible the memory of past happiness – there was yet *ignorance* of the future, there was yet Hope. But at Macquarie Harbour was poured out the very dregs of this cup of desolation. The worst had come, and the worst must for ever remain. That pit of torment was so deep that one could not even see Heaven. There was no hope there as long as life remained. Death alone kept the keys of that island prison.

Is it possible to imagine, even for a moment, what an innocent man, gifted with ambitions and disgusts, endowed with power to love and to respect, must have suffered during one week of such a punishment? We ordinary men, leading ordinary lives – walking, riding, laughing, marrying and giving in marriage – can form no notion of such misery as this. Some dim ideas we may have about the sweetness of liberty and the loathing that evil company inspires; but that is all. We know that were we chained and degraded, fed like dogs, employed as beasts of burden, driven to our daily toil with threats and blows, and herded with wretches among whom all that savoured of decency and manliness was an open mock and scorn, we would – what? Die, perhaps, or go mad. But we do not know, and can never know, how unutterably loathsome life must become when shared with such beings as those who dragged the tree trunks to the banks of the Gordon, and toiled, blaspheming, in their irons, on the dismal sandspit of Sarah Island. No human creature could describe to what depth of personal abasement and self-loathing one week of such a life would plunge him. Even if he had the power to write, he dared not. As one who, in a desert, seeking for a face, comes to a pool of blood, and, seeing his own reflection, flies – so would such a one hasten from the contemplation of his own degrading agony. Imagine such an agony endured for six years!

Ignorant that the sights and sounds about him were the symptoms of the final abandonment of the settlement, and that the *Ladybird* was but sent down to bring away the prisoners, Rufus Dawes decided upon getting rid of that burden of life which pressed upon him so heavily. For six years he had hewn wood and drawn water; for six years he had hoped against hope; for six years he had lived in the valley of the shadow of Death. He dared not recapitulate to himself what he had suffered. Indeed, his senses were deadened and dulled by torture. He cared to remember only one thing – that he was a Prisoner for Life. In vain had been his first dream of freedom. He had done his best, by good conduct, to win release; but the villany of Vetch and Rex had deprived him of the fruit of his labour. Instead of gaining credit by his exposure of the plot on board the *Malabar,* he was himself deemed guilty, and condemned despite his asseverations of innocence. The knowledge of his 'treachery,' for so it was deemed among his associates, while it gained for him no credit with the authorities, procured for him the detestation and ill-will of the monsters among whom he found himself. On his arrival at Hell's Gates he was a marked man – an outcast among outcasts, a Pariah among those beings that were Pariahs to all the world beside.

Thrice his life was attempted; but he was not then quite tired of living, and he defended it. This defence was construed by an overseer into a brawl, and the irons from which he had been relieved were replaced. His strength – brute attribute that would alone avail him – made him respected after this, and he was left at peace. No one spoke to him. At first this treatment was congenial to his temperament; but by-and-bye it became annoying, then painful, then almost unendurable. Tugging at his oar, digging, up to his waist in slime, or bending beneath his burden of pine-wood, he looked greedily for some excuse to be addressed. He would take double weight when forming part of that human caterpillar along whose back lay a pine-tree, for a word of fellowship. He would work double tides to gain a kindly sentence from a comrade. In his utter desolation he agonised for the friendship of robbers and murderers.

Then the reaction came, and he hated the very sound of their voices. He never spoke, and refused to answer when spoken to. He would even take his scanty supper alone, did his chain so permit him. He gained the reputation of a sullen, dangerous, half-crazy ruffian. Captain Barton, the superintendent, took pity on him, and made him his gardener. He accepted the pity for a week or so, and then Barton, coming down one morning, found the few shrubs pulled up by the roots, the flower-beds trampled into barrenness, and his gardener sitting on the ground among the fragments of his gardening tools. For this act of wanton mischief he was flogged.

At the triangles his behaviour was considered curious. He wept and prayed to be released, fell on his knees to Barton, and implored pardon. Barton would not listen, and at the first blow the prisoner was silent. From that time he became more sullen than ever, only at times he was observed, when alone, to fling himself on the ground and cry like a child. It was generally thought that his brain was affected.

When Vickers came, Dawes sought an interview, and begged to be sent back to Hobart Town. This was refused of course, but he was put to work on the *Osprey*. After working there for some time, and being released from his irons, he concealed himself on the slip, and in the evening swam across the harbour. He was pursued, retaken, and flogged. Then he ran the dismal round of punishment. He burnt lime, dragged timber, and tugged at the oar. The heaviest and most degrading tasks were always his. Shunned and feared by his companions, hated by the convict overseers, and regarded with unfriendly eyes by the authorities, Rufus Dawes was at the very bottom of that abyss of woe into which he had voluntarily cast himself. Goaded to desperation by his own thoughts, he had joined with Gabbett and the unlucky three in their desperate attempt to escape; but, as Vickers stated, had been recaptured almost instantly. He was lamed by the heavy irons he wore, and though Gabbett – with a strange eagerness for which after events accounted – insisted that he could make good his flight, the unhappy creature fell in the first hundred yards of the terrible race, and was seized by two volunteers before he could rise again. His capture helped to secure the short freedom of his comrades; for Mr Troke, content with one prisoner, checked a pursuit which the nature of the ground rendered dangerous, and triumphantly brought Dawes back to the settlement as his peace-offering for the negligence which had resulted in the loss of the other four. For this madness he had been condemned to the solitude of Grummet Rock.

In this dismal hermitage, his mind, preying on itself, had become disordered. He saw visions, and dreamt dreams. He would lie for hours motionless, staring at the sun or the sea. He held converse with imaginary beings. He enacted his trial over again, and once more repeated his own defence. He harangued the rocks, and called upon the stones about him to witness his innocence. He was visited by the phantoms of his early friends, and sometimes thought his present life a dream. Whenever he awoke, however, he was commanded by a voice within himself to leap into the surges that washed the walls of his prison, and dream these sad dreams no more.

In the midst of this lethargy of body and brain, the unusual occurences along the shore of the settlement roused in him a still fiercer hatred of life. He saw in them something incomprehensible and terrible, and drew from them conclusions of an increase of misery. Had he known that the *Ladybird* was preparing for sea, and that it had been already decided to fetch him from his rock and iron him with the rest, for safe passage to Hobart Town, he might have paused; but he knew nothing, save that the burden of life was insupportable, and that the time had come for him to be rid of it.

In the meantime the settlement was in a fever of excitement. It had been finally resolved by Governor Arthur that the establishment should be broken up. A succession of murders and escapes had called public attention to the horrors of the place, and its distance from Hobart Town rendered it inconvenient and expensive. Arthur had fixed upon Tasman's Peninsula – the earring we have spoken of – as the future convict depôt, and the prisoners of Macquarie Harbour were to be removed to Port Arthur.

In less than three weeks from the announcement made by Vickers, all had been got ready. Everthing portable had been stowed on board the *Ladybird*; indeed, several cargoes of bulky material had been already quietly dispatched by Vickers, and the surrounding stations were denuded of all that could be broken, burned, or carried away. Hell's Gates was to be abandoned; and had honest Vickers his wish, he would not have left one stone upon another.

He had finally arranged with Frere as to his course of action. He himself would accompany the *Ladybird* with the main body. His wife and daughter were to remain until the sailing of the *Osprey* which Mr Frere – charged with the task of final destruction – was to bring up as soon as possible.

'I will leave you a corporal's guard, and ten prisoners as crew,' Vickers said. 'You can work her easily with that number.' To which, Frere, smiling at Mrs Vickers in a self-satisfied way, had replied that he could do with five prisoners if necessary, for he knew how to get double work out of the lazy dogs.

We need not pause to expatiate upon the extravagant joy with which the news of the coming departure was received by the convicts. When we remember that there are instances on record of Macquarie Harbour prisoners who committed murder in order to be *sent to Hobart Town for trial*, we can readily understand with what rapture the poor wretches looked forward to leaving their place of doom for ever.

Among the incidents which took place during the breaking up, was one which it is necessary to chronicle. Near Phillip's Island, on the north side of the harbour, is situated Coal Head, where a party had been lately at work. This party, hastily withdrawn by Vickers to assist in the business of devastation, had left behind it some tools and timber, and at the eleventh hour, a boat's crew was sent to bring away the *débris*. The men, in high spirits at their projected change of scene, set about the work with something as nearly akin to jollity as could be found in convict composition. Even the coxswain, Mr Troke, was in good humour, and forbore to enforce that strict silence which, by virtue of his carbine and pistols, he usually succeeded in maintaining. The tools were duly collected, and the pine logs – worth twenty-five shillings apiece in Hobart Town – duly rafted and chained, ready for towing, when one of the men lighted upon a sackcloth bag containing salt-meat and bread – the provisions of the coal party. The bag was worth keeping, and, lifting it on his shoulders, the man prepared to carry it to the boat, when one of his comrades cried, with a laugh,

'Let the meat rip; we shall have plenty of fresh tack in old Hobart Town.'

And chiming in with the humour of the hour, the bag was emptied of its contents.

'They'll feed the molly-hawks,' said another, as the loaves and salt meat rolled in a corner of the deserted hut – 'that is, if the birds don't leave the place now we're goin' out of it.' An utterance which was considered almost equal to a witticism.

Mr Troke, dozing in the stern sheets of the boat, had noticed nothing of this conversation, and accepted the empty sack without a murmur. The timber was secured, and, towing it after them, the convicts pulled for the ship just as the sun sank. Now, in the general relaxation of discipline and haste, it fell out that the timber raft was not made with as much care as usual, and the strong current against which the boat was labouring assisted the negligence of the convicts. The logs began to loosen, and though the ownward motion of the boat kept the chains taut, when the rowers slackened their exertions, the mass parted, and Mr Troke, hooking himself on to the side of the *Ladybird,* saw a huge log slip out from its fellows and disappear into the darkness. Gazing after it with an indignant and disgusted stare, as though it had been a refractory prisoner and merited two days' 'solitary,' he thought he heard a cry from the direction in which it had been borne. He would have paused to listen, but all his attention was needed to save the timber, and prevent the boat being swamped by the struggling mass at her stern.

The cry had proceeded from Rufus Dawes. From his solitary rock he had watched the boat pass him and make for the *Ladybird* in-channel, and he had decided – with that curious childishness into which the mind relapses on such supreme occasions – that the moment when the gathering gloom swallowed her up, should be the moment when he would plunge into the surge below him. The heavily-labouring boat grew dimmer and dimmer, as each tug of the oars took her farther from him. Presently only the figure of Mr Troke in the stern sheets was visible; then that also disappeared, and as the nose of the timber raft rose on the swell of the next wave, Rufus Dawes flung himself into the sea.

Heavily ironed as he was he sank like a stone. He had resolved not to attempt to swim, and for the first moment kept his arms raised above his head, in order to sink the quicker. But, as the short, sharp agony of suffocation caught him, and the shock of the icy water dispelled the mental intoxication under which he was labouring, he desperately struck out, and, despite the weight of his irons, gained the surface for an instant. As he did so, all bewildered, and with the one savage instinct of self-preservation predominant over all other thoughts, he became conscious of a huge black mass surging upon him out of the darkness. An instant's buffet with the current, an ineffectual attempt to dive beneath it, a horrible sense that the weight at his feet was dragging him down, and the huge log, loosened from the raft, was upon him, crushing him beneath its rough and ragged sides. All thought of self-murder vanished with the presence of actual peril, and uttering that despairing cry which had been faintly heard by Troke, he flung up his arms to clutch the monster that was thus pushing him down to death. The log passed completely over him, thrusting him beneath the water, but his hand, scraping along the splintered side, came in contact with the loop of hide-rope that yet hung round the mass, and clutched it with the tenacity of a death grip. In another instant he got his head above water, and making good his hold, twisted himself, by a violent effort, across the log.

For a moment he saw the lights from the stern windows of the anchored vessels low in the distance, Grummet Rock disappeared on his left, then, exhausted, breathless, and bruised, he closed his eyes, and the drifting log bore him swiftly and silently away into the darkness.

At daylight the next morning, Mr Troke, landing on the prison rock, found it deserted. The prisoner's cap was lying on the edge of the little cliff, but the prisoner himself had disappeared. Pulling back to the *Ladybird,* the intelligent Troke pondered on the circumstance, and in delivering his report to Vickers, mentioned the strange cry he had heard the night before.

'It's my belief, sir, that he was trying to swim the bay when the log struck him,' he said. 'He must ha' gone to the bottom anyhow, for he couldn't swim five yards with them irons.'

Vickers, engaged in commending his wife and child to the care of Mr Frere, accepted this very natural supposition without question. The prisoner had met his death either by his own act, or by accident. It was either a suicide or an attempt to escape, and the former conduct of Rùfus Dawes rendered the latter explanation the more probable one. In any case, he was dead. As Mr Troke rightly surmised, no man could swim the bay in irons; and when the *Ladybird,* an hour later, passed the Grummet Rock, all on board her believed that the corpse of its late occupant was lying beneath the waves that seethed at its base.

8

THE LAST OF MACQUARIE HARBOUR

IF Rufus Dawes was believed to be dead by the party on board the *Ladybird*, his strange escape was unknown to those still at Sarah Island. Maurice Frere, if he bestowed a thought upon the refractory prisoner of the Rock, believed him to be safely stowed in the hold of the schooner, and already half way to Hobart Town; while not one of the seventeen persons on board the *Osprey* suspected that the boat which had put off for the marooned man had returned without him. Indeed the party had but little leisure for thought; Mr Frere, eager to show his ability and energy, was making strenuous exertions to get away, and kept his unlucky ten so hard at work that within a week from the departure of the *Ladybird* the *Osprey* was ready for sea. Mrs Vickers and the child, having watched with some excusable regret the process of demolishing their old home, had settled down in their small cabin in the brig, and on the evening of the 11th of January, Mr Bates, the pilot, who acted as master, informed the crew that Lieutenant Frere had given orders to weigh anchor at daybreak.

At daybreak accordingly the brig set sail, with a light breeze from the south-west, and by three o'clock in the afternoon, anchored safely outside the Gates. Unfortunately the wind shifted to the north-west, which caused a heavy swell on the bar, and prudent Mr Bates, having consideration for Mrs Vickers and the child, ran back ten miles into Wellington Bay, and anchored there again at seven o'clock in the evening. The tide was running strongly, and the brig rolled a good deal. Mrs Vickers kept her cabin, and sent Dora to entertain Lieutenant Frere. Dora went, but was not entertaining. She had conceived for Frere one of those violent antipathies which children sometimes own without reason, and since the memorable night of the apology had been but barely civil to him. In vain did he pet her and compliment her, she was not to be flattered into liking him. 'I do not like you, Sir,' she had said in her stilted fashion, 'but that need make no difference to you. You occupy yourself with your prisoners; I can amuse myself without you, thank you.' 'Oh, all right!' said Frere, 'I don't want to interfere;' but he felt a little nettled nevertheless. On this particular evening the young lady relaxed her severity of demeanour. Her father away, and her mother sick, the little maiden felt lonely, and as a last resource accepted her mother's commands and went to Frere.

He was walking up and down the deck, smoking.

'Mr Frere, I am sent to entertain you.'

'Are you? All right – go on.'

'Oh dear no. It is the gentleman's place to entertain. Be amusing!'

'Come and sit down then, and we'll talk,' said Frere, who was in good humour at the success of matters up to this point. 'What shall we talk about?'

'You stupid man! As if I knew! It is your place to talk. Tell me a fairy story.'

'Jack and the Beanstalk,' suggested Frere.

'Jack and the Grandmother! Nonsense! Make one up out of your head, you know.'

Frere guffawed.

'I can't,' he said, 'I never did such a thing in my life.'

'Then why not begin? I shall go away if you don't begin.'

Frere rubbed his brows.

'Well, have you read – have you read – Robinson Crusoe?' – as if the idea was the most brilliant one in the world.

'Of *course* I have,' returned Dora, pouting. 'Read it? – yes. Everybody's read Robinson Crusoe!'

'Oh, have they? – Well, I didn't know; let me see now.' And pulling hard at his pipe, he plunged into literary reflection.

Dora sitting beside him, eagerly watching for the happy thought that never came, pouted and said, 'What a stupid, stupid man you are! I shall be so glad to get back to papa again. He knows all sorts of stories, nearly as many as old Danny.'

'Danny knows some, then?'

'Danny!' – with as much surprise as if she said 'Walter Scott!' 'Of course he does. I suppose now,' putting her head on one side, with an amusing expression of superiority, 'you never heard the story of the Banshee?'

'No, I never did.'

'Nor the White Horse of the Peppers?'

'No.'

'No, I suppose not. Nor the Changeling? nor the Leprechaun?'

'No.'

Dora got off the skylight on which she had been sitting, and surveyed the smoking animal beside her with profound contempt.

'Mr Frere, you are really a most Ignorant person. Excuse me if I hurt your feelings. I have no wish to do that, but really you are a *most* Ignorant person – for your age, of course.'

Maurice Frere grew a little angry.

'You are very impertinent, Dora,' said he.

'Miss Vickers is *my* name, Lieutenant Frere, and I shall go and talk to Mr Bates.'

Which threat she fulfilled on the spot; and Mr Bates, who had filled the dangerous office of Pilot, told her about Divers and Coral reefs; and some adventures of his – a little apocryphal – in the Chinese Seas. Frere resumed his smoking half angry with himself and half angry with the provoking little fairy that buzzed so pertinaciously about him. He confessed that this elfin creature had a fascination for him which he could not easily account for.

However, he saw her no more that evening, and at breakfast the next morning she received him with a quaint haughtiness.

'When shall we be ready to sail, Mr Frere? I'll take some marmalade, thank you.'

'I don't know, Missy,' said Bates. 'It's very rough on the bar; me and Mr Frere was a soundin' of it this marnin' and it ain't safe yet.'

'Well,' said Dora, 'I do hope and trust we shan't be shipwrecked and have to swim miles and miles for our lives.'

'Ho, ho!' laughed Frere; 'don't be afraid. I'll take care of you.'

'Can you swim, Mr Bates?' asked Dora.

'Yes, Miss, I can.'

'Well, then, *you* shall save me; I like you. Mr Frere can take mamma. We'll go and live on a desert island, Mr Bates, won't we, and grow cocoanuts and bread-fruit, and – what nasty hard biscuits! – I'll be Robinson Crusoe and you shall be Man Friday. I'd like to live on a desert island, if I was sure there were no savages, and plenty to eat and drink.'

'That would be right enough, my dear, but you don't find them sort of islands every day.'

'*Then*,' said Dora, with a decided nod, 'we won't be ship-wrecked, will we?'

'I hope not, my dear.'

'Put a biscuit in your pocket, Dora, in case of accidents,' suggested Frere, with a grin.

'Oh! you know my opinion of *you*, sir. Don't speak; I don't want any argument.'

'Don't you? – that's right.'

'Mr Frere,' said Dora, gravely pausing at her mother's cabin door, 'If I was Richard the Third, do you know what I'd do with you?'

'No,' says Frere, eating complacently; 'what would you do?'

'Why, I'd make you stand at the door of St Paul's Cathedral in a white sheet, with a lighted candle in your hand, until you gave up your wicked aggravating ways – you Man!'

The picture of Mr Frere in a white sheet, with a lighted candle in his hand, at the door of St Paul's Cathedral, was too much for Mr Bates's gravity, and he roared with laughter.

'She's a queer child, ain't she, sir? A born natural, and yet a good natured little soul.'

'When shall we be able to get away, Mr Bates?' asked Frere, whose dignity was wounded by the mirth of the pilot.

Bates felt the change of tone, and hastened to accommodate himself to his officer's humour.

'I hopes by evening, sir,' said he, 'if the tide slackens then I'll risk it; but it's no use trying it now.'

'The men were wanting to go ashore to wash their clothes,' said Frere. 'If we are to stop here till evening you had better let them go after dinner.'

'All right, sir,' said Bates.

The afternoon passed off auspiciously. The ten prisoners went ashore and washed their clothes. Their names were James Barker, James Lesly, John Lyon, Benjamin Riley, William Cheshire, Henry Shiers, William Russen, James Porter, John Fair, and John Rex.

This last scoundrel had come on board last of all. He had behaved himself a little better of late, and during the work attendant upon the departure of the *Ladybird*, had been conspicuously useful. His intelligence and influence among his fellow prisoners, combined to make him a somewhat important personage, and Vickers had allowed him privileges from which he had been hitherto debarred. Mr Frere, however, who superintended the shipment of some stores, seemed to be delighted to take advantage of Rex's evident willingness to work. He never ceased to hurry and find fault with him. He vowed that he was lazy, sulky, or impertinent. It was 'Rex, come here! Do this! Do that!' As the prisoners declared among themselves, it was evident that Mr Frere had a 'down' on the Dandy. The day before the *Ladybird* sailed, Rex – rejoicing in the hope of speedy departure – had suffered himself to reply to some more than usually galling remark, and Mr Frere had complained to Vickers.

'The fellow's too ready to get away,' said he. 'Let him stop for the *Osprey*, it will be a lesson to him.'

Vickers assented, and John Rex was informed that he was not to sail with the first party. His comrades vowed that this order was an act of tyranny; but he himself said nothing. He only redoubled his activity, and – despite all his wish to the contrary – Frere was unable to find fault. He even took credit to himself for 'taming' the convict's spirit, and pointed out Rex – silent and obedient – as a proof of the excellence of severe measures. To the convicts, however, who knew John Rex better, this silent activity was ominous.

He returned with the rest however on the evening of the 13th, in apparently cheerful mood. Indeed Mr Frere, who, wearied by the delay, had decided to take the whaleboat in which the prisoners had returned, and catch a few fish before dinner, observed him laughing with some of the others, and again congratulated himself.

The time wore on. Dark was closing in, and Mr Bates, walking the deck, began to keep a look-out for the boat, with the intention of weighing anchor and making for the bar.

All was secure. Mrs Vickers and the child were safely below, the two remaining soldiers (two had gone with Frere) were upon deck, and the prisoners in the forecastle were singing. The wind was fair and the sea had gone down. In less than an hour the *Osprey* would be safely outside the Harbour.

⊁ 9 ⊁

THE POWER OF THE WILDERNESS

THE drifting log that had so strangely served as a means of escape for Rufus Dawes swam with the current that was running out of the harbour. For some time the burden that it bore was an insensible one. Exhausted with his desperate struggle for life, the convict lay along the rough back of this Heaven-sent raft without motion, almost without breath. At length a violent shock awoke him to consciousness, and he perceived that the log had become stranded on a sandy point, the extremity of which was lost in darkness. Painfully raising himself from his uncomfortable posture, he staggered to his feet, and crawling a few paces up the beach, flung himself upon the ground and slept.

When morning dawned, he perceived his position. The log had, in passing under the lee of Phillip Island, been cast upon the southern point of Coal Head, and some three hundred yards from him were the mutilated sheds of the coal-gang.

For some time he lay still, basking, as it were, in the warm rays of the rising sun, and scarcely caring to move his bruised and fettered limbs. The sensation of rest was so exquisite, that it overpowered all other considerations, and he did not even trouble himself to conjecture the reason for the apparent desertion of the huts close by him. If there was no one there, – well and good. If the coal party had not gone, he would be discovered in a few moments and returned to his island prison. In his exhaustion and misery, he accepted the alternative and slept again.

As he laid down his aching head, Mr Troke was reporting his death to Vickers, and while he still slept, the *Ladybird* passed him on her way out, so closely, that anyone on board her could with a good glass have espied his slumbering figure as it lay upon the sand.

When he woke again, it was past mid-day, and the sun poured upon him its full rays. His clothes were dry in all places save the side on which he had been lying, and he rose to his feet refreshed by his long sleep. He scarcely comprehended, as yet, his true position. He had escaped, it was true, but not for long. He was versed in the history of escapes, and knew that a man alone on that barren coast was face to face with starvation or recapture. Glancing up at the sun, he wondered, indeed, how he had been free so long. Then the coal sheds caught his eye, and he understood that they were untenanted. This astonished him, and he began to tremble with vague apprehension. Entering, he looked around, expecting every moment to see appear some lurking constable, or armed soldier. Suddenly his glance fell upon the loaves that lay in the corner where the convicts had flung them the night before. At such a moment, this discovery seemed like a direct revelation from Heaven. He would not have been surprised had they disappeared. Had he lived in another age, he would have looked round for the angel that had brought them.

By and bye, having eaten of this miraculous provender, the poor creature began to understand what had taken place. The coal workings were abandoned; the new Commandant had probably other work for his beasts of burden to execute, and he would be safe here for a few hours at least. But he must not stay. For him there was no rest. If he thought to escape, it behoved him to commence his journey at once.

As he contemplated the meat and bread, something like a ray of hope entered his gloomy soul. Here was provision for his needs. The food before him represented the rations of six men. Was it not possible to cross the desert that lay between him and freedom on such fare? The very supposition made his heart beat faster. It surely was possible. He must husband his resources; walk much and eat little; spread out the food for one day into food for three. Here was six men's food for one day, or one

man's food for six days. He would live on a third of this, and he
would have rations for eighteen days. Eighteen days! What
could he not do in eighteen days! He could walk thirty miles a
day – forty miles a day – that would be six hundred miles and
more. Yet stay; he must not be too sanguine; the road was difficult, the scrub was in places impenetrable. He would have to
make *détours*, to turn upon his tracks, to waste precious time.
He would be moderate, and say twenty miles a day. Twenty
miles a day was very easy walking.

Taking a piece of stick from the ground he made the calculation in the sand. Eighteen days and twenty miles a day – three
hundred and sixty miles. More than enough to take him to freedom. It could be done! With prudence it could be done! He
must be careful and abstemious. Abstemious! He had already
eaten too much, and he hastily pulled a barely-tasted piece of
meat from his mouth, and placed it with the rest. The action,
which at any other time would have seemed disgusting, was, in
the case of this poor creature, merely pitiable.

Having come to this resolution, the next thing to do was to
disencumber himself of his irons. This was easier done than he
expected. He found in the shed an iron gad, and with that and
a stone drove out the rivets. The rings were too strong to be
'ovalled',[1] or he would have been free long ago. He packed the
meat and bread as a sort of 'swag', and then pushing the gad
into his belt – it might be needed as a weapon of defence – he
set out on his journey.

His intention was to get round the settlement to the coast,
and then to reach the settled districts, and by some tale of shipwreck or wandering, procure assistance. As to what was particularly to be done *when* he found himself among free men, he did
not pause to consider. At that point his difficulties, though they
really but began, seemed to him to end. Let him but once traverse the desert that was before him, and he would trust to his
own ingenuity, or the chance of fortune, to avert suspicion. The
peril of immediate detection seemed so imminent, that beside it
all other fears were dwarfed into insignificance.

[1]. *Ovalled*. – 'To oval', is a term in use among prisoners, and means to
so bend the round ring of the ankle fetter that the *heel* can be drawn up
through it.

Before dawn next morning he had travelled ten miles, and, husbanding his food, succeeded by the night of the fourth day in accomplishing forty more. Footsore and weary, he lay in a thicket of the thorny melaleuca, and at last felt that he was beyond pursuit. The next day he advanced more slowly. The bush was unpropitious. Dense scrub and jungle impeded his path; barren and stony mountain ranges arose before him. He was lost in gullies, entangled in thickets, bewildered in morasses. The sea that had hitherto gleamed, salt, glittering, and hungry upon his right hand, now shifted to his left. He had mistaken his course, and he must turn round again. Two days did this bewilderment last, and on the third he came to a mighty cliff, that pierced with its blunt pinnacle the clustering bush. He must go over or round this obstacle, and he decided to go round it. A sort of natural pathway wound about its foot. Here and there branches were broken, and it seemed to the poor wretch, fainting under the weight of his lessening burden, that his were not the first footsteps that had trodden there. The path terminated in a glade, and at the bottom of this glade was something that fluttered. Rufus Dawes pressed forward, and stumbled over a corpse.

In the terrible stillness of that solitary place he felt suddenly as though a voice had called to him. All the hideous fantastic tales of murder which he had read or heard seemed to take visible shape in the person of the loathly carcase before him, clad in the yellow dress of a convict, and lying flung together on the ground as though struck down. Stooping over it, impelled by an irresistible impulse to know the worst, he found the body was mangled. One arm was missing, and the skull had been beaten in by some heavy instrument. The first thought, – that this heap of rags and bones was a mute witness to the folly of his own undertaking, the corpse of some starved absconder – gave place to a second more horrible suspicion. He recognized the number imprinted on the coarse cloth as that which had designated the younger of the two men who had escaped with Gabbett. He was standing on the place where a murder had been committed. A murder! – and what else? What was the terrible mystery of this lonely spot? He turned and fled, looking back fearfully as he went. He could not breathe in the shadow of that awful mountain.

Crashing through scrub and brake, torn, bleeding, and wild with terror, he reached a spur of the range and looked around him. Above him rose the iron hills, below him lay the panorama of the bush. The white cone of the Frenchman's Cap was on his right hand, on his left a succession of ranges seemed to bar further progress. A gleam as of a lake streaked the bush to the eastward. Gigantic pine trees reared their graceful heads against the opal of the evening sky, and at their feet the dense scrub through which he had so painfully toiled spread without break and without flaw. It seemed as though he could leap from where he stood upon a solid mass of tree-tops. He raised his eyes, and right against him, like a dull sword, lay the long blue reach of the harbour, from which he had escaped. One darker speck moved on the dark water. It was the *Osprey* making for the Gates. It seemed that he could throw a stone upon her deck. A faint cry of despair escaped him. During the last three days in the bush he must have retraced his steps, and returned upon his own track to the settlement. More than half his allotted time had passed, and he was not yet thirty miles from his prison. Death seemed to have waited to overtake him in this barbarous wilderness. As a cat allows a mouse to escape her for a while, so had he been permitted to trifle with his fate, and lull himself with a sense of false security. Escape was hopeless now. He could never escape; and as the unhappy man raised his despairing eyes, he saw that the sun, redly sinking behind a lofty pine that topped the opposite hill, shot a ray of crimson light into the glade below him. It was as though a bloody finger pointed at the corpse that lay there, and shuddering at the dismal omen, Rufus Dawes, averting his face, plunged again into the forest.

For four days he wandered aimlessly through the bush. He had given up all hopes of making the overland journey, and yet as long as his scanty supply of food held out, he strove to keep away from the settlement. Unable to resist the pangs of hunger, he had increased his daily ration, and though the salted meat, exposed to the rain and heat, had begun to turn putrid, he never looked at it, but he was seized with the desire to eat his fill. The coarse lumps of carrion and the hard rye-loaves were to him delicious morsels fit for the table of an emperor. Once or twice he was constrained to pluck and eat the tops of tea-tree and pepper-mint shrubs. These had an aromatic taste, and sufficed to stay the cravings of hunger for a while, but they induced a raging thirst, which he slaked at the icy mountain springs. Had it not been for the frequency of these streams, he would have died in a few days. At last, on the twelfth day from his departure from the Coal Head, he found himself at the foot of Mount Direc-tion, at the head of the peninsula which makes the western side of the harbour. His terrible wandering had but led him to make a complete circuit of the settlement, and the next night brought him round the shores of Birches Inlet to the landing-place oppo-site to Sarah Island. His stock of provisions had been exhausted for two days, and he was savage with hunger. He no longer thought of suicide. His dominant idea now was to get food. He would do as many others had done before him, and give himself up to be flogged and fed.

When he reached the landing-place, however, the guardhouse was empty. He looked across at the island prison, and saw still no sign of life. The settlement was deserted! The shock of this discovery almost deprived him of reason.

For days, that had seemed centuries, he had kept life in his jaded and lacerated body solely by the strength of his fierce determination to reach the settlement; and now that he had reached it, after a journey of unparalleled horror, he found it deserted. He struck himself to see if he was not dreaming. He refused to believe his eyesight. He shouted, screamed, and waved his tattered garments in the air. Exhausted by these paroxysms, he said to himself, quite calmly, that the sun beating on his unprotected head had dazed his brain, and that in a few moments he should see the well-remembered boats pulling to-wards him. Then, when no boat came, he argued that he was mistaken in the place; that the island yonder was not Sarah Island, but some other island like it, and that in a second or so he would be able to detect the difference. But the inexorable mountains, so hideously familiar for six weary years, made mute reply, and the sea, crawling at his feet, seemed to grin at him with its thin-lipped, hungry mouth. Yet the fact of the de-sertion seemed so inexplicable that he could not realize it. De-serted by man, it seemed as though Heaven also had abandoned him. He felt as might have felt that wanderer in the enchanted mountains, who, returning in the morning to look for his companions, found them turned to stone.

At last the dreadful truth forced itself upon him; he retired a few paces, and then, with a horrible cry to that God whose laws he was about to outrage, stumbled forwards towards the edge of the little reef that fringed the shore. Just as he was about to fling himself off for the second time into the dark water, his despairing eyes, sweeping in a last long look around the bay, caught sight of a strange appearance on the left horn of the sea beach. A thin, blue streak, uprising from behind the western arm of the little inlet, hung in the still air. It was the smoke of a fire!

The dying wretch felt inspired with new hope. It was as though God, whom he had invoked, had sent him a direct sign from Heaven. The tiny column of blueish vapour seemed to him as glorious as the Pillar of Fire that led the Israelites.

There were yet human beings near him! – and turning his face from the hungry sea, he tottered with the last effort of his failing strength towards the blessed token of their presence.

⋆ 10 ⋆

THE SEIZURE OF THE OSPREY

WE left the *Osprey* on the evening of the 14th, riding securely at anchor, waiting only for the return of Mr Maurice Frere to quit Macquarie Harbour for ever.

Frere's fishing expedition had been unsuccessful, and in consequence prolonged. The obstinacy of his character appeared in the most trifling circumstances, and though the fast deepening shades of an Australian evening warned him to return, yet he lingered, unwilling to come back empty-handed. At last a peremptory signal seemed to warn him. It was the sound of a musket fired on board the brig. Mr Bates was evidently getting impatient, and with a scowl, Frere pulled up his lines, and ordered the two soldiers to pull for the vessel.

The *Osprey* yet sat motionless on the gleamless water, and her bare masts gave no sign of making sail. To the soldiers, pulling with their backs to her, the musket shot seemed the most ordinary occurrence in the world. Eager to quit the dismal prison-bay, they had viewed Mr Frere's persistent fishing with disgust, and had for the previous half hour longed to hear the signal of recall which had just startled them. Suddenly, however, they noticed a change of expression in the sullen face of their commander. Frere, sitting in the stern sheets, with his face to the *Osprey*, had noticed a peculiar appearance on her decks. The bulwarks were every now and then topped by strange figures, who disappeared as suddenly as they came, and a faint murmur as of voices floated across the intervening water. Presently the report of another musket shot echoed among the hills, and something dark was seen to fall from the side of the vessel into the water. Frere, with an imprecation of mingled alarm and indignation, sprang to his feet, and shading his eyes with his hand, looked towards the brig. The soldiers, resting affrightedly on their oars, imitated his gesture, and the whale-boat, thus thrown out of ballast, rocked from side to side dangerously. A moment's anxious pause, and then a shrill scream pealing from the ill-fated brig explained all. It was the voice of a woman calling for help. The prisoners had seized the brig. Two more reports were heard in rapid succession, then all was silent.

'Give way!' cries Frere, pale with rage and apprehension, and the soldiers, realizing at once the full terror of their position, forced the heavy whale-boat through the water as fast as the one miserable pair of oars could take her.

Mr Bates, affected by the insidious influence of the hour, and lulled into a sense of false security, had gone below to tell his little playmate that she would soon be on her way to the Hobart Town of which she had heard so much; and taking advantage of his absence, the soldier not on guard went to the forecastle to hear the prisoners' singing. He found the ten together, in high good humour, listening to a 'shanty' sung by three of their number. The singers were melodious enough, and the words of the ditty – chaunted by many stout fellows in many a forecastle before and since – of that character which pleases the soldier nature. Private Grimes forgot all about the unprotected state of the deck, and sat down to listen.

While he listened, absorbed in tender recollections, James Lesly, William Cheshire, William Russen, John Fair, and James Barker, slipped to the hatchway and got upon deck. Barker reached the aft hatchway as the soldier who was on guard turned to complete his walk, and the convict passing his arm round his neck, pulled him down before he could utter a cry. In the confusion of the moment, the man loosed his grasp of the musket to grapple with his unseen antagonist, and Fair, snatching up the weapon, swore to blow out his brains if he raised a finger. Seeing the sentry thus secured, Cheshire, as if in pursuance of some preconcerted plan, leapt down the after-hatchway, and passed up the muskets from the arm-rack to Lesly and Russen. There were three muskets in addition to the one taken from the sentry, and Barker, leaving his prisoner in charge of Fair, seized one of them, and ran to the companion-ladder. Russen, left by this manoeuvre unarmed, appeared to know his own duty. He came back to the forecastle, and passing behind the listening soldier, touched the singer on the shoulder. This was the appointed signal, and John Rex suddenly terminating his song with a laugh, presented his fist in the face of the gaping Grimes.

'No noise!' he cried. 'The brig's ours,' and ere Grimes could reply, he was seized by Lyon and Riley, and bound securely.

'Come on, lads!' says Rex, 'and pass the prisoner down here. We've got her this time, I'll go bail!' And in obedience to this order, the now gagged sentry was flung down the forecastle hatchway, and the hatch secured.

'Stand on the hatchway, Porter,' cries Rex again; 'and if those fellows come up knock 'em down with a handspike. Lesly and Russen, forward to the companion-ladder! Lyon, keep a look out for the boat, and if she comes too near, fire!'

As he spoke, the report of the first musket rang out. Barker had apparently fired up the companion hatchway.

When Mr Bates had gone below, he found Dora curled up on the cushions of the stateroom, reading.

'Well, Missy!' he said, 'we'll soon be on our way to Papa.'

Dora answered by asking a question altogether foreign to the subject.

'Mr Bates,' said she, pushing the hair out of her blue eyes, 'What's a coracle?'

'A which?' asked Mr Bates.

'A coracle. C-o-r-a-c-l-e,' said she, spelling it slowly. 'I want to know.'

The bewildered Bates shook his head.

'Never heard o' one, Missy,' said he, bending over the book. 'What does it say?'

'The Ancient Britons,' said Dora, reading gravely, 'were little better than Barbarians. They painted their bodies with Woad – that's blue stuff, you know, Mr Bates – and seated in their light coracles of skin stretched upon slender wooden frames, must have presented a Wild and Savage appearance.'

'Hah,' says Mr Bates, when this remarkable passage was read to him, 'That's very mysterious, that is. A corricle, a corry –' a bright light burst upon him. 'A *curri*cle you mean, Miss! It's a carriage! I've seen 'em in Hy' Park, with young bloods a drivin' of 'em.'

'What are young bloods?' asked Dora, rushing at this 'new opening'.

'Oh, nobs! Swell coves, don't you know,' returned poor Bates, thus again attacked. 'Young men o' fortune that is, that's given to doing it grand.'

'I see,' says Dora, waving her little hand graciously. 'Noblemen and Princes and that sort of people. Quite so. But what about coracle?'

'Well,' says the humbled Bates, '*I* think it's a carriage, Missy. A sort of Pheayton, as they call it.'

Dora, hardly satisfied, returned to the book. It was a little mean-looking volume – a 'Child's History of England' – and after perusing it awhile with knitted brows, she burst into a childish laugh.

'Why, my dear Mr Bates!' she cried, waving the History above her head in triumph, 'what a pair of geese we are! A *carriage!* Oh, you silly man! It's a boat!'

'Is it?' says Mr Bates, in admiration of the intelligence of his companion. 'Who'd ha' thought that now? Why couldn't they call it a boat at once then, and ha' done with it?' and he was about to laugh also, when, raising his eyes, he saw in the open doorway the figure of James Barker, with a musket in his hand.

'Hallo! What's this? What do you do here, sir?'

'Sorry to disturb yer,' says the convict, with a grin, 'but you must come along o' me, Mr Bates.'

Bates, at once comprehending that some terrible misfortune had occurred, did not lose his presence of mind. One of the cushions of the couch was under his right hand, and snatching it up, he flung it across the little cabin full in the face of the escaped prisoner. The soft mass struck the man with force sufficient to blind him for an instant. The musket exploded harmlessly in the air, and ere the astonished Barker could recover his feeling, Bates had hurled him out of the cabin, and crying 'Mutiny!' locked the cabin door on the inside.

The noise brought out Mrs Vickers from her berth, and the poor little student of English history ran into her arms.

'Good heavens, Mr Bates, what is it?'

Bates, furious with rage, so far forgot himself as to swear.

'It's a Mutiny, ma'am,' said he. 'Go back to your cabin and lock the door. Those bloody villains have riz on us!'

Julia Vickers felt her heart grow sick. Was she never to escape out of this dreadful life?

'Go into your cabin, ma'am,' says Bates again, 'and don't move a finger till I tell ye. Maybe it ain't so bad as it looks. I've got my pistols with me, thank God, and Mr Frere'll hear the shot any way.'

'Mutiny! On deck there!' he cried at the full pitch of his voice, and his brow grew damp with dismay when a mocking laugh from above was the only response.

Thrusting the woman and child into the state berth, the bewildered pilot cocked a pistol, and snatching a cutlass from the arm-stand fixed to the butt of the mast that penetrated the cabin, he burst open the door with his foot, and rushed to the companion ladder. Barker had retreated to the deck, and for an instant he thought the way was clear, but Lesly and Russen thrust him back with the muzzles of the loaded muskets. He struck at Russen with the cutlass, missed him, and seeing the hopelessness of the attack, was fain to retreat.

In the meanwhile Grimes and the other soldier had loosed themselves from their bonds, and encouraged by the firing which seemed to them a sign that all was not yet lost, made shift to force up the fore hatchway. Porter, whose courage was none of the fiercest, and who had been for years given over to that terror of discipline which servitude induces, made but a feeble attempt at resistance, and forcing the handspike from him, the sentry, Jones, rushed aft to help the pilot. As he reached the mizen, Cheshire, a cold-blooded blue-eyed man, raised the musket he held and shot him dead. Grimes fell over the corpse, and Cheshire clubbing the musket – had he another barrel he would have fired – coolly battered his head as he lay, and then seizing the body of the unfortunate Jones in his arms, tossed it into the sea.

'Porter, you lubber!' he cried, exhausted with the effort to lift the body, 'come and bear a hand with this other one!'

Porter advanced aghast, but just then another occurrence claimed the villain's attention, and poor Grimes's life was spared for that time.

Rex, inwardly raging at this unexpected resistance on the part of the pilot, flung himself on the skylight, and tore it up bodily. As he did so, Barker, who had reloaded his musket, fired down into the cabin. The ball passed through the state-room door, and splintering the wood, buried itself close to the golden curls of poor little Dora. It was this hair's-breadth escape which drew from the agonized mother that shriek which, pealing through the open stern-window, had roused the soldiers in the boat.

Rex, who, by the virtue of his Dandyism, yet possessed some abhorrence of useless crime, imagined that the cry was one of pain, and that Barker's bullet had taken deadly effect.

'You've killed the child, you villain!' he cried.

'Wot's the odds?' asked Barker, sulkily. 'She must die anyway, sooner or later.'

Rex put his head down the skylight, and called on Bates to surrender; but Bates only drew his other pistol.

'Would you commit murder?' he asked, looking round, with desperation in his glance.

'No, no,' cried some of the men, willing to blink the death of poor Jones. 'It's no use making things worse than they are. Bid him come up, and we'll do him no harm.'

'Come up, Mr Bates,' says Rex, 'and I give you my word you shan't be injured.'

'Will you set the major's lady and child ashore, then?' asked Bates, sturdily facing the scowling brows above him.

'Yes.'

'Without injury?' continued the other, bargaining, as it were, at the very muzzle of the muskets.

'Ay, ay! It's all right!' returned Russen. 'It's our liberty we want, that's all.'

Bates, hoping against hope for the return of the boat, endeavoured to gain time.

'Shut down the skylight, then,' said he, with the ghost of an authority in his voice, 'until I ask the lady.'

This, however, John Rex refused to do.

'You can ask well enough where you are,' he said.

But there was no need for Mr Bates to put a question. The door of the state-room opened, and Mrs Vickers appeared trembling, with Dora by her side.

'Accept, Mr Bates,' she said, 'since it must be so. We should gain nothing by refusing. We are at their mercy – God help us!'

'Amen to that,' says Bates under his breath, and then aloud, 'We agree!'

'Put your pistols on the table, and come up, then,' says Rex, covering the table with his musket as he spoke. 'Nobody shall hurt you.'

✦ 11 ✦

JOHN REX'S REVENGE

MRS VICKERS, pale and sick with terror, yet sustained by that strange courage of hers of which we have before spoken, passed rapidly under the open skylight, and prepared to ascend. Dora – her romance crushed by too dreadful reality – clung to her mother with one hand, and with the other pressed close to her little bosom the 'English History'. In her all-absorbing fear she had forgotten to lay it down.

'Get a shawl, ma'am, or something,' says Bates, 'and a hat for Missy.'

Mrs Vickers looked back across the space beneath the open skylight, and shuddering, shook her head. The men above impatiently swore at the delay, and the three hastened on deck.

'Who's to command the brig now?' asked undaunted Bates, as they came up.

'I am,' says John Rex; 'and, with these brave fellows, I'll take her round the world.'

The touch of bombast was not out of place. It jumped so far with the humour of the convicts that they set up a feeble cheer, at which Dora frowned. Frightened as she was, the prison-bred child was as astonished at hearing convicts cheer as a fashionable lady would be to hear her footman quote poetry. Bates, however – practical and calm – took quite another view of the case. The bold project, so boldly avowed, seemed to him a sheer absurdity. The 'Dandy', and a crew of nine convicts, navigate a brig round the world! Preposterous; why, not a man aboard could take a reckoning. His nautical fancy pictured the *Osprey* rolling on the swell of the Southern Ocean, or hopelessly locked in the ice of the antarctic seas, and he dimly guessed at the fate of the deluded ten. Even if they got safe to port, the chances of final escape were all against them, for what account could they give of themselves? Overpowered by these reflections, the honest fellow made one last effort to charm his captors back to their pristine bondage.

'Deluded men!' he cried, 'do you know what you are about to do? You will never escape. Give up the brig, and I will declare, before my God, upon the Bible, that I will say nothing, but give all good characters.'

Lesly and another burst into a laugh at this wild proposition, but Rex, who had weighed his chances well beforehand, felt the force of the pilot's speech, and answered seriously.

'It's no use talking,' he said, shaking his still handsome head. 'We have got the brig, and we mean to keep her. I can navigate her, though I am no seaman, so you needn't talk further about it, Mr Bates. It's liberty we require.'

'What are you going to do with us?' asked Bates.

'Leave you behind.'

Bates's face blanched.

'What, *here*?'

'Yes. It don't look a picturesque spot, does it? And yet *I*'ve lived here for some years;' and he sighed.

Bates was silent. The logic of that sigh was unanswerable.

'Come!' cried the Dandy, shaking off his momentary melancholy, 'look alive there! Lower away the jolly-boat. Mrs Vickers, go down to your cabin and get anything you want. I am compelled to put you ashore, but I have no wish to leave you without clothes.'

Bates listened, in a sort of dismal admiration at this courtly convict. *He* could not have spoken like that had his life depended on it.

'Now, my little lady,' continued Rex, 'run down with your mamma, and don't be frightened.'

Dora flushed burning red at this indignity.

'Frightened! If there was anybody else here but women, you never would have taken the brig. Frightened! Let me pass, *prisoner*!'

The whole deck burst into a great laugh at this, and poor Mrs Vickers paused, trembling for the consequences of the child's temerity. To thus taunt the desperate convict who held their lives in his hands seemed sheer madness. In the boldness of the speech, however, lay its safeguard. Rex – whose politeness was mere bravado – was stung to the quick by the reflection upon his courage, and the bitter accent with which the child had pronounced the word *prisoner* (the generic name of convicts) made him bite his lips with rage. Had he had his will, he would have struck the little creature to the deck, but the horse-laugh of his companions warned him to forbear. There is 'public opinion' even among convicts, and Rex dared not vent his passion on so helpless an object. As men do in such cases, he veiled his anger beneath an affectation of indifference. In order to show that he was not moved by the taunt, he smiled upon the taunter more graciously than ever.

'Your daughter has her father's spirit, madam,' said he to Mrs Vickers, with a bow.

Bates opened his mouth to listen. His ears were not large enough to take in the words of this complimentary convict. He began to think that he was the victim of a nightmare. He absolutely felt that John Rex was a greater man at that moment than John Bates.

As Mrs Vickers descended the hatchway, the boat with Frere and the soldiers came within musket range, and Fair, according to orders, fired his musket over their heads, shouting to them to lay to. But Frere, boiling with rage at the manner in which the tables had been turned on him, had determined not to resign his lost authority without a struggle. Disregarding the summons, he came straight on, with his eyes fixed on the bulwarks of the *Osprey*. It was now nearly dark, and the figures on the deck were indistinguishable. The indignant lieutenant could but guess at the condition of affairs. Suddenly, from out of the darkness a voice hailed him —

'Lay off, sir! Lay off!' it cried, and was then seemingly choked in its owner's throat.

The voice was the property of Mr Bates. Standing near the side, he had observed Rex and Lesly bring up a great pig of iron, erst used as part of the ballast of the brig, and poise it on the weather bulwark. Their intention was but too evident; and honest Bates, like a faithful watch-dog, barked to warn his master.

Bloodthirsty Cheshire caught him by the throat, and Frere, unheeding, ran the boat alongside, under the very nose of the revengeful Rex.

The mass of pig-iron fell, and striking the gunwale of the whaleboat, splintered a plank of two fingers' thickness.

'Villains!' cried Frere, 'would you swamp us?'

'Ay,' laughed Rex, 'and a dozen such of ye! The brig's ours, can't ye see, and *we're* your masters now!'

Frere, stifling an exclamation of rage, made an attempt to cling to the side of the vessel, but the blow had driven the boat backward, and she was already beyond arm's length of the brig. Looking up, he saw Cheshire's savage face, and heard the click of the lock as he cocked his piece. The two soldiers, exhausted by their long pull, made no effort to stay the progress of the boat, and almost before the swell caused by the plunge of the mass of iron had ceased to agitate the water, the deck of the *Osprey* had become invisible in the darkness.

Frere struck his fist upon the smooth plank on which he sat, in sheer impotence of rage.

'The scoundrels!' he said, between his teeth, 'they've outwitted us. What do they mean to do now?'

The answer came pat to the question. From the dark hull of the brig broke a flash and a report, and a musket ball cut the water beside them with a chirping noise. Between the black indistinct mass which represented the brig, and the glimmering water, was visible a white speck, which gradually neared them.

'Come alongside with ye,' hailed a voice, 'or it will be worse for ye!'

'They want to murder us,' says Frere. 'Give way, men!'

But the two soldiers, exchanging glances one with the other, pulled the boat's head round, and made for the vessel.

'It's no use, Mr Frere,' said the man nearest him. 'We can do no good now, and they won't hurt us, I dare say.'

'You dogs, you are in league with them,' bursts out Frere, purple with indignation. 'Do you mutiny?'

'Come, come, sir,' returned the soldier sulkily. 'This ain't the time to bully; and as for mutinising, why, one man's about as good as another just now.'

This speech from the lips of a man who, but a few minutes before, would have risked his life to obey the orders of his officer, did more than an hour's reasoning to convince Maurice Frere of the hopelessness of resistance. His authority – born of circumstance, and supported by adventitious aid – had left him. The musket shot had reduced him to the ranks. He was now no more than anyone else; indeed, he was less than many, for those who held the firearms were the ruling powers. With a groan, he resigned himself to his fate, and looking at the sleeve of the undress uniform he wore, it seemed to him that virtue had gone out of it.

When they reached the brig, they found that the jolly-boat had been lowered and laid alongside. In her eleven persons: Bates, with gashed forehead, and his hands bound with spun yarn, the stunned Grimes, Russen and Fair pulling, Lyon, Riley, Cheshire, and Lesly with muskets, and John Rex in the stern sneets, with Bates's pistols in his trousers' belt, and a loaded musket across his knees. The white object which had been seen by the men in the whaleboat was a large white shawl which wrapped Mrs Vickers and Dora.

Frere gave a sigh of relief, when he saw this white bundle. He had feared that the child had been injured. By the directions of Rex, the whale-boat was brought alongside the jolly-boat, and Cheshire and Lesly boarded her. Lesly then gave his musket to Rex, and bound Frere's hands behind him, in the same manner as had been done for Bates. Frere attempted to resist this indignity, but Cheshire, clapping his musket to his ear, swore he would blow out his brains if he uttered another syllable; and Frere, catching the malignant eye of John Rex, remembered how easily a twitch of the finger would pay off old scores, and was silent.

'Step in here, sir, if you please,' said Rex, with polite irony. 'I am sorry to be compelled to tie you, but I must consult my own safety as well as your convenience.'

Frere scowled, and, stepping awkwardly into the jolly-boat, fell. Pinioned as he was, he could not rise without assistance, and Russen pulled him roughly to his feet with a coarse laugh. In his present frame of mind, that laugh galled him worse than his bonds.

Poor Mrs Vickers, with a woman's quick instinct, saw this, and, even amid her own trouble, found leisure to console.

'The wretches!' she said, under her breath, as Frere was flung down beside her, 'to submit you to such indignity!'

Dora said nothing, and seemed to shrink from the lieutenant. Perhaps, in her childish fancy, she had pictured him as coming to her rescue, armed cap-a-pie, and clad in dazzling mail, or, at the very least, as a muscular hero, who should settle affairs out of hand by sheer force of handspiking. If she had entertained any such notion, the reality must have struck coldly upon her senses. Mr Frere, purple, clumsy, and bound, was not at all heroic.

'Now, my lads,' says Rex — who seemed to have become indued with the cast-off authority of Frere — 'we give you your choice. Stay at Hell's Gates, or come with us!'

The soldiers paused irresolute. To join the mutineers meant a certainty of hard work, with a chance of ultimate hanging. Yet to stay with the prisoners was – as far as they could see – to incur the inevitable fate of starvation on a barren coast.

As is often the case on such occasions, a trifle sufficed to turn the scale. The wounded Grimes, who was slowly recovering from his stupor, dimly caught the meaning of the sentence, and in his obfuscated condition of intellect, must needs make comment upon it.

'Go with him, ye beggars!' said he, 'and leave us honest men! Oh, ye'll get a tying up for this!'

The phrase 'tying-up' brought with it recollection of the worst portion of military discipline, the cat, and revived in the minds of the pair already predisposed to break the yoke that sat so heavy upon them, a train of dismal memories. The life of a soldier on a convict-station was at that time a hard one. He was often stinted in rations, and of necessity deprived of all rational recreation, while punishment for offences was prompt and severe. The companies drafted to the penal settlements were not composed of the best material, and the pair had good precedent for the course they were about to take.

'Come,' says Rex, 'I can't wait here all night. The wind is freshening, and we must make the Bar. Which is it to be?'

'We'll go with you!' says the man who had pulled stroke in the whaleboat, spitting into the water with averted face. Upon which utterance the convicts burst into joyous oaths, and the pair were received with much hand-shaking.

Then Rex, with Lyon and Riley as a guard, got into the whale-boat, and having loosed the two prisoners from their bonds, ordered them to take the places of Russen and Fair. The whale-boat was then manned by the seven mutineers, Rex steering, Fair, Russen, and the two recruits pulling, and the other four standing up, with their muskets levelled at the jolly-boat. Their long slavery had begotten such a dread of authority in these men, that they feared it even when it was bound and menaced by four muskets.

'Keep your distance!' shouted Cheshire, as Frere and Bates, in obedience to orders, began to pull the jolly-boat towards the shore, and in this fashion was the dismal little party conveyed to the mainland.

It was night when they reached it, but the clear sky began to thrill with a late moon as yet unarisen, and the waves breaking gently upon the beach, glimmered with a radiance that seemed born of their own motion.

Frere and Bates, jumping ashore, helped out Mrs Vickers, Dora, and the wounded Grimes. This being done under the muzzles of the muskets, Rex commanded that Bates and Frere should push the jolly-boat as far as they could from the shore, and Riley catching her by a boat-hook as she came towards them, she was taken in tow.

'Now, boys,' says Cheshire, with a savage delight, 'three cheers for Old England and Liberty!'

Upon which a great shout went up, that was echoed by the grim hills that had witnessed so many miseries.

To the wretched five, this exultant mirth sounded like a knell of death.

'Great God!' cries Bates, running up to his knees in water after the departing boats, 'would you leave us here to starve?'

But the only answer was the jerk and dip of the retreating oars.

✦ 12 ✦

LEFT AT 'HELL'S GATES'

THERE is no need to dwell upon the mental agonies of that miserable night. Perhaps, of all the five, the one least qualified to endure it realized the prospect of suffering most acutely. Mrs Vickers – lay-figure and noodle as she was – had all that keen instinct of approaching danger, which is in her sex a sort of sixth sense. She was a woman and a mother, and owned to a double capacity for suffering. Her feminine imagination pictured all the horrors of death by famine, and having realised her own torments, her maternal love forced her to live them over again in the person of her child. And, rejecting Bates's offer of a pea-jacket and Frere's vague tenders of assistance, the poor woman withdrew behind a rock that faced the sea, and, with her daughter in her arms, resigned herself to her torturing thoughts. Dora, recovered from her terror, was almost content, and, curled in her mother's shawl, slept. To her little soul, this midnight mystery of boats and muskets had all the flavour of a romance. With Bates, Frere, and her mother so close to her, it was impossible to be afraid; besides, it was obvious that Papa — the Supreme Being of the settlement — must at once return and severely punish the impertinent prisoners who had dared to ill-use his wife and child, and as Dora dropped off to sleep, she caught herself, with some indignation, pitying the mutineers for the tremendous scrape they had got themselves into. How they *would* be flogged when Papa came back! In the meantime this sleeping in the open air was rather pleasant.

Honest Bates produced a piece of biscuit, and, with all the generosity of his nature, suggested that this should be set aside for the sole use of the two females, but Mrs Vickers would not hear of it. 'We must all share alike,' said she, with something of the spirit that she knew her husband would have displayed under like circumstances; and Frere wondered at her apparent strength of mind. Had he been gifted with more acuteness he would not have wondered; for when a crisis like this happens to one of two persons who have lived much together, the influence of the nobler spirit makes itself felt.

Frere had a tinder-box in his pocket, and made a fire with some dry leaves and sticks; but when he made a place for Mrs Vickers by the side of this cheering blaze, she refused to come — 'I am not fit to be seen,' she said, with a strange vanity.

Grimes fell asleep, and the two men, sitting at their fire, discussed the chances of escape. Neither liked to openly broach the supposition that they were finally deserted. It was concluded between them that, unless the brig sailed in the night — and the now risen moon showed her yet lying at anchor — the convicts would return and bring them food.

This supposition proved correct, for about an hour after daylight, they saw the whale-boat pulling towards them.

A discussion had arisen amongst the mutineers, as to the propriety of at once making sail, but Barker, who had been one of the pilot-boat crew, and knew the dangers of the bar, vowed that he would not undertake to steer the brig through the Gates until morning; and so the boats being secured astern, a strict watch was set, lest the helpless Bates should attempt to rescue the vessel.

During the evening – the excitement attendant upon the outbreak having passed away, and the magnitude of the task before them more fully apparent to their minds – a feeling of pity for the unfortunate party on the mainland took possession of them. It was quite possible that the *Osprey* might be recaptured, in which case five useless murders would have been committed; and however callous to bloodshed were the majority of the ten, not one among them could contemplate in cold blood, without a twinge of remorse, the death of the harmless child of the commandant. John Rex, seeing how matters were going, made haste to take to himself the credit of mercy. He ruled, and had always ruled, his ruffians not so much by suggesting to them the course they should take, but by leading them on the way they had already chosen for themselves.

'I propose,' said he, 'that we divide the provision. There are five of them and ten of us. Then nobody can blame us.'

'Ay,' said timid Porter, 'and if we're taken, we can tell what we have done. Don't let our affair be like that of the *Cyprus*, to leave them to starve.'

'Ay, ay,' says Barker, 'you're right! When Fergusson was topped at Hobart Town, I heard old Troke say that if he'd not refused to set the tucker ashore, he might ha' got off with a whole skin.'

Thus urged by self-interest, as well as sentiment, to mercy, the provision was got upon deck by daylight, and a sort of division made.

The soldiers, with a generosity born of remorse, were for giving half to the marooned men, but Barker exclaimed against this.

'When the schooner finds they don't get to head-quarters, she's bound to come back and look for 'em,' said he; 'and we'll want all the tucker we can get, maybe, afore we sights land.'

This reasoning was admitted excellent, and acted upon. There was in the beef-cask about fifty pounds of salt meat, and a third of this quantity, together with half a small sack of flour, and some tea and sugar mixed together in a bag, and an iron kettle and pannikin, was placed in the whale-boat. Rex, fearful of excesses among his crew, had also lowered down one of the two small puncheons of rum that the store-room contained. Cheshire disputed this, and stumbling over a goat that had been taken on board from Phillip Island, with a half-jesting imprecation, caught the creature by the leg, and threw it into the sea, bidding Rex take that with him also. Rex dragged the poor beast into the boat, and with this miscellaneous cargo pushed off to the shore. The poor goat, shivering, began to bleat piteously, and the men laughed. To a stranger it would have appeared that the boat contained a happy party of fishermen, or coast settlers, returning with the proceeds of a day's marketing.

Laying off as the water shallowed, Rex called to Bates to come for the cargo, and three men with muskets, standing up, as before, ready to resist any attempt at capture, the provisions, goat and all, were carried ashore.

'There!' says Rex, 'You can't say we've used you badly, for we've divided the provisions.'

The sight of this almost unexpected succour revived the courage of the five, and they felt grateful. After the horrible anxiety they had endured all that night, they were prepared to look with kindly eyes upon the men who had come to their assistance.

'Men,' says Bates, with something like a sob in his voice, 'I didn't expect this. You are good fellows, for there ain't much tucker on board, I know.'

'Yes,' affirms Frere, 'you're good fellows.'

Rex burst into a savage laugh.

'Shut your mouth, you tyrant,' said he, forgetting his Dandyism in the recollection of his former suffering. 'It ain't for your benefit. You may thank the lady and child for it.'

Julia Vickers hastened to propitiate the arbiter of her daughter's fate.

'We are obliged to you,' she said, not without a touch of quiet dignity that was all her husband's own; 'and if I ever get back safely, I will take care that your kindness shall be known.'

Rex took off his leather cap with quite an air. It was five years since a lady had spoken to him, and the old time when he was Mr Leopold Craven, etc., a 'gentleman of fortune', came back again for an instant. At that moment, with liberty in his hand and fortune all before him, he felt his self-respect return, and he looked the lady in the face without flinching.

'I sincerely trust, madam,' said he, 'that you *will* get back safely. May I hope for your good wishes for myself and my companions?'

Listening Bates burst into a roar of astonished enthusiasm.

'What a dog it is!' he cried. 'John Rex, John Rex, you were never made to be a convict, man!'

Rex smiled.

'Good-bye, Mr Bates, and God preserve you!'

'Good-bye,' says Bates, rubbing his hat off his face, 'and I – I – damme, I hope you'll get safe off! – there! – for liberty's sweet to every man.'

'Good-bye, prisoners!' says Dora, waving her handkerchief; 'and I hope they won't catch you, too.'

So, with cheers and waving of handkerchiefs, the boat departed.

In the emotion which the apparently disinterested conduct of John Rex had occasioned the exiles, all earnest thought of their own position had vanished, and, strange to say, the prevailing feeling was that of anxiety for the ultimate fate of the mutineers. But as the boat grew smaller and smaller in the distance, so did their consciousness of their own position grow more and more distinct; and when at last the boat had disappeared in the shadow of the brig, all started, as if from a dream, to the wakeful contemplation of their own position.

A sort of council of war was held, with Mr Frere at the head of it, and the possessions of the little party thrown into common stock. The salt meat, flour, and tea were placed in a hollow rock some distance from the beach, and Mr Bates was appointed purser, to apportion to each, without fear or favour, his stated allowance. The goat was tethered with a piece of fishing line sufficiently long to allow her to browse. The cask of rum, by special agreement, was placed in the innermost recess of this rock, and it was resolved that its contents should not be touched unless in case of sickness, or in last extremity. There was no lack of water, for a spring ran bubbling from the rocks within a hundred yards of the spot where they had landed.

They calculated that, with prudence, their provision would last them for nearly four weeks.

It was found, upon a review of their possessions, that they had among them three pocket knives, a ball of string, two pipes and a fig of tobacco, a portion of fishing line, with hooks, and a big jack-knife which Frere had taken to gut the fish he had expected to catch. But they saw with dismay that there was nothing which could be used axe-wise among the party. Mrs Vickers had her shawl, and Bates a pea-jacket, but Frere and Grimes were without extra clothing. It was agreed that each should retain his own property, with the exception of the fishing lines, which were confiscated to the commonwealth.

Having made these arrangements, the kettle, filled with water from the spring, was slung from three green sticks over the fire, and a pannikin of weak tea, together with a biscuit, served out to each of the party, with the exception of Grimes, who declared himself unable to eat. Breakfast over, Bates made a damper, which was cooked in the ashes, and then another council was held as to future habitation.

It was clearly evident that they could not sleep in the open air. It was the middle of summer, and though no annoyance from rain was apprehended, the heat in the middle of the day was most oppressive. Moreover, it was absolutely necessary that Mrs Vickers and the child should have some place to themselves. At a little distance from the beach was a sandy rise, that led up to the face of the cliff, and on the eastern side of this rise grew a forest of young trees. Frere proposed to cut down these trees and make a sort of hut with them. It was soon discovered, however, that the pocket knives were insufficient for this purpose, but, by dint of notching the young saplings and then breaking them down, they succeeded, in a couple of hours, in collecting wood enough to roof over a space between the hollow rock which contained the provisions and another rock, in shape like a hammer, which jutted out within five yards of it. Mrs Vickers and Dora were to have this hut as a sleeping place, and Frere and Bates, lying at the mouth of the larder, would at once act as a guard to it and them. Grimes was to make for himself another hut where the fire had been lighted on the previous night.

When they got back to dinner, inspirited by this resolution, they found poor Mrs Vickers in great alarm. Grimes, who, by reason of the dint in his skull, had been left behind, was walking about the sea-beach talking mysteriously, and shaking his fist at some imaginary foe. On going up to him, they discovered that the blow had affected his brain, for he was evidently delirious. Frere endeavoured to soothe him, without effect; and at last, by Bates's advice, the poor fellow was rolled in the sea. The cold bath quelled his violence, and, being laid beneath the shade of a rock hard by, he fell into a condition of great muscular exhaustion, and slept.

The damper was then proportioned by Bates, and, together with a small piece of meat, formed the dinner of the party. Mrs Vickers reported that she had observed a great commotion on board the brig, and thought that the prisoners were throwing overboard such portions of the cargo as were not absolutely necessary to them, in order to lighten her. This notion Bates declared to be correct, and further pointed out that the mutineers had got out a kedge-anchor, and by hauling on the kedge-line, were gradually warping the brig down the harbour. Before dinner was over a light breeze sprang up, and the *Osprey*, running up the Union-Jack reversed, fired a musket, either in farewell or triumph, and spreading her sails, disappeared round an angle of the harbour.

Mrs Vickers, taking Dora with her, went away a few paces, and leaning against the rugged wall of her future home, wept bitterly. Bates and Frere affected cheerfulness, but each felt with astonishment that he had hitherto regarded the presence of the brig as a sort of safeguard, and that he had never fully realized his own loneliness until now.

The necessity for work, however, admitted of no opportunity for the indulgence of vain sorrow, and Bates setting the example, the pair worked so hard that by nightfall they had torn down and dragged together sufficient brushwood to complete Mrs Vickers's hut. During the progress of this work they were often interrupted by Grimes, who persisted in vague rushes at them, exclaiming loudly against their supposed treachery in leaving him at the mercy of the mutineers. Bates also complained of the pain caused by the wound in his forehead, and said that he was afflicted with a giddiness which he knew not how to avert. By dint of frequently bathing his head at the spring, however, he succeeded in keeping on his legs until the work of dragging together the boughs was completed, when he threw himself on the ground and declared that he could rise no more.

Frere applied to him the remedy that had been so successfully tried upon Grimes, but the salt-water inflamed the wound and rendered his condition worse. Mrs Vickers recommended that a little spirit and water should be used to wash the cut, and the cask was got out and broached for that purpose. Tea and damper formed their evening meal; and by the light of a blazing fire, the condition of things looked more cheerful. Mrs Vickers had set the pannikin on a flat stone, and dispensed the tea with an affectation of dignity which would have been absurd, had it not been heart-rending. She had smoothed her hair, and pinned the white shawl about her coquettishly; she even ventured to lament to Mr Frere that she had not brought more clothes. Dora was in high spirits, and scorned to confess hunger. When the tea had been drunk, she fetched water from the spring in the kettle, and bathed Bates's head with it. It was resolved that, on the morrow, a search should be made for some place from which to cast the fishing-line, and that one of the number should fish daily.

The condition of the unfortunate Grimes now gave cause for the greatest uneasiness. From maundering foolishly, he had taken to absolute violence, and was obliged to be watched by Frere. After much muttering and groaning, the poor fellow at last dropped off to sleep, and Frere, having assisted Bates to his sleeping place in front of the rock, and laid him down on a heap of green brushwood, prepared himself to snatch a few hours slumber.

Wearied by excitement and the labours of the day, he slept heavily, but, towards morning, was awakened by a strange noise. Grimes, whose delirium had apparently increased to madness, had succeeded in forcing his way through the rude fence of brushwood, and had thrown himself upon Bates with the ferocity of insanity. Growling to himself, he had seized the unfortunate pilot by the throat, and the pair were struggling together. Bates, weakened by the sickness that had followed upon his wound in the head, was quite unable to cope with his desperate assailant, but calling feebly upon Frere for help, had made shift to lay hold upon the jack-knife of which we have before spoken. Frere, starting to his feet, rushed to the assistance of the pilot, but was too late. Grimes, enraged by the sight of the knife, tore it from Bates's grasp, and before Frere could catch his arm, plunged it twice into the unfortunate man's breast.

'My God!' cries Bates, 'I'm a dead man!'

The sight of the blood, together with the exclamation of his victim, seemed to recall Grimes to consciousness. He looked bewilderedly at the bloody weapon, and then flinging it from him, rushed away towards the sea, into which he plunged headlong.

Frere, aghast at this sudden and terrible tragedy, gazed after him, and saw, from out the placid water, sparkling in the bright beams of morning, emerge a pair of arms, with hands outstretched; a black spot, that was a head, appeared between these stiffening arms, and then, with a horrible cry, the whole disappeared, and the bright water sparkled as placidly as before. The eyes of the terrified Frere travelling back to the wounded man, saw, midway between this sparkling water and the knife that lay on the sand, an object that went far to explain the maniac's sudden burst of fury. The rum cask lay upon its side by the remnants of last night's fire, and close to it was a clout, with which the head of the wounded man had been bound. It was evident that the poor creature, wandering in his delirium, had fallen across the rum cask, and that the fiery spirit had maddened him.

Frere hurried to the side of Bates, and lifting him up, strove to staunch the blood that flowed from his chest. It would seem that he had been resting himself on his left elbow, and that Grimes, snatching the knife from his right hand, had stabbed him twice in the right breast. He was pale and senseless, and Frere feared that the wound was mortal. Tearing off his neckhandkerchief, he endeavoured to bandage the wound, but found that the strip of silk was insufficient for the purpose. The noise had roused Mrs Vickers, who, stifling her terror, made haste to tear off a portion of her dress, and with this a bandage of sufficient width was made.

Frere went to the cask to see if, haply, he could obtain from it a few drops of spirit with which to moisten the lips of the dying man, but it was empty. Wretched Grimes, after drinking his fill, had overturned the unheaded puncheon, and the greedy sand had absorbed every particle of liquor.

Dora brought some water from the spring, and Mrs Vickers, bathing Bates's head with this, he revived a little. By-and-bye Mrs Vickers milked the goat — she had never done such a thing before in all her life — and the milk being given to Bates in a pannikin, he drank it eagerly, but vomited it again almost instantly. It was evident that he was sinking from some internal injury.

None of the party had much appetite for breakfast, but Frere, whose sensibilities were, perhaps, less acute than the rest, ate a piece of salt meat and damper. It struck him, with a curious feeling of pleasant selfishness, that now Grimes had gone, the allowance of provision could be increased, and that if Bates went also, it could be increased still further. He did not give utterance to his thoughts, however, but sat with the wounded man's head on his knees, and brushed the settling flies from his face. He hoped after all that the pilot would not die, for he would then be left alone to look after the women. Perhaps some such thought was dormant in the brain of Mrs Vickers. As for Dora, she made no secret of her anxiety.

'Don't die, Mr Bates — oh, don't die!' she said, standing piteously near the body she was afraid to touch. 'Don't leave mamma and me alone in this dreadful place!'

Poor Bates, of course, said nothing, but Frere frowned heavily, and Mrs Vickers said, reprovingly, 'Dora!' — just as if they had been in the old house on distant Sarah Island.

In the afternoon, Frere went away to drag together some wood for the fire, and when he returned he found the pilot near his last. Mrs Vickers said that for hours he had laid without motion, and almost without breath. The major's wife had seen more than one death-bed, and was calm enough; but poor little Dora, sitting on a stone hard by, shook with terror. She had some dim sort of notion that death was accompanied with violence. As the sun sank, Bates seemed to rally, but the two watchers knew that it was but the final flicker of the expiring candle.

'He's going!' said Frere at length, under his breath — as though fearful of awaking the half-slumbering soul.

Mrs Vickers, her eyes streaming with silent tears, lifted the honest head, and moistened the parched lips with her soaked handkerchief. A tremor shook the once stalwart limbs, and the dying man opened his eyes. For an instant he seemed bewildered, and then, looking from one to the other, intelligence returned to his glance, and it was evident that he remembered all. His gaze rested upon the pale face of the affrighted Dora, and then turned to Frere. There could be no mistaking the mute appeal of those eloquent eyes.

'Yes, I'll take care of her,' said Frere.

Bates smiled, and then observing that the blood from his wound had stained the white shawl of Mrs Vickers, he made an effort to move his head. It was not fitting that a lady's shawl should be stained with the blood of a poor fellow like himself.

The fashionable fribble, with quick instinct, understood the gesture, and gently drew the head back upon her bosom. In the presence of death there was no room for aught but womanhood.

For a moment all was silent, and they thought he had gone; but all at once he opened his eyes again, and looked round for the sea.

'Turn my face to it once more!' he whispered, and as they raised him, he inclined his ear as though to listen.

'It's calm enough here, God bless it,' he said; 'but I can hear the waves abreaking hard upon the Bar !'

And so his head drooped, and he died.

Dora burst out into a wild fit of weeping, and as Frere caught the corpse in his arms, ran to her mother.

'Oh, mamma, mamma,' she cried, 'why did God let him die when we wanted him so much?'

If there was selfishness in the thought, at how many death-beds has not such selfishness intruded?

Before it grew quite dark, Frere made shift to carry the body to the shelter of some rocks at a little distance, and spreading the jacket over the face, he piled stones upon it to keep it steady. The march of events had been so rapid, that he scarcely realised that since the previous evening two of the five human creatures left in this wilderness had escaped from it. As he did realise it, he began to wonder whose turn it would be next.

Mrs Vickers, worn out by the fatigue and excitement of the day, retired to rest early; and Dora, refusing to speak to Frere, followed her mother. This manifestation of unaccountable dislike on the part of the child, hurt Maurice more than he cared to own. He felt angry with her for not loving him, and yet he took no pains to conciliate her. It was with a curious feeling of pleasure that he remembered how she must soon look up to him as her chief protector. Had Dora been a few years older, Frere would have thought himself in love with her.

The following day passed gloomily. It was hot and sultry, and a dull haze hung over the mountains. Frere spent the morning in scooping in the sand a sort of grave, in which to inter poor Bates. Practically awake to his own necessities, he removed such portions of clothing from the body as he felt would be useful to him, but hid them under a stone, not liking to let Mrs Vickers see what he had done. Having completed his grave by midday, he placed the corpse therein, and rolled as many stones as possible to the sides of the mound. In the afternoon he cast the fishing-line from the point of a rock he had marked the day before, but caught nothing. Passing by the grave, on his return, he noticed that Mrs Vickers had placed at the head of it a rude cross, formed by tying together two pieces of stick.

After supper – the usual salt meat and damper – he lit an economical pipe, and tried to talk to Dora.

'Why won't you be friends with me, Missy?' he asked.

'I don't like you,' said Dora. 'You frighten me.'

'Why?'

'You are not kind. I don't mean that you do cruel things, but you are – Oh, I wish Papa was here!'

'Wishing won't bring him!' says Frere, pressing his hoarded tobacco together with prudent forefinger.

'There! That's what I mean! Is that kind? "Wishing won't bring him!" Oh, if it only would!'

'I didn't mean it unkindly,' said Frere. 'What a strange child you are.'

'There are Persons,' says Dora, 'who have no Affinity for

each other. I read about it in a book Papa had, and I suppose that's what it is. I have no Affinity for you. I can't help it, can I?'

'Rubbish!' Frere returned. 'Come here, and I'll tell you a story.'

Mrs Vickers had gone back to her cave, and the two were alone by the fire, near which stood the kettle and the newly-made damper.

The child, with some show of hesitation, came to him, and catching her, he placed her on his knee. The moon had not yet risen, and the shadows cast by the flickering fire seemed weird and monstrous. The wicked thought to frighten this helpless creature came to Maurice Frere.

'There was once,' said he, 'a Castle in an old wood, and in this Castle there lived an Ogre, with great goggle eyes.'

'You silly man!' said Dora, struggling to be free. 'You are trying to frighten me!'

'And this Ogre lived on the Bones of little girls. One day a little girl was travelling through the wood and she heard the Ogre coming. "Haw! haw! Haw! haw!"'

'Mr Frere, let me down!'

'She was terribly frightened, and she ran, and ran, and ran, until all of a sudden she saw —'

A piercing scream burst from his companion.

'Oh! oh! What's that?' she cried, and clung to her persecutor.

On the other side of the fire stood the figure of a man. He staggered forward, and then, falling on his knees, stretched out his hands, with a hoarse cry.

Frere leaped up, as much amazed as his companion. For a moment he thought that the buried corpse of poor Bates had arisen in defence of the child he meant to torture, and then that the sea had given up its dead, or that Grimes had not perished. Snatching a burning brand from the fire, he made as if to strike the ragged creature that knelt among the ashes.

'What do you want?' he cried.

'Give me food, for the love of God!' was the reply. 'Flog me, but give me food!'

It was Rufus Dawes.

The sound of a human voice broke the spell of terror that was on the child, and as the glow from the flourished brand fell upon the tattered yellow garments, she guessed at once the whole story.

Not so Maurice Frere. He saw before him but a new danger, a new mouth to share the scanty provision, and kept the convict at bay. But Rufus Dawes, glaring round with wolfish eyes caught sight of the damper resting against the iron kettle, and made to clutch it.

Frere dashed the brand in his face.

'Stand back!' he cried. 'We have no food to spare!'

Rufus Dawes uttered a savage cry, and raising the iron gad, plunged forward desperately to attack this new enemy; but, quick as thought, the child glided past Frere, and snatching the loaf, placed it in the hands of the starving man.

'Here, poor prisoner,' said she, 'eat!' and then, turning to Frere, who stood with hand upraised in very act to strike, she cast upon him a glance so full of horror, indignation, and surprise, that the man blushed in the darkness.

'Oh,' said she, as she turned to meet her mother, 'I did not know that men could be so wicked!'

As for Rufus Dawes, the sudden apparition of this golden-haired girl frightened him. Weak from his prolonged fast, and sick with hope deferred, the brutal refusal of succour and unexpected vision of childish beauty unmanned him. Hungry as he had been the previous instant, he felt that he could not touch a morsel. Letting the loaf slip through his fingers, he gazed with haggard eyes at the retreating figure of the child, and as it seemed to vanish into the darkness outside the circle of fire-light, the unhappy man sank his face upon his blackened, horny hands, and burst into tears.

'MR' DAWES

T H E coarse tones of Maurice Frere roused him.

'What do you want?' he asked.

Rufus Dawes, raising his head, contemplated the figure before him, and recognized it.

'Is it *you*?' he said, slowly.

'What do you mean? Do you know me?' asked Frere, drawing back.

But the convict did not reply. His momentary emotion passed away, the pangs of hunger returned, and greedily seizing upon the piece of damper, he began to eat in silence.

'Do you hear, man?' repeated Frere, at length. 'What are you?'

'An escaped prisoner. You can give me up in the morning. I've done my best, and I'm beat.'

This sentence struck Frere with dismay. The man did not know that the settlement had been abandoned.

'I cannot give you up. There is no one but myself and a woman and child on the settlement.'

Rufus Dawes, pausing in his eating, stared at him bewilderedly.

'The prisoners have gone away in the schooner. If you choose to remain free, you can do so – as far as I am concerned. I am as helpless as you are.'

'But how do *you* come here?'

Frere laughed bitterly. To give explanations to convicts was foreign to his experience, and he did not relish the task. In this case, however, there was no help for it.

'The prisoners mutinied and seized the brig.'

'What brig?'

'The *Osprey*.'

A terrible light broke upon Rufus Dawes, and he began to understand how he had again missed his chance.

'Who took her?'

'That double-dyed villain, John Rex,' says Frere, giving vent to his passion. 'May she sink, and burn, and –'

'Have they *gone*, then?' cried the miserable man, clutching at his hair with a gesture of hopeless rage.

'Yes; two days ago, and have left us here to starve.'

Rufus Dawes burst into a laugh so discordant that it made the other shudder.

'We'll starve together, Maurice Frere,' said he: 'for while you've a crust, I'll share it. If I don't get liberty, at least I'll have revenge!'

The sinister aspect of this famished savage, sitting with his chin resting on his ragged knees, rocking himself to and fro in the light of the fire, gave Mr Maurice Frere a new sensation. He felt as might have felt that African hunter who, returning to his camp fire, found a lion there.

'Wretch!' said he, shrinking from him, 'why should you wish to be revenged on me?'

The convict turned upon him with a snarl.

'Take care what you say! I'll have no hard words. Wretch! If I am a wretch, who made me one? If I hate you and myself and the world, who made me hate it? I was born free – as free as you are. Why should I be sent to herd with beasts, and condemned to this slavery, worse than death? Tell me that, Maurice Frere – tell me that!'

'I didn't make the laws,' says Frere; 'why do you attack me?'

'Because you are what I was. You are FREE! You can do as you please. You can love, you can work, you can think. I can only *hate*!'

He paused, as if astonished at himself, and then continued, with a low laugh,

'Fine words for a convict, eh! But, never mind, it's all right, Mr Frere; we're equal now, and I shan't die an hour sooner than you, though you are a "free man!" '

Frere began to think that he was dealing with another madman.

'Die! There's no need to talk of dying,' he said, as soothingly as it was possible for him to say it. 'Time enough for that by-and-bye.'

'There spoke the *free* man. We convicts have an advantage

over you *gentlemen*. You are afraid of death; we pray for it. It is the best thing that can happen to us. Die! They were going to hang me once. I wish they had. My God, I wish they had!'

There was such a depth of agony in this terrible utterance that Maurice Frere was appalled at it.

'There, go and sleep, my man,' he said. 'You are knocked up. We'll talk in the morning.'

'Hold on a bit!' cries Rufus Dawes, with a coarseness of manner altogether foreign to that he had just assumed. 'You don't catch old birds with chaff! Who's with ye?'

'The wife and daughter of the Commandant,' replied Frere, half afraid to refuse an answer to a question so fiercely put.

'No one else?'

'No.'

'Poor souls!' says the convict. 'I pity them.'

And then he stretched himself, like a dog, before the blaze, and seemed to go off to sleep instantly.

Maurice Frere, looking at the gaunt figure of this addition to the party, was completely puzzled how to act. Such a character as this had never before come within the range of his experience. He knew not what to make of this fierce, ragged, desperate man, who wept and threatened by turns – who was now snarling in the most repulsive bass of the convict gamut, and now calling upon heaven in tones which were little less than eloquent.

At first he thought of precipitating himself upon the sleeping wretch and pinioning him, but a second glance at the sinewy, though wasted, limbs forbade him to follow out this rash suggestion of his own fears. Then a horrible prompting – arising out of his former cowardice – made him feel for the jack-knife, with which one murder had already been committed. The stock of provision was so scanty, and, after all, the lives of the woman and child were worth more than that of this unknown desperado! But, to do him justice, the thought no sooner shaped itself than he crushed it out.

'We'll wait till morning and see how he shapes,' said he to himself: and pausing at the brushwood barricade, behind which the mother and daughter were clinging to each other, he whis-.

pered that he was on guard outside, and that the absconder slept.

But when morning dawned, he found that there was no need for alarm. The convict was lying in almost the same position as that in which he had left him, and his eyes were closed. His threatening outbreak of the previous night had been produced by the excitement of his sudden rescue, and he was now quite incapable of violence.

Frere advanced and shook him by the shoulder.

'Not alive!' cried the poor wretch, waking with a start, raising his arm to strike. 'Keep off!'

'It's all right,' says Frere. 'No one's going to harm you. Wake up.'

Rufus Dawes glanced around him stupidly, and then seemed to remember what had happened, for, with a great effort, he staggered to his feet.

'I thought they'd got me!' he said; 'but it's the other way, I see. Come, let's have breakfast, Maurice Frere. I'm hungry.'

'You must wait,' says Frere. 'Do you think there is no one here but yourself?'

Rufus Dawes, swaying to and fro from weakness, passed his shred of a cuff over his eyes.

'I don't know anything about it. I only know I'm hungry.'

Frere stopped short. Now or never was the time to settle future relations. Lying awake in the night, with the jack-knife ready to his hand, he had decided on the course of action that must be adopted. The convict should share with the rest, but no more. If he rebelled at that, there must be a trial of strength between them.

'Look you here,' he said. 'We have but barely enough food to serve us until help comes – if it does come. I have the care of that poor woman and child, and I will see fair play for their sakes. You shall share with us to our last bit and drop: but, by Heaven, you shall get no more.'

The convict, stretching out his wasted arms, looked down upon them with the uncertain gaze of a drunken man.

'I am weak now,' he said. 'You have the best of me;' and then he sank suddenly down upon the ground exhausted. 'Give me drink,' he said, feebly motioning with his hand.

Frere got him water in the pannikin, and having drank it, he smiled almost comically, and lay down to sleep again.

Mrs Vickers and Dora coming out while he still slept, recognised him as the desperado of the settlement.

'He was the most desperate man we had,' said Mrs Vickers, identifying herself with her husband. 'Oh, what shall we do?'

'He won't do much harm,' says Frere, looking down at the notorious ruffian with curiosity. 'He's as near dead as can be.'

Dora looked up at him with her clear child's look of disgust.

'We mustn't let him die,' said she. 'That would be murder.'

'No, no,' returned Frere, hastily; 'no one wants him to die. But what can we do?'

'I'll nurse him!' says Dora.

Frere broke into one of his coarse laughs, the first one that he had indulged in since the mutiny, and even poor Mrs Vickers could not restrain a smile.

'*You* nurse him!' cried Frere. 'By George, that's a good one!'

The poor little child, weak and excitable, felt the contempt in the tones, and burst into a passion of sobs.

'Why do you insult me, you wicked man? The poor fellow's ill, and he'll – he'll die, like Mr Bates. Oh, mamma, mamma, let's go away by ourselves. I am afraid of him.'

Frere swore a great oath. 'Nurse him, then, yourselves,' said he, and walked away.

He went into the little wood under the cliff, and sat down. He was full of strange thoughts, which he could not express, and which he never had before. The dislike the child bore to him made him miserable, and yet he took delight in tormenting her. He was conscious that he had acted the part of a coward the night before in endeavouring to frighten her, and that the detestation she bore him was well earned; but he had fully determined to stake his life in her defence, should the savage who had thus come upon them out of the desert attempt violence, and he was unreasonably angry at the pity she had shown. It was not fair to be thus misinterpreted. Then he had done wrong to swear, and, worse still, in leaving so abruptly. But the consciousness of his wrong-doing only made him more confirmed in it. His native obstinacy would not allow him to retract what he had said – even to himself.

Walking along, he came to Bates's grave, and the cross upon it. Here was another evidence of ill-treatment. She had always preferred Bates. Now that Bates had gone, she must needs transfer her childish affections to a convict.

'Oh,' said Frere to himself, with pleasant recollections of many coarse triumphs in love-making, 'if you were a woman, you little vixen, I'd *make* you love me!' When he had said this, he laughed at himself for his folly — 'He was getting romantic!'

When he got back, he found Dawes stretched upon the brushwood, with Dora sitting near him.

'He is better,' says Mrs Vickers, disdaining to refer to the scene of the morning. 'Sit down and have something to eat, Mr Frere.'

'Are you better?' asked Frere, abruptly.

To his surprise, the convict answered quite civilly. 'I shall be strong again in a day or two, and then I can help you, sir,' he said.

'Help me to what?'

'To build a hut here for the ladies,' says Dawes. 'And we'll live here all our lives, and never go back to the sheds any more.'

'He has been wandering a little,' says Mrs Vickers. 'Poor fellow, he seems quite well-behaved.'

The convict here began to sing a little German song, and to beat the refrain with his hand. Frere looked at him with curiosity.

'I wonder what the story of that man's life has been,' he said. 'A queer one, I'll be bound.'

Nurse Dora looked up at him, with a forgiving smile.

'I'll ask him when he gets well,' she said, 'and if you are good, I'll tell you, Mr Frere.'

Frere accepted the proffered friendship.

'I am a great brute, Dora, sometimes, ain't I?' he said, 'but I don't mean it.'

'You are,' returned Dora, frankly, 'but let's shake hands and be Friends. It's no use quarrelling when there are only four of us, is it?'

And in this way was Rufus Dawes admitted a member of the family circle.

Within a week from the night on which he had seen the smoke of Frere's fire, the convict had recovered his strength, and had become an important personage. The distrust with which he had been at first viewed had worn off, and he was no longer an outcast, to be pointed at behind his back, or to be referred to in whispers. He had abandoned his rough manner, and no longer threatened or complained. Indeed, he seemed almost cheerful, and though at times a profound melancholy would oppress him, his spirits were, as a rule, more even than those of Frere's, who was often moody, sullen, and overbearing.

Rufus Dawes was no longer the brutalised wretch that had plunged into the dark waters of the bay to escape a life he loathed, and had alternatively cursed and wept in the solitudes of the forests. He was an active member of society – a society of four – and had begun to regain an air of independence and authority. This change had been wrought by the influence of little Dora. Recovered from the weakness consequent upon his terrible journey, Rufus Dawes had experienced for the first time in five years the soothing power of kindness. He had now an object to live for beyond himself. He was of use to somebody. Had he died, he would have been regretted. To us this means but little, to this unhappy man it meant everything. He found to his astonishment that he was not despised, and that, by the strange concurrence of circumstances, he had been brought into a position in which his convict experiences gave him authority. He was skilled in all the mysteries of the prison sheds. He knew how to sustain life on as little food as possible. He could fell trees without an axe, bake bread without an oven, build a weatherproof hut without bricks or mortar. From the patient, he became the adviser; and from the adviser, the commander. In the semi-savage state to which these four human beings had been brought, he found that savage accomplishments were of most value. Might was right, and Maurice Frere's authority of gentility soon succumbed to Rufus Dawes's authority of knowledge.

As the time wore on, and the scanty stock of provisions decreased, he found that his authority grew more and more powerful. Did a question arise as to the qualities of a strange plant, it was Rufus Dawes who could pronounce upon it. Were fish to be caught, it was Rufus Dawes who caught them. Did Mrs Vickers complain of the instability of her brushwood hut, it was Rufus Dawes who worked a wickershield, and plastering it with clay, produced a wall that defied the keenest wind. He made cups out of pine-knots, and plates out of bark-strips. He worked harder than any three men. Nothing daunted him, nothing discouraged him. When Mrs Vickers fell sick, from anxiety and insufficient food, it was Rufus Dawes who gathered fresh leaves for her couch, who cheered her by hopeful words, who voluntarily gave up half his own allowance of meat that she might grow the stronger on it. The poor woman and her child called him 'Mr' Dawes.

Frere watched all this with a dissatisfaction that amounted at times to positive hatred. Yet he could say nothing, for he could not but confess that, beside Dawes, he was incapable. He even submitted to take orders from this escaped convict – it was so evident that the escaped convict knew better than he. Dora began to look upon Dawes as a second Bates. He was, moreover, all her own. She had a sort of interest in him, as it were, for she had nursed and protected him. If it had not been for her, this prodigy would not have lived. He felt for her an absorbing affection that was almost a passion. She was his good angel, his protectress, his glimpse of Heaven. She had given him food when he was starving, and had believed in him when the world – the world of four – had looked coldly on him. He would have died for her, and, for love of her, *hoped* for the vessel which should take her back to freedom and give him again to bondage.

But the days stole on, and no vessel appeared. Each day they eagerly scanned the watery horizon; each day trembled to behold the bowsprit of the returning *Ladybird* glide past the jutting rock that shut out the view of the harbour – but in vain. Mrs Vickers's illness increased, and the stock of provision began to run short. Dawes talked of putting himself and Frere on half allowance. It was evident that, unless succour came in a few days, they must starve.

Frere started all sorts of wild plans for obtaining food. He would make a journey to the settlement, and, swimming the estuary, search if haply any casks of biscuit had been left behind in the hurry of departure. He would set springes for the sea-gulls, and snare the pigeons at Liberty Point. He would even catch the wild goats that bred about the Pilot Station. But all these schemes proved impracticable, and, with blank faces, they watched their bag of flour grow smaller and smaller daily.

Then the notion of escape was broached. Could they construct a raft? Impossible without nails or ropes. Could they build a boat? Equally impossible for the same reason. Could they raise a fire sufficient to signal a ship? Easily; but what ship would come within reach of that doubly-desolate spot? Nothing could be done but wait for the vessel, which was sure to come for them sooner or later; and, growing weaker day by day, they waited.

One day Dora was sitting in the sun reading the 'English History', which, by the accident of fright, she had brought with her on the night of the mutiny.

'Mr Frere,' said she, suddenly, 'what is an alchemist?'

'A man who makes gold,' was Frere's not very accurate definition.

'Did you ever know one?'

'No.'

'Did you, Mr Dawes?'

'It means a chemist, Miss. I did know one once.'

'What! A man who made gold?'

'No, not exactly gold.'

'Where did you know him?'

'In Germany.'

Frere started.

'Were you ever in Germany?' he asked.

'Yes, I lived there some years,' said the other, quietly.

'But *did* he make gold?' persisted Dora.

'No, not exactly gold. He did try; but he was, in his own idea, an alchemist for all that.'

'What became of him?'

'He – he died,' said Dawes, with so much grief in his tone that the child instinctively turned the subject.

'Then, alchemy is a very old art?'

'Oh, yes.'

'Did the Ancient Britons know it?'

'No, not so old as that.'

Dora suddenly gave a little scream. The remembrance of the evening when she read about the Ancient Britons to poor Bates came vividly into her mind, and though she had since re-read the passage that had then attracted her attention a hundred times, it had never before presented itself to her in its full significance. Hurriedly turning the well-thumbed leaves, she read aloud the passage which had provoked remark:

The Ancient Britons were little better than Barbarians. They painted their bodies with Woad, and, seated in their light coracles of skin stretched upon slender wooden frames, must have presented a Wild and Savage appearance.

'A coracle! That's a boat! Can't we make a coracle, Mr Dawes?'

Four days after this, anybody passing the eastern point of Macquarie Harbour would have seen a strange spectacle.

A little girl was sitting on a rock watching two ragged, famine-stricken men fixing a mast into a curious structure of goat-skins stretched across a framework of saplings.

⊷ 14 ⊶

WHAT THE SEAWEED SUGGESTED

THE question asked by Dora – it seemed like an inspiration at the moment – had given the marooned party new hopes. Maurice Frere, with his usual impetuosity, had declared that the project was a most feasible one, and wondered – as such men will wonder – that it had never occurred to him before.

'It's the simplest thing in the world!' he cried. 'Dora, you have saved us!'

But upon taking the matter into more earnest consideration, it became but too apparent that they were as yet a long way from the realisation of their hopes. To make a coracle of skins seemed sufficiently easy, but how to obtain the skins! The one miserable hide of the unlucky she-goat was utterly inadequate for the purpose.

Dora – her face beaming with hope of escape, and delight at having been the means of suggesting it – watched narrowly the countenance of Rufus Dawes, and felt her little heart sink as she marked no answering gleam of joy in those downcast eyes.

'Can't it be done, Mr Dawes?' she asked, trembling for the reply.

The convict knitted his brows gloomily.

'Come, Dawes!' cries Frere, forgetting his enmity for an instant, in the flash of new hope, 'can't you suggest something?'

Rufus Dawes, thus appealed to as the acknowledged Head of the little society, felt a pleasant thrill of self-satisfaction. It was long since he had felt such.

'I don't know,' he said. 'I must think of it. It looks easy, and yet –' He paused as something in the water caught his eye. It was a mass of bladdery seaweed that the returning tide was wafting slowly to the shore. This object, which would have passed unnoticed at any time, seemed at this instant to suggest to Rufus Dawes a new idea. 'Yes,' he added slowly, with a change of tone, 'it may be done. I think I see my way.'

The others preserved a respectful silence until he should speak again.

'How far do you think it is across the bay?' he asked of Frere.

'What, to Sarah Island?'

'No, to the Pilot Station.'

'About four miles.'

The convict sighed.

'Too far to swim now, though I might have done it once. But this sort of life weakens a man. It must be done, after all.'

'What are you going to do?' asked Frere.

'To kill the goat.'

Dora uttered a cry; she had become fond of her dumb companion.

'Kill Nanny! Oh, Mr Dawes! What for?'

'I am going to make a boat for you,' he said; 'and I want hides, and thread, and tallow.'

A few weeks back, Maurice Frere would have laughed at such a sentence, but he had begun now to comprehend that this escaped convict was not a man to be laughed at, and though he detested him for his superiority, he could not but admit that he was superior.

'You can't get more than one hide off a goat, man?' he said, with an inquiring tone in his voice — as though it was just possible that such a marvellous being as Dawes *could* so get a second hide, by virtue of some secret process known only to himself.

'I am going to catch other goats.'

'Where?'

'At the Pilot Station.'

'But how are you going to get there?'

'Float across. Come, there is no time for questioning! Go and cut down some saplings, and let us begin!'

The lieutenant-master looked at the convict-prisoner with astonishment, and then gave way to the power of knowledge, and did as he was ordered.

Before sundown that evening, the carcase of poor Nanny, broken into various most unbutchery fragments, was hanging on the nearest tree; and Frere, returning with as many young saplings as he could drag together, found Rufus Dawes engaged in a curious occupation. He had killed the goat, and, having cut off its head close under the chin, and its legs at the knee-joint, had extracted the carcase through a slit made in the lower portion of the belly, which slit he had now sewn together with string.

This proceeding gave him a rough bag, and he was busily engaged in filling this bag with such coarse grass as he could collect. Frere observed also that the fat of the animal was carefully preserved, and the intestines had been placed in a pool of water to soak.

Rufus Dawes, however, declined to give information as to what he intended to do.

'It's my notion,' he said. 'Let me alone. I may make a failure of it.'

Frere, on being pressed by Dora, affected to know all about the scheme, but to impose silence on himself. He was galled to think that a convict brain should contain a mystery which he might not share.

On the next day, by Rufus Dawes' directions, Frere cut down some rushes that grew about a mile from the camping ground, and brought them in on his back. This took him nearly half a day to accomplish. Short rations were beginning to tell upon his physical powers. The convict, on the other hand, trained, by a woeful experience in the Boats, to endurance of hardship, had almost recovered his original strength.

'What are they for?' asked Frere, as he flung the bundles down.

His master condescended to reply.

'To make a float.'

'Well?'

The other shrugged his broad shoulders.

'You are very slow, Mr Frere. I am going to swim over to the Pilot Station and catch some of those goats. *I* can get across on the stuffed skin, but I must float *them* back on the reeds.'

'How the doose do you mean to catch 'em?' asked Frere, wiping the sweat from his brow.

The convict motioned to him to approach.

He did so, and saw that his companion was cleaning the intestines of the goat. The outer membrane having been peeled off, Rufus Dawes was turning the gut inside out. This he did by turning up a short piece of it as though it were a coat-sleeve, and catching hold of the turned-up cuff, dipping the whole into a pool of water. The weight of the water pressing between the cuff and the rest of the gut, bore down a further portion; and so, by repeated dippings, the whole length was turned inside out. The inner membrane having been then scraped away, there remained a fine transparent tube, which was tightly twisted and set to dry in the sun.

'There is the catgut for the noose,' said Dawes. 'I learnt *that* trick at the settlement. Now come here.'

Frere, following, saw that a fire had been made between two stones, and that the kettle was partly sunk in the ground near it. On approaching the kettle, he found it full of smooth pebbles.

'Take out those stones,' said Dawes.

Frere, more bewildered still, obeyed, and saw that at the

bottom of the kettle was a quantity of sparkling white powder, while the sides of the vessel seemed crusted with the same material.

'What's that?' he asked.

'Salt. I could have distilled the fresh water, if I had wanted it.'

'Distilled! How?'

'I filled the kettle with salt-water, and then heating those pebbles red-hot in the fire, dropped them into it. We could have caught the steam in a cloth and wrung out fresh-water, had we wished to do so. But, thank God, we have plenty.'

Frere stared.

'Did you learn that at the settlement, too?' he asked.

Rufus Dawes laughed, with a sort of bitterness in his tone.

'Do you think I have been at the "settlement" all my life? The thing is very simple. It is merely evaporation.'

'Oh!'

'A fine word for a convict, isn't it? A convict is not supposed to know anything about chemistry. But, then, I have lived with a chemist.'

Frere burst out in sudden, fretful admiration, 'What a fellow you are, Dawes! What are you – I mean, what *have* you been?'

A triumphant light came into the other's face, and for the instant he seemed about to reply by some startling revelation. But the light faded, and he checked himself with a gesture of pain.

'I *am* a convict. Never mind what I *have* been. A sailor, ship-builder, chemist's assistant, vagabond – what does it matter. It won't alter my fate, will it?'

'If we get safely back,' says Frere, 'I'll ask for a free pardon for you. You deserve it.'

'Come,' returned Dawes, with his discordant laugh. 'Let us wait until we do get back.'

'You don't believe me?'

'I don't want favours at *your* hands,' he said, with a return of the old fierceness. 'Let us get to work. Bring up the rushes here, and tie them with the fishing-line.'

At this instant Dora came up.

'Good afternoon, Mr Dawes. Hard at work? Oh; what's this in the kettle?'

The voice of the child acted like a charm upon Rufus Dawes. He smiled quite cheerfully.

'Salt, Miss. I am going to catch the goats with that.'

'Catch the goats! How?'

'Goats are fond of salt, and when I get over to the Pilot-station, I shall set traps for them baited with this salt. When they come to lick it, I shall have a noose of catgut ready to catch them – do you see?'

'But how will you get across?'

'You will see, tomorrow.'

❖ 15 ❖

A WONDERFUL DAY'S WORK

THE next morning, Rufus Dawes was stirring by daylight. He first got his catgut wound upon a piece of stick, and then having moved his frail floats alongside the little rock that served as a pier, he took a fishing-line and a larger piece of stick and proceeded to draw on the sand a sort of diagram. This diagram when completed represented a rude outline of a punt, eight feet long and three broad, with eight points – four on each side – into which small willow rods were driven. He then awoke Frere and showed him this.

'Get eight stakes of celery-top pine,' he said. 'You can burn them where you cannot cut them – and drive a stake into the place of each of these willow wands. When you have done that, collect as many willows as you can get. I shall not be back until tonight. Now give me a hand with the floats.'

Frere, coming to the pier, saw Dawes strip himself, and piling his clothes upon the stuffed goat-skin, stretch himself upon the reed bundles, and, paddling with his hands, push off from the shore. The clothes floated high and dry, but the reeds, depressed by the weight of the body, sank so that the head and shoulders of the convict alone appeared above water. In this fashion he gained the middle of the current, and the out-going tide swept him down towards the mouth of the harbour.

Frere, sulkily admiring, went back to prepare the breakfast – they were on half rations now, Dawes having forbidden the slaughtered goat to be eaten, lest his expedition should prove unsuccessful – and wondering at the chance which had thrown this convict in his way.

'Parsons would call it "a special providence",' he said to himself. 'For if it hadn't been for him, we should never have got thus far. If his "boat" succeeds, we're all right, I suppose. He's a clever dog. I wonder who he is.'

Then his training as a master of convicts made him think how dangerous such a man would be on a convict station. It would be difficult to keep a fellow of such resources.

'They'll have to look pretty sharp after him, if ever they get him back,' he thought. 'I'll have a fine tale to tell of his ingenuity.' Then the conversation of the previous day occurred to him. 'I promised to ask for a free pardon. He wouldn't have it though. Too proud to accept it at *my* hands! How confoundedly impudent a little liberty makes these beggars! Wait until we get back. I'll teach him his place; for, after all, it is his own liberty that he is working for as well as mine – I mean, ours.' Then a thought came into his head that was in every way worthy of him. 'Suppose we took the boat, and left him behind!' The notion seemed so ludicrously wicked, that he laughed involuntarily.

'What is it, Mr Frere?'

'Oh, it's you, Dora, is it? Ha, ha, ha! I was thinking of something – something funny.'

'Indeed,' says Dora, 'I am glad of that. Where's Mr Dawes?'

Frere was displeased at the interest with which she asked the question.

'You are always thinking of that fellow. It's Dawes, Dawes, Dawes, all day long. He has gone.'

'Oh!' with a sorrowful accent. 'Mamma wants to see him.'

'What about?' says Frere, roughly.

'Mamma is ill, Mr Frere.'

'Dawes isn't a doctor. What is the matter with her?'

'She is worse than she was yesterday. I don't know what is the matter.'

Frere, somewhat alarmed, strode over to the little cavern.

The 'lady of the Commandant' was in a strange plight. The cavern was lofty, but narrow. In shape it was three cornered, having two sides open to the wind. The ingenuity of Rufus Dawes had closed these sides with wicker-work and clay, and a sort of door of interlaced brushwood hung at one of them. Pushing open this door, Frere entered.

The poor woman was lying on a bed of rushes strewn over young brushwood, and was moaning feebly. From the first she had felt the privation to which she was subjected most keenly, and the mental anxiety from which she had suffered increased her physical debility. The exhaustion and lassitude to which she had partially succumbed soon after Dawes's arrival, had now completely overcome her, and she was unable to rise.

'Cheer up, ma'am,' says Maurice, with an assumption of his fine old English manner. 'It will be all right in a day or two.'

'Is it you? I sent for Mr Dawes.'

'He is away just now, ma'am. We are making a boat. Did not Dora tell you?'

'She told me that *he* was making one.'

'Well, I – that is *we* – are making it. He will be back again tonight. Can I do anything for you?'

'No, thank you. I only wanted to know how he was getting on. I must go soon – if I am to go. Thank you, Mr Frere, I am much obliged to you. This is a – he-he – dreadful place to receive visitors, isn't it?'

'Never mind,' says Frere, again, 'you will be back in Hobart Town in a few days now. We are sure to get picked up by a ship. But you must cheer up. Have some tea or something.'

'No, thank you – I don't feel well enough to eat. I am tired.'

Dora began to cry.

'Don't cry, dear. I shall be better by and by. Oh, I wish Mr Dawes was back.'

Maurice Frere went out, indignant. This 'Mr' Dawes was everybody, it seemed, and he himself nobody. Let them wait a little.

All that day, working hard to carry out the convict's directions, he meditated a thousand plans by which he could turn the tables. He would accuse Dawes of violence. He would demand that he should be taken back as an 'absconder'. He would insist that the law should take its course, and that the 'death' which was the doom of all who 'were caught in the act of escape from a penal settlement' should be enforced. Yet if they got safe to land, the marvellous courage and ingenuity of the prisoner would tell strongly in his favour. The woman and child would bear witness to his tenderness and skill, and plead for him. As he himself had said, the man deserved a pardon. Then Maurice Frere, burning with wounded vanity and an undefined jealousy, waited for some method to suggest itself, by which he might claim the credit of the escape, and snatch from the convict, who had dared to rival him, the last hope of freedom.

Rufus Dawes, drifting with the current, had allowed himself to coast along the eastern side of the harbour until the Pilot-station appeared in view on the opposite shore. By this time it was nearly seven o'clock. He landed on a sandy cove that the action of the waves had made, and drawing up his raft, proceeded to unpack from among his garments a piece of damper.

Having eaten sparingly, and dried himself in the sun, he replaced the remains of his breakfast, and pushed his floats again into the water. The Pilot-station lay some distance below him, on the opposite shore. He had purposely made his second start from a point which should give him this advantage of position; for had he attempted to paddle across at right angles, the strength of the current would have swept him out to sea.

As it was, indeed, he had some difficulty in steering his frail craft. The eddies were many and violent, and though the tide was at the slack, the water rushed through the narrow 'Gates', as through the mouth of a bottle. He knew that, once cast into the midst of that white line that marked the Bar, his fate was certain. Weak as he was, he several times nearly lost his hold of the reeds. The clumsy bundle presenting too great a broad-side to the stream, whirled round and round, and was once or twice nearly sucked under altogether. At length, however, breathless and exhausted, he gained the opposite bank, some half a mile below the point he had attempted to make, and carrying his floats out of reach of the tide, made off across the hill to the Pilot-station.

Arrived there about midday, he set to work to lay his snares. The goats, with whose hides he hoped to cover the coracle, were sufficiently numerous and tame, to encourage him to exert all his efforts. He carefully examined the tracks of the animals, and found that they converged to one point – on the track to the nearest water. With much labour, he cut down bushes, so as to mask the approach to the waterhole, on sides save where these tracks immediately conjoined. Close to the water, and at certain unequal distances along the various tracks, he scattered the salt he had obtained by his rude distillation of sea-water. Between this scattered salt and the points where he judged the animals would be likely to approach, he set his traps, made after the following manner.

He took several pliant branches of young trees, and having stripped them of leaves and twigs, dug with his knife and the end of the rude paddle he had made for the voyage across the inlet, a succession of holes, about a foot deep. At the thicker end of these saplings he fastened, by a piece of fishing-line, a small cross-bar, which swung loosely, like the stick handle which a schoolboy fastens to the string of his pegtop. Forcing the ends of the saplings thus prepared into the holes, he filled in and stamped down the earth all around them. The saplings, thus anchored as it were by the cross-pieces of stick, not only stood firm, but resisted all his efforts to withdraw them. No goat, however powerful, could uproot them unless by lowering the earth around the wooden cross-bar.[1]

To the thin ends of these saplings he bound tightly, into notches cut in the wood, and secured by a multiplicity of twisting, the catgut springes he had brought from the camping ground. The saplings were then bent double, and the gutted ends secured in the ground by the same means as that employed

1. This method, well known to travellers in the Arabian deserts, is called by the Arabs *Dàteràm*. The Bedouins picket their horses thus, in sand of the driest description. It has been used with success in the Australian deserts; and has been known to the convict mind – given to keep such matters 'quiet' – for a very long time.

to fix the butts. This was the most difficult part of the business, for it was necessary to discover precisely the amount of pressure that would hold the bent rod without allowing it to escape by reason of its elasticity, and which would yet 'give' to a slight pull on the gut. After many failures, however, this happy medium was discovered; and Rufus Dawes, setting up his springes by means of twigs, smoothed the disturbed sand with a branch, and retired to watch the effect of his snare.

About two hours after he had gone, the goats came to drink. There were five goats and two kids, and they trotted calmly along the path to the water. The watcher soon saw that his precautions had been in a manner wasted. The leading goat marched gravely into the springe, which, catching him round the neck, released the bent rod, and sprang him off his legs into the air. He uttered a comical bleat, and then hung kicking. Rufus Dawes, though the success of the scheme was a matter of life and death, burst out laughing at the antics of the beast.

The other goats bounded off at this sudden elevation of their leader, and three more were entrapped at a little distance. Rufus Dawes now thought it time to secure his prize, though three of the springes had been as yet unsprung. He ran down to the old goat, knife in hand, but before he could reach him, the treacherous catgut gave way, and the old fellow, shaking his head with grotesque dismay, made off at full speed. The others, however, were secured and killed.

The loss of the springe was not a serious one, for three traps yet remained unsprung, and before sundown Rufus Dawes had caught four more goats. Removing with care the catgut that had done such good service, he dragged the carcases to the shore, and proceeded to pack them upon his floats. He discovered, however, that the weight was too great, and that the water, entering through the loops of the stitching in the hide, had so soaked the rush-grass as to render the floats no longer buoyant. He was compelled, therefore, to spend two hours in restuffing the skin with such materials as he could find. Some light and flock-like seaweed, that the action of the water had swathed after the fashion of haybands along the shore, formed an excellent substitute for grass, and having bound his bundle of rushes lengthwise, with the goat-skin as a centre-piece, he succeeded in forming a sort of rude canoe, upon which the carcases floated securely.

He had eaten nothing since the morning, and the violence of his exertions had exhausted him. Still, sustained by the excitement of the task he had set himself, he dismissed with fierce impatience the thought of rest, and dragged his weary limbs along the sand, endeavouring to kill fatigue by further exertion. The tide was now running in, and he knew that it was imperative that he should regain the further shore while the current was in his favour. To cross from the Pilot-station at low-water was impossible. If he waited until the ebb, he must spend another day on the shore, and he could not afford to lose an hour.

Cutting a long sapling, he fastened to one end of it the floating bundle, and thus guided it to a spot where the beach shelved into deep water. It was a clear night, and the risen moon, large and low, flung a rippling streak of silver across the sea. On the other side of the bay, all was bathed in a violet haze, which veiled the inlet from which he had started in the morning. The fire of the exiles, hidden behind a point of rock, cast into the air a red glow. The ocean breakers, rolling in upon the cliffs outside the Bar, filled the air with a hoarse and threatening murmur; and the rising tide rippled and lapped with treacherous melody along the sand. He touched the chill water and drew back. For an instant he determined to wait until the beams of morning should illumine that beautiful but treacherous sea, and then the thought of the helpless child, who was, without doubt, waiting and watching for him on the shore, gave new strength to his wearied frame; and fixing his eyes on the tiny glow that, hovering above the dark tree line, marked her presence, he pushed the raft before him into the sea.

The reeds sustained him bravely, but the strength of the current sucked him underneath the water, and for several seconds he feared that he would be compelled to let go his hold. But his muscles, steeled in the slow fire of convict-labour, withstood this last strain upon them, and, half-suffocated, with bursting chest and paralyzed fingers, he preserved his position; until the mass, getting out of the eddies along the shore line, drifted steadily down the silvery track that led to the settlement. After a few moments' rest, he set his teeth and urged his strange canoe towards the shore. Paddling and pushing, he gradually edged it towards the fire-light; and at last, just when his stiffened limbs refused to obey the impulse of his will, and he began to drift onwards with the onward tide, he felt his feet strike firm ground. Opening his eyes – closed in the desperation of his last efforts – he found himself safe under the lee of the rugged promontory that hid the fire. It seemed that the waves, tired of persecuting him, had, with disdainful pity, cast him ashore at the very goal of all his hopes. Looking back, he for the first time realised the frightful peril he had escaped, and shuddered. Then to this shudder succeeded a thrill of triumph. 'Why had he stayed so long, when escape was so easy?'

Dragging the carcases out of reach of the advancing tide he rounded the little promontory and made for the fire. The recollection of the night when he had first approached it came upon him and increased his exultation. How different a man was he now to then! Passing up the sand, he saw the stakes which he had directed Frere to cut, whiten in the moonshine. His officer worked for him! In his own brain alone lay the secret of escape. He – Rufus Dawes – the scarred, degraded 'prisoner', could alone get these three beings back to civilization. Did he refuse to aid them, they would for ever remain in that prison, where he had so long suffered. The tables were turned – he had become a Gaoler!

He had gained the fire before the solitary watcher there heard his footsteps, and spread his hands to the blaze in silence. He felt as Frere would have felt had their positions been reversed – disdainful of the man who had stopped at home.

Frere, starting, cries, 'It is you! Have you succeeded?'

Rufus Dawes nodded.

'Ah!'

'Of course!'

'What! Did you catch them?'

'There are six carcases down by the rocks. You can have meat for breakfast tomorrow!'

The child, at the sound of the voice, came running down from the hut.

'Oh, Mr Dawes! I am so glad! We were beginning to despair – mamma and I.'

Dawes snatched her from the ground, and bursting into a laugh, swung up the little body in the air.

'Tell me,' he cried, holding up the child with two dripping arms above him — 'what you will do for me if I bring you and mamma safe home again?'

'Give you a free pardon,' says Dora, 'and Papa shall make you his servant!'

Frere burst out laughing at this reply; and Dawes, with a choking sensation in his throat, put the child upon the ground, and walked away.

This was in truth all he could hope for. All his scheming, all his courage, all his peril, would but result in the patronage of a great man like Major Vickers. His heart, big with love and self-denial, and hopes of a fair future, would have this flattering unction laid to it. He had performed a prodigy of skill and daring, and for his reward he was to be made — a servant to the creatures he had protected. Yet what more could a convict expect?

Dora saw how deeply her unconscious hand had driven the iron, and ran up to the man she had wounded.

'And, Mr Dawes, remember that I shall love you always.'

The miserable man, however, his momentary excitation over, motioned her away; and she saw him stretch himself wearily under the shadow of a rock.

Frere heard the sentence, and frowned. The child had never spoken to *him* in such tender tones.

↔ *16* ↔

THE CORACLE

IN the morning, however, Rufus Dawes was first at work, and made no allusion to the scene of the previous evening. It was evident that if he felt at all, his pride would not let him show any outward sign of annoyance; but Frere fancied that his manner was gruffer than usual.

He had already skinned one of the goats, and motioned to Frere to set to work upon another.

'Cut down the rump to the hock, and down the brisket to the knee,' he said. 'I want the hides as square as possible.'

By dint of hard work they got the four goats skinned, and the entrails cleaned ready for twisting, by breakfast time; and having boiled some of the flesh, made a hearty meal.

Mrs Vickers being still no better, Dawes went to see her, and seemed to have made friends again with Dora, for he came out of the hut with the child's hand in his. Frere, who was cutting the meat in long strips to dry it in the sun, saw this, and it added fresh fuel to the unreasonable fire of envy and jealousy that he had kindled for himself. However, he said nothing, for his enemy had not yet shown him how the boat was to be made. Before midday, however, he was a partner in the secret, which, after all, was a very simple one.

Rufus Dawes took first two of the straightest and most taper of the celery-top pines which Frere had cut on the previous day, and lashed them tightly together, with the butts outwards. He thus produced a spliced stick about twelve feet long. About two feet from either end, he notched the young tree until he could bend the extremities upwards, and having so bent them, he secured the bent portions in their places by means of lashings of raw hide. The spliced trees now presented a rude outline of the section of a boat, having the stem, keel and stern all in one piece.

This having been placed lengthwise between the stakes, four more poles, notched in two places, were lashed from stake to stake, thus running crosswise to the keel, and forming the knees.

Four more saplings were now bent from end to end of the upturned portions of the keel that represented stem and stern. Two of these four were placed above, as gunwales; two below, as bottom rails. At each intersection the sticks were lashed firmly with fishing-line. The whole framework being complete, the stakes were drawn out, and there lay upon the ground the skeleton of a boat eight feet long by three broad.

Frere, whose hands were blistered and sore, would fain have rested; but the convict would not hear of it.

'Let us finish,' he said, regardless of his own fatigue. 'The skins will be dry if we stop.'

'I can work no more,' says Frere sulkily; 'I can't stand. You've got muscles of iron, I suppose. I haven't.'

'They *made* me work when I couldn't stand, Maurice Frere. It is wonderful what spirit the cat gives a man. There's nothing like work to get rid of aching muscles – so they used to tell me.'

'Well, what's to be done now?'

'Cover the boat. There, you can set the fat to melt, and sew those hides together. Two and two, do you see? and then sew the pair at the necks. There is plenty of catgut yonder.'

'Don't talk to me as if I was a dog!' says Frere suddenly. 'Be civil, can't you?'

But the other, busily trimming and cutting at the projecting pieces of sapling, made no reply. It is possible that he thought the fatigued lieutenant beneath his notice.

About an hour before sundown the hides were ready, and Rufus Dawes, having in the meantime interlaced the ribs of the skeleton with wattles, stretched the skins over it with the hairy side inwards. Along the edges of this covering he bored holes at intervals, and passing through these holes thongs of twisted skin, he drew the whole to the top rail of the boat. One last precaution remained. Dipping the pannikin into the melted tallow, he plentifully anointed the seams of the sewn skins. The boat, thus turned topsy-turvy, looked like a huge walnut-shell covered with red and reeking hide, or the skull of some Titan who had been scalped.

'There!' cried Rufus Dawes, triumphant. 'Twelve hours in the sun to tighten the hides, and she'll swim like a duck.'

Maurice Frere, tired and sulky, did not echo the enthusiasm.

'Don't cry till you're out of the wood,' said he, flinging himself upon the sand. 'You've not got over the Bar yet.'

The next day was spent in minor preparations. The jerked meat was packed securely into as small a compass as possible. The rum barrel was filled with water, and water-bags were improvised out of portions of the intestines of the goats. Rufus Dawes, having filled these last with water, ran a wooden skewer through their mouths, and twisted it tight, tourniquet fashion.

He also stripped cylindrical pieces of bark, and, having sewn each cylinder at the side, fitted to it a bottom of the same material, and caulked the seams with gum and pine-tree resin. Thus four tolerable buckets were obtained. One goatskin yet remained, and out of that it was determined to make a sail.

'The currents are strong,' said Rufus Dawes, 'and we shall not be able to row far with such oars as we have got. If we get a breeze it may save our lives.'

It was impossible to 'step' a mast in the frail basket structure, but this difficulty was overcome by a simple contrivance. From thwart to thwart two poles were bound, and the mast lashed between these poles with thongs of raw hide, was secured by shrouds of twisted fishing-line running fore and aft. Sheets of bark were placed at the bottom of the craft, and made a safe flooring. It was late in the afternoon of the fourth day when these preparations were completed, and it was decided that on the morrow they should adventure the journey.

'We will coast down to the Bar,' said Rufus Dawes, 'and wait for the slack of the tide. I can do no more now.'

Dora had seated herself on a rock at a little distance, and called to them. Her strength was restored by the fresh meat, and her childish spirits had risen with the hope of safety. The mercurial little creature had wreathed seaweed round her head, and holding in her hand a long twig decorated with a tuft of leaves to represent a wand, she personified one of the heroines of her books.

'I am the Queen of the Island,' she said merrily, 'and you are my Humble Servants. Pray, Sir Eglamour, is the Boat ready?'

'It is, your Majesty,' says poor Dawes.

'Then we will see it. Come, walk in front of me. I won't ask you to rub your Nose upon the ground, like Man Friday, because that would be uncomfortable. Mr Frere, you don't Play?'

'Oh, yes!' says Frere, unable to withstand the charming pout that accompanied the words. 'I'll play. What am I to do?'

'You must walk on *this* side, and be Respectful. Of course it is only Pretend, you know,' she added, with a quick consciousness of Frere's conceit. 'Now, then, the Queen goes to the Seashore surrounded by her Nymphs! There is no occasion to laugh, Mr Frere. Of course, Nymphs are very different to *you*, but then we can't help that.'

Marching in this pathetically ridiculous fashion across the sand, they halted at the coracle.

'So that is the Boat!' says the Queen, fairly surprised out of her assumption of dignity. 'You are a Wonderful Man, Mr Dawes!'

Rufus Dawes smiled sadly.

'It is not much to do, after all,' said he. 'I have seen more wonderful things than that done.'

'Have you?' says Dora, with open eyes.

'The chemist I was telling you about – he did more wonderful things than that. Such wonderful things, that I would not believe them when I saw them.'

'And what were they?'

'They seemed as simple as this.'

'Do you call this simple?' says Frere, who in the general joy had shaken off a portion of his sulkiness. 'By George, I don't! This is ship-building with a vengeance, this is. There's no chemistry about this – it's all sheer hard work.'

'Yes!' echoed Dora, 'sheer hard work – sheer hard work by good Mr Dawes!' And she began to sing a sort of childish chant of triumph, drawing lines and letters in the sand the while, with the sceptre of the Queen.

> 'Good Mr Dawes!
> Good Mr Dawes!
> This is the work of Good Mr Dawes!'

Maurice could not resist a sneer.

> 'See-saw, Margery Daw,
> Sold her bed, and lay upon straw!' said he.

'Good Mr Dawes!' repeated Dora, 'Good Mr Dawes! Why shouldn't I say it? You are Disagreeable, Sir. I won't play with you any more,' and she went off along the sand.

'Poor little child,' said Rufus Dawes. 'You speak too harshly to her.'

Frere – now that the boat was made – had regained much of

his self-confidence. Civilization seemed now brought sufficiently close to him to warrant his assuming the position of authority to which his social position entitled him.

'One would think that a boat had never been built before, to hear her talk,' he said. 'If this washing-basket had been one of my uncle's three-deckers, she couldn't have said much more. By the lord,' he added with a coarse laugh, 'I ought to have a natural talent for ship-building; for if the old villain hadn't died when he did, I should have been a ship-builder myself.'

Rufus Dawes turned his back, and seemed to be occupied with the fastenings of the hides. Could the other have seen his face, he would have been struck by its sudden pallor.

'Ah!' continued Frere, half to himself, and half to his companion, 'that's a sum of money to lose, isn't it?'

'What do you mean?' asked the convict, without turning his face.

'Mean! Why, my good fellow, I should have been left a quarter of a million of money, but the old hunks who was going to give it me died before he could alter his will, and every shilling went to a scapegrace son, that hadn't been near the old man for years. That's the way of the world, isn't it?'

Rufus Dawes, still keeping his face away, did not reply for a second or two, and then he said, in a harsh voice,

'A fortunate fellow – that son!'

'Fortunate!' cries Frere, with another oath. 'Yes, d—d fortunate! He was burnt to death in the *Hydaspes,* and never heard a word about his luck. His brother has got the money, though. I never saw a shilling of it.'

And then seemingly displeased with himself for having allowed his tongue to get the better of his dignity, he walked away to the fire, musing, doubtless, upon the difference between Maurice Frere with a quarter of a million disporting himself in the best Old English society that could be procured, with command of dog-carts, prize-fighters, and game-cocks galore; and Maurice Frere, a penniless lieutenant, marooned on the barren coast of Macquarie Harbour, and acting as boatbuilder to a runaway convict.

Rufus Dawes was also lost in reverie. He leant upon the gunwale of the much vaunted boat, and his eyes were fixed upon the sea, weltering golden in the sunset, but it was evident that he saw nothing of the scene before him.

He was looking far away – across the glittering harbour and the wide sea beyond it – looking at the old house at Harwich, with its well-remembered and gloomy garden. He pictured himself escaped from his present peril, and freed from the sordid thraldom which so long had held him. He saw himself returning, with some plausible story of his wanderings to take possession of the wealth which was his. He saw himself, by the aid of the power of wealth, plucking out the heart of the mystery which had condemned him to the felon's chain, and living once more, rich, free, and respected, in the world from which he had been so long an exile. To this vision succeeded others. Pictures of foreign dresses and foreign manners, of houses with high-peaked gables and fantastic extravagance of outline, of cheery, simple 'home life', of great thoughts shaped in the wreathing smoke of a meerschaum pipe-bowl, and taking visible form in a dusty room littered with strange machinery, and instruments of shape unknown to the vulgar. He saw himself – received with tears of joy and marvelling affection – entering into this home circle, as one risen from the dead, and bringing with him the key to a mystery from beyond the grave. A new life – as he had once pictured it – opened radiant before him, and he felt himself lost, as it were, in the contemplation of his own happiness.

So absorbed was he in these reflections, that he did not hear the light footstep of the child across the sand. Mrs Vickers, having been told of the success which had crowned the convict's efforts, had overcome her weakness so far as to hobble down the beach to the boat, and now, heralded by Dora, approached, leaning on the arm of Maurice Frere.

'Mamma has come to see the Boat, Mr Dawes!' cried Dora, but Dawes did not hear her.

The child reiterated her words, but still the silent figure did not reply.

'Mr Dawes!' she cried again, and pulled him by the coat-sleeve.

The touch aroused him, and looking down, he saw the pretty, thin face upturned to his. Scarcely conscious of what he did, and still following out the imagining which made him free, wealthy, and respected, he caught the little creature in his arms – as he might have caught his own daughter – and kissed her.

Dora said nothing; but Mr Frere – arrived, by *his* chain of reasoning, at quite another conclusion as to the state of affairs – was astonished at the presumption of the man. The lieutenant regarded himself as already reinstated in his old position, and with Mrs Vickers on his arm, reproved the apparent insolence of the convict as freely as he would have done had they both been at his own little kingdom of Maria Island.

'You insolent beggar!' he cried. 'Do you dare! Keep your place, sir!'

The sentence recalled Rufus Dawes to reality. His place was that of a convict. What business had he with tenderness for the daughter of his master! Yet, after all he had done, and proposed to do, this harsh judgment upon him seemed cruel. He saw the two looking at the boat he had built. He marked the flush of hope on the cheek of the poor lady, and the full-blown authority that already made hard the eye of Maurice Frere, and all at once he understood the result of what he had done. He had, by his own act, given himself again to bondage. As long as escape was impracticable, he had been useful, and even powerful. Now he had pointed out the way of escape, and he had sunk into the beast of burden once again. In the desert he was 'Mr' Dawes, the saviour; in civilized life he would become once more Rufus Dawes, the murderer, the prisoner, the absconder. He stood mute, and let Frere point out the excellencies of the craft in silence; and then, feeling that the few words of thanks uttered by the lady were chilled by her consciousness of the ill-advised freedom he had taken with the child, he turned on his heel and strode up into the bush.

'A queer fellow,' said Frere, as Mrs Vickers followed the retreating figure with her eyes. 'Always in an ill temper.'

'Poor man! he has behaved very kindly to us,' said Mrs Vickers.

Even she felt the change of circumstances, and knew that, without any reason that she could name, her blind trust and hope in the convict who had saved their lives had been transformed into a patronising kindliness which was quite foreign to esteem or affection.

'Come, let us have some supper,' says Frere. 'The last we shall eat here, I hope. He will come back when his fit of passion is over.'

But he did not come back, and, after a few expressions of wonder at his absence, Mrs Vickers and her daugher, rapt in the sweet hopes and fears of the morrow, almost forgot that he had left them. With marvellous credulity they looked upon the terrible stake they were about to play for as already won. The possession of the boat seemed to them so wonderful, that the perils of the voyage they were to make in it were altogether lost sight of.

As for Maurice Frere, he was only rejoiced that the convict was out of the way. He wished that he was out of the way altogether.

⤛ 17 ⤜

THE WRITING ON THE SAND

HAVING got out of eye shot of the ungrateful creatures he had befriended, Rufus Dawes had thrown himself upon the ground in an agony of mingled rage and regret. He was at the best but of a savage temper, and his long residence among the infamous ruffians of the settlement had increased his natural ferocity. For the first time for six years, he had tasted the happiness of doing good, the delight of self-abnegation. For the first time for six years, he had broken through the selfish misanthropy he had taught himself. For the first time in six years he had placed his own desires second in importance to those of others. And this was his reward !

He had held his temper in check, in order that it might not offend others. He had banished the galling memory of his degradation, lest haply some shadow of it might seem to fall upon the fair child whose lot had been so strangely cast with his. He had stifled the agony he suffered, lest its expression should give pain to those who seemed to feel for him. He had forborne retaliation, when retaliation would have been most sweet. Having all these years waited and watched for a chance to strike his persecutors, he had held his hand now that an unlooked for accident had placed the weapon of destruction in his grasp. He had risked his life, forgone his enmities, almost changed his nature, and his relief had come in the shape of cold looks and harsh words, so soon as his skill and courage had paved the way to freedom.

This knowledge coming upon him while the thrill of exultation he had felt at the astounding news of his riches yet vibrated in his brain, made him grind his teeth with rage at his own hard fate. Cast out, as he imagined, from his home and kindred, he had sought fresh affections; and, strong in the knowledge of those affections, had sacrificed himself to preserve some secret born of the new responsibilities he had undertaken. Believing himself abandoned and disowned, and disdaining in his sore need to crave help from the father whose sternness had driven him from his door, he had condemned himself to a living death, rather than buy his liberty by a revelation which would injure the friends who trusted him. By a strange series of accidents, fortune had assisted him to maintain the deception he had practised. His cousin had not recognized him. His intentional change of handwriting, had baffled the roused suspicions of the lawyer. The very ship in which he was believed to have sailed, had been lost with every soul on board. His identity had been completely destroyed – no link remained which could connect Rufus Dawes the convict, with Richard Devine the vanished heir to the wealth of the dead ship-builder.

Oh, if he had only known! If, while in the gloomy prison, distracted by a thousand fears, and weighed down by crushing evidence of circumstance, he had but guessed that he owned gold enough to blunt the keenest lance of Justice, and to hire the sharpest of those human ferrets trained to hunt guilt through all its burrowing windings, he might have spared himself the sacrifice he had made. No need for him then to reveal whatever mystery it behoved him to guard so jealously. No need for him to tell who and what was his murdered companion. He had been tried and condemned as a nameless sailor, who could call no witnesses in his defence, and give no particulars as to his previous history. He could not but confess that he might have adhered to his statement of ignorance concerning the murdered man, and preserved inviolate the secret of his name and story, and have yet been free. Judges are just, but popular opinion is powerful, and it was not impossible that Richard Devine would have escaped the fate which had overtaken Rufus Dawes.

Into his calculations in the prison — when, half crazed with terror and despair he had counted up his chances of life — the wild supposition that he had inherited the wealth of the father who had disowned him, had never entered. The knowledge of that one fact would have altered the whole current of his life, and he learnt it for the first time now — too late.

Now, lying prone upon the sand; now, wandering aimlesssly up and down among the stunted trees that bristled white beneath the mist-barred moon; now, sitting — as he had sat in the prison so long ago — with his head gripped hard between his hands, swaying his body to and fro, he thought out the frightful problem of his bitter life. Of little use was the heritage that he had gained. A convict-absconder, whose hands were hard with menial service, and whose back was scarred with the lash, could never be received among the gently nurtured. Let him lay claim to his name and rights, what then? He was a convicted felon, and his name and rights had been taken from him by the law. Let him go and tell Maurice Frere that he was his lost cousin. He would be laughed at. Let him proclaim aloud his birth and innocence, and the convict-sheds would grin, and the convict overseer set him to harder labour. Let him even, by dint of re-iteration, get this wild story believed, what would happen? Who would take up the thread where he had broken it, and turn again that hour-glass of Death, whose sands were doubt-less long since blown away and dispersed on a thousand shores? Who would take the trouble to hunt up the personages of the drama that had played itself out six years ago at the Old Bailey?

If it was heard in England — after the lapse of years, perhaps — that a convict in the chain-gang of Macquarie Harbour — a man held to be a murderer, and whose convict career was one long record of mutiny and punishment — claimed to be the heir to an English fortune, and to own the right to dispossess staid and worthy English gentlemen of their land and station, with what feeling would the announcement be received? Certainly not with a desire to redeem this ruffian from his bonds and place him in the honoured seat of his ousted brother. Such intelligence would be regarded as a calamity, an unhappy blot upon a fair reputation, a disgrace to an honoured and unsullied name. Let him succeed, he would be at the best but a living shame.

But success was almost impossible. He did not dare to retrace his steps through the hideous labyrinth into which he had plunged. Was he to show his scarred shoulders as a proof that he was a gentleman and an innocent man? Was he to relate the nameless infamies of Macquarie Harbour as a proof that he was entitled to receive the hospitalities of the generous, and to sit, a respected guest, at the tables of men of refinement? Was he to quote the horrible slang of the prison-ship, and retail the filthy jests of the chain gang and the hulks, to prove that he was a fit companion for pure-minded women and innocent children? All the wealth in the world could not buy back that blissful ignorance of evil he once had owned. All the wealth in the world could not purchase the self-respect that had been cut out of him by the lash, or banish from his brain the memory of his degradation.

For hours this agony of thought racked him. He cried out, as though with physical pain, and then lay in a stupor, as though exhausted with actual physical suffering. It was hopeless to think of freedom and honour. Let him keep silence, and pursue the life fate had marked out for him. He would return to bondage. The law would claim him as an absconder, and would mete out to him such punishment as was fitting. Perhaps he might escape punishment, as a reward for his exertions in saving the child. He might consider himself fortunate if such was permitted to him. Fortunate!

Suppose he did not go at all, but wandered away into the wilderness and died! Better death than such a doom as his. Yet need he die? He had caught goats, he could catch fish. He could build a hut. There was, perchance, at the deserted settlement some remnant of seed corn that, planted, would give him bread. He had built a boat, he had made an oven, he had fenced in a hut. Surely he could contrive to live alone, savage and free.

Alone! Why *live* alone? Was not the boat he had built below

him on the shore? Why not escape in her, and leave to their fate
the miserable creatures who had treated him with such ingratitude?

The idea flashed into his brain, as though someone had spoken
the words into his ear. He had a boat at hand. Twenty strides
would place him in possession of her, and half an hour's drifting with the current would take him beyond pursuit. Once outside the Bar, he would make for the westward, in the hopes of
falling in with some whaler. He would doubtless meet with one
before many days, and he was well supplied with provision and
water in the meantime. A tale of shipwreck would satisfy the
sailors, and – he paused – he had forgotten that the yellow rags
he wore would betray him.

With an exclamation of despair, he started from the posture
in which he was lying. He thrust out his hands to raise himself,
and felt his fingers come in contact with something soft. He had
been lying at the foot of some loose stones that were piled cairn-
wise beside a low-growing bush; and the object that he had
touched was protruding from beneath these stones. He caught it
and dragged it forth. It was the shirt of poor Bates. With
trembling hands he tore away the stones, and pulled forth the
rest of the garments. They seemed as though they had been left
purposely for him. Heaven had sent him the very disguise he
needed!

The night had passed during his reverie, and the first faint
streaks of dawn began to lighten in the sky. Haggard and pale,
he rose to his feet, and scarcely daring to think about what he
proposed to do, ran towards the boat. As he ran, however, the
voice that he had heard seemed to encourage him. 'Your life is
of more importance to you than theirs. You have been falsely
accused; you have the chance to discover the guilty man, and
bring him to justice. They will die, but they have been ungrateful, and deserve death. You will escape out of this Hell, and
become rich as you ought to be. You can do so much good with
your riches. You can do more good to mankind than by saving
the lives of these people who despise you. Besides, they may not
die. They are sure to be sent for. Think of what awaits you
when you return – an absconded convict!'

He was within three feet of the boat, when he suddenly

checked himself, and stood motionless, staring at the sand with as much horror as though he saw there the Writing which foretold the doom of Belteshazzar.

He had come upon the sentence traced by Dora the evening before, and in the grey uncertain light of morning it seemed to him that the letters had shaped themselves at his very feet.

GOOD MR DAWES

'Good Mr Dawes!' What a frightful reproach there was to him in that simple sentence! What a world of cowardice, baseness and cruelty, had not those eleven letters opened to him! He seemed to hear the voice of the child who had nursed him, calling on him to save her. He seemed to see her at that instant standing between him and the boat, as she had stood when she held out to him the loaf, on the night of his return to the settlement.

He reached the cavern, and seizing the sleeping Frere by the arm, shook him violently.

'Awake! awake!' he cried, 'and let us leave this place!'

Frere, starting to his feet, looked at the white face and blood-shot eyes of the wretched man before him with blunt astonishment.

'What's the matter with you, man!' he said. 'You look as if you'd seen a ghost!'

At the sound of his voice, Rufus Dawes gave a long sigh, and drew his hand across his eyes.

'Perhaps I have,' he said.

'Come, Dora!' shouted Frere, 'it's time to get up. I am ready to go!'

The convict turned away, and two great, glistening tears rolled down his rugged face, and fell upon the sand.

AT SEA

An hour after sunrise, the frail boat that was the last hope of these four human beings drifted with the outgoing current towards the mouth of the Harbour.

When first launched she had come nigh swamping, through being overloaded, and it was found necessary to leave behind a great portion of the dried meat. With what pangs this was done can be easily imagined, for each atom of food represented an hour of life. Yet there was no help for it. As Frere said, it was 'neck or nothing with them'. They must get away at all hazards.

That evening they camped at the mouth of the Gates, Dawes being afraid to risk a passage until the slack of the tide, and about ten o'clock at night adventured to cross the Bar. The night was lovely, and the sea calm. It seemed as though Providence had taken pity on them; for, notwithstanding the insecurity of the craft and the violence of the breakers, the dreaded passage was made with safety. Once indeed, when just entered upon the surf, a mighty wave, curling high above them, seemed about to overwhelm the frail structure of skins and wickerwork; but, Rufus Dawes keeping the nose of the boat to the sea, and Frere baling with his hat, they succeeded in reaching deep water. A great misfortune, however, occurred. Two of the bark buckets, left by some unpardonable oversight uncleated, were washed overboard, and with them nearly a fifth of their scanty store of water. In the face of the greater peril this accident seemed trifling; and as, drenched and chilled, they gained the open sea, they could not but admit that Fortune had almost miraculously befriended them.

Having made tedious way with their rude oars, a light breeze from the north-west sprung up with the dawn, and, hoisting the goatskin sail, they crept along the coast.

It was resolved that the two men should keep watch and

watch; and Frere for the second time enforced his authority, by giving the first watch to Rufus Dawes.

'I am tired,' he said, 'and shall have a sleep for a little while.'

Rufus Dawes, who had not slept for two nights, and who had done all the harder work, said nothing. He had suffered so much during the last few days that his senses were becoming dulled to pain.

Frere slept until late in the afternoon, and, when he woke, found the boat still tossing on the sea, and Dora and her mother both seasick. This seemed strange to him. Seasickness appeared to be a malady which belonged exclusively to civilization. Moodily watching the great green waves that curled incessantly between him and the horizon, he marvelled to think how curiously events had come about. A slice had been taken out his life, as it were. It seemed a lifetime since he had done anything else but so moodily scan the sea or shore. Yet, on the morning of leaving the settlement, he had counted the notches on a calendar-stick he carried, and had been astonished to find them but twenty-two in number. Taking out his knife, he cut two nicks in the wicker gunwale of the coracle. That brought him to twenty-four days. The mutiny had taken place on the 13th of January; it was now the 6th of February. 'Surely,' thought he, 'the *Ladybird* might have returned by this time.' Unfortunately, there was no one to tell him that the *Ladybird* had been driven into Port Davey by stress of weather, and detained there for seventeen days.

That night the wind fell, and they had to take to their oars. Rowing all night, they seemed to have made but little progress, and Rufus Dawes suggested that they should put into the shore and wait until the breeze sprang up. But, upon getting under the lee of a long line of basaltic rocks, which rose abruptly out of the sea, they found the waves breaking furiously upon what seemed to be a horse-shoe reef, six or seven miles in length. There was nothing for it but to coast again.

They coasted for two days, without a sign of a sail, and on the third day a great wind broke upon them from the south-east, and drove them back thirty miles. The coracle began to leak, and required constant baling. What was almost worse, the rum-cask, that held the best part of their water had leaked also, and was now half empty. They caulked it, by cutting out the leak and plugging the hole with linen.

'It's lucky we ain't in the tropics,' says Frere, with a sort of desperate consolation.

Poor Mrs Vickers, lying at the bottom of the boat, wrapped in her wet shawl, and chilled to the bone with the bitter wind, had not the heart to reply. Surely the stifling calm of the tropics could not be worse than this bleak and barren sea.

The position of the four poor creatures was now most desperate. Mrs Vickers, indeed, seemed completely prostrated; and it was evident that unless some help came she could not long survive the continued exposure to the weather. The child was in somewhat better case. Rufus Dawes had wrapped her in his woollen shirt, and, unknown to Frere, had divided with her daily his allowance of meat. She lay in his arms at night, and in the day crept by his side for shelter and protection. As long as she was near him, she seemed safe. They spoke little to each other, but when Rufus Dawes felt the pressure of her tiny hand in his, or sustained the weight of her head upon his shoulder, he almost forgot the cold that froze him, and the hunger that gnawed him.

So two more days passed, and yet no sail! On the tenth day after their departure from Macquarie Harbour, they came to the end of their provisions. The salt water had spoiled the meat, and soaked the bread into a nauseous paste. The sea was still running high, and the wind, having veered to the north, was blowing off shore with increased violence. The long low line of coast that still stretched upon their left hand, was at times obscured by a blue mist. The water was the colour of mud, and the sky threatened rain. The wretched craft to which they had entrusted themselves was leaking in four places. If caught in one of the frequent storms that ravaged that iron-bound coast, she could not live an hour. The two men, wearied, hungry and cold, almost hoped for the end to come quickly. To add to their distress, the child was seized with something that resembled fever. She was hot and cold by turns, and in the intervals of moaning talked deliriously. Rufus Dawes, holding her in his arms, watched the suffering he was unable to alleviate, with a savage despair at his heart. Was she to die after all?

Frere had retired to the fore part of the boat, and watched these two with the old selfish jealousy. In the midst of his own torments, he felt the additional pang of seeing the convict preferred before him to the last.

So another day and night passed, and the eleventh morning saw the boat yet alive, rolling in the trough of the same deserted sea. The four exiles lay in her almost without breath.

All at once Dawes uttered a cry, and, seizing the sheet, put the clumsy craft about.

'A sail! a sail!' he cried. 'Do you not see her?'

Frere staggered to his feet, but his hungry eyes ranged the dull water in vain.

'There is no sail, fool!' he said. 'You mock us!'

The boat, no longer following the line of coast, was running nearly due south, straight into the great Southern Ocean. Frere came aft, and tried to wrest the thong from the hand of the convict, and bring the boat back to her course.

'Are you mad,' he asked, in fretful terror, 'to run us out to sea?'

'Sit down!' returned the other, with a menacing gesture, and his eyes staring across the grey water. 'I tell you I see a sail!'

Frere was overawed by the strange light that gleamed in the eyes of his companion, and shifted sulkily back to his place.

'Have your own way,' he said, 'madman! It serves me right for putting off to sea in such a Devil's craft as this.'

After all, what did it matter? As well be drowned in mid-ocean, as in sight of land.

The long day wore out, and no sail appeared. The wind freshened towards evening, and the boat, plunging clumsily into the long brown waves, staggered as though drunk with the water she had swallowed. At one place near the bows the water ran in and out as through a slit in a wine-skin. The coast had altogether disappeared, and the huge ocean – vast, stormy and threatening – heaved and hissed all around them. It seemed impossible that they should live until morning. But Rufus Dawes, with his eyes fixed as if on some object visible alone to him, hugged the child in his arms, and drove the quivering coracle into the black waste of night and sea.

To Frere, sitting sullenly in the bows, this aspect of this grim immovable figure, with its back-blown hair and staring eyes, had in it something supernatural and horrible. He began to think that privation and anxiety had driven the unhappy convict mad.

Thinking and shuddering over his fate, he fell – as it seemed to him – into a momentary sleep, in the midst of which someone called to him. He started up, with shaking knees and bristling hair. The day had broken, and the dawn, in one long pale streak of sickly saffron, lay low on the left hand. Between this streak of saffron-coloured light and the bows of the boat, gleamed for an instant a white speck.

'A sail! a sail!' cries Rufus Dawes, with a wild light gleaming in his eyes, and a strange tone vibrating in his voice. 'Did I not tell you that I saw a sail?'

Frere, utterly confounded, looked again, with his heart in his mouth, and again did the white speck glimmer. For an instant he felt almost safe, and then a blanker despair than before fell upon him.

From the distance at which she was, it was impossible for the ship to sight the boat.

'They will never see us!' he cried. 'Dawes – Dawes! Do you hear? They will never see us!'

Rufus Dawes started as if from a trance. Lashing the sheet to the pole which served as a gunwale, he laid the sleeping child by her mother, and tearing up the strip of bark on which he had been sitting, sprang to the bows of the boat.

'They will see *this*! Tear up that board! So! Now, place it thus across the bows. Hack off that sapling end! Now that dry twist of osier! Never mind the boat, man; we can afford to leave her now. Give me your pea-jacket! Tear off that outer strip of hide! See the wood beneath is dry! Quick – you are so slow.'

'What are you going to do?' cries Frere, aghast, as the convict tore up all the dry wood he could find, and heaped on the sheet of bark on the bows.

'To make a fire! See!'

And he scraped with his knife the hairy lining of the peajacket, collecting the tindery fluff thus obtained, and placing it carefully beneath the shreds and chips of bark.

Frere began to comprehend.

'I have three matches left,' he said, fumbling, with trembling fingers, in his pocket. 'I wrapped them in one of the leaves of the book to keep them dry.'

The word 'book' was a new inspiration. Rufus Dawes sprang back to the stern sheets, and seizing upon the 'English History', which had already done such service, he tore out the drier leaves in the middle of the volume, and carefully added them to the little heap of touchwood.

'Now, steady!'

The match was struck and lighted. The paper, after a few obstinate curlings, caught fire, and Frere blowing the young flame with his breath, the bark began to burn.

He piled upon the fire all that was combustible, the hides began to shrivel, and a great column of black smoke rose up over the sea.

'Dora!' cried Rufus Dawes, 'Dora! My darling! You are saved!'

The child opened her blue eyes and looked at him, but there was no sign of recognition. Delirium had succeeded to fever, and in the hour of safety the child had forgotten her preserver.

Rufus Dawes, overcome by this last cruel stroke of fortune, sat down in the stern of the boat, with the child in his arms, speechless.

Frere, feeding the fire, thought that the chance he had so longed for had come. With the mother at the point of death, and the child delirious, who could testify to this hated convict's skilfulness. No one but Mr Maurice Frere, and Mr Maurice Frere, as a commandant of convicts, could not but give up an 'absconder' to justice.

The ship changed her course, and came towards this strange

fire in the middle of the ocean. The boat, the fore part of her blazing like a pine torch, could not float above an hour. The little group of the convict and the child remained motionless. Mrs Vickers was lying senseless, ignorant even of the approaching succour.

The ship – a brig, with American colours flying – came within hail of them. Frere could almost distinguish figures on her deck. He walked aft to where Dawes was sitting, unconscious, with the child in his arms, and stirred him roughly with his foot.

'Go forward,' he said, in tones of command, 'and give the child to me.'

Rufus Dawes raised his head with a snarl, and then seeing the approaching vessel, seemed to awake to the consciousness of his duty. With a low laugh, that was full of unutterable bitterness, he placed the burden he had borne so tenderly, in the arms of the lieutenant, and moved to the blazing bows.

The brig was close upon them. Her canvas loomed large and dusky, shadowing the sea. Her wet decks shone in the morning sunlight. From her bulwarks peered bearded and eager faces, looking with astonishment at this burning boat and its haggard company, alone on that barren and stormy ocean.

Frere, with Dora in his arms, waited for her.

BOOK FOUR

++ 2 ++

A LABOURER IN THE VINEYARD

'SOCIETY in Hobart Town, in the year of grace 1838, is, my dear lord, composed of very curious demands.'

So ran a passage in the sparkling letter which the Rev. Mr Meekin, newly-appointed chaplain, and seven-days' resident in Van Diemen's Land, was carrying to the post-office, for the delectation of his patron in England.

As the reverend gentleman tripped daintily down the summer street that lay between the blue river and the purple mountain, he cast his mild eyes hither and thither upon human nature, and the sentence he had just penned recurred to him with pleasurable appositeness. Elbowed by well-dressed officers of garrison, bowing sweetly to well-dressed ladies, shrinking from ill-dressed, ill-odoured ticket-of-leave men, or hastening across a street to avoid being run down by the hand-carts that, driven by little gangs of grey-clothed convicts, rattled and jangled at him unexpectedly from behind corners, he certainly felt that the society through which he moved was composed of curious elements. Now passed, with haughty nose in the air, a newly-imported government official, relaxing for an instant his rigidity of demeanour to smile languidly at the chaplain whom Sir John Franklin delighted to honour; now swaggered, with coarse defiance of gentility and patronage, a wealthy ex-prisoner, grown fat on the profits of rum. The population that was abroad on that sunny December afternoon had certainly an incongruous appearance to a dapper clergyman lately arrived from London, and missing, for the first time in his sleek, easy-going life, those social screens which in London civilisation decorously conceal the frailties and vices of human nature. Clad in glossy black of the most fashionable clerical cut, with dandy boots, and gloves of lightest lavender, – a white silk overcoat encouragingly hinting that its wearer was not wholly free from fleshly weaknesses of sun and heat – the Reverend Meekin tripped daintily to the post-office and deposited his letter. Two ladies met him as he turned.

'Mr Meekin!'

Mr Meekin's elegant hat was raised from his intellectual brow and hovered in the air, like some courteous black bird, for an instant.

'Mrs Jellicoe! Mrs Protherick! Me dear leddies, this *is* an unexpected pleasure.'

'We were coming to post our letters for the mail,' said Mrs Jellicoe, a fat and merry woman, not without a twang of vulgarity in her fatness and merriment, 'and I thought I recognized your Back! I said to Mrs Protherick, that's Mr Meekin's Back among a thousand! Didn't I, Mrs Protherick?'

Mrs Protherick, a tall and stately lady, the widow of a late Comptroller of Customs, and, as such, of loftier rank than Mrs Jellicoe, who was only the wife of a Superintendent of Convicts' Barracks, bent an iron neck in reply.

'*I* recognized you at once, dear Mr Meekin. We were just talking of you.'

'Indeed! And here I am!' returned Mr Meekin, smiling with prim sweetness. 'Ah! how often in our wondrous life do such coincidences occur?'

'Talk of the – ahem, you know,' says Mrs Jellicoe, cheerfully, 'and he's sure to appear!'

The comparison was a little out of place, and, perhaps, the Reverend Meekin felt it to be so, for he hastened to change the conversation.

'And where, my dear leddies, are you going on this lovely afternoon? To stay in the house is positively sinful. Ah! what a climate, – but the Trail of the serpent, my dear Mrs Protherick – the Trail of the serpent –'

Mrs Protherick evidently did not understand the allusion, and the Reverend Meekin, in no wise abashed, added, by way of explanation.

'Is over it all. You remember the delightful lines of Moore? Poor Thomas!'

'I do not admire Moore,' said Mrs Protherick, corrugating

her iron, so to speak. 'I am afraid he was an Unbeliever, Mr Meekin.'

The Reverend Meekin sighed.

'He moved in the best society,' said he, as though that fact was enough to stamp Moore as orthodox – 'the best society. But, then, his temperament was ardent. He burnt his candle at both ends, dear leddies – at both ends. Indeed, I am afraid that the Flight of Fancy induced him to melt it in the middle.'

The sentence seemed to please him, for he repeated again, softly, 'melt it in the middle.'

'Bless my soul!' said honest Mrs Jellicoe. 'What extravagance! Did you know him, Mr Meekin?'

'Oh yes,' said Mr Meekin, with an air as though an affirmative reply was unnecessary, 'I met him at the Bishop's,' and he sighed again.

'It must be a great trial to you to come to the colony,' said Mrs Jellicoe, sympathizing with the sigh, as Meekin intended that she should sympathize. 'To leave all your friends, and – Bishops, Mr Meekin.'

Meekin smiled, as a gentlemanly martyr might have smiled.

'The Lord's work, dear leddies – the Lord's work. I am but a poor labourer in the vineyard, toiling through the heat and burden of the day.'

The aspect of him, as he stood under the post-office verandah, with his faultless tie, his airy coat, his natty boots, and his self-satisfied Christian smile, was so unlike a poor labourer toiling through the heat and burden of the day, that good Mrs Jellicoe felt a horrible thrill of momentary heresy.

'I would rather have remained at home,' continued Mr Meekin, smoothing one lavender finger with the tip of another, and arching his elegant eyebrows in mild deprecation of any praise for his self-denial, 'but I felt it my duty not to refuse the offer made me through the kindness of his lordship. Here is a field, leddies – a field for the Christian pastor. They appeal to me, leddies, these lambs of our Church – these lost and outcast lambs of our Church.'

A rumbling hand-cart, half dragged half pushed by six leather-capped ironed convicts, halted opposite to them as he spoke, as though to point the illustration he had made.

'Here they are, leddies,' said Mr Meekin, indicating them with lavender finger. 'Poor dreadful creatures; and yet Souls, dear leddies – Souls.'

The hand-cart, coming in violent contact with a stone, had precipitated the foremost Soul – a Soul in parti-coloured livery – at the feet of the Christian pastor, and the fall jerked out from the Soul's lips a torrent of blasphemy.

'Now, then!' says the convict constable, with an admonitory oath. 'None o' that! No swearin'. Don't yer see the gentlefolks, d—n yer?'

'Dear, dear,' said the Reverend Meekin, feeling called upon by this accident to vindicate his holy office. 'This is very dreadful. My good man, why this uncalled-for profanity?'

The good man, picking at a pebble that had been driven into his palm by the fall, touched his cap and said nothing.

'A trifling accident like this,' went on the dainty labourer in this dreary and unpromising vineyard, 'to cause such horrible language! I am astonished! Do you know that not a sparrow falls to the ground without the direct permission of Providence? Have you ever *heard* of Providence? Do you know that Providence is at this moment watching over you?'

The gang leant up against their cart, grateful for the chance of breathing, and grinned to each other. The overseer scowled furiously at the Soul, but the Soul, pulling off his cap as he had been taught to do, and wiping the sweat from his brow with the back of the uninjured hand, only looked up into the sky, as if he expected to see a visible and material Providence watching there. Failing to perceive anything but blinding blue, his eyes came down again, and after wandering a little, settled upon the convict constable as the nearest approach to a Providence that they could discover.

'Are you not aware of a Beneficent Being,' went on Mr Meekin, with a pulpit glance at the two ladies, 'who loves you and guards you?'

The convict's great mouth slowly widened, and into his dull eyes, resting upon the constable's loaded carbine, came a lurid gleam of brutal scorn, but still he did not answer.

'Come,' says Mr Meekin, in sprightly annoyance at the Soul's stupidity, 'do you ever think of God, my good fellow?'

The newly-enlightened eyes, looking from the constable to Mr Meekin and from Mr Meekin to the hand-cart, appeared to take in the position of things. The new parson was 'gaffering' to his friends.

'Bless yer,' says the Soul, with a sort of pitying insolence, '*we* ain't got no time for such things as them.'

Mr Meekin, horrified into graceful uplifting of the lavender gloves, turned to the overseer.

'This is very dreadful, overseer,' he said. 'Have these poor creatures *no* religious instruction? I understood that *all* the prisoners attended Divine Service, and were made acquainted with the rites of our Holy Church?'

'So they does, your reverence,' said the overseer, with a lambent grin flickering over his features, 'but this one's a regular bad one. He won't confess to nothing, he won't. He has his Sunday prayers like the rest of 'em; but what good do they do *him*?'

'Don't speak like that, my good man,' returns Meekin, with a sidelong shake of the head. 'They are consoling – most consoling. Oh! this is very dreadful. Take him away.'

Mrs Jellicoe, accustomed to the ways of convicts, shook her gay bonnet ribbons at Mr Meekin, with a hearty smile.

'You don't know our convicts,' she said (from the tone of her jolly voice, it might have been 'our cattle'). 'They are horrible creatures. And as for servants – my goodness, I have a fresh one every week. When you have been here a little longer, you will know them better, Mr Meekin.'

'They are quite unbearable at times,' said Mrs Protherick, with a stately indignation mantling in her sallow cheeks. 'I am ordinarily the most patient creature breathing, but I *do* confess that the stupid, vicious wretches that one gets are enough to put a saint out of temper.'

'We have all our crosses, dear leddies – all our crosses,' said Mr Meekin, piously. 'Heaven send us strength to bear them! *Good*-morning.'

'Why, you are going our way,' says Mrs Jellicoe. 'We can walk together.'

'Delighted! I am going to call on Major Vickers.'

'And I live within a stone's throw,' returned the wife of the

Superintendent of Convict Barracks. 'What a charming little creature she is, isn't she?'

'Who?' asked Mr Meekin, as they walked.

'Dora – my Pet. You don't know her! Oh, a dear little thing.'

'I have only met Major Vickers at Government House,' says Meekin. 'I haven't yet had the pleasure of seeing his daughter.'

'A sad thing,' says Mrs Jellicoe. 'Quite a romance, if it was not so sad, you know. His wife, poor Mrs Vickers.'

'Indeed! What of her?' asked Meekin, bestowing a condescending bow on a passer-by. 'Is she an invalid?'

'She is dead, poor soul,' returned jolly Mrs Jellicoe, with a fat sigh. 'You don't mean to say that you haven't heard the story, Mr Meekin?'

'My dear leddies, I have only been in Hobart Town a week, and I have not heard the story.'

'You don't say so!' says Mrs Protherick.

'It's about the mutiny, you know,' said Mrs Jellicoe, as the trio neared a low but roomy house in Macquarie-street. 'The mutiny at Macquarie Harbour. The prisoners took the ship, and put Mrs Vickers and Dora ashore somewhere. Captain Frere was with them, too. The poor things had a dreadful time, and nearly died. Captain Frere made a boat at last, and they were picked up by a ship. Poor Mrs Vickers only lived a few hours, and little Dora – she was only eleven years old then – was quite light-headed, the little soul. They thought she wouldn't recover.'

'How dreadful! And has she recovered?'

'Oh yes, she's quite strong now, but her memory's gone.'

'Her memory?'

'Yes,' struck in Mrs Protherick, eager to have a share in the story-telling. 'She doesn't remember anything about the three or four weeks they were ashore – at least not distinctly. And she says the most extraordinary things at times. Quite an Original, Mr Meekin, I assure you.'

'She's a Dear!' interrupted Mrs Jellicoe, determined to keep the post of honour, 'and it's a great Mercy. Who wants her to remember these horrors? From Captain Frere's account, it was positively awful.'

'You don't say so!' said Mr Meekin, dabbing his nose with dainty handkerchief.

'A "bolter" – that's what we call an escaped prisoner, Mr Meekin – happened to be left behind, and he found them out, and insisted on sharing the provisions – the wretch! Captain Frere was obliged to watch him constantly for fear he should murder them. Even in the boat, he tried to run them out to sea, and escape. He was one of the worst men in the Harbour, they say; but you should hear Captain Frere tell the story.'

'And where is he now?' asked Mr Meekin, with interest.

'Captain Frere?'

'No, the prisoner.'

'Oh goodness, I don't know – at Port Arthur, I think. I know that he was tried for bolting, and would have been hanged but for Captain Frere's exertions.'

'Dear, dear! a strange story, indeed,' said Mr Meekin. 'And so the young lady doesn't know anything about it?'

'Only what she has been told, of course, poor dear. She's engaged to Captain Frere.'

'Really! To the man who saved her. How charming – quite a romance!'

'Isn't it?' said Mrs Jellicoe, her good-humoured face in a flame with the exertion of walking. 'Everybody says so. And Captain Frere's so much older than she is.'

'But her girlish love clings to her heroic protector,' says Meekin, pausing at the door, and beaming mildly poetical again. 'Remarkable and beautiful. Quite the – hem! – the ivy and the oak, dear leddies. Ah, in our fallen nature, what sweet spots – I think *this* is the gate.'

'Give her my love,' says Mrs Jellicoe, holding out a fat hand.

'And Mrs Protherick's kind regards,' says that majestic creature.

'I will, dear leddies – I will. Love and kind regards. Once more, then, *good* morning.'

'A most superior man!' said the widow of the Comptroller of Customs.

'So aristocratic!' said the wife of the Superintendent of Convict Barracks.

'One seldom sees so aristocratic a clergyman.'

'He was chaplain to the Bishop of Brandywine, I believe,'

said vulgar Mrs Jellicoe. 'It is so nice to have such men in the colonies.'

'Yes, indeed; they should raise the moral tone of society,' said aristocratic Mrs Protherick.

And as they spoke, the convict cart, which had attracted the attention of the Reverend Mr Meekin, jangled round the opposite corner.

The man who 'had no time to think about them things,' saw the two ladies, and their presence seemed to remind him of his recent interview, for he turned to his next neighbour, and a silent laugh ran round the gang.

↤ 2 ↦

MR MEEKIN FEELS OUT OF PLACE

THE smart convict-servant – he had been a pickpocket of note in days gone by – left the Reverend Mr Meekin to repose in a handsomely furnished drawing-room, whose sunblinds revealed a wealth of bright garden flecked with shadows, while he went in search of Miss Vickers.

The Major was out, it seemed, his duties as Superintendent of Convicts rendering such absences necessary; but Miss Vickers was in the garden, and could be called in at once.

The Reverend Meekin, wiping his heated brow, and pulling down his spotless wristbands, laid himself back on the soft sofa, soothed by the elegant surroundings no less than by the coolness of the atmosphere. Having no better comparison at hand, he compared this luxurious room, with its soft couches, brilliant flowers, and opened piano, to the chamber in the house of a West India planter, where all was glare and heat and barbarism without, and all soft and cool and luxurious within. He was so charmed with this comparison – he had a knack of being easily pleased with his own thoughts – that he commenced to turn a fresh sentence for the Bishop, and to sketch out an eloquent description of the oasis in his desert of vineyard. While at this occupation, he was disturbed by the sound of voices in the garden; and it appeared to him that someone near at hand was sobbing and crying. Softly stepping on to the broad verandah, he saw, on the grass-plat, two persons – an old man and a young girl. The sobbing proceeded from the old man.

' 'Deed, Miss, it's the truth, on my soul. I've but jest come back to yez this morning. O my! but it's a cruel thrick to play an ould man.'

He was a white-haired old fellow, in a grey suit of convict frieze, and stood leaning with one venous hand upon the pedestal of a vase of roses.

'But it is your own fault, Danny – we all warned you against her,' said the young lady, softly.

'Sure ye did. But oh! how did I think it, Miss? This is the second time she served me so. Sure an' she let me alone, I wouldn't ha' throubled her long, the creature.'

'How long was it, Danny?'

'Six months, Miss. She said I was a drunkard, and beat her. Beat her, God help me!' stretching forth two trembling hands. 'And they believed her, o' coorse. Now, when I kem back, there's me little place all thrampled by the boys, and she's away wid a ship's captain, saving your presence, miss, dhrinking in the George the Fourth. O my, but it's hard on an auld man!' and he fell to sobbing again.

The girl sighed.

'I can do nothing for you, Danny. I dare say you can work about the garden as you did before. I'll speak to the Major when he comes home.'

Danny, lifting his bleared eyes to thank her, caught sight of Mr Meekin, and saluted abruptly.

The girl turned round, and Mr Meekin, bowing his apologies, became conscious that her eyes were very large and soft, and her hair very plentiful and bright, and that the hand which held a little book she had been reading was very white and small.

'Miss Vickers, I think. My name is Meekin – the Reverend Arthur Meekin.'

'How do you do, Mr Meekin?' says Dora, putting out one of the small hands, and looking straight at him. 'Papa will be in directly.'

'His daughter more than compensates for his absence, my dear Miss Vickers,' says Meekin, smiling, with all the whiteness of his teeth, at her.

Dora pouted.

'I don't like flattery, Mr Meekin, so don't use it. At least,' she added, with a delicious frankness, that seemed born of her very brightness and beauty, 'not *that* sort of flattery. Young girls *do* like flattery, of course. Don't you think so?'

This rapid attack quite disconcerted Mr Meekin, and he could only bow and smile at the self-possessed young lady.

'Go into the kitchen, Danny, and tell Pagthorne to give you some tobacco. Say *I* sent you. Mr Meekin, won't you come in?'

Mr Meekin getting leisure by this to observe the whiteness of her muslin dress, and the youthful curves of her slight figure, felt emboldened to remark upon the conversation he had heard.

'A strange old gentleman that, Miss Vickers,' he said. 'A faithful retainer, I presume?'

'An old convict servant of ours,' said Dora. 'He was with papa many years ago. He has got into trouble lately, though, poor old man.'

'Into trouble?' asked Mr Meekin, as Dora took off her hat and motioned him to a seat.

'On the roads, you know. That's what they call it here. He married a free woman much younger than himself, and she makes him drink and then gives him in charge for insubordination.'

'For insubordination! Pardon me, my dear young lady, did I understand you rightly?'

'Yes, insubordination. He is her assigned servant, you know,' said Dora, as if such a condition of things was the most ordinary in the world; 'and if he misbehaves himself she sends him back to the road-gang.'

The Reverend Mr Meekin opened his blue eyes very wide indeed.

'What an extraordinary anomaly! I am beginning, my dear Miss Vickers, to find myself indeed at the antipodes.'

'Society here is different from society in England, I believe. Most new arrivals say so,' returned Dora, quietly.

'But for a wife to imprison her husband, my dear young lady !'

'She can have him flogged if she likes,' says Dora, with a smile. 'Danny has been flogged. But then his wife is a bad woman, and lives with other men half the time. She is younger than he. He was very silly to marry her; but you can't reason with an old man in love, Mr Meekin.'

Mr Meekin's christian brow had grown crimson, and his decorous blood tingled to his finger tips. To hear a young lady, apparently of the best breeding and education, talk of the seventh commandment in such an open way, was terrible. Why, in reading the Decalogue from the altar, Mr Meekin was accustomed to soften that indecent prohibition, lest its uncompromising plainness of speech might offend the delicate sensibilities of his female Souls !

He turned from the dangerous theme without an instant's pause for wonder at the strange power accorded to Hobart Town 'free' wives.

'You have been reading?'

' "Paul et Virginie." I have read it before in English.'

'Ah, you read French, then, my dear young lady?'

'Not very well. I had a master for some months, but papa had to send him back to the jail again. He stole a silver tankard out of the dining-room, and pawned it.'

'A French master ! Pawn – !'

'He was a prisoner, you know. A clever man. He wrote for the *London Magazine*. I have read his writings. Some of them are beautiful.'

'And how did he come to be transported?' asked Mr Meekin, feeling that his vineyard was getting larger than he had anticipated.

'Poisoning his niece, I think, but I forget the particulars. He was a gentlemanly man, but, oh, such a drunkard !'

Mr Meekin, more astonished at this strange country, where beautiful young ladies talked of poisoning and flogging as matters of little moment, where wives imprisoned their husbands, and murderers taught French, perfumed the air with his London-bought cambric in silence.

'You have not been here long, Mr Meekin,' says Dora.

'No, only a week,' says Meekin; 'and, I confess, I am surprised. A lovely climate, but, as I said just now to Mrs Jellicoe, the Trail of the Serpent – the Trail of the Serpent – my dear young lady.'

'If you send all the wretches in England here, you must expect the trail of the serpent,' says Dora. 'It isn't the fault of the colony.'

'Oh, no; certainly not,' returns Meekin, hastening to apologize. 'But it is very shocking.'

'But you gentlemen should make it better. I don't know what the penal settlements are like, but the prisoners here have not much inducement to become good men.'

'They have the beautiful Liturgy of our Holy Church read to them twice every week, my dear young lady,' says Mr Meekin, as who should solemnly say, 'If that doesn't reform them, what will?'

'Oh, yes,' returned Dora, 'they have that, certainly; but that is only on Sundays. But don't let us talk about this, Mr Meekin,' she added, pushing back a stray curl of golden hair. 'Papa says that I am not to talk about these things, because they are all done according to the Rules of the Service, as he calls it.'

'An admirable notion of papa's,' says Meekin, with pious patronage, condescendingly changing the conversation. 'And what do you think of Paul? Is he not charming?'

'No,' says Dora, 'I don't think he is.'

'No! Why, my dear young lady, it is a lovely story – one of the most pure and delightful books that can be imagined. Not like Paul! I *am* surprised.'

'It doesn't strike me as pure, at all,' says Dora – 'all that nonsense about not carrying the girl over the water because she must show her legs. Girls *have* legs, I suppose?'

'I – I – I suppose so,' says Meekin, jerking his chair a little further back, as if the fact had never occurred to him before, and had come upon him now with the force of an alarming and terrible discovery. 'Of course they have legs, my dear Miss Vickers. Oh, decidedly!'

'Well,' says Dora, 'it being necessary to show them, why not show them? There was no need for her to Flourish them at people, you know – I don't mean that.'

Mr Meekin, with an agonised smile, intimated that he never thought that she could have meant anything so improper.

'But to make the fuss that is made here,' says Dora, tapping the book, 'is silly, I think – more than silly, it's rude. I mean it makes a great mystery out of a very innocent matter. I don't think St Pierre was an innocent-minded man – do you, Mr Meekin?'

Mr Meekin, driven into a corner by this question, said from out his handkerchief, that he had not given 'that consideration to the subject which it merited,' and prepared to take his leave. This colonial-bred young lady, who didn't see any harm in showing her legs, and thought the author of 'Paul and Virginia' a nasty-minded man, was a being quite foreign to his experience. He felt as if he was in that room with a bombshell, which might explode at any moment. What might not this self-possessed young person say next?

Just as he had arisen, and with his hat held as a sort of shield before him, prepared to shake hands with her, the door opened, and Vickers and Frere entered.

Vickers's hair had grown white, but Frere carried his thirty years as easily as some men carry five-and-twenty.

'My dear Dora,' cries Vickers, 'here's an extraordinary thing!' and then, becoming conscious of the presence of the agitated Meekin, he paused.

'You know Mr Meekin, papa?' says Dora. 'Mr Meekin, Captain Frere.'

'I have that pleasure,' says Vickers. 'Glad to see you, sir. Pray sit down.'

Upon which, Mr Meekin witnessed Dora unaffectedly kiss both gentlemen; but became strangely aware that the kiss bestowed upon her father was warmer than that which greeted her affianced husband.

'Warm weather, Mr Meekin,' says Frere. 'Dora, my darling, I hope you have not been out in the heat. You have! My dear, I've begged you –'

'It's not hot at all,' says Dora, pettishly. 'Nonsense! I'm not made of Butter – I shan't melt. Thank you, dear, you needn't pull the blind down.' And then, as though angry with herself for her anger, she added, 'You are always thinking of me, Maurice,' and gave him her little hand affectionately.

'It is very oppressive, Captain Frere,' says Meekin; 'and to a stranger, quite enervating.'

'Have a glass of wine,' says Frere, as if the house was his own. 'One wants bucking up a bit in a day like this.'

'Ay, to be sure,' repeated Vickers. 'A glass of wine. Dora, dear, some sherry. I hope she has not been attacking you with her strange theories, Mr Meekin?'

'Oh, dear no; not at all,' returned Meekin, feeling that this charming young lady was evidently regarded as a creature who was not to be judged by ordinary rules. 'We got on famously, my dear Major – quite famously.'

'That's right,' said Vickers. 'She is very plain-spoken is my little girl, and strangers can't understand her sometimes. Can they, Poppet?'

Poppet tossed her head saucily.

'I don't know,' she said. 'Why shouldn't they? But you were going to say something Extraordinary when you came in. What is it, dear?'

'Ah!' says Vickers, with grave face. 'Yes, a most extraordinary thing. They've caught those villains.'

In that little family there were, for conversational purposes, but one set of villains in the world – the Mutineers of the *Osprey*.

'What, you don't mean – ? No, papa!' says Dora, turning round with alarmed face.

'They've got four of them in the bay at this moment – Rex, Barker, Shiers, and Lesly. They are on board the *Lady Jane*. The most extraordinary story I ever heard in my life. The fellows got to China and passed themselves off as shipwrecked sailors. The merchants in Canton got up a subscription, and sent them to London. They were recognized there by old Pine – you remember Doctor Pine, Dora? – who had been surgeon aboard the ship they came out in.'

Dora sat down on the nearest chair, with heightened colour.

'And where are the others?'

'Two were executed in England; the other six have not been taken. These fellows have been sent out for trial.'

'To what are you alluding, dear sir?' asked Meekin, eyeing the sherry with the gaze of a fasting saint.

'The piracy of a convict brig five years ago,' says Vickers. 'The scoundrels put my poor wife and child ashore, and left them to starve. If it hadn't been for Frere — God bless him — they would have starved. They shot the pilot and a soldier — and — but it's a long story to tell now.'

'I have heard of it already,' said Meekin, sipping the sherry, which another convict servant had brought for him; 'and of your gallant conduct, Captain Frere.'

'Oh, that's nothing,' says Frere, reddening. 'We were all in the same boat. Poppet, have a glass of wine?'

'No,' says Dora, 'I don't want any.'

She was staring at the strip of sunshine between the verandah and the blind, as though the bright light might enable her to remember something.

'What's the matter?' says Frere, bending over her.

'I was trying to recollect, but I can't, Maurice. It is all confused. I only remember a great shore and a great sea, and two men, one of whom — that's you, dear — carried me in his arms.'

'Dear, dear,' said Mr Meekin.

'She was quite a baby,' said Vickers, hastily, as though unwilling to admit that her illness had been the cause of her forgetfulness.

'Oh, no; I was eleven years old,' says Dora; 'that's not a baby, you know. But I think the fever made me stupid.'

Frere, looking at her uneasily, shifted in his seat.

'There, don't think about it now,' he said.

'Maurice,' asked she suddenly, 'what became of the other man?'

'Which other man?'

'The man who was with us; the other one, you know.'

'Poor Bates?'

'No, not Bates. The prisoner. What was his horrible name?'

'Oh, ah — the prisoner,' said Frere, as if he, too, had forgotten. 'Why, you know darling, he was sent to Port Arthur.'

'Horrible man!' says Dora, with a shudder. 'And is he there still?'

'I believe so,' said Frere, with a frown, as if the subject was distasteful to him.

'By-the-bye,' said Vickers, 'I suppose we shall have to get some of these fellows up for the trial. We have to identify the villains.'

'Can't you and I do that?' says Frere, uneasily

'I am afraid not. I wouldn't like to swear to a man after five years.'

'By George,' says Frere, 'I'd swear to him! When once I see a man's face – that's enough for me.'

'Yes, I know,' said Vickers, with a smile. 'Your memory is proverbial among them.'

'Then there's Troke!'

'We had better get up a few prisoners who were at the Harbour at the time,' says Vickers, as if wishing to terminate the discussion. 'I wouldn't let the villains slip through my fingers for anything.'

'And are the men at Port Arthur old men?' asked Meekin.

'Old convicts,' returned Vickers. 'It's our place for "colonial sentence" men. The worst we have are there. It has taken the place of Macquarie Harbour. What excitement there will be among them when the schooner goes down on Monday!'

'Excitement! Indeed? How charming! Why?' asked Meekin.

'To bring up the witnesses, my dear sir. Most of the prisoners are "lifers," you see, and a trip to Hobart Town is like a holiday for them.'

'And do they never leave the place when sentenced for life?' said Meekin, nibbling a biscuit. 'How distressing!'

'Never, except when they die,' says Frere, with a laugh; 'and then they are buried on an island. Oh, it's a fine place! You should come down with me and have a look at it, Mr Meekin. Picturesque, I can assure you.'

'My dear Maurice,' says Dora, going to the piano, as if in protest to the turn the conversation was taking, 'how can you talk like that?'

'I should much like to see it,' said Meekin, still nibbling, 'for Sir John was saying something about a chaplaincy there, and I understand that the climate is endurable.'

The convict servant, who had entered with some official

paper for the Major, stared at the dainty clergyman, and rough Maurice laughed again.

'Oh, it's a stunning climate,' he said; 'and nothing to do. Just the place for you. There's a regular little colony there. All the scandals in Van Diemen's Land are hatched at Port Arthur.'

This agreeable chatter about scandal and climate seemed a strange contrast to the grave-yard island and the men who were prisoners for life. Perhaps Dora thought so, for she struck a few chords, which, compelling the party, out of sheer politeness, to cease talking for the moment, caused the conversation to flag, and hinted to Mr Meekin that it was time for him to depart.

'Good afternoon, dear Miss Vickers,' he said, rising with his sweetest smile. 'Thank you for your delightful music. That piece is an old, old friend of mine. It was quite a favourite of dear Lady Jane at the Bishop's. Pray excuse me, my dear Captain Frere, but this strange occurrence – of the capture of the wreckers, you know – must be my apology for touching on a delicate subject. How charming to contemplate! Yourself and our dear young lady! The preserved and preserver, dear Major. "None but the brave, you know, none *but* the brave, none but the *brave,* deserve the fair!" You remember glorious John, of course. Well, good afternoon.'

'It's rather a long invitation,' said Vickers, always well disposed to anyone who praised his daughter, 'but if you've nothing better to do, come and dine with us on Christmas Day, Mr Meekin. We usually have a little gathering then.'

'Charmed,' said Mr Meekin – 'charmed, I am sure. It *is* so refreshing to meet with persons of one's own tastes in this delightful colony. "Kindred souls together knit," you know, dear Miss Vickers. Indeed, yes. Once more – *good* afternoon.'

Mercurial Dora burst into laughter as the door closed.

'What a ridiculous creature!' said she. 'Bless the man, with his gloves and his umbrella, and his hair and his scent! Fancy that mincing noodle showing me the way to Heaven! I'd rather have old Mr Bowes, papa, though he is as blind as a beetle, and makes you so angry by Bottling up his Trumps – whatever that is.'

'My dear Dora,' says Vickers, seriously, 'Mr Meekin is a clergyman, you know.'

'Oh, I know,' says Dora; 'but, then, a clergyman can talk like a man, can't he? I felt inclined to scream at him two or three times, with his "dear Miss Vickers." Why do they send such people here? I am sure they could do much better at home. Oh, by the way, papa dear, poor old Danny's come back again. I told him he might go into the kitchen. May he, dear?'

'You'll have the house full of these vagabonds, you little Puss,' says Vickers, kissing her. 'I suppose I must let him stop. What has he been doing now?'

'His wife,' says Dora, 'locked him up, you know, for being drunk. Wife! What do people want with wives, I wonder.'

'Ask Maurice!' said her father, smiling.

Dora jumped away, and tossed her head.

'What does he know about it? Maurice, you are a great Bear; and if you hadn't saved my life, you know, I shouldn't love you a bit. There, you may kiss me' (her voice grew softer). 'This convict business has brought it all back; and I *should* be an ungrateful Wretch if I didn't love you, dear.'

Maurice Frere, with suddenly crimsoned face, accepted the proffered caress. 'God bless you, darling,' he said, and then turned away to the window. A grey-clothed man was working in the garden, and whistling as he worked. 'They're not so badly off, after all,' he said.

'What's that, sir?' asked Dora.

'That I'm not half good enough for you,' says Frere, with sudden vehemence. 'I – I –'

'If you think so, why not give someone else a chance?' says Dora. 'It's *my* happiness that you've got to think of, Captain Bruin. You've saved my life, haven't you, Gruffy? and that's enough for me. I should be a Beast if I didn't love you! No, no more kisses,' she added, putting out her hands. 'Come, Pappy, love, it's cool now, let's walk in the garden, and leave Maurice to think of his own unworthiness.'

Maurice watched the retreating pair with a puzzled expression. 'She always leaves me for her father,' he said to himself. 'I wonder if she really *loves* me, or if it's only gratitude, after all?'

He had often asked himself the same question during the five years of his wooing, but he had never satisfactorily answered it.

⊷ 3 ⊶

SARAH PURFOY THREATENS

THE evening passed as it had passed a hundred times before; and, having smoked a pipe at the barracks, Captain Frere returned home.

His home was a cottage on the New Town road – a cottage which he had occupied since his appointment as Assistant Police Magistrate, an appointment given to him as a reward for his exertions in connection with the *Osprey* mutiny.

Captain Maurice Frere had risen in life. Quartered in Hobart Town, he had assumed a position in society, and had held several of those excellent appointments which in the year 1834 were bestowed upon officers of garrison. He had been Superintendent of Works at Bridgewater, and, when he got his captaincy, Assistant Police Magistrate at Bothwell. The affair of the *Osprey* made a noise; and it was tacitly resolved that the first 'good thing' that fell vacant should be given to the gallant preserver of Major Vickers's child.

Major Vickers also had prospered. He had always been a careful man, and, having saved some money, had purchased land on favourable terms. The 'assignment system' enabled him to cultivate portions of it at a small expense, and, following the usual custom, he stocked his run with cattle and sheep. He had sold his commission, and was now a comparatively wealthy man. He owned a fine estate; the house he lived in was purchased property. He was in good odour at Government House, and his office of Superintendent of Convicts caused him to take an active part in that local government which keeps a man constantly before the public. Major Vickers, a colonist against his will, had become, by force of circumstances, one of the leading men in Van Diemen's Land.

His daughter was a good match for any man; and many ensigns, and lieutenants cursing their hard lot in 'country quarters,' many sons of settlers living on their father's station among the mountains, and many dapper clerks on the civil establishment, envied Maurice Frere his good fortune. Some went so far as to say that the beautiful daughter of 'Regulation Vickers' was too good for the coarse, red-faced Frere, whose past life had not been the most moral, and who was noted for his fondness for low society, and overbearing, almost brutal demeanour. No one denied, however, that Captain Frere was a valuable officer. It was said that, in consequence of his tastes, he knew more about the tricks of convicts than any man on the island. It was said, even, that he was wont to disguise himself, and mix with the pass-holders and convict servants, in order to learn their signs and mysteries. It was his open boast that he knew more convict slang than many of the convicts themselves, and that he was familiar with the names and sentences of the most noted offenders. When in charge at Bridgewater, it had been his delight to rate the chain-gangs in their own hideous jargon, and to astound a new-comer by his knowledge of his previous history. For the rest, he was foremost in all that savoured of old English pastime. A bold rider, and an excellent shot, he rejoiced in all violent exertion. His 'terriers' were the finest-bred on the island; his gamefowls were a proverb among the manumitted poachers and rick-burners who frequented the taverns of Bathurst-street; he was honorary secretary to the racing club; and Mr Nat Facer, of the Three Skittles (lately transported for burglary), sampled the noble science of self-defence under his direct patronage. The convict population hated and cringed to him, for, with his brutality and violence, he mingled a ferocious good humour, that resulted sometimes in tacit permission to go without the letter of the law. Yet, as the convicts themselves said, 'a man was never safe with the Captain;' for, after drinking and joking with them, as Sir Oracle of some public-house whose hostess he delighted to honour, he would disappear through a side-door just as the constables burst in at the back, and show himself as remorseless, in his next morning's sentence of the captured, as if he had never entered a tap-room in all his life. His superiors called this 'zeal;' his inferiors, 'treachery.' For himself, he laughed. 'Everything is fair with those wretches,' he was accustomed to say.

As the time for his marriage approached, however, he had in a measure given up these exploits, and strove, by his demeanour, to make his acquaintances forget several remarkable scandals concerning his private life, for the promulgation of which he had once cared little. As we have said, when Maurice Frere first landed in the colony, certain license was permitted in relation to convict servants, and he had taken full advantage of such license for his own gratification. The Factory Laundry (the 'Suds,' as the women called it) was not in every case a mere place of punishment; and if an officer of garrison chose to hire a convict housemaid from the 'Nelson' hulk, there was nobody to say nay to such a natural proceeding. Moreover, when the assignment system came into force, any person who wanted a female domestic could obtain one by the making of certain depositions, not a whit more restrictive than such checks upon immorality have ever been. Certain houses in Hobart Town – notably the George the Fourth, which Captain Frere had taken under his especial patronage – gave shelter to a larger number of female prisoners than a stranger would judge necessary to the requirements of its domestic service, and it is to be feared that transportation to a country where the males exceeded the females in number by more than a third, and where social obligations were necessarily less stringent than in settled England, did not always give encouragement to sinners to return to virtue.

Before Frere had been Commandant at Maria Island, and for the first two years after his return from the unlucky expedition to Macquarie Harbour, he had not suffered any fear of society's opinion to restrain his natural coarseness of disposition; but, as the affection for the pure young girl, who looked upon him as her saviour from a dreadful death, increased in honest strength, he had resolved to shut up those dark pages in his colonial experience, and to read therein no more. He was not repentant, he was not remorseful, he was not even disgusted. He merely came to the conclusion that when a man married, he was to consider certain extravagances common to all bachelors as at an end. He had 'had his fling, like all young men;' perhaps he had been a fool, like most young men, but no reproachful ghosts of past misdeeds arose to haunt him. His fine old English nature was far too prosaic to admit of the existence of such phantoms. Dora, in her purity and excellence, was so far above him, that in raising his eyes to her, he lost sight of all the sordid creatures to whose level he had once debased himself, and had come in part to regard the sins he had committed, before his redemption by the love of this bright young creature, as sins committed by him under a past condition of existence, and for the consequences of which he was not called upon to be responsible.

One of the consequences, however, was very close to him at this moment. His convict servant had, according to his instructions, sat up for him, and as he entered, handed him a letter, bearing a superscription in a clear and even elegant female hand.

'Who brought this?' asked Frere, hastily tearing it open to read.

'The groom, sir. He said that there was a gentleman at the George the Fourth that wished to see you.'

Frere smiled, as if in admiration of the intelligence which had dictated such a message, and then frowned, as if in anger at the contents of the letter.

'You needn't wait,' he said to the man. 'I shall have to go back again, I suppose.'

Changing his forage cap for a soft hat, and selecting a stick from a miscellaneous collection in a corner, he prepared to retrace his steps.

'What does she want now?' he asked himself fiercely, as he strode down the moonlit road; but beneath the fierceness there was an under current of petulance, which seemed to imply that, whatever she did want, she had a fair right to expect to get.

The George the Fourth was a long, low house, situated in Elizabeth-street. Its front was painted a dull red, and the narrow panes of glass in its windows, and the ostentatious affectation of red curtains and homely comfort, gave to it a spurious appearance of old English jollity. A knot of men round the door melted into air as Captain Frere approached, for it was now past eleven o'clock, and all persons found in the streets after eight could be compelled to 'show their pass' or explain their business. The convict constables were not scrupulous in the exercise of their duty, and the bluff figure of Frere, clad in the blue serge which he affected as a summer costume, looked not unlike that of a convict constable.

Pushing open the side-door with the confident manner of one well acquainted with the house, Frere entered, and made his way along a narrow passage, past a parlour full of noisy drinkers and smokers, to a glass door at the further end. A tap upon this door brought a white-faced, pock-pitted Irish girl, who curtsied with servile recognition of the visitor, and ushered him into a parlour, where a peacock's feather, suspended over a black-framed looking glass, kept watch above a horse-hair sofa and two horse-hair chairs.

'Tell your mistress I'm here,' says Frere, seating himself, 'and look sharp.'

He had not long to wait, for in an instant the servant returned and ushered him upstairs.

The room into which he was now shown was a large one. It had three windows looking into the street, and was handsomely furnished. The carpet was soft, the candles were bright, and a supper tray gleamed invitingly from a table between the windows. As Frere entered, a little terrier ran barking to his feet. It was evident that he was not a constant visitor. The rustle of a silk dress behind the terrier betrayed the presence of a woman; and Frere, rounding the promontory of an ottoman, found himself face to face with Sarah Purfoy.

'Thank you for coming,' she said. 'Pray, sit down.'

This was the only greeting that passed between them, and Frere sat down, in obedience to a motion of a plump hand that twinkled with rings.

The eleven years that had passed since we last saw this woman had dealt gently with her. Her foot was as small and her hand as white as of yore. Her hair, bound close about her head, was plentiful and glossy, and her eyes had lost none of their dangerous brightness. Her figure was certainly coarser, and the white arm that gleamed through a muslin sleeve showed an outline that a fastidious artist might wish to thin. The most noticeable change was in her face. The cheeks owned no longer that delicate purity which they once boasted, but had become thicker, while here and there showed those faint red streaks – as though the rich blood throbbed too painfully in the veins – which are the first signs of the decay of 'fine' women. With middle age had come that fullness of figure to which most creatures of her class are prone; and with it had come also that indescribable vulgarity of speech and manner which habitual absence of moral restraint never fails to produce. With all her sensuous beauty, with all her daring provocation of gesture, glance, and speech, with all the appreciation for colour that was shown in her dress, with all the undeniable talent that lived in her eyes and voice, one felt instinctively that the woman was dangerous, and that the very beauty which gave breadth to her temples, suppleness to her figure, and fire to her eye, was the beauty that would intoxicate, not soothe – would kill, not make alive. A greater contrast than Sarah Purfoy and Dora Vickers could not be imagined. Yet both were women, and in that sad similarity lay the sum of the awful difference between them.

Maurice Frere spoke first, as if anxious to bring his visit to as speedy a termination as possible.

'What do you want of me?' he asked.

Sarah Purfoy laughed. A forced laugh, that sounded so unnatural, that Frere turned to look at her.

'I want you to do me a favour – a very great favour; that is, if it will not put you out of the way.'

'What do you mean?' asks Frere, roughly, pursing his lips with a sullen air. 'Favour! What do you call *this*?' striking the sofa on which he sat. 'Isn't *this* a favour? What do you call your precious house and all that's in it? Isn't that a favour? What do you mean?'

To his utter astonishment, the woman replied by bursting out crying. For some time he regarded her in silence, as if unwilling to be softened by such shallow device, but eventually felt constrained to say something.

'Have you been drinking again?' he asked, 'or what's the matter with you? Tell me what it is you want, and have done with it. I don't know what possessed me to come here at all.'

Sarah sat upright, and dashed away her tears with one passionate hand.

'I am ill, can't you see, you fool,' said she. 'The news has unnerved me. If I have been drinking, what then? It's nothing to you, is it?'

'Oh no,' returned the other, 'it's nothing to me. You are the principal party concerned. If you choose to bloat yourself with brandy, do it by all means.'

'*You* don't pay for it, at any rate,' said she, with that quickness of retaliation which showed that this was not the only occasion on which they had quarrelled.

'Come,' says Frere, impatiently brutal, 'get on. I can't stop here all night.'

She suddenly rose and crossed to where he was standing.

'Maurice, you were very fond of me once.'

'Once,' says Maurice.

'Not so very many years ago.'

'Hang it!' says he, shifting his arm from beneath her hand, 'don't let us have all that stuff over again. It was before you took to drinking and swearing, and going raving mad with passion, any way.'

'Well, dear,' said she, with her great glittering eyes belying the soft tones of her voice, 'I suffered for it, didn't I? Didn't you turn me out into the streets? Didn't you lash me with your whip like a dog? Didn't you put me in gaol for it, eh? It's hard to struggle against you, Maurice.'

The compliment to his obstinacy seemed to please him — perhaps the crafty woman intended that it should — and he smiled.

'Well, there; let old times be old times, Sarah. You haven't done badly, after all,' and he looked round the well-furnished room. 'Is this all yours?'

'All mine?' she laughed. 'No, Captain Frere; nor half of it. I don't know rightly whose it is, but I expect that Abbaddee owns the best part of it. The patronage of the garrison is something, my dear sir, but it is not everything; and there is less money in the town than there used to be.'

'All gone to Port Phillip, I suppose,' says Frere with a sneer. 'If they stop transportation, there'll be less money than ever.'

'There was a transport came in this morning.'

'Well?'

'*You* know who was on board her, Maurice!'

Maurice brought one hand into the palm of the other with a great laugh.

'Oh, that's it, is it? 'Gad, what a flat I was not to think of it before! You want to see him, I suppose?'

She came close to him, and, in her earnestness, took his hand.

'I want to save his life.'

'Oh, that be hanged, you know! Save his life! It can't be done.'

She sank her voice lower.

'You can do it, Maurice.'

'I save John Rex's life?' cried Frere. 'Why, you must be mad!'

'He is the only creature that loves me, Maurice – the only man that cares for me. He has done no harm. He has only wanted to be free – is it not natural? You can save him if you like. I don't ask for his freedom – though I thought he *had* escaped until I heard this afternoon – I only ask for his life. What does it matter to you? – a miserable prisoner – his death would be of no use. Let him live, Maurice.'

Maurice laughed.

'What have I to do with it?'

'You are the principal witness against him. If you say that he behaved well – and he did behave well, you know, many men would have left you to starve – they won't hang him.'

'Oh, won't they! That won't make any difference.'

'Ah, Maurice, be merciful!'

She bent towards him, and tried to retain his hand, but he withdrew it.

'You're a nice sort of woman, to ask me to work for your lover – a man who left me on that cursed coast to die, for all he cared,' he said, with a galling recollection of his humiliation of five years back. 'Save him! Confound him, not I!'

'Ah, Maurice, you will.' She spoke with a suppressed sob in her voice. 'What is it to you? You don't care for me now. You beat me, and turned me of doors, though I never did you wrong. This man was a husband to me – long, long before I met you. He never did you any harm, he never will. He will bless you if you save him, Maurice.'

Frere jerked his head impatiently.

'*Bless* me!' he said. 'I don't want his blessings. Let him swing. Who cares?'

Still she persisted, with tears streaming from her eyes, with white arms upraised, on her knees even, catching at his coat, and beseeching him in broken accents. In her wild fierce beauty, and passionate abandonment, she might have been a deserted Ariadne – a suppliant Medea. Anything rather than what she was – a dissolute, half-maddened woman, praying for the pardon of her convict paramour.

Maurice Frere flung her off with an oath.

'Get up!' he cried brutally, 'and stop that nonsense. I tell you the man's as good as dead for all I do to save him.'

At this repulse, her pent-up passion broke forth. She sprang to her feet, and, pushing back the hair that in her frenzied pleading had fallen about her face, poured out upon him a torrent of abuse.

'You! Who are you, that you dare to speak to me like that? His little finger is worth your whole body. He is a man, a brave man, not a coward like you are. A coward! Yes, a coward! a coward! a coward! You are very brave with defenceless men and weak women. You have beaten me until I was bruised black, you cur; but who ever saw you attack a man unless he was chained or bound? Do not I know you? I have seen you taunt a man at the triangles, until I wished the screaming wretch could get loose, and murder you as you deserved. You will be murdered one of these days, Maurice Frere – take my word for it. Men are flesh and blood, and flesh and blood won't endure the torments you lay on it.'

'There, that'll do,' says Frere, growing paler. 'Don't excite yourself.'

He might have spoken to the chair by which she held, with as much hope of answer.

'I know you, you brutal coward; sensual, malignant, stupid. I have not been your mistress – God forgive me! – without learning you by heart. I've seen your ignorance and your conceit. I've seen the men who ate your food and drank your wine laugh at you. I've heard what your friends say; I've heard the comparisons they make. Learn to spell! learn to write! learn to read! A *magistrate*! A pretty magistrate! How do you spell magistrate? One of your dogs has more brain than you, and twice as much heart. And these are the men they send to *rule* us! Oh, Heaven! And such an animal as this has life and death in his hands! He may hang, may he? I'll hang with him, then, and God will forgive me for murder, for I will kill *you*.'

Frere had cowered ghastly pale before this frightful torrent of blasphemous rage, but, at the scream which accompanied the last words, he stepped forward as though to seize her.

In her desperate courage in her own weakness, she flung herself before him.

'Strike me! You daren't! I defy you! Bring up the wretched creatures who learn the way to Hell in this cursed house, and let them see you do it! Call them! They are old friends of yours. They all know Captain Maurice Frere.'

'Sarah!'

'You remember Lucy Barnes − poor little Lucy Barnes that was "lagged" for stealing sixpennyworth of calico. She is downstairs now. Would you know her if you saw her? She isn't the bright-faced baby she was when they sent her here to "reform," and when Lieutenant Frere wanted a new house-maid from the Factory! Call for her! − call! do you hear? Send for her and your child! Ask any of those beasts whom you lash and chain, for Lucy Barnes. He'll tell you all about her − ay, and about many more − many more poor souls that are at the bidding of any drunken brute that has stolen a pound note to fee the Devil with! Oh, you good God in Heaven, will you not judge this man?'

Frere trembled. He had often witnessed this creature's whirlwinds of passion, but never had he seen her so violent as this. Her horrible frenzy frightened him.

'For Heaven's sake, Sarah, be quiet. What is it you want? What would you do?'

'Do! I'll tell yŏu what I'll do. I'll go to this girl you want to marry, and tell her of your infamy. I've seen her in the streets − seen her look the other way when I passed her − seen her gather up her muslin skirts when my silks touched her − I, that nursed her, that heard her say her baby-prayers, O Jesus pity me! − and I know what she thinks of women like me. She is good − and virtuous − and cold. She would shudder at you if she knew what I know. Shudder! She would hate you! Hate and loathe you! And I will tell her! Ay, I will! You will be *respectable*, will you? A model husband! Wait till I tell her my story, – till I send poor Lucy to tell hers! You kill my love; I'll blight and ruin yours! Dora –'

Frere caught her by both wrists, and with all his strength forced her to her knees.

'Don't speak *her* name,' he said, in a hoarse voice, 'or I'll do you a mischief. I know all you mean to do. I'm not such a fool as not to see that. Be quiet! I have heard that men have murdered women like you, and now I know how they came to do it.'

For a few minutes a silence fell upon the pair, and at last Frere, releasing her hands, fell back from her.

'I'll do what you want, on one condition.'

'What?'

'That you leave this place.'

'Where for?'

'Anywhere – the farther the better. I'll pay your passage to Sydney, and you go or stay there as you choose.'

She had grown calmer, hearing him thus relenting.

'But this place, Maurice?'

'You are not in debt?'

'No.'

'Well, leave it. It's your own affair, not mine. If I help, you must go.'

'May I see *him*?'

'No.'

'Ah! Maurice.'

'You can see him in the dock if you like,' says Frere, with a laugh, cut shortly by a flash of her eyes. 'There, I didn't mean to offend you.'

'Offend me! Go on.'

'Listen here,' said he doggedly. 'If you will go away, and promise never to interfere with me or mine by word or deed, I'll do what you want.'

'What will you do?' she asked, unable to suppress a smile at the victory she had won.

'I will not say all I know about this man. I will say he befriended me. I will do my best to save his life.'

'You *can* save it if you like.'

'Well, I will try. On my honour, I will try.'

'I must believe you, I suppose?' said she, doubtfully; and then with sudden pitiful pleading, that was in strange contrast to her former violence, 'You are not deceiving me, Maurice?'

'No. Why should I? You keep your promise, and I'll keep mine. Is it a bargain?'

'Yes.'

He eyed her steadfastly for some seconds, and then turned on his heel. As he reached the door, she called him back. Knowing him as she did, she felt that he would keep his word, and her feminine nature could not resist a parting sneer.

'There is nothing in the bargain to prevent me helping him to escape!' she said, with a smile.

'Escape! He won't escape again, I'll go bail. Once get him in double irons at Port Arthur, and he's safe enough.'

The smile on her face seemed infectious, for his own sullen features relaxed.

'Good night, Sarah!' he said.

She put out her hand, as if nothing had happened.

'Good night, Captain Frere. It's a bargain then?'

'A bargain.'

'You have a long walk home. Will you have some brandy?'

'I don't care if I do,' he said, advancing to the table and filling his glass. 'Here's a good voyage to you!'

Sarah Purfoy, standing watching him, burst into a laugh.

'Human beings are queer creatures,' she said. 'Who would have thought that we had been calling each other names just now; I say, I'm a vixen when I'm roused, ain't I, Maurice?'

'Remember what you've promised,' said he, with a hint of a threat in his voice, as he moved to the door. 'You must be out of this by the next boat.'

'Never fear, I'll go.'

Getting into the cool street directly, and seeing the calm stars shining and the placid water sleeping with a peace in which he had no share, he strove to cast off the nervous fear that was on him. The interview had frightened him, for it had made him think. It was hard that, just as he had turned over a new leaf, this old blot should seem to stain the page. It was hard that, having comfortably forgotten the past, he should be thus rudely reminded of it. Curse it! why could he not leave his burden behind him in the room he had quitted? Why could he not, in shutting the door of the house, shut in the memory of his misdeeds?

Two constables, who had stopped a girl at the corner, saluted him as he passed, and the salute was pleasant to him. He was, after all, respected and feared. His position went for something, let the world say what it might. He paused in this friendly glow of respect, to warm himself at it.

'What's the matter now?'

'A prisoner, y'r honour, out without her pass. Come on, my girl.'

'No! For the love of mercy! I'm going for med'cin — med'cin for my sick child. He's ill, gentlemen. This is the bottle. See! — Ah!'

One of the constables had dashed the phial from her hand, and it was shivered to fragments on the pavement.

'Who told you to do that?' asked Frere, in a voice so suddenly fierce that it made the girl shrink back against the wall. 'Let her go? Do you hear?'

The men obeyed, and, with an affrighted look at her protector, the poor creature sped away.

Frere, with a heavier scowl than before, strode away up the street, swinging his stick, as if by violent motion to banish unpleasant thoughts. As he passed the Prisoners' Barracks in Campbell-street, the sentry presented arms, and some late-returning brother-officer, speeding past on the opposite side of the road, shouted a cheery good-night. He was once more Captain Frere, the man of position and consequence.

'Curse her and her brat!' he muttered. 'What are they to me?'

And before he reached his house he had relapsed again into his old complacent repudiation of the past, and determination to enjoy the future.

'THE NOTORIOUS DAWES'

THE amusements of Hobart Town were not so numerous but that the trial of the mutineers of the *Osprey* was hailed as a pleasant subject of conversation in all family circles.

The unfortunate wretches had been long since given up as dead, and the story of their desperate escape had become indistinct to the general mind. Now that they had been recaptured in this remarkable manner, popular belief invested them with all sorts of strange surroundings. They had been – according to popular belief – kings over savage islanders, chiefs of lawless and ferocious pirates, respectable married men in Java, merchants in Singapore, and swindlers in Hong Kong. Their adventures had been dramatised at a London theatre, and the popular novelist of that day was engaged in a work descriptive of their wondrous fortunes.

John Rex, the ringleader, was the younger son of a noble family, and a special message, it was reported, had come out to Sir John Franklin concerning him. He had every prospect of being satisfactorily hung, however, for even the most outspoken admirers of his skill and courage could not but admit that he had committed an offence which was death by the law. The Crown would leave nothing undone that could help to convict him, and the already crowded prison was re-crammed with some half-dozen life-sentence men, brought up specially from Port Arthur to identify the prisoners beyond all question of error. Amongst these half-dozen was stated, by the *Mercury*, to be 'the notorious Dawes.'

This statement gave fresh food for recollection and invention. It was remembered that 'the notorious Dawes' was the absconder who had been brought away by Captain Frere, and who owed such fettered life as he possessed to the fact that he had in a measure assisted Captain Frere to make that wonderful boat in which the escape of the marooned party had been effected. It was remembered, also, how sullen and morose he had been on his trial five years before, and how he had laughed when the commutation of his death sentence was announced to him. The *Mercury* published a little biography of this horrible villain – a biography setting forth how he had been engaged in a mutiny on board the convict-ship, how he had twice escaped from Macquarie Harbour, how he had been repeatedly flogged for violence and insubordination, and how he was now double-ironed at Port Arthur after two more ineffectual attempts to regain his freedom. Indeed, the *Mercury*, discovering that the wretch had been originally transported for murder, argued very ably against such nauseous humanity, and urged that it would be far better to hang such wild beasts in the first instance, rather than suffer them to burden the ground and grow confirmed in villany. 'Of what use to society,' asked the *Mercury*, quite pathetically, 'has this scoundrel been during the last eleven years?' And everybody agreed that he had been of no use whatever.

Miss Dora Vickers also received an additional share of public attention. Her romantic salvation by the heroic Frere, who was shortly to reap the reward of his devotion in the good old fashion, made her almost as famous as the villain Dawes, or his confederate monster, John Rex. It was reported that she was to give evidence on the trial, together with her affianced husband, they being the only two living witnesses who could speak to the facts of the mutiny. It was reported also that her lover was naturally most anxious that she should not so give evidence, she being – an additional point of romantic interest – affected deeply by the illness consequent on the suffering she had undergone, and in a state of pitiable mental confusion as to the whole business.

These reports caused the Court, on the day of the trial, to be crowded with spectators; and as the various particulars of the marvellous history of this double escape were detailed, the excitement grew more intense. The aspect of the four heavily-ironed prisoners caused a sensation which, in that city of the ironed, was quite novel, and bets were offered and taken as to the line of defence which they would adopt. At first it was thought that they would throw themselves on the mercy of the Crown, seeking, as it were, in the very extravagance of their story, to excite public sympathy; but a little study of the demeanour of the chief prisoner dispelled all thought of that conjecture. Calm, placid, and defiant, he seemed prepared to accept his fate, or to meet his accusers with some plea which should be sufficient to secure his acquittal on the capital charge. Only when he heard the indictment, setting forth that he had 'feloniously pirated the brig *Osprey*,' he smiled a little.

Mr Meekin, sitting in the body of the Court, felt his religious prejudices sadly shocked by that smile.

'A perfect wild beast, my dear Miss Vickers,' he said, returning, in a pause during the examination of the convicts who had been brought to identify the prisoner, to the little room where Dora and her father were waiting. 'He has quite a tigerish look about him.'

'Poor man,' said Dora, with a shudder.

'Poor! My *dear* young lady, you do not pity him?'

'I do,' said Dora, twisting her hands together as if in pain. 'I pity them all, poor creatures.'

'Charming sensibility!' says Meekin, with a glance at Vickers. 'The true woman's heart, my dear Major.'

The Major tapped his fingers impatiently at the ill-timed twaddle. Dora was too nervous for sentiment of that kind to be poured out upon her.

'Come here, Poppet,' he said, 'and look through this door. You can see them from here, and if you do not recognise any of them, I can't see what is the use of putting you in the box; though, of course, if it is necessary, you must go.'

The raised dock was just opposite to the door of the room in which they were sitting, and the four manacled men, each with an armed warder behind him, were visible above the heads of the crowd.

The girl had never before seen the ceremony of trying a man for his life, and the silent and antique solemnities of the business affected her, as it affects all who see it for the first time. The atmosphere was heavy and distressing. The chains of the prisoners clanked ominously. The crushing force of judge, jailors, warders, and constables assembled to punish the four men, appeared cruel. The familiar faces that, in her momentary glance, she recognised, seemed to her evilly transfigured. Even the countenance of her promised husband, bent eagerly forward towards the witness-box, appeared tyrannous and bloodthirsty.

Her eyes hastily followed the pointing finger of her father and sought the men in the dock. Two of them lounged, sullen and inattentive; one nervously chewed a straw, or piece of twig, pawing the dock with restless hand; the fourth scowled across the Court at the witness-box, which she could not see. The four faces were all strange to her.

'No, papa,' she said, with a sigh of relief, 'I can't recognise them at all.'

As she was turning from the door, a voice from the witness-box behind her made her suddenly pale and pause to look again.

The Court itself appeared, at that moment, affected, for a murmuring shudder ran through it, and some official cried, 'Silence!'

The notorious criminal, the wild beast whom the *Mercury* had judged not fit to live, the desperado of Port Arthur, had just entered the witness-box. He was a man of thirty, in the prime of life, with a torso whose muscular grandeur not even the ill-fitting yellow jacket could altogether conceal, with strong, embrowned, and nervous hands, an upright carriage, and a pair of fierce, black eyes, that roamed the Court hungrily. Not all the weight of the double irons, swaying from the leathern thong around his massive loins, could mar that elegance of attitude which comes only from perfect muscular development, not all the frowning faces bent upon him, could frown an accent of respect into the contemptuous tones in which he answered to his name,

'Rufus Dawes, prisoner of the Crown.'

'Come away, my darling,' said Vickers, alarmed at his daughter's blanched face and eager eyes.

'Wait,' she said, impatiently, listening for the voice whose owner she could not see. 'Rufus Dawes! Oh, I have heard that name before!'

'You are a prisoner of the Crown at the penal settlement of Port Arthur?'

'Yes.'

'For life?'

'For life.'

A murmur ran through the Court again.

'A thundering long life, too,' says some one to his neighbour.

Dora turned to her father with breathless inquiry in her eyes.

'Oh, papa! who is that speaking? I know the name! I know the voice!'

'That is the man who was with you in the boat, dear,' says Vickers, gravely. 'The prisoner.'

The eager light died out of her eyes, and in its place came a look of disappointment and pain.

'I thought it was a good man,' she said, holding by the edge of the doorway. 'It sounded like a good voice.'

And then she pressed her hands over her eyes and shuddered.

'There, there,' says Vickers, soothingly. 'Don't be afraid, Poppet; he can't hurt you now.'

'No, ha! ha!' says Meekin, with great display of off-hand courage, 'the villain's safe enough now.'

The colloquy in the Court went on.

'Do you know the prisoners in the dock?'

'Yes.'

'Who are they?'

'John Rex, Henry Shires, James Lesley, and, and — I'm not sure about the last man.'

'You are not sure about the last man. Will you swear to the three others?'

'Yes.'

'You remember them well?'

'I was in the chain gang at Liberty Point with them for three years.'

Dora, hearing this hideous reason for acquaintance, gave a low cry, and fell into her father's arms.

'Oh, papa, take me away! I feel as if I was going to remember something terrible!'

Amid the deep silence that prevailed, the cry of the poor girl was distinctly audible in the Court, and all heads turned to the door. In the general wonder, no one noticed the strange change that had seized Rufus Dawes. His face had flushed scarlet, great drops of sweat stood on his forehead, and his black eyes glared in the direction from whence the sound came, as though they would pierce the envious wood that separated him from the woman whose voice he had heard.

Maurice Frere sprang up and pushed his way through the crowd under the Bench.

'What's this?' he said to Vickers, almost brutally. 'What did you bring her here for? She is not wanted. I told you that.'

'I considered it my duty, sir,' says Vickers, with stately rebuke.

'What has frightened her? What has she heard? Who has she seen?' asked Frere, with strangely white face. 'Dora! Dora!'

She opened her eyes affrightedly at the sound of his voice.

'Take me home, papa; I'm ill. Oh, what thoughts!'

'What does she mean?' cried Frere, looking in alarm from one to the other.

'That ruffian, Dawes, frightened her,' said Meekin. 'A gush of recollection, poor child. There, there, calm yourself, Miss Vickers. He is quite safe.'

'Frightened her, eh?'

'Yes,' said Dora, faintly, 'he frightened me, Maurice. I needn't stop any longer, dear, need I?'

'No,' says Frere, the cloud passing from his face. 'Go home, darling. Major, I beg your pardon, but I was hasty. Take her home at once. This sort of thing is too much for her.'

And so he went back again, wiping his brow, and breathing hard, as one who has just escaped some near peril.

Rufus Dawes had remained in the same attitude until the figure of Frere, passing through the doorway, roused him.

'Who is she?' he said, in a low, hoarse voice, to the constable behind him.

'Miss Vickers,' said the man, shortly flinging the information at him as one might fling a bone to a dangerous dog.

'Miss Vickers!' repeated the convict, still staring in a sort of bewildered agony. 'Why, man, she's dead!'

The constable snuffed contemptuously at this preposterous conclusion, as who should say, 'If you know all about it, animal, why did you ask?' and then feeling that the fixed gaze of his interrogator demanded some sort of reply, added,

'You thort she was, I've no doubt. You did your best to make her so, I've heard.'

The convict raised both his hands with sudden action of

wrathful despair, as though he would seize the other, despite the loaded muskets; but checking himself with sudden impulse, wheeled round to the Court.

'Your Honour! – Gentlemen! – I want to speak a moment.'

The change in the tones of his voice, no less than the sudden loudness of the exclamation, made the faces, hitherto bent upon the door through which Mr Frere had passed, turn round again.

To many in the Court it seemed that the 'notorious Dawes' was no longer in the box, for, in place of the defiant, upright, and easy-mannered ruffian who had stood there an instant back, was a white-faced, nervous, agitated creature, bending forward in an attitude almost of supplication, one hand grasping the rail, as though to save himself from falling, the other outstretched towards the bench.

'Your Honour, there has been some dreadful mistake made. I want to explain about myself. I have explained before, when first I was sent to Port Arthur, but the letters were never forwarded by the Commandant; of course that's the rule, and I can't complain. I've been sent there unjustly, your Honour. *I* made that boat, your Honour. *I* saved the Major's wife and daughter. *I* was the man; I did it all myself, and my liberty was sworn away by a villain who hated me. I thought, until now, that no one knew the truth, for they told me that she was dead.'

It would have been a curious experiment for one who had been in the Old Bailey Court, eleven years before, to compare how different was this speech with the one made by the same man then, and to speculate through what course of brutalisation his intellect must have passed to reduce his eloquence to this level.

The rapid utterance seemed to have taken the Court so much by surprise that no one interrupted him.

'I was sentenced to death for bolting, sir, and they reprieved me because I helped them in the boat. Helped them! Why, I *made* it! She will tell you so. I nursed her! I carried her in my arms! I starved myself for her! She was fond of me, sir; she was indeed. She called me "Mr Dawes."'

At this, a coarse laugh broke out, that was instantly checked.

The judge bent over to ask, 'Does he mean Miss Vickers?' and in this interval, Rufus Dawes, looking down into the Court, saw Maurice Frere staring up at him with savage terror in his eyes.

'I see you, Maurice Frere, you coward and liar! Put him in the box, gentlemen, and make him tell his story. She'll contradict him, never fear. Oh, and I thought she was dead all this while!'

The judge had got his answer by this time.

'Miss Vickers had been seriously ill, had fainted just now in the Court. Her only memories of the convict who had been with her in the boat were those of terror and disgust. The sight of him just now had most seriously affected her. The convict himself was an inveterate liar and schemer, and his story had been already disproved by Captain Frere.'

The judge, a man inclining by nature to humanity, but forced by experience to receive all statements of prisoners with caution, said all he could say, and the sight-seers in the Court heard the following dialogue: —

Judge. This is not the place for an accusation against Captain Frere, nor the place to argue upon your alleged wrongs. If you have suffered injustice, the authorities will hear your complaint, and redress it.

Rufus Dawes. I have complained, your Honour. I wrote letter after letter to the Government, but they were never sent. Then I heard she was dead, and they sent me to the coal mines after that, and we never hear anything there.

Judge. I can't listen to you. Mr Mangles, have you any more questions to ask the witness?

But Mr Mangles not having any more, some one called 'Matthew Gabbett,' and Rufus Dawes, still endeavouring to speak, was clanked away with, amid a buzz of remark and surmise.

This episode was food for much conversation during the adjourning of the Court, and the scheme of the 'notorious Dawes' was rather admired for its ingenuity. Some few people seemed to be at first of opinion that there might be something of truth in his statement; but Captain Frere, bluff and loud-voiced, soon bore down that notion.

'The fellow was always saying that. The biggest liar and villain unhung. You have no notion of the powers of acting these fellows have. Unluckily for him, there were *proofs* – unmistakeable proofs – and if he insisted on an inquiry, he would get the worst of it. But they'd do anything for a week in Hobart Town these fellows would.'

The principal anxiety of Captain Frere, however, was to keep the knowledge of this untoward event from his affianced bride.

'It would agitate her dreadfully if she knew it,' he said to his friends. 'Any attempt to remember anything about the thing always made her ill,' and with this notion, perhaps, he decided to go down to Vickers, and warn him against talking on the subject.

On his way, he was met by a man who touched his hat, and asked to speak with him an instant. This man was past middle age, owned a red and brandy-beaten face, and had in his gait and manner that nameless salt-water something that denotes the seaman.

'Well, Blunt,' says Frere, pausing, with the impatient air of a man who expects to hear bad news, 'what is it now?'

'Only to tell you that it is all right, sir,' says Blunt. 'She's come aboard again this morning.'

'Come aboard again!' ejaculated Frere. 'Why, I didn't know that she had been ashore. Where did she go?'

He spoke with an air of confident authority, and Blunt – no longer the bluff tyrant of old – seemed to quail before him.

The trial of the mutineers of the *Malabar* had, so to speak, ruined Phineas Blunt. Make what excuses he might, there was no concealing the fact that Pine found him drunk in his cabin when he ought to have been attending to his duties on deck, and the 'authorities' could not, or would not, pass over such a heinous breach of discipline. Captain Blunt – who, of course, had his own version of the story – transferred his able seamanship to the merchant service, and, deprived of the honour of bringing His Majesty's prisoners to His Majesty's colonies of New South Wales and Van Diemen's Land, went on a whaling cruise to the South Seas. It would seem, however, that the influence which Sarah Purfoy had acquired over him had irretrievably injured him. It was as though she had poisoned the man's moral nature. Perhaps the influence of a clever and wicked woman over a sensual and dull-witted man would have

that effect. Blunt gradually sank lower and lower. He began to
gain a reputation as a drunkard, and to be known as a man
with a 'grievance against the Government.' Captain Frere, having had occasion for him in some capacity, had become in a
manner his patron, and had got him the command of a schooner
trading from Sydney. On getting this command – not without
some wry faces on the part of the owner resident in Hobart
Town – Blunt had taken the pledge for the space of twelve
months, and was as miserable as a dog in consequence. He was,
however, a faithful henchman, for he hoped by Frere's means
to get some 'Government billet' – the *ultima Thule* of all
colonial sea captains of that epoch.

'Well, sir, she went ashore to see a friend,' says Blunt, looking
at the sky and then at the earth – 'a friend who was sick.'

'What friend?'

'A female, sir. One of the gals at the George the Fourth. She
was dying, and she sent for Mrs Purfoy to see her.'

'Who was she?'

'Lucy, she called herself. I don't know any other name. A
fair girl, with—'

'There, I don't want her description,' Frere interrupted, with
quick anger. 'And she saw her, I suppose?'

'Well, no,' says Blunt. 'The girl was dead before she got
there.'

There was a pause for a few seconds, during which Frere
ground his heel into the earth, as though he would grind out
and destroy some unpleasant memory that had suddenly arisen
to torment him.

'I thought I'd better tell you, sir,' says Blunt.

'Of course; quite right,' returned the other, rousing himself.
'You had better start at once. It's no use waiting.'

'She wished to hear about the trial,' said Blunt, with a coarse
timidity.

'Well, she can't hear about the trial, then. It may last for
days.'

'As you wish, sir. I can sail to-morrow morning – or this
evening, if you like.'

'This evening,' says Frere, turning away; 'as soon as possible.'

'Captain Frere.'

'Well?'

'There's a situation in Sydney I've been looking after, if you could help me to it.'

'How can I help you to it?'

'Your recommendation, sir.'

'As what?'

'One of the Government vessels, sir.'

'Well, keep sober then,' says Frere, 'and I'll see what I can do. And keep that woman's tongue still if you can.'

The pair looked at each other, and Blunt grinned slavishly.

'I'll do my best.'

'Take care you do.'

'You may rely on me,' says Blunt, seemingly relieved at having delivered his report without further question.

And they parted.

'Thank heaven, that she-devil's going at all events,' was Maurice's thought, as he strode towards the Major's cottage. 'Now, I must shut that fellow's mouth once for all.'

⤙ 5 ⤚

MAURICE FRERE'S GOOD ANGEL

He found Vickers in the garden, and at once began to beg him not to talk about the 'business' to his daughter.

'You saw how bad she was to-day, Vickers. For goodness sake, don't make her ill again.'

'My dear sir,' says poor Vickers, '*I* won't refer to the subject again. She's been very unwell ever since. Nervous and unstrung. Go in and see her.'

So Frere went in and soothed the excited girl, with real sorrow at her suffering.

'It's all right now, Poppet,' he said to her. 'Don't think of it any more. Put it out of your mind, dear.'

'It was foolish of me, Maurice, I know, but I could not help it. The sound of – of – that man's voice seemed to bring back to me some great pity for something or some one. I don't explain what I mean, I know, but I felt that I was just on the verge of remembering a story of some great wrong, just about to hear some dreadful revelation that should make me turn from all the people I feel most love for. Do you understand?'

'I think I know what you mean,' says Frere, with sulkily averted face. 'But that's all nonsense, you know.'

'Of course,' returned she, with a touch of her old childish manner of disposing of questions out of hand. 'Everybody knows it's all nonsense. But then we *do* think such things. It seems to me that I am Double, that I have lived somewhere before, and have had another life – a Dream-life.'

'What a romantic little puss you are,' says the other, dimly comprehending her meaning. 'How could you have a dream-life?'

'Of course, not Really, Stupid! But in thought, you know. I dream such strange things now and then. I am always falling down precipices and into cataracts, and being pushed into great caverns in enormous rocks. Horrible dreams!'

'Indigestion,' says practical Frere. 'You don't take exercise enough. You shouldn't read so much. Have a good five-mile walk.'

'And in these dreams,' continued Dora, not heeding his interruption, 'there is one strange thing. You are always there, Maurice.'

'Come, that's all right,' says Maurice.

'Ah, but not kind and good as you *are*, Captain Bruin, but scowling, and threatening, and angry, so that I am afraid of you.'

'But that is only in a dream, darling.'

'Yes, but—' playing with the button of his coat.

'But what?'

'But you looked just so, to-day, in the Court, Maurice, and I think that's what made me so silly.'

'My darling! There! Hush – don't cry!'

But she had burst into a passion of sobs and tears, that shook her slight figure in his arms.

'Oh, Maurice, I am a wicked girl! I don't know my own mind. I think sometimes I don't love you as I ought – you who have saved me and nursed me.'

'There, never mind about that,' says Maurice Frere, with a sort of choking in his throat.

She grew more composed presently, and said, after a while, lifting her face,

'Tell me, Maurice, did you ever, in those days of which you have spoken to me, – when you nursed me as a little child in your arms, and fed me, and starved for me – did you ever think we should be married?'

'I don't know,' says Maurice. 'Why?'

'I think you must have thought so, because – it's not vanity, dear – you would not else have been so kind, and gentle, and devoted.'

'Nonsense, Poppet,' he said, with his eyes resolutely averted.

'No, but you have been, and I am very pettish sometimes. Papa has spoiled me. You are always affectionate, and those Worrying Ways of yours, which I get angry at, all come from love for me, don't they?'

'I hope so,' says Maurice, with an unwonted moisture in his eyes.

'Well, you see, that is the reason why I am angry with myself for not loving you as I ought. I want you to like the things I like, and love the books and the music and the pictures and the – the World I love; and I forget that you are a man, you know, and that I am only a girl; and I forget how nobly you behaved, Maurice, and how unselfishly you risked your life for mine. Why, what is the matter, dear?'

He had put her away from him suddenly, and gone to the window, gazing across the trees of the sloping garden at the bay below, sleeping in the soft evening light. The schooner which had brought the witnesses from Port Arthur lay off the shore, and the yellow flag at her mast fluttered gently in the cool evening breeze. The sight of this flag appeared to anger him, for, as his eyes fell on it, he uttered an impatient exclamation, and turned round again.

'Maurice!' she cried, 'I have wounded you!'

'No, no. It is nothing,' said he, with the air of a man

surprised in a moment of weakness. 'I – I did not like to hear you talk in that way, – about not loving me.'

'Ah, forgive me, dear; I did not mean to hurt you. It is my silly way of saying more than I mean. How could I do otherwise than love you – after all you have done?'

Some sudden desperate whim caused him to exclaim,

'But suppose I had not done all you think, would you not love me still?'

Her eyes, raised to his face with anxious tenderness for the pain she had believed herself to have inflicted, fell at this speech.

'What a question! I don't know. I suppose I should, – yet – but what is the use, silly man, of *supposing*? I know you *have* done it, and that is enough. How can I say what I might have done if something else had happened? Why,' with coquettish surprise, 'you might not have loved *me*.'

If there had been for a moment any sentiment of remorse in his selfish heart, the hesitation of her answer went far to dispel it.

'To be sure, that's true;' and he placed his arm round her.

She lifted her face again with a bright laugh.

'We are a pair of Geese – supposing! How can we help what has past? We have the Future, darling – the Future, in which I am to be your little wife, and we are to love each other all our lives, like the people in the Story-books.'

Temptation to evil had often come to Maurice Frere, and his selfish nature had succumbed to it when in far less witching shape than this fair and innocent child luring him with wistful eyes to win her. What hopes had he not built upon her love; what good resolutions had he not made – or seemed to make – by reason of the purity and goodness she was to bring him? As she said, the past was beyond recall; the future – in which she was to love him all her life – was only before them. With the consummate hypocrisy of that supreme selfishness which deceives even itself, he laid the little head upon his heart with a veritable glow of virtue.

'God bless you, darling! You are my good angel.'

'What, Poetical! The Poet Gruffy! I hope I am. Don't, sir! Do you think I have nothing to do but to put on clean collars for you to tumble?'

Then, with that quaint mingling of sentiment and drollery which characterized her, the laughing expostulation at his rough caress was followed by a heartfelt prayer for his welfare –

'God bless you, darling! I *will* be your Good Angel if you will let me.'

⊷ 6 ⊶

MR MEEKIN ADMINISTERS CONSOLATION

THE trial of the mutineers progressed without further incident. Every effort was being made to hurry it to an end before Christmas, and this hurry was beneficial to the accused. Some persons indeed expressed regret that the matter had not been put off until spring, and accused Captain Frere, by whose instrumentality the trial had taken place so immediately, of undue haste to secure a conviction. Such persons, however, changed their tone when Captain Frere went into the witness-box and honestly spoke in favour of John Rex. 'He might have left us to starve,' Frere said – 'he might have murdered us; we were completely in his power. The stock of provisions on board the brig was not a large one, and I consider that, in dividing it with us, he showed great generosity for one in his situation.' This piece of evidence told strongly in favour of the prisoners, for Captain Frere was known to be such an uncompromising foe to all rebellious convicts, that it was understood that nothing but the sternest sense of justice and truth could lead him to speak in such terms. The defence set up by Rex, moreover, was most ingenious. He was guilty of absconding, but his moderation might plead an excuse for that. His only object was his freedom, and having gained it, he had lived honestly for nearly three years, as he could prove. He was charged with piratically seizing the brig *Osprey,* and he urged that the brig *Osprey,* having been built by convicts at Macquarie Harbour, and never entered in any shipping list, could not be said to be 'piratically seized,' in the strict meaning of the term. The Court admitted the force of this objection, and, influenced doubtless by Captain Frere's evidence, the fact that five years had passed since the mutiny, and that the two most guilty (Cheshire and Barker) had been executed in England, sentenced the four to transportation for life to the penal settlements of the colony.

Rex told Mr Meekin, who had done him the honour to visit him, that, 'under Providence, he owed his escape from death to the kind manner in which Captain Frere had spoken of him.'

'I hope your escape will be a warning to you, my man,' said Mr Meekin, 'and that you will endeavour to make the rest of your life, thus spared by the Mercy of Providence, an atonement for your early errors.'

'Indeed, I will, sir,' said John Rex, who had taken Mr Meekin's measure very accurately, 'and it is very kind of you to condescend to speak so to a wretch like me.'

'Not at all,' said Meekin, with affability. 'It is my duty. I am a Minister of the Gospel.'

'Ah! sir, I wish I had attended to the Gospel's teachings when I was younger. I might have been saved from all this.'

'You might indeed, poor man; but the Divine Mercy is infinite – quite infinite, and will be extended to all of us – to you as well as to me.' (This with the air of saying, 'What do you think of *that*?') 'Remember the penitent thief, Rex – the penitent thief.'

'Indeed, I do, sir.'

'And read your Bible, Rex, and pray for strength to bear your punishment.'

'I will, Mr Meekin. I need it sorely, sir – physical as well as spiritual strength, sir – for the Government allowance is sadly insufficient.'

'I will speak to the authorities about a change in your dietary scale,' returned Meekin, patronizingly. 'In the meantime just collect together in your mind those particulars of your adventures of which you spoke, and have them ready for me when next I call. Such a remarkable history ought not to be lost.'

'Thank you kindly, sir. I will, sir. Ah! I little thought when I occupied the position of a gentleman, Mr Meekin' – the cunning scoundrel had been piously grandiloquent concerning his past career – 'that I should be reduced to this. But it is only just, sir.'

'The mysterious workings of Providence are always just,

Rex,' returned Meekin, who preferred to speak of the Almighty with well-bred vagueness. 'I am glad to see you so conscious of your errors. Good morning.'

'Good morning, and Heaven bless you, sir,' says Rex, with his tongue in his cheek, for the benefit of his yard-mates; and so Mr Meekin tripped gracefully away, with the happy notion that he was labouring most successfully in the Vineyard, and that the convict Rex was really a most superior person.

'I will send this narrative to the Bishop,' said he to himself. 'It will amuse him. There must be many strange histories here, if one could but find them out.'

As the thought passed through his brain, his eye fell upon the 'notorious Dawes', who, waiting for the schooner to take him back to Port Arthur, had been permitted to amuse himself by breaking stones.

The prison-shed in which Mr Meekin was labouring was long and low, roofed with iron, and terminating at each end in the stone wall of the gaol. At one side rose the cells, at the other the outer wall of the prison. From the outer wall projected a weatherboard under roof, and beneath this were seated some forty heavily-ironed convicts. Two constables, with loaded carbines, walked up and down the clear space in the middle, and another watched from a sort of sentry-box built against the main wall. Every half hour a third constable went down the line and examined the irons.

The admirable system of solitary confinement – which in average cases produces insanity in the space of twelve months – was as yet unknown in Hobart Town, and the forty heavily-ironed men had the pleasure of seeing each other's faces every day for six hours. The other inmates of the prison were at work on the roads, or otherwise bestowed in the day time, but the forty were judged too desperate to be let loose. They sat, three feet apart, in two long lines, each man with a heap of stones between his outstretched legs, and cracked the pebbles in leisurely fashion. The double row of dismal woodpeckers tapping at this terribly hollow beech-tree of penal discipline had a semi-ludicrous appearance. It seemed so painfully absurd that forty muscular men should be ironed and guarded for no better purpose than the cracking of a cartload of flint-stones. In the meantime the air was heavy with angry glances shot from one to the other, and the passage of the parson was hailed by a grumbling under-tone of blasphemy. It was considered fashionable to grunt when the hammer came in contact with the stone, and under cover of this mock exclamation of fatigue, it was convenient to launch an oath. A fanciful visitor, seeing the irregularly rising hammers, now here now there, along the line, might have likened the shed to the interior of some vast piano, whose notes an unseen hand was erratically fingering.

Rufus Dawes was seated last of the line – his back to the cells, his face to the gaol wall. This was the place nearest the watching constable, and was allotted on that account to the most ill-favoured. Some of his companions envied him that melancholy distinction.

'Well, Dawes,' says Mr Meekin, measuring with his eye the distance between the prisoner and himself, as one might measure the chain of some ferocious dog. 'How are you this morning, Dawes?'

Dawes, scowling in a parenthesis between two stones, was understood to say that he was very well.

'I am afraid, Dawes,' says Mr Meekin, reproachfully, 'that you have done yourself no good by your outburst in court on Monday. I understand that public opinion is quite incensed against you.'

Dawes, busily arranging one large fragment of bluestone in a comfortable basin of smaller fragments, made no reply.

'I am afraid you lack patience, Dawes. You do not repent of your offences against the law, I fear.'

The only answer vouchsafed by the ironed man – if answer it could be called – was a blow which split the stone into fragments, and made the clergyman skip a step backward.

'You are a hardened ruffian, sir! Do you not hear me speak to you?'

'I hear you,' said Dawes, picking up another stone.

'Then listen respectfully, sir,' said Meekin, roseate with celestial anger. 'You have all day to break those stones.'

'Yes, I have all day,' returned Rufus Dawes, with a dogged look upward, 'and all next day, for that matter. Ugh!' and again the hammer descended.

'I came to console you, sir — to console you,' says Meekin, indignant at the contempt with which his well meant overtures had been received. 'I wanted to give you some good advice, sir!'

The self-important annoyance of the tone seemed to appeal to whatever vestige of appreciation for the humorous, chains and degradation had suffered to linger in the convict's brain, for a faint smile crossed his features.

'I beg your pardon, sir,' he said. 'Pray go on.'

'I was going to say, my good fellow, that you had done yourself a great deal of injury by your ill-advised accusation of Captain Frere, and the use you made of Miss Vickers's name.'

A frown, as of pain, contracted the prisoner's brows, and he seemed with difficulty to put a restraint upon his speech.

'Is there to be no inquiry, Mr Meekin?' he asked, at length. 'What I stated was the truth — the truth, so help me God!'

'No blasphemy, sir,' says Meekin, solemnly. 'No blasphemy, wretched man. Do not add to the sin of lying the greater sin of taking the Name of the Lord thy God in vain. He will not hold him guiltless, Dawes. He will not hold him guiltless, remember. No, there is to be no inquiry.'

'Are they not going to ask her for *her* story?' asked Dawes, with a pitiful change of manner. 'They told me that she was to be asked. Surely they will ask her.'

'I am not, perhaps, at liberty,' says Meekin, placidly unconscious of the agony of despair and rage that made the voice of the strong man before him quiver, 'to state the intentions of the authorities, but I can tell you that Miss Vickers will not be asked anything about you. You are to go back to Port Arthur on the 24th, and to remain there.'

A groan burst from Rufus Dawes; a groan so full of torture, that even the comfortable Meekin was thrilled by it.

'It is the Law, you know, my good man. I can't help it,' he said. 'You shouldn't break the Law, you know.'

'Curse the Law!' cries Dawes. 'It's a Bloody Law! It's — there, I beg your pardon,' and he fell to cracking his stones again, with a laugh that was more terrible in its bitter hopelessness of winning attention or sympathy, than any outburst of passion could have been.

'Come,' says Meekin, feeling uneasily constrained to bring forth some of his London-learnt platitudes. 'You can't complain. You have broken the Law, and you must suffer. Civilized Society says you shan't do certain things, and if you do them, you must suffer the penalty Society imposes. You are not wanting in intelligence, Dawes — more's the pity — and you can't deny the justice of that.'

Rufus Dawes, as if disdaining to answer in words, cast his eyes round the yard with a glance that seemed to ask grimly, if Civilized Society was progressing quite in accordance with justice, when its civilisation created such places as that stone-walled, carbine-guarded prison-shed, and filled it with such creatures as those forty human beasts, doomed to spend the best years of their manhood cracking pebbles in it.

'You don't deny *that*?' asked the smug parson, 'do you Dawes?'

'It's not my place to argue with you, sir,' said Dawes, in that tone of indifference which, born of lengthened suffering, was so nicely balanced between contempt and respect, that the inexperienced Meekin could not for the life of him tell whether he had made a convert or subjected himself to an impertinence; 'but I'm a prisoner for life, sir, and don't look at it in the same way that you do.'

This view of the question did not seem to have occurred to Mr Meekin, for his mild cheek flushed. Certainly the fact of being a prisoner for life did make some difference. The sound of the noonday bell, however, warned him to cease argument, and to take his consolation out of the way of the mustering prisoners.

With a great clanking and clashing of irons, the forty got erect, and stood each by his stone-heap. The third constable came round, rapping the leg-irons of each man with easy nonchalance, and roughly pulling the coarse trowsers (made with buttoned flaps at the sides, like Mexican *calzoneros*, in order to give free play to the ankle fetters), so that he might assure himself that no tricks had been played since his last visit. As each man passed this ordeal, he saluted, and clanked, with widespread legs, to his place in the double line. Mr Meekin, though not a patron of field sports, found something in the scene that reminded him of a blacksmith picking up horses' feet to examine the soundness of their shoes.

'Upon my word,' he said to himself, with a momentary pang of genuine compassion, 'it *is* a dreadful way to treat human beings. I don't wonder at that wretched creature yonder groaning under it.'

At that instant, however, the wretched creature was not groaning; indeed, something like a smile hovered about his lips, if Mr Meekin had been near enough to have seen it. Having mechanically risen, and held out his leg-irons to be tapped, and pulled up his short yellow jumper, in order that his leather belt might be inspected, he had become absorbed in watching a little incident that was just taking place in the yard.

A wandering parrot, a little blue and green bird, had made its appearance in the centre of the open space, and was sitting contentedly pluming itself upon a fragment of bluestone. Some one of the forty – as if brutally unwilling to see any of God's creatures vaunting its liberty unchecked in that place of chains and bolts – slyly flung a pebble at it. The bird flew away a few paces, and then perched on a large heap of metal which had been thrown beneath the wall the day before. From this vantage ground it twittered defiance, and then hopping to the roof of the weatherboard shed, gave a pert sidelong glance into the yard, fluttered to the top of the wall, and disappeared.

Rufus Dawes had paused, in rapt contemplation of this trifling incident, and stood gazing at the place where the parrot had perched, as though it possessed for him some peculiar fascination.

'Thinking of his liberty, perhaps. "Oh, that I had wings like a Dove!"' said Meekin to himself, unable, even in his thoughts, to resist such a familiar illustration, '"for then would I flee away and be at rest." Bless me, it is nearing one o'clock, and I promised to lunch with Major Vickers at two. How time flies, to be sure!'

RUFUS DAWES' IDYLL

That afternoon – while Meekin was digesting his lunch and chatting airily with Dora – Rufus Dawes began to brood over a desperate scheme.

The intelligence that the investigation he had hoped for was not to be granted to him, had rendered doubly bitter those galling fetters of self-restraint and contempt which he had laid upon himself. For five years of desolation he had waited and hoped for a chance which might bring him to Hobart Town, and enable him to denounce the treachery of Maurice Frere. He had, by an almost miraculous accident, obtained that chance of open speech, and, having obtained it, he found that he was not allowed to speak. All the hopes he had formed were dashed to earth. All the calmness with which he *had* forced himself to bear his fate was now turned into bitterest rage and fury. Instead of one enemy, he had twenty. All – judge, jury, gaoler, and parson – all were banded together to work him evil and deny him right. The whole world was his foe, there was no honesty or truth in any living creature – save one.

During the dull misery of his convict life at Port Arthur, one bright memory shone upon him like a star. In the depth of his degradation, at the height of his despair, he cherished one pure and ennobling thought – the thought of the child whom he had saved, and who loved him. When, on board the whaler that had rescued him from the burning boat, he had felt that the sailors, believing in Frere's bluff lies, shrunk from the moody convict-murderer, he had gained strength to be silent, by thinking of the suffering child. When poor Mrs Vickers died, making no sign, and he saw the chief witness of his heroism perish before his eyes, the thought that the child was left, had restrained his selfish regrets. When Frere, handing him over to the authorities as an absconder, ingeniously twisted the details of the boat-building to his own glorification, the knowledge that Dora would assign to these pretensions their true value had given him courage to keep silence. So strong was his belief in her gratitude, that he scorned to *beg* for the pardon he had taught himself to believe that she would ask for him. So utter was his contempt for the coward and boaster who, drest in brief authority, bore insidious false witness against him, that, when he heard his sentence of life banishment, he disdained to make known the true part he had played in the matter, preferring to wait for the more exquisite revenge, the more complete justification which would follow upon the recovery of the child from her illness.

But when, hurried to Port Arthur, day after day passed over, and brought no word of pity or justification, he began, with a sickening feeling of despair to comprehend that something strange must have happened. He heard, from newcomers, that the child of the Commandant lay still sick and near to death. Then he heard that she and her father had left the colony, and that all prospect of her righting him by her evidence was at an end. This piece of news gave him a terrible pang; and at first he was inclined to break out into upbraidings of her selfishness. But, with that depth of love which was in him, albeit crusted over and concealed by the harshness of speech and manner which his sufferings, working upon his violent temper, had produced, he found excuses for her even then. She was ill. She was in the hands of friends who loved her, and disregarded him; perhaps, even her entreaties and explanations were put aside as childish babblings. She would free him if she had the power. Then he wrote 'statements', agonised to see the Commandant, pestered the gaolers and warders with the story of his wrongs, and inundated the Government with letters, which, containing as they did always denunciations of Maurice Frere, were never suffered to reach their destination. The authorities, willing at the first to look kindly upon him in consideration of his strange experience, grew weary of this perpetual reiteration of what they believed to be a series of malicious falsehoods, and ordered him heavier tasks and more continuous labour. They mistook his gloom for sullenness, his impatient outbursts of passion at his fate for ferocity, his silent endurance for dangerous cunning. As he had been at Macquarie Harbour, so did he become at Port Arthur – a marked man.

Despairing of winning his coveted liberty by fair means, and oppressed at the hideous thought of a life in chains, he twice attempted to escape, but escape was even more hopeless than it had been at Hell's Gates. The Peninsula was admirably guarded, signal stations drew a chain round the prison, an armed boat's crew watched each bay, and across the narrow isthmus of Hawks Neck was a cordon of watch-dogs, in addition to the soldier guard. He was retaken, of course, flogged, and weighted with heavier irons. The second time, they sent him to the Coal Mines — where the prisoners lived underground, worked half naked, and dragged their inspecting gaolers in waggons upon iron tramways when such great people condescended to visit them. The day on which he started for this place he learnt that Dora was dead, and with the news his last hope went from him.

Then began with him a new religion. He worshipped the dead. For the living, he had but hatred and evil words; for the dead, he had love and tender thoughts. Instead of the phantoms of his vanished youth which were once wont to visit him, he saw now but one vision — the vision of the child who had loved him. Instead of conjuring up for himself pictures of that home circle in which he had once moved, and those creatures who in the past years had thought him worthy of esteem and affection, he placed before himself one idea, one embodiment of happiness, one being who was without sin and without stain among all the monsters of that pit into which he had fallen. Around the figure of the innocent child who had lain in his breast, and laughed at him with her red young mouth, he grouped all the phantasmata of happiness and love.

Having banished from his thoughts all hope of resuming his name and place, he pictured to himself some quiet nook in the world's end — a deep-gardened house in a German country town, or remote cottage by the English sea-shore, where he and his dream-child might have lived together, happy in a purer affection than the love of man for woman. He bethought him how he could have taught her out of the strange store of learning his roving life had won for him, how he could have tried again with her the experiments he had once made, how he could have confided to her the secret, for the keeping of which he had sold himself into bondage, and purchase for her wealth and honour by reason of it. Yet, – he thought, she would not care for wealth or honour, she would prefer a quiet life, – a life of unassuming usefulness, a life devoted to good deeds, and charity and love. He could see her – in his visions – reading by a cheery fire-side, wandering in summer woods, or lingering by the marge of the slumbering mid-day sea. He could feel – in his dreams – her soft arms about his neck, her innocent kisses on his lips, he could hear her light laugh, and see her sunny ringlets float, back-blown, as she ran to meet him. Conscious that she was dead, and that he did to her gentle memory no disrespect by linking her fortunes to those of a wretch who had seen so much of evil as himself, he loved to think of her as still living, and to plot out for her and for himself impossible plans of future happiness. In the foetid darkness of the mine, in the glaring light of noon-day, dragging at his loaded waggon, he could see her ever with him, her calm eyes fixed lovingly on his, as they had been in the boat so long ago. She never seemed to grow older, she never seemed to wish to leave him. It was only when his misery became too great for him to bear, and he cursed and blasphemed, mingling for a time in the hideous mirth of his companions, that the little figure fled away.

Thus dreaming, he had shaped out for himself a sorrowful comfort, and in his dream-world found a compensation for the terrible affliction of living. An indifference to his present sufferings took possession of him; only at the bottom of this indifference lurked a fixed hatred of the man who had brought these sufferings upon him, and a determination to demand at the first opportunity a reconsideration of that man's claims to be esteemed a hero.

It was in this mood that he had intended to make the revelation which he had made in court, but the intelligence that Dora had not died unmanned him, and his prepared speech had been usurped by a passionate torrent of complaint and invective, which convinced no one, and gave to Frere the very argument he needed. It was decided that the prisoner Dawes was a malicious and artful scoundrel, whose only object was to gain a brief respite of the punishment which he had so justly earned. Against this injustice he had resolved to rebel. It was monstrous, he thought, that they should refuse to hear the witness who was so ready to speak in his favour, infamous that they should send him back to his doom without allowing her to say a word in his defence. But he would defeat that scheme. The incident of the bird had given him an idea of a method of escape, and he would break from his bonds, fling himself at her feet, and pray her to speak the truth for him, and save him. Strong in his faith of her, and with his love for her brightened by the love he had borne to her dream-image, he felt sure in her power to rescue him now, as he had rescued her before. 'If she knew I was alive, she would come to me,' he said. 'I am sure she would. Perhaps, they told her that I was dead.'

Meditating that night in the solitude of his cell – his evil character had gained him the poor luxury of loneliness – he almost wept to think of the cruel deception that had doubtless been practised on her.

'They have told her that I was dead, in order that she might learn to forget me; but she could not do that. I have thought of her so much all these years, that she must have thought of me. Five years! She must be a woman now. Dora a woman! Yet she is sure to be childlike, sweet, and gentle. How she will shudder when she hears of my sufferings. Oh! my little darling, you are not dead.'

And then looking hastily about him in the darkness, as though fearful of being seen, he pulled from out his breast a sort of packet, and felt it lovingly with his coarse, toil-worn fingers, reverently raising it to his lips, and sitting dreaming over it, with a smile on his face, as though it were a sacred talisman that should open to him the doors of freedom.

⊷ 8 ⊶

AN ESCAPE

A few days after this – that is to say, on the 23rd of December – Maurice Frere was alarmed by a piece of startling intelligence. The notorious Dawes had escaped from gaol!

The Captain had in the morning superintended certain fine old English arrangements touching the distribution of beef and pudding on the ensuing Christmas Day, with his accustomed growling as to the 'luxuries permitted by Government to these fellows,' and had found everything as it should be. The influence of Christmas time, showing itself in a variety of pleasant ways in the town – making green booths of the butchers' shops, and transforming the solitary confectioner – himself a convict once – into a sort of presiding genius of rich jellies and unsubstantial sugar temples, bringing into the city an unwonted influx of browned and bearded 'settlers' from the country districts, and turning Major Vickers's house out of windows with preparation for Christmas festivities – had even shed a little of its kindliness upon the ironed prisoners in the gaol. The customary soup and bread – diversified by carefully-weighed portions of meat – was soon to be replaced by such substitute for Christmas pudding as the 'authorities' judged expedient to permit, and the universal holiday in honour of the birth of Him whose mission was to preach 'Peace and goodwill to men,' was to be celebrated by twelve hours' cessation from stone breaking and barrow dragging. The knowledge of this coming holiday, assisted perhaps by heaven knows what sorrowful recollection of *other* Christmas days, before the retribution of outraged Society had been merited, inspired the prisoners with something like cheerfulness, and it seemed to Captain Frere that the hammers had never fallen so briskly, or the chains clanked so gaily, as on the occasion of his visit.

'Thinking of their Christmas holiday, the dogs!' he had said to the patrolling warder – 'Thinking of their Christmas pudding, the luxurious scoundrels!' and the convict nearest him had laughed appreciatively, as convicts and schoolboys do laugh at the jests of the man in authority. All seemed contentment; moreover, he had – by way of a pleasant stroke of wit – tormented Rufus Dawes with his ill fortune. 'The schooner sails tomorrow, my man,' he had said. 'You'll spend *your* Christmas at the mines,' and congratulated himself upon the fact that Rufus Dawes merely touched his cap and went on with his stone-cracking in silence. Certainly double-irons and hard labour were fine things to break a man's spirit.

So that when in the afternoon of the same day he heard the astounding news that Rufus Dawes had freed himself from his fetters, climbed the gaol wall in broad daylight, run the gauntlet of Macquarie-street, and was now supposed to be safely hidden in the mountains, he felt dumbfounded.

'How the deuce did he do it, Jenkins?' he asked as soon as he reached the yard.

'Well, I'm blessed if I rightly know, your honour,' says Jenkins. 'He was over the wall before you could say "knife". Scott fired and missed him, and then I heard the sentry's musket, but he missed him too.'

'Missed him!' cries Frere. 'Pretty fellows you are, all of you! I suppose you couldn't hit a haystack at twenty yards? Why the man wasn't three feet from the end of your carbine!'

The unlucky Scott, standing in melancholy attitude by the empty irons, muttered something about the sun having been in his eyes.

'I don't know how it was, sir. I ought to have hit him, for certain. I think I did touch him, too, as he went up the wall.'

A stranger to the customs of the place might have imagined that he was listening to a conversation about a pigeon match.

'Tell me all about it,' says Frere, with an angry curse.

'I was just turning, your honour, when I hears Scott sing out "Hullo!" and when I turned round I saw Dawes's irons on the ground and him a scrambling up the heap o' stones yonder. The two men on my right jumped up, and I thought it was a made-up thing among 'em, so I covered 'em with my carbine, according to instructions, and called that I'd shoot the first that stepped out. Then I heard Scott's piece, and the men give a shout like. When I looked round, he was gone.'

'Nobody else moved?'

'No, sir. I was confused at first, and thought they were all in it, but Parton and Haines they runs in and gets between me and the wall, and then Mr Short he come, and we examined their irons.'

'All right?'

'All right, your honour; and they all swore they knowed nothing of it. The Dandy — Rex, sir — said that Dawes's irons was all right when he went to dinner; but you can't believe what he says , of course.'

'Of course not. Well?'

'That's all, sir. Mr Short he says, "They'll get him outside," and then we heard the sentry's musket, but he missed him, too, your honour.'

'Were his irons examined when he went to dinner, Mr Short?'

'Parton examined them, sir '

'They was all right, sir, then. I'll take my h'oath,' says Parton. Frere stooped and examined the irons.

'All right be hanged,' he said. 'If you don't know your duty better than this, the sooner you go somewhere else the better, my man. Look here !'

The two ankle fetters were severed. One had been evidently filed through, and the other broken transversely. The latter was bent, as from a violent blow.

'It's as plain as a pikestaff, you precious beggars ! He found out the weak point in this jimcrack thing long ago, depend upon it. That must have taken a week to file and more.'

'Don't know where he got the file from,' says Warder Short.

'Know ! Of course you don't know. You sort of men never do know anything until the mischief's done. You want me here for a month or so. By God, I'd teach you your duty. Don't know – with things like *this* lying about? I wonder the whole yard isn't loose and dining with the Governor.'

'*This*' was fragment of delf which Frere's quick eye had detected among the broken metal.

'I'd cut the biggest iron you've got with this; and so would he and plenty more, I'll go bail. You ought to have lived with me at Sarah Island, Mr Short. Don't know !'

'Well, Captain Frere, it's an accident,' says Short, 'and can't be helped now.'

'An accident !' roared Frere. 'What business have you with *accidents*? How, in the Devil's name, you let the man get over the wall, *I* don't know.'

'He ran up that stone-heap,' says Scott, 'and seemed to me to jump at the roof of the shed. I fired at him, and he swung his legs over the top of the wall and dropped.'

Frere measured the distance with his eye, and an irrepress-sible feeling of admiration, arising out of his own skill in athletics, took possession of him for the instant.

'By the Lord Harry, but it's a big jump!' he said; and then the instinctive fear with which the consciousness of the hideous wrong he had done the now escaped convict inspired him, made him add – 'A desperate devil like that wouldn't stick at a mur-der if you pressed him hard.'

Taking advantage of the momentary pause in the torrent of vilification, Mr Short hastened to interject a word of comfort.

'They expect to take him before night, sir. There's six men out after him now.'

'Which way did he go!'

'Right up Macquarie-street, and then made for the Moun-tain. There were few people about, but Mr Mays, of the Star Hotel, tried to stop him, and was knocked head over heels. He says the fellow runs like a deer.'

'We'll have the reward out if we don't get him tonight,' says Frere, turning away; 'and you'd better put on an extra warder. This sort of game is catching.'

'It reminds a man of the old bushranging days, Captain Frere,' says Jenkins, with a grin. 'I remember the time when there was forty-two bolters out at once, and pretty nearly two thousand pounds on 'em altogether. Ah, them days is gone by, sir.'

'If you'd attend to your duty, sir, and not pitch quite so much, it would be better for you,' returned Frere, with a scowl. 'We don't want escaped murderers running about the streets in day-light. Mr Short, you'll be good enough to send in an official re-port of this business, and I shall take care that Major Vickers makes an inquiry into it.'

'Yes, sir,' says Short, and presently relieved his feelings by vehemently spitting on the ground.

'The Captain's in a nice humour,' says Jenkins, with an eye to his master's indignation. 'One'd think a man was dog to hear him talk!'

'What rum go, ain't it!' says Scott, staring at the wall.

'You'd a thought a fly couldn't a walked up that now.'

'Wait till the Captain ketches 'im,' returned Jenkins; 'he'll make him walk up, I fancy.'

'Ay,' says the other, with an oath, 'he's a nipper, he is. Did yer notice how he dropped to that bit o' chaney, Tom? There ain't a dodge going that he ain't fly to.'

'My colonial oath!' says Tom.

Fully conscious of the admiration his acuteness had excited, but yet too full of wrath to permit such consciousness to make itself apparent, Frere strode away to the Barracks. The whole town was babbling of the escape, and he was at once assailed with questions.

The Hobart Town of those days was but a small place, and its interests all focussed in the great centre of convict discipline. From the oilman who supplied the material for the lamps in the dormitories, to His Excellency Sir John Franklin himself, the astounding and daring action of the notorious Dawes was canvassed and commented upon. Rumour reported a general rising in the prison, and an indiscriminate slaughter of young and old, only put down by the valour and determination of Captain Frere; and well-to-do merchants, dozing after dinner in the warehouses on the wharf, were awakened by fearful accounts of murderous gangs let loose to pillage and to ravish.

From right to left, from east to west, through the prison city, flew the signal of alarm, and the patrol, clattering out along the road to New Norfolk, made hot haste to strike the trail of the fugitive. But night came and found him yet at large, and patrols returning, weary and disheartened, protested that he must be lying hid in some gorge of the purple mountain that o'er-gloomed the town, and would have to be starved into submission.

Meanwhile, the usual message ran through the island, and so admirable were the arrangements which reforming Arthur had initiated, that, before noon of the next day, not a signal station on the coast but knew that No. 8942, etc., etc., prisoner for life, was illegally at large. This intelligence, further aided by a paragraph in the *Mercury* anent the 'Daring Escape', once noised abroad, the world seemed to care but little that the *Mary Jane,*

Government schooner, had sailed for Port Arthur without Rufus Dawes.

But two or three people cared a good deal. Major Vickers, for one, was indignant that his boasted security of bolts and bars should have been so easily defied, and, in proportion to his indignation, was the grief of Messieurs Jenkins, Scott, and Co., suspended from office, and threatened with absolute dismissal. Mr Meekin was reasonably frightened at the fact that so dangerous a monster should be roaming at large within murdering reach of his own saintly person. Dora had shown symptoms of a nervous terror, none the less injurious because carefully repressed; and Captain Maurice Frere was, to all appearance, a prey to the most cruel anxiety. He had ridden off at a hand-gallop within ten minutes that he had been inspecting the prison, a few hours before the escape took place, and his efforts were therefore attributed to zeal, not unmixed with chagrin.

'Our dear friend feels his reputation at stake,' the future chaplain of Port Arthur said to Mrs Protherick. 'He is so proud of his knowledge of these unhappy men that he dislikes to be outwitted by any of them.'

Notwithstanding all this, however, Dawes had disappeared. The fat landlord of the Star Hotel was the last person who saw him, and the flying yellow figure would seem to have been as completely swallowed up by the warm summer's afternoon as if it had run headlong into the blackest night ever hung above the earth.

ⵌ 9 ⵌ

JOHN REX'S LETTER HOME

THE little gathering, of which Major Vickers had spoken to Mr Meekin, had swelled into something larger than he had anticipated. Instead of a quiet dinner at which his own household, his daughter's betrothed, and the stranger clergyman should alone be present, the Major found himself entangled with the ladies

Protherick and Jellicoe, Mr McNab of the garrison, and Mr Pounce of the civil list. His family dinner had grown into an evening party.

Dora was rather pleased at this. She delighted in music and laughter and excitement. She was not without a certain healthy liking for admiration, and looked forward to the somewhat uncouth compliments of young Ensign McNab - 'the Mock Nob', as he called himself - with interest. Not that she liked the Mock Nob, but that she was pleased at the offerings he brought. The sanctity of the rite, say the Fathers, is in no wise affected by the unworthiness of the priest, and honest admiration is pleasant to a girl of eighteen, even though the admirer be but a freckled subaltern with a strong Scotch accent.

'Hoo d'ye do, Meejor Veekers?' says the Mock Nob on entering, 'Mees Veekers, a marry Chreestmas t'ye and hoppy New Yeear!'

'Thank you, Mr McNab,' says Dora, with a reproving glance at Maurice Frere, who seemed about to grin, 'I'm much obliged to you I'm sure.'

'This is better than Scotland, eh Mac?' says Frere; 'something like a climate this; none of your hail and mist, eh?'

'The cleemat o' Scautlan, sir, is a varry exallant cleemat, and maist suited for the keepin' o' Chreestmas time in the faushion o' oor auncestors.'

'Give me old England,' says Frere, 'that's the place for me. Confound your porridge and sheep's paunches.'

'Come, Maurice, the Haggis is Mr McNab's National dish,' says Dora, willing to spare the young Scotchman a pang, 'and is sung of by his national Poet.'

'Ay, ay, Meess Dora, Rrrabbie Burrrns sings o't. Th'immortal Rab! and in faith 'tis a varry exallant deesh wun prauperly cookit, I can assure ye.'

'Never mind, McNab; you'll get some Roast Beef and Plumpudding today,' said Vickers.

'The Roast Beef of Old England,' says Mrs Jellicoe, as if she was quoting poetry.

'Ay, the Old English Roast Beef,' says the Rev. Meekin cheerfully, taking up the strain. 'Nothing like it leddies, nothing like it.'

'You won't get much at Port Arthur,' says Frere, incapable of uttering a sentence without a blundering sting in it. 'Salt meat, Meekin, is the rule there, except when the schooner brings down fresh provisions. You might get a bit of dog now and then.'

'Dog? What do you mean?' says Meekin, astonished.

'They've got nine dogs chained across the Isthmus at Eagle-hawk Neck,' replied Frere, 'and when any of 'em die, don't you know, the guard have a change of diet.'

'My dear Maurice,' says Dora, 'how can you say such horrid things?'

'Upon my soul!' says Maurice. 'The sea washes up pretty close, don't you see, and some of the dogs are set out on stages in the water. The cold kills 'em.'

Mr Meekin's countenance expressed some surprise.

'My dear fellow,' continued the agreeable Frere, regardless of Vickers's frown, 'that's nothing. They've got a shark down there, "Government Billy", they call him; and he swims about the bay, ready for any adventurous bolter.'

'Captain Frere, you're not in earnest?'

'Oh yes, I am. They ration old Billy like any other warder. So many pounds of pork, you know, and so on. Don't they, Vickers?'

'I believe that there *is* a shark down there,' says Vickers abruptly, 'but Mr Meekin will find out all about Port Arthur for himself, I've no doubt. Mr Meekin, will you take my daughter; Maurice, give Mrs Jellicoe your arm.'

And with such arranging of guests the party moved into the dining-room.

But the conversation, thus started into the convict track, would not leave it.

'Heard anything about that fellow Dawes?' asked Mr Pounce, before the soup was removed.

'Not yet,' says Frere, sulkily, 'but he won't be out long. I've got a dozen men up the mountain.'

'I suppose it is not easy for a prisoner to make good his escape?' says Meekin.

'Oh, he needn't be caught,' says Frere, 'if that's what you mean, but he'll starve instead. The bushranging days are over now, and it's a precious poor look out for any man to live upon luck in the bush.'

'Indeed yes,' says Mr Pounce, carefully mingling sauces for his fish; 'this island seems specially adapted by Providence for a convict settlement; for, with an admirable climate, it carries little indigenous vegetation which will suffice to support human life.'

'Wull,' said the Mock Nob to Dora, 'I don't think Prauvidence had any thocht o' caunveect deeciplin whun He created the cauleny o' Van Deemen's Lan'.'

'Neither do I,' said Dora.

'A most acute remark of yours, Mr Pounce,' says Mrs Protherick. 'Poor Protherick used often to say that it seemed as if some Almighty Hand had planned the Penal Settlements round the coast, for the country is so delightfully barren.'

'Ay, Port Arthur couldn't have been better if it had been made on purpose,' says Frere; 'and all up the coast from Tenby to St Helens there isn't a scrap for human being to make a meal on. The West Coast is worse. By George, sir, in the old days, I remember –'

'Jellicoe was at Hell's Gates for a while before you went there, Major,' put in Mrs Jellicoe, 'and the accounts he gave of the place terrified me.'

'By the way,' says Meekin, 'I've got something to show you. Rex's confession. I brought it down on purpose.'

'Rex's confession!'

'His account of his adventures after he left the Macquarie Harbour. I am going to send it to the Bishop.'

'Oh, I should like to see it,' said Dora, with heightened colour. 'The story of these unhappy men has a personal interest for me, you know.'

'A forbidden subject, Poppet.'

'No, papa, not altogether forbidden, for it does not affect me now like it used to do. You must let me read it, Mr Meekin.'

'A pack of lies, I expect,' says Frere, with a scowl. 'That scoundrel Rex couldn't tell the truth to save his life.'

'You misjudge him, Captain Frere,' said Meekin. 'All the prisoners are not hardened in iniquity like Rufus Dawes. Rex is, I believe, truly penitent, and has written a most touching letter to his father.'

'A letter!' said Vickers. 'You know that, by the King's – no, the Queen's – Regulations, no letters are allowed to be sent to the friends of prisoners without first passing through the hands of the authorities.'

'I am aware of that, Major, and for that reason have brought it with me, that you may read it for yourself. It seems to me to breathe a spirit of true piety.'

'Let's have a look at it,' says Frere.

'Here it is,' returned Meekin, producing a packet: 'and when the cloth is removed, I will ask the permission of the ladies to read it aloud. It is most interesting.'

A glance of surprise passed between the ladies Protherick and Jellicoe. The idea of a convict's letter proving interesting! But, then, Mr Meekin was new to the ways of the place.

Frere, turning the packet between his fingers, read the address:

> John Rex, sen.,
> Care of Mr Blick
> 38 Bishopgate Street Within
> London.

'Why can't he write to his father direct?' said he. 'Who's Blick?'

'A worthy merchant, I am told, in whose counting-house the unfortunate Rex passed his younger days. He has tolerable education, as you are aware.'

'Educated prisoners are always the worst,' says Vickers. 'James, some more wine. We don't drink toasts here, but as this is Christmas Eve – "Her Majesty the Queen!"'

'Hear, hear, hear!' says Maurice. '"Her Majesty the Queen!"'

Having drunk this loyal toast with due fervour, Vickers proposed 'His Excellency Sir John Franklin', which toast was likewise duly honoured.

'Here's a Merry Christmas and a Happy New Year to you, sir,' says Frere, with the letter still in his hand. 'God bless us all.'

'Amen!' says Meekin, piously. 'Let us hope He will; and now, leddies, the letter. I will read you the Confession afterwards.'

Opening the packet with the religious ecstasy of a Gospel

vineyard labourer who sees his first vine sprouting, the good creature began:

'Hobart Town, Dec. 27th, 1838.

'MY DEAR FATHER, Through all the chances, changes, and vicissitudes of my chequered life, I never had a task so painful to my mangled feelings as the present one, of addressing you from this doleful spot – my sea-girt prison, on the beach of which I stand a monument of destruction; driven by the adverse winds of fate to the confines of black despair and into the vortex of galling misery.'

'Poetical!' says Frere.

'I am just like a gigantic tree of the forest which has stood many a wintry blast and stormy tempest, but now, alas! I am become a withered trunk with all my greenest and tenderest branches lopped off. Though fast attaining middle-age, I am not filling an envied and honoured post with credit and respect. No – I shall be soon wearing the garb of degradation and the badge and brand of infamy, at P.A., which is, being interpreted, Port Arthur, the "Villain's Home."'

'Poor fellow!' says Dora.
'Touching, is it not?' says Meekin.

'I am, with heart-rending sorrow and anguish of soul, ranged and mingled with the outcasts of Society. My present circumstances and picture you will find well and truly drawn in the 88th Psalm and the 102nd, commencing with the 3rd verse to the 12th inclusive, which, my dear father, I request you will read attentively before you proceed any further.'

'Hullo!' says Frere, pulling out his pocket-book, 'what's that? Read those numbers again.'

Mr Meekin complied, and Frere grinned.

'Go on,' he said. 'I'll show you something in that letter directly.'

'Oh, my dear father, avoid, I beg of you, the reading of profane books. Let your mind dwell upon holy things, and assiduously study to grow in grace. Isaiah xli. 10, 11, 12; Ps. lxxiii. 2. Yet I have hope even in this my desolate condition. – Ps. xxxv. 18. For the Lord God is merciful, and inclineth his ear unto pity.'

'Blasphemous dog!' says Vickers. 'You don't believe all that, Meekin, do you?'

The parson reproved him gently.

'Wait a moment, sir, until I have finished.'

'Party spirit runs high, even in prison Van Diemen's Land. I am sorry to say that a licentious press invariably evinces a great degree of contumely, while the authorities are held in respect by all well-disposed persons, though it is endeavoured by some to bring on them the hatred and contempt of prisoners. But I am glad to tell you that their efforts are without avail; but, nevertheless, do not read in any colonial newspaper. There is so much scurrility and vituperation in their productions.'

'That's for your benefit, Frere,' said Vickers, with a smile. 'You remember what was said about your presence at the race meetings?'

'Of course,' said Frere. 'Artful scoundrel! Go on, Mr Meekin, pray.'

'I am aware that you will hear accounts of cruelty and tyranny, said, by the malicious and the evil-minded haters of Government and Government officials, to have been inflicted by gaolers on convicts. To be candid, this is not the "hell" it has been represented to be by vindictive writers. Severe flogging and heavy chaining is used, no doubt, but only in rare cases; and nominal punishments are marked out by law for slight breaches of discipline. So far as I have an opportunity of judging the lash is never bestowed unless merited.'

'As far as he is concerned, I don't doubt it!' says Frere, cracking a walnut.

'The texts of Scripture quoted by our chaplain have comforted me much, and I have much to be thankful for; for after the rash attempt I made to secure my freedom, I have reason to be thankful for the mercy shown to me. Death – dreadful death of soul and body – would have been my portion, but, by the mercy of Omnipotence, I have been spared to repentance – John iii. I have now come to bitterness. The chaplain, a pious gentleman, says it but rarely pays to steal. "Lay up for yourself treasures in heaven, where neither moth nor rust doth corrupt." Honesty is the best policy, I am convinced, and I would not for £1000 repeat my evil courses – Ps. xxx. viii., 14. When I think of the happy days I passed with good Mr Blick in the old house in Blue Anchor Yard, and reflect that since that happy time I have plunged in sin, and stolen goods and watches, studs, rings, and jewellery, become, indeed, a common thief, I tremble with remorse, and fly to prayer – Ps. v. O what sinners we are! Let me hope that now I, by God's blessing placed beyond temptation, will live safely, and that some day I even may, by the will of the Lord Jesus, find mercy for my sins. Some kind of madness has method in it, but madness of sin holds us without escape. Such is, dear father, then, my hope and trust for my remaining life here – Ps. c., 75. I owe my bodily well-being to Captain Maurice Frere, who was good enough to speak of my conduct, in reference to the *Osprey*, when, with Shires, Barker, and others, we captured that vessel. Pray for Captain Frere, my dear father. He is a good man, and though his public duty is painful and trying to his feelings, yet, as a public functionary, he could not allow his private feelings, whether of mercy or revenge, to step between him and his duty.'

'Confound the rascal!' says Frere, growing crimson.

'Remember me most affectionately to Sarah and little William, and all friends who yet cherish the recollection of me, and bid them take warning by my fate and keep from evil courses. A good conscience is better than gold, and no amount can compensate for the misery incident to a return to crime. Whether I shall ever see you again, dear father, is more than uncertain. For my doom is life, unless the Government alter their plans concerning me, and allow me an opportunity to earn my freedom by hard work.

'The blessing of God rest with you, my dear father; and that you may be washed white in the blood of the Lamb, is the prayer of your

'Unfortunate Son,

JOHN REX.'

' "Though your sins be as scarlet they shall be whiter than snow." '

'Is that all?' says Frere.

'That is all, sir, and a very touching letter it is.'

'So it is,' says Frere. 'Now, let me have it a moment, Mr Meekin.'

He took the paper, and referring to the numbers of the texts which he had written in his pocket-book, began to knit his brows over Mr John Rex's impious and hypocritical production.

'I thought so,' he said at length. 'Those texts were never written for nothing. It's an old trick, but cleverly done.'

'What do you mean?' said Meekin.

'Mean!' cries Frere, with a smile at his own acuteness. 'This precious composition contains a very gratifying piece of intelligence for Mr Blick, whoever he is. Some receiver, I've no doubt. Look here, Mr Meekin. Take the letter and this pencil, and begin at the second text. The 102nd Psalm, from the 3rd verse to the 12th inclusive, doesn't he say? Very good; that's nine verses, isn't it? Well now, underscore nine consecutive words from the second word immmediately following the second text quoted, "I have hope", &c. Have you got it?'

'Yes,' says Meekin, astonished, while all heads bent over the table.

'Well now, his text is the eighteenth verse of the thirty-*fifth* Psalm, isn't it? Count eighteen words on, then, and underscore *five* consecutive ones. You've done that?'

'A moment – eight, nine, ten, eleven – yes.'

'Go on then in the same way until you come to the word "Texts" somewhere. Vickers, I'll trouble you for the claret.'

'Yes,' says Meekin, after a pause. Here it is – "the texts of Scripture quoted by our chaplain." But surely, Mr Frere –'

'Hold on a bit now,' cries Frere. 'What's the next quotation? – John iii. That's every third word. Score away now until you come to a quotation. Got it? How many words in it?'

'"Lay up for yourselves treasures in Heaven, where neither moth nor rust doth corrupt,"' says Meekin, a little scandalized. 'Fourteen words.'

'Count fourteen words on, then, and score the fourteenth. I'm up to this text-quoting business.'

'The word "£1,000",' says Meekin. 'Yes.'

'Then there's another text. Thirty-eighth – isn't it? – Psalm and the fourteenth verse. Do that the same way as the other. Count fourteen words, and then score eight in succession. Where does that bring you?'

'The fifth Psalm.'

'Every fifth word then. Go on, my dear sir – go on. "Method" of "escape", yes. The hundredth Psalm means a full stop. What verse? Seventy-fifth. Count seventy-four, and score.'

There was a pause for a few minutes while Mr Meekin counted. The letter had really turned out interesting.

'Read out your marked words now, Meekin. Let's see if I'm right.'

Mr Meekin read, with gradually crimsoning face.

'I have hopes even in this my desolate condition ... in prison Van Diemen's Land ... the authorities are held in ... hatred and contempt of prisoners ... read in any colonial newspaper ... accounts of cruelty and tyranny ... inflicted by gaolers on convicts ... severe flogging and heavy chaining ... for slight breaches of discipline I ... come ... the ... pious ... it ... pays ... £1,000 ... in the old house in Blue Anchor Yard ... stolen goods and watches studs rings and jewellery ... are ... now ... placed ... safely ... I ... will ... find ... some ... method of ... escape ... then ... for ... revenge.'

'Well,' says Maurice, looking round, with a grin, 'what do you think of that?'

'Marvellous!'

'Most remarkable!' said Mr Pounce.

'Extraordinary!'

'How did you find it out, Frere?'

'Oh, it's nothing,' says Frere; meaning that it was a great deal. 'I've studied a good many of these things, and this one is clumsy to some I've seen. But it's pious, isn't it, Meekin?'

Mr Meekin arose in wrath.

'It is very ungracious on your part, Captain Frere. A capital joke, I have no doubt; but permit me to say I do not like jesting on such matters. This poor fellow's letter to his aged father to be made the subject of heartless merriment, I confess I do not understand. It was confided to me in my sacred character as a Christian pastor.'

'That's just it. The fellows play upon the parsons, excuse me, don't you know, and under cover of your "sacred character", play all kinds of pranks. How the dog must have chuckled when he gave you that!'

'Captain Frere,' said Mr Meekin, changing colour like a chameleon with indignation and rage, 'your interpretation is, I am convinced, an incorrect one. How could the poor man compose such an ingenious piece of cryptography?'

'If you mean, fake up that paper,' returned Frere, unconsciously dropping into prison slang, 'I'll tell you. He had a Bible, I suppose, while he was writing?'

'I certainly permitted him the use of the Sacred Volume,

Captain Frere. I should have judged it inconsistent with the character of my Office to have refused it to him.'

'Of course. And that's just where you parsons are always putting your foot into it. If you'd put your "Office" into your pocket and open your eyes a bit –'

'Maurice! My dear Maurice!'

'I beg your pardon, Meekin,' says Maurice, with clumsy apology; 'but I *know* these fellows. I've lived among 'em, I came out in a ship with 'em, I've talked with 'em, and drank with 'em, and I'm down to all their moves, don't you see. The Bible is the only book they get hold of, and texts are the only bits of learning ever taught 'em, and being chockful of villainy and devilment and plots and conspiracies, what other book should they make use of to aid their infernal schemes *but* the one that the chaplain has made a text-book of for 'em.' And Maurice rose in disgust, not unmixed with self-laudation.

'Dear me, it is really very terrible,' said Meekin, who was not ill-meaning, but only self-complacent – 'very terrible indeed.'

'But unhappily true,' said Mr Pounce. 'An olive? Thanks.'

'Upon me soul!' burst out honest Mock Nob, 'the hail seestem seems to be maist ill-calculated tae advance the wark o' reformation.'

'Mr McNab, I'll trouble you for the port,' says equally honest Vickers, bound hand and foot in the chains of the 'rules of the service'.

'I beg your pardon, Kornel,' says Mock Nob, blushing scarlet at reflection upon his heretical outburst.

'It is really most melancholy and distressing,' says Mrs Protherick, turning a black bracelet on an iron wrist. 'Dora, my love, you promised to show me those charming things you received from Paris.'

And so, what seemed likely to become a dangerous discussion upon convict discipline, was stifled judiciously at the birth. But Dora, prompted, perhaps, by curiosity, perhaps by a desire to modify the parson's chagrin, in passing Mr Meekin, took up the 'confession', that lay unopened beside his wine glass, and bore it off.

'I *must* read this,' she whispered, with an arch look at her stately father. 'I will give it to you before you go.'

'Come, Mr Meekin,' says Vickers, when the door closed, 'help yourself. I am sorry the letter turned out so strangely, but you may rely on Frere, I assure you. He knows more about convicts than any man on the island.'

'You think that this man Rex has really tried to communicate intelligence to his friends,' says Meekin, playing with the letter irresolutely.

'Judge for yourself, my dear fellow. I dare say there's more, if I had time to make it out. Can't you see,' continued Frere, whose baleful experience stood in the place of analytical ability, 'that Blick is the fence to the gang, and Master Rex has planted a swag in some house of meeting, and warns his mates of it.'

'Ah!' says Meekin, wishing now to appear as cunning of knowledge as his teacher, 'thinking they may as well have it, now that he is in prison, I suppose.'

'Not a bit,' returned Frere, with a mental oath. 'Don't you see he says he hopes to escape, and enjoy it. He wants Blick to keep it for him.'

'Honour among thieves?'

'Just that. Don't you believe that these fellows are robbed by their pals. It's precious seldom, I can tell you. A fence will keep a swag for a good man for years.'

'Indeed! I thought –'

'I know you did; but don't. It don't *pay* a fence to steal, any more than it pays a banker to break, unless he goes in for a very heavy sum.'

'Feefty thoosan' sattled on his wife, and paying a penny in the pund,' says the Mock Nob, who refuted ten times a day the calumny that the Scotch have no sense of humour.

'Honesty is a fence's capital, Mr Meekin. It's all he lives upon.'

'I see, Captain Frere, that you have made a study of the criminal classes.'

'So I have, my dear sir, and know every turn and twist among 'em. I'll tell you my maxim. It's some French fellow's, too, I believe, but that don't matter – *divide to conquer*. Set all the dogs spying on each other.'

'Oh!' says Meekin.

'It's the only way. Why, my dear sir, if the prisoners were as faithful to each other as the fences are to them, we couldn't hold the island a week. It's just because no man can trust his neighbour that every mutiny falls to the ground.'

'I suppose it must be so,' says poor Meekin.

'It is so; and, by George, sir, if I had my way, I'd have it so that no prisoner should say a word to his right hand man, but his left hand man should tell me of it. I'd promote the men that peached, and make the beggars their own warders. Ha, ha!'

'But such a course, Captain Frere, though perhaps useful in a certain way, would surely produce harm. It would excite the worst passions of our fallen nature, and lead to endless lying and tyranny. I'm sure it would.'

'Wait a bit,' cries Frere. 'Perhaps, one of these days, I'll get a chance, and then I'll try it. Convicts! By the Lord Harry, sir, there's only one way to treat 'em; give 'em tobacco when they behave 'emselves, and flog 'em when they don't.'

'Terrible!' says the clergyman, with a shudder. 'You speak of them as if they were wild beasts.'

'So they are,' said Maurice Frere, calmly.

That was the general opinion in those days.

❧ 10 ❧

WHAT BECAME OF THE MUTINEERS OF THE OSPREY

LEFT to entertain the ladies, Miss Dora felt wearied. The usual chit-chat concerning servants and wages, and marryings and givings in marriage – small-beer brewed infinitely small in that town where every one knew his neighbour's affairs better than his own – did not interest her. She longed to read the manuscript she had borne off from Meekin, and searched for an opportunity. By and by one offered itself. Good Mrs Jellicoe, who had assumed the position of a gratuitous mother to the Major's daughter, commenced an interminable story concerning an incident in the life of the late Joseph Jellicoe; and Dora, after skirmishing from the piano to the book-case, effected an escape by the open window into the garden.

The 'good old custom' of early dining was preserved by Major Vickers, and the sun had not set yet. The gentlemen were sure to linger over their wine until light failed them, Dora thought; and excess of ceremony with an old friend like Mrs Protherick would be out of place. She reasonably might calculate upon an hour of loneliness.

'I am going for a stroll in the garden,' she said. 'My head aches.'

'Do dear,' replied Mrs Jellicoe, scarcely pausing in her narration. 'Don't mind us – And so, you see, when I heard *that,* I said, "Joseph! I may be a woman, Joseph, but *still –*" '

At the bottom of the long luxuriant garden-ground was a rustic seat, abutting upon the low wall that topped the lane. The branches of the English trees (planted long ago) hung above it, and between their rustling boughs one could see the reach of the silver river. Sitting with her face to the bay and her back to the house, Dora opened the manuscript and began to read. It was written in a firm, large hand, and headed –

A NARRATIVE

Of the sufferings and adventures of certain of the ten convicts who piratically seized the brig Osprey, *at Macquarie Harbour, in Van Diemen's Land, related by one of the said convicts while lying under sentence for this offence in the gaol at Hobart Town.*

Dora, having read this grandiloquent sentence, paused for a moment. The story of the mutiny, which had been the epoch of her childhood, lay before her, and it seemed to her that, were it related truly, she would comprehend a something strange and terrible, which had been for many years but a shadow upon her memory. Longing, and yet fearing, to proceed, she held the paper, half unfolded, in her hand, as, in her childhood, she had held ajar the door of some dark room, into which she longed and yet feared to enter. Her timidity lasted but an instant.

'When orders arrived from head-quarters to break up the penal settlement of Macquarie Harbour, the Commandant (Major Vickers, —th Regiment) and most of the prisoners embarked on board a colonial vessel, and set sail for Hobart Town, leaving behind them a brig that had been built at Macquarie Harbour, to be brought round after them, and placing Captain Maurice Frere in command, left aboard her Mr Bates, who had acted as pilot at the settlement, four soldiers, and ten prisoners, as a crew to work the vessel. The Commandant's wife and child were also aboard.'

'How strangely it reads,' thought the girl.

'On the 12th of January, 1834, we set sail, and in the afternoon anchored safely outside the Gates, but a breeze setting in from the north-west, caused a swell on the bar, and Mr Bates ran back to Wellington Bay. We remained there all next day; and in the afternoon Captain Frere took two soldiers and a boat, and went a fishing. There were then but Mr Bates and the other two soldiers aboard, and it was proposed by William Cheshire to seize the vessel. I was at first unwilling, thinking that loss of life might ensue, but Cheshire and the others, knowing that I was acquainted with navigation – having in happier days lived much on the sea – threatened me if I refused to join. A song was started in the folksle, and one of the soldiers coming to listen to it, was seized, and Lyon and Riley then made prisoner of the sentry. Forced thus into a project with which I had at first but little sympathy, I felt my heart leap at the prospect of freedom, and would have sacrificed all to obtain it. Maddened by the desperate hopes that inspired me, I from that moment assumed the command of my wretched companions; and honestly think, that however culpable I may have been in the eyes of the law, I prevented them from the display of a violence to which their savage life had unhappily made them but too accustomed.'

'Poor fellow,' says Dora, beguiled by Master Rex's specious paragraphs, 'I think he was not to blame.'

Mr Bates was below in the cabin, and on being summoned by Cheshire to surrender, with great courage attempted a defence. Barker fired at him through the skylight, but fearful of the lives of the Commandant's wife and child, I struck up his musket, and the ball passed through the mouldings of the stern windows. At the same time the soldiers whom we had bound in the folksle forced up the hatch and came on deck. Cheshire shot the first one, and struck the other with his clubbed musket. The wounded man lost his footing, and the brig lurching with the rising tide, he fell into the sea. This was – by the blessing of God – the only life lost in the whole affair.

'Mr Bates, seeing now that we had possession of the deck, surrendered, upon promise that the Commandant's wife and child should be put ashore in safety. I directed him to take such matters as he needed, and prepared to lower the jolly-boat. As she swung off the davits, Captain Frere came alongside in the whale-boat, and gallantly endeavoured to board us, but the boat drifted past the vessel. I was now determined to be free – indeed, the minds of all on board were made up to carry through the business – and hailing the whale-boat, swore to fire into her unless she surrendered. Captain Frere refused, and was for boarding us again, but the two soldiers joined in with us, and prevented his intention. Having now got the prisoners into the jolly-boat, we transferred Captain Frere into her, and being ourselves in the whale-boat, compelled Captain Frere and Mr Bates to row ashore. We then took the jolly-boat in tow, and returned to the brig; a strict watch being kept for fear that they should rescue the vessel from us.

'At break of day every man was upon deck, and a consultation took place concerning the parting of the provisions. Cheshire was for leaving them to starve, but Lesley, Shires, and I held out for an equal division. After a long and violent controversy, Humanity gained the day, and the provisions were brought on deck. The pieces of meat were divided as evenly as possible, also a good portion of the tea, sugar, and biscuit, a small puncheon of rum, and a live goat. They were all put into the whale-boat, and taken ashore. Upon the receipt of the provisions, Mr Bates thus expressed himself, "Men, I did not for one moment expect such kind treatment from you, regarding the provisions you have now brought ashore for us, out of so little which there was on board. When I consider your present undertaking, without a competent navigator, and in a leaky vessel, your situation seems most perilous, therefore I hope God will prove kind to you, and preserve you from the manifold dangers you may have to encounter on the stormy ocean.[1]" Mrs Vickers also was pleased to say that I had behaved kindly to her, that she wished me well, and that when she returned to Hobart Town she would speak in my favour. They then cheered us on our departure, wishing we might be prosperous on account of our humanity in sharing the provisions with them.

'Having had breakfast, we commenced throwing overboard the light cargo which was in the hold, which employed us until dinner time. After dinner we ran out a small kedge-anchor with about 100 fathoms of line, and having weighed anchor, and the tide being slack, we hauled on the kedge-line, and succeeded in this manner by kedging along, and we came to two islands called the Cap and Bonnet.

1. We know what Bates really *did* say. Book III, chap. 12.

The whole of us then commenced heaving the brig short, sending the whale-boat to take her in tow after we had tripped the anchor. By this means we got her safe across the bar. Scarcely was this done when a light breeze sprang up from the south-west, and firing a musket to apprize the party we had left of our safety, we made sail and put out to sea.'

Having read thus far, Dora paused in an agony of recollection. She remembered the firing of the musket, and that a female figure, that was her mother, had wept over her. But beyond this all was uncertainty. Memories slipped across her mind like shadows – she caught at them, and they were gone. Yet the reading of this strange story made her nerves thrill. Despite the hypocritical grandiloquence and affected piety of the narrative, it was easy to see that, save some warping of facts to make for himself a better case, and to extol the courage of the gaolers who had him at their mercy, the narrator had not attempted to better his tale by the invention of perils. The history of the desperate project that had been planned and carried out five years before was related with that grim simplicity which (because it at once bears the stamp of truth, and forces the imagination of the reader to supply the omitted details of horror), is more effective to inspire sympathy than the most elaborate of descriptions. The very barrenness of the narration was hideously suggestive, and the girl felt her heart beat quicker as her poetic intellect rushed to complete the terrible picture sketched by the convict. She saw it all – the blue sea, the burning sun, the slowly moving ship, the wretched company on the shore, she heard – Was that a rustling in the bushes below her? A bird! How nervous she was growing!

'Being thus fairly rid – as we thought – of our prison life, we cheerfully held consultation as to our future course. It was my intention to get among the islands in the South Seas, and scuttling the brig, to pass ourselves off among the Natives as shipwrecked seamen, trusting to God's mercy that some homeward bound vessel might at length rescue us. With this view, I made James Lesley first mate, he being an experienced mariner, and prepared myself with what few instruments we had to take our departure from Birches Rock. Having hauled the whale-boat alongside, we stove her, together with the jolly-boat, and cast her adrift. This done, I parted the landsmen with the seamen, and, steering east south-east, at eight p.m. we set our first watch.

'In little more than an hour after this, came on a heavy gale from the south-west. I, and others of the landsmen, were violently sea-sick, and Lesley had some difficulty in handling the brig, as the boisterous weather called for two men at the helm. In the morning, getting upon deck with difficulty, I found that the wind had abated, but upon sounding the well discovered much water in the hold. Lesley rigged the pumps, but the starboard one only could be made to work. From that time there were but two businesses aboard – from the pump to the helm. The gale lasted two days and a night, the brig running under close reefed topsails, we being afraid to shorten sail, lest we might be overtaken by some pursuing vessel, so strong was the terror of our prison upon us.

'On the 16th, at noon, I again forced myself on deck, and taking a meridian observation, altered the course of the brig to east and by south, wishing to run to the southward of New Zealand, out of the usual track of shipping; and having a notion that, should our provisions hold out, we might make the South American coast, and fall into Christian hands. This done, I was compelled to retire below, and for a week lay in my berth as one at the last gasp. At times I repented of my resolution, Fair urging me to bestir myself, as the men were not satisfied with our course. On the 21st, a mutiny occurred, headed by Cheshire, who asserted we were heading into the Pacific, and must infallibly perish. This disaffected man, though ignorant of navigation, insisted upon steering to the south, believing that we had run to the northward of the Friendly Islands, and was for running the ship ashore and beseeching the protection of the Natives. Lesley in vain protested that a southward course would bring us into icefields. Barker, who had served on board a whaler, strove to convince the mutineers that the temperature of such latitudes was too warm for such an error to escape us. After much noise, Cheshire rushed to the helm, and Russen, drawing one of the pistols taken from Mr Bates, shot him dead, upon which the others returned to their duty. This dreadful deed was, I fear, necessary to the safety of the brig; and had it occurred on board a vessel manned by free-men, would have been applauded as a stern but needful measure.

'Forced by these tumults upon deck, I made a short speech to the crew, and convinced them that I was competent to perform what I had promised to do, though at the time my heart inwardly failed me, and I longed for some sign of land. Supported at each arm by Lesley and Barker, I took an observation, and altered our course to north by east, the brig running eleven knots an hour under single-reefed topsails, and the pumps hard at work. So we ran until the 31st of January, when a white squall took us, and nearly proved fatal to all aboard.

'Lesley now committed a great error, for, upon the brig righting (she was thrown upon her beam ends, and her spanker boom carried away), he commanded to furl the foretopsail, strike topgallant yards, furl the main course, and take a reef in the maintopsail, leaving her to scud under single-reefed maintopsail and fore-sail. This caused the vessel to leak to that degree that I despaired of reaching land in her, and prayed to the Almighty to send us speedy assistance. For nine days and nights the storm continued, the men being utterly exhausted. One of the two soldiers whom we had employed to fish the two pieces of the spanker boom with some quartering that we had, was washed overboard and drowned. Our provision was now nearly done, but the gale abating on the ninth morning, I gave orders to cross topgallant yards and make sail; and on the 25th of February, about a quarter of an hour before dark, we sighted land. Lesley swore roundly that we were mistaken, as, by his reckoning, we were five hundred miles from Chili; but, notwithstanding, I gave orders to shorten sail, keeping a good look-out at each cathead, and at nightfall, in much anxiety, we hove to the brig. At daybreak, we saw land clearly under our lee, and held consultation as to our course, being scarcely able to keep the brig free. Though believing the land to be the coast of Valparaiso, I was fearful of our reception, and urged that we should not abandon the brig. I was overruled, however, and as, during our discussion, the leak had gained on us, we hastened to put provisions on the launch. The sea was heavy, and we were compelled to put a purchase on the fore and main yards, with preventers to windward, to ease the launch in going over the side. We got her fairly afloat at last, the others battening down the hatches in the brig. Having dressed ourselves in the clothes of Captain Frere and the pilot, we left the brig at sundown, lying with her channel plates nearly under water.

'The wind freshening during the night, our launch, which might, indeed, be termed a longboat, having been fitted with mast, bowsprit, and main boom, began to be very uneasy, shipping two seas one after the other. The only plan we could devise was to sit four of us about in the stern sheets, with our backs to the sea, to prevent the water pooping us. This itself was enough to exhaust the strongest men. The day, however, made us some amends for the dreadful night. Land was not more than ten miles from us; approaching as nearly as we could with safety, we hauled our wind, and ran along it, trusting to find some harbour. At half-past two we sighted a bay of very curious appearance, having two large rocks at the entrance, resembling pyramids. Shires, Russen, and Fair landed, in hopes of discoverng fresh water, of which we stood much in need. Before long they returned, stating that they had found an Indian hut, inside of which were some rude earthenware vessels. Fearful of surprise, we lay off the shore all that night, and putting into the bay very early in the morning, killed a seal. This was the first fresh meat I had tasted for four years. It seemed strange to eat it under such circumstances. We cooked the flippers, heart, and liver for breakfast, giving some to a cat which we had taken with us out of the brig, for I would not, willingly, allow even that animal to perish.

'After breakfast, we got under weigh; and here I cannot help remarking, that it seemed as if we were especially assisted by Providence, never having yet been without a favourable wind, for we had scarcely been out half an hour when we had a fresh breeze, which carried us along at the rate of seven knots an hour, running from bay to bay to find inhabitants. Steering along the shore, as the sun went down, we suddenly heard the bellowing of a bullock, and James Barker, whom, from his violent conduct, I thought incapable of such sentiment, burst into tears.

'In about two hours we perceived great fires on the beach, and let go the anchor in nineteen fathoms of water. We lay awake all that night. In the morning, we rowed further inshore and moored the boat to some seaweed. As soon as the inhabitants caught sight of us, they came down to the beach. A tall man, wearing a poncho, or cloak, formed of a square piece of a good size, with a hole in the middle, through which he put his head, and a pair of worsted trousers dyed blue with indigo, and a large knife suspended from his side, the hilt of which he kept continually in his hand, seemed to be their chief. I offered to this chief a hatchet, of which he well seemed to know the use. He brandished it about his head, and invited us to come ashore. Barker, Fair, Shires, and Russen, armed with a cutlass and three of Mr Bates's pistols, went ashore; and returning in about an hour, informed me that they had been treated kindly. I distributed needles and thread among the Indians, and on saying "Valdivia," a woman instantly pointed towards a tongue of land to the southward, holding up three fingers and crying "*leaghos!*" which I conjectured to be three leagues; the distance we afterwards found it to be.

'About three o'clock in the afternoon, we weathered the point pointed out by the woman, and perceived a flagstaff and a twelve-gun battery under our lee. I now divided among the men the sum of six pounds ten shillings that I had found in Captain Frere's cabin, and made another and more equal distribution of the clothing. There were also two watches, one of which I gave to Lesley, and kept the other for myself. It was resolved among us to say that we were part of the crew of the brig *Eliza,* bound for China and wrecked in the South Seas. Upon landing at the battery, we were received with the greatest civility by the Spaniards, and were heartily entertained, though we did not understand one word of what they said. Next morning, it was agreed that Lesley, Barker, Shires, and Russen, should pay for a canoe to convey them to the town, which was nine miles up the river; and on the morning of the 6th March they took their departure. On the 7th March, a boat, commanded by a lieutenant, came down with orders that the rest of us should be conveyed to town; and we accordingly launched the boat under convoy of the soldiers, and reached the town the same evening, in some trepidation. I feared lest the Spaniards had obtained a clue as to our real character, and was not deceived – the surviving soldier having betrayed us. This fellow was thus doubly a traitor; first, in deserting his officer, and then in betraying his comrades.

'We were immediately escorted to prison, where we found our four companions. Some of them were for brazening out the story of shipwreck, but knowing how confused must necessarily be our accounts, were we examined separately, I persuaded them that open confession would be our best chance of safety. The following morning we were taken before the Judge, and I gave a statement of our escape and how we came there, telling him also the names we were known by in Van Diemen's Land. The Judge informed us that the Intendente, or Governor, would visit us shortly, and that if we gave the same statement to him, we should all be released without doubt, as it appeared there had been no bloodshed. We remained in prison five days. I, as captain, was allowed by the Government one dollar; Lesley, as mate, half a dollar; the remainder, a quarter dollar per diem; and provisions being cheap, this money was amply sufficient for our support. On the 13th, we were all taken before the Governor, Don Fernando Martelle, and examined. Being asked why we had landed on that coast, I said, "Because we knew that they were patriots, and had declared their independence, and that we had thrown ourselves under the protection of their flag, relying on their mercy."

'The Governor replied, "Englishmen, I am informed, and believe, that you have spared life and committed no murder, and on that account I shall use my influence with the President at Santiago, the capital of Chili, that you remain here free subjects, being punished if you commit yourselves, under our laws, which are severe." We then returned to the guardhouse, where I made interest with Captain Lawson, our interpreter (a gentleman of great respectability), to draw up a petition, which was signed by a great number of the inhabitants.

'On the 14th, we were again taken before the Governor, who informed us that we were free, on condition that we chose to live within the limits of the town. At this intelligence I felt my heart grow light, and only begged in the name of my companions that we might not be given up to the British Government; "rather than which," said I, "I would beg to be shot dead in the palace square." The Governor regarded us with tears in his eyes, and spoke as follows: "My poor men, do not think that I would take that advantage over you. Do not make an attempt to escape, and I will be your friend; and should a vessel come to-morrow to demand you, you shall find I will be as good as my word. All I have to impress upon you is, to beware of intemperance, which is very prevalent in this country, and when you find it convenient, to pay Government the money that was allowed you for subsistence while in prison."

'The following day we all procured employment in launching a vessel of three hundred tons burden, and my men showed themselves so active that the owner said he would rather have us than thirty of his own countrymen; which saying pleased the Governor, who was there with almost the whole of the inhabitants and a whole band of music, this vessel having been nearly three years on the stocks. After she was launched, the seamen amongst us helped to fit her out, being paid fifteen dollars a month with provisions on board. As for myself, I speedily obtained employment in the shipbuilders' yard, and subsisted by honest industry, almost forgetting, in the unwonted pleasures of freedom, the sad reverse of fortune which had befallen me. To think that I, who had mingled among gentlemen and scholars, should be thankful to labour in a shipwright's yard by day, and sleep on a bundle of hides by night! But this is personal matter, and need not be obtruded. In the same yard with me worked the soldier who had betrayed us, and I could not but regard it as a special judgment of Heaven, when he one day fell from a great height and was taken up for dead, dying in much torment in a few hours. The days thus passed on in comparative happiness until the 20th of May, 1836, when the old Governor took his departure, regretted by all the inhabitants of Valdivia, and the *Achilles*, a one-and-twenty-gun brig of war, arrived with the new Governor. One of the first acts of this gentleman (Governor Thompson) was to sell our boat, which was moored at the back of Government-house. He sold mast, oars, sails, and all belonging to her; also, a compass, spy-glass, two small coils of inch rope, an anchor and cable of about 30 fathoms, with about 3 cwt. of large composition nails which I had put into the boat to ballast her before we took our departure from the *Osprey*. This proceeding looked to my mind indicative of ill-will; and upon Fair, Lyon, and Porter taking their departure from Valdivia in a schooner with one Captain West, we were ordered to present ourselves to the officer of the guard every evening at six o'clock. I knew that British vessels often cruised in those waters, and, fearful lest Governor Thompson should deliver us again into bondage, I resolved to make my escape from the place. Having communicated my plans to Barker, Lesley, Riley, Shires, and Russen, I offered the Governor to get built for him a handsome whaleboat, making the iron work myself. The Governor consented, and in little more than a fortnight we had completed a four-oared whaleboat, capable of weathering either sea or storm. We fitted her with sails and provisions in the Governor's name, and on the 4th of July, being a Saturday night, we took our departure from Valdivia, dropping down the river shortly after sunset. Whether the Governor, disgusted at the trick we had played him, decided not to pursue us, or whether — as I rather think — our absence was not discovered until the Monday morning, when we were beyond reach of capture, I know not, but we got out to sea without hazard. Some months before, and in part view of such an enterprise, I had purchased from Captain Lawson our interpreter a sextant and quadrant, and taking accurate bearings ran for the Friendly Islands, as had been agreed upon amongst us.

'But now it seemed that the good fortune which had hitherto attended us had deserted us. After crawling four days in sultry weather, there fell a dead calm, and we lay like a log upon the sea for forty-eight hours. Gloom began to settle upon our faces, when, about eight o'clock in the evening of the 10th there sprang up a light breeze from the westward, and we hastened to set all sail. Towards night the wind shifted, and a small dark cloud was observed hovering over the land. Lesley assured us that this appearance was the precursor of a squall, and begged us to take in our sails. We had scarcely done so, when the cloud increased in size and density. The breeze fell, and a boding stillness reigned around. Suddenly, a rushing noise was heard, the surface of the water, which was before almost without a ripple, became one huge sheet of foam, and in an instant the boat capsized, and we were struggling in the water. The darkness was intense; and for a few moments I thought I was alone; but on calling, I heard a reply not far from me. The wind fell as suddenly as it had risen, and swimming in the direction of the voice, I found my five companions alive clinging to the boat. It seems that she had partially righted; but in the first panic several had attempted to board her once, and she had heeled over, floating now keel uppermost. In this dreadful condition I strove to rally my comrades, beseeching them to work for the general good. Moved by my urgent entreaties, those clinging to the keel relinquished their hold, and we succeeded after much trouble in righting the boat. Barker and Lesley now got into her, and commenced bailing with two dippers of tin, which (together with the instruments) I had fortunately secured in a locker at the bows. We remained in the water clinging to the gunwale.

'The two men, however, had scarcely commenced bailing, when Russen cried, "A shark! a shark!" All order was at once at an end, the boat again capsized, and, a prey to feelings of the most terrible apprehension, we were all again struggling in the water. No sharks, however, appeared, and we summoned up our courage to again right the boat. The night passed, and it was the morning of the 11th. The bailing had proceeded but slowly, for Lesley lost his hold of the dipper when the boat overturned. In an hour or so I calculated the boat would have been cleared, when I heard again the cry, "The sharks! the sharks!" This time it was no false alarm; the boat capsized for the second time, and we were literally cast amid a shoal of these ferocious monsters. For some minutes we remained uninjured, though not untouched, for the sharks actually rubbed against us, and frequently passed over the boat and between us, while resting on the gunwale. This did not last long. A shark soon seized Riley by the leg, and he disappeared, dying the water with his blood He had not time for more than one shriek, when the savages were fighting for his body under our very feet. Each expected his own would be the next life taken, but by the mercy of God we succeeded, by superhuman exertions, in righting the boat before the shoal reappeared. We resumed our efforts, and though nearly exhausted, did not desist until the boat was nearly dry. Then, in spite of agony of mind, thirst, and hunger, I fell into a sound sleep which lasted until daybreak.

'For three days we remained in the midst of the ocean, exposed to the burning rays of the sun, in a boat without oars, sails, or provisions. On the fourth day, just as we had resolved to draw lots to determine who should die for the sustenance of the others, we were picked up by an opium clipper returning to Canton. The captain, an American, was most kind to us, and on our arrival at Canton, a subscription was got up for us by the British merchants of that city, and a free passage to England obtained for us. Russen, however, getting in drink, made statements which brought suspicion upon us. I had imposed upon the Consul with a fictitious story of a wreck, but had stated that my name was Wilson, forgetting that the sextant which had been preserved in the boat had Captain Lawson's name engraved upon it. These circumstances together caused sufficient doubt in the Consul's mind to cause him to give directions that, on our arrival in London, we were to be brought before the Thames Police Court. There being no evidence against us, we should have escaped, had not a Dr Pine, who had been surgeon on board the *Malabar* transport, being in the Court, recognised me and swore to my identity. We were remanded, and, to complete the chain of evidence, Mr Capon, the Hobart Town gaoler, was, strangely enough, in London at the time, and identified us all. Our story was then made public, and Barker and Lesley turning king's evidence against Russen, he was convicted of the murder of Cheshire, and executed. We were then placed on board the *Leviathan* hulk, and remained there until shipped in the *Lady Jane*, which was chartered, with convicts, for Van Diemen's Land, in order to be tried in the colony, where the offence was committed, for piratically seizing the brig *Osprey*, and arrived here on the 15th December, 1838.'

Coming, breathless, to the conclusion of this wonderful relation, Dora suffered her hands to fall into her lap, and sat meditative. The history of this desperate struggle for liberty, was to her full of a vague terror. She had never before realized among what manner of men she had lived. The sullen creatures who worked in the chain gangs, or pulled in the boats – their faces brutalised into a uniform blankness – must be very different men to John Rex and his companions. Her imagination pictured for her the voyage in the leaky brig, the midnight escape, the desperate rowing, the sudden squall, the horror of the sharks, the long, slow agony of starvation, and the heart-sickness that must have followed upon recapture and imprisonment. Surely the punishment of 'penal servitude' must have been made very terrible, for men to dare such hideous perils to escape from it. Surely John Rex, the convict, who, alone, and prostrated by sickness, navigated a vessel through a storm-ravaged ocean, quelled a mutiny, and secured the protection of a Spanish Governor, must possess qualities which could be put to better use than stone-quarrying. Was the opinion of Maurice Frere the correct one after all, and were these convict monsters gifted with unnatural powers of endurance, only to be subdued and tamed by unnatural and inhuman punishments of lash and chain?

Her fancies growing amid the fast gathering gloom, she shuddered as she guessed to what extremities of evil might such men proceed did an opportunity ever come to them to retaliate upon their gaolers. Perhaps beneath each mask of servility and sullen fear, that was the ordinary prison face, lay hid a courage and a despair as mighty as that which sustained those ten poor wanderers over the Pacific Sea. Maurice had told her that these people had their secret signs, their secret language. She had just seen a specimen of the skill with which this very Rex – still bent upon escape – could send a hidden message to his friends beneath the eyes of his gaolers. What if the whole island was but one smouldering volcano of revolt and murder – the whole convict population but one incarnated conspiracy, engendered and bound together by the hideous Freemasonry of crime and suffering! Terrible to think of, – yet not impossible.

Oh, how strangely must the world have been civilised, that this most lovely corner of it must needs be set apart as a place of banishment for the monsters that civilization had brought forth and bred!

She cast her eyes around, and all beauty seemed blotted out from the scene before her. The graceful foliage melting into indistinctness in the gathering twilight, appeared to her horrible and treacherous. The river seemed to flow sluggishly, as though thickened with blood and tears. The shadow of the trees seemed to hold lurking shapes of cruelty and danger. Even the whispering breeze bore with it sighs, and threats, and mutterings of revenge. Oppressed by a terror of loneliness, she hastily caught up the manuscript and turned to seek the house, when, as if summoned from the earth by the power of her own fears, a ragged figure barred her passage.

To the excited girl this apparition seemed the embodiment of the unknown evil she had dreaded. She recognised the yellow clothing, and marked the eager hands outstretched to seize her. Instantly upon her flashed the story that had set the prison-town agog. The desperado of Port Arthur, the escaped mutineer and murderer was before her, with unchained arms, free to wreak his will of her!

'Dora! It is you! Oh, at last! I have escaped, and come to ask – What? Do you not know me?'

Pressing both hands to her bosom, she stepped back a pace, speechless with terror.

'I am Rufus Dawes,' he said, looking in her face for the grateful smile of recognition that did not come. 'Rufus Dawes.'

The party at the house had finished their wine, and, sitting on the broad verandah, were listening to some gentle dulness of the clergyman, when there broke upon their ears a cry.

'What's that?' said Vickers.

Frere sprang up, and looked down the garden. He saw two figures that seemed to struggle together. One glance was enough, and, with a shout, he leapt the flower-beds, and made straight at the escaped prisoner.

Rufus Dawes saw him coming, but, secure in the protection of the girl who owed to him so much, he advanced a step nearer and caught her dress.

'Oh, help, Maurice, help!' cried Dora again.

Into the face of Rufus Dawes came an expression of horror-stricken bewilderment. For three days the unhappy man had contrived to keep life and freedom, in order to get speech with the one being who, he thought, cherished for him some affection. Having made an unparalleled escape from the midst of his warders, he had crept to the place where lived the idol of his dreams, braving recapture, that he might hear from her two words of justice and gratitude. Not only did she refuse to listen to him, and shrink from him as from one accursed, but, at the sound of his name, she summoned his deadliest foe to capture him. Such monstrous ingratitude was almost beyond belief. She, too – the child he had nursed and fed, the child for whom he had given up his earned chance of freedom and fortune, the child of whom he had dreamed, the child whose image he had worshipped – she, too, against him! Then was there no justice, no heaven, no God!

He loosed his hold of her dress and, regardless of the approaching footsteps, stood speechless, shaking from head to foot.

In an instant Frere and McNab launched themselves upon him and he was borne bleeding to the gound. Though weakened by starvation he shook them off with scarce an effort, and despite the servants who came hurrying from the alarmed house, might even then have turned and made good his escape. But he seemed unable to fly. His chest heaved convulsively, great drops of sweat beaded his white face, and from his eyes tears seemed about to break. For an instant his features worked convulsively, as if he fain would invoke upon the girl weeping on her father's shoulder some hideous curse. But no words came – only thrusting his hand into his breast, with a supreme gesture of horror and aversion, he made as if he flung something from him. Then a profound sob escaped him, and he held out his hands to be bound.

There was something so pitiable about this silent grief, that, as they led him away, the little group instinctively averted their faces, lest they should seem to triumph over him.

← 11 →

A RELIC OF MACQUARIE HARBOUR

'You must try and save him from further punishment,' said Dora, next day, to Frere. 'I did not mean to betray the poor creature, but I had made myself nervous by reading that convict's story.'

'You shouldn't read such rubbish,' says Frere. 'What's the use? I don't suppose a word of it's true.'

'It must be true. I am sure it's true. Oh, Maurice, these are dreadful men. I thought I knew all about convicts, but I had no idea that such men as these were among them.'

'Thank God, you know very little,' says Maurice. 'The servants you have here are very different sort of fellows to Rex and Company.'

'Maurice, do you think there will ever be a Mutiny?'

'Where – here? Not a bit of it.'

'What ever should we do if there was one! I was thinking last night, Maurice, how few *we* are in comparison with *them*.'

'Don't be alarmed, Poppet.'

'Oh, Maurice, I am so tired of this place. It's wrong, perhaps, with poor papa and all, but I do wish I was somewhere out of the sight of chains and yellow cloth. I don't know what has made me feel like I do.'

'Come to Sydney,' says Frere. 'There are not so many convicts there. It was arranged that we should go to Sydney, you know.'

'For our Honeymoon? Yes,' said Dora, simply. 'I know it was. But we are not married yet.'

'That's easily done,' says Maurice.

'Oh, nonsense, sir! But I want to speak to you about this poor Dawes. I don't think he meant any harm. It seems to me now that he was rather going to ask for food or something, only I was so nervous. They won't hang him, Maurice, will they?'

'No,' says Maurice. 'I spoke to your father this morning. If the fellow is tried, you may have to give evidence, and so we think that Port Arthur again and heavy irons will meet the case. We gave him another life sentence this morning. That will make the third he's had.'

'What did he say?'

'Nothing. I sent him down aboard the schooner at once. He ought to be out of the river by this time.'

'Maurice, I have a strange feeling about that man.'

'Eh?' says Maurice.

'I seem to fear him, as if I knew some story about him, and yet didn't know it.'

'That's not very clear,' says Maurice, forcing a laugh; 'but don't let's talk about him any more. We'll soon be far from Port Arthur and everybody in it.'

'Alone with my Bruin, – my good, kind, brave Maurice. Maurice, I love you, dear. You'll always protect me against these men, won't you?'

Delighted Maurice kissed her.

'You have not got over your fright, Dora,' he said. 'I see I shall have to take a great deal of care of my wife.'

'Of course,' replied Dora.

And then the pair began to make love, or rather Maurice made it, and Dora suffered him.

Suddenly her eye caught something. 'What's that – there, on the ground by the fountain?'

They were near the spot where Dawes had been seized the night before. A little stream ran through the garden, and a Triton – of convict manufacture – blew his horn in the middle of a – convict built – rockery. Under the lip of the fountain lay a small packet.

Frere picked it up. (It was made of soiled yellow cloth, and stitched evidently by a man's fingers.)

'It looks like a needle-case,' said he.

'Let me see. What a strange-looking thing! Yellow cloth, too. Why, it must belong to a prisoner. Oh, Maurice, the man who was here last night!'

'Ay,' says Maurice, turning over the packet, 'it might have been his, sure enough.'

'He seemed to fling something from him, I thought. Perhaps this is it?' said she, peering over his arm, in delicate curiosity.

Frere, with something of a scowl on his brow, tore off the outer covering of the mysterious packet, and displayed a second envelope, of grey cloth – the 'good-conduct' uniform. Beneath this was a piece, some three inches square, of stained and discoloured merino, that had once been blue.

'Hullo!' says Frere. 'Why, what's this?'

He had expected a letter, at the very least.

'It is a piece of a woman's dress,' said Dora.

It was a portion of the frock she had worn at Macquarie Harbour, and which the unhappy convict had cherished as a relic for five weary years.

Frere made an impatient movement, and flung it into the water. The running stream whirled it away.

'Why did you do that?' cried the girl, with a sudden pang of remorse for which she could not well account.

The shred of cloth, caught by a weed, lingered for an instant on the surface of the water.

Almost at the same moment, the pair, raising their eyes, saw the schooner which bore Rufus Dawes glide past the opening of the trees and disappear.

When they looked again for the strange relic of the desperado of Port Arthur, it also had vanished.

'It grows cold,' said Dora, with a shudder. 'Let us go in.'

AT PORT ARTHUR

THE usual clanking and hammering was prevalent upon the stone jetty of Port Arthur when the schooner bearing Rufus Dawes ran alongside.

On the heights above the stone esplanade rose the grim front of the soldiers' barracks; beneath the soldiers' barracks was the long range of prison buildings, with their workshops and tan-pits; to the left lay the Commandant's house, authoritative by reason of its embrasured terrace and guardian sentry; while the jetty, that faced the purple length of the 'Island of the Dead,' swarmed with parti-coloured figures, clanking about their enforced business, under the muskets of their gaolers.

Rufus Dawes had seen this prospect before, had learnt by heart each beauty of rising sun, sparkling water, and wooded hill. From the hideously clean jetty at his feet, to the signal station, that, embowered in bloom, reared its slender arms upwards into the cloudless sky, he knew it all. There was no charm for him in the exquisite blue of the sea, the soft shadows of the hills, or the soothing ripple of the waves, that crept voluptuously to the white breast of the shining shore. He sat with his head bowed down, and his hands clasped about his knees, disdaining to look until they roused him.

'Hallo, Dawes!' says Warder Troke, halting his train of ironed yellow-jackets. 'So you've come back again! Glad to see yer, Dawes! It seems an age since we had the pleasure of your company, Dawes!'

At this pleasantry the train laughed, so that their irons clanked more than ever. They found it inconvenient not to laugh at Mr Troke's humour.

'Step down here, Dawes, and let me introduce yer to your hold friends. They'll be glad to see yer, won't yer, boys? Why, bless me, Dawes, we thort we'd lost yer! We thort yer'd given us the slip altogether, Dawes. They didn't take care of yer in

Hobart Town, I expect, eh, boys? We'll look after yer here, Dawes, though. You won't bolt any more.'

'Now, Mr Troke,' said a warning voice, 'you're at it again! Let the man alone!'

By virtue of an order transmitted from Hobart Town, they had begun to attach the dangerous prisoner to the last man of the gang, rivetting the leg-irons of the pair by means of an extra link, which could be removed when necessary, but Dawes had never given sign of consciousness.

At the sound of the friendly tones, however, he looked up, and saw a tall, gaunt man, dressed in shabby pepper-and-salt raiment, and wearing a black handkerchief knotted round his throat. He was a stranger to him.

'I beg yer pardon, Mr North,' says Troke, sinking at once the bully in the sneak. 'I didn't see yer reverence.'

'A parson!' thought Dawes, with disappointment, and dropped his eyes.

'I know that,' returned Mr North, coolly. 'If you had, you would have been all butter and honey. Don't trouble yourself to tell a lie; it's quite unnecessary.'

Dawes looked up again. This was a strange parson.

'What's your name, my man?' says Mr North, suddenly, catching his eye.

Rufus Dawes had intended to scowl, but the tone, sharply authoritative, roused his automatic convict second-nature, and he answered, almost despite himself.

'Rufus Dawes!' said Mr North, 'Oh, this is the man, is it? I thought he was to go to the Coal Mines.'

'So he is,' says Troke, 'but we hain't a goin' to send there for a fornit, and in the meantime I'm to work him on the chain.'

'Oh!' says Mr North again. 'Lend me your knife, Troke.'

And then, before them all, this curious parson took a piece of tobacco out of his ragged pocket, and cut off a 'chaw' with Mr Troke's knife.

Rufus Dawes felt what he had not felt for three days – an interest in something. He stared at the parson in unaffected astonishment.

Mr North perhaps mistook the meaning of his fixed stare, for he held out the remnant of tobacco to him.

The chained line vibrated at this, and bent forward to enjoy the vicarious delight of seeing another man chew tobacco. Troke grinned with a silent mirth that betokened retribution for the favoured convict.

'Here,' said Mr North, holding out the dainty morsel upon which so many eyes were fixed.

Rufus Dawes took the tobacco; looked at it hungrily for an instant, and then – to the astonishment of everybody – flung it away with a curse.

'I don't want your tobacco,' he said; 'keep it.'

From convict mouths went out a respectful roar of amazement, and Mr Troke's eyes snapped with pride of outraged janitorship.

'You ungrateful dog!' he cried, raising his stick.

Mr North put up a hand.

'That will do, Troke,' he said, 'I know your respect for the cloth. Move the men on again.'

'Get on!' said Troke, rumbling oaths beneath his breath, and Dawes felt his newly-rivetted chain tug. It was some time since he had been in a chain gang, and the sudden jerk nearly overbalanced him. He caught at his neighbour, and looking up, met a pair of black eyes which gleamed recognition. His neighbour was John Rex.

Mr North, watching them, was struck by the resemblance the two men bore to each other. Their height, eyes, hair, and complexion were similar. Despite the difference in name they might be related.

'They may be brothers,' thought he. 'Poor devils! I never knew a prisoner refuse tobacco before.' And he looked on the ground for the despised portion. But in vain. John Rex, oppressed by no foolish sentiment, had picked it up and put it in his mouth.

So Rufus Dawes was relegated to his old life again, and came back to his prison with the hate to his kind, that his prison had bred in him, increased a hundred fold. The last hope had vanished. The last phantom of human love and affection had faded. His dreams were broken. He was awake at last, awake to the consciousness that he had been deceiving himself, that his idol was – like the rest of the world – ungrateful, and that for the future his relief must be to loathe her, and himself, and all mankind.

It seemed to him that the sudden awakening had dazed him, that the flood of light so suddenly let in upon his slumbering soul had blinded his eyes, used so long to the sweetly-cheating twilight. He was at first unable to apprehend the details of his misery. He knew only that his dream-child was alive and shuddered at him, that the only thing he loved and trusted had betrayed him, that all hope of justice and mercy had gone from him for ever, that the beauty had gone from the earth, the brightness from heaven, and that he was doomed still to live.

He went about his work, unheedful of the jests of Troke, ungalled by his irons, unmindful of the groans and laughter about him. His magnificent muscles saved him from the lash; for the amiable Troke tried to break him down in vain. He did not complain, he did not laugh, he did not weep. In the gang he was viewed with respect, and the popular voice, always eager to exaggerate the merits of its heroes, credited him with a murder. His 'mate' Rex tried to converse with him, but did not succeed. In the midst of one of Rex's excellent tales of London dissipation, Rufus Dawes would sigh wearily.

'There's something on that fellow's mind,' thought Rex, prone to watch the signs by which the soul is read. 'He has some secret which weighs upon him.'

Perhaps he was right, but it was in vain that he attempted to discover what this secret might be. To all questions concerning his past life – however artfully put – Rufus Dawes was dumb; and the utmost that Rex, skilled to worm secrets from his coarser comrades, could elicit was, that he had been a sailor, and had lived in Germany. One evening, by some correction that Dawes made to a statement of a forging Jew, Rex discovered that he was not unacquainted with chemistry, and he began to wonder more and more in his mind what manner of man this was. In vain he practised all his arts, called up all his graces of manner and speech – and these were not few – to fascinate the silent man and win from him some confidence. Rufus Dawes met all his advances with a cynical carelessness that revealed nothing; and, when not addressed, held a gloomy silence. Galled by this indifference, John Rex had attempted to practise those ingenious arts of torment by which Gabbett, Vetch, or other leading spirits of the gang asserted their superiority over their quieter comrades. But he soon ceased.

'I have been longer in this hell than you,' said Rufus Dawes, 'and I know more of the devil's tricks than you can show me. You had best be quiet.'

Rex neglected the warning, and Rufus Dawes took him by the throat one day, and would have strangled him, but that watchful Troke beat off the angered man with a favourite bludgeon. Rex had a wholesome respect for personal prowess, and had the grace to admit the provocation to Troke.

Even this instance of self-denial did not move the stubborn Dawes. He only laughed.

Then Rex came to a conclusion. His mate was plotting an escape. He himself cherished a notion of the kind, as did Gabbett and Vetch, but by common distrust no one ever gave utterance to thoughts of this nature. It would be too dangerous. 'He would be a good comrade for a "rush,"' thought Rex, and resolved more firmly than ever to ally himself to this dangerous and silent companion.

One question Dawes had asked which Rex had been able to answer.

'Who is that North?'

'A chaplain. He is only here for a week or so. There is a new one coming. North goes to Sydney. He is not in favour with the Bishop.'

'How do you know?' asked Dawes, opening his eyes.

'By deduction,' says Rex, with a smile that was peculiar to him. 'He wears coloured clothes, and smokes, and doesn't patter Scripture. The Bishop dresses in black, detests tobacco, and quotes the Bible like a Concordance. North is sent here for a month, as a warming-pan for that ass Meekin. *Ergo,* the Bishop don't care about North.'

Jemmy Vetch, who was next to Rex, let the full weight of his portion of tree-trunk rest upon Gabbett, in order to express his unrestrained admiration of Mr Rex's sarcasm.

'Ain't the Dandy a one'er?' said he.

'Are you thinking of coming the pious?' asked Rex. 'It's no good with North. He's a —! Wait until the highly intelligent

Meekin comes. You can twist that worthy successor of the Apostles round your little finger.'

'Silence there!' cries the overseer. 'Do you want me to report yer?'

And so the subject dropped.

Then the versatile Rex began to retail ingenious experiences of past frolics with parsons, and was notable and facetious concerning a certain marriage that was no marriage, at which he had officiated as chaplain. Unluckily for the story-teller, Troke, peering round on the look-out for something to vent his official spleen upon, observed the clustered heads, and falling straightway into the belief that a conspiracy was hatching, scattered the audience with blows. Rex himself was dragged out upon hands and knees, and 'searched' for tobacco; a process which did not add to his dignity. But at Port Arthur the dignity of a convict was not always considered, and John Rex's gaoler only smiled when his efforts proved fruitless. Troke – who, by virtue of his position, claimed right of search at any moment – thereupon searched the whole gang, making two men strip to the skin; and finding nothing, reported the two unlucky ones for 'insubordination and talking on the chain,' easing his conscience by getting them five-and-twenty lashes in consequence.

Amid such diversions the days rolled on, and Rufus Dawes almost longed for the Coal Mines. To be sent from the settlement to the Coal Mines, and from the Coal Mines to the settlement, was to these unhappy men a 'trip'. At Port Arthur one went to an out station as more fortunate people go to Brighton or Schnapper Point now-a-days for 'change of air'.

↤ 13 ↦

THE COMMANDANT'S BUTLER

RUFUS DAWES had been a fortnight at the settlement when a new-comer appeared on the chain gang.

This was a young man of about twenty years of age, thin, fair, and delicate. His name was Kirkland, and he belonged to what were known as the 'educated' prisoners. He had been a clerk in a banking house, and was transported for embezzlement, though, by some, grave doubts as to his guilt were entertained. The Commandant, Captain Burgess, had employed him as a butler in his own house, and his fate was considered a 'lucky' one. So, doubtless, it was, and might have been, had not an untoward accident occurred. Captain Burgess, who was a bachelor of the 'old school,' confessed to an amiable weakness for blasphemy, and was given to condemning the convicts' eyes and limbs with indiscriminate violence. Kirkland belonged to a Methodist family, and owned to a piety utterly out of place in that region. The language of Burgess made him shudder, and one day he so far forgot himself and his place as to raise his hands to his ears.

'My blank!' cries Burgess. 'You blank blank, is that your blank game? I'll blank soon cure you of that!' and forthwith ordered him to the chain gang for 'insubordination.'

The groom — an oldish man, made older by his convict experience — looked at him with some pity as he was led away. Kirkland did not quite comprehend this pitying glance.

He was received with suspicion by the gang, who did not like white-handed prisoners. Troke, by way of an experiment in human nature, perhaps, placed him next to Gabbett. The day was got through in the usual way, and Kirkland felt his heart revive. The toil was severe, and the companionship uncouth, but, despite his blistered hands and aching back, he had not experienced anything so very terrible after all. When the muster bell rang, and the gang broke up, Rufus Dawes, on his silent way to his separate cell, observed a notable change of custom in the disposition of the new convict. Instead of placing him in a cell by himself, Troke was turning him into the yard with the others.

'I'm not to go in there?' says the ex-bank clerk, drawing back in dismay from the cloud of foul faces that lowered upon him.

'By God, but you are, then!' says Troke. 'The Governor says a night in there'll take the starch out of yer. Come, in yer go!'

'But Mr Troke —'

'Stow yer gaff,' says Troke, with another oath, and impatiently striking the lad with his thong – 'I can't argue here all night. Get in.'

So Kirkland, aged twenty-two, and the son of Methodist parents, went in.

Rufus Dawes, among whose sinister memories this yard was numbered, sighed. So fierce was the glamour of the place, however, that, when locked into his cell, he felt ashamed of that sigh, and strove to erase the memory of it. 'What is he more than anybody else?' said the wretched man to himself, as he hugged his misery close.

In the night, the watchman at the gate of the yard dormitory heard scuffling and loud breathing. Being an experienced man, he smiled. The old hands were doubtless amusing themselves with the innocence of the educated convict. About dawn, Mr North – who, amongst other vagaries not approved of by his bishop, had a habit of prowling about the prison at unofficial hours – was attracted by a dispute at the door of the dormitory.

'What's the matter here?' he asked.

'A prisoner refractory, your reverence,' says the watchman. 'Wants to come out.'

'Mr North! Mr North!' cries a voice; 'for the love of God, let me out of this place!'

Kirkland, ghastly pale, bleeding, with his woollen shirt torn, and his blue eyes wide open with terror, was clinging to the bars.

'Oh, Mr North! Mr North! Oh, Mr North! Oh! for God's sake, Mr North!'

'What, Kirkland!' cries North, who was ignorant of the vengeance of the Commandant. 'What do you do here?'

But Kirkland could do nothing but cry, 'Oh, Mr North! For God's sake, Mr North!' and beat on the bars with white and sweating hands.

'Let him out, watchman,' says North.

'Can't sir, without an order from the Commandant.'

'I order you, sir,' North cries, indignant.

'Very sorry, your reverence; but your reverence knows that I daren't do such a thing.'

'Mr North!' screamed Kirkland. 'Would you see me perish, body and soul, in this place? Mr North! Oh, you ministers of

Christ — wolves in sheep's clothing — you shall be judged for this! Mr North,. I say.'

'Let him out,' cries North again, stamping his foot.

'It's no good,' returned the gaoler, 'I *can't*. If he was dying, I can't.'

North rushed away to the Commandant, and the instant his back was turned, Hailes, the watchman, flung open the door, and rushed into the dormitory.

'Take that, you —!' he cried, dealing Kirkland a blow on the head with his keys, that stretched him senseless. 'There's more trouble with you bloody aristocrats than enough. God damn ye, lie quiet.'

The Commandant, roused from slumber, told Mr North that Kirkland might stop where he was, and that he'd thank the chaplain not to wake him up in the middle of the night because a blank prisoner set up a blank howling.

'But, my good sir,' protested North, restraining his impulse to overstep the bounds of modesty in his language to his superior officer, 'you know the character of the men in that ward. You can guess what that unhappy boy has suffered.'

'Impertinent young beggar!' says Burgess. 'Do him good, curse him! Mr North, I'm sorry you should have had the trouble to come here, but *will* you let me go to sleep?'

North returned to the prison disconsolately, found the dutiful Hailes at his post, and all quiet.

'What's become of Kirkland?' he asked.

'Fretted hisself to sleep, yer reverence,' says Hailes, in accents of parental concern. 'Poor young chap! It's hard for such young 'uns as he, sir.'

In the morning, Rufus Dawes, coming to his place on the chain gang, was struck by the altered appearance of Kirkland. His face was of a greenish tint, and wore an expression of bewildered horror.

'Cheer up, mate!' says Dawes, touched with momentary pity. 'It's no good being in the mopes, you know.'

'What do they do if you try to bolt?' whispered Kirkland.

'Kill you,' returned Dawes, in a natural tone of surprise at so preposterous a question.

'Thank God!' says Kirkland.

'Now, then, Miss Nancy,' says one of the men, 'what's the matter with *you?*'

Kirkland shuddered, and his pale face grew crimson.

'Oh, Lord,' he said, 'that such a wretch as I am should live!'

'Silence!' cries Troke. 'Number 44, if you can't hold your tongue I'll give you something to talk about. March!'

The work of the gang that afternoon was the carrying of some heavy logs to the water-side, and Rufus Dawes observed that Kirkland was exhausted long before his task was accomplished.

'They'll kill you, you little beggar!' said he, not unkindly. 'What have you been doing to get into this scrape?'

'Have you ever slept in that — that place I was in last night?' asked Kirkland.

Rufus Dawes nodded.

'Does the Commandant know what goes on there?'

'I suppose so. What does he care?'

'Care! Man, do you believe in a God?'

'No,' says Dawes, 'not here. Hold up, my lad. If you fall, we must fall over you, and then you're done for.'

He had hardly uttered the words, when the boy flung himself beneath the log. In another instant the train would have been scrambling over his crushed body had not Gabbett stretched out an iron hand and plucked the would-be suicide from death.

'Hold on to me, Miss Nancy,' says the giant, smirking his huge lips. 'I'm big enough to carry double.'

There seemed to be something in the tone or manner of the speaker which affected Kirkland to disgust, for, spurning the offered hand, he uttered a cry, and then, holding up his irons with his hands, he started to run for the water.

'Halt! you young fool,' roars Troke, raising his carbine. But Kirkland kept steadily on for the river. Just as he reached it, however, the figure of Mr North rose from behind a pile of stones. Kirkland jumped for the jetty, missed his footing, and fell into the arms of the chaplain.

'You young vermin — you shall pay for this,' says Troke. 'You'll see if you won't remember this day.'

'Oh, Mr North,' says Kirkland, 'why did you stop me? I'd better be dead than stay another night in that place.'

'You'll get it, my lad,' says Gabbett, when the runaway was brought back. 'Your blessed hide'll feel for this, see if it don't.'

Kirkland only breathed harder, and looked round for Mr North, but Mr North had gone. The new chaplain was to arrive that afternoon, and it was incumbent on him to be present to receive him.

Troke reported the ex-bank clerk that night to Burgess; and Burgess, who was about to go to dinner with the new chaplain, disposed of his case out of hand.

'Tried to bolt, eh! Must stop that. Fifty lashes, Troke. Tell Macklewain to be ready – or stay, I'll tell him myself – I'll break the young devil's spirit, blank him.'

'Yes, sir,' says Troke. 'Good evening, sir.'

'Troke – pick out some likely man, will you? That last fellow you had ought to have been tied up himself. His flogging wouldn't have killed a flea.'

'You can't get 'em to warm one another, your honour,' says Troke. 'They *won't* do it.'

'Oh yes they will, though,' says Burgess, 'or I'll know the reason why. I won't have my men knocked up with flogging these rascals. If the scourger won't do his duty, tie him up and give him five-and-twenty for himself. I'll be down in the morning myself if I can.'

'Very good, yer honour,' says Troke.

Kirkland was put into a separate cell that night; and considerate Troke, by way of assuring him a good night's rest, told him that he was to have 'fifty' in the morning. 'And Dawes'll lay it on,' he added. 'He's one of the smartest men I've got, and he won't spare yer, yer may take your oath of that.'

MR NORTH'S INDISPOSITION

'You will find this a terrible place, Mr Meekin,' said North to his supplanter, as they walked across to the Commandant's to dinner. 'It has made me heart-sick.'

'I thought it was a little paradise,' says Meekin. 'Captain Frere says that the scenery is delightful.'

'So it is,' returned North, looking askance; 'but the prisoners are not delightful.'

'Poor, abandoned wretches,' says Meekin, 'I suppose not. How sweet the moonlight sleeps upon that bank ! Eh !'

'Abandoned, indeed, by God and man – almost.'

'Mr North, Providence never abandons the most unworthy of his servants. Never have I seen the righteous forsaken, nor his seed begging their bread. In the valley of the shadow of death He is with us. His staff, you know, Mr North. Really, the Commandant's house is charmingly situated !'

Mr North sighed again.

'You have not been long in the colony, Mr Meekin, I doubt – forgive me for expressing myself so freely – if you quite know our convict system.'

'An admirable one ! A most admirable one !' says Meekin. 'There were a few matters I noticed in Hobart Town that did not quite please me – the frequent use of profane language for instance – but, on the whole, I was delighted with the scheme. It is so complete.'

North pursed his lips.

'Yes, it is very complete,' he said; 'almost too complete. But I am always in a minority when I discuss the question, so we will drop it, if you please.'

'If you please,' said Meekin, gravely.

He had heard from the Bishop that Mr North was an ill-conditioned sort of person, who smoked clay pipes, had been detected in drinking beer out of a pewter pot, and had been heard to state that white neckcloths were of no consequence.

The dinner went off successfully. Burgess – desirous perhaps, of favourably impressing the chaplain whom the Bishop delighted to honour – shut off his blasphemy for a while, and was urbane enough.

'You'll find us rough, Mr Meekin,' he said, 'but you'll find us "all there" when we're wanted. This is a little kingdom in itself.'

'Like Beranger's?' asked Meekin, with a smile. Captain Burgess had never heard of Beranger, but he smiled as if he had learnt his works by heart.

'Or like Sancho Panza's island,' said North. 'You remember how justice was administered there?'

'Not at this moment, sir,' said Burgess, with dignity. He had been often oppressed by the notion that the Reverend Mr North 'chaffed' him. 'Pray, help yourself to wine.'

'Thank you, none,' says North, filling a tumbler with water. 'I have a headache.'

His manner of speech and action was so awkward that a silence fell upon the party, caused by each one wondering why Mr North should grow confused, and drum his fingers on the table, and stare everywhere but at the decanter. Meekin – ever softly at his ease – was first to speak.

'Do you have many visitors, Captain Burgess?'

'Very few. Sometimes a party come over with a recommendation from the Governor, and I show them over the place; but, as a rule, we see no one but ourselves.'

'I asked,' says Meekin, 'because some friends of mine were thinking of coming.'

'And who may they be?'

'Do you know Captain Frere?'

'Frere! I should say so!' returned Burgess, with a laugh, modelled upon Maurice Frere's own. 'I was quartered with him at Sarah Island. So he's a friend of yours, eh?'

'I had the pleasure of meeting him in society. He is just married, you know.'

'Is he?' says Burgess. 'The devil he is! I heard something about it, too.'

'Miss Vickers, a charming young person. They are going to Sydney, where Captain Frere has some interest, I believe, and Frere thinks of taking Port Arthur on his way down.'

'A strange fancy for a honeymoon trip,' said North.

'Captain Frere takes a deep interest in all relating to convict discipline,' went on Meekin, unheeding the interruption, 'and is anxious that Mrs Frere should see this place.'

'Yes, one oughtn't to leave the colony without seeing it,' says Burgess, 'it's worth seeing.'

'So Captain Frere thinks. A romantic story, Captain Burgess. He saved her life, you know.'

'Ay! that was a queer thing, that mutiny,' says Burgess. 'We've got the fellows here, you know.'

'I saw them tried at Hobart Town,' said Meekin. 'In fact, the ringleader, John Rex, gave me his confession, and I sent it to the Bishop.'

'A great rascal,' put in North. 'A dangerous, scheming, cold-blooded villain.'

'Well now!' says Meekin, with asperity; 'I don't agree with you. Everybody seems to be against that poor fellow – Captain Frere tried to make me think his letters contained a hidden meaning, but I don't believe they did. He seems to me to be truly penitent for his offences – a misguided but not a hypocritical man; if my knowledge of human nature goes for anything.'

'I hope he is,' said North. 'I wouldn't trust him.'

'You keep him securely I hope, Captain Burgess.'

'Oh! there's no fear of him,' says Burgess, cheerily; 'if he grows uproarious we'll soon give him a touch of the cat.'

'I suppose severity is necessary,' returned Meekin; 'though to my ears a flogging sounds a little distasteful. It is a brutal punishment.'

'It's a punishment for brutes,' said Burgess, and laughed; pleased with one of the nearest approaches to an epigram he ever made in his life.

Here attention was called by the strange behaviour of Mr North. He had risen, and without apology, flung wide the window as though he gasped for air.

'Hullo, North! what's the matter?' cries Burgess.

'Nothing,' said North, recovering himself with an effort, 'A spasm. I have these attacks at times.'

'Have some brandy,' says Burgess.

'No, no, it will pass. *No,* I say. Well, if you insist.' And seizing the tumbler offered to him, he half-filled it with raw spirit, and swallowed the fiery draught at a gulp.

The Reverend Meekin eyed his clerical brother with horror. The Reverend Meekin was not accustomed to clergymen who wore black neckties, smoked clay pipes, chewed tobacco, and drank neat brandy out of tumblers.

'Ha!' says North, looking wildly round upon them. 'That's better.'

'Let us go on the verandah,' says Burgess. 'It's cooler than in the house.'

So they went on the verandah, and looked down upon the lights of the prison, and listened to the sea lapping the shore. The Reverend Mr North, in this cool atmosphere, seemed to recover himself, and conversation progressed with some sprightliness. By and by, a short figure, smoking a cheroot, came up out of the dark, and proved to be Dr Macklewain, who was prevented from attending the dinner by reason of an accident to a constable at Norfolk Bay, which had claimed his professional attention.

'Well, how's Forrest?' cried Burgess. 'Mr Meekin — Dr Macklewain.'

'Dead,' says Macklewain. 'Delighted to see you, Mr Meekin.'

'Confound it — another of my best men,' grumbled Burgess. 'Macklewain, have a glass of wine.'

But Macklewain was tired, and wanted to get home.

'I must also be thinking of repose,' says Meekin; 'the journey — though most enjoyable — has fatigued me.'

'Come on, then,' said North. 'Our roads lie together, doctor.'

'You *won't* have a nip of brandy before you start?' asked Burgess. 'No? Then I shall send round for you in the morning, Mr Meekin. Good-night. Macklewain, I want to speak with you a moment.'

Before the two clergymen had got halfway down the steep path that led from the Commandant's house to the flat on which the cottages of the doctor and chaplain were built, Macklewain rejoined them.

'Another flogging to-morrow,' said he, grumblingly. 'Up at daylight, I suppose, again?'

'Who is he going to flog now?'

'That young butler-fellow of his.'

'What, Kirkland?' cries North. 'You don't mean to say he's going to flog Kirkland?'

'Insubordination,' says Macklewain. 'Fifty lashes.'

'Oh, this must be stopped,' cries North, in great alarm. 'He can't stand it. I tell you he'll die, Macklewain.'

'Perhaps you'll have the goodness to allow me to be the best judge of that', returned Macklewain, drawing up his little body to its least insignificant stature.

'My dear sir,' replied North, alive to the importance of conciliating the surgeon, 'you haven't seen him lately. He tried to drown himself this morning.'

Mr Meekin expressed some alarm; but Dr Macklewain reassured him.

'*That* sort of nonsense must be stopped,' said he. 'A nice example that, to set. I wonder Burgess didn't give him a hundred.'

'He was put into the long dormitory,' said North, 'you know what sort of a place that is. I declare to Heaven his agony and shame terrified me.'

'Well, he'll be put into the hospital for a week or so to-morrow,' says Macklewain, 'and that'll give him a spell.'

'If Burgess flogs him I'll report it to the Governor,' cries North, in great heat. 'The condition of those dormitories is infamous.'

'If the boy has anything to complain of, why don't he complain. We can't do anything without evidence.'

'Complain! Would his life be safe if he did? Besides, he's not the sort of creature to complain. He'd rather kill himself than say anything about the matter.'

'That's all nonsense,' said Macklewain. 'We can't flog a whole dormitory on suspicion. *I* can't help it. The boy's made his bed and he must lie on it.'

'I'll go back and see Burgess,' says North. 'Mr Meekin, here's the gate, and your room is on the right hand. I'll be back shortly.'

'Pray don't hurry,' said Meekin politely. 'You are on an errand of mercy, you know. Everything must give way to that. I shall find my portmanteau in my room, you said.'

'Yes, yes. Call the servant if you want anything. He sleeps at the back,' and North hurried off.

'An impulsive gentleman,' said Meekin to Macklewain, as the sound of Mr North's footsteps died away in the distance.

Macklewain shook his head seriously.

'There is something wrong about him, but I can't make out what it is. He has the strangest fits at times. Unless it's cancer in the stomach, I don't know what it can be.'

'Cancer in the stomach! dear me, how dreadful!' says Meekin. 'Ah! Doctor, we all have our crosses, have we not? How delightful the grass smells! This seems a very pleasant place, and I think I shall enjoy myself very much. Good-night.'

'Good-night, sir. I hope you will be comfortable.'

'And let us hope poor Mr North will succeed in his labour of love,' said Meekin, shutting the little gate, 'and save the unfortunate Kirkland. Good night, once more.'

'A civil sort of beggar,' thought Macklewain, as he sat down to mix himself a glass of grog before retiring, 'and not likely to make himself officious. That fellow North is always poking his nose into everything. I dare say he is right about Kirkland, but, God bless me, that sort of thing has been going on for years. *I* can't stop it.'

Captain Burgess was shutting his verandah-window when North hurried up.

'Captain Burgess, Macklewain tells me you are going to flog that young Kirkland.'

'Well, sir, what of that?' says Burgess.

'I have come to beg you not to do it, sir. The lad has been cruelly punished already. He attempted suicide to-day – unhappy creature.'

'Well, that's just what I'm flogging him for. I'll teach my prisoners to attempt suicide.'

'But he can't stand it, sir. He's too weak.'

'That's Macklewain's business.'

'Captain Burgess,' protested North, 'I assure you that he does not deserve punishment. I have seen him, and his condition of mind is pitiable.'

'Look here, Mr North, I don't interfere with what you do to the prisoner's souls, don't you interfere with what I do to their bodies.'

'Captain Burgess, you have no right to mock at my office.'

'Then don't you interfere with me, sir.'

'Do you persist in having this boy flogged?'

'I've given my orders, sir.'

'Then, Captain Burgess,' cries North, his pale face flushing, 'I tell you the boy's blood will be on your head. I am a Minister of God, sir, and I forbid you to commit this crime.'

'Damn your impertinence, sir,' burst out Burgess. 'You're a dismissed officer of the Government, sir. You've no authority here in any way; and by God, sir, if you interfere with my discipline, sir, I'll have you put in irons until you're shipped out of the island.'

This, of course, was mere bravado on the part of the Commandant. North knew well that he would never dare to attempt any such act of violence, but the insult stung him like the cut of a whip. He made a stride towards the Commandant, as though to seize him by the throat, but, checking himself in time, stood still, with clenched hands, flashing eyes, and beard that bristled.

The two men looked at each other, and presently Burgesss' eyes fell before those of the chaplain.

'Miserable blasphemer,' said North, 'I tell you that you shall not flog the boy.'

Burgess, white with rage, rang the bell that summoned his convict servant.

'Show Mr North out,' he said, 'and go down to the barracks and tell Troke that Kirkland is to have *a hundred* lashes to-morrow. I'll show you who's master here, my good sir.'

'I'll report this to the Government,' said North, aghast. 'This is murderous.'

'The Government may go to —, and you, too!' roared Burgess. 'Get out!'

And God's viceregent at Port Arthur slammed the door.

North returned home in great agitation.

'They shall not flog that boy,' he said. 'I'll shield him with my own body, if necessary. I'll report this to the Government. I'll see Sir John Franklin myself. I'll have the light of day let into this den of horrors.'

He reached his cottage, and lighted the lamp in the little sitting-room. All was silent, save that from the adjoining chamber came the sound of Meekin's gentlemanly snore. North took down a Bible from the shelf and tried to read, but the letters ran together.

'I wish I hadn't taken that brandy,' he said. 'Fool that I am.'

Then he began to walk up and down, to fling himself on the sofa, to read, to pray.

'Oh God, give me strength! Aid me! Help me! I struggle, but I am weak! Oh Lord, look down upon me!'

To see him rolling on the sofa in agony, to see his white face, his parched lips, and his contracted brow, to hear his moans and muttered prayers, one would have thought him suffering from the pangs of some terrible disease.

He opened the Bible again, and forced himself to read, but his eyes wandered to the cupboard. It seemed that there lurked something that fascinated him. He got up at length, went into the kitchen, and found a packet of red pepper. He mixed a teaspoonful of this in a pannikin of water and drank it. It seemed to relieve him for a while.

'I *must* keep my wits for to-morrow. The life of that lad depends upon it. Meekin here, too, will suspect. I will lie down.'

He went into his bedroom and flung himself on the bed, but only to toss from side to side. In vain he repeated texts of Scripture and scraps of verse; in vain counted imaginary sheep, or listened to imaginary clock-tickings. Sleep would not come to him. It was as though he had reached the crisis of some disease which had been for days gathering force.

'I *must* have a teaspoonful,' he said, 'just to allay the craving.'

Twice he paused on his way to the sitting-room, and twice did he seem driven on by a power stronger than his will.

He reached it at length, and opening the cupboard, pulled out what he sought.

A brandy bottle!

With this in his hand, all thoughts of moderation vanished.

He raised it to his lips and eagerly drank. Then, ashamed of what he had done, he thrust the bottle back, and made for his room. Still he could not sleep. The taste of the liquor maddened him for more. He saw in the darkness the brandy bottle,— vulgar and terrible apparition! He saw its amber fluid sparkle. He heard it gurgle as he poured it out. He smelt the nutty aroma of the spirit. He pictured it standing in the corner of the cupboard, and imagined himself seizing it and quenching the fire that burned within him. He wept, he prayed, he fought with his desire as with a madness. He told himself that another's life depended on his exertions, that to give way to his fatal passion was unworthy of an educated man and a reasoning being, that it was degrading, disgusting, and bestial. That, at all times debasing, at this particular time it was infamous; that a vice, unworthy of any man, was doubly sinful in a man of education and a minister of God. In vain. In the midst of his arguments he found himself at the cupboard, with the bottle at his lips, in an attitude that was at once ludicrous and horrible.

He had no cancer. His disease was a more terrible one. The Rev. Mr North – gentleman, scholar, and Christian priest – was a confirmed drunkard.

✦ 15 ✦

ONE HUNDRED LASHES

THE morning sun, bright and fierce, looked down upon a curious sight. In a stone yard, not far from where the black gibbet erected its hideous arms, was a little group of persons, – Troke, Burgess, Macklewain, Kirkland, and Rufus Dawes.

Three wooden staves, seven feet high, were fastened together in the form of a triangle. The structure looked not unlike that made by gipsies to boil their kettles. To this structure Kirkland was bound. His feet were fastened with thongs to the base of the triangle, his wrists, bound above his head, at the apex. His body was then extended to its fullest extent, and his white back shone in the sunlight. During his tying up he had said nothing – only when Troke roughly pulled off his shirt he shivered.

'Now, prisoner,' said Troke to Dawes, 'do your duty.'

Rufus Dawes looked from the three stern faces to Kirkland's white back, and his sullen face grew purple. In all his experience he had never been asked to flog before. He had been flogged often enough.

'You don't want me to flog him, sir?' he said to the Commandant.

'Pick up the cat, sir,' says Burgess, astonished; 'what is the meaning of this?'

Rufus Dawes picked up the heavy cat, and drew its knotted lashes between his fingers.

'Go on, Dawes,' whispered Kirkland, without turning his head. 'You are no more than another man.'

'What does he say?' asked Burgess.

'Telling him to cut light, sir,' says Troke, eagerly lying; 'they all do it.'

'Cut light, eh! We'll see about that. Get on, my man, and look sharp, or I'll tie you up and give you fifty for yourself, as sure as God made little apples.'

'Go on, Dawes,' whispered Kirkland again. 'I don't mind.'

Rufus Dawes lifted the cat, swung it round his head, and brought its knotted cords down upon the white back.

'Wonn!' cries Troke.

The white back was instantly striped with six crimson bars. Kirkland stifled a cry. It seemed to him that he had been cut in half.

'Damn you, you scoundrel,' roared Burgess; 'separate your cat! What do you mean by flogging a man that fashion?'

Rufus Dawes drew his crooked fingers through the entangled cords, and struck again. This time the blow was more effective, and the blood beaded on the skin.

The boy did not cry; but Macklewain saw his hands clutch the staves tightly, and the muscles of his naked arms quiver.

'Tew!'

'That's better,' said Burgess.

The third blow sounded as though it had been struck upon a piece of raw beef, and the crimson turned purple.

'My God!' said Kirkland, faintly; and then bit his lips.

The flogging proceeded in silence for ten strikes, and then Kirkland gave a screech like a wounded horse.

'Oh! ... Captain Burgess! ... Dawes! ... Mr Troke! ... Oh, my God! ... Oh! Oh! ... Mercy! ... Oh, Doctor! ... Mr North! ... Oh, you're cutting my bowels out! ... Oh! Oh! Oh!'

'Ten!' cried Troke, impassibly counting to the end of the first twenty.

The lad's back, swollen into a hump, now presented the appearance of a ripe peach which a wilful child has scored with a pin.

Dawes, turning away from his bloody handiwork, drew the cats through his fingers twice. They were beginning to get clogged a little.

'Go on,' said Burgess, with a nod; and Troke cried 'Wonn!' again.

Roused by the morning sun streaming in upon him, Mr North opened his bloodshot eyes, rubbed his forehead with hands that trembled; and suddenly awaking to a consciousness of his promised errand, rolled off the bed and rose to his feet. He saw the empty brandy-bottle on his wooden dressing-table, and remembered what had passed.

With shaking hands, he dashed water over his aching head, and proceeded to smooth his garments. The debauch of the previous night had left its usual effects behind it. His brain seemed on fire, his hands were hot and dry, his tongue clove to the roof of his mouth. He shuddered as he viewed his pale face and red eyes in the little looking-glass, and hastily tried the door. He had retained sufficient sense in his madness to lock it, and his condition had been unobserved. Stealing into the sitting-room, he saw that the clock pointed to half-past six. The flogging was to have taken place at half-past five. Unless some accident had favoured him, he was too late. Fevered with remorse and anxiety, he hurried past the room where Meekin yet slumbered, and made his way to the prison.

As he entered the yard, Troke called 'Ten!' Kirkland had just got his fiftieth lash.

'Stop!' cried North. 'Captain Burgess, I call upon you to stop.'

'You're rather late, Mr North,' retorted Burgess. 'The punishment is nearly over.'

'Wonn!' cries remorseless Troke again; and North stood by, biting his nails and grinding his teeth, during six more lashes.

Kirkland had ceased to yell now, and merely moaned. His back was like a bloody sponge, while, in the interval between the lashes, the swollen flesh twitched like that of a newly-killed bullock. Suddenly, experienced Macklewain saw his head droop on his shoulder.

'Throw him off! Throw him off!' he cried, and Troke hurried to loosen the thongs.

'Fling some water over him,' says Burgess, 'he's shamming.'

A bucket of water made Kirkland open his eyes.

'I thought so,' says Burgess. 'Tie him up again.'

'No. Not if you are Christians!' cries North.

He met with an ally where he least expected one.

Rufus Dawes flung down the dripping cat.

'I'll flog no more,' said he.

'What?' roared Burgess, furious at this gross insolence.

'I'll flog no more. Get some one else to do your bloody work for you. I won't.'

'Tie him up!' cries Burgess, foaming. 'Tie him up. Here, constable, fetch a man here with a fresh cat. I'll give you that beggar's fifty, and fifty more to the back of 'em; and he shall look on while his back cools.'

Rufus Dawes, with a glance at North, pulled off his shirt without a word, and stretched himself at the triangle. His back was not white and smooth, like Kirkland's had been, but hard and seamed. He had been flogged before.

Troke appeared with Gabbett – grinning. Gabbett liked flogging. It was his boast that he could flog a man to death on a place no bigger than the palm of his hand. He could use his left hand equally with his right, and if he got hold of a 'favourite,' would 'cross the cuts.'

Rufus Dawes planted his feet firmly on the ground, took fierce grasp of the staves, and drew in his breath.

Macklewain spread the garments of the two men upon the

ground, and, placing Kirkland upon them, turned to watch this new phase in the morning's amusement. He grumbled a little below his breath, for he wanted his breakfast, and when the Commandant once began to flog, there was no telling where he would stop.

Rufus Dawes took five-and-twenty lashes without a murmur, and then Gabbett 'crossed the cuts.' This went on up to fifty lashes, and North felt himself stricken with admiration at the courage of the man.

'If it had not been for that cursed brandy,' thought he, with bitterness of self-reproach, 'I might have saved all this.'

At the hundredth lash, the giant paused, expecting the order to throw off, but Burgess was determined to 'break the man's spirit.'

'I'll make you speak, you dog, if I cut your heart out,' he cried. 'Go on, prisoner.'

For twenty lashes more Dawes was mute, and then the agony forced from his labouring breast a hideous cry. But it was not a cry for mercy, as that of Kirkland had been. Having found his tongue, the wretched man gave vent to his boiling passion in a torrent of curses. He shrieked imprecations upon Burgess, Troke, and North. He cursed all soldiers for tyrants, all parsons for hypocrites. He blasphemed his God and his Saviour. With a frightful outpouring of obscenity and blasphemy, he called on the earth to gape and swallow his persecutors, for heaven to open and rain fire upon them, for hell to yawn and engulf them quick. It was as though each blow of the cat forced out of him a fresh burst of beast-like rage. He seemed to have abandoned his humanity. He foamed, he raved, he tugged at his bonds until the strong staves shook again, he writhed himself round upon the triangles and spit impotently at Burgess, who jeered at his torments.

North, with his hands to his ears, crouched against the corner of the wall, palsied with horror. It seemed to him that the passions of hell raged around him. He would fain have fled, but a horrible fascination held him back.

In the midst of this – when the cat was hissing its loudest – Burgess laughing his hardest, and the wretch on the triangles filled the air with his cries, North saw Kirkland looking at him with what seemed a smile. Was it a smile? He leapt forward, and uttered a cry of dismay so loud that all turned.

'By God!' says Troke, running to the heap of clothes, 'the young 'un's slipped his wind!'

Kirkland was dead.

'Throw him off!' says Burgess, aghast at the unfortunate accident; and Gabbett reluctantly untied the thongs that bound Rufus Dawes. Two constables were alongside him in an instant, for sometimes newly tortured men grew desperate. This one, however, was silent with the last lash, only in taking his shirt from under the body, he muttered, 'Dead!' and his tone seemed to be not without a touch of envy. Then flinging his shirt over his bleeding shoulders, he walked out – defiant to the last.

'Game, ain't he?' said one constable to the other, as they pushed him, not ungently, into an empty cell; there to wait for the hospital guard.

The body of Kirkland was taken away in silence, and Burgess turned rather pale when he saw North's threatening face.

'It isn't my fault, Mr North,' he said. 'I didn't know that the lad was chicken-hearted.'

But North turned away in disgust, and Macklewain and Burgess pursued their homeward route together.

'Strange that he should drop like that,' said the Commandant.

'Yes, unless he had any internal disease,' said the surgeon.

'Disease of the heart, for instance,' said Burgess.

'I'll *post mortem* him and see.'

'Come in and have a nip, Macklewain. I feel quite qualmish,' said Burgess.

And the two went into the house amid respectful salutes from either side.

Mr North, in agony of mind at what he considered the consequences of his neglect, slowly, and with head bowed down, as one bent on a painful errand, went to see the prisoner who had survived. He found him kneeling on the ground, prostrated.

'Rufus Dawes.'

At the low tone, Rufus Dawes looked up, and, seeing who it was, waved him off.

'Don't speak to me,' he said, with an imprecation that made

North's flesh creep. 'I've told you what I think of you – a bloody hypocrite, who stands by while a man is cut to pieces, and then comes and whines religion to him.'

North stood in the centre of the cell, with his arms hanging-down and his head bent.

'You are right,' he said, in a low tone. 'I must seem to you a hypocrite! *I* a servant of Christ? A besotted beast rather! I am not come to whine religion to you. I am come to – to ask your pardon. I might have saved you from punishment, – saved that poor boy from death. I wanted to save him, God knows. But I have a vice, I am a drunkard, I yielded to my temptation, and – I was too late. I come to you, as one sinful man to another, to ask you to forgive me.'

And North suddenly flung himself down beside the convict, and caught his blood-bespotted hands in his own, crying, 'Forgive me, brother!'

Rufus Dawes, too astonished to speak, bent his black eyes upon the man that crouched at his feet, and a ray of divine pity penetrated his gloomy soul. He seemed to catch a glimpse of a misery more profound than his own, and his stubborn heart felt a human sympathy with this erring brother.

'Then in this hell there is yet a man,' said he; and a hand grasp passed between these two unhappy beings.

North arose, and, with averted face, passed quickly from the cell. Rufus Dawes looked bewilderedly at the hand which his strange visitor had taken, and something glittered there. It was a tear.

He broke down at the sight of it, and when the guard came to fetch him, they found him on his knees in a corner, sobbing like a child.

↢ 16 ↣

KICKING AGAINST THE PRICKS

THE morning after this, the Rev. Mr North departed in the returning schooner for Hobart Town. Between the officious chaplain and the Commandant, the events of the previous day had fixed a great gulf. Burgess knew that North meant to report the death of Kirkland, and guessed that he would not be backward in relating the story to such persons in Hobart Town as would most readily repeat it. 'Blank awkward his dying,' he confessed to himself. 'If he hadn't died, nobody would have bothered about him.' A sinister truth.

North, on the other hand, comforted himself with the belief that the fact of the convict's death under the lash would cause indignation and subsequent inquiry. 'The truth must come out if they only *ask*,' thought he. Self-deceiving North! Four years a Government chaplain, and not yet attained to a knowledge of a Government's method of 'asking' about such matters! Kirkland's mangled flesh would be food for worms before the ink on the last 'minute' from deliberating Authority was dry.

Burgess, however, touched with selfish regrets, determined to burk the parson at the outset. He would send down an official 'return' of the unfortunate occurrence by the same vessel that carried his enemy, and thus get the ear of the Office. Meekin, walking on the evening of the flogging past the wooden shed where the body lay, saw Troke bearing buckets filled with dark-coloured water, and heard a great splashing and sluicing going on inside the hut.

'What is the matter?' he asked.

'Doctor's bin post morticing the prisoner who was flogged this morning, sir,' says Troke, 'and we're cleanin' up.'

English-bred Meekin sickened, and walked on. He had heard that unhappy Kirkland possessed, unknown, disease of the heart, and had unhappily died before receiving his allotted punishment. His duty was to comfort Kirkford's soul, he had nothing to do with Kirkland's slovenly unhandsome body, and so he went for a walk on the pier that the breeze might blow his momentary sickness away from him. On the pier he saw North talking to Father Flaherty, the Roman Catholic chaplain. Meekin had been taught to look upon a priest as a shepherd might look upon a wolf, and passed with a distant bow. The pair were apparently talking of the occurrence of the morning, for he heard Father Flaherty say, with a Douay shrug of his round shoulders, 'He woas not one of moi people, Mr North, and the Govermint would not suffer me to interfere with mathers relating to Prhotestint prisoners.' 'The wretched creature was a Protestant,' thought Christian Meekin. 'At least then his immortal soul was not endangered by belief in damnable heresies of the Church of Rome.' So he passed on, giving good-humoured Denis Flaherty, the son of the butter-merchant of Kildrum, a wide berth and sea-room, lest he should pounce down upon him unawares, and, with Jesuitical argument and silken softness of speech, convert him by force to his own state of error,—as was the well-known custom of those intellectual gladiators, the Priests of the Catholic Faith. North, on his side, left Flaherty with regret. He had spent many a pleasant hour with him, and knew him for a narrow-minded, conscientious, yet laughter-loving creature, whose God was neither his belly nor his breviary, but sometimes in one place and sometimes in the other, according to the hour of the day, and the feasts appointed for due mortification of the flesh. 'A man who would do Christian work in a jog-trot parish, or where men lived too easily to sin harshly, but utterly unfit to cope with Satan, as the British Government has transported him,' had been North's sadly satirical reflection upon Father Flaherty, as Port Arthur faded into indistinct beauty behind the swift-sailing schooner. 'God help those poor villains, for neither parson nor priest can.'

He was right. North, the drunkard and self-tormented, had a power for good, of which Meekin and the other knew nothing. Not merely were the men incompetent and self-indulgent, but they understood nothing of that frightful capacity for agony which is deep in the soul of every evil doer. They might strike the rock as they chose with sharpest-pointed machine-made pick of warranted Gospel-manufacture, stamped with the approval of eminent divines of all ages, but the water of repentance and remorse would not gush for them. They possessed not the frail Wand that alone was powerful to charm. They had no sympathy, no knowledge, no experience. He who would touch the hearts of men must have had his own heart seared. The missionaries of mankind have ever been great sinners before they earned the divine right to heal and bless. Their weakness was made their strength, and out of their own agony of repentance came the knowledge which made them masters and saviours of their kind. It was the Agony of the Garden and the Cross that gave to the world's Preacher his kingdom in the hearts of men. The crown of Divinity is a crown of thorns.

North, on his arrival, went straight to the house of Major Vickers.

'I have a complaint to make, sir,' he said. 'I wish to lodge it formally with you. A prisoner has been flogged to death at Port Arthur. I saw it done.'

Vickers bent his brow.

'A serious accusation, Mr North. I must, of course, receive it with respect coming from you, but I trust that you have fully considered the circumstances of the case. I always understood that Captain Burgess was a most humane man.'

North shook his head. He would not accuse Burgess. He would let events speak for themselves.

'I only ask for an enquiry,' said he.

'Yes, my dear sir, I know. Very proper indeed on your part, if you think any injustice had been done; but have you considered the expense, the delay, the immense trouble and dissatisfaction all this will give?'

'No trouble, no expense, no dissatisfaction should stand in the way of humanity and justice,' cries North.

'Of course not. But will justice be done? Are you sure you can prove your case? Mind, I make no charge against Captain Burgess, whom I have always considered a most worthy and zealous officer; but, supposing your charge to be true, can you prove it?'

'I don't know. Yes. If the witnesses speak the truth.'

'Who are they?'

'Myself, Dr Macklewain, the constable, and two prisoners, one of whom was flogged himself. *He* will speak the truth, I believe. The other man I have not much faith in.'

'Very well; then there is only a prisoner and Dr Macklewain; for if there has been foul play, the convict-constable will not accuse the authorities. I have lived a long time with such people, Mr North, and I know their ways. Now, the doctor does not agree with you.'

'No!' cries North, amazed.

'No. You see, then, my dear sir, how necessary it is not to be hasty in matters of this kind. I really think – pardon me for my plainness – that your goodness of heart has misled you. Captain Burgess sends a report of the case. He says the man was sentenced to a hundred lashes for gross insolence and disobedience of orders, that the doctor was present during the punishment, and that the man was thrown off by his directions, after he had received fifty-six lashes. That, after a short interval, he was found to be dead, and that the doctor made a *post-mortem* examination of the body and found disease of the heart.'

North started.

'A *post-mortem*? I never knew there had been one held.'

'Here is the medical certificate,' said Vickers, holding it out, 'accompanied by the copies of the evidence of the constable and a letter from the Commandant.'

Poor North took the papers and read them slowly. They were apparently straightforward enough.

'Aneurism of the ascending aorta was given as the cause of death; and the doctor frankly admitted that had he known the deceased to be suffering from that complaint, he would not have permitted him to receive more than twenty-five lashes.'

'I think Macklewain is an honest man,' said North. 'He would not dare to return a false certificate. Yet the circumstances of the case – the horrible condition of the prisoners – the frightful story of that boy –'

'My dear Mr North,' said Vickers, gravely. 'I know the horrible condition of the prisoners; so does every thinking person on this island. What can we do?'

'Hold an enquiry.'

'To what end?'

'Increase the number of gaolers.'

'That means spend more money, and we have no more to spend.'

'Petition the Crown, and have the light let in to these dark places. The whole system is monstrous. It is wrong from beginning to end. It is not punishment; it is torment.'

'I felt as strongly as you do, Mr North, when I came here first,' said Vickers, 'but I have seen so much of it. There are convicts who are nothing but wild beasts, and must be punished like wild beasts.'

'Ay, but what makes them beasts?' cried North.

Major Vickers rose. He was getting a little wearied by the discussion.

'I cannot enter into these questions, Mr North. My position here is to administer the law to the best of my ability, not to question it.'

North bowed his head to the reproof. In some sort of justly unjust way, he felt that he deserved it.

'I can say no more, sir. I am afraid I am helpless in this matter – as I have been in others. I see that the evidence is against me; but it is my duty to carry my efforts as far as I can, and I will do so.'

Vickers bowed stiffly, and wished him good morning. Authority – however well-meaning in private life – has in its official capacity a natural dislike to those dissatisfied persons who persist in pushing enquiries to extremities.

North, going out with saddened spirits, met in the passage a beautiful young girl. It was Dora – glowing with the bright beauty of a week's marriage – coming to 'call' upon her father.

He lifted his hat and looked after her. He guessed that she was the daughter of the man he had left – the wife of the Captain Frere, concerning whom he had heard so much. He was a man whose morbidly excited brain was prone to strange fancies; and it seemed to him that beneath the clear blue eyes that flashed upon him for a moment, lay a hint of future sadness, in which, in some strange way, he himself was to bear part. He stared after her figure until it disappeared; and long after the dainty presence of the young bride – rustling in whitest lawn and stiffest silk, trimly-booted, tight-waisted, and neatest-gloved – had faded, with all its sunshine of gaiety and health from out of his mental vision, he still saw those two blue eyes and that cloud of golden hair.

CAPTAIN AND MRS FRERE

DORA had become the wife of Maurice Frere. The wedding created excitement in the convict settlement, for Maurice Frere, though oppressed by the secret shame at open matrimony which affects men of his character, could not in decency – seeing how 'good a thing for him' was this wealthy alliance – demand unceremonious nuptials. So, after the fashion of the town – there being no 'Continent' or Scotland adjacent as a hiding place for bridal blushes – the alliance was entered into with due pomp of ball and supper; bride and bridegroom departing through the golden afternoon to the nearest of Major Vickers's stations. Thence it had been arranged they should return after a fortnight or so, and take ship for Sydney.

Major Vickers, affectionate though he was to the man whom he believed to be the saviour of his child, had no notion of allowing him to live on Dora's fortune. He had settled Dora's portion – ten thousand pounds it was currently reported to be – upon herself and children, and had informed Frere that he expected him to live upon an income of his own earning. After many consultations between the pair, it had been arranged that a civil appointment in Sydney would suit the bridegroom, who was to sell out of the service. This notion was Frere's own. He never cared for military duty, and had, moreover, private debts to no inconsiderable amount. By selling his commission he would be enabled at once to pay these debts, and render himself eligible for any well-paid post under the Colonial Government that the interest of his father-in-law and his own reputation as a convict disciplinarian might procure. Vickers would fain have kept his daughter with him, but he unselfishly acquiesced in the scheme, admitting that Frere's plea as to the comforts she would derive from the 'Society' to be found in Sydney was a valid one.

'You can come over and see us when we get settled, Papa,'

said Dora, with all a young matron's pride of place, 'and we can come and see you. Hobart Town is very pretty, but I want to see the World.'

'You should go to London, Poppet,' says Maurice, 'that's the place. Isn't it, sir?'

'Oh, London!' cries Dora, clapping her hands. 'And Westminster Abbey, and the Tower, and St James's Palace, and Hyde Park, and Fleet-street! "Sir," said Doctor Johnson, "let us take a walk down Fleet-street." Do you remember, in Mr Croker's book, Maurice? No you don't, I know, because you only looked at the pictures, and then read Pierce Egan's account of the Topping Fight between Bob Gaynor and Ned Neal, or some such person.'

'*Tom* Gaynor,' corrected Frere, gravely.

'A *Tom* was he? Well, he was a horror, I know, and I wasn't sorry when Mr Neal fell upon him, and he came up *groggy* and with *bellows to mend*.'

'My dear Dora!' says Vickers, astonished.

'Oh, I saw it in the book, papa. Such a funny account!' she returned, smiling at her husband, and affecting a charming pomposity of utterance. 'Gaynor, though *piping*, was on his *mettle*, and *milling* was the order of the day. Gaynor's *nob* soon showed the *handiwork* of the *plucky* Neal, and his left *peeper* was put on the *winking* list. That is the sort of thing, isn't it, Maurice?'

Maurice thinks it's as eloquent as Burke.

'Little girls should be seen and not heard,' says Maurice, between a laugh and a blush. 'You have no business to read my books.'

'Why not? Husband and Wife should have no secrets from each other, sir. Besides, I want you to read *my* books. I am going to read Shelley to you.'

'Don't, my dear,' says honest Maurice, simply. 'I can't understand him.'

Dora's face clouded a little, but her spirits were too high to be easily dashed.

'Well, I'll explain to you,' she said. 'You shall be my Pupil. Papa, lend me your spectacles. Maurice, sit up straight, and don't laugh. Oh-h-h! you Stupid old Stupid!'

With which outburst, she took him by the ears and kissed him, with a display of much apparent violence.

This little scene took place at the dinner table of Frere's cottage, in New Town, to which Major Vickers had been invited, in order that future plans might be discussed.

'I don't want to go to Port Arthur,' said the bride, later in the evening. 'Maurice, there can be no necessity to go there.'

'Well,' says Maurice, 'I want to have a look at the place. I ought to be familiar with all phases of convict discipline, you know.'

'There is likely to be a Report ordered upon the death of a prisoner,' said Vickers. 'The chaplain, a fussy but well-meaning person, has been memorialising about it. You may as well do it as anybody else, Maurice.'

'Ay. And save the expenses of the trip,' says Maurice.

'But it is so melancholy,' cried Dora.

'The most delightful place in the island, my dear. I was there for a few days once, and I really was charmed.'

It was remarkable — so Vickers thought — how each of these newly-mated ones had caught something of the other's manner of speech. Dora was less choice in her mode of utterance, Frere more so. He caught himself wondering which of the two methods both would finally adopt.

'But those dogs, and sharks, and things. My goodness, Maurice, haven't we had enough of convicts?'

'Enough! Why, I'm going to make my living out of 'em,' says Maurice, with his most natural manner.

'Dreadful man! As if you were a Slave-trader, like the man in the Arabian Nights, and sold your fellow-creature for thirty Tomauns apiece. What's a Tomaun?'

'*I* don't know. A piece of money, I suppose, Goose.'

'Yes, but how much? Why don't you know? Men ought to know everything. Never mind, your Wife shall find it out for you. Do you hear, Captain Bruin? Your Lovely, Accomplished, and Intellectual Wife shall find it out for you.'

'She'll spoil you, Maurice,' said Vickers, looking at the bright young creature with overflowing eyes.

'I take a deal of spoiling, Poppet, eh?'

'You're a Base Wretch, sir! "Men were deceivers ever. One foot on sea" – you Monster – "and one on shore, To one thing constant never." '

'Play something, darling,' said her father; and so Dora, setting down to the piano – specially hired by Maurice in the plenitude of his primal uxoriousness – trilled and warbled in her pure young voice, until the Port Arthur question floated itself away upon waves of melody, and was heard of no more for that time.

But upon pursuing the subject, Dora found her husband firm. He wanted to go, and he would go. Having once assured himself that it was advantageous to him to do a certain thing, the native obstinacy of the animal urged him to do it despite all opposition from others, and Dora, having had her first 'cry' over the question of the visit, gave up the point with a sort of fear that, unless she did so, she might find her Idol the least bit in the world selfish.

This was the first difference of their short married life, and she hastened to condone it. In the sunshine of Love and Marriage – for Maurice really loved her; and love, curbing the worst part of him, brought to him, as it brings to all of us, that gentleness and abnegation of self which is the only token and assurance of a love that is aught but animal. Dora had seen her fears and doubts melt away, as the mists melt in the beams of morning. A young girl, healthy, warm-hearted, and not without romance, Marriage had opened to her the gate of the Beautiful Land she had seen in her dreams. A young girl, with passionate fancy, with honest and noble aspirations, but with the dark shadow of her early mental sickness brooding upon her childlike nature, Marriage had made her a woman, by developing in her a woman's trust and pride in the man to whom she had voluntarily given herself. Maurice loved her. She loved Maurice. One was necessary to the other. She belonged to him, and – oh! wonder and pride! – he belonged to her. If she provoked his anger, it was but that she might have the exquisite bliss of being forgiven. If she affected anger with him, it was but that she might enjoy the still more exquisite bliss of bestowing forgiveness. Into such a Heaven as this, what thoughts of past distrust, of past horrors but dimly remembered, could enter?

She was a woman. She loved, and was loved. What was the whole world to her beside that marvellous happiness?

Yet out of this new delight, by-and-by, arose a new source of anxiety.

Having accepted her position as a wife, and put away from her all doubts as to her own capacity for loving the man to whom she had allied herself, she began to be haunted by a dread lest he might do something which would lessen the affection she bore him.

On one or two occasions she had been forced to confess that her husband was more of an egotist than she cared to think. He demanded of her no great sacrifices – had he done so she would have found, in making them, that pleasure that women of her nature always find in such self-mortifications – but he now and then intruded on her that disregard for the feelings of others which was part of his character. He was fond of her – almost too passionately fond, for her staider liking – but he was unused to thwart his own will in anything, least of all in those seeming trifles, for the consideration of which true unselfishness bethinks itself. Did she want to read when he wanted to walk, he good-humouredly put aside her books, with an assumption that a walk with him must, of necessity, be the most pleasant thing in the world. Did she want to walk when he wanted to rest, he laughingly set up his laziness as an all-sufficient plea for her remaining within doors. He was at no pains to conceal his weariness when she read her favourite books to him. If he felt sleepy when she sang or played, he slept without apology. If she talked about a subject in which he took no interest, he turned the conversation remorselessly. He would not have wittingly offended her; but it seemed to him so natural to yawn when he was weary, to sleep when he was fatigued, and to talk only about those subjects he understood. Had anybody told him that he was selfish, he would have been astonished.

Thus it came about that Dora one day discovered that she led two lives – one in the body, and one in the spirit; and that with her spiritual existence her husband had no share. This discovery alarmed her, and then she smiled at it. 'As if Maurice could be expected to take interest in all my silly fancies,' said she; and, despite a harassing thought that these same fancies were not foolish, but were the best and brightest portion of her, she succeeded in overcoming her uneasiness. 'A man's thoughts are different from a woman's,' she said; 'he has his business and his worldly cares, of which a woman knows nothing. I must comfort him, and not afflict him with my follies.' Poor little sophist!

Yet, perhaps, it will not seem inconsistent to some people that she should have been all this time happier than she had ever been before.

As for Maurice, he grew sometimes rather troubled in his mind. He could not understand his wife. Her nature was an enigma to him; her mind a puzzle which would not be pieced together with the rectangular correctness of ordinary life. He had known her from a child, loved her from a child, and had committed a mean and cruel crime to obtain her; but having got her, he was no nearer to the mystery of her thoughts than before. She was all his own, he thought. Her golden hair was free for his fingers, her lips were warm for his caress, her eyes looked love upon him alone. Yet there were times when her lips seemed to be cold to his kisses, and her eyes to look disdainfully upon his coarser passion. He would catch her musing when he spoke to her, much as she would catch him sleeping when she read to him, – but she awoke with a start and a blush of remorse at her forgetfulness, which he never did. He was not a man to brood much over these things; and, after some reflective pipes and ineffectual rubbings of his head, he 'gave it up.' How was it possible, indeed, for him to solve the mental enigma when the woman herself was to him a physical riddle? It was extraordinary to find that the child he had seen growing up by his side day by day should be a young woman with little secrets, now to be revealed to him for the first time. He found that she had a mole on her neck, and remembered that he had noticed it when she was a child. Then it was a thing of no moment, now it was a marvellous discovery. He was in daily wonderment at the treasure he had obtained. He marvelled at her feminine devices of dress and adornment. Her dainty garments seemed to him perfumed with the odour of sanctity. The fact that she habitually wore night-caps tied with pink ribbon was a thing to be seriously noted.

The fact was, that the patron of Sarah Purfoy had not met with many virtuous women, and the Minotaur had just discovered what a dainty morsel Modesty was.

⊷ 18 ⊷

IN THE HOSPITAL

THE Hospital of Port Arthur was not a cheerful place, but to the tortured and unnerved Rufus Dawes it seemed a Paradise. There at least – despite the roughness and contempt with which his gaolers ministered to him – he felt that he was *considered*. There at least he was free from the enforced companionship of the men whom he loathed, and to whose level he felt, with mental agony unspeakable, he was daily sinking. Throughout his long term of degradation he had, as yet, aided by the memory of his sacrifice and his love, preserved something of his self-respect, but he felt that he would not preserve it long. Little by little, he had come to regard himself as one out of the pale of love and mercy, as one tormented of fortune, plunged into a deep into which the eye of Heaven did not penetrate. Since his capture in the garden at Hobart Town, he had given loose rein to his hatred and despair. 'I am forgotten or despised; I have no name in the world; what matter if I become like *one of these*?' It was under the influence of this feeling that he had picked up the cat at the command of Captain Burgess. As the unhappy Kirkland had said, 'As well you as another;' and truly, what was *he* that he should cherish sentiments of honour or humanity?

But he had miscalculated his own capacity for evil. As he flogged, he blushed; and when he had flung down the cat and stripped his own back for punishment, he felt a fierce joy at the thought that his baseness would be atoned for in his own blood. Even when unnerved and faint from his hideous ordeal, he flung himself upon his knees in the cell, he regretted only the impotent ravings that the torture had forced from him. He could have bitten out his tongue for its blasphemous utterings

– not because they were blasphemous, but because their utterance, by revealing his agony, gave their triumph to his tormentors. When North had found him, he was in the very depth of this abasement, and he repulsed his comforter – not so much because he had seen him flogged, but because he had heard him cry. The ruthless self-reliance and force of will which had hitherto sustained him through his self-imposed trial had failed him – he felt – at the moment when he needed it most; and the man who had with unflinched front faced the gallows, the desert, and the sea, confessed his debased humanity beneath the physical torture of the lash. He had been flogged before, and had wept in secret at his degradation, but he now for the first time comprehended how terrible that degradation might be made, for the first time understood the full punishment of the 'cat,' as he realised how the agony of the wretched body can force the soul to quit its last poor refuge of unarmed Indifference, *and confess itself conquered*.

Not many months before, one of the companions of his chain, suffering under Burgess's tender mercies, had killed his mate when at work with him, and, carrying the body on his back to the nearest gang, had surrendered himself – going to his death thanking God he had at last found a way of escape from his miseries, which no one would envy him – save his comrades. His heart had been filled with horror at a deed so bloody, and he had – with others – commented on the cowardice of the man that would thus shirk the responsibility of that state of life in which it had pleased Man and the Devil to place him. Now he understood how and why the crime had been committed, and felt only pity. Lying awake, with back that burned beneath its lotioned rags, when lights were low, in the breathful silence of the hospital, he registered in his heart a terrible oath that he would die ere he would again be made such hideous sport for his enemies. In this frame of mind, with whatever shreds of honour and worth that had formerly clung to him seemingly blown away in the whirlwind of his passion, he bethought him of the strange man who had deigned to clasp his hand and call him 'brother.' He had wept with no unmanly tears at this sudden flow of tenderness in one whom he had thought callous as the rest. He had been touched with a wondrous sympathy at the confession of weakness made to him, in a moment when his own weakness had overcome him to his shame.

Soothed by the momentary rest that his fortnight of hospital seclusion had afforded him, he had begun, in a languid and speculative way, to turn his thoughts to religion. He had read of martyrs who had borne agonies unspeakable, upheld by their confidence in Heaven and God. In his old wild youth he had scoffed at prayers and priests; in the hate to his kind that had grown upon him with his later years he had despised a creed that told men to love one another. 'God is love, my brethren,' said the chaplain on Sundays, and all the week the thongs of the overseer cracked, and the cat hissed and swung. Of what practical value was a piety that preached but did not practice? It was admirable for the 'religious instructor' to tell a prisoner that he must not give way to evil passions, but must bear his punishment with meekness. It was only right that he should advise him to 'put his trust in God.' But, as a hardened prisoner, convicted of getting drunk in an unlicensed house of entertainment, said 'God was so terrible far from Port Arthur.'

Rufus Dawes had smiled at the spectacle of a priest admonishing men who knew what *he* knew and had seen what *he* had seen against the crimes of lying and stealing. He had believed all priests imposters or fools, all religion a mockery and a lie. But now, finding how utterly his own strength had failed him when tried by the rude test of physical pain, he began to think that this Religion which was talked of so largely was not a mere bundle of legends and formulas, but had in it something vital and sustaining. Broken in spirit, and weakened in body, with faith in his own will shaken, he longed for something to lean upon; and turned – as all men turn when in such case – to the Unknown. Had, now, there been at hand some Christian priest, some Christian man even, no matter of what faith, to pour into the ears of this poor wretch words of comfort and grace; to rend away from him the garment of sullenness and despair in which he had wrapped himself; to drag from him a confession of his unworthiness, his obstinacy, and his hasty judgment, and to cheer his fainting soul with promise of immortality and justice, he might have been saved from his after fate; but there was no such man.

He asked for the Chaplain. North was battling with the Convict department, seeking vengeance for Kirkland, and (victim of 'clerks with the cold spurt of the pen') was pushed hither and thither, referred here, snubbed there, bowed out in another place. Rufus Dawes, half ashamed of himself for his request, waited a long morning, and then saw, respectfully ushered into his cell as his soul's physician – Meekin!

⊹ 19 ⊹

THE CONSOLATIONS OF RELIGION

'WELL, my good man,' says Meekin, soothingly, 'so you wanted to see me.'

'I asked for the chaplain,' says Rufus Dawes, his anger with himself growing apace.

'I am the chaplain,' returned Meekin, with dignity, as who should say, none of your brandy-drinking, pea-jacketted Norths, but a Respectable Chaplain who is the friend of a Bishop!

'I thought that Mr North was –'

'Mr North has left, sir,' said Meekin, drily, 'but I will hear what you have to say. There is no occasion to go, constable; wait outside the door.'

Rufus Dawes shifted himself on the wooden bench, and resting his scarcely-healed back against the wall, smiled bitterly.

'Don't be afraid, sir; I am not going to harm you,' he said. 'I only wanted to talk a little.'

'Do you read your Bible, Dawes?' asked Meekin, by way of reply. 'It would be better to read your Bible than to talk, I think. You must humble yourself in prayer, Dawes.'

'I have read it,' says Dawes, still lying back and watching him.

'But is your mind softened by its teachings? Do you realize the Infinite Mercy of God, who has compassion, Dawes, upon the greatest sinners.'

The convict made a movement of impatience. The old sickening, barren cant of piety was to be recommended then. He came asking for bread, and they gave him the usual stone.

'Do you believe there is a God, Mr Meekin?'

'Abandoned sinner! Do you insult a clergyman by such a question?'

'Because I think sometimes that, if there is, He must be preparing a terrible vengeance for the bloody deeds done here,' said Dawes, half to himself.

'I can listen to no mutinous observations, prisoner,' says Meekin. 'Do not add blasphemy to your other crimes. I fear that all conversation with you, in your present frame of mind, would be worse than useless. I will mark a few passages in your Bible, that seem to me appropiate to your condition, and beg you to commit them to memory. Hailes, the door, if you please.'

So, with a bow, the 'consoler' departed.

Rufus Dawes felt his heart grow sick. North had gone, then. The only man who had seemed to have a heart in his bosom had gone. The only man who had dared to clasp his horny and blood-stained hand, and call him 'brother,' had gone. Turning his head, he saw through the window — wide open and unbarred, for Nature, at Port Arthur, had no need of bars — the lovely bay, smooth as glass, glittering in the afternoon sun, the long quay, spotted with groups of parti-coloured chain-gangs, and heard, mingling with the soft murmur of the waves, and gentle rustling of the trees, the never-ceasing clashing of irons and the eternal click of hammers. Was he to be for ever buried in this whited sepulchre, shut out from the face of Heaven and mankind?

The appearance of Hailes broke his reverie.

'Here's a book for you,' said he, with a grin. 'Parson sent it.'

Rufus Dawes took the Bible, and, placing it on his knee, turned to the places indicated by slips of paper. There were some three or four of these slips of paper, embracing some twenty marked texts.

'Parson says he'll come and hear you to-morrer, and you're to keep the book clean.'

'Keep the book clean!' and 'hear him!' Did Meekin think that he was a charity school boy? The utter incapacity of the chaplain to understand his wants was so sublime that it was nearly ridiculous enough to make him laugh. He turned his eyes downwards to the texts. Good Meekin, in the fulness of his stupidity, had selected the fiercest denunciations of bard and priest. The most notable of the Psalmist's curses upon his enemies, the most furious of Isaiah's ravings anent the forgetfulness of the national worship, the most terrible thunderings of apostle and evangelist against idolatry and unbelief, were grouped together and presented to Dawes to soothe him. All the material horrors of Meekin's faith — stripped, by force of dissociation from the context, of all poetic feeling and local colouring — were launched at the suffering sinner by Meekin's ignorant hand. The miserable man, seeking for consolation and peace, turned over the leaves of the Bible only to find himself threatened with 'the pains of Hell,' 'the never-dying worm,' 'the unquenchable fire,' the bubbling of brimstone, the 'bottomless pit,' from out of which the 'smoke of his torment' should ascend for 'ever and ever.' Before his eyes was held the image of no tender Saviour, (with hands soft to soothe, and eyes brimming with ineffable pity), dying crucified that he and other malefactors might have hope, by thinking on His marvellous humanity. The worthy Pharisee who was sent to him to teach him how mankind is to be redeemed with Love, preached only that harsh Law whose barbarous power died with the gentle Nazarene on Calvary.

Repelled by this unlooked for ending to his hopes, he let the book fall to the ground.

'Is there, then, nothing but torment for me in this world or the next?' he groaned, shuddering.

Presently his eyes sought his right hand, resting upon it as though it were not his own, or had acquired some secret virtue which made it different from the other. '*He* would not have done this! *He* would not have thrust upon me these savage judgments, these dreadful threats of Hell and Death. He called me 'Brother!' And filled with a strange wild pity for himself, and, yearning love towards the man who befriended him, he fell to nursing the hand on which North's tears had fallen, moaning, and rocking himself to and fro.

Good Meekin, coming in the morning, found his pupil more sullen than ever.

'Have you learnt these texts, my man?' said he, cheerfully, willing not to be angered with this uncouth and unpromising convert.

Rufus Dawes pointed with his foot to the Bible, which still lay on the floor as he had left it the night before.

'No!'

'No! Why not?'

'I want to learn no such words as those. I would rather forget them.'

'Forget them! My good man, I –'

Rufus Dawes sprang up in sudden wrath, and, pointing to his cell door with a gesture that, chained and degraded as he was – had something of dignity in it, cried,

'What do you know about the feelings of such as I? Take your book and yourself away! When I asked for a priest, I had no thought of *you*. Begone!'

Meekin, despite the halo of sanctity that he felt should surround him, found his gentlemanliness melt all of a sudden. Adventitious distinctions had disappeared for the instant. The pair had become simply man and man, and the sleek priest-master quailed before the outraged manhood of the convict-penitent. He picked up his Bible and went out.

'That man Dawes is very insolent,' said to Burgess the insulted Chaplain. 'He was brutal to me to-day – quite brutal.'

'Was he?' says Burgess. 'Had too long a spell, I expect. I'll send him back to work to-morrow.'

'It would be well,' said gentle Meekin, 'if he had some employment.'

✦ 20 ✦

'A NATURAL PENITENTIARY'

THE 'employment' at Port Arthur consisted of agriculture, ship-building, tanning, etc. Dawes, who was in the chain-gang, was put to chain-gang labour; that is to say, bringing down logs from the forest, or 'lumbering' timber on the wharf. This work was not light; an ingenious calculator has discovered that the pressure of the log upon the shoulder was wont to average from 50 to 200 lbs. Members of the chain-gang were dressed in yellow, and – by way of encouraging the others – had the word 'Felon' stamped upon conspicuous parts of their raiment.

This was the sort of life Rufus Dawes led.

In the summer he rose at half-past five in the morning, and worked until six in the evening, getting three quarters of an hour for breakfast, and one hour for dinner. His breakfast consisted of one pint of gruel, made with two ounces of oatmeal and half an ounce of molasses, and six ounces of bread; to this was added, three times a week, one pint of soup, made with three ounces of mixed vegetables, half an ounce of flour, half an ounce of barley, and one-hundredth part of an ounce of pepper. On Sunday – blessed day of rest – he got no meat, but twelve ounces of potatoes, and twelve ounces of a pudding made of one and a half ounces of suet, six ounces of flour, and four and a half ounces of water. Rufus Dawes, being a healthy, refractory, and ill-conditioned fellow, swore that the pudding was uneatable, and 'swopped' it, for more bread. Once a week he had a clean shirt, and once a fortnight clean socks. If he felt sick, he was permitted to 'report his case to the medical officer.' If he wanted to write a letter he could ask permission of the Commandant, and send the letter, open, through that Almighty Officer, who could stop it if he thought necessary. If he felt himself aggrieved by any order, he was 'to obey it instantly,' but might complain 'afterwards, if he thought fit, to the Commandant.' In making any complaint against an officer or constable, it was strictly ordered that a prisoner 'must be most respectful in his manner and language, when speaking of or to such officer or constable.' He was held responsible only for the safety of his chains, and for the rest was at the mercy of his gaoler.

These gaolers – owning rights of search, entry into cells at all hours, and other *droits* of seigneury – were responsible only to the Commandant, who was responsible only to the Governor, that is to say, to nobody but God and his own conscience.

The jurisdiction of the Commandant included the whole of Tasman's Peninsula, with the islands and waters within three miles thereof; and, 'save the making of certain returns to head-quarters,' his power was unlimited. At Port Arthur the Commandant occupied the position of God's vicegerent upon earth.

A word as to the position and appearance of this place of punishment. Tasman's Peninsula is, as we have said before, in the form of an earring with a double drop. The lower drop is the larger, and is ornamented, so to speak, with bays. At its southern extremity is a deep indention called Maingon Bay, bounded east and west by the organ-pipe rocks of Cape Raoul, and the giant form of Cape Pillar. From Maingon Bay an arm of the ocean cleaves the rocky walls in a northerly direction. On the western coast of this sea-arm was the settlement; in front of it was a little island where the dead were buried, called *The Island of the Dead.* Ere the in-coming convict passed the purple beauty of this convict Golgotha, his eyes were attracted by a point of grey rock covered with white buildings, and swarming with life. This was Point Puer. It was astonishing – many honest folks averred – how ungrateful were these juvenile convicts for the goods the Government had provided for them.

From the extremity of Long Bay, as the extension of the sea-arm was named, a convict-made tramroad ran due north through the nearly impenetrable thicket to Norfolk Bay. In the mouth of Norfolk Bay was Woody Island. This was used as a signal station, and an armed boat's crew was stationed there. To the north of Woody Island lay One-tree Point – the southernmost projection of the drop of the earring; and the sea that ran between narrowed to the eastward, until it struck on the sandy bar of Eaglehawk-Neck.

Eaglehawk-Neck was the link that connected the two drops of the earring. It was a strip of sand twenty yards wide and one hundred yards long. On its eastern side the blue waters of Pirate's Bay, that is to say, of the Southern Ocean, poured their unchecked force. The isthmus itself emerged from a wild and terrible coast-line, into whose bowels the ravenous sea had bored strange caverns, resonant with perpetual roar of tortured billows. At one spot in this wilderness the ocean had penetrated the wall of the rock for two hundred feet, and in stormy weather the salt spray rose through a perpendicular shaft more than five hundred feet. This place was called the Devil's Blow-hole.

The upper drop of the earring was named Forrester's Penin-sula, and was joined to the mainland by another isthmus called East Bay Neck. Forrester's Peninsula was an almost impene-trable thicket growing to the brink of a perpendicular cliff of basalt.

Eaglehawk-Neck was the door to the prison, and it was kept bolted. On the narrow strip of land was built a guard-house, where soldiers from the barrack on the mainland relieved each other, night and day; and on stages, set out in the water on either side, were chained watch-dogs. The station officer was charged 'to pay especial attention to the feeding and care' of these useful beasts, being ordered 'to report to the Commandant whenever any one of them became useless.' It may be added that the Bay was not innocent of sharks.

Westward from Eaglehawk-Neck and Woody Island, lay the dreaded Coal Mines. Sixty of the 'marked men' were sta-tioned here under a strong guard. At the Coal Mines was the northernmost of that ingenious series of semaphores which rendered escape almost impossible. The wild and mountainous character of the peninsula offered peculiar advantages to the signalmen. On the summit of the hill which overlooks the guard-tower of the settlement was a gigantic gum-tree stump, upon the top of which was placed a semaphore. This semaphore communicated with the two wings of the prison – Eaglehawk-Neck and the Coal Mines – by sending a line of signals right across the peninsula. Thus, the settlement communicated with Mount Arthur, Mount Arthur with One-Tree Hill, One-Tree Hill with Mount Communication, and Mount Communication with the Coal Mines. On the other side, the signals would run thus – the settlement to Signal Hill, Signal Hill to Woody Island, Woody Island to Eaglehawk. Did a prisoner escape from the Coal Mines, the guard at Eaglehawk-Neck could be aroused, and the whole island informed of the 'bolt' in less than twenty minutes.

With these advantages of nature and art, the prison was held to be the most secure in the world. Colonel Arthur reported to the Home Government that the spot which bore his name was 'a natural penitentiary.' The worthy disciplinarian probably took as a personal compliment the polite forethought of the Almighty, in thus considerately providing for the carrying out of the 'Regulations for Convict Discipline.'

⇥ 21 ⇤

A VISIT OF INSPECTION

ONE afternoon the ever-active semaphores transmitted a piece of intelligence which set the peninsula agog. Captain Frere, having arrived from head-quarters, with orders to hold an Inquiry, was not unlikely to make a progress through the stations, and it behoved the keepers of the Natural Penitentiary to produce their Penitents in good case.

Burgess was in high spirits at finding so congenial a soul selected for the task of reporting upon him.

'It's only a nominal thing, old man,' Frere had said to his old comrade, when they met. 'That parson has been meddling, and they want to close his mouth.'

'I am only glad to have the opportunity of showing you and Mrs Frere the place,' returned Burgess. 'I must try and make your stay as pleasant as I can, though I'm afraid that Mrs Frere will not find much to amuse her.'

'Frankly, Captain Burgess,' said Dora, 'I would rather have gone straight to Sydney. My husband, however, was obliged to come, and, of course, I accompanied him.'

'You will not have much society,' said Meekin, who, necessarily, was of the welcoming party. 'Mrs Datchett, the wife of one of our stipendiaries, is the only lady here, and I hope to have the pleasure of making you acquainted with her this evening at the Commandant's. Mr McNab, whom you know, is down at the Neck, and cannot leave very well, or you would have seen him.'

'I had planned a little party,' said Burgess, 'but I fear that it will not be as successful as I could wish.'

'You jolly old bachelor,' says Frere, 'you should get married, like I am.'

'Ah!' says Burgess, with a bow, 'that would be difficult.'

Dora was compelled to smile at the compliment, made in the presence of some twenty prisoners, who were carrying the various trunks and packages up the hill, and remarked that the said prisoners grinned — so to speak — with their eyes at the Commandant's clumsy courtesy.

'I don't like Captain Burgess, Maurice,' she said, in the interval before dinner. 'I dare say he did flog that poor fellow to death. He looks as if he could do it.'

'Nonsense!' says Maurice, pettishly. 'He's a good fellow enough. Besides, I've seen the doctor's certificate. It's all a trumped-up story. I can't understand your absurd sympathy with prisoners.'

'Don't they deserve sympathy?'

'No, certainly not — a set of lying scoundrels. You are always whining over them, Dora. I don't like it, and I've told you before about it.'

Dora sighed, but said nothing. Maurice was often guilty of these small brutalities, and she had learnt that the best way to meet them was by silence. Unfortunately, silence did not mean indifference, for the reproof was unjust, and nothing stings a woman's finer sense like an injustice.

'I hope Burgess will give us a good dinner,' said Maurice, turning the conversation; 'I am as hungry as a hunter.'

Burgess had prepared a feast, and the 'Society' of Port Arthur was present.

Father Flaherty, the Reverend Meekin, Doctor Macklewain, and Mr and Mrs Datchett had been invited, and the dining-room was resplendent with glass and flowers.

'I've a fellow who was a professional gardener,' said Burgess to Dora during the dinner, 'and I make use of his talents.'

'We have a professional artist also,' said Macklewain, with a sort of pride. 'That picture of the "Prisoner of Chillon" yonder was painted by him. A very meritorious production, is it not?'

'I've got the place full of curiosities,' said Burgess; 'quite a collection. I'll show them to you to-morrow. Those napkin rings were made by a prisoner.'

'Ah!' cries Frere, taking up the daintily-carved bone, 'very nice!'

'That is some of Rex's handiwork,' said Meekin. 'He is very clever at these trifles. He made me a paper-cutter that was really a Work of Art.'

At this point, Mr Datchett, the 'stipendiary,' who had been informed that Mrs Frere was 'clever,' and had, in consequence, primed himself with topics of literary and artistic interest, burst out with,

'What do you think of Michael Angelo, Mrs Frere?' And upon Dora replying, in a somewhat confused way, that she had not seen any of that great man's works, said 'Ah!' with intense satisfaction, and relapsed again into nothingness. Mr Datchett, indeed, distinguished himself a good deal at this dinner. Not quite satisfied with Dora's reply, he got ready to fire another shot, and presently discharged:

'Which do you admire most, Mrs Frere, Milton or Shakspeare?'

'Well, I think Shakspeare,' says poor Dora, after some hesitation, during which Mr Datchett, lost in expectation, held a morsel suspended midway to his lips. When she had given her opinion, he cried 'Ah!' again, and nodded, as if to express that the great question of his life was now at rest.

So in the intervals of eating, he returned to the charge with such generalities as, 'Are you fond of Pictures?' 'Do you like Music?' and receiving Dora's answers with 'Ahs!' of much vehemence. Indeed, upon coming into the drawing-room, after the feast was over, he attempted higher flights, occasionally saying, in a solemn tone, from the other end of the room, 'I am an admirer of Sir Walter Scott!' or, 'I have read Campbell's poetry, Mrs Frere, with much interest!' His conversation, however, not getting beyond these observations, could hardly be called thoroughly satisfactory.

Mrs Datchett, a care-worn, ill-dressed lady, who seemed to bear that relation to ordinary people that slop-made clothes bear to legitimately-tailored garments, said nothing at all, but contented herself with smiling feebly when addressed, and saying 'Oh, yes!' or 'Oh, no!' as she thought would best satisfy her interlocutor. Of 'Society' as assembled, Dora liked Father

Flaherty best. He sat beside her after dinner, and — while Frere loudly argued concerning convict discipline — told her stories of foreign manners and customs, and revealed to her his pet scheme for planting olive trees at the side of all the highways in the colony.

'We will go down to the Neck to-morrow or next day, Mrs Frere,' said Burgess, 'and you shall see the Blow-hole. It is a curious place.'

'Is it far?' asked Dora.

'Oh no! We shall go in the train.'

'The train!'

'Yes — don't look so astonished. You'll see it to-morrow. Oh, you Hobart Town ladies don't know what we can do here.'

'What about this Kirkland business?' Frere asked. 'I suppose I can have half an hour with you in the morning, and take the depositions?'

'Any time you like, my dear fellow,' says Burgess. 'It's all the same to me.'

'*I* don't want to make more fuss than I can help,' Frere said, apologetically — the dinner had been good — 'but I must send these people up a "full, true, and particular," don't you know.'

'Of course,' cried Burgess, with friendly *nonchalance*. 'That's all right. I want Mrs Frere to see Point Puer.'

'Where the boys are?' asked Dora.

'Exactly. Nearly three hundred of 'em. We'll go down to-morrow, and you shall be my witness, Mrs Frere, as to the way they are treated.'

'Indeed,' said Dora, 'I would rather not. I — I don't take the interest in these things that I ought, perhaps. They are very dreadful to me.'

'Nonsense!' cries bluff Frere, with a scowl. 'We'll come. Burgess, of course.'

So the next two days were devoted to sight-seeing. Dora was taken through the Hospital and the Workshops, shown the semaphores, and shut up, by laughing Maurice, in a 'dark cell.' Her husband and Burgess seemed to regard the prison as some tame animal, whom they could handle at their leisure, and whose natural ferocity was kept in check by their superior intelligence. This bringing of a young and pretty woman into immediate contact with bolts and bars had about it an incongruity which pleased them. Maurice penetrated everywhere, questioned the prisoners, jested with the jailers, even, in the munificence of his heart, bestowed tobacco on the sick. Dora was perpetually compelled to listen to such conversations as this:

Frere. What's *your* name?

Prisoner. John Jones. Marpelia.

Frere. Offence and sentence?

Prisoner. Burning hayricks. Seven years.

Frere. Colonial sentence?

Prisoner. Fourteen years.

Frere (to Burgess). What's he been doing?

Burgess (to Frere). Absconding from his hired service.

Frere. Oh! *(To Prisoner).* Are you comfortable?

Prisoner (with great readiness). Yes, your honour.

Frere. Plenty to eat and drink?

Prisoner. Yes, your honour.

Frere. Any complaints?

Prisoner. No, your honour.

Frere (encouragingly). Don't be afraid to speak out, you know. Have you nothing to complain of?

Prisoner (with his eye on Burgess). Nothing at all, your honour.

Frere (pompously). Have I your permission, Captain Burgess, to give this man a piece of tobacco?

Burgess (solemnly). Certainly, Captain Frere.

Frere. Here's some tobacco for you, my man.

Prisoner (touching his forehead). Much obliged to you sir.

And then, turning his back, he would grin among his comrades.

Sometimes Meekin took part in the farce, by calling out a prisoner to quote Scripture. Thus:

Meekin. Come here, No. 422, and let me see if you can recite to the gentlemen any of the texts I have taught you.

No. 422 (with immense volubility). Though I walk through the valley of the shadow of death I will fear no evil for thou art with me thy rod and thy staff they comfort me *(gasp)* thou preparest a table before me in the presence of mine enemies thou anointest my 'ead with hoil my cup runneth over (*gasp*) surely goodness and mercy shall follow me all the days of my life and I shall dwell in the 'ouse of the Lord for ever (*touches forehead*).

Meekin (*looking round with delight*). And you can tell me who wrote those verses?

No. 422. David.

Meekin. And who was David?

No. 422. A king of Israel. He was a shepherd, and killed Goliath with a sling, Anno Mundi Two thousand nine hundred and fifty-six.

Meekin. Very good, indeed. Thank you. (*Aside to Dora*) A most intelligent man. I have great hopes of him.

No. 422. (*aside to his friends on retiring*). No blank tobacco! Blank 'em, do they think a blank blank is going to spout their blank texts for nothing! Blank and space and (etc., etc.).

With such grateful rattlings of dry bones, they got by-and-by to Point Puer, where a luncheon had been provided.

◄◄ 22 ►►

AN EPISODE OF THREE CHILDREN

An unlucky accident had occurred at Point Puer that morning, however, and the place was in a suppressed ferment. A refractory little thief named Peter Brown, aged ten years, had jumped off the high rock and drowned himself in full view of the constables. These 'jumpings off' had become rather frequent lately, and Burgess was enraged at one happening on this particular day of all days. If he could by any possibility have brought the corpse of poor little Peter Brown to life again, he would have soundly whipped him for his impertinence.

'It is most unfortunate,' he said to Frere, as they stood in the cell where the little body was laid, 'that it should have happened to-day.'

'Oh,' says Frere, looking down upon the young face that seemed to frown at him. 'It can't be helped. I know those young devils. They'd do it out of spite. What sort of character had he?'

'Very bad. Johnson, the book.'

Johnson bringing it, the two saw Peter Brown's iniquities set down in the neatest of running-hand, and the record of his punishments ornamented in quite an artistic way with flourishes of red ink.

'20th November, disorderly conduct, 12 lashes. 24th November, insolence to hospital attendant, diet reduced. 4th December, stealing cap from another prisoner, 12 lashes. 15th December, absenting himself at roll call, two days' cells. 23rd December, insolence and insubordination, two days' cells. 8th January, insolence and insubordination, 12 lashes. 20th January, insolence and insubordination, 12 lashes. 22nd February, insolence and insubordination, 12 lashes and one week's solitary. 20th February, insolence and insubordination, 20 lashes.'

'That was the last?' asked Frere.

'Yes, sir,' says Johnson.

'And then he – hum – did it?'

'Just so, sir. That was the way of it.'

Just so! The magnificent system starved and tortured a child of ten until he killed himself. That was the way of it.

After luncheon, the party made a progress. Everything was most admirable. There was a long schoolroom, where such men as Meekin taught how Christ loved little children; and behind the schoolroom were the cells and the constables and the little yard where they gave their 'twenty lashes.' Dora shuddered at the array of faces. From the stolid fifteen years old booby of the Kentish hop fields, to the wizened, shrewd six years' old Bohemian of the London streets, all degrees and grades of juvenile vice grinned, in untameable wickedness, or snuffled in affected piety. 'Suffer little children to come unto Me, and forbid them not, for of such is the Kingdom of Heaven.' Of such it seemed that a large number of Honourable Gentlemen, together with Her Majesty's faithful Commons in Parliament assembled, had done their best to create a Kingdom of Hell.

After the Farce had been played again, and the children had stood up and sat down, and sung a hymn, and told how many twice five were, and repeated their belief in 'One God the Father Almighty, maker of Heaven and Earth,' the party reviewed the workshops, and saw the church, and went everywhere but into the room where the body of Peter Brown, aged ten, lay starkly on its wooden bench, staring at the gaol roof which was between it and Heaven.

Just outside this room Dora met with a little adventure. Meekin had stopped behind, and Burgess, being suddenly summoned for some official duty, Frere had gone with him, leaving his wife to rest on a bench that, placed at the summit of the cliff, overlooked the sea. While resting thus, she became aware of another presence, and, turning her head, beheld a small boy, with his cap in one hand and a hammer in the other. The appearance of the little creature, clad in a uniform of grey cloth that was too large for him, and holding in his withered little hand a hammer that was too heavy for him, had something pathetic about it.

'What is it, you Mite?' asked Dora.

'We thought you might have seen Him, mum,' says the little figure, opening its blue eyes with wonder at the kindness of the tone.

'Him! Whom?'

'Cranky Brown, mum,' returned the child; 'him as did it this morning. Me and Billy knowed him, mum; he was a mate of ours, and we wanted to know if he looked Happy.'

'What do you mean, child?' said she, with a strange terror at her heart; and then, filled with pity at the aspect of the little being, she drew him to her, with sudden womanly instinct, and kissed him.

He looked up at her with joyful surprise.

'Oh!' he said.

Dora kissed him again.

'Does nobody ever kiss you, poor little Mite?' said she.

'Mother used to,' was the reply, 'but she's dead. Oh, mum,' with a sudden crimsoning of the little face, 'may I fetch Billy?'

And taking courage from the bright young face, he gravely marched to an angle of the rock, and brought out another little creature, with another grey uniform and another hammer.

'This is Billy, mum,' he said. 'Billy never had no mother. Kiss Billy.'

The young wife felt the tears rush to her eyes.

'You two poor Babies!' she cried.

And then, forgetting that she was a 'lady,' dressed in silk and lace, she fell on her knees in the dust, and, folding the friendless pair in her arms, wept over them.

'What is the matter, Dora?' said Frere, when he came up. 'You've been crying.'

'Nothing, Maurice; at least, I will tell you by-and-bye.'

So, when they were alone that evening, she told him of the two boys, and he laughed.

'Artful little humbugs,' he said, and supported his argument by so many illustrations of the precocious wickedness of juvenile felons, that the young woman was half convinced against her will.

Unfortunately, when Dora went away, Tommy and Billy put into execution a plan which they had carried in their poor little heads for some weeks.

'I can do it now,' said Tommy. 'I feel strong.'

'Will it hurt much, Tommy?' said Billy, who was not so courageous.

'Not so much as a whipping.'

'I'm afraid! Oh, Tom, it's so deep! Don't leave me, Tom!'

The bigger baby took his little handkerchief from his neck, and with it bound his left hand to his companion's right.

'Now I can't leave you.'

'What was it the Lady that kissed us said, Tommy?'

'Lord have pity on them two fatherless children!' repeated Tommy.

'Let's say it, Tom.'

And so the two babies knelt down on the brink of the cliff, and, raising the bound hands together, looked up at the sky, and said, 'Lord have pity on us two fatherless children!' And then they kissed each other, and 'did it.'

The intelligence, transmitted by the ever-active semaphore, reached the Commandant in the midst of dinner, and in his agitation, he blurted it out.

'These are the two poor things I saw in the morning,' cried Dora. 'Oh, Maurice, those two poor babies driven to suicide!'

'Condemning their young souls to everlasting fire,' said Meekin, piously.

'Mr Meekin! How can you talk like that! Poor little mortals! Oh, it's horrible! Maurice, take me away.'

And she burst into a passion of weeping.

'I can't help it, mam,' says Burgess, rudely. 'It ain't my fault.'

'She's nervous,' says Frere, leading her away. 'You must excuse her. Come and lie down, dearest.'

'I will not stop here longer,' said she. 'Let us go to-morrow.'

'We can't,' said Frere.

'Oh, yes, we can. I insist. Maurice, if you love me, take me away.'

'Well,' says Maurice, moved by her evident grief, 'I'll try.'

He spoke to Burgess.

'Burgess, this matter has unsettled my wife, so that she wants to leave at once. I must visit the Neck, you know. How can we do it?'

'Well,' says Burgess, 'if the wind only holds, the brig could go round to Pirates' Bay and pick you up. You'll only be a night at the barracks.'

'I think that would be best,' said Frere. 'We'll start to-morrow, please, and if you'll give me a pen and ink I'll be obliged.'

'I hope you are satisfied,' said Burgess.

'Oh, quite,' said Frere. 'I must recommend more careful supervision at Point Puer though. It will never do to have these young blackguards slipping through our fingers in this way.'

So a neatly written statement of the occurrence was appended to the ledgers in which the names of William Tomkins and Thomas Grove were entered. Macklewain held an inquest, and nobody troubled about them any more. Why should they? The prisons of London were full of such Tommys and Billys.

THE END OF THE ENQUIRY

DORA passed through the rest of her journey in a sort of dream of terror. The incident of the children had shaken her nerves, and she longed to be away from the place and its associations. Even Eaglehawk Neck, with its curious dog stages and its 'natural pavement,' did not interest her. Honest McNab's blandishments were wearisome. She shuddered as she gazed into the boiling abyss of the Blow-hole, and shook with fear as the Commandant's 'train' rattled over the dangerous tramway that wound across the precipice to Long Bay.

The 'train' was composed of a number of low waggons pushed and dragged up the steep inclines by convicts, who drew themselves up in the waggons when the trucks dashed down the slope, and acted as drags. Dora felt degraded at being thus drawn by human beings, and trembled when the lash cracked and the convicts answered to the sting – like cattle. Moreover, there was among the foremost of these beasts of burden, a face that she knew – a face that had haunted her girlhood, and only lately vanished from her dreams. This face looked on her – she thought – with bitterest loathing and scorn, and she felt relieved when at the midday halt its owner was ordered to fall out from the rest, and with four others re-chained for the homeward journey. Frere, struck with the appearance of the five, said, 'By Jove, Poppet, there are our old friends Rex and Dawes and the others. They won't let 'em come all the way, because they are such a desperate lot, they might make a rush for it.' Dora comprehended now: the face was the face of Dawes; and as she looked after him, she saw him suddenly raise his hands above his head with a motion that terrified her. She seemed to dimly remember some place or time when that action, or one like it, had startled her. She felt for an instant a great shock of pitiful recollection. Staring at the group, she strove to recall when and how Rufus Dawes, the wretch from whose clutches her husband had saved her, had ever merited her pity, but her clouded memory could not complete the picture, and as the waggons swept round a curve and the group disappeared, she awoke from her reverie with a sigh.

'Maurice,' she whispered, 'how is it that the sight of that man always makes me sad?'

Her husband frowned, and then caressing her, bid her forget the man and the place and her fears.

'I was wrong to have insisted on your coming,' he said, when standing on the deck of the Sydney-bound vessel, the next morning, they watched the 'Natural Penitentiary' grow dim in the distance. 'You were not strong enough.'

'Oh, Maurice,' she whispered, laying her head upon his breast. 'Think of those two poor children! Think if *our* children should ever come to suffer such misery as that.'

'Rubbish, my darling,' says Maurice, cheerfully. 'Our children won't be convicts, I hope. Let us think no more of it.'

And so resolving, they looked their last upon Port Arthur.

'Dawes,' said John Rex, that same evening, seeming to take up the thread of a conversation where he had dropped it. 'You love that girl! Now that you've seen her another man's wife, and have been harnessed like a beast to drag him along the road, while he held her in his arms! – now that you've seen and suffered that, perhaps you'll join us.'

Rufus Dawes made a movement of agonized impatience.

'You'd better. You'll never get out of this place any other way. Come, be a man; join us!'

'No!'

'It is your only chance. Why refuse it? Do you *want* to live here all your life?'

'I want no sympathy from you or any other. I will *not* join you.'

Rex shrugged his shoulders and walked away.

'If you think to get any good out of that "inquiry," you are mightily mistaken,' said he, as he went. 'Frere has put a stopper upon that, you'll find.'

He spoke truly. Nothing more was heard of it, only that, some six months afterwards, Mr North, when at Parramatta, received an official letter (in which the expenditure of wax and printing and paper was as large as it could be made), and which informed him that the 'Comptroller-General of the convict department had decided that further inquiry concerning the death of the prisoner named in the margin was unnecessary,' and that some gentleman with an utterly illegible signature 'had the honour to be his most obedient servant.'

⊷ 24 ⊶

IN SYDNEY

MAURICE found his expectations of Sydney fully realised.

His notable escape from death at Macquarie Harbour, his alliance with the daughter of so respected a colonist as Major Vickers, and his reputation as a convict disciplinarian, rendered him a man of note. He and his wife were received at once into the highest Sydney society, and at balls and public gatherings formed part of that select circle that revolved round the orbit of the 'Governor's party.' Mrs Frere – though she once committed the almost unpardonable sin of addressing the grandson of an Emancipist at a governor's ball – was voted 'charming.'

'He is a very nice person,' Dora had said. 'Why shouldn't I speak to him?' Sydney society, however, soon convinced her 'why' not, being in the habit of assembling itself at one end of a room and leaving the 'cross' to its degradation at the other.

'My dear creature,' said Mrs Bibtuckett, of Bullocksferry – Mrs *Captain* Bibtuckett, she styled herself – whose worthy grandfather had been a swindling contractor for beef in the Peninsula, 'he may be all you say. I know he has £30,000 a-year, and has travelled all over Europe; but, my dear' – whispering hum, hum, hum –

'Sent out for duelling! Well, there is nothing so *very* bad in that; and beside *he* can't help it!'

'Oh, we never recognise such persons in *society*, my love,' says Mrs Captain Bibtuckett. 'We are very strict in Sydney, I assure you.'

Maurice – who had been to dine with a gentleman who gave

bachelor parties, at which his emancipist mistress presided –
supported Mrs Captain Bibtuckett in her assurance of the strict-
ness of prevailing morality.

'For goodness sake, Dora, take care,' he said to her when at
home. 'You've no notion how these people mark the line between "bond" and "free." Van Diemen's Land is nothing to
it.'

'And yet,' said Dora, 'they seem to be most careless about
their servants. When I was at Mrs Pratt's yesterday, I heard the
children using the most dreadful language, which they could
only have learnt from the lowest people. I am sure in Hobart
Town we were most particular.'

'Your father was,' said Maurice, with a laugh; 'others were
not, though. Why, my dear child, I've known –' but he stopped,
as if what he *did* know would scarcely bear narration. 'However, that's nothing, but be careful.'

'I don't think *you* were very careful, Maurice, dining with
that wretched woman,' she retorted.

'My dear, what was I to do? Everybody goes there.'

'Did you speak to the Creature?' asked Dora, with that
bitterness that the best of women evince toward sinful sisters.

'Yes,' says Maurice, grinning, 'of course. I took wine with
her.'

'How did you address her? You didn't say Mrs Smith, I
suppose?'

'No, Smith would have been offended at that. She had been
his assigned servant, you know. It *was* rather awkward. But I
took a glass, like this, see,' imitating the action, 'waited till I
caught her eye, and then said, "Shall I have the pleasure?" But,
however, that has nothing to do with it. The people here are
most sensitive, and you must not offend their prejudices. It
would do me harm as well as yourself.'

'Oh,' says Dora, with as much spite as her sweetness of nature
permitted her, 'if that's the case, I will be most careful.'

'That is right,' said Maurice, gravely. 'I expect to get a magistracy if old Jupp goes, and I don't want to run my head against
the wall, you know.'

Old Jupp did go, and Frere, receiving the vacant post, became even more noted for hardness of heart and artfulness of

prison knowledge than before. The convict population spoke of him as 'that — Frere,' and registered vows of vengeance against him, which he laughed – in his fine old English bluffness – to scorn.

One example of the method by which he shepherded his flock will suffice, out of many that might be quoted.

It was his custom to visit the prison yard at Hyde Park Barrack twice a week. Visitors to convicts were, of course, armed, and the two pistol-butts that peeped from Frere's waistcoat attracted many a longing eye. How easy it would be for some quick fellow to pluck one forth and shatter the smiling, hateful face of the noted disciplinarian! But Frere, brave to rashness, never would bestow his weapons more safely, but lounged through the yard with his hands in the pockets of his shooting-coat, and the deadly butts ready to the hand of any one bold enough to take them.

One day, a man named Kavanagh, a captured absconder, who had openly sworn in the dock the death of the magistrate, walked quickly up to him as he was passing through the yard, and snatched a pistol from his belt. The yard caught its breath, and the attendant warder, hearing the click of the lock, instinctively turned his head away, so that he might not be blinded by the flash. But Kavanagh did not fire. At the instant his hand was on the pistol, he felt Frere's cold, imperious eyes on his. An effort, and the spell would have been broken. A twitch of the finger and his enemy would have fallen dead. There was an instant when that twitch of the finger could have been given, but Kavanagh let that instant pass. The dauntless eyes fascinated him. He played with the pistol-butt nervously, while all remained stupefied. Frere stood, never withdrawing his hands from the pockets into which they were plunged.

'That's a fine pistol, Jack,' he said at last.

Kavanagh, down whose white face the sweat was pouring, burst into a hideous laugh of relieved terror, and thrust the weapon, cocked as it was, back again into the belt.

Frere slowly drew one hand from his pocket, took the cocked pistol and levelled it at his recent assailant.

'That's the best chance *you'll* ever get, Jack,' said he.

Kavanagh fell on his knees.

'For Gord's sake, Captain Frere !'

Frere looked down upon the trembling wretch, and then uncocked the pistol, with a laugh of ferocious contempt.

'Get up, you dog,' he said. 'It takes a better man than you to best [1] me. Bring him up in the morning, Hawkins, and we'll give him five and twenty.'

As he went out – so great is the admiration for Power – the poor devils in the yard cheered him.

One of the first things that Frere did upon his arrival in Sydney was to enquire for Sarah Purfoy. To his astonishment, he discovered that she was proprietor of large export warehouses in Pitt-street, owned a neat cottage on one of the points of land that jutted into the bay, and was reputed to possess a banking account of no inconsiderable magnitude.

He in vain applied his brains to solve this mystery. She was not rich when she left Van Diemen's Land – at least, so she had assured him, and appearances bore out her assurance. How had she accumulated this sudden wealth? Above all, why had she invested it in such a business? He made enquiries at the banks, but was snubbed at for his pains. Sydney banks in those days did some queer business.

'Mrs Purfoy had come to them fully accredited,' said the manager, with a smile.

'But where did she get the money?' asked the magistrate. 'I am suspicious of these sudden fortunes. The woman was a notorious character in Hobart Town, and when she left hadn't a penny.'

'My dear Captain Frere,' said the acute banker – his father had been one of the builders of the "Rum Hospital" – 'it is not the business of a bank to make these enquiries into the previous history of its customers. The bills were good, you may depend, or we should not have honoured them. Good morning.'

The bills! Frere saw but one explanation. Sarah had received the proceeds of some of Rex's rogueries. The remembrance of Rex's letter home to his father, and the mention of the sum of money 'in the Old House in Blue Anchor Yard,' flashed

1. *Best* – get the better of.

across him. Perhaps Sarah had got the money from the receiver and appropriated it. But why invest it in an oil and tallow warehouse? He had always been suspicious of the woman, because he had never understood her, and his suspicions redoubled. Convinced that there was some plot hatching, he determined to use all the advantages that his position gave him to discover the secret and bring to light the mystery. The name of the man to whom Rex's letter had been addressed was 'Blick.' He would find out if any of the convicts under his care had heard of Blick.

Prosecuting his enquiries in the proper direction, he soon obtained a reply. Blick was a noted receiver of stolen goods, known to at least a dozen of the black sheep of the Sydney fold. He was reputed to be enormously wealthy, had often been tried, but never convicted. One of the prisoners – it was the murderous Kavanagh – stated, moreover, that a lad who had been in the employment of Blick, and who was known among his friends by the name of 'Gammy,' had been transported within the last five years, and was, so Kavanagh believed, now at Point Puer. Frere wrote to Burgess to make enquiry of this youth, and was informed in reply that 'Gammy' was the nickname of Edward Davis, a boy of nineteen, one of the worst of the juvenile prisoners. He had been recently placed in the chain-gang for an attempt to abscond; Burgess had sent for him, and interrogated him in vain. He professed to know nothing of Blick, and neither threats nor promises could induce him to alter his statement. 'A bad case,' wrote Burgess.

Frere was thus not much nearer enlightenment than before, and an incident that occurred a few months afterwards increased his bewilderment.

He had not been long established in his magistracy, when Blunt came to claim his payment for the voyage of Sarah Purfoy.

'There's that brig going begging, one may say, sir,' said Blunt, when the office door was shut.

'What brig?'

'The *Franklin*.'

The *Franklin* was a vessel of 320 tons, which plied between Norfolk Island and Sydney, as the *Osprey* had plied in the old days between Macquarie Harbour and Hobart Town.

'I am afraid that is rather stiff, Blunt,' says Frere. 'That's one of the best billets going, you know. I doubt if I have enough interest to get it for you. Besides,' he added, eyeing the sailor critically, 'you are getting rather oldish for that sort of thing, ain't you?'

Phineas Blunt stretched his arms wide, and opened his mouth full of sound white teeth.

'I am good for twenty years more yet, sir,' he said. 'My father was trading to the Indies at seventy-five years of age. *I'm* hearty enough, thank God; for, barring a drop of rum now and then, I've no vices to speak of. However, I ain't in a hurry, Captain, for a month or so; only I thought I'd jog your memory a bit, d'ye see.'

'Oh, you're not in a hurry; where are you going then?'

'Well,' says Blunt, shifting on his seat, uneasy under Frere's eye, 'I've got a job on hand.'

'Glad of it, I'm sure. What sort of a job?'

'A job of whaling,' says Blunt, more uneasy than before.

'Oh, that's it, is it. Your old line of business. And who employs you now?'

There was no suspicion in the tone, and had Blunt chosen to evade the question, he might have done so without difficulty, but he seemed to reply as one who had anticipated such questioning, and had been advised to answer it straight.

'Mrs Purfoy.'

'What!' cries Frere, scarcely able to believe his ears.

'She's got a couple of ships now, Captain, and she made me skipper on one of 'em. We look for beshdellamare,[1] and take a turn at harpooning sometimes.'

Frere stared at Blunt, who stared at the window. There was – the inner conscience of the magistrate told him – some strange project a-foot. Yet that common sense which so often misleads us, urged that it was quite natural that enriched Sarah should employ whaling vessels to increase her trade. Granted that there was nothing wrong about her obtaining the business, there was nothing strange about her owning a couple of whaling vessels. There were people in Sydney of no better origin who owned half-a-dozen.

1. Bêche-de-la-mer.

'Oh,' said he. 'And when do you start?'

'I'm expecting to get the word every day,' returned Blunt, apparently relieved, 'and I thought I'd just come and see you first in *case* of anything falling in.'

Frere played with a penknife on the table in silence for awhile, allowing it to fall through his fingers with a series of sharp clicks, and then he said,

'Where does she get the money from?'

'Blest if I know,' says Blunt, in unaffected simplicity. 'That's beyond me. She says she saved it. But that's all my eye, you know.'

'*You* don't know anything about it, then,' cries Frere, suddenly fierce.

'No, not I.'

'Because, if there's any game on, she'd better take care,' he cried, relapsing in his excitement into the vernacular. 'She knows me. Tell her that I've got my eyes on her. Let her remember her bargain. If she runs any rigs on me, let her take care.'

In his suspicious wrath he so savagely struck downwards and unwarily with the open penknife that it shut upon his fingers and cut him to the bone.

'I'll tell her,' said Blunt, wiping his brow. 'I'm sure she wouldn't go to sell you. But I'll look in when I come back, sir.'

When he got outside he drew a long breath.

'By the Lord Harry, but it's a ticklish game to play,' he said to himself, with a lively recollection of the dreaded Frere's vehemence; 'and there's only one woman in the world I'd be fool enough to play it for.'

Maurice Frere, oppressed with suspicions, ordered his horse one afternoon, and rode down to see the cottage which the owner of 'Purfoy's Stores' had purchased.

He found it a low white building, situated some four miles from the city, at the extreme end of a tongue of land which ran into the deep waters of the harbour. A garden, carefully cultivated, stood between the roadway and the house, and in this garden he saw a nurse-maid in charge of a boy some two years of age.

'Does Mrs Purfoy live here?' he asked, pushing open one of the iron gates.

The nurse-maid replied in the affirmative, staring at the visitor with some suspicion.

'Is she at home?'

'No.'

'You are sure?'

'If you don't believe me, ask at the house,' was the uncourteous reply.

Frere pushed his horse through the gate, and walked up the broad and well-kept carriage drive. A man-servant in livery answering his ring, told him that Mrs Purfoy had gone to town, and then shut the door in his face. Frere, more astonished than ever at these outward and visible signs of independence, paused indignant, feeling half inclined to enter despite opposition. As he looked through a break in the trees, he saw the masts of a brig lying at anchor off the extremity of the point on which the house was built, and understood that the cottage commanded communication by water as well as by land. Could there be a special motive in choosing such a situation, or was it mere chance? Baffled but not relieved from his uneasiness, he turned, determined to cross-question the nurse. Seemingly alarmed by his presence, she was already making for the house by a side-walk.

'Whose child is that?' he asked.

'The mistress's of course. Whose should it be?'

Here was a new mystery. He had never heard that Sarah was a mother, though he confessed to himself, with a grin, that it was not improbable she might have been one without his necessarily hearing of it.

However, she had kept faith with him so far. She had entered upon a new and more reputable life, and why should he seek to imagine evil where perhaps no evil was. Blunt was evidently honest. Women like Sarah Purfoy often emerged from penury and childlessness into a condition of comparative riches and apparent domestic virtue. It was likely that, after all, some wealthy merchant was the real owner of house and garden, child, pleasure yacht, and tallow warehouse.

There was, after all, no need for alarm.

RUFUS DAWES AND JOHN REX

THE substance of the conversation which Rex had with Rufus Dawes was often repeated.

From the instant John Rex heard his sentence of life banishment, he had determined upon escaping, and had brought all the powers of his acute and unscrupulous intellect to the consideration of the best method of achieving his purpose. His first care was to procure money, This he thought to do by writing to Blick, but when informed by Meekin of the fate of his letter, he adopted the – to him – less pleasant alternative of procuring it through Sarah Purfoy.

It was peculiar to the man's hard and ungrateful nature that, despite the attachment of the woman who had followed him to his place of durance, and had made it the object of her life to set him free, he had cherished for her no affection.

It was her beauty that attracted him, when as Mr Leopold Craven, he swaggered in the night-society of London. Her talents, and her devotion were secondary considerations – useful to him as attributes of a creature he owned, but not to be thought of when his fancy wearied of its choice. During the twelve years that had passed – since his rash disregard of her advice had delivered him into the hands of the law at the house of Green the coiner – he had been oppressed with no regrets for her fate. He had, indeed, seen and suffered so much, that the old life appeared to have been put away from him. A new set of impressions had been stamped upon his memory, and so sharp were they, that the old ones were almost effaced by them. When he heard that Sarah Purfoy was still in Hobart Town he was glad, for he knew that he had an ally who would do her utmost to help him – she had shown that on board the *Malabar*. But he was also sorry, for he remembered that the price she would demand for her services was his affection, and that had cooled long ago. However, he would make use of her. There might be a way to discard her if she proved troublesome.

His pretended piety had accomplished the end he had designed for it. Despite Frere's exposure of his cryptograph, he had won the confidence of Meekin; and into that worthy creature's ear he poured a strange and sad history.

He was the son — he said — of a clergyman of the Church of England, whose real name, such was his reverence for the Cloth, should never pass his lips. He was transported for a forgery which he did not commit. Sarah Purfoy was his wife — his erring, lost, and yet loved wife. She, an innocent and trusting girl, had determined, strong in the remembrance of that promise she had made at the altar, to follow her husband to his place of doom, and hired herself as ladies-maid to Mrs Vickers. Alas! fever prostrated that husband on a bed of sickness, and Maurice Frere, the profligate and the villain, had taken advantage of the wife's unprotected state to ruin her! Rex darkly hinted how the seducer made his power over the sick and helpless husband a weapon against the virtue of the wife; and so terrified poor Meekin, that, had it not 'happened so long ago', he would have thought it necessary to look with some social disfavour upon the boisterous son-in-law of Major Vickers.

'I bear him no ill-will, sir,' said Rex. 'I did at first. There was a time when I could have killed him, but when I had him in my power, I forbore to strike. No, sir! I could not commit murder.'

'Very proper,' says Meekin.

'God will punish him, in His own way, and His own time,' continued Rex. 'My great sorrow is for the poor woman. She is in Sydney, I have heard, living respectably, sir; and my heart bleeds for her.'

Here Rex heaved a sigh that would have made his fortune on the boards.

'My poor fellow,' said Meekin. 'Do you know where she is?'

'I do, sir.'

'You might write to her.'

John Rex appeared to hesitate, to struggle with himself and to finally take a deep resolve.

'No, Mr Meekin, I will not write.'

'Why not?'

'You know the orders, sir — the Commandant *reads* all the

letters sent. Could I write to my poor Sarah what other eyes were to read?' and he watched the parson slyly.

'N – no, you could not,' said Meekin, at last.

'It is true, sir,' said Rex, letting his head sink on his breast.

The next day, Meekin, blushing with the consciousness that what he was about to do was wrong, said to him,

'If you will promise to write nothing that the Commandant *might* not see, Rex, *I* will send your letter to your wife.'

'Heaven bless you, sir,' says Rex, and took two days to compose an epistle which should tell Sarah Purfoy how to act.

The letter was a model of composition in one way. It stated everything clearly and succinctly. Not a detail that could assist was omitted – not a line that could embarrass was suffered to remain. John Rex's scheme of six months' deliberation was set down in the clearest possible manner.

He brought his letter unsealed to Meekin. Meekin looked at it with an interest that was half suspicion.

'Have I your word that there is nothing in this that might not be read by the Commandant?'

John Rex was a bold man, but, at the sight of the deadly thing fluttering open in the clergyman's hand, he felt his knees knock together. Strong in his knowledge of human nature, however, he pursued his desperate plan.

'Read it, sir,' he said, turning away his face reproachfully. 'You are a gentleman. I can trust *you.*'

'No, Rex,' said Meekin, walking loftily into the pitfall, 'I do not read private letters.'

It was sealed, and John Rex felt as if somebody had withdrawn a match from a powder barrel.

In a month Mr Meekin received a letter, beautifully written, from 'Sarah Rex', stating briefly that she had heard of his goodness, that the enclosed letter was for her husband, and that if it was against the rules to give it him, she begged it might be returned to her unread.

Of course, Meekin gave it to Rex, who next morning returned to Meekin a most touching and pious production, begging him to read it. Meekin did so, and any suspicions he may have had were at once disarmed.

He was ignorant of the fact that the pious letter contained

another intended for John Rex's private eye, which latter John Rex thought so highly of that, having read it twice through most attentively, he *ate* it.

The plan of escape which had been contrived was after all a simple one. Sarah Purfoy was to obtain from Blick the moneys he held in trust, and to embark the sum thus obtained in any business which would suffer her to keep a vessel hovering round the southern coast of Van Diemen's Land without exciting suspicion. The escape was to be made in the winter months – if possible, in June or July. The watchful vessel was to be commanded by some trustworthy person; who was to frequently land on the south-eastern side, and keep a look-out for any extraordinary appearance along the coast. Rex himself must be left to run the gauntlet of the dogs and guards unaided.

'This seems a desperate scheme,' wrote Rex, 'but it is not so wild as it looks. I have thought over a dozen others, and rejected them all. This is the only way. Consider it well. I have my own plan for escape, which is easy if rescue be at hand. All depends upon placing a trustworthy man in charge of the vessel. You ought to know a dozen such. I will wait eighteen months, to give you time to make all arrangements.'

The eighteen months had now nearly passed over, and the time for the desperate attempt drew near. Faithful to his cruel philosophy, John Rex had provided scape-goats who, by their vicarious agonies, should assist him to his salvation.

He had discovered that of the twenty men in his gang eight had already determined on an effort for freedom. The names of these eight were Gabbett, Vetch, Bodenham, Cornelius, Greenhill, the 'Moocher', Cox, and Travers. The leading spirits were Vetch and Gabbett, who, with profound reverence, requested the 'Dandy' to join.

John Rex, ever suspicious, and feeling repelled by the giant's strange eagerness, at first refused, but by degrees allowed himself to appear to be drawn into the scheme. He would urge these men to their fate, and take advantage of the excitement attendant on their absence to effect his own escape.

'While all the island is looking for these eight boobies, I shall have a good chance to slip away unmissed.'

He wished, however, to have a companion. Some strong man, who, if pressed hard, would turn and keep the pursuers at bay, would be useful without doubt; and this comrade-victim he sought to find in the person of Rufus Dawes.

Beginning, as we have seen, from a purely selfish motive, to urge his fellow-prisoner to abscond with him, John Rex gradually found himself attracted into something like friendliness by the very sternness with which his overtures were repelled. Always a keen student of human nature, the scoundrel saw beneath the roughness with which it had pleased the unfortunate man to shroud his agony, how faithful a friend and how ardent and undaunted a spirit was concealed. There was, moreover, a mystery about Rufus Dawes which Rex, the reader of hearts, longed to fathom.

'Have you *no* friends whom you would wish to see?' he asked, one evening, when Rufus Dawes had proved more than usually deaf to his arguments.

'No,' said Dawes, gloomily. 'My friends are all dead to me.'

'Have you no enemies, then?' asked the other. 'Most men have *someone* whom they wish to see.'

Rufus Dawes laughed a slow, heavy laugh.

'My enemies are out of my reach,' he said. 'My friends would be made my enemies if I returned to them. I am better here.'

'Then, are you content to live this dog's life?'

Again Rufus Dawes laughed.

'Ay; why not? I can never right myself – never prove that I should not have been made the monster they have made me.'

'Who knows!' cried Rex, clutching at the straw thus held out. 'A free man can do much to prove his innocence, and I believe you are innocent.'

'Why?' asked Dawes, eyeing him with quick suspicion.

'Gammy says that Jerry Mogford killed the man for whose death you suffered.'

Rufus Dawes's mind went back at a leap to that night when, ere the fever clutched him, he had overheard the conversation of the three miscreants who were now his comrades.

'Gammy says so!'

'Ay. That Point Puer lad who came in two days ago. Here, Gammy!'

'Vot is it?' asked Ned Davis.

'Didn't you say that the Lurker did the job that Dawes was spun for?' said Rex, adopting his phraseology to the comprehension of his hearer.

'I didn't say he did the job. I said I thought he did. I was at old Blick's when Jerry came there. A precious taking he was in, too. He gave me a bull[1] to fetch his brother to him, and his brother sent him down five quid[2] next day, and twenty more through Blickses.'

'What became of him?' asked Dawes. 'He couldn't be found at the trial.'

'In course not,' returned Davis, with a grin. 'He would ha' been a soft 'un to ha' stopped there. He went away from old Blick quick sticks; where, I don't know.'

Rufus Dawes caught the boy's arm with sudden vehemence.

'There's more in that murder than has ever been told yet. It was *not* Jerry!'

'All right,' says the young man peevishly, resettling the handkerchief that he wore under the cap that surmounted his sallow, effeminate face. '*I* don't want to argue. P'r'aps it wasn't. Folks thought it was *you* – some of 'em.'

John Rex laughed at this sally, but Dawes continued, excitedly,

'I'd give half my – a thousand pounds, if I had it – to find out the murderer. Quaid – you know Quaid, Rex?'

John Rex nodded.

'– Quaid slept there that night, and he said that he saw Mogford's brother look in at the window, and then slide down the water-pipe and run off.'

'Jonathan Bradford business,' said Rex. 'Bosh! It was Master Jerry, for fifty pounds, if it wasn't our amiable friend here.'

Rufus Dawes loosed his hold of Gammy's arm, and the boy, with a grin of wondering contempt for any man who could desire to be innocent of so glorious an achievement as a murder, lounged off. Dawes sat, with his chin on his hands, thinking. Rex saw that he had aroused in him some interest, and strove to press his point.

1. *A bull* – five shillings.
2. *Quid* – a sovereign.

'You'd better come with us,' he said. 'It can't fail. I've been thinking of it for eighteen months, and it *can't* fail.'

'Who are going?' asked the other, his eyes still fixed on the ground.

John Rex enumerated the eight, and Dawes raised his head.

'I won't go. I have had two trials at it; I don't want another. I would advise you not to attempt it either.'

'Why not?'

'Gabbett bolted twice before,' said Rufus Dawes, shuddering at the resemblance of the ghastly object he had seen in the sun-lit glen at Hell's Gates. 'Others went with him, but each time he returned *alone.*'

'What do you mean?' asked Rex, struck by the tone of his companion.

'What became of the others?'

'Died, I suppose,' said the 'dandy', with a forced laugh.

'Yes; but how? They were all without food. How was it that monster lived six weeks?'

John Rex grew a shade paler, and did not reply. He recollected the sanguinary legend that pertained to Gabbett's rescue. But he did not intend to make the journey in his company, so, after all, he had no cause for fear.

'Come with me,' he said, at length. 'We will try our luck to-gether.'

'No. I have resolved. I stay here.'

'And leave your innocence unproved.'

'How can I prove it?' cried Rufus Dawes, fiercely impatient. 'There are crimes committed which are never brought to light, and this is one of them.'

'Well,' said Rex, rising, as if weary of the discussion, 'have it your own way, then. You know best. The private detective game *is* hard work. I, myself, have gone on a wild-goose chase before now. There's a mystery about a certain Harwich ship-builder that took me four months to unravel, and *then* I lost the thread.'

'*A Harwich shipbuilder!* Who was he?'

John Rex paused in wonderment at the eager interest with which the question was put, and then hastened to take advantage of this new opening for conversation.

'A well-known character in my time — Sir Richard Devine. A miserly old curmudgeon, with a scapegrace son.'

Rufus Dawes bit his lips to avoid showing his emotion. This was the second time that the name of his dead father had been spoken in his hearing.

'I think I remember something of him,' he said, with a voice that sounded strangely calm in his own ears. 'What was the story?'

'A curious one,' said Rex, plunging into past memories. 'Amongst other matters, I dabbled a little in the Private Inquiry line of business, and the old man came to me. He had a son who had disappeared abroad — a wild young dog, by all accounts — and he wanted particulars of him.'

'Did you get them?'

'To a certain extent. I hunted him through Paris into Brussels, and from Brussels to Antwerp. There I found he had taken up with a German chemist, a half-mad fellow who had ridiculous dreams of the philosopher's stone, and other absurdities. The chemist was supposed to have gone to Amsterdam, but I lost him there. A miserable end to a long and expensive search. I sent the particulars to the ship-builder, and by all accounts the news killed him, for he died a day or so after.'

'And the son?'

'Came to the queerest end of all. The old man had left him his fortune — a large one I believe — but he'd left Europe, it seems, for India, and was lost in the *Hydaspes*. She was burnt on the Line. Frere was his cousin.'

'Ah!'

'By Gad, it annoys me when I think of it,' continued Rex, feeling, by force of memory, once more the adventurer of fashion. 'With the resources I had too! Oh, a miserable failure! The days and nights I've spent walking about looking for Mr Richard Devine, and never catching a glimpse of him. The old man gave me his portrait, with full particulars of his early life, and I suppose I carried that ivory gimcrack in my breast pocket for nearly three months, pulling it out to refresh my memory every half-hour. By Gad, if the young gentleman was anything like his picture, I could have sworn to him if I'd met him in Timbuctoo.'

'Do you think you'd know him again?' asked Rufus Dawes in a low voice, turning away his head.

There may have been something in the attitude in which the speaker had put himself that awakened memory, or perhaps the subdued eagerness of the tone, contrasting so strangely with the comparative inconsequence of the theme, had caused John Rex's brain to perform one of those feats of automatic analysis at which we afterwards wonder. The German chemist – the profligate son – the motive for murder – the question of the portrait! The chain of thought, joining its two ends in magnetic circle, produced an idea that struck him as with a blow.

'THIS IS THE MAN!'

He had sufficient self-command to reply with a laugh, 'I'm not likely to meet him, poor devil.'

Warder Troke coming up, put his hand on Rex's shoulder.

'Dawes,' he said, 'you're wanted at the yard,' and then, seeing his mistake, added with a grin, 'Curse you two; you're so much alike one can't tell t'other from which.'

Rufus Dawes walked off moodily as though in thought, but John Rex's evil face brightened with a strange smile.

'Gad, Troke's right,' he said; 'We are alike. *I'll not press him to escape any more.*'

⊹ 26 ⊹

RUNNING THE GAUNTLET

THE *Pretty Mary* – as ugly and evil-smelling a tub as ever pitched under a southerly burster – had been lying on and off Cape Surville for nearly three weeks. Captain Blunt was getting wearied. He made the most strenuous endeavours to find the oyster-beds of which he was in search, but no success attended his efforts. In vain did he take boat and pull into every cove and nook between the Hippolyte Reef and Schouten's Island. In vain did he run the *Pretty Mary* as near to the rugged cliffs as he dared to take her, and make perpetual expeditions to the shore. In vain did he – in his eagerness for the interests of Mrs

Purfoy – clamber up the rocks, and spend hours in solitary soundings in Blackman's Bay. He never found an oyster.

'If I don't find something in three or four days more,' said he to his mate, 'I shall go back again. It's too dangerous cruising here.'

On the same evening that Captain Blunt made this resolution, the watchman at Signal Hill saw the arms of the semaphore at the settlement make three motions, thus:

The semaphore was furnished with three revolving arms, fixed one above the other. The upper one denoted units, and marked by six motions, numbers ONE TO SIX. The middle one denoted tens, and marked, in similar manner, numbers TEN to SIXTY. The lower one marked numbers ONE HUNDRED to SIX HUNDRED.

The lower and upper arms whirled out.

That meant THREE HUNDRED AND SIX.

A ball ran up to the top of the post.

That meant ONE THOUSAND.

Number 1306, or being interpreted, 'Prisoners absconded.'

'By George, Harry,' said he, 'there's a bolt!'

The semaphore signalled again:

Number 1411.

'With arms!' he said, translating as he read. 'Come here, Harry; here's a go!'

But Harry did not reply, and looking down, the watchman saw a dark figure suddenly fill the doorway. The boasted semaphore had failed *this* time at all events. The 'bolters' had arrived as soon as the signal!

The man sprang at his carbine, but the intruder had already possessed himself of it.

'It's no use making a fuss, Jones; there are eight of us. Oblige me by attending to your signals.'

Jones knew the voice. It was John Rex.

'Reply, can't you?' said Rex, coolly. 'Captain Burgess is in a hurry.'

The arms of the semaphore at the settlement were, in fact, gesticulating with comical vehemence.

Jones took the strings in his hands, and, with his signal-book open before him, was about to acknowledge the message, when Rex stopped him.

'Send *this* message,' he said. 'NOT SEEN! SIGNAL SENT TO EAGLEHAWK!'

Jones paused irresolutely. He was himself a convict, and dreaded the inevitable cat, that he knew would follow this false message.

'If they finds me out –' he said.

Rex cocked the carbine, with so decided a meaning in his

black eyes, that Jones – who could be brave enough on occasions – banished his hesitation at once, and began to signal eagerly.

There came up a clinking of metal, and a murmur from below.

'What's keeping yer, Dandy?'

'All right. Get those irons off, and then we'll talk, boys. I'm putting salt on old Burgess's tail.'

The rough jest was received with a roar, and Jones, looking momentarily down from his window on the staging, saw, in the waning light, a group of men freeing themselves from their irons with a hammer taken from the guard-house; while two, already freed, were casting buckets of water on the beacon wood-pile. The sentry was lying bound at a little distance.

'Now,' said the leader of this surprise party, 'signal to Woody Island.'

Jones perforce obeyed.

'Say, "AN ESCAPE AT THE MINES! WATCH ONE-TREE POINT! SEND ON TO EAGLEHAWK!" Quick, now!'

Jones – comprehending at once the force of this manoeuvre, which would have the effect of distracting attention from the Neck – executed the order with a grin.

'You're a knowing one, Dandy Jack,' said he.

John Rex acknowledged the compliment by uncocking the carbine.

'Hold out your hands! – Jemmy Vetch!'

'Ay, ay,' replied the Crow, from beneath.

'Come up and tie our friend Jones. Gabbett, have you got the axes?'

'There's only one,' says Gabbett, with an oath.

'Then bring that, and any tucker you can lay your hands on. Have you tied him? On we go, then.'

And in the space of five minutes from the time when unsuspecting Harry had been silently clutched by two forms, who rushed upon him out of the shadow of the huts, the Signal Hill Station was deserted.

At the settlement, Burgess was foaming.

Nine men to seize the Long Bay boat, and get half an hour's start of the alarm-signal, was an unprecedented achievement!

What could Warder Troke have been about? Warder Troke, however, found eight hours afterwards, disarmed, gagged and bound in the scrub, had been guilty of no negligence. How could he tell, that at a certain sign from Dandy Jack, the nine men he had taken to Stewart's Bay would 'rush him'; and, before he could draw a pistol, truss him like a chicken? The worst man of the gang, Rufus Dawes, had volunteered for the hated duties of pile-driving, and Troke felt himself quite secure. How could he possibly guess that there was a plot, in which Rufus Dawes, of all men, had refused to join.

Constables, mounted and on foot, were dispatched to scour the bush round the settlement. Burgess, confident by the reply of the Signal Hill semaphore, that the alarm had been given at Eaglehawk, promised himself the re-capture of the gang before many hours; and giving orders to keep the communications going, retired to dinner.

His convict servant had barely removed the soup when the result of John Rex's ingenuity became manifest.

The semaphore at Signal Hill had stopped working.

'Perhaps the fools can't see,' said Burgess. 'Fire the beacon — and saddle my horse.'

The beacon was fired.

All right at Mount Arthur, Mount Communication, and the Coal Mines. To the westward, the line was clear. But at Signal Hill was no answering light.

Burgess stamped with rage.

'Get me my boat's crew ready; and tell the Mines to signal to Woody Island.'

As he stood on the jetty, a breathless messenger brought the reply.

'A BOAT'S CREW GONE TO ONE-TREE POINT! FIVE MEN WENT FROM EAGLEHAWK, IN OBEDIENCE TO ORDERS!'

'Give way, men!' And the boat, shooting into the darkness, made for Long Bay.

'I won't be far behind 'em,' said Burgess, 'at any rate.'

Between Eaglehawk and Signal Hill were, for the absconders, other dangers.

Along the indented-shaped coast of Port Bunche were four

constables' stations. These stations – mere huts within signalling distance – fringed the shore, and to avoid them, it would be necessary to make a circuit into the scrub. Unwilling as he was to lose time, John Rex saw that to attempt to run the gauntlet of these four stations would be destruction. The safety of the party depended upon the reaching of the Neck while the guard was weakened by the absence of some of the men along the southern shore, and before the alarm could be given from the eastern arm of the peninsula.

With this view, he ranged his men in single file; and, quitting the road near Norfolk Bay, made straight for the Neck.

The night had set in with high westerly wind, and prospect of rain. It was pitch dark; and the fugitives were guided only by the dull roar of the sea as it beat upon Descent Beach. Had it not been for the accident of a westerly gale, they would not have had that bodeful assistance.

The Crow walked first, as guide, carrying a musket taken from Harry. Then came Gabbett, with the axe; followed by the other six, sharing between them such provisions as they had obtained at Signal Hill. John Rex, with the carbine, and Troke's pistols, walked last. It had been agreed that if attacked, they were to run each one his own way. In their desperate case, disunion was strength.

At intervals, on their left, gleamed the lights of the constables' stations, and as they stumbled onward they heard plainer and more plainly the hoarse murmur of the sea, beyond which was liberty or death.

After nearly two hours of painful progress, Jemmy Vetch stopped, and whispered them to approach. They were on a sandy rise. To the left was a black object that was a constable's hut; to the right was a dim white *sound* that was the ocean; in front was a row of lamps, and between every two lamps leapt and ran a dusky indistinct body. Jemmy Vetch pointed with his lean forefinger.

'The dogs!'

Instinctively they crouched down, lest even at that distance the two sentries, so plainly visible in the red light of the guard-house fire, should see them.

'Well, bo's,' says Gabbett, 'wot's to be done now?'

As he spoke a long low howl broke from one of the chained hounds, and the whole kennel burst into hideous outcry.

John Rex, who perhaps was the bravest of the party, shuddered.

'They've smelt us,' he said. 'We must go on now.'

Gabbett spit on his hands, and took firmer hold of the axe-handle.

'Right you are,' said he. 'I'll leave my mark on some of them – before this night's out.'

On the opposite shore lights began to move, and the fugitives could hear the hurrying tramp of feet.

'Make for the right-hand side of the jetty,' said Rex in a fierce whisper. 'I think I see a boat there. It is our only chance now.'

'Now! All together!'

Gabbett was fast outstripping the others by some three feet of distance. There were eleven dogs, two of whom were placed on stages set out in the water, and they were so chained that their muzzles nearly touched. The giant leapt into the line, and with a blow of his axe split the skull of the beast on his right hand. This action unluckily took him within reach of the other dog, who seized him by the thigh.

'Fire!' cried McNab from the other side of the lamps.

The giant uttered a cry of rage and pain, and fell with the dog under him. It was, however, the dog who had pulled him down, and the musket-ball intended for him struck Travers in the jaw. The unhappy villain fell – like Virgil's *Dares* – 'spitting blood, teeth, and curses.'

Gabbett clutched the mastiff's throat with iron hand, and forced him to loose his hold; then, bellowing with fury, seized his axe and sprang forward, mangled as he was, upon the nearest soldier.

Jemmy Vetch had been beforehand with him. Uttering a low snarl of hate, he fired, and shot the sentry through the breast. The others rushed through the now broken cordon, and made headlong for the boat.

'Fools!' cried a voice behind them. 'You have wasted a shot! LOOK TO YOUR LEFT!'

Burgess, hurried down the tram-road by his men, had tarried at Signal Hill but long enough to loose the surprised guard from their bonds, and taking the Woody Island boat, was pulling with a fresh crew to the Neck.

The reinforcement was not ten yards from the jetty.

The Crow saw the danger, and flinging himself into the water pulled the boat to shore.

'In with you for your lives!' he cried.

Another volley from the guard spattered the water around the fugitives, but in the darkness the ill-aimed bullets fell harmless. Gabbett swung himself over the sheets, and seized an oar.

'Cox, Bodenham, Greenhill! Now push her off! Jump, Tom, jump!' and as wrathful Burgess leapt to land, Cornelius was dragged over the stern, and the whale-boat floated into deep water.

McNab ran down to the water side.

'Lift her over the bar, men!' he shouted. 'With a will – So!'

And raised in twelve strong arms, the pursuing craft slid across the isthmus.

'We've five minutes start,' said Vetch coolly, as he saw the Commandant take his place in the stern sheets. 'Pull away, my jolly boys, and we'll best 'em yet.'

The soldiers on the Neck fired again almost at random, but the blaze of their pieces only served to show the Commandant's boat a hundred yards astern of that of the mutineers, which had already gained the deep water of Pirates' Bay.

Then, for the first time, the six prisoners became aware that John Rex was not among them.

⤙ 27 ⤚

IN THE NIGHT

JOHN REX put into execution the first part of his scheme.

At the moment when, seeing Burgess's boat near the sand-spit, he had uttered the warning cry heard by Vetch, he turned back into the darkness, and made for the water's edge at a point some distance from the Neck.

His desperate hope was that, the attention of the guard being concentrated on the escaping boat, he might – favoured by the darkness and the confusion – *swim* to the peninsula.

It was not a very marvellous feat to accomplish, and he had confidence in his own powers. Once safe on the peninsula, his plans were formed.

But, owing to the strong westerly wind, that caused a sort of incoming tide upon the isthmus, it was necessary for him to attain some point sufficiently far to the southward to enable him, on taking the water, to be assisted, not impeded, by the current. With this view, he hurried over the sandy hummocks at the entrance to the Neck, and ran backwards towards the sea.

In a few strides he had gained the hard and sandy shore, and, pausing to listen, heard behind him the sound of footsteps. He was pursued. The footsteps stopped, and then a voice cried –

'Surrender !'

It was McNab, who, seeing Rex's retreat, had daringly followed him.

John Rex drew from his breast Troke's pistol, and waited.

'Surrender !' cried the voice again, and the footsteps advanced two paces.

At the instant he raised the weapon to fire, a vivid flash of lightning showed him, on his right hand, a sort of path. On the ghastly and pallid sea were two boats, the hindermost one apparently within a few yards of him. The men looked like corpses. In the distance rose Cape Surville, and beneath Cape Surville was the hungry sea. The scene vanished in an instant – swallowed up almost before he had realized it. But the shock it gave him made him miss his aim, and flinging away the pistol with a curse, he turned down the path and fled. McNab followed.

The path seemed to have been made by frequent passage from the Station, and Rex found it tolerably easy running. He had acquired – like most men who live much in the dark – that cat-like perception of obstacles, which is due rather to increased sensitiveness of touch than increased acuteness of vision. His feet seemed to accommodate themselves to the inequalities of the ground; his hands to instinctively outstretch themselves towards the overhanging boughs; his head to duck of its own accord to any obtrusive sapling that seemed to obstruct his progress.

His pursuer was not so fortunate. Twice did John Rex laugh mentally, at a crash and scramble that told of a fall, and once — in a valley where trickled a little stream that he had cleared almost without effort — he heard a splash, that made him laugh outright.

The track now began to go uphill, and Rex redoubled his efforts, trusting to his superior muscular energy to finally shake off his pursuer. He breasted the rise and paused to listen. The crashing of branches behind him had ceased, and it seemed that he was alone.

He had gained the summit of the cliff. The lights of the Neck were invisible. Below him lay the Sea. Out of the black emptiness· came puffs of sharp salt wind. The tops of rollers that broke below were blown off and whirled away into the night — white patches, swallowed up immediately in the increasing darkness. From the north side of the bay was borne the hoarse roar of the breakers as they dashed against the perpendicular cliffs that guarded Forestier's Peninsula. At his feet arose a frightful shrieking and whistling, broken at intervals by reports like claps of thunder. Where was he? Exhausted and breathless, he sank down into the rough scrub and listened.

All at once, on the track over which he had passed, he heard a sound that made him bound to his feet in deadly fear.

It was the bay of a dog!

He thrust his hand to his breast for the remaining pistol, and uttered a cry of alarm. He had dropped it. He felt round about him in the darkness for some stick or stone that would serve as a weapon. In vain. His fingers clutched nothing but the prickly scrub and the coarse grass.

The sweat ran down his face. With staring eyeballs, and bristling hair, he stared into the darkness, as if he would dissipate it by the very intensity of his gaze.

The noise was repeated, and, piercing through the roar of

wind and water, above and below him, seemed to be close at hand. He heard a man's voice cheering the dog, in accents that the gale blew away from him before he could recognize them. It was probable that some of the soldiers had been sent to the assistance of McNab. Capture, then, was certain. In his agony, the wretched man almost promised himself repentance should he escape this peril.

The dog, crashing through the underwood, gave one sharp howl, and then ran mute.

The darkness had increased with the gale. The wind, ravaging the hollow heaven, had spread between the lightnings and the sea an impenetrable curtain of black cloud. It seemed possible to seize upon this curtain and draw its edge yet closer, so dense was it. The white and raging waters were blotted out, and even the lightning seemed unable to penetrate that intense blackness.

A large, warm drop of rain fell upon Rex's outstretched hand, and far overhead rumbled a wrathful peal of thunder. The shrieking which he had heard a few moments ago had ceased, but every now and then dully-heard but immense shocks, as of some mighty bird flapping the cliff with monstrous wings, reverberated around him, and seemed to shake the ground where he stood.

He looked back, and seemed to see rise behind him a tall, misty Form that – grey against the all-pervading blackness – beckoned and bowed to him. He saw it distinctly for an instant, and then, with an awful shriek, as of wrathful despair, it sank and vanished.

Maddened with a terror he could scarce define, the hunted man turned to meet the material peril that was so close at hand.

With a ferocious gasp, the dog flung himself upon him. John Rex was borne backwards, but, in his desperation, he clutched the beast by the throat and belly, and exerting all his strength, flung him off.

The brute uttered one howl, and seemed to lie where he had

fallen; while above his carcase again hovered that white and vaporous column.

It was strange that McNab and the soldier did not follow up the advantage they had gained. Courage – perhaps he should defeat them yet! He had been lucky to dispose of the dog so easily. With a fierce thrill of renewed hope, he ran forwards; when at his feet, in his face, arose that misty Figure, breathing chill warning, as though to wave him back. The terror at his heels drove him on. A few steps more, and he should gain the summit of the Cliff. He could feel the sea roaring in front of him in the gloom.

The Figure disappeared; and in a lull of wind, uprose from the place where it had been such a hideous medley of shrieks, laughter, and exultant wrath, that John Rex paused in horror. Too late. The ground gave way – it seemed – beneath his feet. He was falling – clutching, in vain, at rocks, shrubs, and grass.

The cloud-curtain lifted, and by the lightning that leapt and played about the ocean, John Rex found an explanation of his terrors, more terrible than they themselves had been.

'The Blow-hole!'

Clinging to a tree that, growing half way down the precipice, had arrested his course, he stared into the abyss.

Before him – already high above his head – was a gigantic arch of cliff. Through this arch he saw, at an immense distance below him, the raging and pallid ocean. Beneath him was an abyss splintered with black rocks, turbid and raucous with tortured water. Suddenly the bottom of this abyss seemed to advance to meet him; or, rather, the black throat of the chasm vomited up a torrent of leaping, curling water, which mounted to drown him. Was it fancy that showed him on the surface of the rising column the mangled body of the dog?

The lightning vanished; but, even in the darkness that followed, John Rex shut his eyes that he might not see the cold and cruel death which rose shrieking to swallow him.

A LEAP FOR LIFE

THE chasm into which John Rex had fallen was in the shape of a huge funnel set up on its narrow extremity. The sides of this funnel were living rock, and out of banks of earth lodged here and there upon projecting portions, grew trees and shrubs. The scanty growth paused abruptly half way down the gulf, and the rock below was perpetually damp from the upthrown spray.

Accident – had the convict been an escaping clergyman, we might term it Providence – had lodged him on the lowest of these banks of earth. In calm weather he would have been out of danger, but the lightning flash revealed to his terror-sharpened senses a black patch of dripping rock on the side of the chasm some ten feet above his head. Upon the next rising of the water-spout the place where he stood would be covered with water.

The roaring column mounted with the swiftness of thought. Rex felt it rush at him and swing him upward. With both arms round the tree, he clutched the sleeves of his jacket with either hand. Perhaps if he could maintain his hold, he might outlive the shock of that suffocating torrent. He felt his feet rudely seized, as though by the hand of a giant, and plucked upwards. Water gurgled in his ears. His arms seemed about to be torn from their sockets. Had the strain lasted another instant, he must have loosed his hold; but, with a wild, hoarse shriek, as though it was some sea-monster baffled of its prey, the column sank, and left him gasping, bleeding, half drowned, but alive.

It was impossible that he could survive another shock, and in his agony he unclasped his stiffened fingers, determined to resign himself to his fate. At that instant, however, he saw on the wall of rock that hollowed on his right hand, a red and lurid light, in the midst of which fantastically bobbed hither and thither the gigantic shadow of a man. He cast his eyes upwards and saw, slowly descending into the gulf, a blazing bush tied to a rope.

McNab was taking advantage in the pause in the spouting to examine the sides of the Blow-hole.

A despairing hope seized John Rex. In another instant the light would reveal to those above his figure, clinging like a limpet to the rock. He must be detected in any case; but if they could lower the rope sufficiently quickly, he might clutch it and be saved. His dread of the horrible death that was beneath him overcame his resolution to avoid recapture. The long-drawn agony of the retreating water as it was sucked back again into the throat of the whirlpool had ceased, and he knew that the next tremendous pulsation of the sea below would hurl the spuming destruction up upon him. The gigantic torch slowly descended, and he had already drawn in his breath for a shout which should make itself heard above the roar of the wind and water, when a strange appearance in the face of the cliff made him pause.

About six feet from him – glowing like molten gold in the gusty glow of the burning tree – a round, sleek stream of water slipped from the rock into the darkness, like a serpent from its hole. Above this stream a dark spot defied the torch-light, and John Rex felt his heart leap with one last desperate hope as he comprehended that close to him was one of those tortuous drives which the worm-like action of the sea bores in such caverns as that in which he found himself. The drive, opened first to the light of day by the natural convulsion which had raised the cliff itself above ocean level, probably extended into the bowels of the cliff. The stream ceased to let itself out of the crevice; it was then likely that the rising column of water did not penetrate far into this wonderful hiding-place.

Endowed with wisdom, which in one placed in a less desperate position would have been madness, John Rex shouted to his pursuers,

'The rope! the rope!'

The words, projected against the sides of the enormous funnel, were pitched high above the blast, and reduplicated by a thousand echoes, reached the ears of those above.

'He's alive!' cried McNab, peering into the abyss. 'I see him. Look!'

The soldier – a grim Waterloo veteran – whipped the end of

the bullock-hide lariat round the tree to which he held, and began to oscillate it, so that the blazing bush might reach the ledge on which the daring convict sustained himself.

The groan which preceded the fierce belching forth of the torrent was cast up to them from below.

'God be gude to the puir felly!' says the pious young Scotchman, catching his breath.

A white spume seemed visible at the bottom of the gulf, and the groan changed into a rapidly increasing bellow.

John Rex, eyeing the blazing pendulum, that with longer and longer swing momentarily neared him, looked up to the black heaven for the last time, with a muttered prayer. The bush – the flame fanned by the motion – flung a crimson glow upon his frowning features, that as he caught the rope seemed to have a sneer of triumph on them.

'Slack out! slack out!' he cried; and then, drawing the burning bush towards him, attempted to stamp out the fire with his feet.

The Waterloo-man set his body against the tree trunk and gripped the rope hard, turning his head away from the fiery pit below him.

'Hold tight, your honour,' he muttered to McNab. 'She's coming!'

The bellow changed into a roar, the roar into a shriek, and with a gust of wind and spray the boiling torrent leapt up out of the gulf.

John Rex, unable to extinguish the flame, twisted his arm about the rope, and the instant before the surface of the rising torrent made a momentary floor to the mouth of the cavern, he spurned the cliff desperately with his feet and flung himself across the chasm. He had already clutched the rock, and thrust himself forward when the tremendous volume of water struck him.

McNab and the soldier felt the sudden pluck of the rope and saw the light swing across the abyss. Then the fury of the water-spout burst with a triumphant scream, the tension ceased, the light was blotted out, and when the column sank, there dangled at the end of the lariat nothing but the drenched and blackened skeleton of the sheoak bough.

Amid a terrific peal of thunder, the long pent-up rain descended, and a sudden ghastly rending asunder of the clouds showed far below them the heaving ocean, high above them the jagged and glistening rocks, and at their feet the black and murderous abyss of the Blow-hole – empty!

They pulled up the useless rope, in silence; and another deadtree lighted and lowered, showed them nothing.

'God rest his puir soul,' said McNab, shuddering. 'He's oot o' our hands.'

⊷ 29 ⊷

THE WORK OF THE SEA

THE violence of the water-spout had saved John Rex's life. At the moment when it struck him, he was on his hands and knees at the entrance to the cavern. The wave, gushing upwards, at the same time expanded laterally, and this lateral force drove the convict into the mouth of the subterlapian passage. The passage seemed to trend downwards, and for some seconds he was rolled over and over, the rush of water wedging him at length into a crevice between two enormous stones, which seemed to overhang a still more formidable abyss. Fortunately for the preservation of his hard-fought-for life, this very fury of incoming water prevented him from being washed out again with the recoil of the wave. He could hear the water dashing with frightful echoes far down into the depths beyond him, but it was evident that the two stones against which he had been thrust acted as breakwaters to the torrent poured in from the outside, and repelled the main body of the stream in the fashion he had observed from his position on the ledge. In a few seconds the cavern was empty.

Painfully extricating himself, and feeling as yet but half doubtful of his safety, John Rex essayed to climb the twinblocks that barred the unknown depths below him. The first movement he made caused him to shriek aloud. His left arm – with which he clung to the rope – hung powerless. Ground against the ragged entrance, it was momentarily paralyzed. For

an instant the unfortunate wretch sank despairingly upon the
wet and rugged floor of the cave; then a terrible gurgling beneath his feet warned him of the approaching torrent, and collecting all his energies, he scrambled up the incline. Though
nigh fainting with pain and exhaustion, he pressed desperately
higher and higher. He heard the hideous shriek of the whirlpool which was beneath and around him grow louder and
louder. He saw the darkness grow darker as the rising water-
spout covered the mouth of the cave. He felt the salt spray sting
his face, and the wrathful tide lick the hand that hung over the
shelf on which he fell.

But that was all. He was out of danger at last! And as the
thought blessed his senses, his eyes closed, and the wonderful
courage and strength which had sustained the villain so long,
exhaled in stupor.

When he awoke the cavern was filled with the soft light of
dawn. Raising his eyes, he beheld, high above his head, a roof of
rock, on which the reflection of the sunbeams, playing upwards
through a pool of water, cast flickering colours. On his right
hand was the mouth of the cave, on his left a terrific abyss, at
the bottom of which he could hear the sea faintly rumbling and
washing.

He raised himself and stretched his stiffened limbs. Despite
his injured shoulder, it was imperative that he should bestir himself. He knew not if his escape had been noticed, or if the cavern
had another inlet, by which returning McNab could penetrate.
Moreover, he was wet and famished. To preserve the life he had
torn from the sea, he must have fire and food.

First he examined the crevice by which he had entered. It
was shaped like an irregular triangle, the base of which was
hollowed by the action of the water which in such storms as
that of the preceding night was forced into it by the rising of the
sea. John Rex dared not crawl too near the edge lest he should
slide out of the damp and slippery orifice, and be dashed upon
the rocks at the bottom of the Blow-hole. Craning his neck he
could see, two hundred feet below him, the sullenly frothing
water, gurgling, spouting, and creaming, in huge turbid eddies,
occasionally leaping upwards as though it savagely longed for

another storm to send it raging up to the man who had escaped its fury. It was impossible to get down that way.

He turned back into the cavern, and began to explore in that direction.

The twin-rocks against which he had been hurled were, in fact, pillars which supported the roof of the water-drive. Beyond them lay a great grey shadow which was emptiness faintly illumined by the sea-light cast up through the bottom of the gulf. Midway across the grey shadow fell a strange beam of dusky brilliance which cast its flickering light upon a wilderness of waving sea-weeds. Great stalactites – or rocks which, in their monstrous aping of nature, seemed stalactites – hung from the immense roof. Giant sponges clung to the rising stones like mosses to an old wall. Pulpy and jelly-like creatures, cylinders of rose-coloured crystal, from which grew living flowers, floated in the deep pools of water left by the retired tide. John Rex comprehended that he was standing where no human creature had ever stood before – on the edge of another Blow-hole *inside the cliff*!

Even in the desperate position in which he found himself, there survived in the Vagabond's nature sufficient poetry to make him value the natural marvel upon which he had so strangely stumbled. The immense promontory, which, viewed from the outside, seemed as solid as a mountain, was in reality but a hollow cone, reft and split into a thousand fissures by the unsuspected action of centuries of sea. The Blow-hole was but an insignificant cranny compared with this enormous chasm.

Descending with difficulty the steep incline, he found himself on the brink of a gallery of rock, which, jutting out over the pool, bore on its moist and weed-bearded edges signs of frequent submersion. It must be low tide without the rock. Beyond this gallery fell the soft beam of light whose influence spiritualised the coralines and polypes of this submarine grotto. Clinging to the rough and root-like algae that fringed the ever-moist walls, John Rex crept round the projection of the gallery, and passed at once from dimness to daylight.

There was a broad loophole in the side of the honey-combed and wave-perforated cliff. The cloudless heaven expanded above him; a fresh breeze kissed his cheek, and, a hundred feet below him the sea wrinkled all its lazy length, sparkling in myriad wavelets beneath the bright beams of morning.

Not a sign of the recent tempest marred the exquisite harmony of the picture. Not a sign of human life gave evidence of the grim neighbourhood of the prison. From the recess out of which he peered nothing was visible but sky of torquoise smiling upon a sea of sapphire.

This placidity of Nature was, however, to the hunted convict a new source of alarm. It was a reason why the Blow-hole and its neighbourhood should be thoroughly searched. He guessed that the favourable weather would be an additional inducement to McNab and Burgess to satisfy themselves as to the fate of their late prisoner.

He turned from the opening and prepared to descend still further into the rocky pathway. The sunshine had revived and cheered him, and a sort of instinct told him that the cliff so honey-combed above, could not be without some gully or chink at its base, which at low tide would give upon the rocky shore. It grew darker as he descended, and twice he almost turned back in dread of the gulfs on either side of him. It seemed to him, also, that the gullet of weed-clad rock through which he was crawling doubled upon itself and let only in to the bowels of the mountain. Gnawed by hunger and conscious that in a few hours at most the rising tide would fill the subterranean passage and cut off his retreat, he pushed desperately onwards. He had descended some ninety feet, and had lost in the devious windings of his downward path all but the reflection of the light from the gallery, when he was rewarded by a glimpse of sunshine striking upwards. He parted two enormous masses of seaweed, whose bubble-beaded fronds hung curtain-wise across his path, and found himself in the very middle of the narrow cleft of rock through which the sea was driven to the Blow-hole.

At an immense distance above him was the arch of cliff. Beyond that arch appeared a segment of the ragged edge of the circular opening down which he had fallen. He looked in vain for the funnel-mouth whose friendly shelter had received him. It was not indistinguishable. At his feet was a long reft in the solid rock, so narrow that he could almost have leapt across it. This reft was the channel of a swift black current which ran from the sea for fifty yards under an arch eight feet high, until it broke upon the jagged rocks that lay glistering in the sunshine at the bottom of the circular opening in the upper cliff.

An uncontrollable shudder shook the limbs of the adventurous convict. He comprehended that at high tide the place where he stood was under water, and that the narrow cavern became a subaqueous pipe of solid rock forty feet long, through which were spouted the league-long rollers of the Southern Sea.

The narrow strip of rock at the base of the cliff was as flat as a table. Here and there were enormous hollows like pans, which the retreating tide had left, full of clear, still water. The crannies of the rock were full of small white crabs, and John Rex found to his delight that there were on this little *plateau* abundance of mussels, which, though lean and acrid, were sufficiently grateful to his famished stomach. Attached to the flat surfaces of the numerous stones, moreover, were coarse limpets. These, however, John Rex found too salt to be palatable, and was compelled to reject them. A larger variety, however, having a succulent body as thick as a man's thumb contained in long razor-shaped shells, were in some degree free from this objection, and he soon collected the materials for a meal.

Having eaten and sunned himself, he began to examine the enormous rock to the base of which he had so strangely penetrated. Ragged and worn, it raised its huge breast against wind and wave, secure upon a broad pedestal, which probably extended as far beneath the sea as the massive column itself rose above it. Rising thus, with its shaggy drapery of sea-weed clinging about its knees, it seemed to be a motionless but sentient being — some monster of the deep, a Titan of the ocean condemned ever to front in silence the fury of that illimitable and untravelled sea. Yet — silent and motionless as he was — the hoary ancient gave hint of the mysteries of his revenge. Standing upon the broad and seagirt platform where surely no human foot but his had ever stood in life, the convict saw many feet above him, pitched into a cavity of the huge and slimy boulders, an object that his sailor eye told him at once was part of the top hamper of some large ship. Crusted with shells, and its ruin so over-run with the ivy of the ocean, that its ropes could barely be distinguished from the weeds with which they were encumbered, this relic of human labour attested the triumph of nature over human ingenuity. Perforated by the relentless sea, exposed above to the full fury of the tempest; set in solitary defiance to the waves, that rolling from the ice-volcano of the Southern pole, hurled their gathered might unchecked upon its iron front, the great rock drew from its lonely warfare the materials of its own silent vengeances. Clasped in its iron arms, it held its prey, snatched from the jaws of the all-devouring sea. One might imagine that, when the doomed ship, with her crew of shrieking souls, had splintered and gone down, the deaf, blind giant had clutched this fragment, upheaved from the seething waters, with a thrill of grim and terrible joy.

John Rex, gazing up at this memento of a forgotten agony, felt a sensation of pleasure. 'There's wood for my fire!' thought he; and mounting to the spot, he essayed to fling down the splinters of timber upon the platform. Long exposed to the sun, and flung high above the water-mark of recent storms, the timber had dried to the condition of touchwood, and would burn fiercely. It was precisely what he required. Strange accident that had for years stored, upon a desolate rock, this fragment of a vanished and long-forgotten vessel, that it might aid at last to warm the limbs of a villain escaping from justice!

Striking the disintegrated mass with his iron-shod heel, John Rex broke off convenient portions; and making a bag of his shirt, by tying the sleeves and neck, he was speedily staggering into the cavern with a supply of fuel. He made two trips, flinging down the wood in the floor of the gallery that overlooked the sea, and was returning for a third, when his quick ear caught the dip of oars. He had barely time to lift the sea-weed curtain that veiled the entrance to the chasm, when the Eagle-hawk boat rounded the promontory. Burgess was in the stern-sheets, and seemed to be making signals to some one on the top of the cliff. Rex, grinning behind his veil, divined the manoeuvre. McNab and his party were to search above, while the Commandant examined the gulf below. The boat headed direct for the passage, and, for an instant, John Rex's undaunted soul shivered at the thought that, perhaps after all, his pursuers might be aware of the existence of the cavern. Yet that was unlikely. He kept his ground, and the boat passed within a foot of him, gliding silently into the gulf. He observed that Burgess's usually florid face was pale, and that his left sleeve was cut open, showing a bandage on the arm. There had been some fighting, then, and it was not unlikely that his fellow-desperadoes had been captured! He chuckled at his own ingenuity and good sense.

The boat, emerging from the archway, entered the pool of the Blow-hole, and, held with the full strength of the party, remained stationary. John Rex watched Burgess scan the rocks and eddies, saw him signal to McNab, and then, with much relief, beheld the boat's head brought round to the seaboard.

He was so intent upon watching this dangerous and difficult operation, that he was oblivious of an extraordinary change which had taken place in the interior of the cavern. The water, which, an hour ago, had left exposed a long reef of black hummock-rocks, was now spread in one foam-flecked sheet over the ragged bottom of the rude staircase by which he had descended. The tide had turned, and the sea, apparently sucked in through some deeper tunnel in the portion of the cliff which was below the water, was being forced into the vault with a rapidity which bid fair to shortly submerge the mouth of the cave. The convict's feet were already wetted by the incoming waves, and as he turned for one last look at the boat, he saw a green, glassy billow heave up against the entrance to the chasm, and, almost blotting out the daylight, roll majestically through the arch. It was high time for Burgess to take his departure if he did not wish his whale-boat to be cracked like a nut against the roof of the tunnel.

Alive to his danger, the Commandant abandoned the search after his late prisoner's corpse, and hastened to gain the open sea. The boat, carried backwards and upwards on the bosom of a monstrous wave, narrowly escaped destruction, and John Rex, climbing to the gallery, saw with much satisfaction the broad back of his outwitted gaoler disappear round the sheltering promontory. The last effort of his pursuers had failed, and in another hour the only accessible entrance to the convict's retreat was hidden under three feet of furious sea-water.

They were convinced of his death, and would search for him

no more. So far, so good. Now for the last desperate venture – the escape from the wonderful cavern which was at once his shelter and his prison. Piling his wood together, and succeeding after many efforts, by aid of a flint and the ring that yet clung to his ankle, in lighting a fire and warming his chilled limbs in its cheering blaze, he set himself to meditate upon his course of action. He was safe for the present, and the supply of food that the rock afforded was amply sufficient to sustain life in him for many days, but it was impossible that he could remain many days concealed. He had no fresh water, and though by reason of the soaking he had received he had hitherto felt little inconvenience from this cause, the salt and acrid mussels speedily induced a raging thirst, which he could not alleviate. It was imperative that within forty-eight hours at farthest he should be on his way to the peninsula. He remembered the little stream into which – in his flight of the previous night – he had so nearly fallen, and hoped to be able under cover of the darkness to steal round the reef and reach it unobserved. His desperate scheme was then to commence. He had to run the gauntlet of the dogs and guards, gain the peninsula, and await the rescuing vessel. He confessed to himself that the chances were terribly against him. If Gabbett and the others had been recaptured – as he devoutly trusted – the coast would be comparatively clear; but if they had escaped, he knew Burgess too well to think that he would give up the chase while hope of re-taking the absconders remained to him. If indeed all fell out as he had wished, he had still to sustain life until Blunt found him – if haply Blunt had not returned, wearied with useless and dangerous waiting.

As night came on, and the firelight showed strange shadows waving from the corners of the enormous vault, while the dismal abysses beneath him murmured and muttered with uncouth and ghastly utterances, there fell upon the lonely man the terror of Solitude. Was this marvellous hiding place that he had discovered to be his sepulchre? Was he – a monster among his fellow-men – to die some monstrous death, entombed in that mysterious and terrible cavern of the sea?

He tried to drive away these gloomy thoughts by sketching

out for himself a plan of action – but in vain. In vain he strove
to picture in its completeness that – as yet vague design – by
which he promised himself to wrest from the vanished son of
the wealthy shipbuilder his name and heritage. His mind, filled
with forebodings of shadowy horror, could not give to the subject that calm consideration which it needed. In the midst of his
schemes for the baffling of the jealous love of the woman who
was to save him, and the getting to England, in ship-wrecked
and foreign guise, as the long lost heir to the fortune of Sir
Richard Devine, there arose ghastly and awesome shapes of
death and horror, with whose terrible unsubstantiality he must
grapple in the lonely recesses of that dismal cavern.

He heaped fresh wood upon his fire, that the bright light
might drive out the grewsome things that lurked above, below,
and around him. He became afraid to look behind him, lest
some shapeless mass of mid-sea-birth – some voracious polyp
with far reaching arms and jellied mouth ever open to devour –
might not slide up over the edge of the dripping caves below
and fasten upon him in the darkness. His imagination – always
sufficiently vivid and spurred to unnatural effect by the exciting
scenes of the previous night – painted the most outrageous
monsters as dwelling in the vermicular labyrinths that twined
beneath him. Each patch of shadow, clinging bat-like to the
humid wall, seemed to him some globular sea-spider ready to
drop upon him with its viscid and clay-cold body, and drain out
his chilled blood, enfolding him in rough and hairy arms. Each
moist bulb of sea-weed seemed to hold within it the germ of a
ropy and mucilaginous monster which should put forth clammy
and grumous tentacles to entwine him to a slimy death. Each
splash in the water beneath him, each sigh of the multitudinous
and melancholy sea, seemed to prelude the laborious advent of
some misshapen and ungainly abortion of the ooze. Each of the
living paunches that, detached from the parent cyst, floated in
the pools and hollow places of the rocks, seemed endowed with
greedy life to crawl to him. All the sensations induced by lapping water and regurgitating sea took material shape and surrounded him. All creatures that could be ingendered by slime
and salt crept forth into the firelight to stare at him. Red dabs
and splashes that were living beings, having a strange phos-

phoric light of their own, glowed upon the floor like red-hot coals that had been quenched in blood. The livid incrustations of a hundred years of humidity slipped from off the walls and painfully heaved their mushroom surfaces to the blaze. The red glow of the unwonted fire, crimsoning the wet sides of the cavern, seemed to attract countless blisterous and transparent shapelessnesses, which elongated themselves towards him. Creatures which were nothing but gelatinous stomachs supported upon fleshy stalks, blushed and throbbed in the circle of radiance. Monstrous mouths, borne by flower-like fungi, opened and shut. Bloodless and bladdery things ran hither and thither noiselessly. Strange carapaces crawled from out the rocks. All the horrible unseen life of the ocean was rising up and surrounding him.

He rushed to the entrance of the gallery, and his shadow, thrown into the opening, seemed to take the shape of an avenging phantom, with arms upraised to warn him back.

He retreated to the brink of the gulf, and the glare of the upheld brand fell upon a rounded hummock, whose coronal of silky weed out-floating in the water looked like the head of a drowned man.

The naturalist, the explorer, or the shipwrecked seaman would have found nothing frightful in this exhibition of the harmless life of the Australian ocean. But the convict's guilty conscience, long suppressed and derided, asserted itself in this hour when it was alone with Nature and Night. The bitter intellectual power which had so long supported him succumbed beneath imagination – the unconscious religion of the soul. If ever he was nigh repentance it was then. He deemed all the phantoms of his past crimes arising to gibber at him, and covering his eyes with his hands, he fell shuddering upon his knees. The brand, loosening from his grasp, dropped into the gulf, and was extinguished with a hissing noise.

As if the sound had called up some spirit that lurked below, a whisper ran through the cavern.

'John Rex!'

The hair of the convict's flesh stood up, and he cowered to the earth.

'Who calls?'

'John Rex!'

It was a *human* voice! Whether of friend or enemy he did not pause to think. His terror over-mastered all other considerations.

'Here! here!' he cried, and waving a log snatched from the fire, he sprang to the opening of the vault.

⊶ 30 ⊷

THE FLIGHT

Burgess had not overtaken the absconders. Favoured by their start, and the darkness of the night, they had eluded the pursuing boat, but Burgess had – in his own opinion – achieved a triumph nevertheless. He returned to the Neck with the firm conviction that the seven men in the whaleboat had perished before his eyes.

Gabbett, guided by the Crow, had determined to beach the boat on the southern point of Cape Surville. It will be seen by those who have taken the trouble to follow our description of the topography of Colonel Arthur's Penitentiary, that nothing but the desperate nature of the attempt could have justified so desperate a measure. The perpendicular cliffs seemed to render such an attempt certain destruction; but Vetch, who had been employed in building the pier at the Neck, knew that on the southern point of the promontory was a strip of beach, upon which the company might, by good fortune, land in safety. With something of the decision of his leader – Rex – the Crow determined at once that in their desperate plight this was the only measure, and setting his teeth as he seized the oar that served as a rudder, he put the boat's head straight for the huge rock that formed the northern horn of Pirates' Bay.

Save for the faint phosphorescent radiance of the foaming waves, the darkness was intense, and Burgess for some minutes pulled almost at random. The same tremendous flash of lightning which had saved the life of McNab, by causing Rex to miss his aim, showed to the Commandant the whale-boat balanced on the summit of an enormous wave, and apparently about to be flung against the wall of rock which – magnified in the sudden flash – seemed frightfully near to them. The next instant Burgess himself – his boat lifted by the swiftly advancing billow – beheld at his feet a sort of panorama. Suspended on the brink of the wave, the Commandant seemed on the summit of a cliff, from which he saw a wild waste of raging sea scooped into abysmal troughs, in which the bulk of a leviathan might wallow. At the bottom of one of these valleys of water lay the mutineers' boat, looking, with its out-spread oars, like some six-legged insect floating in a pool of ink. The great cliff, whose every scar and crag was as distinct as though its huge bulk was but a yard distant, seemed to shoot out from its base towards the struggling insect, a broad, flat straw, that was a strip of dry land. The next instant the rushing water, carrying the six-legged atom with it, creamed up over this strip of beach; the giant crag, amid the thunder-crash that followed upon the lightning, appeared to stoop down over the ocean, and as it stooped the billow rolled onwards, the boat glided down into the depths, and the whole phantasmagoria was swallowed up in the tumultuous darkness of the tempest.

Burgess – his hair bristling with terror – shouted to put the boat about, but he might with as much reason have shouted at an avalanche. The wind blew his voice away, and emptied it violently into air. A snarling billow jerked the oar from his hand. Despite the desperate efforts of the soldiers, the boat was whirled up the mountain of water like a leaf on a water-spout, and a second flash of lightning showed what seemed a group of dolls struggling in the surf, and a walnut-shell bottom upwards was driven by the recoil of the wave towards them. For an instant all thought that they must share the fate which had overtaken the unlucky convicts; but Burgess succeeded in trimming the boat, and, awed by the peril he had so narrowly escaped, gave the order to return. As the men set the boat's head to the welcome line of lights that marked the neck, a black spot balanced upon a black line was swept under their stern and carried out to sea. As it swooped past them this black spot emitted a cry, and they knew that it was one of the shattered boat's crew clinging to an oar.

'He was the only one of 'em alive,' said Burgess, bandaging his sprained wrist two hours afterwards at the Neck, 'and he's food for the fishes by this time!'

He was mistaken, however. Fate had in reserve for the crew of villains a less merciful death than that of drowning. Aided by the lightning, and that wonderful 'good luck' which urges villany to its destruction, Vetch beached the boat, and the party, bruised and bleeding, reached the upper portion of the shore in safety. Of all this number only Cox was lost. He was pulling stroke-oar, and being something of a laggard, stood in the way of the Crow, who, seeing the importance of haste in preserving his own skin, plucked the man backwards by the collar, and passed over his sprawling body to the shore. Cox, grasping at anything to save himself, clutched his oar, and the next moment found himself borne out with the overturned whale-boat by the under-tow. He was drifted past his only hope of rescue – the guard-boat – with a velocity that forbade all attempts at rescue, and almost before the poor scoundrel had time to realize his condition, he was in the best possible way of escaping the hanging that his comrades had so often humorously prophesied for him. Being a strong and vigorous villain, however, he clung tenaciously to his oar, and even unbuckling his leather belt, passed it round the slip of wood that was his salvation, girding himself to it as firmly as he was able. It was in this condition, *plus* a swoon from exhaustion, in which he was descried by the helmsman of the *Pretty Mary*, a few miles from Cape Surville, at daylight next morning. Blunt, with a wild hope that this waif and stray might be the lover of Sarah Purfoy *dead*, lowered a boat and picked him up. Nearly bisected by the belt, gorged with salt-water, frozen with cold, and having two ribs broken, the victim of Vetch's murderous quickness retained sufficient life to survive Blunt's remedies for nearly two hours. During that time he stated that his name was Cox, that he had escaped from Port Arthur with eight others, that John Rex was the leader of the expedition, that the others were all drowned, and that he believed John Rex had been retaken. Having placed Blunt in possession of these particulars, he further said that it pricked him to breathe, cursed Jemmy Vetch, the settlement, and the sea, and so impenitently died.

Blunt smoked two pipes, and then altered the course of the *Pretty Mary* two points to the eastward, and ran for the coast. It was possible that the man for whom he was searching had not been retaken, and was now awaiting his arrival. It was clearly his duty – hearing of the planned escape having been actually attempted – not to give up the expedition while hope remained.

'I'll take one more look along,' said he to himself.

The *Pretty Mary*, hugging the coast as closely as she dared, crawled in the thin breeze all day, and saw nothing. It would be madness to land at Cape Surville, for the whole station would be on the alert, so Blunt as night was falling stood off a little across the mouth of Pirates' Bay.

He was walking the deck, groaning at the folly of the expedition, when a strange appearance on the southern horn of the bay made him come to a sudden halt.

There was a furnace blazing in the bowels of the mountain!

Blunt rubbed his eyes and stared. He looked at the man at the helm.

'Do you see anything yonder, Jem?'

Jem – a Sydney man, who had never been round that coast before – briefly remarked,

'Lighthouse!'

Blunt stumped into the cabin and got out his charts. No lighthouse laid down there, only a mark like an anchor, and a note, 'remarkable hole at this point.'

A remarkable hole indeed; a remarkable 'lime kiln' would have been more to the purpose.

Blunt called up his mate, William Staples, a fellow whom Sarah Purfoy's gold had bought body and soul. William Staples looked at the waxing and waning glow for a while, and then said, in tones trembling with greed,

'It's a fire. Lie to, and lower away the jolly-boat. Old Man, that's our bird, for a thousand pounds!'

The *Pretty Mary* shortened sail, and Blunt and Staples got into the jolly-boat.

'Goin' a hoysterin', sir?' said one of the crew, with a grin, as Blunt threw a bundle into the stern-sheets.

Staples thrust his tongue into his cheek. The object of the voyage had got to be pretty well understood among the carefully-picked crew. Blunt had not chosen men who were likely to betray him, though, for that matter, all-thoughtful Rex had suggested a precaution which rendered betrayal almost impossible.

'What's in the bundle, Old Man?' asked Will Staples, after they had got clear of the ship.

'Clothes,' returned Blunt. 'We can't bring him off, if it *is* him, in his canaries. He puts on these duds, d'ye see, sinks Her Majesty's livery, and comes aboard, a "ship-wrecked mariner!"'

'That's well thought of. Whose notion's that? The Madam's, I'll be bound.'

'Ay.'

'She's a knowing one.'

And the sinister laughter of the pair floated across the violet water.

'Go easy, man,' says Blunt, as they neared the shore. 'They're all awake at Eaglehawk; and if those — dogs give tongue, there'll be a boat out in a twinkling. It's lucky the wind's off shore.'

Staples lay on his oar and listened.

The night was moonless, and the ship had already disappeared from view. They were approaching the promontory from the south-east, and the isthmus of the guarded Neck was hidden by the outlying cliff. In the south-western angle of this cliff, about midway between the summit and the sea, was an arch, which vomited a red and flickering light, that faintly shone upon the sea in the track of the boat. The light was lambent and uncertain, now sinking almost into insignificance, and now leaping up with a fierceness that caused a deep glow to throb in the very heart of the mountain. Sometimes a black figure would pass across this gigantic furnace-mouth, stooping and rising, as though feeding the fire. One might have imagined that a door in Vulcan's Smithy had been left inadvertently open, and that the old hero was forging arms for a demigod.

Superstitious Blunt turned pale.

'It's no mortal,' he whispered, 'Let's go back.'

'And what will the Madam say?' returned dare-devil Will

Staples, who would have plunged into Mount Erebus had he been paid for it.

Thus appealed to in the name of his ruling passion, Blunt turned his head, and the boat sped onward.

Arrived at the foot of the cliff, the pair found themselves in almost complete darkness, for the light of the mysterious fire, which had hitherto guided them, had necessarily disappeared. Calm as was the night, and still as was the ocean, the sea yet ran with silent but dangerous strength through the channel which led to the Blow-hole; and Blunt, instinctively feeling the boat drawn towards some unknown peril, held off the shelf of rocks out of reach of the current. A sudden flash of fire, as from a flourished brand, burst out above them, and floating downwards through the darkness, in erratic circles, came an atom of burning wood. Surely no one but a hunted man would lurk in such a savage retreat.

Blunt, in desperate anxiety, determined to risk all upon one venture.

'John Rex!' he shouted up through his rounded hands.

The light flashed again at the eye-hole of the mountain, and on the point above them appeared a wild figure, holding in its hands a burning log, whose fierce glow illumined a face so contorted by deadly fear and agony of expectation, that it was scarce human.

'Here! here!'

'The poor devil seems half-crazy,' says Will Staples, under his breath; and then aloud, 'We're FRIENDS!'

'Thank God!'

⊷ 31 ⊷

THE 'DANDY' HIMSELF AGAIN

A FEW moments sufficed to explain matters. The terrors which had oppressed John Rex disappeared in human presence, and the villain found his coolness return.

Kneeling on the rock platform, he held parley.

'It is impossible for me to come down now,' he said. 'The tide covers the only way out of the cavern.'

'Can't you dive through it?' says Will Staples.

'No, nor you neither,' says Rex, shuddering at the thought of trusting himself to that horrible whirlpool.

'What's to be done? You can't come down that *wall*.'

'Wait until morning,' returned Rex, coolly. 'It will be dead low tide at seven o'clock. You must send a boat at six, or thereabout. It will be low enough for me to get out, I daresay, by that time.'

'But the Guard?'

'— Won't come here, my man. They've got their work to do in watching the Neck and exploring after my mates. They won't come here. Besides, I'm dead.'

'Dead!'

'Thought to be so, which is as well — better for me, perhaps. If they don't see your ship, or your boat, you're safe enough.'

'I don't like to risk it,' says Blunt. 'It's Life if we're caught, remember.'

'It's Death if *I'm* caught!' returned the other, with a sinister laugh. 'But there's no danger if you are cautious. No one looks for rats in a terrier's kennel, and there's not a station along the beach from here to Cape Pillar. Take your vessel out of eyeshot of the Neck, bring the boat up Descent Beach, and the thing's done.'

'Well,' says Blunt, 'I'll try it.'

'You wouldn't like to stop here till morning? It is rather lonely,' suggested Rex, absolutely making a jest of his late terrors.

Will Staples laughed. 'You're a bold boy!' said he. 'We'll come at day-break.'

'Have you got the clothes as I directed?'

'Yes.'

'Then goodnight. I'll put my fire out, in case somebody else might see it, who wouldn't be as kind as you are.'

'Good night.'

'Not a word for the Madam,' said Staples, when they reached the vessel.

'Not a word, the ungrateful dog,' assented Blunt, adding with some heat, 'That's the way with women. They'll go through fire and water for a man that doesn't care a snap of his fingers for 'em; but for any poor fellow who risks his neck to pleasure 'em they've nothing but sneers! I wish I'd never meddled in the business.'

'There are no fools like old fools,' thought Will Staples, looking back through the darkness at the place where the fire had been, but he did not utter his thoughts aloud.

At eight o'clock the next morning the *Pretty Mary* stood out to sea with every stitch of canvas set, alow and aloft. The skipper's fishing had come to an end. He had caught a shipwrecked seaman, who had been brought on board at daylight, and was then at breakfast in the cabin. The crew winked at each other when the haggard mariner, attired in garments that seemed remarkably well preserved, mounted the side. But they, none of them, were in a position to controvert the skipper's statement.

'Where are we bound for?' asked John Rex, smoking Staples' pipe in lingering puffs of delight. 'I'm entirely in your hands, my worthy Blunt.'

'My orders are to cruise about the whaling grounds until I meet my consort,' returned Blunt, sullenly, 'and put you aboard her. She'll take you back to Sydney. I'm victualled for a twelve-month's trip.'

'Right!' cries Rex, clapping his preserver on the back. 'I'm bound to get to Sydney somehow; but, as the Philistines are abroad, I may as well tarry in Jericho till my beard be grown. Don't stare at my scriptural quotation, Mr Staples,' he added, inspirited by creature-comforts, and secure amid his purchased friends. 'I assure you that I've had the very best religious instruction. Indeed, it is chiefly owing to my worthy spiritual pastor and master that I am enabled to smoke this very villainous tobacco of yours at the present moment!'

THE VALLEY OF THE SHADOW OF DEATH

IT was not until they had scrambled up the beach to safety that the absconders became aware of the loss of another of their companions. As they stood on the break of the beach, wringing the water from their clothes, Gabbett's small eye counting their number missed the stroke oar.

'Where's Cox?'

'The fool fell overboard,' said Jemmy Vetch, shortly. 'He never had as much sense in that skull of his as would keep it sound on his shoulders.'

Gabbett scowled.

'That's three of us gone,' he said in the tones of a man suffering some personal injury.

They summed up their means of defence against attack. The 'Moocher' (Alexander Dalton) and Greenhill had knives. Gabbett still retained the axe in his belt. Vetch had dropped his musket at the Neck; and Bodenham and Cornelius were unarmed.

'Let's have a look at the tucker,' said Vetch.

There was but one bag of provisions. It contained a piece of salt pork, two loaves, and some uncooked potatoes. Signal Hill station was not rich in edibles.

'That's ain't much,' said the Crow, with rueful face. 'Is it, Gabbett?'

'It must do, anyway,' returned the giant carelessly.

The inspection over, the six proceeded up the shore, and encamped under the lee of a rock. Bodenham was for lighting a fire, but Vetch, who by tacit consent had been chosen leader of the expedition, forbade it, saying that the light might betray them. 'They'll think we're drowned, and won't pursue us,' he said.

So all that night the miserable wretches crouched fireless together.

Morning breaks clear and bright, and they comprehend that their terrible journey has begun.

'Where are we to go? – How are we to live?' asks Bodenham, scanning the barren bush that stretched to the barren sea. 'Gabbett, you've been out before – how's it done?'

'We'll make the shepherds' huts, and live on their tucker till we get a change o' clothes,' says Gabbett, evading the main question. 'We can follow the coast line.'

'Steady, lads,' says Prudent Vetch; 'we must sneak round yon sandhills, and so creep into the scrub. If they've a good glass at the Neck, they can see us.'

'It does seem close,' says Bodenham; 'I could pitch a stone on to the guard-house. Good-bye, you Bloody Spot,' he adds, with sudden rage, shaking his fist vindictively at the Penitentiary. 'I don't want to see you no more till the Day o' Judgement.'

Vetch divides the provisions, and they travel all that day until dark night. The scrub is prickly and dense. Their clothes are torn, their hands and faces bleeding. Already they feel outwearied. No one seeming to pursue, they light a fire, and sleep.

The second day they come to a sandy spit that runs out into the sea, and find that they have got too far to the eastward, and must follow the shore line to East Bay Neck. Back through the scrub they drag their heavy feet. That night they eat the last crumb of the loaf.

The third day – at high noon – after some toilsome walking they reach a big hill, now called Collins' Mount, and see the upper link of the earring, the isthmus of East Bay Neck, at their feet. A few rocks are on their right hand, and blue in the lovely distance lies hated Maria Island.

'We must keep well to the eastward,' says Greenhill, 'or we shall fall in with the settlers and get taken.'

So, passing the isthmus, they strike into the bush along the shore, and tightening their belts over their gnawing bellies, camp under some low-lying hills.

The fourth day is notable for the indisposition of Bodenham, who is a bad walker, and, falling behind, delays the party by frequent cooeys. Gabbett threatens him with a worse fate than sore feet if he lingers. Luckily that evening Greenhill espies a hut, but not trusting to the friendship of the occupant, they wait until he quits it in the morning, and then send Vetch to forage. Vetch, secretly congratulating himself on having by his counsel prevented violence, returns bending under half a bag of flour.

'You'd better carry the flour,' says he to Gabbett, 'and give me the axe.'

Gabbett eyes him for a while as if struck by his puny form, but finally gives the axe to his mate Dalton. That day they creep along cautiously between the sea and the hills, camping at a creek. Vetch, after much search, finds a handful of berries, and adds them to the main-stock. Half of this handful is eaten at once, the other half reserved for 'tomorrow'.

The next day they come to an arm of the sea, and struggling northward, Maria Island disappears, and with it all danger from telescopes. That evening they reach the camping ground by twos and threes; and each wonders – between the paroxysms of hunger – if his face is as haggard, and his eyes as bloodshot, as those of his neighbour.

The seventh day, Bodenham says his feet are so bad he can't walk, and Greenhill, with a meaning look at the berries, bids him stay behind. Being in a very weak condition, he takes his companion at his word, and drops off about noon the next day. Gabbett, discovering this defection, however, goes back, and in an hour or so appears, driving the wretched creature before him with blows, as a sheep is driven to the shambles. Greenhill remonstrates at another mouth being thus forced upon the party, but the giant silences him with a hideous glance. Jemmy Vetch remembers that Greenhill accompanied Gabbett once before, and feels uncomfortable. He gives hint of his suspicions to Dalton, but Dalton only laughs. It is horribly evident that there is an understanding among the three.

The ninth sun of their freedom, rising upon sandy and barren hillocks, bristling thick with cruel scrub, sees the six famine-stricken wretches cursing their God, and yet afraid to die. All around is the fruitless, shadeless, shelterless bush. Above, the pitiless heaven. In the distance, the remorseless sea. Something terrible must happen. That grey wilderness, arched by grey heaven, stooping to grey sea, is a fitting keeper of hideous secrets. Vetch suggests that Oyster Bay cannot be far to the eastward – the line of ocean is deceitfully close, – and though such a proceeding will take them out of their course, they resolve to make for it. After hobbling five miles, they seem no nearer than before, and, nigh dead with fatigue and starvation, sink despairingly upon the ground. Vetch thinks Gabbett's eyes have a wolfish glare in them, and instinctively draws off from him. Says Greenhill, in the course of a dismal conversation, 'I am so weak I could eat a piece of a man.'

On the tenth day, Bodenham refuses to stir, and the others being scarce able to drag along their limbs, sit on the ground about him. Greenhill eyeing the prostrate man, says, slowly,

'I have seen the same done before, boys, and it tasted not unlike a little pork.'

Vetch, hearing his savage comrade give utterance to a thought all had secretly cherished, speaks out, crying,

'It would be murder to do it, and then perhaps we couldn't eat it.'

'Oh,' says Gabbett, with a grin, 'I'll warrant you that, but you must all bear a hand, that you may all be equal in the crime.'

Gabbett, Dalton, and Greenhill then go aside, and presently Dalton coming to the Crow, says, 'He consented to act as flogger. We'll kill him.'

'So did Gabbett, for that matter,' shudders Vetch.

'Ay, but Bodenham's feet are sore,' says Dalton, 'and 'tis a pity to leave him.'

Having no fire, they make a little break-wind; and Vetch, half-dozing behind this at about three in the morning, hears some one call out 'Christ!' and awakes, sweating ice.

'I've done it. I hit him with the axe, and Gabbett cut his throat.' It is Greenhill, running up, who says this.

'Why cut his throat?' asks Vetch, in terror.

'To *bleed* him, you fool!' says practical Greenhill.

No one but Gabbett and Greenhill would eat that night. That savage pair, however, make a fire, fling ghastly fragments on the embers, and eat the broil before it is right warm. In the morning the frightful carcase is divided.

That day's march takes place in silence, and at the midday halt Cornelius volunteers to carry the billy, affecting great restoration from the food. Vetch gives it him, and in half an hour afterwards Cornelius is missing. Gabbett and Greenhill pursue him in vain, and return with curses.

'He'll die like a dog,' says Greenhill, 'alone in the bush.'

Jemmy Vetch, with his intellect acute as ever, thinks that Cornelius prefers such a death to the one in store for him, but says nothing.

The twelfth morning dawns wet and misty, but Vetch, seeing the provision running short, strives to be cheerful, telling stories of men who have escaped greater peril. Vetch feels with dismay that he is the weakest of the party, but has some sort of ludicro-horrible consolation in remembering that he is also the thinnest. They come to a creek that afternoon, and look, until nightfall, in vain for a crossing-place. The next day Gabbett and Vetch swim across, and Vetch directs Gabbett to cut a long sapling, which, being stretched across the water, is seized by Greenhill and the Moocher, who are dragged over.

'What would you do without me!' says the Crow, with a ghastly grin.

They cannot kindle a fire, for Greenhill, who carries the tinder, has allowed it to get wet. The giant swings his axe in savage anger at enforced cold, and Vetch takes an opportunity to remark what a *big* man Greenhill is.

On the fourteenth day they can scarcely crawl, and their limbs pain them. Greenhill, who is the weakest, sees Gabbett and the Moocher go aside to consult, and crawling to the Crow, whimpers:

'For God's sake, Jemmy, don't let 'em murder me!'

'I can't help you,' says Vetch, looking about in terror. 'Think of poor Tom Bodenham.'

'But he was no murderer. If they kill me, I shall go to hell with Tom's blood on my soul.'

He writhes on the ground in sickening terror, and Gabbett arriving, bids Vetch bring wood for the fire. Vetch, going, sees Greenhill clinging to wolfish Gabbett's knees, and Dalton calls after him,

'You will hear it presently, Jem.'

The nervous Crow puts his hands to his ears, but is conscious, nevertheless, of a dull crash and a groan. When he comes back, there is something hanging on a little tree, and some sputtering over the fire that makes him shudder. Gabbett is putting on the dead man's shoes, which are better than his own.

'We'll stop here a day or so and rest,' says he, *now we've got provisions.*

Two more days pass, and the trio, eyeing each other suspiciously, resume their march. The third day – the sixteenth of their ghastly journey – such portions of the carcase as they have with them prove unfit to eat. Dalton boils some, but the repulsive mess makes him vomit. They look into each other's famine-sharpened faces, and wonder 'who next?'

'We must all die together,' says Dalton quickly, 'before anything else must happen.'

Vetch marks the terror that lies concealed in the words, and when the dreaded giant is out of earshot, says,

'For God's sake, let's go on alone, Alick. You see what sort of a cove that Gabbett is – he'd kill his father before he'd fast one day.'

They make for the bush, when the giant turns and strides towards them. Vetch skips nimbly on one side, but Gabbett strikes the Moocher on the forehead with the axe. 'Help! Jem, help!' cries the victim, cut, but not fatally, and in the strength of his desperation tears the axe from the monster who bears it, and flings it to Vetch.

'Keep it, Jemmy,' he cries – 'let's have no more murder done!'

They fare again through the horrible bush until nightfall, when Vetch, in a strange voice, calls the giant to him.

'He must die.'

'Either you or he,' laughs Gabbett. 'Give me the axe.'

'No, no,' says the Crow, his thin, malignant face distorted by a horrible resolution. '*I'll keep the axe. Stand back! You shall hold him, and I'll do the job.*'

Dalton, seeing them approach, knows his end has come, and submits, crying,

'Give me half an hour to pray for myself.'

They consent, and the bewildered wretch kneels down and

folds his hands like a child. His big, stupid face works with emotion. His great cracked lips move in desperate agony. He wags his head from side to side, in pitiful confusion of his brutalized senses.

'*I can't think o' the words, Jem!*'

'Pah,' snarls Vetch, swinging the axe, 'we can't starve here all night.'

Four days have passed, and the two survivors of this awful journey sit watching each other. The gaunt giant, his eyes gleaming with hate and hunger, sits sentinel over the dwarf. The dwarf, chuckling to himself at his superior sagacity, clutches the fatal axe. Armed Cunning is pitted against brute Strength. For two days they have not spoken to each other. For two days each has promised himself that on the next his companion must *sleep* – and die. Vetch comprehends the devilish scheme of the monster who has entrapped five of his fellow-beings to aid him by their deaths to his own safety, and holds aloof. Gabbett watches to snatch the weapon from his companion, and make the odds even for once and for ever. In the daytime they travel on, seeking each a pretext to creep behind the other. In the night-time they feign slumber, and each stealthily raising a head catches the wakeful glance of his companion. Vetch feels his strength deserting him, and his brain overpowered by fatigue. Surely the giant, muttering, gesticulating, and slavering at the mouth, must be on the road to madness. Will the monster find opportunity to rush at him, and, braving the blood-stained axe, kill him by main force; or will he sleep, and be himself a victim? Unhappy Vetch! It is the terrible privilege of insanity to be sleepless.

On the fifth day, Vetch, creeping behind a tree, takes off his belt, and makes a noose. He will hang himself. He gets one end of the belt over a bough, and then his cowardice bids him pause. Gabbett approaches; he tries to evade him, and steal away into the bush. In vain. The insatiable giant, ravenous with famine, and sustained by madness, is not to be shaken off. Vetch tries to run, but his legs bend under him. The axe that has drunk so much blood feels heavy as lead. He will fling it away. He dares not.

Night falls again. He must rest, or go mad. His limbs are powerless. His eyelids are glued together. He sleeps as he stands. This horrible thing must be a dream. He is at Port Arthur, or will wake on his pallet in the penny lodging-house he slept at when a boy. Is that the Deputy come to wake him to the torment of living? It is not time – surely not time yet.

He sleeps – and the giant, grinning with ferocious joy, approaches on clumsy tiptoe and seizes the coveted axe.

On the north-east coast of Van Diemen's Land is a place called St Helen's Point, and a certain skipper, being in want of fresh water, landing there with a boat's crew, finds on the banks of the creek a gaunt and blood-stained man, clad in tattered yellow, who carries on his back an axe and a bundle.

When the sailors come within sight of him, he makes signs to them to approach, and opening his bundle with much ceremony offers them some of its contents.

Filled with horror at what the maniac displays, they seize and bind him.

At Hobart Town he is recognized as the only survivor of the nine desperadoes who had escaped from Colonel Arthur's 'Natural Penitentiary'.[1]

1. While this story has been passing through the press, I have been so often accused of exaggerating facts to create 'sensation,' that I would ask leave to say a word in reference to this episode.

I would not have introduced so repulsive an incident as this cannibalism of escaping convicts, were not such incidents hideously frequent among absconders; and no writer, professing to give a truthful picture of the results of the old convict system, can afford to ignore them.

The story of Gabbett and his companions is a story which can be found in print. The real name of the convict who ate his comrades was Pierce. He escaped from Macquarie Harbour in 1822, and I have taken his own confession as the basis of the narrative, shifting the scene to Port Arthur.

That such an occurrence was not unlikely to take place there, may be shown, by the following well-known anecdote, related by Mr James Bonwick in his 'Bushrangers:' – 'Among the few successful bolters were two men and a boy, who contrived to get across the mainland in a bark boat. Landing upon an unsettled part of the coast, wholly unprovided with food . . . they had recourse to murder and cannibalism . . . Not long after, they were captured . . . and when their dreadful account was doubted, they exhibited a portion of the roasted body which they had retained for another meal.' – M.C.

BOOK FIVE

Extracted from the Diary of the Rev. James North

Bathurst, February the 11th, 1846.

In turning over the pages of my journal, to note the good fortune that has just happened to me, I am struck by the barrenness of my life for the last seven years.

Can it be possible that I, James North, the college-hero, the poet, the prizeman, the heaven knows what else, have been content to live on at this dreary spot – an animal, eating and drinking, for tomorrow I die? Yet it has been so. My world, that world of which I once dreamt so much, has been – here. My fame – which was to reach the ends of the earth – has penetrated to the neighbouring stations. I am considered a 'good preacher' by my sheep-feeding friends. It is kind of them.

Yet, when now on the eve of leaving it, this solitary life of mine has not been without its charms. I have had my books and my thoughts – though at times the latter were but grim companions. I have striven with my familiar sin, and have not always been worsted. Melancholy reflection. 'Not always!' '*But yet*' is as a gaoler to bring forth some monstrous malefactor. I vowed, however, that I would not cheat myself in this diary of mine, and I will not. No evasions. No glossings over of my own sins. This journal is my confessor, and I bare my heart to it.

It is curious the pleasure I feel in setting down here in black and white these agonies and secret cravings of which I dare not speak. Outwardly a man of God, pious and grave, softly spoken, with a mien calculated to impress my sanctity upon the beholder. Inwardly – what? The mean, cowardly, weak sinner that this book knows me. ... Imp! I could tear you in pieces! ... One of these days I will. In the meantime, I will keep you under lock and key, and you shall hug my secrets close. No, old friend, with whom I have communed so long, forgive me, forgive me. You are to me instead of wife or priest. I tell to your cold blue pages – how much was it I bought you for in Paramatta, rascal? – these stories, longings, remorses, which I would fain tell to human ear could I find a human being as discreet as thou. It has been said that a man dare not *write* all his thoughts and deeds; the words would blister the paper. Yet your sheets are smooth enough, you fat rogue! Our neighbours of Rome know human nature. A man *must* confess. One reads of wretches who have carried secrets in their bosoms for years, and blurted them forth at last. I, shut up here without companionship, without sympathy, without letters, cannot lock up my soul and feed on my own thoughts. They will out, and so I whisper them to thee.

> What art thou, thou tremendous power
> Who does inhabit us without our leave,
> And art, within ourselves, another self,
> A master self that loves to domineer?

What? Conscience? That is a word to frighten children with. The conscience of each man is of his own making. My friend the shark-toothed cannibal whom Staples brought in his whaler to Sydney would have found his conscience reproach him sorely did he refuse to partake of the feasts made sacred by the customs of his ancestors. A spark of divinity? The divinity that, according to received doctrine, sits apart enthroned amid sweet music, and leaves poor humanity to earn its condemnation as it may? I'll have none of that – though I preach it. One must soothe the vulgar senses of the people. Priesthood has its 'pious frauds'. The Master spoke in parables. Wit? The wit that sees how ill-balanced are our actions and our aspirations? The devilish wit born of our own brain, that sneers at us for our own failings? Perhaps madness? More likely, for there are few men who are not mad one hour of the waking twelve. Yet I can 'the matter reword which madness would gambol from.' If madness be the differing from the judgment of the majority of mankind in regard to familiar things, I suppose *I* am mad – or too wise. The speculation draws to hair splitting. James North, let thy *alter ego* address thee through the pages of this *socius* of thine. Bring your mind back to earth. Circumstances have made you what you are, and will shape your destiny for you without your interference.

That's comfortably settled!

Now supposing – to take another canter on my night-mare – that man is the slave of circumstances (a doctrine which I am not uninclined to believe, though unwilling to confess), what circumstance can have brought about the sudden awakening of the powers that be to James North's fitness for duty?

Hobart Town, Jan. 12th.

DEAR NORTH, I have much pleasure in informing you that you can be appointed Protestant chaplain at Norfolk Island, if you like. It seems that they did not get on well with the last man, and when my advice was asked, I at once recommended you for the office. The pay is small, but you have a house and so on. It is certainly better than Bathurst, and indeed is considered rather a prize in the clerical lottery.

There is to be an investigation into affairs down there. Poor old Pratt – who went down, as you know, at the earnest solicitation of the Government – seems to have become absurdly lenient with the prisoners, and it is reported that the island is in a frightful state. Sir Eardley is looking out for some disciplinarian to take the place in hand.

In the meantime the chaplaincy was vacant, and I thought of you. Have I done right?

Yours very faithfully,
GEORGE FREDERICK DE LA VERE.

The Rev. James North, Bathurst.

'And so I thought of you?' Yes. But why? Did any lingering memory of the day I saved your baby-face from the fists of the bargee haunt you, O most elegant George Frederick? You have been private secretary to His Excellency for the last three years, and you never 'thought of me'. You didn't even answer my note, most official and delicate de la Vere. However, it seems ungrateful to abuse you! Yet my *socius* here – my book of confessions – knows I don't like you, dainty George.

February 19th. I accept. There is work to be done among those unhappy men that may be my purgation. They shall hear me yet – though inquiry was stifled at Port Arthur. By the way, a

Pharaoh has arisen who knows not Joseph. It is evident that the meddlesome parson who complained of men being flogged to death is forgotten. Like the men are! How many ghosts must haunt the dismal loneliness of that prison shore! Poor Burgess is gone the way of all flesh. I wonder if *his* spirit revisits the scene of its violences? I have written 'poor' Burgess. It is strange how we pity a man that has gone out of this life. The Stagyrite says 'we do not hate the dead'. One's enmity is extinguished when one can but *remember* injuries. If a man had injured me, the fact of his living at all would be sufficient grounds for me to hate him, – if I had injured *him* I should hate him still more. Is that the reason I hate myself at times – my greatest enemy and one whom I have injured beyond forgiveness. There are offences against one's own nature that are not to be forgiven. Isn't it Tacitus that says 'the hatred of those most nearly related is most inveterate?' But – I am taking flight again.

No more, my sleek confidant. I will write to de la Vere. I remember doing the puppy's Alcaics for him in the fourth form – and accept his offer.

February 27th, 11.30 p.m. – Nine Creeks Station. I like to be accurate in names, dates, etc. Accuracy is a virtue.

To exercise it, then. Host's name Carr. Station ninety miles from Bathurst. I should say about 4,000 head of cattle. Luxury without refinement. Plenty to eat, drink, and, yes – read. Host likes books, and can talk. I don't like him, though. A black-a-vised sneering fellow, and though easy in his manners, *not* a gentleman. The wife is a puzzle. She is a well-preserved creature, about thirty-four years of age I should say, and is a clever woman – not in a poetical Byronic sense, but in the widest acceptation of the term. Her conversation was a pleasure I had not thought to experience. At the same time, I should be sorry to be her husband. Women have no business with a brain like hers – that is, if they wish to be women and not sexual monsters. A woman should own just sufficient intellect to *appreciate*. One don't want them to do original things. At least, I don't. A 'help meet' (good old word), is never a genius – she sometimes has a genius for a son, though, which is more satisfactory to her.

Mrs Carr is not a lady, though she might have been one. I don't think she is a good woman either. It is possible, indeed, that she has known the Factory before now. One never knows in this excellent colony — so many men marry their assigned servants. There is a boy — a son, I suppose — who rides like Alexander. There is a mystery about the pair — or I am no judge of character. A word or so at dinner gave me a notion of much bickering and unhappiness. I wonder if that big-bearded Carr beats her? I don't think she would suffer indignity calmly. After all, what business is it of mine? I was beguiled into taking more wine at dinner than I wanted. Confessor! — do you hear me? But I will not allow myself to be carried away. You grin, you fat familiar! So may I, but I shall be eaten with remorse to-morrow.

March 3rd. A place called Jerrilang, where I have a headache and a heartache. 'One that hath let go himself from the hold and stay of reason, and lies open to the mercy of all temptations.'

March 20th. Seventeen days since I have opened you, beloved and detested companion of mine. I have more than half a mind to never open you again! To read you is to recall to myself all I would most willingly forget; yet not to read you would be to forget all that I should for my sins remember.

The last week has made a new man of me. I am no longer morose, despairing, and bitter, but genial and on good terms with fortune.

It is strange that a mere accident should have induced me to stay a week under the same roof with that vision of brightness which has haunted me so long. A meeting in the street, an introduction, an invitation — the thing is done.

These circumstances that form our fortunes are curious things. I had thought never again to meet the bright young face to which I felt so strange an attraction — and lo! here it is smiling on me daily. Captain Frere should be a happy man. The picture of his wife bending over her three-year-old lassie was charming. '*O matre pulchrâ filia pulchrior!*' A picture that makes an old bachelor like me sigh. There seems a skeleton in this house also. That young girl, by nature so loveable and so mirthful, ought not to have the sadness on her face that twice today has clouded it. He seems a passionate and bearish creature this wonderful convict disciplinarian. His convicts – poor devils – are doubtless disciplined enough. Charming little Dora, with your quaint wit and weird beauty, he is not good enough for you – and yet it was a love match.

March 21st. I have read family prayers every night since I have been here – my black coat and white tie give me the natural preeminence in such matters – and I feel guilty every time I read. I wonder what Mrs Frere, the little lady of the devotional eyes, would say if she knew that I was a miserable hypocrite, preaching what I did not practise, exhorting others to believe those marvels which my own heart laughs to scorn? I am a coward not to throw off the saintly mask and appear as a Freethinker. Yet, am I a coward? I urge upon myself that it is for the glory of God I hold my peace. The scandal of a Priest turned Infidel would do more harm than the reign of reason would do good. Imagine this trustful woman for instance – she would suffer anguish at the thoughts of such a sin, though another were the sinner. 'If any one offend one of these little ones it were better for him that a mill-stone be hanged about his neck and that he be cast into the sea.' Yet truth is truth, and should be spoken – should it not, malignant monitor, that reminds me how often I fail to speak it? Surely among all his army of black-coats our worthy bishop must have some men like me, who cannot bring their reason to believe in things contrary to the experience of mankind and the laws of nature and physics. I can see him in my mind's eye rubbing his comfortable hands in perplexed anger at the insult to his cloth. Poor spiritual lord of mine. Thou hast a wife. I have met her, and can forgive thee much.

March 22nd. There is a romantic story connected with Captain Frere's marriage. He told me after dinner tonight, how his wife had been wrecked when a child, and how he had saved her life, and defended her from the rude hands of an escaped convict – one of these monsters that our monstrous system breeds.

'That was how we fell in love,' said he, tossing off his wine complacently.

'An auspicious opportunity,' said I.

To which he nodded. He is not overburdened with brains, I fancy.

Let me see if I can set down some account of this lovely place and its people.

A long low white house, surrounded by a blooming garden. Wide windows opening on a lawn. The ever glorious, ever changing bay beneath. It is evening. I am talking with Mrs Frere, of London, and picture galleries, and new books. There comes a sound of wheels on the gravel. It is the magistrate returned from his convict-discipline – how I hate the term. We hear him come briskly up the steps, but we go on talking. (I fancy there was a time when the lady would have run to meet him.) He enters, coldly kisses his wife, and disturbs at once the current of our thoughts.

'It has been hot today. What, still no letter from Headquarters, Mr North! I saw Mrs Golightly in town, Dora, and she asked for you. There is to be a ball at Government House. We must go.'

Then he departs, and is heard in the distance dimly cursing because the water is not hot enough, or because Dawkins, his convict servant, has not brushed his trousers sufficiently.

We resume our chat, but he returns all hungry, and bluff, and whisker-brushed.

'Dinner! Ha-ha! I'm ready for it. North, take Mrs Frere.' By and bye it is, 'North, some sherry? Dora, the soup is ruined again. Did you go out today? No?' His eyebrows contract here, and I know he says inwardly, 'Reading some trashy novel, I suppose.' However he grins, and obligingly relates how the police have captured Cockatoo Bill the noted bushranger.

After dinner comes Dora the younger, a fair-haired little wonder, with dark eyes. She is 'old-fashioned'. She is placed in a high chair near mamma, and is pleased to converse with me.

Her conversation is not brilliant, but it is amusing from its intense gravity of tone.

'Dive Dotty pear! Dive Dotty fig! Mamma! Papa!'

This is all she says, but her pudgy hands grasp everything, and remorsely smear her mother's laces with jam.

Dotty is the idol of her mother. Captain Frere condescends to patronize her in a lofty way, saying, 'Dotty, have some grapes?' or, 'Dotty, take a piece of apple?' But he soon grows weary of her, and snubs her. Then the mother fondles and purrs over the pretty little brat, and the two heads go together.

After dinner the disciplinarian and I converse – of dogs and horses, game cocks, convicts, and moving accidents by flood and field. I remember old college feats, and strive to keep pace with him in the relation of athletics. What hypocrites we are! – for all the time I am longing to get to the drawing-room, and finish my criticism of the new poet, Mr Tennyson, to Mrs Frere. (I have asserted that the 'Owl' is an imitation of Shakespeare, and I'll prove it too!) Frere does not read Tennyson – nor anybody else.

Adjourned to the drawing-room, we chat – Mrs Frere and I – until supper. (He eats supper.) She is a charming companion, and when I talk my best – I *can* talk, you must admit, O Familiar – her face lightens up with an interest I rarely see upon it at other times. I feel cooled and soothed by this companionship. The quiet refinement of this house, after bullocks and Bathurst, is like the shadow of a great rock in a weary land. That is a metaphor, by the way, which A. Tennyson, Esq, never approached.

Mrs Frere seems about five and twenty. She is rather beneath the middle height, with a slight, girlish figure. This girlish appearance is enhanced by the fact that she has bright fair hair and blue eyes. Upon conversation with her, however, one sees that her face has lost much of that delicate plumpness that it probably owned in youth. Her cheeks are thin, and her eyes have a tinge of sadness, which speaks of some physical or mental grief. This thinness of face makes the eyes appear larger and the brow broader than they really are. Her hands are white and painfully thin. They must have been plump and pretty once. Her lips are red with perpetual fever.

Captain Frere seems to have absorbed all his wife's vitality. Who is it quotes the story of Lucius Claudius Hermippus, who lived to a great age by being constantly breathed on by young girls? I suppose Burton – who quotes everything. In proportion as she has lost her vigour and youth he has gained strength and heartiness. Though he is at least forty years of age, he does not look more than thirty. His face is ruddy, his eyes bright, his voice firm and ringing. He must be a man of considerable strength and – I should say – of more than ordinary animal courage. There is not a nerve in his body which does not twang like a piano wire. In appearance, he is tall, broad, and bluff, with red whiskers and reddish hair slightly touched with grey. His manner is loud, coarse, and imperious; his talk of dogs, horses, cocks, and convicts.

What a strangely mated pair !

March 30th. A letter from Van Diemen's Land. 'There is a row in the pantry,' says de la Vere, with his accustomed slang. The Comptroller-General of Convicts has appointed a Mr Pounce to go down and make a report on the state of Norfolk Island. I am to go down with him, and shall receive instructions to that effect from the Comptroller-General. I have informed Frere of this, and he has written to Pounce to come and stay on his way down. There has been nothing but convict discipline talked since.

Frere is great upon this point, and wearies me with his explanations of convict tricks and wickedness. He is celebrated for his knowledge of such matters. Detestable wisdom ! His servants hate him, and yet they obey him without a murmur. I have observed that habitual criminals – like all savage beasts – cower before the man who has once mastered them. I should not be surprised if the Van Diemen's Land Government selected Frere as their 'disciplinarian'.

I hope they won't, and yet I hope they will.

April 4th. Nothing worth recording until today. Eating, drinking, and sleeping. Despite my forty-seven years, I begin to feel almost like the James North who fought the bargee and took the gold medal. What a drink water is ! The *fons Bandusiæ splendidior vitro* was better than all the Massic, Master Horace ! I doubt if your celebrated liquor bottled when Manlius was consul could compare with it.

But to my notable facts. I have found out tonight two things which surprise me.

One is that the convict who attempted the life of Mrs Frere is none other than the unhappy man whom my fatal weakness caused to be flogged at Port Arthur, and whose face comes before me to reproach me even now.

The other that Mrs Carr is an old acquaintance of Frere's.

The latter piece of information I obtained in a curious way.

Sitting after Mrs Frere and Dotty had retired, we were talking of clever women. I broached my theory, that intellect in women went far to destroy their womanly nature.

'Desire in man,' said I, 'should be Volition in woman; Reason, Intuition; Reverence, Devotion; Morality, Conscience; Thought, Ideality; Passion, Love; Impression, Perception. The woman should strike a lower key note, but a sharper sound. Man has vigour of reason, woman quickness of feeling. The woman who possesses masculine force of intellect is abnormal.'

He did but half comprehend me, I could see, but he agreed with the broad view of the case.

'I only knew one woman who was really "strong-minded", as they call it,' he said, 'and she was a regular bad one.'

'It does not follow that she should be *bad*,' said I.

'This one was, though – stock, lock, and barrel. But as sharp as a needle, sir, and as immovable as a rock. A fine woman too.'

I saw by the expression of the man's face that he owned ugly memories, and pressed him further.

'She's up country somewhere,' he said. 'Married her assigned servant, I believe, a fellow named Carr. I haven't seen her for years, and don't know what she may be like now, but in the days when I knew her she was just what you describe.' (Let it be noted that I had described nothing.) 'She came out in the ship with me as maid to my wife's mother.'

It was on the tip of my tongue to say that I had met her, but I don't know what induced me to be silent. There are passages in the lives of most men of Captain Frere's complexion that don't bear descanting on. I expect there was in this case, for he changed the subject very abruptly as his wife came in.

Is it possible that these two creatures – the wife of the assigned servant and the notable disciplinarian – could have been more than friends in youth? Quite possible. He is the sort of man for gross amours. (A pretty way I am abusing my host!)

And the supple woman with the dark eyes would have been just the creature to enthral him. Perhaps some such story as this may account in part for Mrs Frere's sad looks.

Why do I speculate on such things? I seem to do violence to myself and to insult *her* by writing such suspicions. If I was a Flaggelant now, I would don hair-shirt and up flail. 'For this sort cometh not out but by prayer and fasting.'

April 7th. Mr Pounce has arrived – full of the importance of his mission. He seems to walk with the air of a minister of state on the eve of a vacant garter, hoping, wondering, fearing, and dignified even in his dubitancy.

I am as flippant as a school-girl concerning this fatuous official, and yet – Heaven knows – I feel deeply enough the importance of the task he has before him. One relieves one's brain by these whirlings of one's mental limbs. I remember that a prisoner at Hobart Town, twice condemned and twice reprieved, jumped and shouted with frenzied vehemence when he heard his sentence of death finally pronounced. He told me if he had not so shouted, he believed he would have gone mad.

We had a state dinner last night. The conversation was about nothing in the world but convicts. I never saw Mrs Frere to less advantage. Silent, *distraite*, and sad. She told me after dinner that she disliked the very name of 'convict' from early associations.

'I have lived among them all my life,' she said, 'but that does not make it the better for me. I have terrible fancies at times, Mr North, that seem half-memories. I dread to be brought in contact with prisoners again. I am sure that some evil awaits me at their hands.'

I laughed, of course, but it would not do. She holds to her own opinion, and looks at me with eyes that seem to have a rising horror in them. This *unborn terror* in her face is perplexing.

'You are nervous,' I said. 'You want rest.'

'I *am* nervous,' she replied, with that candour of voice and manner I have before remarked in her, 'and I have presentiments of evil.'

We sat silent for a while, and then she suddenly turned her

large eyes on me, and stroking Dotty's curls with one hand, said calmly,

'Mr North, what death shall I die?'

The question was an echo of my own thoughts – I have some foolish (?) fancies as to physiognomy – and made me start. What death, indeed? What sort of death would one meet with widely-opened eyes, parted lips, and brows bent as though to rally fast-flying courage? Not a peaceful death surely. I brought my black-coat to my aid.

'My dear lady, you must not think of such things. Death is but a sleep you know. Why anticipate a nightmare?'

She sighed, slowly awaking as though from some momentary trance. Her eyes fell on the child, and she burst into tears. This ended in an hysterical fit. I heard her husband afterwards recommending sal volatile. He is the sort of man who would recommend sal volatile to the Pythoness if she consulted him.

April 26th. All has been arranged, and we start tomorrow. Mr Pounce is in a condition of painful dignity. He seems afraid to move lest motion should thaw his official ice. Having found out that I am the 'chaplain', he has refrained from familiarity. My self-love is wounded, but my patience relieved. *Query:* Would not the majority of mankind rather be bored by people in authority than not noticed by them? James North declines to answer for his part.

I have made my farewells to my friends, and on looking back on the pleasant hours I have spent, feel saddened. It is not likely that I shall have many such pleasant hours. I feel like a vagabond who having been allowed to sit by a cheerful fireside for a while is turned out into the wet and windy streets, and finds them colder than ever. What were the lines I wrote in her album?

> As some poor tavern-haunter flushed with wine,
>   With staggering footsteps through the streets returning,
> – Seeing through blinding rain a beacon shine
>   From household lamp in happy window burning, –
> Pauses an instant at the reddened pane
>   To gaze on that sweet scene of love and duty,
> Then turns into the wild wet night again,
>   Lest his sad presence mar its homely beauty.

Um! Yes, those were the lines. With more of truth in them than she expected; and yet what business have I sentimentalising? My *socius* thinks 'What a puling fool this North is!'

So, that's over! Now for Norfolk Island and my purgation.

⤙ 2 ⤚

AT 'CARR'S'

It is evening at Nine Creeks Station. The sun going down behind the hill sends a last ray of light to illumine the white dress of a woman seated on the broad verandah that overlooks the swamp. From the 'men's huts' on the brow of the hill comes faintly a clinking of pannikins and pails. A lad is carrying a bucket of water to the stable. Derwent Jack is plaiting a rawhide girth. Tom, Joe, and Harry, and the half-dozen others who have been 'mustering' the cattle, walk their reeking horses slowly to water at the dam. A cloud of dust heavily hangs above the 'yards'.

There is heard a crashing of scrub and undergrowth, and a white bullock, with head down and tail in air, bursts out of the gum-saplings near the huts. A boy mounted on a smart chestnut appears following the bullock, and deftly heading him, wheels him towards the yards.

Tom and Harry set spurs to their jaded horses, and gallop down the hill. The rails rattle to the ground. Two or three of the imprisoned beasts rush out, only to be penned against the wing fence, and in company with the white bullock to be yarded amid a fusillade of stock-whips.

'Confound you!' cries the lad on the chestnut. 'Didn't you hear me cooee? A nice job I've had with the brute. He bested me twice by the crossing-place, and I might have followed him all night for all you cared.' And here follow a shower of oaths that sound more than ordinarily hideous from such young lips.

The men reply in the same strain, and an interchange of curses takes place which bids fair to end in mischief to somebody, when a tall man mounted on a strong low grey rides up at a canter, and puts an end to the controversy by lashing the lad savagely with his stock-whip.

'Squabbling again, young imp!' cries he in high wrath. 'You'll go to bed without supper again this night.'

The lad, flinching but not cowed, reins back his horse, and as the pair ride together towards the stables the stockmen grin at each other. They would laugh aloud, but John Carr, the assigned servant who married his mistress, is not a man to be trifled with, and they know it.

'He don't bear no good-will to his step-son,' says Tom, flinging the lash of his whip out in the air and catching it dexterously between finger and thumb.

'No, nor his step-son to him,' returns the other, pegging the rails and climbing to saddle. 'He's a true son of his mother whoever his father is.'

'Some swell in Sydney they *do* say?' puts the other inquiringly.

'So I've heard,' says Harry. 'I suppose the "cove" knows, and if he don't I can't tell him. They're a bright lot altogether.'

Meanwhile John Carr – late John Rex – has flung his bridle to the black boy, and is making for the house.

The lad – Dick Purfoy – follows him. He is a slim wiry young animal of about nine years of age. If he is not the son of John Carr he might be, for he owns the same black hair and eyes, and the same reckless and defiant bearing.

At the little gate that leads to the garden John Carr wheels upon him angrily.

'Go down to the men's hut,' he says. 'You don't come in here tonight. Be off now!'

The boy goes without a word, and John Carr steps on to the verandah where the woman is sitting.

'Where's Dick?' is her first inquiry.

'Gone down to the men's hut. Is tea ready?'

'Yes. I've been waiting.'

'So have I – ever since breakfast.'

All that is known in the district about Mrs John Carr is that some five years ago Mrs Sarah Purfoy, the widow of a wealthy whaling captain, purchased Nine Creeks Station, and in the space of twelve months more wedded one of her assigned servants named John Carr. Rumour did not speak too well of Mrs Purfoy's past history, hinting even that the whaling captain and the widowhood were alike fictions, and that the boy whom she called her son had no legal father. It was not to be expected, however, that John Carr, transported for forgery and with three years of his time of assigned service yet to run, would be particular. As soon as his mistress brought him from Sydney as storekeeper she seemed to take a fancy to him, and when she offered him herself and station he refused neither. He was an 'expiree' now, and master of a fine wife and a fine fortune. A man to be envied.

It is not necessary to say that he was hated intensely by his servants. The major part of them had been 'government' themselves, and resented the fact that one of their number had been raised up to rule over them. This hatred, however, was a matter of small moment to John Carr, who ruled the huts with a rod of iron. The only satisfaction that the victims of his wrath possessed was the suspicion that he himself was in his turn browbeaten by his wife. Their rude guess was not far short of the mark. Much as she loved the scoundrel, Sarah Purfoy held him to her by fear, not affection. He knew that if he made any attempt to escape from his marriage-bonds, the woman who had risked so much to save him would not hesitate to deliver him over to the authorities, and state how the opportune death of fever-stricken John Carr had enabled her to give name and employment to absconded John Rex. He had thought once that the fact of her being his wife would prevent her from giving evidence against him, and that he could thus defy her. But she reminded him that a word to Blunt would be all sufficient.

'I know you don't care for me now, John,' she said, with grim complacency; 'but your life is in my hands, and if you desert me I will bring you to the gallows.'

In vain he raged and chafed. He was tied hand and foot. She held his money, and her shrewd wit had more than doubled it. She was all-powerful, and he could but wait until her death or some lucky accident would rid her of him, and leave him free to follow out the scheme he had matured.

'Once rid of her,' he thought, in his solitary rides over the station of which he was the nominal owner, 'and the rest is easy. I shall become a man of fortune and family, and shall doubtless be received with open arms by the dear brother and sister from whom I have been so long parted. If Mr Francis is of a fraternal nature he will give up his estate without trouble, and I will be munificent towards him. If he is suspicious, we will fight it out. Richard Devine shall have his own again.'

Full of this devilish plot, he tried twice to escape from his thraldom, and was twice brought back.

'I have bought you, John,' his partner had laughed, 'and you don't get away from me. Surely you can be content with these comforts. You were content with less once. I am not so ugly and repulsive, am I?'

'I am home-sick,' John Carr retorted. 'Let us go to England, Sarah.'

She tapped her strong white fingers sharply on the table.

'Go to England? No, no. That is what you would like to do. You would be master there. You would take my money, and leave me to starve. I know you, Jack. We stop here, dear. Here, where I can hand you over to the first trooper as an escaped convict if you are not kind to me.'

'She-devil!'

'Oh, I don't mind your abuse. Abuse me all night if you like, Jack. Beat me if you will, but don't leave me, or it will be the worse for you.'

'You are a strange woman,' he cries, in sudden petulant admiration.

'To love such a villain? I don't know that. I love you because you are a villain. A better man would be wearisome to such as I am.'

'What objection you can have to England I can't think. I live here like a man on the drop with the rope round his neck.'

'Ay Jack, but I hold the end of it. Why you want to go to England I don't know — unless you have some scheme in your head.'

'What if I have?'

'Then tell it to me.'

'No: you would use it against me.'

'Then you don't go.'

'Then you don't know.'

'Very well. I am content.'

'I wish to Heaven I'd never left Port Arthur. Better there than this dog's life.'

'Go back, then. You only have to say the word!'

And so they would wrangle, she glorying in her power over the man who had so long triumphed over her, and he consoling himself with the hope that the day was not far distant which should bring him at once freedom and fortune.

She felt a rapture in this unnatural love-and-hate, and would not have let her convict-husband escape her for the world. He kept his secret close and waited, venting his ill-humour upon the boy.

This lad was an additional source of quarrel between the pair. Though he bore her name, Sarah Purfoy would never acknowledge him as her son, and had been accustomed to lash her husband to violence by ambiguous givings out respecting the lad's birth. At first John Rex, torn by a sensual jealousy, demanded explanations with threats, but as detestation took the place of ardour he apparently ceased to trouble himself about the matter, and allowed her to keep her own secrets. He rarely, however, spoke to Dick in tones of kindness, and the boy, who had a fierce spirit of his own, hated his step-father.

Neither was Sarah's conduct towards him of a kind to win his affection. She seemed to regard him as a curious creature whose development was, for some cause best known to herself, worthy of being watched with care. It was not in her woman's nature, bad as it was, to be cruel to the boy; but she never troubled herself as to his morals or his manners, and, as long as he continued to live and grow, seemed to care little what become of him.

At times she would look at him as though half-terrified as to what he might become. At times she would urge him by jest and sneer to the performance of the maddest pranks. No one, save passing travellers, came near the station, and poor Dick grew up in familiar companionship with the half-dozen ruffians who had found their way through the convict sieve to the 'men's huts'. His mother neglected or sneered at him. His step-father neglected or beat him. He was never happy save when in the rude company of the 'hands', or galloping down the ranges after cattle. The consequence of all this was that at nine years old he could drink rum, smoke tobacco, curse like a bullock-driver, and ride – as North had said – like Alexander. He could not repeat the Ten Commandments correctly, but he could sit a buck-jumper with any 'currency flash' in the colony. In the company of anything above a bullock-driver he was sulky and ill-at-ease, but in the smoky atmosphere of the huts he could tell a rough story, or sing a rough song, without a blush, and at a 'cutting-out' or a 'general muster' was often foremost in prowess.

On this particular evening the 'huts' are unusually silent. The day's work has been hard, and the men are tired. Tom in a corner tailing a stock-whip, says nothing. Joe, twisting an old silk handkerchief – stolen, or I'm much mistaken, Joe! – into 'crackers', is silent also. Bob and Harry are playing all-fours by the light of a cotton wick protruding from a pannikin of fat, – playing with a pack of cards so greasy and begrimed with filth that the pips are barely distinguishable; and as they play they curse at intervals.

'Larry, give me some supper,' says little Dick, walking in.

'Sent down to us, Master Dick?' enquires Bob, wetting his gigantic thumb previous to dealing.

'Yes,' retorts Dick, with an oath; 'that's about it.'

The chorus blasphemously sympathize.

In the meantime Larry rattles on to the table a shallow tin dish, in which a lump of salted beef swelters in its own grease, tilts some tea into a pannikin, and slapping down a brown tin plate and a black-handled knife and fork, bids his guest fall to.

'Have a puffterlooner, Master Dick,' suggests Derwent Jack, 'or a bit o' sweetcake. Why, what's come to your face, boy?'

'A cut,' says Dick, shortly. 'He did it.'

In fact, a livid weal scores the lad's brown cheek. There is another outburst of good-hearted blasphemy, and some one suggests that a knife in the ribs of the 'cove' would be a sight acceptable to the eyes of mankind in general.

'A jumped up – wretch,' says Tom, emphatically, alluding to Mr Carr's rise in life. 'Who's he, I should like to know?'

'He'll do you a mischief some day, my kiddy,' says Derwent Jack.

'No fear, cocky!' returns poor Dick, with his mouth full of sweetcake.

Harry says that 'he wouldn't stand it' if he were in Dick's shoes; and the hut generally begins to revile its master. It is a favourite sport this setting of the 'young cove' against the 'boss'.

Encouraged by the applause, Dick reviles his step-father in the choicest of convict-slang, and promises himself to speedily rebel against the harsh rule of his unhappy home.

So the evening passes, and in the bright, pure moonlight Dick steps out of the hut to seek his own bed-chamber. He staggers somewhat, and walks hesitatingly. Derwent Jack has a bottle of rum in his blankets.

In the room that serves as dining-room his step-father is seated moodily smoking. He hears the footsteps in the passage, and calls out, 'Who's there?'

Dick answers huskily, and is presently confronted by John Carr, irate and fierce.

'Drunk, you young dog!' he cries, and seizing a whip from the corner of the room, beats the little wretch until he writhes and begs for mercy.

Whoever is poor Dick's father, it is certain that his son has not a happy time.

❧ 3 ❧

Extracted from the Diary of the Rev. James North

May 12th, 1846. Landed today at Norfolk Island, and have been introduced to my new abode.

The first aspect of the place fills me with horror. There seems neither discipline nor order. On our way to the Commandant's house we passed a low dilapidated building where the men were at work grinding maize, and at the sight of us they commenced whistling, hooting, and shouting, using the most disgusting language. Three warders were by, but no attempt was made to check this unseemly exhibition. N.B. – The clothing of the men is rags.

I was introduced to the commandant, Major Pratt. He seems a gentlemanly person, but weak and excitable. He defended his conduct in an elaborate way to Mr Pounce at dinner – a proceeding which I thought in bad taste.

I expected prayers in the evening, but we had none. Pounce insisted on going through the wards, and I went with him. Bad as I remember Port Arthur to have been, this is infinitely worse. The men are locked up from six in the evening until sunrise, without supervision of any kind. No lights are allowed, and on opening the doors the hot foul air rushed out like a blast from a furnace. The only means of ventilation is to open the windows, and as these are situated immediately over the heads of the sleepers (among whom a hideous kind of ophthalmia is prevalent), they are usually kept closed.

But tomorrow we begin our inspection of the island.

May 13th. I sit down to write with about as much reluctance as I would sit down to relate my experience of a journey through a sewer.

I am mentally sick at the recollection of what I have seen today. First, however, to describe the place.

The island is about seven miles long and four broad. The most remarkable natural object is of course the Norfolk Island pine, which rears its stately head a hundred feet above the surrounding forest. The appearance of the place is very wild and beautiful, bringing to my mind the description of the romantic islands of the Pacific, which old geographers dwell upon so fondly. Lemon, lime, and guava trees abound, also oranges, grapes, figs, bananas, peaches, pomegranates, and pine apples. The climate just now is hot and muggy.

The approach to Kingstown – as the barracks and huts are called – is properly difficult. A long low reef – probably originally a portion of the barren rocks of Nepean and Phillip Islands, which rise east and west of the settlement – fronts the bay (*Sydney* Bay they call it!) and obstructs the entrance of vessels. We were landed in boats through an opening in this reef, and our vessel stands on and off within signalling distance. The surf washes almost against the walls of the military roadway that leads to the barracks.

Our journey yesterday was as follows: — First to the prisoners' barracks, which stand on an area of about three acres, surrounded by a lofty wall. A road runs between this wall and the sea. The barracks are three storeys high, and hold 790 men (let me remark here that there are more than 2,000 men on the island). There are 22 wards in this place. Each ward runs the depth of the building, viz., 18 feet, and in consequence is simply a funnel for hot or cold air to blow through. When the ward is filled the men's heads lie under the windows. The largest ward contains 100 men, the smallest 15. They sleep in hammocks, slung close to each other as on board ship, in two lines, with a passage down the centre. There is a wardsman to each ward. He is selected by the prisoners, and is generally therefore a 'colonial sentence' man of the worst character. He is supposed to keep order, but of course he never attempts to do so; indeed, as he is locked up in the ward every night from six o'clock in the evening until sunrise, *without light*, it is possible that he might get maltreated did he make himself obnoxious.

The barracks look upon the Barrack Square, which is filled with lounging prisoners. On the west side of the square stands the Roman Catholic Chapel, the sleeping wards of the (convict) sub-overseers, and a hospital ward. The windows of the hospital ward look upon the barrack-yard, and the prisoners are in constant communication with the patients. On the east side of the square is the Church of England Chapel, the stores, and the 'school-room', which is also, I am informed, used as a Courthouse when the Commissioners for the trial of offenders visit the island.

Close to the beach stand the Gaols and the Hospital. The latter is a low stone building capable of containing about twenty patients. I placed my hands on the wall, and found it damp. An ulcerous prisoner also said it was so, owing to the heavy surf constantly rolling so close beneath the building. There are two gaols, the old and the new. The old gaol stands near the sea, close to the landing-place. Outside it, at the door, is the Gallows. I touched it as I passed in. This horrible engine is the first thing that greets the eyes of a newly-arrived prisoner. The new gaol is barely completed, is of a pentagonal shape, and has eighteen radiating cells of a pattern approved by some wiseacre in England, who thinks that to prevent a man seeing his fellow-men is *not* the way to send him mad. In the old gaol are twenty-four prisoners, all heavily ironed, awaiting trial by the visiting Commission. Some of these poor ruffians, having committed their offences just after the last sitting of the Commission, have already been in gaol upwards of eleven months!

The prisoners are thrust four and five together in a cell. As well as I can reckon, there are only twenty-six cells – including the eighteen in the pentagon – at the settlement, and there are upwards of 1,000 men here, most of them doubly convicted villains from all parts of the colonies.

At six o'clock we saw the men mustered. I read prayers before the muster, and was surprised to find that some of the prisoners attended and some did not, but strolled about the yard, whistling, singing, and joking. The muster is a farce. The prisoners are not mustered outside and then marched to their wards, but they rush into the barracks indiscriminately, and place themselves dressed or undressed in their hammocks. A convict sub-overseer then calls out the names, and somebody replies. If an answer is returned to each name all is considered right. The lights are taken away, and save for a few minutes at eight o'clock, when the good-conduct men are let in, the ruffians are left to their own devices until morning. Anything more calculated to breed mutiny and encourage insubordination I cannot imagine. Knowing what I know of the customs of convicts, my heart sickens when I in imagination put myself in the place of a newly-transported man, plunged from six at night until daybreak into that foetid den of worse than wild beasts.

Complaint of violence would be out of the question. A terrorism is sternly and resolutely maintained to revenge not only exposure but even complaint, and threats of murder – often carried into effect – are rendered more alarming by the fact that the prisoners are in the general habit of carrying knives!

May 15th. There is a place enclosed between high walls adjoining the convict barracks, called the Lumber Yard. This is where the prisoners mess. It is roofed on two sides, and contains tables and benches. 600 men can mess here perhaps, but as 700 are always driven into it, it follows that the weakest men are compelled to sit on the ground. A more disorderly sight than this yard at meal times I never beheld. The cook-houses are adjoining it, and the men bake their meal-bread there. Outside the cook-house door the firewood is piled, and fires are made in all directions on the ground, round which sit the prisoners, frying their rations of fresh pork, baking their hominy cakes, chatting, and even smoking.

Owing to the lax state of discipline, tobacco and spirits are easily obtained by such of the prisoners as can afford to fee the sub-overseers. The principal objects of exchange are, portions of rations, carved boxes made out of the pine-wood, shoes, or cabbage-tree hats, at the manufacture of which the prisoners secretly work. Pounce discovered a roll of tobacco and several pairs of boots in one of the hammocks, and it appears that the pilfering of Government stores is perpetual.

The Lumber Yard is a sort of Alsatia, to which the hunted prisoner retires. I don't think that the boldest constable on the island would venture into that place to pick out a man from the seven hundred. If he did go in I don't think he would come out again alive.

And this in a place of restraint!

16th May. An intelligent sub-overseer, a man named Ferris, has been talking to me. He says that the sub-overseers' lives are not safe if they do their duty, and that he has been often threatened. I can believe him readily. Three or four men have been disposed of in this way, and the murderers have escaped. Ferris says that there are some forty of the oldest and worst prisoners who form what he calls the 'ring', and that the members of this ring are bound by an oath taken with hideous ceremony to support each other, and to avenge the punishment of any of their number. In proof of his assertions he instanced two cases of English prisoners who had refused to join in some crime, and had informed the stipendiary magistrate, Mr Earle, of the proceedings of the 'ring'. They were found in the morning strangled in their hammocks. An enquiry was held, but not a man out of the ninety in the ward would speak a word.

I am convinced that this mixing of English and colonial prisoners is very bad. Young men sentenced in England are sent directly to this pit of infamy. The 'old hands' contaminate the young by every means in their power. The day before yesterday some of these ruffians refused to go out to work, and nearly one hundred remained in the lumber yard. Several newly-joined prisoners were among them, and I am convinced that these last would have never attempted any such insubordination of their own accord.

I dread the task that is before me. How can I attempt to preach piety and morality to these men. How can I attempt even to save the less villainous?

17th May. Visited the wards today, and returned in despair. The condition of things is worse than I expected. It is not to be written. The English prisoners — and some of their histories are most touching ones — are insulted by the language and demeanour of these miscreants. The vilest crimes are perpetrated as jests. These are creatures who openly defy authority, whose language and conduct is such as was never before seen or heard out of Bedlam. There are men who are known to have murdered their comrades, and who boast of it. With these the English farm labourer, the tempted and fallen mechanic, the suspected but innocent victim of perjury or mistake, are indiscriminately herded. With them are mixed Chinamen from Hong Kong, the aborigines of New Holland, West Indian blacks, Greeks, Caffres, and Malays, soldiers for desertion, idiots, madmen, pigstealers, and pickpockets.

The dreadful place seems set apart for all that is hideous and vile in our common nature. In its recklessness, its insubordination, its filth, and its despair it realises to my mind the notion of hell.

May 20th. Dined at the Commandant's today, and see no reason to repent of my opinion of him. He is a weak, but impetuous good-natured man. The newly appointed stipendiary magistrate, Mr Earle, seems to have taken all power out of his hands, and to manage the island as he likes. Pounce is much taken with

Earle, and owns that he is a most efficient and valuable officer, and that, had it not been for his severity, the prisoners would have mutinied long since.

Earle has established a sort of secret police by raising the most infamous ruffians in the place to the rank of constables, and giving them power to do as they please to prisoners. His severity is as ill-timed as Pratt's leniency is ill-considered. I am anxious for Pounce's report, for the lives of the wretched convict sub-overseers promoted to their dangerous posts *against their own wishes* are not safe for one day.

By the way, let me apologize to Mr Pounce for not seeing his good qualities sooner. Though pompous and saturated with official snobbery, he is courageous, honest, and acute. He smells an abuse at once, knows to an ounce how many sweet potatoes 'balance' the loss of 2 lbs. of meat, and is provided with an official remedy, consisting usually of 'forms', 'requisitions', and 'approvals' for any and every evil.

From what he said at dinner, I gather that his report will be unfavourable to Pratt, as, indeed, how should it not. I wish things were settled.

May 21st. Entered today officially upon my duties as Religious Instructor at the Settlement. Let me set down the instructions issued by Her Majesty's Government.

'The duties of the Religious Instructor,' says the Comptroller General of Convicts,

are of that nature that they cannot be minutely defined. In most instances they will depend on the circumstances around him, and these must be taken advantage of at his discretion.

His prescribed duties will be as follows: – He will perform divine service to the assembled gang twice on every Sunday. He will also twice on every Sunday instruct the convicts in the fundamental truths of religion on the Sunday School principle. This duty will be under his sole direction, and such educated convicts of good conduct as can be selected by the superintendent for monitors will be employed under his orders.

The gang is to be assembled for morning and evening prayers before going out to work and at sunset, and at these times the religious instructor will perform such services as he may think most suitable.

He will daily visit the sick in hospital, for the purpose of affording them instruction and advice. He will likewise daily visit the separate apartments and solitary cells, and afford instruction and advice to their inmates.

The Religious Instructor should assiduously study the disposition and character of the individual characters composing the gang, to enable him in conjunction with the superintendent to make the report prescribed in the regulations of the first stage of probation.

A school will be established at each station under the immediate superintendence and care of the religious instructor.

The libraries established at the various stations are to be under his care and management.

Let me pause to observe here that the 'library' is a mockery and a farce. With the exception of some odd volumes of *Chambers' Journal*, some numbers of the *Penny Magazine*, the *Saturday Magazine*, and a few historical and geographical works of the dryest and most uninteresting nature, the 'library' consists of doctrinal pamphlets. There are but 500 volumes altogether, and 200 are collections of penny tracts of a virulently sectarian character. I can imagine Mooney, who told me today that his Maker was the Virgin Mary, puzzling his brain over 'Henry, the little Anglo-Indian', which relates how a boy of eight years of age attacked, and defeated, his Dissenting aunt on the question of Infant Baptism! I must try and get some of this rubbish removed, and a few readable and amusing books substituted. In support of my course of action, if any support is needed, I may cite poor Markham, whom I saw this morning. This man was a London solicitor in large practice, and a leading member of several literary and scientific institutions. He says that a client introduced some fraudulent business to his office, and that for a supposed guilty knowledge of these transactions he was transported for life. He assures me of his innocence, and his friends are trying hard to obtain a pardon for him. This man – criminal or not – is a highly cultivated, quiet, and inoffensive person. I found him in solitary confinement in the new gaol. He implored me to get him some book to read, showing the one the gaoler had brought him. It was an odd volume of Blair's sermons. Markham was undergoing four days' solitary for having tobacco. I asked Hailey, one of Earle's new police, how he came to find tobacco on Markham, as he had assured me that he did not smoke. Hailey replied that he had not found any tobacco, but that he saw the traces of it on Markham's tongue! Hailey was a burglar, and previous to Jackman's arrival, bore a very bad character.

There seems no medium between extreme violence towards unoffending prisoners, and extreme indulgence towards desperadoes.

An occurrence took place today which shows the dangerous condition of the 'Ring'. I accompanied Mr Pounce this morning to the Lumber Yard, and, on our entry, we observed a man in the crowd round the cook-house deliberately smoking. The Chief Constable of the Island – my old friend Troke – seeing that this exhibition attracted Pounce's notice, pointed out the man to an assistant. The assistant, Jacob Gimblett, advanced and desired the prisoner to surrender the pipe. The man plunged his hands into his pockets, and, with a gesture of the most profound contempt, walked away to that part of the mess-shed where the 'Ring' congregate.

'Take the scoundrel to gaol,' cries Troke.

No one moved.

The man at the gate that leads through the carpenters' shop into the barracks called to us to come out, saying that the prisoners would never suffer the man to be taken.

Pounce, however, with more determination than I gave him credit for, kept his ground, and insisted that so flagrant a breach of discipline should not be suffered to pass unnoticed. Thus urged, Mr Troke pushed through the crowd, and made for the spot whither the man had withdrawn himself.

The yard was now buzzing like a disturbed hive, and I momentarily expected that a rush would be made upon us. In a few moments the prisoner appeared, attended by, rather than in the custody of, the Chief Constable of the island. He advanced to the unlucky assistant constable, who was standing close to me, and asked,

'What have you ordered me to gaol for?'

The man made some reply advising him to go quietly, when the convict raised his fist and deliberately felled the man to the ground.

'You had better retire, gentlemen,' says Troke. 'I see them getting out their knives.'

We made for the gate, and the crowd closed in like a sea upon the two constables. I expected murder, but in a few moments Troke and Gimblett appeared, borne along by a mass of men, dusty, but unharmed, and having the convict between them.

He sulkily raised a hand as he passed me, either to rectify the position of his straw hat, or to offer a tardy apology. A more wanton, unprovoked, and flagrant outrage than that of which this man was guilty I never witnessed. It is customary for 'the old dogs' to use the most opprobrious language to their officers, and to this a deaf ear is usually turned, but I never before saw a man wantonly strike a constable. I fancy that the act was done out of bravado. Troke informed me that the man's name is Rufus Dawes, and that he is considered the worst man on the island; that to secure him, he (Troke) was obliged to use the language of expostulation; that he dared not have seized him, and that, but for the presence of an officer accredited by His Excellency, he dared not have acted as he had done.

This is the same man, then, whom I injured at Port Arthur. Seven years of 'discipline' don't seem to have done him much good. His sentence is 'life' — a lifetime in this place! Troke says that he was the terror of Port Arthur, and that they sent him here when a 'weeding' of the prisoners was made. He has been here four years. Poor wretch!

24th May. After prayers, I saw Dawes. He was confined in the Old Gaol, and seven others were in the well with him. He came out at my request, and stood leaning against the door-post. He has much changed from the man I remember. Seven years ago, he was a stalwart, upright, *handsome* man. He has become a beetle-browed, sullen, slouching ruffian. His hair is grey, though he cannot be more than forty years of age, and his frame has lost that just proportion of parts which, despite his muscularity, made him almost graceful. His face also has grown like other convict faces — how hideously alike they all are ! — and, save for his black eyes and a peculiar trick he has of compressing his lips, I should not have recognised him. Yet at one time his features were as marked as those of my host Carr, whom I should recognise anywhere. How habitual sin and misery suffice to tantalise 'the human face divine!' I said but little, for the other prisoners were listening, eager, as it appeared to me, to witness my discomfiture. It is evident that Rufus Dawes has been accustomed to meet the ministrations of my predecessor with insolence. I spoke to him for a few minutes about mundane matters, saying how foolish it was to rebel against an authority superior in strength to himself. He did not answer, and the only emotion he evinced during the interview was when I reminded him that we had met before. He shrugged one shoulder as if in pain or anger, and seemed about to speak, but casting his eyes upon the group in the cell, relapsed into silence again. I must get speech with him alone. One can do nothing with a man if seven other devils worse than himself are locked up with him.

I sent for Ferris and asked him about cells. He says that the gaol is crowded to suffocation. 'Solitary confinement' is a farce. There are six men, each sentenced to solitary confinement, in a cell together. This cell is called the 'nunnery'. It is small, and the six men were naked to the waist when I entered, the perspiration pouring in streams off their naked bodies! It is disgusting to write of such things. It is rumoured that Earle, fearful of the result of the Report, is about to make strenuous efforts to subdue the men before the new Commandant arrives — for everybody takes it for granted that we shall have a new Commandant.

26th June. Pounce departed in the *Lady Franklin* for Hobart Town. The *Lady Franklin* is commanded by an old man named Blunt, a fellow to whom I have taken one of my inexplicable and unreasoning dislikes.

28th June. Earle is making himself most oppressive to the prisoners. He has organised three parties of police. One patrols the fields, one is on guard at stores and public buildings, and the third is employed as a detective force. There are two hundred soldiers on the island, and the officer in charge, Captain McNab, has been induced by Earle to increase their duties in many ways. The cords of discipline are suddenly drawn tight. For the disorder which prevailed when I landed, Jackman has substituted a sudden and excessive rigour. Any officer found giving the smallest piece of tobacco to a prisoner is liable to removal from the island. The tobacco which grows wild has been rooted up and destroyed lest the men should obtain a leaf of it. The privilege of having a pannikin of hot water when the gangs came in from field labour in the evening has been withdrawn. The shepherds, hut-keepers, and all other prisoners, whether at the stations of Longridge or the Cascades (where the English convicts are stationed), are forbidden to keep a parrot or any other bird. The plaiting of straw hats during the prisoners' leisure hours is also prohibited. At the settlement where the 'old hands' are located railed boundaries have been erected, beyond which no prisoner dare pass unless to work. Two days ago Job Dodd, a negro, let his jacket fall over the boundary rails, crossed them to recover it, and was severely flogged. The floggings are hideously frequent. On flogging mornings I have seen the ground where the men stood at the triangles saturated with human gore, as if a bucket of blood had been spilled on it, covering a space three feet in diameter, and running out in various directions, in little streams of two or three feet long. I examined the punishment record yesterday, and found that during the last sixteen months *twenty thousand six hundred and twenty-four* lashes have been inflicted! Miscreants of the worst character are appointed to the offices of warders and constables, and their activity in 'getting up charges' knows no bounds. No prisoner in gang is allowed to have a knife, pipe, book, bit of thread, half-penny, or even a needle in his possession. All this has produced an outward show of regularity and order, but unless I much mistake a mutiny is brewing.

June 29th. I discovered today the reason why the men refused to work for two days, as I noted on the 16th May. It was because they had not been fed! It appears that in January last their potato gardens were taken from them and ploughed up, and for ten days *half a pint of island grown peas* was issued to them in lieu of the regulation allowance of 2 lbs. of sweet potatoes. On the 10th of January the peas were all consumed, and until the 20th of January half a pound of biscuit was issued. On the

21st they got nothing but their usual ration, to wit 1 lb. of salt beef (*boiled down to 8 oz.*), 1 lb. of maize meal, and ½ oz. of sugar (frequently bad) daily. The men refused to work unless they received full ration, and so, instead of the 2 lbs. of potatoes, *half a pound of inferior wheaten flour* was issued. On the 5th May there was no meal in store (owing to official negligence in providing supplies), and the prisoners were informed that 2 *oz. of salt pork* would be in future issued instead of 2 lbs. of potatoes! Ferris says that the mingled indignation and ridicule with which this order was received by the convicts was terrible. When the morsel of salt pork was brought into the mess-yard it was flung against the wall with fierce execrations. Victims of bad management and official negligence, the men were filled with disgust and hatred.

That they are for the most part execrable villains and scoundrels cannot be denied, but it is true the boasted system of convict management as applied to them has proved not only utterly useless for good, but horribly provocative of the most frightful evil.

June 30th. Saw Rufus Dawes this morning. He still continues sullen and morose. His papers are very bad. He seems to be perpetually up for punishment. I am informed that he and a man named Eastwood, nicknamed Jacky Jacky, glory in being the leaders of the 'Ring', and that they openly avow themselves weary of life. Can it be that the flogging which the poor creature got at Port Arthur was instrumental in bringing him to this horrible state of mind? It is quite possible. Oh, James North, pray Heaven to let you redeem one soul at least, to plead for your own sinful one at the Judgment Seat.

I took a holiday this afternoon, and walked in the direction of Mount Pitt. The scenery was lovely. The island lay at my feet like a gorgeous bouquet dropped upon a bed of heliotrope. No, the simile is tame. Like a gem floating on a purple ocean. Like – as sings Mrs Frere's favourite poet – 'a summer's isle of Eden lying in dark purple sphere of sea.' Sophocles has the same idea in the *Philoctetes*, but I can't quote it. Note: I measured a Pine twenty-three feet in circumference. I followed a little brook that runs from the hills, and winds through thick undergrowths of creeper and blossom, until it reaches a lovely valley surrounded by lofty trees, whose branches, linked together by the luxurious grape-vine, form an arching bower of bloomy verdure. Here stands the ruin of an old hut, formerly inhabited by the early settlers; lemons, figs, and guavas are thick; while amid the scrub and cane a large convolvulus is intertwined, and stars the green with its purple and crimson flowers.

I sat down here, and had a smoke.

It seems that the former occupant of my rooms at the settlement read French; for in searching for a book to bring with me – I never walk without a book – I found and pocketed a volume of Balzac. It proved to be a portion of the *Vie Privée* series, and I stumbled upon a story called *La Fausse Maîtresse*. With that calm belief in the Paris of his imagination – where Marcas was a politician, Macingen a banker, Gobseck a money-lender, and Vautrin a candidate for Cayenne – Balzac introduces me to a Pole by name Paz, who, loving the wife of his friend, devotes himself to watch over her happiness and her husband's interest. The husband gambles and is profligate. Paz informs the wife that the leanness which hazard and debauchery have caused to the domestic exchequer is due to *his* extravagance, the husband having lent him money. She does not believe, and Paz feigns an intrigue with a circus-rider in order to lull all suspicions. She says to her adored spouse, 'Get rid of this extravagant friend! Away with him! He is a profligate, a gambler! A drunkard!' Paz finally departs, and when he has gone the lady finds out the poor Pole's worth. The story ends unsatisfactorily of course. Balzac was too great a master of his realistic art to *finish* his books. In real life the curtain never falls on a comfortably finished drama. The play goes on eternally.

I have been thinking of the story all the evening. A man who loves his friend's wife, and devotes his energies to increase her happiness by concealing from her her husband's follies! Surely none but Balzac would have hit upon such a notion. 'A man who loves his friend's wife.' – Asmodeus, I write no more. I have ceased to converse with thee for so long that I blush to confess all that I have in my heart. – I will *not* confess it, so that shall suffice.

July 2nd. My prediction has been fulfilled. There has been a fatal and disastrous outbreak of the prisoners.

⊷ *4* ⊶

THE RIOT OF THE 1ST JULY, 1846

On the 30th June, 1846, Mr Earle, the stipendiary magistrate, signified to Mr Anthony Troke, the acting chief constable, his pleasure that all pots and kettles hitherto used by prisoners in the Lumber Yard should be removed.

'But,' says Troke, 'they have been accustomed for so long to use them that they have come to consider it a right.'

'Perhaps, Mr Troke,' remarks Earle, 'you will be good enough to do your duty.'

'Oh certainly,' says Troke; and taking Ferris and Gimblett with him, he proceeded that evening to the Lumber-yard, and carried off the kettles.

'I am afraid there will be a row, Jack,' said Troke, 'for as these things have been made by prisoners they regard them as their own property.'

'If there is,' says Ferris, 'I wash my hands of it. Earle's coming it too strong, and so he'll find.'

In the morning the prisoners were mustered as usual, and after prayers marched to the Lumber Yard to breakfast.

'Hullo!' says Cavan, a notorious bushranger, 'where's our kettles?'

The overseer Smith, in the Cook-house, made some feeble reply, but the murmurs and the crowd increased.

'Send for Troke,' says Smith to a constable named Stevens, 'or there'll be murder done!'

Stevens slips through the crowd, and runs to Troke's quarters. In the meantime the mass of men are angrily talking among themselves. Patrick Sullivan, assistant superintendent over doubly-convicted prisoners, goes to the Cook-house and consults with Smith. As he comes out the men set up a great yell, and call upon him to 'come on,' taunting him in their convict slang.

Sullivan, who is not without courage, steps among them. A man named Edwards has apparently been haranguing them.

'What is the matter, Eastwood?' asks Sullivan of Jacky-Jacky.

'Something's the matter; I don't know what!' he replies, and then heading the main body of prisoners, rushes out of the Lumber-yard to the convict Barrack-stores. There they possess themselves of the kettles, and, flushed with success, return to the yard.

'What now, boys?' cries Edwards.

'To — with all these tyrants,' says Eastwood. 'Follow me; I'll lead you; but you follow me to death!'

Smith, crouching behind the Cook-house, looks in vain for Stevens, and hears some one call to Ryder, the constable at the gate, 'Save yourself, Ryder! They have sworn to have your life! They remember you at Port Arthur!'

Ryder, who had been an overseer at that place, and who was noted for his treachery to prisoners, made an effort to escape into the Barrack-yard, but seeing that place also a-buzz drew back.

At that moment Eastwood, followed by some twenty of the Ring, armed with poles and splinters of wood, rushed into the Cook-house.

Smith ran to the far end, crying 'Spare me!'

Eastwood struck him, and he fell dead. In an instant his body was mangled beyond recognition.

'To the Gate!' cries the frantic wretch, brandishing his bloody cudgel – 'to the Gate!'

Ryder makes no effort to prevent the passage of the stream through the covered archway, but sits crouching against the wall, paralysed with terror.

Jacky-Jacky, maddened for blood, wantonly spatters his brains against the wall with a furious blow, and, screaming, makes for a group of constables, who stand, terror-stricken, outside the yard.

'Let's begin with these,' cries Eastwood, 'we'll settle them first!' and aims a tremendous blow at Ferris.

Ferris leaps aside, and the stake strikes his comrade, Pinkney, on the shoulder.

Pinkney attempts to clutch the maniac's arm, but is overwhelmed and borne down in a moment.

Triumphant Eastwood sees an axe standing against the hut wall, seizes it, and rushes into the hut crying,

'Where's Dog Brown?'

A constable, named Saxton, says,

'Not here, you bloody villain!' and strikes at Eastwood with his bare hands.

'Kill him, Jack!' cries an old man, named Donovan; and Eastwood fells him with the axe.

Sub-constable Quin, who is in bed, raises himself, and rubbing his eyes, says,

'Eastwood, I saw who did that!'

'Did you?' says Eastwood, with an oath. 'That's all you will see, then,' and strikes him in the jaw with the axe.

In the meantime, Stevens, running to Troke's quarters, cries,

'The men are rushing the Barrack-store. Come down!'

'Have you sent to the Commandant?' asked Troke.

'Yes. Come down; there's murder doing.'

Troke runs into the Barrack-yard, and sees several of the convict constables jumping out of the windows.

'They've taken the barracks!' he cries. 'Let's go back!'

A man named Douglas calls out of the window,

'Run, Mr Troke; they're looking out for you.'

'Where's Smith?' says Troke to Stevens.

Stevens, pointing to the Cook-house, fancies he hears a cry, but Troke declares it may be a ruse of the prisoners to get him and murder him, and declines to go.

The prisoners in the yard cluster round angrily, but a party of military appear at the gate. The drums roll at the barracks, and the tramp of soldiers is heard on the road. The men sulkily retreat towards the barracks, and presently Eastwood and his party, driven in at the point of the bayonet, are surrounded and made prisoners. Troke and others, searching for blood-stains, arrest six men.

'Why did you do it, Eastwood?' asks Ferris, as the dead bodies of Smith and Ryder are borne past the manacled group.

'Because I am tired of my life!' says desperate Eastwood. 'They must hang me now.'

Troke did not venture to contradict a proposition so self-evident, but contented himself with observing,

'The Commission's due in a day or so, so you won't have long to wait.'

During the next three days, two hundred men were lodged in the gaols and boat-houses, awaiting trial for participation in the riots.

'It's a good thing for you that we have you in quod,' says Troke to Dawes.

'If you hadn't,' says Dawes, 'you wouldn't be here now. Had I been in Jacky's shoes, I wouldn't have left one of ye alive!'

Troke reported this speech to Earle, who ordered Rufus Dawes to the chain-gang. 'The whole island is in a state of mutiny,' said Earle. 'A pretty condition of things for the new Commandant!'

◄◄ 5 ►►

Extracted from the Diary of the Rev. James North

August 4th. The new Commandant has arrived with his family. – He is no less a person than Captain Maurice Frere!

Have I reason to be glad or sorry?

◄◄ 6 ►►

Extracted from the Diary of the Rev. James North

August 24th. There has been but one entry in my journal since the fatal second of July, and that but to record the advent of our Commandant.

So great have been the changes which have taken place, that I scarcely know how to record them. Captain Frere has realised my worst anticipations. He is brutal, vindictive, and domineering. His knowledge of prisons and prisoners gives him an advantage over Burgess, otherwise he much resembles that murderous animal. He has but one thought – to keep the prisoners in subjection. As long as the island is quiet, he cares not whether the men live or die.

'I was sent down here to keep order,' said he to me, a few days after his arrival, 'and by God, sir, I'll do it.'

He has done it, I must admit; but at a cost of a legacy of hate to himself, that he may some day regret to have earned.

Earle was bad enough; but Frere, having the excuse of the mutiny of July, is fifty times worse. It seems that the most exaggerated notions of the liberality of Major Pratt got abroad in Hobart-town and Sydney. Mrs Frere tells me that the people there were under the impression that the prisoners did as they pleased, were never locked up, and roamed the island at will.

'My husband,' said she (how women defend their husbands!) 'received the most peremptory orders from the Van Diemen's Land authorities to bring the prisoners under subjection, and his measures are all taken for the best, I am sure.'

I could but sigh and say nothing. I have long ago discovered that the notions of Captain Frere and his wife do not agree in many points. At the same time, let me say, with that strict justice I love to mete out to those I hate, that the island is in a condition of abject submission. There is not much chance of another mutiny. The men go to their work without a murmur, and slink to their dormitories like whipped hounds to kennel. The gaols, and solitary (!) cells are crowded with prisoners, and each day sees fresh sentences for fresh crimes. It is crime here to do anything but live.

The method by which Captain Frere has brought about this repose of desolation is characteristic of him. He sets on every man to spy upon his neighbour, awes the more daring into obedience by the display of a ruffianism more outrageous than their own, and raising the worst scoundrels in the place to office, compels them to find 'cases' for punishment.

His reason for this mode of proceeding is also characteristic.

'It is impossible, Captain Frere,' said I, one day, during the initiation of this system, 'to think that these villains whom you have made constables will do their duty.'

His reply was,

'They *must* do their duty. If they are indulgent to the prisoners, they know I shall flog 'em. If they do what I tell 'em, they'll make themselves so hated that they'd have their own father up to the triangles to save themselves being sent back to the ranks.'

'You treat them then like slave keepers of a wild beast den. They must flog the animals to avoid being flogged themselves.'

'Ay,' said he, with his coarse laugh, 'and having once flogged 'em, they'd do anything rather than be put in the cage, don't ye see.'

It is horrible to think of this sort of logic being used by a man who has a wife and child, and friends and enemies. It is the logic that the Keeper of the Tormented would use, I should think.

One good thing he has done. He has settled the 'ration' question. On my representing to him what I believed to be the true reason of the mutiny, namely, insufficient food and wanton interference with the men's meat and drink, he yesterday gave notice that in future 18 ounces of flour would be served out daily to each man. This is only gaol allowance in Van Diemen's Land, but it is a welcome boon to the gangs here. Nevertheless, the monstrous method of *espionage* and brutality by far outbalances this act of justice. The worst villains are made constables. Perfidy is rewarded. It has been made part of a convict-policeman's duty to search a fellow-prisoner anywhere and at any time. This searching is often conducted in a wantonly rough, and disgusting manner; and if resistance is offered, the man resisting can be knocked down by a blow from the searcher's bludgeon. Inquisitorial vigilance and indiscriminating harshness prevail everywhere, and the lives of hundreds of prisoners are reduced to a continual agony of terror and self-loathing.

I am sick unto death of the place. It makes me think less of my fellow-creatures. It makes me a disbeliever in the social charities. It takes out of penal science anything it may possess of nobility or worth. It is cruel, debasing, inhuman.

August 26th. Saw Rufus Dawes again to-day. His usual bearing is ostentatiously rough and brutal. He seems to have sunk to that pitch of self-abasement in which one takes a delight in one's misery. This condition is one familiar to me.

He is working in the chain-gang to which Ferris was made sub-overseer. Blind Mooney, an ophthalmic prisoner, who was removed from the gang to hospital, told me that there was a plot to murder Ferris, on account of the evidence he had given against Eastwood, but that Dawes had prevented it.

I saw Ferris and told him of this, asking him if he had been aware of the plot.

He said 'No,' falling into a great tremble. 'Major Pratt promised me a removal if I would give evidence,' said he. 'I expected it would come to this.' I asked him why Dawes defended him; and, after some trouble, he told me, exacting from me a promise that I would not acquaint the Commandant. It seems that one morning last week Ferris had gone up to the Commandant's house with a return from Troke, and coming back through the garden had plucked a flower. Dawes had asked him for this flower, offering two days' ration for it. Ferris, who is not a bad-hearted man, gave him the sprig. 'There were tears in his eyes as he took it,' said Ferris.

There must be some way to get at this man's heart, bad as he seems to be.

August 28th. Ferris was murdered yesterday. He applied to be removed from the gaol gang, but Frere refused.

'I never let my men "funk",' he said. 'If they've threatened to murder you, I'll keep you there another month in spite of 'em.'

Someone who overheard this, reported it to the gang, and they set upon the unfortunate gaoler yesterday and beat his brains out with their shovels. Troke says that the wretch who was foremost cried,

'There's for you; and if your master don't take care, he'll get served the same one of these days!'

The gang were employed at building a reef in the sea, and were working up to their armpits in water. Ferris fell into the surf, and never moved after the first blow. I saw the gang, and Dawes said,

'It was Frere's fault; he should have let the man go!'

'I am surprised you did not interfere,' said I.

'I've done all I can,' was the man's answer. 'What's a life more or less *here*!'

This occurrence has spread consternation among the overseers, and they have addressed a 'round-robin' to the Commandant. This document sets forth the dreadful condition of the place better than I could describe it by the writing of a dozen pages.

Norfolk Island, August 28th, 1846[1]

SIR, It is the wish of the prisoner sub-overseers to draw your attention to the man Ferris, that lost his life yesterday in doing his duty as a sub-overseer. He was tried for saying a few words to Mr T—, a free overseer, and got detained on the island, or else he would have gone up by the last ship. Now, we wish to show you the way we are situated; that we are not safe from one hour to another; but we may share the same fate as Ferris.

We can assure you, sir, the ration is not sufficient for us who are doing nothing, and we have not lost all feelings of humanity towards our fellow-prisoners. But if we drive them at work on a hungry belly, we may rest assured some very serious consequences will result from our doing so. The men may work on a fair scale of rations, but on a hungry belly they cannot work. You must be well aware that a *sub-overseer on this island is thought as bad as a hangman*; and if anyone offends the men in our gangs, they vent their spleen on the sub-overseers; and if we speak ever so civilly to them about their work, they answer, 'We are as well off dead as alive.' And we, the sub-overseers, get nothing but frowns from everyone, and if there is not proper steps taken to better our situations, we shall, against our inclination, be forced to give up our billets as sub-overseers.

Sir, if you will be pleased to take this into consideration before it is too late, the men here mentioned will feel thankful. Sir, we do not write this to give offence, or in any saucy way, but only what we think we are in duty bound for the safety of our lives.

(Signed)

> P. STEVENS,
> J. JOYCE,
> C: NORTON,
> N. MATHEWS,
> J. GIMBLETT,

And ten other sub-overseers, prisoners of the Crown.

To Captain Maurice Frere, etc., etc.

1. An authentic document.

To me, this document, which mingles so strangely courage and servility, terror and humanity, speaks volumes. To what a condition must men have been brought when, under a conviction that their lives were in danger, they could write such a letter as this!

The way Frere has dealt with it was characteristic, and fills me with abomination and disgust. He came down with it in his hand to the gaol-gang, walked into the yard, shut the gate, and said, 'I've just got this from my overseers. They say they're afraid *you'll* murder them, as you murdered Ferris. Now, if you want to murder, murder *me*. Here I am. Step out one of you.' All this, said in a tone of the most galling contempt, did not move them. I saw a dozen pairs of eyes flash hatred, but the bull-dog courage of the man overawed them here, as, I am told, it had done in Sydney. It would have been easy to kill him then and there, and his death, I am told, is sworn among them; but no one raised a finger. The only man who moved was Rufus Dawes, and he checked himself instantly. Frere, with a recklessness of which I did not think him capable, stepped up to this terror of the prison, and ran his hands lightly down his sides, as is the custom with constables when 'searching' a man. Dawes – who is of a fierce temper – turned crimson at this bravado, and I thought would have struck him, but he did not. Frere then – still unarmed and alone – proceeded to taunt the man, saying, 'How are you, Dawes? Do you think of bolting again, Dawes? Have you made any more boats?'

'You Devil!' said the chained man, in voice pregnant with such weight of unborn murder, that the gang winced.

'You'll find me one,' said Frere, with a laugh; and, turning to me, continued, in the same jesting tone, 'There's a penitent for you, Mr North – try your hand on him.'

I was speechless at his audacity, and must have shown my disgust in my face, for he coloured slightly, and as we were leaving the yard, endeavoured to excuse himself, by saying that it was no use preaching to stones, and such doubly-dyed villains as this Dawes were past hope. 'I know the ruffian of old,' said he. 'He came out in the ship with me, and tried to raise a mutiny on board. He was the man who nearly murdered my wife.

He has never been out of irons – except then and when he escaped – for the last eighteen years; and as he's three life sentences, he's like to die in 'em.'

'What was he transported for?' I asked.

'Murder.'

A monstrous wretch and criminal evidently, and yet I feel a strange sympathy with this outcast.

⊷ 7 ⊶

IN WHICH THE CHAPLAIN IS TAKEN ILL

THOUGH the Commandant's house was comfortable and well furnished, and though, of necessity, all that was most hideous in the 'discipline' of the place was hidden, Dora felt the loathing with which she had approached the last and most dreaded abiding place of the elaborate convict system, under which it had been her misfortune to live, had not decreased. The sights and sounds of pain and punishment surrounded her. She could not look out of her windows without a shudder. She dreaded each evening when her husband returned, lest he should blurt out some fresh atrocity. She feared to ask him in the morning whither he was going, lest he should thrill her with the expectation of some fresh punishment.

'I wish, Maurice, we had never come here,' said she, piteously, when he recounted to her the scene of the gaol-gang. 'These unhappy men will do you some frightful injury one of these days.'

'Stuff!' said her husband. 'They've not the courage. I'd take the best man among them and dare him to touch me.'

'I cannot think how you like to witness so much misery and villany. It is horrible to me to think of.'

'Our tastes differ, my dear. – Jenkins! Confound you! Jenkins, I say.'

The convict-servant entered.

'Where is the charge-book? I've told you always to have it ready for me. Why don't you do as you are told? You loafing, lazy scoundrel. I suppose you were yarning in the cook-house, or –'

'If you please, sir –'

'Don't answer me, sir. Give me the book.' Taking it and running his finger down the leaves, he commented on the list of offences to which he would be called upon in the morning to mete out judgment.

Meer-a-Seek, having a pipe – the rascally Hindoo scoundrel! – *Benjamin Pellett, having fat in his possession. James Howarth, W. Colman, and N. Mar, malingering* – I'll cure their complaint for them without a doctor. *M. Byrne, not walking fast enough* – We must enliven Mr Byrne. *John Tree, absent from muster. Thomas Twist, having a pipe and striking a light. W. Barnes, not in place at muster; says he was 'washing himself'* – I'll wash him! *John Richards, missing muster and insolence. F. Mackintosh, misconduct in refusing to work. John Gateby, insolence and insubordination. J. McCullen, insolence and foul language* – I'll make that scoundrel jump it yet, or I'll know the reason why.[1] *Rufus Dawes, gross insolence, refusing to work* – Ah! we must look after you. You are a parson's man, are you? I'll break your spirit my man, or I'll – Dora!'

'Yes.'

'Your friend Dawes is doing credit to his bringing up.'

'What do you mean?'

'That infernal villain and reprobate Dawes. He is fitting himself faster for —'

She interrupted him.

'Maurice, I wish you would not use such language. You know I dislike it.'

She spoke coldly and sadly, as one who knows that remonstrance is vain, and is yet constrained to remonstrate.

'Oh,' returned her husband. 'It's only a fashion of speaking. I didn't mean anything.'

'It is an offensive fashion. There is no necessity to use such words.'

'Oh, dear! My Lady Proper! can't bear to hear her husband swear. How refined we're getting!'

1. *To jump it*, in convict slang, means to turn informer.

'There, I did not mean to annoy you,' said she, wearily. 'Don't let us quarrel, for goodness sake. Dinner will be ready in a minute; you had better change your clothes.'

'What have we got to-day? That everlasting pork, I suppose.'

'I really don't know, dear. I suppose so.'

He went away noisily, and she sat looking at the carpet wearily, waiting for his return. Was she thinking of the mistake she had made in marrying the admirable convict disciplinarian? It was fortunate, perhaps, for her peace that she had had few opportunities of comparing him with other men of a nature more suited to her own. A noise startled her. She looked up and saw North. Her face beamed instantly.

'Ah! Mr North, I did not expect you. What brings you here? You'll stay to dinner, of course.' (She rang the bell without waiting for a reply). 'Mr North dines here; place a chair for him. And have you brought me the book? I have been looking for it.'

'Here it is,' said North, producing a volume of 'Monte Cristo.' 'I envy you.'

She seized the book with avidity, and, after running her eyes over the pages, turned to the fly-leaf.

'It belongs to my predecessor,' says North, as though in answer to her thought. 'He seems to have been a great reader of French. I have found many French novels of his.'

'I thought clergymen never read French novels,' said Dora, with a smile.

'There are French novels and French novels,' said North. 'Stupid people confound the good with the bad. I remember a worthy friend of mine in Sydney who soundly abused me for reading "Rabelais," and when I asked him if *he* had read it, he said that he would sooner cut his hand off than open it. Admirable judge of its merits!'

'But is this really good? Papa told me it was rubbish.'

'It is a romance, but, in my opinion, a very fine one. The notion of the sailor being taught in prison by the priest, and sent back into the world, an accomplished gentleman, to work his vengeance, is superb.'

'Now, now — you are telling me,' laughed she; and then, with feminine perversity, 'Go on, what is the story?'

'Only that of an unjustly imprisoned man, who escaping by a marvel, and becoming rich – as Dr Johnson says, "beyond the bounds of avarice," – devotes his life and fortune to revenge himself.'

'And does he?'

'Read –!'

'No, but – you provoking man – tell me.'

'He does, upon all his enemies save one.'

'And he –?'

'*She* – was the wife of his greatest enemy, and Dantes spared her because he loved her.'

Dora turned away her head with a slight blush.

'It seems common-place enough,' said she, coldly.

'Of course; such matters are too common-place.'

There was a silence for a moment, which each seemed afraid to break. North bit his lips, as though regretting what he had said. Mrs Frere beat her foot on the floor, and at length raising her eyes, and meeting those of the clergyman fixed upon her face, rose hurriedly.

'Dotty!'

The child, who was in the next room, gravely occupied in some infantile absurdity, ran in, and the mother, kissing her, regained her composure.

'Here is Mr North, Dotty,' said she.

North took the child on his knee, and pressed his lips upon the same spot where the mother's had rested an instant before.

She slipped from his arms quickly, as though the caress had pained her.

Frere entered at that moment, and the infatuated clergyman felt his knees shake under him, and he stammered, as though his host had caught him in the act of pocketting one of the numerous knicknacks that lay scattered over the tables.

'Come to dinner, of course!' said Frere, who, though he found himself unaccountably beginning to dislike the clergyman, yet was glad of anybody who would help him to pass a cheerful evening. 'Take Mrs Frere. Come, Dot!'

'I – I came to bring Mrs Frere a book.'

'Ah. She reads too many books. She's always reading books.

It is not a good thing to be always poring over print, is it, North? You have some influence with her. Tell her so.'

He spoke with that affectation of jollity with which husbands of his calibre veil their bad temper.

Dora had her defensive armour on in a twinkling.

'Of course, you two men will be against me. When did two men ever disagree upon the subject of wifely duties? However, I shall read in spite of you. Do you know, Mr North, that when I married I made a special agreement with Captain Frere that I was not to be asked to sew buttons on for him?'

'Indeed!' says blind North, not understanding this change of humour.

'And she never has from that hour,' says Frere. 'I never have a shirt fit to put on. Upon my word – there are a dozen in the drawer now.'

'Mrs Frere, I don't believe that,' says North, constrained to say something. 'He is calumniating you.'

'No, he never does that. He only swears dreadfully when his collars won't fasten – Dotty, put down that spoon.'

'It is a woman's mission to sew on buttons,' says Frere, tossing off his wine. 'What is it Shakspeare says, "To – to" –'

'– Sew on buttons and chronicle small beer,' says Dora.

'Something of that sort. And, by Jove, he's right! Household duties, by Jove! That's the sphere for women!'

North perused his plate uncomfortably. A saying of omniscient Balzac occurred to him. 'Le grand écueil est le ridicule,' and his mind began to sound all sorts of philosophical depths, not of the most clerical character. In fact, as the reader has seen, this unfortunate priest had fallen in love with another man's wife, and had not the courage to confess it even to himself.

After dinner, Maurice launched out into his usual topic – convict discipline. It was pleasant for him to get a listener; for his wife, cold, statuesque, and unsympathetic, tacitly declined to enter into his schemes for the subduing of the refractory villains. 'You insisted on coming here,' she would say. 'I did not wish to come. I don't like to talk of these things. Talk of something else.' When she adopted this method of procedure, he had no alternative but to submit, for he was afraid of her, after a fashion. In this ill-assorted match he was apparently the master.

He was a physical tyrant. For him, a creature had but to be weak to be an object of contempt; and his gross nature seemed to triumph over the finer one of his wife. It may be admitted at once that all love had long since become eliminated from their social relations. The young, impulsive, delicate girl, who had given herself to him seven years before, had been changed into a weary, suffering woman. The wife is what her husband makes her, and his rude animalism had made her what she was. Instead of love, he had awakened a distaste which at times amounted to disgust. We have neither the skill nor the boldness of that profound philosopher whose hideously-brilliant analysis of human passion awoke North's contemplation, and we will not presume to set forth in bare English the story of this marriage of the Minotaur. Let it suffice to say that Dora liked her husband least when he loved her most. In this repulsion lay her power over him. When the animal and spiritual natures cross each other, the nobler triumphs in fact if not in appearance. Maurice Frere, though his wife obeyed him, knew that he was inferior to her, and was afraid of the statue he had created. She was ice, but it was the artificial ice that chemists make in the midst of a furnace. Her coldness was at once her strength and her weakness. When she chilled him, she commanded him.

Unwitting of the thoughts that possessed his guest, Frere chatted amicably. North said little, but drank a good deal. The wine, however, rendered him silent, instead of talkative. He seemed to drink as though to forget unpleasant memories, and to drink without accomplishing his object. When the pair proceeded to the room where Mrs Frere awaited them, Frere was boisterously good humored, North silently misanthropic.

'Sing something, Dora!' says Frere, with the ease of possession, as one who should say to a living musical-box, 'Play something.'

'Oh, Mr North doesn't care for music, and I'm not inclined to sing.'

What could North do but vow that he agonised for harmony, and yet beg that she would not disturb herself?

'Oh, if *you* wish it, Mr North!' cries she, and forthwith warbles deliciously.

North feels a pang at this open preference to his wishes, but Captain Frere – if any half-formed notion arises in his brain that the action of his wife means more than courtesy – imagines that she is coquetting to pique *him*, and so affects lordly indifference.

North, hanging over the piano, grows pale, and gasps, on a sudden,

'Excuse me, but – but – a sudden faintness!'

The windows are thrown open, and the clergyman gradually recovers, much in the same manner as he did in Burgess's parlour, at Port Arthur, seven years ago.

'I am liable to these attacks. A touch of heart disease, I think. I shall have to rest for a day or so.'

'Take a spell,' says Frere; 'you overwork yourself.'

North, sitting, gasping and pale, smiles in a ghastly manner.

'I – I will. If I do not appear for a week, Mrs Frere, you will know the reason.'

'A week! Surely it will not last as long as that,' exlaims Dora.

The ambiguous 'it' appears to annoy him, for he flushes painfully, replying,

'Sometimes longer. It is a – um – uncertain,' in a confused and shame-faced manner.

Dora glanced at her husband, and then, with a woman's quickness of perception, dashed into pleasant prattle, endeavouring to give her visitor time to recover himself. He does recover himself at length – sufficiently to join in the conversation, to promise the second volume of the French romance, to drink a glass of brandy with Frere, and to depart, walking painfully erect, and picking his way among the furniture with carefully-deliberated accuracy.

An hour afterwards, Mrs Frere, brushing her long hair before her looking-glass contemplatively, said to her husband,

'I wonder what was the matter with Mr North.'

'Something wrong with his heart, didn't he say?' suggested her husband, from his dressing-room.

The lady at the glass blushed, and observing that her dressing-gown was open at the neck, closed it with a hurried movement, as though some other eyes than those of her legal owner were upon her.

'He'll be right enough in the morning,' continued Frere, tugging at his boots, which presently fell off with two great bangs. 'I never met a parson yet who had a digestion worth a button.'

'You haven't met many, perhaps,' says Mrs Frere, softly.

'No; that's true. Not in my way much – psalm-singing, devil-dodging old humbugs. North ain't a bad sort, though. He's a manly beggar is old North. Seems a great admirer of yours, Dora.'

'You think everybody an admirer of mine,' says Dora, with unnecessary heat. 'I don't suppose Mr North thinks any more of me than he does of anybody else.'

There was just enough of interrogation in the tone to cause Frere to answer.

'He's always talking about you, and quoting what you say. At least he used to be.'

'And he doesn't now. Rude man!' said Mrs Frere, with a laugh, that sounded very forced, to her own ears at all events.

A knock at the door interrupted this matrimonial conversation.

'A messenger, sir. The chaplain's compliments, and he's not well, and would you be good enough to lend him a bottle of brandy?'

'Of course,' cries Frere, appearing in shirt and trousers. 'Where are the keys, Dora? Tell the messenger to wait.'

'I wonder if Dr Field knows,' says Dora. 'Perhaps he's very ill.'

'Not he!' says Frere, opening the door and following the servant down the passage.

'Did you see him, Sam?'

'No, sir. His servant give me the message. I was coming to you from Mr Troke, sir.'

'Troke! What's the matter now?'

'Dawes, sir, 's been violent and assaulted Mr Troke, Mr Troke said you'd left orders to be told at once of the insubordination of prisoners.'

– It is remarked by a variety of intelligent strangers, visitors, and journalists, how familiar prisoners – otherwise uneducated – grow with the stereotyped expressions of the convict code. –

'Quite right. Where is he?'

'In the cells, I think, sir. They had a hard fight to get him there, I'm told, your honour.'

'Had they? Give my compliments to Mr Troke, and tell him I shall have the pleasure of breaking Mr Dawes's spirit to-morrow morning at nine sharp. Here is the brandy. Will you have a nip?'

'Thank you, sir,' says the man, with watering lips.

'No, I don't think it's good for you,' says Frere, grinning at the poor fellow's discomfiture. 'Take it to Mr North as it is. See, the cork's drawn already, but if you're found drinking any of it, don't come to me to protect you.'

And so, with a laugh at his own wit, the Commandant departed to bed, leaving Sam to trudge back with bitter wrath. It was the custom of the Commandant to frequently condescend to be witty after this fashion.

'Dora,' said he, when he got back, 'your friend Dawes is in for it this time.'

But Dora was apparently fast asleep.

⇥ 8 ⇤

DICK PURFOY IN SEARCH OF A FATHER

THE morning after little Dick Purfoy got his thrashing – which, by the way, let us hasten to admit he thoroughly deserved – he saddled his grey horse Badger and galloped up into the ranges.

These ranges, big, long, and bristling with the grotesque vegetation of the Australian mountain ridges, were his father and mother, his confidant and familiar friend. Whenever he was beaten or maltreated, he would disappear into the sombre gullies, and forcing his mountain-bred horse up all sorts of devious paths, would spend hours stretched upon some lofty crag, staring alternately into the blue sky above him and the grey bush below him. Not that there was anything poetical in the boy – save that natural poetry inherent in children – but that in these solitudes lay all he had known of peace and ease. Alone amid the mountain gorges, with his fleet horse tethered close at hand, ready to bear him where he liked, and with no living creature else visible but the floating eagle-hawks, he realised something of that calm happiness which more fortunate children find in well-ordered homes and the caresses of loving parents. Lying there a solitary little soul, he could form wild boyish plans of the future, beat his sorrows into the kindly earth with passionate hands, catch — from the rustling of the branches and the soughing of the mountain airs — something of a better and holier thought than was vouchsafed to him in the gross revelry of the huts, or the fierce excitement of the dusty yards. The trees were his companions, the boulders and crags his trusty friends. *They* never laughed at him, nor lashed him. On this giant gum he had cut his initials, by that rough stone he had sat and wept. It was in this creek he had been nearly drowned in the last winter's flood. It was in that gully he had found the brindled bullock, for whom the whole station had hunted in vain. It was into that pool he had hurled fragments of earth, measuring the future greatness of his righteous vengeance by the widening eddies. It was against yonder tree that he had flung stones, deciding if he should find his father — that momentous and absorbing question — by his success in striking the gnarled and knotted target.

The lonely boy had been inoculated by his putative mother with two ideas — first, that he was the son of a Gentleman; second, that there was a certain creature existent in that unknown 'world' of which he had heard so much, which creature merited the contempt and hatred of all honest and bold men. This unknown monster was Captain Maurice Frere. At ten years of age, Dick Purfoy had two objects in life — to find his magnificent and to-be-beloved father, and to execute justice upon that monster and villain, Captain Maurice Frere.

Lying among the scrub, on this particular day, sore in body and sick at heart, he shaped out for himself a course of action. He would remain to be beaten and abused no longer. He would run away to seek his fortune and find his fate.

Many boys of ten years of age make such resolutions; few, however, have the advantages of climate and education which had fallen to the lot of John Carr's stepson, and therefore few carry out their intentions.

When Dick reached the house, he found his mother – as he called her – reading in the verandah, and forthwith burst out upon her.

'Mother, I want to know who my father is.'

The face of the woman flushed, and placing her book on her knees, she flung her shapely arms above her head, looking at the slight, bold figure, with a sort of sleepy admiration.

'You are growing curious, Dick. That is the third time this week you have asked me that question.'

'I want to know, mother. Don't be angry. I do so want to know.'

'A gentleman, Dick.'

'Yes, so you've said; but what sort of a gentleman?'

'A very fine, handsome, noble, accomplished, good-natured gentleman,' was the reply, each adjective slowly enunciated, as though carefully selected.

'Tell me his name, mother.'

'By-and-bye, Dick, when you are older.'

'No; now, mother.'

'You are too young,' says she, swinging herself slowly backwards and forwards on the low rocking-chair. 'You would not comprehend his nobleness, Dick. He is not one of the animals who drink brandy, and curse, and beat helpless women, like – like –'

'– Like that Frere!' cries Dick, desirous to propitiate his mother by showing that he was mindful of the lessons she had taught him.

'Like that villain, Frere, as you say,' continued Sarah. 'Not one of that sort, but a Gentleman, Dick – a thorough true blue, fine old English Gentleman!'

And she finished the sentence with a low, self-congratulating laugh.

'Won't you tell me his name?'

'No.'

'Mother!' cried Dick, seized with a sudden desire to pour out his bursting little heart.

'Well my dear son!'

Children – albeit as precocious as Dick Purfoy – are painfully sensitive to sarcasm. They comprehend ridicule in an instant. The poor lad detected the icy sneer in her tone, and the opening blossom of confidence withered at once.

'I want to go over to Joyce's to-night. He has promised me one of his kangaroo [1] pups. Will you tell father?'

'Are you going to stop all night?'

'Yes.'

'Don't be late in the morning, then. Goodbye.'

The boy descended the steps slowly, and then, as if prompted by a sudden impulse, ran back.

'Kiss me, mother!'

The beautiful woman, a little astonished, stooped and touched the boy's forehead with her soft, firm lips.

'Don't get into mischief,' said she, with a tenderness born of some latent good yet left in her.

And Dick, nodding quickly (his wretched little heart was too full to suffer him to speak), bounded down the steps, and made for the kitchens.

Larry's back being turned, Dick hastily pushed some bread and meat into the breast of his little jumper, and glided to the stables. There was no one there, unless Badger, champing his chaff, could be called someone. Dick unsaddled his horse, wiped his back, patted him, (with a strong desire to burst out crying), and then, taking his saddle on his head, and a nose-bag full of filched oats in his hand, made for the yards. Tom had 'run the horses up' an hour before, and Dick selected a strong bay nag out of the 'mob' before him. Just as he got him saddled and girthed, he heard his step-father's voice below the hill. The well-known and hated sound dispelled any lingering desire to forego his purpose, and hastily replacing the rails, he sprang to saddle, and walked his horse rapidly to the paddock gate.

Ten minutes afterwards, he was cantering under the newly-risen moon, in an exactly opposite direction to Joyce's. The boy had, in fact, set out upon a journey of two hundred miles. He was making for Sydney.

By the time that the fully-risen moon looked down upon the sleeping station of Nine Creeks, Dick was twenty miles away,

1. *Subaudite* – 'dog.'

fairly out upon the lightly-timbered country which ran between the Plains and the Mountains. He had slackened his pace, and the bay cob, thoroughly warm to his work, walked briskly, cocking first one ear and then the other, and sweating pleasantly, getting his second wind. The gaunt gum-trees cast grotesque shadows on the cold grass, the laughing jackasses shouted at the moon, and the sweet, clear, piney odours of the bush penetrated his senses. Now and then sleeping cattle stampeded, or a grey mass, which was a mob of camping sheep, broke and dispersed with a scurrying noise. A distant bullock bell gave token of some strayed beast, and here and there a foraging opossum slipped across the path, clattering up a tree-trunk to safety. Dick began to feel rather lonely and chilly.

He ate a piece of bread and meat, and then, to check his thoughts, tightened the rein, and broke into a hand-gallop. The moon made a misty daylight, and the panorama of the bush flitted past him in two long grey streaks. In less than twenty minutes he was on the edge of the great Plains, which billowed away before him for ninety miles. He halted, and looked back. The ranges rose magnificent. The station was just below that cleft peak, that pierced the blue, like a bishop's mitre. It was cold. What a snug blanket he would have had at Joyce's! What a goose he had been not to wait for supper! It was only thirty miles back; he could get home by daylight. He loosened the rein, and the cob – knowing beast – edged off the track directly, with intent to wheel round to his birthplace. Dick jerked him sharply back to obedience, and just as the cuckoo-clock in his step-father's house chirrupped midnight, rode out into the Carrum Plains.

He made twelve miles more, and then lay down, with the bridle round his arm, and slept a dog-sleep. The horse, impatiently feeding, woke him every now and then. The last time he was so awakened, he saw close to him four huge monsters, that slowly advanced. He rose to his feet, and the monsters disappeared. They were wild turkeys, magnified into moas by the mists of morning. It was not far off daylight, for the sky was red above him, and Dick, unbitting the cob, let the bridle hang by the throat-lash, and allowed the horse to feed along the track.

The sun rising at one surge behind the edge of the plains,

flung two immense shadows to the bottom of the timber belt. The shadow of a dumpy creature, with legs twelve miles long, followed by an animal like a camel, that bent an enormous head to pluck immense bristles of herbage.

He mounted, and pushed on until ten o'clock, when he found himself alone, a speck in the middle of a round, straw-coloured plain. The earth seemed to rise up on all sides of him to the horizon, but he knew that when he reached the apparent limit where the brown track seemed to melt into air, he would find yet another sweep of crisp silver grass, and the same straw-coloured barrenness rising all around. He finished the remainder of his bread and meat, gave his horse a feed of oats, and set forward again. The bush-bred boy had no fear of being lost. He would not have feared that in any case. Even if the well-defined ribbon of 'track' ploughed by waggon-wheels, and sharply indented by cloven hoofs, had not been beneath his feet, was there not the sun, that would soon mark mid-day by means of that unerring sun-dial (his own shadow projected over his horse, now to this side, now to that); and would there not by-and-by rise effulgent the southern cross and luminous moon to guide him? To be 'bushed' was simply impossible. Moreover, there was a 'station' ahead somewhere.

'Hey, Fidget! Get on!'

He slept that night at Carrum Plains Station, having done his eighty miles without inconvenience.

He was searching, he said, for a bay mare branded T. C. under P. on the near shoulder; but the stockmen had seen nothing of her. It would have been strange if they had.

All next day through the weary hot plains, to make Glen Tilt – it was wonderful how Scotland was turned upside down in the antipodes! – and 'making it' late in the evening, he found supper over, and nothing but a drink of tea and a bite of bread procurable.

Waking, wearied and sore, late the next morning, he found the assembled 'huts' viewing his horse, and remarking that he must have 'pushed him hard' the day before.

Dick, conscious that he had ridden too fast, walked the best part of the next day, wondering how much further off this wonderful Sydney was.

Towards sundown he found himself entering timber again, and began to dread lest he should not make the next station before nightfall. 'Macgillicuddy's,' as it was called, lay some ten miles off the track; and though he had obtained minute directions as to bearings 'by the Long Waterhole,' and 'turning sharp to the left before entering the Honeysuckle scrub,' he had not a very distinct notion of his way.

As he was jogging on, scarcely daring to spur his jaded horse, his quick ears caught the rapid beat of hoofs behind him. Somebody was approaching at a smart canter. The cob pricked up his ears and neighed. Dick, looking back, saw, black against the grey sky, a figure which he fancied was familiar to him. He drew off into the timber, and waited, his heart thumping against his ribs.

In five minutes more, John Carr passed him at a hand-gallop, and struck without hesitation the track that branched to Macgillicuddy's.

He was pursued then!

His stepfather had evidently tracked him to his last night's resting-place, and, mounted on a fresh horse, was galloping fast to Macgillicuddy's.

This was, in fact, just what had happened. As the boy did not return, Sarah Purfoy, calling to mind his strange conduct, had persuaded her husband to go to Joyce's; and John Rex, learning that Dick had not been there at all, guessed that he had made Sydneywards, and swearing many oaths, started at once on his track.

'I'll teach him to bolt again, the young whelp!' thought he, understanding for the first time in his life the fierce wrath that possessed gaolers hunting for escaped prisoners. Dick, intuitively understanding the meaning of the squared shoulders, and hat pulled down over the brows, dug spurs into the staunch old cob and hurried down the main track.

He galloped in a sweat of terror for nearly an hour, until his wearied beast under him no longer answered to the thrusts of the bloody spurs, and, groaning, subsided into a walk. Just as the boy was about to fling himself from the saddle in sheer despair, he saw a red glow in the dark forest ahead. There was a 'camp' by the track.

The moon had not yet risen, and as he rode up alongside the huge waggons, there was nothing but the lurid light of the fire to show him the faces of the two bullock-drivers.

'Hullo! my young Napoleon,' says one of the two – 'what's *your* little caper?'

The speaker was a tall, gaunt man, with grizzled beard and wild, fierce eyes.

'Looking for a bridled bullock,' says Dick, undauntedly. 'Have you seen him?'

'We've seen a good many, my kiddy,' replied the second man, in good-humoured tones. 'Ain't we, Jerry?'

'My word!' says Jerry.

'Well,' cries Dick, flinging his right leg over his horse's neck, and so springing to earth in the approved stock-riding fashion, 'I'm about dead beat, and may as well camp here with you. Give us a drink o' tea!'

'There you are, my Infant Roscius,' says the thin man, with a sort of barren jocoseness that seemed habitual to him. 'There's a damper in that dish. Hang up your moke, my young Ducrow, sit down, and flash your Dover.'[1]

The jolly companion of the facetious Jerry laughed; and Dick, hearing the clink of hobble-chains, hastily hobbled his own nag with a stirrup-leather, and leading him to the others, left him there, sure of finding him in the morning.

The man called Jerry sat himself down by the logs and meditated, looking sideways at the boy.

'Moke seems rather baked?' says he at length.

'Yes,' returned Dick.

'Had a hard day's work?'

'Yes.'

'Good sort of moke?'

'Not bad.'

'Worth about forty notes I should say?'

1. *Flash your Dover* is essentially *Colonial* slang. The majority of claspknives imported into the Australian colonies twenty years ago were made by one 'Dover.' Hence 'flashing your Dover' is equivalent to 'drawing your Toledo.'

'I dare say he is.'

'Come far?'

'From Glen Tilt.'

'Oh.' A pause. 'Have a nip o' rum?'

'I don't mind.'

So the cheerful companion gets a rum-bottle out of an empty gin-case, that seems to serve the pair as pantry, dressing-closet, wine-cellar, and wardrobe, all combined; and the long man drinks a variety of toasts, with intense affectation of merriment. Dick joining in, and the fire burning brightly, the cheerful man discourses, and, by-and-bye, Dick learns that the pair have been taking tea, sugar, and tobacco to some far-away place beyond the ranges, and are now returning home with empty drays. It further appears that the cheerful man is 'boss,' and that the facetious Jerry is but a servant. As the rum diminishes, however, it becomes evident that Jerry has influence over his companion; who, being a simple-minded fellow himself, looks upon the talkative Cockney as a model of politeness and humour. All this sharp-eyed Dick observes, and gets into his head also that the thin man has 'seen better days,' and was not always a bullock-driver.

The moon gets up and lights the strange scene. The wild wilderness, the huge waggons, the white body of a camping 'poler,' and three ragged figures round the glowing logs.

The cheerful companion suggests a song, and sings one, in which he expresses his opinion that 'Currency Flash' is the 'style for him,' and desires to know forthwith

What will Old England say?

and intimating that in case of any domestic outbreak, she

Will wish she had her sons back ag'in,
Wot she sent to Bottiney Bay!

This ditty rouses Jerry, who, as soon as his features settled into singing, showed himself to be an innately melancholy man, and he hiccupped a ditty, of which the first verse is as follows:—

' 'Twas on an Easter Monday, in the spring time of the year,
When rolling Tom the Drover to Smithfield did repair;

His togs were tight and clever, his dogs were staunch and free,
With a bird's-eye fogle about his squeeze, and his garters below his
  knee.'

This elegant strain concluded, the conversation fell upon
horseflesh, and Jerry, after the interchange of many mysterious
winks and nods with his companion, suggested that a 'swop'
might be made between a certain mare, which was in the distance, and Dick's shapely cob.

Dick, acutely alive to the fact that the cob would be unable
to go ten miles in the morning, demanded to see the animal,
and Jerry — staggering somewhat in his gait — departed into
the bush, presently returning with an old white mare.

Dick, terrified at the proximity of his dreaded stepfather,
would have swopped the bay horse for a jackass, so that he
could keep the start he had gained; and after some bargaining,
and a vain effort at 'loot' on the part of the bullock-driver, the
bargain was concluded.

A parting 'nip' was taken in honour of the exchange, and
the adventurous lad crept under the fly of the waggon to sleep.

He did not relish his company, and for some time endeavoured to keep his eyes fixed on the two figures by the fire. He
saw Jerry produce another rum-bottle, and set to work upon it.
He heard fragments of conversation, scraps of songs, and fag
ends of drunken utterances; but in a short time the moonlit
heaven, looking down so coldly upon the rude debauch, was
veiled from his sight; the trees spun round the fire, the figures
melted away, and the reeling weary boy fell fast asleep.

He had not closed his eyes five minutes — as it seemed to him,
though he had been snoring vigorously for the last two hours —
when he was awakened by a sharp cry. He started up and
looked around in dismay. The scene was unchanged, save that
the moon had sunk lower, and the firelight had waned. The two
figures lay like logs on either side the embers. Whence could
the sound that had awakened him have proceeded?

Suddenly, one of the recumbent figures rose to a sitting
posture, and called out, in accents of terror,

'Joe! Joe! Oh, Lord, it's Joe!'

It was the man called Jerry who spoke. He was sitting up,
with face white in the moonbeams, outstretched arms, and

staring, glassy eyes. For a few frightful seconds he remained thus, gibbering inanely, and then fell flat again, after the manner of a galvanized corpse from which the wire has been suddenly withdrawn.

Dick, terrified at the ghastliness of this apparition, sprang out of the waggon, with intent to wake the sleeper, but, just as he neared it, the prostrate body rose up again; the widely-opened eyes looking with meaningless stare at him, and one long claw outstretched, as though to grasp him.

'I must have money, Joe! Money! do you hear!'

So fierce was the whisper – hinting as it did of some dreadful secret, which, hugged close by day, took advantage of the night to escape from custody, and proclaim itself – that the boy shrank back, afraid to awaken in the sleeper the consciousness of his indiscretion. In a few moments the paroxysm passed as before, and the trembling boy, seeing no sign of another attack, crept back to his dray. Oppressed by the necessity for flight, he woke at dawn, caught his new purchase, saddled her, and prepared to start. When he returned to the waggon, however, Jerry was stirring.

'I got drunk last night,' said he, roughly. 'Did I talk?'

'I don't know,' says Dick, with unblushing face. 'I was asleep.'

'I've got a habit of dreaming,' said the other, 'and talk like a fool sometimes. Have a nip?'

'No,' says Dick. 'I'll have a drink o' tea, though.'

'Here you are. Now, you'd better make a start; it's getting late.'

This proposition so chimed with his own wishes, that the runaway took no notice of the eagerness with which it was made. It was most important that he should get on, lest his stepfather should overtake him, or, perchance, recognize the cob, and continue pursuit. Moreover, he feared lest Jerry, on examination of the animal he had obtained, should find fault with his distressed condition, and insist upon the annulling of the bargain. Waving a 'Good day,' he rode off.

The white mare, though old, was a quick and easy goer, and Dick, making thirty miles before noon, rejoiced at his astuteness in the matter of horse-dealing. He had got 'a good bit of stuff' this time.

That night he fell in with a stockman, who took him to his hut, where he rested till noon of the following day. Pursuit seemed abandoned, and he travelled by easy stages into civilization. The 'track' had long ago changed into a broad metalled road. Ferns and townships increased; houses occurred at shorter and shorter intervals; graceful villas nestled amid bowery trees, girdled by glowing flower-beds and shaven lawns. Churches and public-houses mocked each other. Far away below him, he caught glimpses of a bright blue expanse that was the Sea of his dreams; and presently, on turning an angle, he saw at his feet, stretching out into that exquisite bay of a thousand islands, the fair white city of Sydney, glittering in the sun as did the City of the Beautiful at the feet of Christian. He stopped to gaze, and a gang of convicts mending the roadway cursed him in the familiar slang of the men's huts.

He had no plans for the future, and had thought that Sydney town, being not much bigger than the country townships, he could find his father easily. The unexpected number of the shops, and the people and the carriages, terrified him. It seemed that the streets were endless, and that once entangled in that maze, he would be 'bushed' indeed. What was he to do? He was weary and hungry, and utterly without money. He had nothing to sell save his clothes and his horse. He almost wished himself back again. In the bush he could have lived easily enough, but what was to become of him in that wilderness of a city? The white mare, left by the preoccupation of her rider to her own devices, unconsciously settled the question. She turned now to the right, now to the left, quickening her pace, as if approaching some well-known spot. Dick looked up, and found himself at the entrance to a horse-yard. Two gentlemen were smoking cigars at the entrance, and one of them started as Dick walked the mare under the mighty iron roof over the tan. A low-sized man, standing with his legs apart, was chewing a straw and cracking a huge whip.

'Do you want to buy a mare?' says Dick, uneasily plunging into the subject his heart was hot upon.

The man eyed him from head to heel. 'I might,' said he, slowly. 'What's your figure?'

Dick was about to make some evasive reply proper to the

occasion, when he found himself violently seized by the collar and dragged to earth.

'You infernal young scoundrel!' cries a voice. 'What are you doing with my mare?'

Dick looked up and saw one of the two loungers at the gate bending over him.

'She ain't your mare,' says he, writhing. 'She's mine!'

'Where did you get her?' says the gentleman, still holding him fast.

'Swopped a bay cob for her at Macgillicuddy's station on the Bingabool, a week ago,' says Dick, furiously. 'Let me go!'

The thickset man with the whip, who seemed master of the yards, burst into a loud laugh.

'There's a currency flash for ye, Mr Macgillicuddy!' said he.

Poor Dick understood all at once the eagerness and simplicity of the long bullock-driver. The mare had been stolen out of Macgillicuddy's paddock.

The owner of the mare joined in the laugh good-humoredly, and, turning to his companion, said, 'I've half a mind to let the young scamp go.'

Dick tremblingly awaited his fate, but there was no mercy in the harsh grey eyes that met his own.

'Stuff! Give him in charge, Mac. It's a clear case. You'll be a fool if you don't.'

Macgillicuddy's momentary good-nature evaporated, and, despite Dick's protestations, he flung him to the thickset whip cracker, and, after seeing his regained property fairly bestowed, quitted the wards with his friend.

'Who's that?' Dick asked, pointing to the man who had condemned him to become in the future as one of the chain-gang who had cursed him at his entrance to this fatal city.

The thickset man looked at him with some contempt, mingled with a sort of pity.

'It'd ha' been better for you if it had been anybody else,' said he. 'That's Captain Frere.'

Dick's heart gave a jump. If he had not found his father, he had found his enemy.

In due course the punishment for horse-stealing — five years on the roads – followed, the judge remarking upon the combined youth and iniquity of the culprit.

John Rex, returned to his station after an unsuccessful search, saw in the paper that a boy who gave the name of Richard Purfoy had been sentenced at the criminal sessions, and, rejoiced at having got rid of a nuisance, debated whether he should tell his wife. She had taken the intelligence of Dick's disappearance with such calmness, however, that there seemed but little danger in telling her. He did so, and, to his astonishment, she laughed.

'The Lord has delivered him into my hands,' said she. 'Sit down, Jack, you noodle, and I'll tell you who the boy is!'

The tale was not a long one, but Rex, vagabond and scoundrel as he was, seemed affected by it.

'How you can *hate*, Sarah!' said he, and fell to meditation.

⟶ 9 ⟵

BREAKING A MAN'S SPIRIT

RUFUS DAWES, on being removed to the cells, knew what he had to expect.

The insubordination of which he had been guilty was, in this instance, tolerably insignificant. It was the custom of the newly-fledged constables of Captain Frere to enter the wards at night, armed with cutlasses, tramping about, and making a great noise. Mindful of the report of Pounce, they pulled the men roughly from their hammocks, examined their persons for concealed tobacco, and compelled them to open their mouths to see if any was inside. The men in Dawes's gang – to which Mr Troke had an especial objection – were often searched more than once in a night, searched going to work, searched at meals, searched going to prayers, searched coming out, and this in the roughest manner. Their sleep broken, and what little self-respect they might yet presume to retain harried out of them, the objects of this incessant persecution were ready to turn upon and kill their tormentors.

The great aim of Troke was to catch Dawes tripping, but the leader of the 'Ring' was too wary. In vain had Troke, eager to sustain his reputation for sharpness, burst in upon the convict at all times and seasons. He had found nothing. In vain had he laid traps for him; in vain had he 'planted' figs of tobacco, and attaching long threads to them, waited in a bush hard by until the pluck at the end of his line should give token that the fish had bitten.[1] The experienced 'old hand' was too acute for him. Filled with disgust and ambition, he determined upon an ingenious little trick. He was certain that Dawes possessed tobacco; the thing was to find it upon him.

Now, Rufus Dawes, holding aloof, as was his custom, from the majority of his companions, had made one friend — if so mindless and battered an old wreck could be called a friend — Blind Mooney. Perhaps this oddly-assorted friendship was brought about by two causes — one that Mooney was the only man on the island who knew more of the horrors of convictism than the leader of the Ring; the other, that Mooney was blind, and, to a moody, sullen man, subject to violent fits of passion, and a constant suspicion of all his fellow-creatures, a blind companion was more congenial than a sharp-eyed one.

Mooney was one of the 'First Fleeters.' He had arrived in Sydney fifty-seven years before, in the year 1789, and when he was transported he was fourteen years old. He had been through the whole round of servitude, had worked as a bondsman, had married, had been 'up country,' and had been again sentenced, and was a sort of dismal patriarch of Norfolk Island, having been there at its former settlement. He had no friends. His wife was long since dead, and he stated, without contradiction, that his master, having taken a fancy to her, had despatched the uncomplaisant husband to imprisonment. Such cases were not uncommon.[2]

1. A fact.

2. *Extract from voluntary statement made by Mrs Joseph Smith, Macdonald's River, Hunter Colony, 3d October, 1848, to Mrs Chisholm:* — 'I have seen Dr — take a woman who was in the family-way, tie a rope round her, and duck her in the water at Queen's Wharf. The laws were bad then. If a gentleman wanted a man's wife, he would send the husband to Norfolk Island.'

Mooney was accustomed to relate strange stories of his early life.

'When I first arrived,' said he to Dawes, 'there were but eight houses in the colony. I and eighteen others lay in a hollow tree for seventeen weeks, and cooked out of a kettle with a wooden bottom. We used to stick it in a hole in the ground and make a fire round it. For seventeen weeks we only had five ounces of flour a day. We never got a full ration except when the ship was in harbour. I have taken grass and pounded it, and made soup from a native dog. Any man would have committed murder for a week's provisions. I was chained seven weeks on my back for being out getting greens and wild herbs. I knew a man hung then and there for stealing a few biscuits, and another for stealing a duck frock. A man was condemned – no time – take him to the tree and hang him.

'The motto used to be, "Kill 'em or work 'em, their provisions is in store." I've been yoked like a bullock, with twenty or thirty others, to drag along timber. We used to be taken in large parties to raise a tree; when the body of the tree was raised, the overseer would call some of the men away; then more; the men were bent double; they could not bear it; they fell; the tree on one or two, killed on the spot. "Take him away, put him in the ground." There was no more about it. I've seen a man flogged for pulling six turnips instead o' five. Those were the days! I've seen seventy men flogged at night – twenty-five lashes each. One man came ashore in the *Pitt;* his name was Dixon. He was a guardsman. He was put to the drag; it soon did for him. He began on a Thursday and died on the Saturday, as he was carrying a load down Constitution-hill. How they used to die! There was a great hole for the dead; once a day, men were sent down to collect the corpses of prisoners, and throw them in without ceremony or service. The native dogs used to come down at night, and fight and howl, in packs, gnawing the poor dead bodies. Eight hundred died in six months, at Constitution-hill – or Toongabbie as it was called. I knew a man, so weak that he was thrown into the grave,[1] when he said, "Don't cover me up, I'm not dead; for God's sake don't

---

1. The name of this man was James Glasshouse. In 1845 he was living at Richmond, N.S.W.

cover me up!" The overseer answered, "Damn your eyes, you'll die to-night, and we shall have the trouble to come back again."'

Such dismal recollections as these were Mooney's consolation in his blindness. One would have thought that, having passed through such an ordeal, doomed for life to such a punishment, he would at seventy-one have been glad to slip into his grave; but it was not so. The old blind man believed that he must soon be released on account of his great age. 'What's the good of a blind old fool like me?' he would ask; and he looked forward to his release with the greatest eagerness, for he believed himself master of millions. 'I've found a gold mine,' he used to say, to the amusement of his comrades. Dawes, however, with some dim remembrance of those chemical and metallurgical studies in which he had once delighted, listened to the old man with patience. It was just wildly possible that Australia was auriferous, and that Mooney's story of the gold dust in the bed of the creek was a true one. The old shepherd himself believed it, and would draw to his comrade wonderful pictures of what he meant to do when he got out. 'Mooney's gold mine' was a standing joke in the prison, and the old man, pressed in rough sarcasm to reveal its whereabouts, was incited to paroxysms of rage. Dawes sometimes allowed himself to speculate upon the probable consequences of a similar discovery being made by himself. With money one could do anything.

One of the many ways in which Rufus Dawes had secured the affection of the old blind man was the gift of such fragments of tobacco as he from time to time secured. Troke knew this; and on the evening in question hit upon an excellent plan. Admitting himself noiselessly into the boatshed, where the gang slept, he crept close to the sleeping Dawes, and counterfeiting Mooney's mumbling utterance, asked for 'some tobacco.'[1] Rufus Dawes was but half awake, and on repeating his request, Troke felt something put into his hand. He grasped Dawes's arm and struck a light. He had got his man this time. Dawes had conveyed to his (fancied) friend a piece of tobacco almost as big as the top joint of his little finger.

One can understand the feelings of a man entrapped by such base means. Rufus Dawes no sooner saw the hated face of War-

1. This was a not unfrequent trick among Norfolk Island constables.

der Troke peering over his hammock, than he sprang out, and exerting to the utmost his powerful muscles, slung out his left hand from his hip with such tremendous violence that Mr Troke was knocked fairly off his legs into the arms of the incoming constables. A desperate struggle took place, at the end of which, the convict, overpowered by numbers, was borne senseless to the cells, gagged, and chained to the ring-bolt on the bare flags. While in this condition he was dreadfully beaten by five or six constables.[1]

To this maimed and manacled rebel was the Commandant ushered by Troke the next morning.

'Ha! ha! my man,' says the Commandant. 'Here you are again, you see. How do you like this sort of thing?'

Dawes, glaring, makes no answer.

'You shall have fifty lashes, my man,' says Frere. 'We'll see how you'll feel then!'

The fifty were duly administered, and the Commandant called the next day. The rebel was still mute.

'Give him fifty more, Mr Troke. We'll see what he's made of.'

Fifty more lashes were inflicted in the course of the morning, but still the sullen convict refused to speak. He was then treated to fourteen days' solitary confinement in one of the new cells. On being brought out and confronted with his tormentor, he merely laughed. For this he was sent back for another fourteen days; and still remaining obdurate, was flogged again, and got fourteen days more. Had the chaplain then visited him, he would have found him open to consolation, but the chaplain — so it was stated — was sick. When brought out at the conclusion of his third confinement, he was found to be in so exhausted a condition, that the doctor ordered him to hospital. As soon as he was sufficiently recovered, Frere visited him, and finding his

---

1. *Extract from the Diary of the Rev. T. Rogers, chaplain at Norfolk Island.* – 'April 16, Friday, 1846. Had a long chat with Ditton. He was chained down to the floor by Mr —'s order, and had been gagged. . . . He was gagged, and had been chained down; was then dreadfully beaten by five or six constables. He lay in a puddle of blood. The next day a constable went and jumped upon him, and severely hurt his chest. He pierced his body with a piece of sharp iron or steel. He showed me a scar on his arm he had received on that occasion.'

'spirit' not yet 'broken,' ordered that he should be put to grind maize. Dawes declined the work. So they chained his hand to one arm of the grindstone, and placed another prisoner at the other arm. As the second prisoner turned, the hand of Dawes of course revolved.[1]

'You're not such a pebble as folks seem to think,' grinned Frere, pointing to the turning wheel.

Upon which the indomitable poor devil straightened his sorely-tried muscles, and prevented the wheel from turning at all.

Frere gave him fifty more lashes, and sent him the next day to grind cayenne pepper.

This was a punishment more dreaded by the convicts than any other. The pungent dust filled their eyes and lungs, causing them the most excruciating torments. For a man with a raw back the work was one continued agony. In four days, Rufus Dawes, emaciated, blistered, blinded, broke down.

'For God's sake, Captain Frere, kill me at once!' he said.

'No fear,' said the other, rejoiced at this proof of his power. 'You've given in; that's all I wanted. Troke, take him to the hospital.'[2]

When he was in hospital, North visited him.

'I would have come to see you before,' said the clergyman, 'but I have been very ill.'

In truth, he looked so. He had had a fever, it seemed, and they had shaved his beard and cropped his hair. Dawes could see that the haggard, wasted man had passed through some agony as great as his own.

The next day Frere visited him, complimented him on his courage, and offered to make him a constable.

Dawes turned his scarred back to his torturer, and resolutely declined to answer.

'I am afraid you have made an enemy of the Commandant,' said North, the next day. 'Why not accept his offer?'

Dawes cast on him a glance of quiet scorn.

'And betray my mates? I'm not one of that sort.'

1. Another fact.
2. See the cases of Thomas Williams, mason, and George Armstrong, otherwise called 'Dubbo,' at Norfolk Island, in 1848, as related by Martin Cash, and published in Hobart Town, in 1870, at the *Mercury* office.

'Surely,' thought North, 'there is yet some soft place in this unhappy man's heart.'

The clergyman spoke to him of hope, of release, of repentance and redemption. The prisoner laughed.

'Who's to redeem me?' he said, expressing his thoughts in phraseology that seemed blasphemous. 'It would take a Christ to die again to save such as I.'

North spoke to him of immortality.

'There is another life,' said he. 'Do not risk your chance of happiness in it. You have a future to live for, man.'

'I hope not,' said the victim of the 'system.' 'I want to rest — to sleep, and never be disturbed again.'

His 'spirit' was 'broken' enough by this time. Yet he had resolution enough to refuse Frere's repeated offers.

'I'll never "jump" it,' he said to North, 'if they cut me in half first.'

North pityingly implored the stubborn mind to have mercy on the lacerated body, but without effect. His own wayward heart gave him the key to read the cipher of this man's life. 'A noble nature ruined,' said he to himself. 'What is the secret of his history?'

Dawes, on his part, seeing how different from other black coats was this priest — at once ardent and gloomy, stern and tender — began to speculate on the cause of his monitor's sunken cheeks, fiery eyes, and preoccupied manner, to wonder what grief inspired those agonized prayers, those eloquent and daring supplications, which were daily poured out over his rude bed.

So between these two — the priest and the sinner — was a sort of sympathetic bond.

One day this bond was drawn so close as to tug at both their heart-strings.

The chaplain had a flower in his coat. Dawes eyed it with hungry looks, and, as the clergyman was about to quit the room, said,

'Mr North, will you give me that rosebud?'

North paused irresolutely, and finally, as if after a struggle with himself, took it carefully from his button-hole, and placed it in the prisoner's brown scarred hand.

In another instant, Dawes, believing himself alone, pressed the gift to his lips.

North returned abruptly, and the eyes of the pair met. North flushed crimson, but Dawes turned as white as death. Neither spoke, but each seemed to feel drawn closer to the other, since each had kissed the rosebud plucked by Dora's fingers.

⊰ 10 ⊱

Extracted from the Diary of the Rev. James North

October 21st. I am safe for another six months if I am careful, for my last bout lasted longer than I expected. I suppose one of these days I shall have a paroxysm that will kill me. I shall not regret it.

I wonder if this Familiar of mine – I begin to detest the expression – will accuse me of wantonly endeavouring to make a case for myself if I say that I believe my madness to be a disease? I do believe it. I honestly can no more help getting drunk, than a lunatic can help screaming and gibbering. It would be different with me, perhaps, was I a contented man, happily married, with children about me, and family cares to distract me. But as I am – a lonely, gloomy, fantastic-fancied being, debarred from love, devoured by spleen, and tortured with repressed desires – I become a living torment to myself. I think of happier men, of men who are loved and who love, of men with fair wives and clinging children, of Frere for instance – and a hideous wild beast seems to stir within me, a monster whose cravings cannot be satisfied, can only be drowned in stupefying brandy. I will set down once for all the course of this drunkard's madness which is destroying me.

Penitent and shattered, I vow to lead a new life; to forswear spirits, to drink nothing but water. Indeed, the sight and smell of brandy make me ill. All goes well for some weeks, when I grow nervous, discontented, moody. I smoke, and am soothed. But moderation is not to be thought of; little by little, I increase the dose of tobacco. Five pipes a day become six or seven. Then I count up to ten and twelve, then drop to three or four, then mount to eleven at a leap; then lose count altogether. Much smoking excites the brain. I feel clear, bright, gay. My tongue is parched in the morning, though, and I use liquor to 'moisten my clay.' I drink wine or beer in moderation, and all goes well. My limbs regain their suppleness, my hands their coolness, my brain its placidity. I begin to feel that I have a will. I am confident, calm, and hopeful. To this condition, however, succeeds one of the most frightful melancholy. I remain plunged, for an hour together, in a stupor of despair. The earth, air, sea, all appear barren, colourless – life is a burden. I long to sleep, and sleeping struggle to awake, because of the awful dreams that flap about me in the darkness. At night I cry, 'Would God it were morning!' in the morning, 'Would God it were evening!' I loathe myself, and all around me. I am nerveless, passionless, bowed down with a burden like the burden of Saul. I know quite well what will restore me to life and ease – restore me, but to cast me back again into a deeper fit of despair. I drink. One glass – my blood is warmed, – my heart leaps, my hand no longer shakes. Three glasses, I rise with hope in my soul, – the evil spirit flies from me. I continue – pleasing images flock to my brain, the fields break into flower, the birds into song, the sea gleams sapphire, the warm heaven laughs. Great God! what man could withstand a temptation like this?

By an effort, I shake off the desire to drink deeper, and fixing my thoughts on my duties, on my books, on the wretched prisoners to whom I am a 'saint' (or a 'hypocrite!') I succeed perhaps for a time; but my blood, heated by the wine which is at once my poison and my life, boils in my veins. I drink again, and dream. I feel all the animal within me stirring. In the day my thoughts wander to all monstrous imaginings. The most familiar objects suggest to me loathsome thoughts. Obscene and filthy images surround me. My nature seems changed. By day I feel myself a wolf in sheep's clothing; a man possessed by a devil, who is ready at any moment to break out and tear him to pieces. At night I become a satyr. While in this torment I at once hate and fear myself. One fair face is ever before me, gleaming through my hot dreams like a flying moon in the sultry midnight of a tropic storm. I dare not trust myself in the presence of those I love and respect, lest my wild thoughts should find vent in wilder words. I lose my humanity. I am a beast.

Out of this depth there is but one way of escape. Downwards. I must drench the monster I have awakened until he sleeps again. I drink and become oblivious.

In these last paroxysms there is nothing for me but brandy. I shut myself up alone and pour down my gullet huge draughts of spirit. It mounts to my brain. I am a man again; and as I regain my manhood, I topple over – dead drunk!

But the awakening! Let me not paint it. The delirium, the fever, the self-loathing, the prostration, the despair. I view in the looking-glass a haggard face, with red eyes. I look down upon my shaking hands, flaccid muscles, and shrunken limbs. I speculate if I shall ever be one of the grotesque and melancholy beings, with blear eyes and running noses, swollen bellies and shrunken legs! Ugh! – it is too likely.

October 22nd. Have spent the day with Mrs Frere. She is evidently eager to leave the place – as eager as I am. Frere rejoices in his murderous power, and laughs at her entreaties. I suppose men get tired of their wives. In my present frame of mind, I am at a loss to understand how a man could refuse a wife like that anything.

I do not think she can possibly care for him. I am not a selfish fool, as are the majority of seducers. I would take no woman away from a husband for mere liking. Yet I think there are cases in which a man *who loved* would be justified in making a woman happy at the risk of his own – soul, I suppose.

Making her happy! Ay, that's the point. Would she be happy? There are few men who can endure to be 'cut,' slighted, pointed at, and women suffer more than men in these regards. I, a grizzled man of forty, am not such an arrant ass as to suppose that a brief year of guilty happiness can compensate a gently-nurtured woman for the loss of that social dignity which constitutes her best happiness. I am not such an idiot as to forget that there may come a time when the woman I love may cease to love *me*, and having no tie of self-respect, social position, or family duty, to bind her, may inflict upon her seducer that agony which he has taught her to inflict upon her husband. Apart from the question of the sin of breaking the seventh commandment, I doubt if the worst husband and the most unhappy home are not better, in this social condition of ours, than the most devoted lover. A strange subject this for a clergyman to speculate upon! If this diary should ever fall into the hands of a real God-fearing, honest booby, who never was tempted to sin, by finding that at middle-age he loved the wife of another, how he would condemn me! And rightly, of course.

October 23rd. Visited the chain gang. Ten men in a small room called the 'nunnery,' a room six feet by twelve, the thermometer at 100. The wretches were obliged to pull off their waistcoats and shirts, to prevent their being saturated with the perspiration that ran down their naked bodies in streams. I was seized with vertigo, and was compelled to step out into the open yard to save myself from fainting.

Several applications made out by the men who came by the *King William,* probation prisoner ship (September, 1845), to get them back their bibles, prayer books, hymn books, and tracts, which were taken from them by Captain Frere. It was a pitiless and cruel thing to take their books just then, as the men's minds were, if ever, in the best possible state to profit by them. Many men have asked me for their books, and begged me to get them back for them if I could. Their bibles and prayer books are generally the gifts of broken-hearted relations in England, or else presented to them by the chaplains of gaols at home, when they were removed for embarkation. These books were the sole links that remained to tie their hearts and thoughts by any visible sign or token to home and friends, now lost to them for ever. Several men, whose bibles had been written in by their wives, and given in the farewell agonies of life-long separation, came to me,[1] with streaming eyes, imploring to get their books back, because they had their wives' handwritings in them, or even to *let them see the books,* and they would be satisfied. Some old men have had their spectacles taken from them. All this is done under the plea that prisoners are to have nothing in their possession but the clothing given by the Government.

1. See the case of the prisoners by the *John Calvin*, Sept., 1846.

October 25th. Visited the gaol. Found Bland strapped down, upon suspicion of having prevented his eye from recovering. His back was bad (he had just been flogged), and the cord which laced the strait-waistcoat which they put on him pained him much. His eye was very bad. He was laid on his back, unable to stir hand or foot, and in an agony of pain from the pressure of his lacerated back upon the cord. He said to a turn-key, 'If I am guilty of injuring myself, let me be punished; if not, why am I thus strapped down?' For saying this he was flogged. He told me that Doctor Field did not think that he had done anything to his eye. His back stunk most offensively; and on my intercession, Captain Frere allowed the cord to be removed, but his hands were chained to the foot of the bed.[1] He had received a sentence of 18 months on the reef in chains. N.B. Some of these chains were 36 lbs. weight, and on the reef the men had mostly to work up to the middle in water.

November 12th. A frightful thing has happened. In one of the turnkey's rooms in the new gaol is to be seen an article of harness, that at first sight creates surprise in the mind of the beholder, who considers what animal of the brute creation exists of so diminutive a size as to admit of its use. On inquiry, it will be found to be a bridle,[2] perfect in headband, throat-lash, etc., for a human being.

There is attached to this bridle a round piece of cross wood, of almost four inches in length, and one and a half in diameter. This, again, is secured to a broad strap of leather to cross the mouth. In the wood there is a small hole, and when used, the wood is inserted in the mouth, the small hole being the only breathing space. This being secured with the various straps and buckles, a more complete bridle could not be well imagined.

I was in the gaol last evening at eight o' clock. I had been to see Rufus Dawes, and returning, paused for a moment to speak to Hailey. Gimblett, who robbed Mr Vane of £200, was present; he was at that time a turnkey, holding a third-class pass, and in receipt of 2s. per diem. Everything was quite still. I

1. This man's name was Waters. He was at Norfolk Island in 1847.
2. A fact.

could not help remarking how quiet the gaol was, when Gimblett said,

'There's someone speaking. I know what — that is.'

And forthwith took from its pegs one of the bridles just described, and a pair of handcuffs.

I followed him to one of the cells, which he opened, and therein was a man lying on his straw mat, undressed, and to all appearance fast asleep. Gimblett ordered him to get up and dress himself. He did so, and came into the yard, where Gimblett inserted the iron-wood gag in his mouth. The sound produced by his breathing through it (which appeared to be done with great difficulty) resembled a low, indistinct whistle. Gimblett led him to the lamp post in the yard, and I saw that the victim of this wanton tyranny was the poor blind wretch Mooney. Gimblett placed him with his back against the lamp-post, and his arms being taken round, were secured by handcuffs round the post. I was told that the old man was to remain in this condition for three hours.

The consequences following upon this were as terrible as they were unexpected.

✦ 22 ✦

THE LONGEST STRAW

RUFUS DAWES hearing, when 'on the chain' the next day, of the wanton torture of his friend, uttered no threat of vengeance, but groaned only.

'I am not so strong as I was,' said he, as if in apology for his lack of spirit. 'They have unnerved me.' And he looked sadly down at his gaunt frame and trembling hands.

'I can't stand it no longer,' said Mooney, grimly. 'I've spoken to Bland, and he's of my mind. You know what we resolved to do. Let's do it.'

Rufus Dawes stared at the sightless orbs turned inquiringly to his own. The fingers of his hand, thrust into his bosom, felt the rose that lay there. A shudder thrilled him. 'No, no. Not now,' he said.

'You're not afeard, man?' asked Mooney, stretching out his hand in the direction of the voice. 'You're not going to shirk?'

The other avoided the touch, and shrank away, still staring.

'You ain't going to back out after you swored it, Dawes? You're not that sort. Dawes, speak, man !'

'Is Bland willing?' asked Dawes, looking round, as if to seek for some method of escape from the glare of those unspeculative eyes.

'Ay and ready. They flogged him again yesterday.'

'Leave it till to-morrow,' said Dawes, at length.

'No; let's have it over,' urged the old man, with a strange eagerness. 'I'm tired o' this.'

Rufus Dawes cast a wistful glance towards the wall behind which lay the house of the Commandant.

'Leave it till to-morrow,' he repeated, with his hands still in his breast.

They had been so occupied in this conversation that neither had observed the approach of their common enemy.

'What are you hiding there?' cries Frere, seizing Dawes by the wrist. 'More tobacco, you dog?'

The hand of the convict, thus suddenly plucked from his bosom, opened involuntarily, and a withered rose fell to the earth.

Frere at once indignant and astonished, picked it up.

'Hallo ! What the devil's this? You've not been robbing my garden for a nosegay, Jack?'

The Commandant was wont to call all convicts 'Jack' in his moments of facetiousness. It was a little humorous way he had.

Rufus Dawes uttered one dismal cry, and then stood trembling and cowed. His companions, hearing the exclamation of rage and grief that burst from him, looked to see him snatch back the flower or perform some act of violence. Perhaps such was his intention, but he did not execute it. One would have thought that there was some charm about this rose so strangely cherished, for he stood gazing at it as it twirled between Captain Frere's strong fingers as though it fascinated him.

'You're a pretty man to want a rose for your buttonhole ! Are you going out with your sweetheart next Sunday, Mr Dawes?' The gang laughed. 'How did you get this?' Dawes was silent.

'You'd better tell me.' No answer. 'Troke, let us see if we can't find Mr Dawes's tongue. Pull off your shirt, my man. I expect that's the way to your heart – eh, boys?'

At this elegant allusion to the lash, the gang laughed again, and looked at each other astonished. It seemed possible that the leader of the Ring was going to turn milk-sop.

Such indeed appeared to be the case, for Dawes, trembling and pale, cried, 'Don't flog me again, sir! I picked it up in the yard. It fell out of your coat one day.'

Frere smiled with an inward satisfaction at the result of his spirit-breaking. The explanation was probably the correct one. He was in the habit of wearing flowers in his coat, and it was impossible that the convict should have obtained one by any other means. Had it been a fig of tobacco now, the astute Commandant knew plenty of men who would have brought it into the prison. But who would risk a flogging for so useless a thing as a flower?

'You'd better not pick up any more, Jack. We don't grow flowers for your amusement,' he said. And contemptuously flinging the rose over the wall, he strode away.

The gang, left to itself for a moment, bestowed their attention upon Dawes. Large tears were silently rolling down his face, and he stood staring at the wall as one in a dream. The gang curled their lips. One fellow, more charitable than the rest, tapped his forehead and winked. 'He's going cranky,' said this good-natured man, who could not understand what a sane prisoner had to do with flowers. Dawes recovered himself, and the contemptuous glances of his companions seemed to bring back the colour to his cheeks.

'We'll do it to-night,' whispered he to Mooney, and Mooney smiled with pleasure.

Since the 'tobacco-trick,' Mooney and Dawes had been placed in the new prison, together with the wretched Bland, whose condition was stated by North in his journal of October 25th. Bland had – as had Dawes – twice attempted to kill himself, but had not succeeded. When old Mooney, fresh from the torture of the gag-and-bridle, lamented his hard case, Bland proposed that the three should put in practice a scheme in which two at least must succeed. The scheme was a desperate one, and attempted but in the last extremity. It was the custom of the Ring, however, to swear each of its members to carry out to the best of his ability this last invention of the convict-disciplined mind, should two other members crave his assistance.

The scheme – like all great ideas – was simplicity itself.

That evening, when the cell-door was securely locked, and the absence of a visiting gaoler might be counted upon for an hour at least, Bland produced a straw, and held it out to his companions. Dawes took it, and tearing it into unequal lengths handed the fragments to Mooney.

'The longest is the one,' says the blind man. 'Come on, boys, and dip in the lucky-bag!'

It was evident that lots were to be drawn to determine to whom fortune would grant freedom. The men drew in silence, and then Bland and Dawes looked at each other. The prize had been left in the bag. Mooney – fortunate old fellow – retained the longest straw. Bland's hand shook as he compared notes with his companion. There was a moment's pause, during which the blank eyeballs of the blind man fiercely searched the gloom, as if in that awful moment they could penetrate it.

'I hold the shortest,' said Dawes to Bland. ''Tis you that must do it.'

'I'm glad of that,' said Mooney.

Bland, seemingly terrified at the danger which fate had decreed that he should run, tore the fatal lot into fragments, with an oath, and sat gnawing his knuckles in excess of abject terror.

Mooney stretched himself out upon his plank-bed. 'Come on, mate,' he said.

Bland extended a shaking hand and caught Rufus Dawes by the sleeve.

'You have more nerve than I. You do it.'

'No, no,' says Dawes, almost as pale as his companion. 'I've run my chance fairly. 'Twas your own proposal.'

The coward who, confident in his own luck, would seem to have fallen into the pit he had dug for others sat rocking himself to and fro, holding his head in his hands.

'By Heaven, I can't do it,' he whispered, lifting a white, wet face.

'What are you waiting for?' said fortunate Mooney. 'Come on, I'm ready.'

'I – I – thought you might like to – to – pray a bit,' says Bland.

The notion seemed to sober the senses of the old man, exalted too fiercely by his good fortune.

'Ay,' he said. 'Pray. A good thought!' and he knelt down, and shutting his blind eyes – 'twas as though he was dazzled by some strong light, unseen by his comrades – moved his lips slowly.

The silence was at last broken by the footstep of the warder in the corridor. Bland hailed it as a reprieve from whatever act of daring he dreaded.

'We must wait until he goes,' he whispered eagerly. 'He might look in.'

Dawes nodded, and Mooney, whose quick ear apprised him very exactly of the position of the approaching gaoler, rose from his knees, radiant.

The sour face of Gimblett appeared at the trap of the cell-door.

'All right?' he asked, somewhat – so the three thought – less sourly than usual.

'All right,' was the reply, and Mooney added 'Good-night, Mr Gimblett.'

'I wonder what makes the old man so cheerful,' thought Gimblett, as he got into the next corridor.

The sound of his echoing footsteps had scarcely died away, when upon the ears of the two less fortunate casters of lots, fell the dull sound of rending woollen. The lucky man was tearing a strip from his blanket.

'I think this will do,' said he, pulling it between his hands to test its strength. 'I am an old man.'

It was possible that he debated concerning the descent of some abyss into which the strip of blanket was to lower him.

'Here, Bland, catch hold.' Bland mechanically seized the end of the improvised rope.

'Dawes, come here a minute.' The old man spoke with a sort

of dignity, and Dawes obeyed. 'If ever you get out,' whispered Mooney, 'go to Summerhill Creek, where it joins the Macquarie. Pick out some narrow gully, between the quartz-rocks, and when you come to a bit o' good red earth, dig. D'ye mind now?'

'Yes, yes,' said Dawes, soothingly, as though willing to humour his comrade.

'He don't believe it,' said Mooney, as if to himself. 'I'm giving him my fortune, and he don't believe it.'

'It's no use – I shall never get out,' returned Dawes.

'No, you ain't got my luck. I'm agoing – quick! Good-bye, old chap! Bland – where are ye? – don't be faint hearted, man. It won't take ye long.'

It was quite dark now in the cell, but as Bland advanced, his face seemed a white mask floating upon the darkness, it was so ghastly pale. Dawes pressed his lucky comrade's hand and withdrew to the farthest corner. Bland and Mooney seemed, for a few moments, occupied with the rope – doubtless preparing for escape by means of it. The silence was broken only by the convulsive jangling of Bland's irons – he was shuddering violently. At last Mooney spoke again, in strangely soft and subdued tones.

'Dawes, lad, do you think there is a Heaven?'

'I know there is a Hell,' said Dawes, without turning his face.

'Ay, and a Heaven, lad. I think I shall go there. You will, old chap, for you've been good to me – God bless you, you've been very good to me.'

Dawes uttered a choking sob.

When Troke came in the morning, he saw what had occurred at a glance, and hastened to remove the corpse of the strangled Mooney.

'We drew lots,' said Rufus Dawes, pointing to Bland, who crouched in the corner farthest from his victim, 'and it fell upon him to do it. I'm the witness.'

'They'll hang you, for all that,' said Troke.

'I hope so,' said Rufus Dawes; and then, as the body of the old man was borne past him, the full horror of the crime in which he had participated burst upon him, and he raised his hands to heaven with a dreadful cry — 'Oh! when a man is brought into this place his Man's heart is taken from him and he gets the heart of a Beast!'

The scheme of escape hit upon by the convict intellect was simply this. Three men being together, lots were drawn to determine whom should be murdered. The drawer of the longest straw was the 'lucky' man. He was killed. The drawer of the next longest straw was the murderer. He was hanged. The unlucky one was the witness — necessary to ensure the happiness of number two. The third man had, of course, a chance of being hung also, but his doom was not so certain, and he therefore looked upon himself as unfortunate.

◄◄ 12 ►►

Extracted from the Diary of the Rev. James North

December 7th. I have made up my mind to leave this place, where for I know not — to bury myself again in the bush, I suppose, and await extinction. I try to think that the reason of this determination is the frightful condition of misery existing among the prisoners; that because I am daily horrified and sickened by scenes of torture and infamy, I decide to go away; that, feeling myself useless to save others, I wish to spare myself. But in this journal, in which I bound myself to write nothing but truth, I am forced to confess that these are *not* the reasons. I will write them plainly. '*I covet my neighbour's wife.*' It does not look well thus written; it looks hideous. In my own breast I find numberless excuses for my passion. I say to myself, 'My neighbour does not love his wife, and her unloved life is misery. She is forced to live in the frightful seclusion of this cursed island, and she is dying for want of companionship. She feels that I understand and appreciate her, that I could love her as she deserves, that I could render her happy. I feel that I have met the only woman who has power to touch my heart, to hold me back from the ruin into which I am about to plunge, to make me useful to my fellows – a man, and not a drunkard.' Whispering these conclusions to myself, I am urged to brave public opinion, and make two lives happy. I say to myself, or, rather, my desires say to me – 'What sin is there in this? Adultery? No; for a marriage without love is the coarsest of all adulteries. What tie binds a man and woman together – that formula of license pronounced by the priest, which the law recognised as a "legal bond?" Surely not this only, for marriage is but a partnership – a contract of mutual fidelity – and in all contracts the violation of the terms of the agreement by one of the contracting persons absolves the other. Mrs Frere is, then, absolved by her husband's act. I cannot but think so. But is she willing to risk the shame of divorce or legal sin? Perhaps. Is she fitted by temperament to bear such a burden of contumely as must needs fall upon her? Will she not feel disgust at the man who entrapped her into shame? Do not the comforts which surround her compensate for the lack of affection?'

And so the torturing catechism continues until I am driven mad with doubt, love, and despair.

Of course, I am wrong; of course, I outrage my character as a priest; of course, I endanger – according to the creed I teach – my soul and hers. But priests, unluckily, have hearts and passions as well as other men. Thank God, as yet, I have never expressed my madness in words. I am outwardly innocent, but, says the Master – 'He that looketh at a woman to lust after her, has committed adultery already with her in his heart.' What a fate is mine! When I am in her presence I am in torment; when I am absent from her, my imagination pictures her surrounded by a thousand graces that are not her's, but belong to all the women of my dreams – to Helen, to Juliet, to Rosalind. Fools that we are of our own senses. When I think of her I blush; when I hear her name my heart leaps, and I grow pale. Love! What is the love of two pure souls, scarce conscious of the Paradise into which they have fallen, to this maddening delirium? I can understand the poison of Circe's cup; it was the sweet-torment of a forbidden love like mine! Away gross materialism in which I have so long schooled myself! I, who laughed at passion as the outcome of temperament and easy living – I, who thought, in my intellect, to sound all the depths and shallows of human feeling – I, who analyzed my own soul – scoffed at my own yearnings for an immortality – am forced to deify the senseless Power of my creed, and believe in GOD, *that I may pray to Him*. I know now why men reject the cold Impersonality that reason tells us rules the world – it is because they love. To die, and be no more – to die, and rendered into dust, be blown about the earth – to die, and leave our Love defenceless and forlorn, till the bright soul that smiled to ours is smothered in the earth that made it. No! To love is life eternal. God, I believe in Thee! Aid me! Pity me! Sinful wretch that I am, to have denied Thee! See me on my knees before Thee! Pity me, or let me die!

December 9th. I have been visiting the prisoners and praying with them. O Lord, let me save one soul that may plead with Thee for mine! Let me draw one being alive out of this pit! I weep – I weary Thee with my prayers, O Lord! Look down upon me. Grant me a sign. Thou did'st it in old times to men who were not more fervent in their supplications than am I. So says Thy Book. Thy Book which I believe – which I believe. Grant me a sign – one little sign, O Lord! ... I will not see her. I have sworn it. Thou knowest my grief – my agony – my despair. Thou knowest why I love her. Thou knowest how I strive to make her hate me. Is that not a sacrifice? I am so lonely – a lonely man, with but one creature that he loves – yet, what is mortal love to Thee? Cruel and implacable, Thou sittest in the Heavens men have built for Thee, and scornest them! Will not all the burnings and slaughters of the saints appease Thee? Art Thou not sated with blood and tears, O God of vengeance, of wrath, and of despair? Kind Christ, pity me! *Thou* wilt – for Thou wast human! Blessed Saviour, at whose feet knelt the Magdalen! Divinity, who most divine in Thy despair, called on Thy cruel God to save Thee – by the memory of that moment when Thou did'st deem Thyself forsaken – forsake not me! Sweet Christ, have mercy on Thy sinful servant!

I can write no more. I will pray to Thee with my lips. I will shriek my supplications to Thee. I will call upon Thee so loud

that all the world shall hear me, and wonder at Thy silence –
unjust and unmerciful God!

December 14th. What blasphemies are these that I have uttered
in my despair? Horrible madness that hast left me prostrate, to
what heights of frenzy did'st thou not drive my soul! I have
been mad. Like him of old time, who wandered among the
tombs, shrieking and tearing himself, I have been possessed by
a devil. For a week I have been unconscious of aught save
torture. I have gone about my daily duties as one who in his
dreams repeats the accustomed action of the day, and knows it
not. Men have looked at me strangely. They look at me
strangely now. Can it be that my disease of drunkenness has
become the disease of insanity? Am I mad, or do I but verge on
madness? O Lord, whom in my agonies I have confessed, leave
me my intellect – let me not become a drivelling spectacle for
the curious to point at or to pity! At least, in mercy, spare me
a little. Let not my punishment overtake me *here*. Let *her*
memories of me be clouded with a sense of my rudeness or my
brutality; let me for ever seem to her the ungrateful ruffian I
strive to show myself – but let her not behold me – *that!*

✦ 13 ✦

THE STRANGE BEHAVIOUR OF MR NORTH

ON or about the 8th of December, Mrs Frere noticed a sudden
and unaccountable change in the manner of the chaplain. He
came to her one afternoon, and, after talking for some time, in
a vague and unconnected manner, about the miseries of the
prison and the wretched condition of some of the prisoners, began
to question her abruptly concerning Rufus Dawes.

'I don't remember him,' said she, with a shudder. 'I don't
wish to remember him. He tried to murder me when a child,
and had it not been for my husband, he would have done so. I
have only seen him once since then – at Hobart Town, when he
was taken.'

'He sometimes speaks to me of you,' said North, eyeing her. 'He asked me once to give him a rose plucked in your garden.'

Dora blushed. 'And you gave it him?'

'Yes, I gave it him. Why not?'

'It was valueless, of course, but still – a wretch like that!'

'You are not angry?'

'Oh no! Why should I be angry?' she laughed constrainedly. 'It was a strange fancy for a creature like that to have, that's all.'

'I suppose you would not give me another rose, if I asked you.'

'Certainly,' said she, blushing deeper. 'You are a gentleman.'

'Not I – you don't know me.'

'What do you mean?'

'I mean that it would be better for you if you had never seen me.'

'Mr North!' Terrified at the wild gleam in his eyes, she had risen hastily. 'You are talking very strangely.'

'Oh, don't be alarmed, Madam, I am not *drunk!*' – he pronounced the word with a fierce energy – 'I don't know whether I look so. I had better leave you, I think. Indeed, I think the less we see of each other the better.'

Deeply wounded and astonished at this extraordinary outburst, Dora allowed him to stride away without a word. She saw him pass through the garden and slam the little gate, but she did not see the agony on his face, or the passionate gesture with which – when out of eyesight – he lamented the voluntary abasement of himself before her.

She thought over his conduct with growing fear. It was not possible that he was intoxicated – such a vice was the last one of which she should have believed him guilty. It was more probable that some effects of the fever, which had recently confined him to his house, yet lingered. So she thought – and, thinking, was alarmed to realize of how much importance the wellbeing of this man was to her.

The next day, he met her, and, bowing, passed swiftly. This pained her. Could she have offended him by some unlucky word? She made Maurice ask him to dinner, and, to her astonishment, he pleaded illness as an excuse for not coming. Her pride was hurt, and she sent him back his books and music.

A curiosity that was unworthy of her, compelled her to ask the servant who carried the parcel what the clergyman had said. 'He said nothing – only laughed.' Laughed! In scorn of her foolishness! His conduct was ungentlemanly and intemperate. She would forget, as speedily as possible, that such a being had ever existed. This resolution taken, she was unusually snappish to her husband, and he being in a bad temper also, the pair fell to wrangling. Many bitter words passed between them, and, Maurice flinging coarse oaths at her, the quarrel ended in sulks for him, and hysterics for her.

She passed the next day in her own room, with the blinds drawn down, and Maurice relieved his feelings by flogging three or four men for 'insubordination.' When he came home, he boasted of his achievements, not because he was proud of them, but because he knew that the recitation would wound and annoy his wife. Whenever the ill-mated pair quarrelled, Maurice made a point of asserting his penal authority in the most violent manner. It was a sort of vicarious triumph over his wife. She might sting him into fury by her reproaches, but he knew that the narrative of his own brutality would crush her into horrified silence.

He succeeded so well that she came to him one day and begged to be sent back to Hobart Town. 'I cannot live in this horrible island,' she said. 'I am getting ill. Dotty, too, wants change. Let us go to my father for a few months, Maurice.'

Maurice hummed and hahed over the project, but at last consented. His wife *was* looking ill, and Major Vickers was an old man – a rich old man – who loved his only daughter. It was not undesirable that Mrs Frere should visit her father, indeed, so little sympathy was there between the pair, that the first astonishment over, Maurice felt rather glad to get rid of her for a while.

'You can go back in the *Lady Franklin*, if you like,' he said, 'I expect her every day.'

At this decision – much to his surprise – she kissed him with more show of affection than she had manifested since the birth of her child.

So a week passed, and Mr North did not return. Unluckily, for the poor wretch, the very self-sacrifice he had made brought about the precise condition of things which he was desirous to avoid. It is possible that had the acquaintance between them continued on the same staid footing, it would have followed the lot of most acquaintanceships of the kind – other circumstances and other scenes might have wiped out the memory of all but common civilities between them, and Dora might never have discovered that she had owned for the chaplain any other feeling but that of esteem. But the very fact of the sudden wrenching away of her soul-companion, showed her how barren was the solitary life to which she had been fated. Her husband, she had long ago admitted, with bitter self-communings, was utterly unsuited to her. She could find in his society no enjoyment, and for the mental sympathy which she needed was compelled to turn elsewhere. She understood that his love for her had burnt itself out – she confessed, with intensity of self-degradation, that his apparent affection had been born of sensuality, and had perished in the fires it had itself kindled. Many women have, unhappily, made some such discovery as this, but for most women there is some distracting occupation. Had it been Dora's fate to live in the midst of fashion and society, she would have found relief in the conversation of the witty, or the homage of the distinguished. Had fortune cast her lot in a city, Dora might have become one of those charming women, who collect around their supper-tables whatever of male intellect is obtainable, and who find the husband admirably useful to open his own champagne bottles. The celebrated women who have stepped out of their domestic circles to enchant, or astonish the world, have almost invariably been cursed with unhappy homes. But poor Dora was not destined to become a George Sand or a Mary Montague. Cast back upon herself, she found no surcease of pain in her own imaginings, and meeting with a man sufficiently her elder to encourage her to talk, and sufficiently clever to induce her to seek his society and his advice, she learnt, for the first time, to forget her own griefs, and, for the first time, suffered her nature to expand under the sun of a congenial influence. This sun, suddenly withdrawn, her soul, grown accustomed to the warmth and light, shivered at the gloom, and she looked about her in dismay, at the dull and barren prospect of life which lay before her. In a word, she found that the society of North had become so far a necessary to her, that to be deprived of it was a grief — notwithstanding that her husband remained to console her.

A few weeks passed, and North did not make his appearance. So far, however, from forgetting him, Dora longed the more eagerly for his society. Had it not been a step beneath the dignity of a woman, she would have gone herself and asked him the meaning of his unaccountable rudeness, but there was just sufficient morbidity in the sympathy she had for him to restrain her from an act which a young girl — though not more innocent — would have dared without hesitation. Calling one day upon the wife of the surgeon, however, she met the chaplain face to face, and with the consummate art of acting to which most women are born, rallied him upon his absence from her house. The behaviour of the poor devil, thus stabbed to the heart, was curious. He forgot gentlemanly behaviour and the respect due to a woman, flung one despairing angry glance at her, and abruptly retired. Dora flushed crimson, and endeavoured to excuse North on account of his recent illness. The surgeon's wife, a childless, bitter woman, looked askance, and turned the conversation. The next time Dora bowed to this lady, she got a chilling salutation in return that made her blood boil.

'I wonder how I have offended Mrs Field,' she asked Maurice. 'She almost cut me to-day.'

'Oh, the old cat!' returned Maurice. 'What does it matter if she did?'

However, a few days afterwards, it seemed that it did matter, for Maurice called upon Field and conversed seriously with him. The issue of the conversation being reported to Mrs Frere, the lady wept indignant tears of wounded pride and shame. It appeared that North had watched her out of the house, returned, and related — 'in a stumbling, hesitating way,' Mrs Field said — how he had been often oppressed by the importunities of Mrs Frere, how he did not want to visit her, and how flighty and reprehensible such conduct seemed in a married woman of her rank and station. This act of baseness — or profound nobleness — certainly achieved its purpose. Dora shunned the unhappy priest as if he had a pestilence.

Between the Commandant and the chaplain arose a coolness,

and Frere set himself, by various petty tyrannies, to disgust North, and compel him to a resignation of his office. The convict-gaolers speedily marked the difference in the treatment of the chaplain, and their demeanour changed. For respect was substituted insolence; for alacrity, sullenness; for prompt obedience, impertinent intrusion. The men whom North favoured were selected as special subjects for harshness, and, for a prisoner to be seen talking to the clergyman, was sufficient to ensure for him a series of tyrannies. The result of this was, that North saw the souls he laboured to save slipping back into the gulf; beheld the men he had half won to love him meet him with averted faces; discovered that, to show interest in a prisoner, was to injure him, not to serve him.

The unhappy man grew thinner and paler under this ingenious torment. He had deprived himself of that love which, guilty though it might be, was, nevertheless, the only true love he had known; and he found that, having won this victory, he had gained the hatred of all living creatures with whom he came in contact. The authority of the Commandant was so supreme that men lived but by the breath of his nostrils. To offend him was to perish, and the man whom the Commandant hated must be hated, also, by all those who wished to exist in peace.

There was but one being who was not to be turned from his allegiance – the poor convict murderer, Rufus Dawes, who awaited death. For many days he had remained mute, broken down beneath his weight of sorrow or of sullenness; but North, bereft of other love and sympathy, strove with that fighting soul, if haply he might win it back to Peace. It seemed to the fancy of the priest – a fancy distempered, perhaps, by excess, or superhumanly exalted by mental agony – that this convict, over whom he had wept, was given to him as a hostage for his own salvation. 'I must save him or perish,' he said, 'I must save him, though I redeem him with my blood.'

Frere – unable to comprehend the reason of the calmness with which the doomed felon met his taunts and torments – thought that he was shamming piety to gain some indulgence of meat and drink, and redoubled his severity.

He ordered Dawes to be taken out to work just before the

hour at which the chaplain was accustomed to visit him. He pretended that the man was 'dangerous,' and ordered a gaoler to be present at all interviews, 'lest the chaplain might be murdered.' He issued an order that all civil officers should obey the challenges of convicts acting as watchmen; and North, coming to pray with his penitent, would be stopped ten times by grinning felons, who, putting their faces within a foot of his, would roar out, 'who goes there?' and burst out laughing at the reply. Under the pretence of watching more carefully over the property of the chaplain, he directed that any convict, acting as constable, might at any time 'search everywhere and anywhere,' for property supposed to be in the possession of a prisoner. The chaplain's servant was a prisoner, of course; and North's drawers were ransacked twice in one week by Troke, who wanted to find 'papers belonging to Markham.' North met these impertinences with unruffled brow, and baffled Frere could in no way account for his obstinacy, until the arrival of the *Lady Franklin* explained the chaplain's apparent coolness. He had sent in his resignation two months before, and saintly Meekin was appointed in his stead.

Frere, unable to attack the clergyman, and indignant at the manner in which he had been defeated, revenged himself upon Rufus Dawes.

⤙ *14* ⤚

MR NORTH SPEAKS

THE method and manner of his revenge became a subject of whispered conversation on the island. It was reported that North had been forbidden to visit the convict, but that he had refused to accept such prohibition, and, by a threat of what he would do when the returning vessel had landed him in Hobart Town, had compelled the Commandant to withdraw his order. The Commandant, however, speedily discovered in Rufus Dawes signs of insubordination, and set to work again to reduce still further the 'spirit' he had so ingeniously 'broken.' The unhappy convict was deprived of food, was kept awake at nights, was put to the hardest labour, was loaded with the heaviest irons. Troke, with devilish malice, suggested that, if the tortured wretch would decline to see the Chaplain, some amelioration of his condition might be effected; but his suggestions were in vain. Fully believing that his death was certain, Dawes clung to North as the saviour of his agonised soul, and rejected all such insidious overtures. Enraged at this obstinacy, Frere sentenced his victim to the 'spread eagle' and the 'stretcher.'

These tortures might have been used with success by those good folks who invented the 'scavenger's daughter,' the rack, and the 'press.' The torment of the 'spread eagle,' as described by the Rev. Mr Rogers, chaplain at Norfolk Island, in 1846, was as follows: —[1]

'Two ringbolts, about six feet asunder, and five and a half feet from the floor, are securely fastened in the walls of the cells, and a third to the floor; the three bolts so placed as to form the letter V. The prisoner who has to undergo this punishment is, in several instances, placed with his back to the wall, but oftener with his face. His arms are stretched out and firmly secured to the ringbolts, and his feet, being brought close together, are made fast to the one on the floor. The bridle and iron-wood bit are, in most cases, added to increase the torture.'

The 'stretcher' was an elaboration of this mechanism, and was more painful in its operation. A man is reported to have actually died during its infliction.

Though Dora had not seen or heard of North, the rumour of the obduracy of the convict, whose name had been recalled to her by the clergyman at their strange interview, had reached her ears. She had heard gloomy hints of the punishments inflicted on him by her husband's order; and as — constantly revolving in her mind that last conversation with the chaplain — she wondered at the prisoner's strange fancy for a flower, her

1. Correspondence Relative to the Dismissal of the Rev. T. Rogers from his Chaplaincy at Norfolk Island. Launceston: Henry Dowling. 1849. For private Circulation. Page 43.

brain began to thrill with those undefined and dreadful memories which had haunted her childhood. What was the link between her and this murderous villain? How came it that she felt at times so strange a sympathy for his fate, and that he – who had attempted her life – cherished so tender a remembrance of her as to beg for a flower which her hand had touched?

She questioned her husband concerning the convict's misdoings, but, with that petulant brutality he invariably displayed when the name of Rufus Dawes intruded itself into their conversation, Maurice Frere harshly refused to satisfy her. This but raised her curiosity higher. She reflected how bitter he had always seemed against this man – she remembered how, in the garden at Port Arthur, the hunted wretch had caught her dress with words of assured confidence – she recollected the fragment of cloth he had passionately flung from him, and which her affianced husband had contemptuously tossed into the stream. The name of 'Dawes,' detested as it had become to her, bore yet some strange association of comfort and hope. What secret lurked behind the twilight that had fallen upon her childish memories? Deprived of the advice of North – to whom, a few weeks back, she would have confided her misgivings – she resolved upon a project that, for her, was most distasteful. She would herself visit that mysterious 'prison,' and judge how far the rumours of her husband's cruelty were worthy of credit.

One sultry afternoon, when the Commandant had gone on a visit of inspection, Troke, lounging at the door of the New Prison, beheld, with surprise, the figure of the Commandant's lady.

'What is it, mam?' he asked, scarcely able to believe his eyes.

'I want to see the prisoner Dawes.'

Troke's jaw fell.

'See Dawes?' he repeated.

'Yes. Where is he?'

Troke was preparing a lie. The imperious voice, and the clear, steady gaze, confused him.

'He's here.'

'Let me see him.'

'He's – he's under punishment, mam.'

'What do you mean? Are they flogging him?'

'No; but – but he's dangerous, mam. The Commandant –'

'Do you mean to open the door or not, Mr Troke?'

Troke grew more confused. It was evident that he was most unwilling to open the door.

'The Commandant gave strict orders –'

'Do you wish me to *complain* to the Commandant, Man?' cries Dora, with a touch of her old spirit, and jumping hastily at the conclusion that the gaolers were perhaps torturing the convict for their own entertainment, 'Open the door at once! – at once!'

Thus commanded, Troke, with a hasty growl of its 'being no affair of his, and he hoped Mrs Frere would tell the captain how it happened,' flung open the door of a cell on the right hand of the doorway.

It was so dark that, at first, Dora could distinguish nothing but the outline of some framework, with something stretched upon it that resembled a human body.

Her first thought was that the man was dead, but this was not so – he groaned. Her eyes, accustoming themselves to the gloom, began to see what the 'punishment'[1] was. Upon the floor was placed an iron frame about six feet long, and two and a half feet wide, with round iron bars, placed transversely, about twelve inches apart. The man she came to seek was bound in a horizontal position upon this frame, with his head projecting over the end of it. If he allowed his head to hang, the blood rushed to his brain and suffocated him, while the effort to keep it raised strained every muscle to agony pitch. His face was purple, and he foamed at the mouth. Dora uttered a cry.

'This is no punishment; it is murder! Who ordered this?'

'The Commandant,' says Troke, sullenly.

'I don't believe it. Loose him!'

'I daren't, mam,' says Troke.

'Loose him, I say! Hailey! – you, sir, there!' The noise had brought several warders to the spot. 'Do you hear me? Do you know who I am? Loose him, I say!'

In her eagerness and compassion, she was on her knees by the side of the infernal machine, plucking at the ropes with her delicate fingers.

1. Brit. Parliamentary Papers. 1847.

'Wretches, you have cut his flesh! He is dying! Help! You have killed him!'

The prisoner, in fact, seeing this angel of mercy stooping over him and hearing close to him the tones of a voice that for seven years he had heard but in his dreams, had fainted.

Troke and Hailey, alarmed by her vehemence, dragged the stretcher out into the light, and hastily cut the lashings. Dawes rolled off like a log, and his head fell against Mrs Frere. Troke roughly pulled him aside, and called for water.

Dora, trembling with sympathy, and pale with passion, turned upon the crew.

'How long has he been like this?'

'An hour,' said Troke.

'A lie!' said a stern voice at the door. 'It is nine hours!'

'Wretches!' cried Dora, 'you shall hear more of this. Oh, oh! I am sick!' – she felt for the wall – 'I – I –' North watched her with agony on his face, but did not move – 'I faint! – I –' – she uttered a despairing cry that was not without a touch of anger – 'Mr North! – do you not see? Oh! Take me home – take me home!'

She would have fallen across the body of the tortured prisoner had not North caught her in his arms.

Rufus Dawes, awaking from his stupor, saw, in the midst of a sunbeam which penetrated a window in the corridor, the group of the woman who came to save his body, supported by the priest who came to save his soul; and staggering to his knees, he stretched out his hands with a hoarse cry. Perhaps there was something in the action which brought back to the dimmed remembrance of the Commandant's wife the image of a similar figure stretching forth its hands to a frightened child in the mysterious far-off time. She started, and pushing back her hair, bent a wistful, terrified gaze upon the face of the kneeling man, as though she would fain read there an explanation of the shadowy memory that haunted her. It is possible that she would have spoken, but North – thinking the excitement had produced one of those hysterical crises which were common to her – gently drew her, still gazing, back towards the gate.

The convict's arms fell, and an undefinable presentiment of evil chilled him as he beheld the priest – emotion pallid in his cheeks — slowly draw the fair young creature from out the sunlight into the grim shadow of the heavy archway. For an instant the gloom swallowed them, and it seemed to Dawes that the strange wild man of God had in that instant become a man of Evil — blighting the brightness and the beauty of the innocence that clung to him. For an instant — and then they passed out of the prison archway into the free air of heaven — and the sunlight glowed golden on their faces.

'You are ill,' said North. 'You will faint. Why do you look so wildly!'

'What is it,' she whispered, more in answer to her own thoughts than to his question, 'that links me to that man? What deed — what terror — what memory! I tremble with crowding thoughts, that die ere they can whisper to me. Oh, that prison!'

'Look up; we are in the sunshine.'

She passed her hand across her brow, sighing heavily, as one awaking from a disturbed slumber, shuddered, and withdrew her arm from his.

North interpreted the action correctly, and the blood rushed to his face.

'Pardon me, you cannot walk alone; you will fall. I will leave you at the gate.'

In truth she would have fallen had he not again assisted her. She turned upon him eyes whose reproachful sorrow had almost forced him to a confession, but he bowed his head and held silence. They reached the house, and he placed her tenderly in a chair.

'Now you are safe, madam. I will leave you.'

She burst into tears.

'Why do you treat me thus, Mr North? What have I done to make you hate me?'

'Hate you!' said North, with trembling lips. 'Oh, no, I do not — do not *hate* you. I am rude in my speech, abrupt in my manner. You must forget it, and — and *me*.'

A horse's feet crashed upon the gravel, and an instant after, Maurice Frere burst into the room.

Returning from the Cascades, he had met Troke, and learned

the release of the prisoner. Furious at this usurpation of authority by his wife, his self-esteem wounded by the thought that she had witnessed his mean revenge upon the man he had so infamously wronged, his natural brutality enhanced by brandy, he had made for the house at full gallop, determined to assert his authority. Blind with rage, he saw no one but his wife.

'What the devil's this I hear? *You* have been meddling in my business! *You* release prisoners! *You* –'

'Captain Frere!' said North, stepping forward to assert the restraining presence of a stranger.

Frere started, astonished at the intrusion of the chaplain. Here was another outrage of his dignity, another insult to his supreme authority. In its passion, his gross mind leapt to the worst conclusion.

'You here, too! What do you want here – with my wife! This is your *quarrel*, is it?' His eyes glanced wrathfully from one to the other; and he strode towards North. 'You infernal hypocritical lying scoundrel, if it wasn't for your black coat, I'd –'

'Maurice!' cried Dora, in an agony of shame and terror, striving to place a restraining hand upon his arm.

He turned upon her with so fiercely infamous a curse, that North, pale with righteous horror, seemed prompted to strike the burly ruffian to the earth. For a moment, the two men faced each other, and then Frere, muttering threats of vengeance against each and all – convict, gaolers, wife, and priest – flung the suppliant woman violently from him, and rushed from the room. She fell heavily against the wall, and as the chaplain raised her, they heard the hoof-strokes of the departing horse.

'Oh!' cried Dora, covering her face with trembling hands, 'let me leave this place.'

North, enfolding her in his arms, strove to soothe her with incoherent words of comfort. Dizzy with the blow she had received, she clung to him sobbing. Twice he tried to tear himself away, but had he loosed his hold she would have fallen. He could not hold her – bruised, suffering, and in tears – thus against his heart and keep silence. In a torrent of agonised eloquence the story of his guilty love burst from his lips.

'Why should you be thus tortured?' he cried. 'Heaven never willed you to be mated to that boor – you, whose life should be all sunshine – leave him – leave him, he has cast you off. We have both suffered. Let us leave this dreadful place – this isthmus between earth and hell! I will give you happiness – you and your child.'

'We are going,' she said, faintly. 'We had already arranged to go.'

North trembled. Fate had befriended him. 'We go together!' he cried, and raised the cold hand he held to his lips.

They looked at each other, – she felt the fever of his blood, she read his passion in his eyes, she comprehended the 'hatred' he had affected for her, and, deadly pale, snatched back the hand he would have kissed.

'Go!' she murmured. 'Leave me! Do not see me or speak to me again' – her silence added the words she could not utter, *'till then.'*

⊷ 15 ⊶

GETTING READY FOR SEA

MAURICE FRERE's passion had spent itself in that last act of violence. He did not return to the prison, as he had promised himself, but turned into the road that led to the Cascades. He had been a fool after all. There was nothing strange in the presence of the chaplain. Dora had always liked the man, and an apology for his conduct had doubtless removed her anger. To make a mountain out of a molehill was the act of an idiot. It was natural that she should release Dawes – women *were* so tender-hearted. A few well-chosen, calmly-uttered platitudes anent the necessity for treatment that, to those unaccustomed to the desperate wickedness of convicts, must appear harsh, would have served his turn far better than bluster and abuse. Moreover, North was to sail in the *Lady Franklin*, and might put in execution his threats of official complaint, unless he was carefully dealt with. To put Dawes again to the torture, would be to show to Troke and his friends that the 'Commandant's wife' had acted without the 'Commandant's authority,' and that must not be shown. He would return and patch up a peace. His wife sailed in the same vessel with North, and he would, in a few days, be left alone on the island to pursue his 'discipline' unchecked.

With this intent, he returned to the prison, and gravely informed poor Troke that he was astonished at his barbarity.

'Mrs Frere who, most luckily, had appointed to meet me this evening at the prison, tells me that the poor devil Dawes had been on the stretcher since seven o'clock in the morning.'

'You ordered it fust thing, yer honour,' said Troke.

'Yes, you fool, but I didn't order you to keep the man there for nine hours, did I? Why, you scoundrel, you might have killed him.'

Troke scratched his head in bewilderment.

'Take his irons off, and put him in a separate cell in the old jail. If a man *is* a murderer, that is no reason you should take the law into your own hands, is it? You better take care, Mr Troke.'

On the way back he met the chaplain, who, seeing him, made for a byepath in curious haste.

'Halloo!' roars Frere. 'Hi! Mr North!'

North paused, and the Commandant made at him abruptly.

'Look here, sir, I was rude to you just now – devilish rude. Most ungentlemanly of me. I must apologise.'

North bowed, without speaking, and tried to pass.

'You must excuse my violence,' Frere went on. 'I'm bad tempered, and I didn't like my wife interfering. Women, don't you know, don't see these things – don't understand these scoundrels.'

North again bowed.

'Why, dammit, how ill you look! Quite ghastly, bigod! I must have said most outrageous things. Forget and forgive, you know. Come home and have some dinner. Let's part friends, bigod!'

'I cannot enter your house again, sir,' said North, in tones more agitated than the occasion would seem to warrant.

Frere hunched his great shoulders with a clumsy affectation of good humour, and held out his hand.

'Well, shake hands, parson. You'll have to take care of Mrs Frere on the voyage, and we may as well make up our differences before you start. Shake hands.'

'Let me pass, sir!' cries North, with heightened colour; and so ignoring the proffered hand, strides savagely on.

'You've a d—d fine temper for a parson,' said Frere to himself. 'However, if you won't, you won't. Hang me if I'll ask you again.'

Nor, when he reached home, did he fare better in his efforts at reconciliation with his wife. Dora met him with the icy front of a woman whose pride has been wounded too deeply for tears.

'Say no more about it,' she said. 'I am going to my father. If you want to explain your conduct, explain it to him.'

'Come, Dora,' he urged; 'I was a brute, I know. Forgive me.'

'It is useless to ask me,' she said; 'I cannot. I have forgiven you so much during the last seven years.'

There was a world of desolation and outrage in the sigh which accompanied the words.

He attempted to embrace her. 'My darling –'

She withdrew herself loathingly from his arms. 'Don't touch me, sir! You have killed my love for you, but I have no wish to hate you.'

He swore a great oath at her, and, too obstinate to argue further, royally sulked. Blunt coming in about some ship matters, the pair drank rum.

She went to her room, and occupied herself with some minor details of clothes-packing (it is wonderful how women find relief from thought in household care), while North, poor fool, seeing from his window the light in hers, sat staring at it, alternately cursing and praying.

In the meantime, the unconscious cause of all this – Rufus Dawes – sat in his new cell – wondering at the chance which had procured him comfort, and blessing the fair hands that had brought it to him. He doubted not but that Dora had interceded with his tormentor, and by her gentle pleading bought him ease. 'God bless her,' he murmured. 'I have wronged her all these weary years. She did not know that I suffered.'

He waited anxiously for North to visit him that he might have his belief confirmed. 'I will get him to thank her for me,' he thought. But North did not come for two whole days. No one came but his gaolers; and, gazing from his prison-window upon the sea that almost washed its walls, he saw the schooner at anchor, mocking him with a liberty he could not achieve. On the third day, however, North came. His manner was constrained and abrupt. His eyes wandered uneasily, and he seemed burdened with thoughts which he dared not utter.

'I want you to thank her for me, Mr North,' said Dawes.

'Thank whom?'

'Mrs Frere.'

North shuddered at hearing the name. 'I do not think you owe any thanks to her. Your irons were removed by the Commandant's order.'

'But by her persuasion. I feel sure of it. Ah, I was wrong to think she had forgotten me. Ask her for her forgiveness.'

'Forgiveness!' said North, recalling the scene in the prison. 'What have you done to need her forgiveness?'

'I doubted her,' said Rufus Dawes. 'I thought her ungrateful and treacherous. I thought she delivered me again into the bondage from whence I had escaped. I thought she had betrayed me — betrayed me to the villain whose base life I saved for her sweet sake.'

'What do you mean?' asked North. 'You never spoke to me of this.'

'No — I had vowed to bury the knowledge of it in my own breast — it was too bitter to speak.'

'Saved his life!'

'Ay, and her's! I made the boat that carried her to freedom. I held her in my arms, and took the bread from my own lips to feed her!'

'She cannot know this,' said North, in an undertone.

'She has forgotten it, perhaps — for she was but a child. But you will remind her — will you not? You will do me justice in her eyes before I die? You will get her forgiveness for me?'

North could not explain why such an interview as the convict desired was impossible, and so he promised.

'She is going away in the schooner,' said he. 'I will see her before she goes, and tell her.'

'God bless you, sir,' said poor Dawes. 'Now pray with me;' and the wretched priest mechanically repeated one of the formulae his church prescribed.

The next day he told his penitent that Mrs Frere had forgiven him. This was a lie. He had not seen her; but what should a lie be to him now? Lies were needful in the tortuous path he had undertaken to tread. Yet the deceit he was forced to practice cost him many a pang. He had succumbed to his passion, and to win the love for which he yearned had voluntarily abandoned truth and honour; but, standing thus alone with his sin, he despised and hated himself. To deaden remorse and drown reflection, he had recourse to brandy; and though the fierce excitement of his hopes and fears steeled him against the stupefying action of the liquor, he was rendered by it incapable of calm reflection. In certain nervous conditions our mere physical powers are proof against the action of alcohol, and though ten times more drunk than the toper, who, incoherently stammering, reels into the gutter, we can walk erect and talk with fluency. Indeed, in this artificial exaltation of the sensibilities, men often display a brilliant wit, and an acuteness of comprehension, calculated to delight their friends and terrify their physicians. North had reached this condition of brain-drunkenness. In plain terms, he was trembling on the verge of madness.

The days passed swiftly, and Blunt's preparations for sea were completed. There were two stern cabins in the schooner, one of which was appropriated to Mrs Frere and Dotty, while the other was set apart for North. Maurice had not attempted to renew his overtures of friendship, and the chaplain had not spoken. Mindful of Dora's last words, he had resolved not to meet her until fairly embarked upon the voyage which he intended should link their fortunes together. On the morning of the 19th December, Blunt declared himself ready to set sail, and in the afternoon the three passengers came on board.

Rufus Dawes, gazing from his window upon the schooner that lay outside the reef, thought nothing of the fact that after the Commandant's boat had taken away the Commandant's wife, another boat should put off with the Chaplain. It was quite natural that Mr North should desire to bid his friends farewell, and through the hot still afternoon he watched for the returning boat, hoping that the chaplain would bring him some message from the woman whom he was never to see more on earth. The hours wore on, however, and no breath of wind ruffled the surface of the sea. The day was exceedingly close and sultry, heavy dun clouds hung on the horizon, and it seemed probable that unless a thunderstorm cleared the air before night, the calm would continue. Blunt, however, with a true sailor's obstinacy in regard to weather, swore there would be a breeze, and held to his purpose of sailing. The hot afternoon passed away in a sultry sunset, and it was not until the shades of evening had begun to fall that Rufus Dawes distinguished a boat detach itself from the sides of the schooner and glide through the oily water to the jetty. The chaplain was returning, and in a few moments perhaps would be with him, to bring him the message of comfort for which his soul thirsted. He stretched out his unshackled limbs, and throwing himself upon his stretcher, fell to recalling the past – his boat-building, the news of his fortune, his love, and his self-sacrifice. He could almost form, out of the gathering shadows, the image of the child who held out to him the loaf, and whom he had in his turn preserved from a lingering and cruel death. The stone walls that surrounded him melted into air, he was once more free, the saviour of three lives, the beloved of innocence, 'Good Mr Dawes.'

_{↞ 16 ↠}

THE LAST OF NORFOLK ISLAND

NORTH, as we know, was not returning to bring to the prisoner a message of comfort, but he was returning on purpose to see him, nevertheless. The unhappy man, torn by revenge and passion, had resolved upon a course of action which seemed to him a penance for his crime of deceit. He had determined to confess to Dawes that he had *not* executed his errand, and that the message he brought was wholly fictitious. Then he would tell him that he himself was about to leave the island for ever, and striking him down with a double blow, would earn the curses he felt that he deserved. 'I am no hypocrite,' he fondly thought. 'If I choose to sin, I will sin boldly; and this poor wretch, who looks up to me as an angel, shall know me for my true self.'

The notion of thus destroying his own fame in the eyes of the man whom he had taught to love him, was pleasant to his diseased imagination. It was the natural outcome of the morbid condition of mind into which he had drifted, and he provided for the complete execution of his scheme with that cunning which is born of working mischief in the brain. It was desirable that the fatal stroke should be dealt at the very last possible instant; that he should suddenly unveil his own infamy, and then depart, never to be seen again. To this end he had invented an excuse for returning to the shore at the latest possible moment. He had purposely left in his room a dressing-bag – the sort of article one is so likely to forget in the hurry of departure from one house, and so certain to remember when the time comes to finally prepare for settling in another. He had ingeniously extracted from Blunt the fact that 'he didn't expect a wind before dark, but wanted all ship-shape and aboard,' and then, just as darkness fell, remembered that it was imperative for him to go ashore.

Unsuspecting Blunt cursed, but, if the chaplain insisted upon going, there was no help for it.

'There'll be a breeze in less than two hours,' said he. 'You've plenty of time, but if you're not back before the first puff, I'll sail without you, as sure as you're born.'

North assured him of his punctuality.

'Don't wait for me, Captain, if I'm not here,' said he, with that lightness of tone which men use to mask their anxiety.

'I'd take him at his word, Blunt,' said the Commandant, who was affably waiting to take final farewell of his wife. 'Give way there, men,' he shouted to the crew, 'and wait at the jetty.

If Mr North misses his ship through your laziness, you'll pay for it.'

So the boat set off, North laughing uproariously at the thought of being late. Frere observed with some astonishment that the chaplain wrapped himself in a boat cloak that lay in the stern sheets. 'Does the fellow want to smother himself in a night like this!' was his remark. The truth was that, though his hands and head were burning, North's teeth chattered with cold. Perhaps this was the reason why, when landed and out of eyeshot of the crew, he produced a pocket-flask of rum and eagerly drank. The spirit gave him courage for the ordeal to which he had condemned himself; and, with steadied step, he reached the door of the old prison. To his surprize, Gimblett refused him admission !

'I've got orders to let no one in after sundown.'

'But I have come direct from the Commandant,' said North.

'Got any order, sir?'

'Order ! No.'

'I can't let you in, your reverence,' said Gimblett.

'I want to see the prisoner Dawes. I have a special message for him. I have come ashore on purpose.'

'I am very sorry, sir –'

'The ship will sail in two hours, man, and I shall miss her,' says North, indignant at being thus frustrated in his design. 'Let me pass.'

'Upon my honour, sir, I daren't,' said Gimblett, who was not without his good points. 'You know what authority is, sir, as well as I do.'

North was in despair, but a bright thought struck him – a thought that, in his soberer moments, would never have entered his head – he would buy admission. He produced the rum-flask from beneath the sheltering cloak.

'Come, don't talk nonsense to me, Gimblett. You don't suppose I would come here *without* authority. Here, take a pull at this, and let me through.'

Gimblett's features relaxed into a smile.

'Well, sir, I suppose it's all right, if you say so,' said he.

And clutching the rum-bottle with one hand, he opened the door of Dawes's cell with the other.

North entered, and as the door closed behind him, the prisoner, who had been lying apparently asleep upon his bed, leapt up, and made as though to catch him by the throat.

Rufus Dawes had dreamt a dream.

He thought that he was once more upon that barren strand where he had first met with the sweet child he loved. He lived again his life of usefulness and honour. He saw himself working at the boat, embarking, and putting out to sea. The fair head of the innocent girl was again pillowed on his breast; her young lips again murmured words of affection in his greedy ear. Frere was beside him, watching him, as he had watched before. Once again the grey sea spread around him, barren of succour. Once again, in the wild, wet morning, he beheld the American brig bearing down upon them, and saw the bearded faces of the astonished crew. He saw Frere take the child in his arms and mount upon the deck; he heard the shout of delight that went up, and pressed again the welcoming hands that greeted the rescued castaways. The deck was crowded. All the folk he had ever known were there. He saw the white hairs and stern features of his miser-father, and beside him stood sleek Quaid, rubbing together his white hands with a fat smile. Mr Mogford, the landlord of the Bell, bowed at the hatchway, as though it were the entrance to his respectable and ill-omened posting-house. Holding in his hand the black valise of the murdered man, he invited Dawes to enter; but Jerry, with grotesque and ghastly terror in his thin face, thrust out a bony hand of warning. The dreamer would have pressed onward, but Hans, in whose arm leant a pale-faced, blue-eyed girl, pointed to his blood-bedabbled breast, and barred the pathway. Then Burgess strode forward, and after him John Rex, the convict, who, roughly elbowing through the crowd of prisoners and gaolers, would have reached the spot where stood Sir Richard Devine, but that the pale-faced girl shrieked out his name and crimes. How the hammers clattered in the shipbuilder's yard! Was it a coffin they were making? No; not for Dora — surely not for her! The air grows heavy, lurid with flame, and black with smoke. The *Hydaspes* is on fire! Dora clings to her husband. Base wretch, would you shake her off! Look up; the midnight heaven is glittering with stars; above the smoke the air breathes delicately! One step – another; fix your eyes on mine – so – to my heart! Alas! she turns; he catches at her dress. What! It is a priest – an apostate priest – who, smiling with infernal joy, would drag her to the flaming gulf that yawns for him. The dreamer leaps at the wretch's throat, and crying, 'Villain, was it for *this* fate I saved her!' – awakes to find himself struggling with the monster of his dream, the idol of his waking senses.

'Mr North!'

North, paralyzed no less by the suddenness of the attack than by the words with which it was accompanied, had let fall his cloak, and stood trembling before the prophetic accusation of the man whose curses he had come to earn.

'I was dreaming,' said Rufus Dawes, 'a terrible dream! But it has passed now. The message – you have brought me a message, have you not? Why – what ails you? You are pale – your knees tremble. Did my violence –?'

North recovered himself with a great effort.

'It is nothing. Let us talk, for my time is short. You have thought me a good man – one blessed of God, one consecrated to a holy service; a man honest, and pure, and truthful. I have returned to tell you the truth. I am none of these things.'

Rufus Dawes sat staring, unable to comprehend this madness.

'I told you that the woman you loved – for you *do* love her – sent you a message of forgiveness. I lied.'

'Great Heaven –'

'I never told her of your confession. I never mentioned your name to her.'

'And she will go without knowing – Oh, Mr North, what have you done?'

'Wrecked my own soul!' cries North, wildly, stung by the reproachful agony of the tone. 'Do not cling to me. My task is done. You will hate me now. That is my wish – I merit it. Let me go, I say. I will be late.'

'Too late! For what?' He looked at the cloak – through the open window came the murmured voices of the men in the boat – the memory of the rose, of the scene in the prison, flashed across him, and he understood it all. *'You go together?'*

'Let me go!' repeats North, in a hoarse voice.

'No, madman, I will not let you go, to do this great wrong, to kill this innocent young soul, who – God help her – loves you!'

North, confounded at this sudden reversal of their positions towards each other, crouched bewildered against the wall.

'I say you shall *not* go! You shall *not* destroy your own soul and hers! You love her! So do I; and my love is mightier than yours, for it shall save her!'

'In God's name –' cries the unhappy priest, striving to stop his ears.

'Ay, in God's name! In the name of that God whom in my torments I had forgotten! In the name of that God whom you taught me to remember! That God who sent you to save me from despair, gives me strength to save you in my turn! ... Oh, Mr North – my teacher – my friend – my brother – by the sweet hope of mercy which you preached to me, be merciful to this erring woman!'

North lifted an agonized face. 'What do *you* know of love?'

'What do *I* know?' said Dawes, his pale face radiant as an angel's. 'I will tell you the secret I thought to have carried to the grave. Twenty years ago, I was condemned for a crime for which I was innocent. I could have saved myself by a confession of my projects and my name, but that confession would have brought shame upon a loving woman – would have torn the heart of one who, when my own flesh and blood forsook me, cherished and wept over me. I was silent.'

'Ah! – You loved her.'

'No,' said Rufus Dawes. '*Then* would there have been no sacrifice. I loved her not; 'twas she – poor soul – loved me.'

'What do you mean?' asked North, unable to grasp on the instant the idea of so sublime a sacrifice. 'I do not comprehend.'

'Come closer.'

Nearly an hour had passed since the chaplain had placed the rum-flask in his hand, and Gimblett observed, with semi-drunken astonishment, that it was not yet empty. He had intended, in the first instance, to have taken but one nip in payment of his courtesy – for Gimblett was conscious of his own weakness in the matter of strong waters – but as he waited and waited, the one sup became two, the two, three, and at length more than half the contents of the bottle had moistened his gullet, and maddened him for more. Gimblett was in a quandary. If he didn't finish the flask, he would be oppressed with an everlasting regret. If he did finish it, he would be drunk; and to be drunk on duty, was the one unpardonable sin. He looked across the darkness of the sea, to where the rising and falling light marked the anchored schooner. The Commandant was a long way off! A faint breeze, which had – according to Blunt's prophecy – arisen with the night, brought up to him the voices of the boat's crew from the jetty below him. His friend Jack Mannix was coxswain of her. He would give Jack a drink. Leaving the gate, he advanced to the edge of the embankment, and putting his head over, called out to his friend. The breeze, however, which was momentarily freshening, carried his voice away; and Jack Mannix, hearing nothing, continued his conversation.

Gimblett was just drunk enough to be virtuously indignant at this incivility, and seating himself on the edge of the bank, swallowed the remainder of the rum at a draught. The effect upon his enforcedly-temperate stomach was very touching. He made one feeble attempt to get upon his legs, cast a reproachful glance at the rum-bottle, essayed to drink out of its spirituous emptiness, and then, with a smile of reckless contentment, d—d the island and all its contents, and fell asleep.

North, coming out of the prison, however, did not notice the absence of the gaoler; indeed, he was not in a condition to notice anything. Bare-headed, without his cloak, with staring eyes, and clenched hands, he rushed through the gates into the night as one who flies headlong from some fearful vision. It seemed that, absorbed in his own thoughts, he took no heed to his steps, for, instead of taking the path that led to the sea, he kept along the more familiar one that led to his own cottage on the hill.

'This man a convict!' he cried. 'Great heaven, he is a hero – a martyr! *He* worthy of death! Worthy of worship rather! Oh,

James North, consecrated minister of Christ, how base art thou in the eyes of God beside this despised, degraded outcast! Love! Yes, that is love indeed! My pride falls from me, my delusions are shrivelled up in the fervent heat of this man's terrible relation!'

And so muttering, tearing out his grey hair, and beating his aching temples with clenched hands, he reached his own room, and saw, by the light of the new-born moon, the dressing-bag and candle standing on the table as he had left them. They brought again to his mind the recollection of the task that was before him. He lighted the candle, and, taking the bag in his hand, cast one last look round the chamber which had witnessed his futile struggles against that baser part of himself which had at last triumphed. It was so. Fate had condemned him to sin, and he must now fulfil the doom he might once have averted. Already he fancied he could see the speck that was the schooner move slowly away from the prison shore. He must not linger; they would be waiting for him at the jetty. As he turned, the moonbeams – as yet unobscured by the rapidly-gathering clouds – flung a silver streak across the sea, and across that streak North saw pass a boat. Was his distracted brain playing him false? In the stern sat, wrapped in a cloak, the figure of a man! A fierce gust of wind drove the sea-rack over the moon, and the boat disappeared, as though swallowed up by the gathering storm. North staggered back as the truth struck him.

He remembered how he had said, 'I will redeem him, if I redeem him with my own blood!' Was it possible that a just heaven had thus decided to allow the innocent to escape, and punish the guilty? Oh, this man deserved freedom; he was honest, noble, truthful! How different from himself – a hateful self-lover, an unchaste priest, a drunkard. The looking-glass, in which the saintly face of Meekin was soon to be reflected, stood upon the table, and North, peering into it, with one hand mechanically thrust into the bag, started in insane rage, at the pale face and bloodshot eyes he saw there.

What a hateful wretch he had become!

That last fatal impulse of the insanity which seeks relief from its own hideous self came upon him, and his fingers closed convulsively upon the subject they had been seeking.

'It is better so,' he muttered, addressing, with fixed eyes, his own detested image. 'I have examined you long enough. I have read your heart, and written out your secrets! You are but a shell — the shell that holds a corrupted, and sinful heart. *He* shall live; *you* shall die!'

The rapid motion of his arm overturned the candle, and all was dark.

Rufus Dawes had remained for a few moments motionless in his cell, expecting to hear the heavy clang of the outer door, which should announce to him the departure of the chaplain. But he did not hear it, and it seemed to him that the air in the cell had grown suddenly cold. He went to the door, and looked into the narrow corridor, expecting to see the scowling countenance of Gimblett. To his astonishment the door of the prison was wide open, and not a soul in sight. His first thought was of North. Had the story he had told, coupled with the entreaties he had lavished, sufficed to turn him from his purpose?

He looked around. The night was growing dismal; the wind was mounting; from beyond the bar came the hoarse murmur of an angry sea. If the schooner was to sail that night, she had best get out to deep waters. Where was the chaplain? Pray heaven the delay had been sufficient, and they had sailed without him. Yet they would be sure to meet. He advanced a few steps nearer, and looked about him. Was it possible that, in his madness, the chaplain had been about to commit some violence which had drawn the trusty Gimblett from his post?

'Gr-r-r-r! Ouph!'

The trusty Gimblett was lying at his feet — dead drunk!

'Hi! Hoho! Hillo there!' roars somebody from the jetty below. 'Be that you, Muster Noarth! We ain't too much tiam, sur!'

From the uncurtained windows of the chaplain's house on the hill beamed the newly-lighted candle. They in the boat did not see it, but it brought to the prisoner a wild hope that made his heart bound. He ran back to his cell, clapped on North's wideawake, and flinging the cloak hastily about him, came quickly down the steps. If the moon should shine out now!

'Jump in, sir,' says unsuspecting Mannix, thinking only of the flogging he had been threatened with. 'It'll be a dirty night this night! Put this over your knees, sir. Shove her off! Give way!' And they were afloat.

But one glimpse of moonlight fell upon the slouched hat and cloaked figure, and the boat's crew, engaged in the dangerous task of navigating the reef in the teeth of the rising gale, paid no attention to the chaplain.

'By George, lads, we're but just in time!' cries Mannix; and they laid alongside the schooner, black in blackness.

'Up ye go, yer honour, quick!'

The wind had shifted, and was now off the shore. Blunt, who had begun to repent of his obstinacy, but would not confess it, thought the next best thing to riding out the gale was to get out to open sea. 'Dam the parson,' he had said in all heartiness; 'we can't wait all night for him. Heave ahead, Mr Johnson!' And so the anchor was a-trip as Rufus Dawes ran up the side.

The Commandant, already pulling off in his own boat, roared a coarse farewell.

'Good-bye, North! It was touch and go with ye!' adding, 'Curse the fellow, he's too proud to answer.'

The chaplain indeed spoke to no one, and plunging down the hatchway, made for the stern cabins.

'Close shave, your reverence!' said a respectful boy, opening a door.

It was; but the clergyman did not say so. He double-locked the door, and hardly realizing the danger he had escaped, flung himself on the bunk, panting. Over his head he heard the rapid tramp of feet and the cheery

Yo hi-oh! and a rumbelow!

of the men at the capstan. He could smell the fresh sea breeze, and through the open window of the cabin could distinguish the light in the chaplain's house on the hill. The trampling ceased, the vessel began to move swiftly. The Commandant's boat appeared below him for an instant, making her way back. The *Lady Franklin* had set sail.

With his eyes fixed on the tiny light, he strove to think what was best to be done. It was hopeless to think that he could maintain the imposture which, favoured by the darkness and confusion, he had hitherto successfully attempted. He was certain to be detected at Hobart Town, even if he could lie concealed during his long and tedious voyage. He had, however, saved Dora, for Mr North had been left behind. Poor Mr North! As the thought of pity came to him, the light he looked at was suddenly extinguished, and Rufus Dawes, compelled thereto by an irresistible power, fell upon his knees, and prayed for the pardon and happiness of the sinner who had redeemed him.

'That's a gun from the shore,' says Partridge, the mate, 'and they're burning a red light. There's a prisoner escaped. Shall we lie-to?'

'Lie-to be —!' returns old Blunt, with a tremendous oath. 'We'll have suthin else to do. Look there!'

The sky to the northward was streaked with a belt of livid green colour, above which rose a mighty black cloud, whose shape was ever changing.

A hurricane was approaching.

✦ 17 ✦

THE HURRICANE

HURRICANE is a word considered to signify one of those terrible outbursts of wind and rain which devastate the islands of the tropics.

'There are in tropical latitudes, and as far as 50° or 55° N. and S. of the equator,' says Piddington, 'two kinds of tempests, or storms. The monsoon, or trade wind, or winter gales, in which the barometer remains high and the wind steady, and the hurricanes, or typhoons (cyclones), often blowing with irresistible fury, and almost invariably accompanied by a falling barometer.'

The terms hurricane and typhoon are really interchangable. The word hurricane was originally a Carib or Indian one; for

in the *Relacion summaria de la Historia Natural de las Indias,
&c.*, addressed to the Emperor Charles V. by Captain Fernando
de Oviedo, speaking of the superstitions of the Indians (Caribs)
of Tierra Firme, probably about Yucatan, the author says:

'So when the devil wishes to terrify them (the Indians) he
promises them the *huracan*, which means tempest. This he
raises so powerfully that it overturns houses and tears up many
and very large trees; and I have seen in thick forests, and those
of very large trees, for the space of half a league, and continuing
for a quarter of a league in length, the forest quite overthrown,
and all the trees, large and small, torn up by the roots; the roots
of many being uppermost, and the whole so fearful to see, that
it doubtless appeared to be the devil's work, and could not be
looked on without terror.'

The author here exactly describes the passage of a tornado in
a thick forest, and by the explanation he gives of the word
huracan, we see that it was an Indian one. The dictionary of
the Spanish Academy does not give the derivation of words.
Indeed, Oviedo, speaking of the San Domingo hurricane in
1508, says:

'Hurricane (*huracan*), in the language of this island, means
properly an excessively tempestuous storm, for indeed it is
nothing but a violent gale, together with rain. Now it happened
that on Tuesday, the 3rd of August, 1508 (Father Nicolas Oviedo being then governor of the island), about noon, an exceeding
great wind with rain came on at once, which was felt at the
same time in many sites in the island, and there arose from it
suddenly great damage, and many estates were ruined. In this
city of St Domingo, all the straw houses were prostrated, and
some even of those of stone were much shaken and damaged.
At Buena Ventura, all the houses were destroyed, so that for
the many who were ruined there, it might more properly be
called Mala Ventura. And, what was worse and more grievous
was, that in the harbour of the city more than twenty ships,
caravels, and other vessels were lost. The northerly wind was
so strong that as soon as it began to blow hard, the seamen
did everything in their power, by laying out more anchors and
fastening by more ropes, to secure their vessels; but the wind
was so violent that no precautions could withstand it, every

thing was carried away, and the force of the wind drove all the vessels, large and small, out of the port, down the river, and they perished in various ways. But the wind changing suddenly to the opposite quarter, and with not less impetus and fury, blew from the south as violently as before from the north, when some vessels were driven furiously back into the port, and as the north wind had driven them out to sea, so this opposite one drove them back to the port and up to the river. They were afterwards seen drifting down again with only the tops in sight above water. Many persons perished in this calamity, and the most violent part of the tempest lasted twenty-four hours, until the next day at noon, but it did not cease all at once as suddenly as it came on.'

The author then goes on to describe the frightful appearances and damage occasioned by the storm, and adds, that the Indians (and they were then a numerous people) said that they had frequently experienced hurricanes, but that neither they nor their fathers had ever before experienced the like for its extreme violence.

Tyfoon is a Chinese word. Dr Morrison, in his Notices on China and the Port of Canton, says:

'At Hainam and the peninsula opposite (to the north of it), they have temples dedicated to the Tyfoon, the god (goddess?) of which they call *ƙeu woo,* "the tyfoon mother," in allusion to its producing a gale from every point of the compass; and this mother-gale, with her numerous offspring or a union of gales from the four quarters of heaven, make conjointly a *taefung,* or tyfoon. In a work called *"Kw'an Tung Sin yu,"* the typhoon is called *ƙow-fung* or *fung-ƙow.* A severe one is called *teé hwuy* or *Teó ƙeu* – an iron whirlwind. They have also separate names for whirlwinds, which, I am informed, are called *yung-ƙeƙ-foong* and *suing-foong.'*

The peculiarity of the hurricane and tyfoon, as described by these authorities, is the fact that the wind suddenly shifts, appearing to blow from all parts of the compass. In Bermuda, gales of this kind are called 'roundabouts,' and the Spanish navigators termed them 'tourbillons.' Modern science, investigating the law of storms, has given to these circular tempests the name of cyclones. It has been ascertained, by the examination and analysis of the logs of innumerable ships, that the wind in these 'hurricanes' has two motions. It turns or blows round a focus, in a more or less circular form; and at the same time has a straight or curved motion forward, so that, like a great whirlwind, it is both turning round and, as it were, rolling forward at the same time.

Next, it is considered to be proved that when such a hurricane occurs on the north side of the equator, it turns from the east towards the west, with a motion contrary to that of the hands of a watch, but that, in the southern hemisphere, its motion is the other way. That is, its expression for the northern hemisphere would be S.E.N.W.; for the southern hemisphere, N.E.S.W.

The chronicler of the wreck of the *Idhao* in the year 1867 by one of these gigantic whirlwinds, likens the storm to a 'cartwheel turning upon its axletree while rolling over the ground.' Now, if we suppose the storm to be thus rolling over the bosom of the ocean as a wheel rolls over a muddy road, we shall see, as Piddington remarks, that while the whole wheel (or the body of the cyclone) moves forward on the track, the dirt on the upper rim is thrown forward, and that on the lower rim backward; so that, if we imagine windarrows painted as the felloe of the wheel, and that the said wheel is really a disk of air a mile or two high, moving horizontally over a mass of water, we can understand how the different changes take place to ships on opposite sides of the storm circle.

Thus we have in a hurricane three parts. The outer disk of air, the inner circle, or furious wind, and the calm focus, or centre.

The operation of this revolving tempest is terrible. For its duration it is master of the ocean. The sea is tortured by it into madness. Volumes of water are gathered up and discharged. Birds and insects, caught in the centre of the hurricane, are borne with incredible velocity out to sea, and fall exhausted upon the decks of ships miles from land. The tormented ocean glows phosphorescent, boiling like a cauldron. Waterspouts rush upward. Lightnings traverse the intense blackness. The wind shrieks like a monster in pain. Mr Macqueen, master of the ship *Rawlins*, says, of a hurricane which caught his vessel, 'The wind represented numberless voices elevated to the highest tone of screaming.' Captain Biden, in his remarks on the log of H.C.S. *Princess Charlotte of Wales*, says, 'The gusts from noon until seven p.m. were like to successive discharges of artillery, or the roaring of wild beasts.' In truth, in such storms, the old navigators might well suppose the direct 'Wrath of God' was at hand. The clouds open and shut. The waters appear 'piled upon each other.' The power of electricity works its inexplicable marvels. Many-coloured lights appear in the heavens. The rays of the sun, having to force their way through strata of clouds, lose their character. The white rays are absorbed, and the sky swelters in a horrible bloodiness. Mr Lynn, of the H.C.S. *Buccleugh*, says, 'At sunset, the clouds predicted another severe typhoon. This appearance was that of remarkably dense and large clouds surrounding the horizon at an altitude of about 10° or 15°, having thin edges tinged with a deep crimson border, and reflecting an awful redness on the sails.' In the *Nautical Magazine* for 1841, page 666, occurs the following:—

'Sometimes there appears first like a flaming cloud in the horizon from whence proceeds the fiery tempest, in a most astonishing manner, and some of these hurricanes and whirlwinds have seem'd so very terrible, as if there had happened one entire conflagration of the air and seas. I was inform'd by Captain Proud of Stepney, a person of great experience and integrity, that in one of his voyages to the East Indies about the 17th degree of south latitude, he met with a tempest of this nature, towards the coast of India; of which I had some particulars extracted from his journal: First, contrary to the course of the winds, which they expected to be at south-east, or between the south and east, they found them between the east and north, the sea extremely troubl'd, and, which was most remarkable and dreadful, in the N.N.W., N. and N.N.E. parts of the horizon, the sky became wonderfully red and inflam'd, the sun being then upon the meridian. These were thought omens of stormy weather, which afterwards happen'd according to their suspicions; and as the darkness of the night increas'd, so did the violence of the wind, till it ended in an hurricane; which, an hour after midnight, came to such an height, that no canvas or sayles would hold; and seven men could scarce govern the helme. But that which I mention as the most considerable to our purpose was, that the whole atmosphere, both the heavens and raging seas, appeared but as one entire flame of fire; and those who are acquainted with the reputation of this grave person will find no just reason to distrust the truth of the relation.'

Captain Norman McLeod, of the *John McViccar*, who was in the ship *Albion* in the *London's* cyclone of October, 1832, says:

'At sunset the sea and sky became all on a sudden of a bright scarlet colour; I do not remember ever seeing it so red before, even to the very zenith, and all round the horizon was of this colour. The sea appeared an ocean of cochineal, and the ship and every thing on board looked as if it were dyed with that colour; the sky kept this appearance till nearly midnight, and it only diminished as it came on to rain. No sooner was this phenomenon over, than the sea became as if it were all on fire with phosphoric matter. We took up several buckets of water, but even with the microscope few or no animalcules were detected. Having lost my log, I cannot give you the temperature of the water.'

This red light is a forewarning of the cyclone, appearing sometimes for eighteen hours before the tempest bursts. Sometimes, however, a solitary white spot heralds the tornado. This white spot is called by the Portugese *olho de bove*, or the 'eye of the bull.' Victor Hugo, in his description of the hurricane in 'Les Travailleurs de la Mer,' refers, with his frequent magnificent inaccuracy, to this appearance as occurring in the height of the storm. This is not the case. The 'eye' appears like a white spot near the zenith in a perfectly clear sky, and in fine weather. M. Goldsberry ('Purdy's Atlantic Memoir,' Part I., page 70), describing a tornado between Cape Verga and Cape Palmas, says: 'The sky is clear, a perfect calm has prevailed for several hours, and the weight of the air is oppressive. Suddenly, in the most elevated region of the atmosphere, is perceived a little round and white cloud, the diameter of which does not appear to exceed five or six feet. This cloud, which seems to be perfectly fixed and motionless, is the indication of a tornado.'

Though the home – the lair – of these awful tempests is the

tropic seas, cyclones are not unfrequent around the Australian coast. Mariners seldom speak of them, however, for a very excellent reason. When a cyclone occurs in these latitudes, it is so violent that a ship rarely escapes to bear intelligence.

'From the N.W. point of Australia southward to Cape Leuwin,' says Piddington, 'it would appear that storms of great violence, and these often rotatory, occur.' Lieutenant Wickam, of H.M.S. *Beagle,* writing in the *Nautical Magazine* for 1841 (page 725) has the following passage:

'The west coast of New Holland is at times visited by sudden squalls, resembling hurricanes, as I was told by the master of an American whaler, that in March, 1839, when in company with several whalers off Shark's Bay, he experienced some very bad weather without any previous warning, but it was not of long continuance. The gusts of wind were very violent, shifting to all points of the compass; some of the ships lost topmasts, sails, &c.; I think the first squall was from N.E. of the land.'

On the west coast of Australia, off Rottnest Island, the French ship *Le Geographe* experienced, in June, 1801, a cyclone, whose track was from the S. by W. to N. by E.

Along the south coast, though the usual westerly winds and gales of the higher latitudes in both hemispheres prevail during the greater part of the year, cyclones are not unfrequent. Gales commence at N.W. with a low barometer, and thick rainy weather, increasing at W. and S.W., and gradually veering and moderating to the South, and even S.S.E., with the barometer rising to above 30 inches. Sometimes also they return to west or more northerly, with a fall in the barometer, but the gale is not then over, though it may diminish or die away for a day or two. Sometimes the wind flies round suddenly from N.W. to S.W., and the rainy thick weather then continues a longer time.

Commander Stokes, of H.M.S. *Beagle*, says:

'The gales in Bass's Straits begin at N.N.W., and draw gradually by W. to S.W., when they subside. If it backs it will continue, but the barometer will indicate its duration; it is seldom fine with a pressure of 29.95 inches, and always bad if it falls to 29.70 inches. This exactly represents the northern half of a cyclone travelling through the Strait from the westward. The "backing" would be the case of a cyclone passing from the S.W. to the N.E., and lasting longer, either because its diameter was greater, or because its motion was slower, having been checked in its passage over the N.W. part of Van Diemen's Land; for the passage of a cyclone over high land certainly checks, for a time, its rate of travelling.'

There is no doubt but that true cyclones occur at New Zealand. The log of the *Adelaide*, for 29th February, 1840, describes one which travelled at the rate of ten miles an hour, and had all the veerings – calm centre, etc. – of a true tropical hurricane.

The Rev W. B. Clarke, of Sydney, writing in the *Sydney Herald* in 1851, says:

'So completely does the law of rotation appear to be from left to right, in gales of wind off the coasts of Australia and on the neighbouring ocean, that it is scarcely possible to escape the observation, in perusing the log books of any extended cruise. One further example, to show this, shall now be quoted. "The whaler *Merope* left Sydney 22nd March, 1840, with wind at the South, steering for Lord Howe's Islands. On 27th, she was in lat. 35 deg. 4 min. S., long. 158 deg. 35 min. E. The order of the wind's changes was as follows: 23rd, at S.E., veering N.E.; 24th, N.N.E. and N.E.; 25th, increasing from N.E., N.N.E., E.N.E. with a tempest; 26th, N.E. to N., with confused sea, N.W. and drawing to W.; 27th, S.W.S., S.S.E., and back to S. The wind thus completed a revolution in five days, on a direct course, from left to right. Between Australia and America a similar course is pursued by the winds to that which is followed between the Cape of Good Hope and Cape Leuwin, and more than one instance has come before us of vessels having been driven *all round the compass before the wind* during a gale not far from Cape Horn." '

These rotatory storms occur principally in spring and November, commencing at E., and after suddenly changing from N.E. to N.W. and S.W., end within a few points of where they commenced. Beecher's 'Pacific Ocean' gives an account of one of these cyclones, and a further and fuller description of the same storm can be found in a paper published for Captain

Byron Drury, R.N., by the Meteorological Department of the Board of Trade, in 1856.

It would appear, from a comparison of these records, that a cyclone occurring off the west coast of New Zealand would have travelled from the New Hebrides – where such manifestations are hideously frequent – (for an account of a destructive hurricane in these latitudes, see the *Sydney Herald* of 30th March, 1848), and enveloping Norfolk Island, pass directly across the track of vessels coming from South America to Sydney. Having expended its fury in the ugly strip of ocean between Sydney and New Zealand, it would pass under the southern point of Tasmania, and cause the storm-currents which have wrecked so many emigrant ships at the western entrance to Bass's Straits.

It was one of these rotatory storms – an escaped tempest of the tropics – which threatened the *Lady Franklin*.

⋆ 18 ⋆

WRECKED

BLUNT, accustomed to the appearance of the phenomena which heralded the approaching danger, began to regret his obstinacy. It was now, however, too late for such reflections. The ominous calm which had brooded over the island during the day had given place to a smart breeze from the north-east, and though the schooner had been sheltered at her anchorage under the lee of the island – the 'harbour' looked nearly due south – when once fairly out to sea, Blunt saw it would be impossible to put back in the teeth of the gale. Haply, however, the full fury of the storm would not overtake them until they had gained sea-room.

Rufus Dawes, exhausted with the excitement through which he had passed, had slept for some two or three hours, when he was awakened by the motion of the vessel going on the other tack.

He rose to his feet, and found himself in complete darkness.

Overhead was the noise of trampling feet, and he could distinguish the hoarse tones of Blunt bellowing orders. Astonished at the absence of the moonlight which had so lately silvered the sea, he flung open the cabin window, and looked out.

As we have said, the cabin allotted to North was one of the two stern-cabins, and from it the convict had a full view of the approaching storm.

The sight was one of terrible grandeur.

The huge black cloud which hung in the horizon had changed its shape. Instead of a curtain it was an arch. Beneath this vast and magnificent portal, shone a dull phosphoric light, resembling that transmitted through oiled paper by a candle. Across this livid space pale flashes of sheet-lightning passed noiselessly. Behind it was a dull and threatening murmur, made up of the grumbling of thunder, the falling of rain, and the roar of contending wind and water. The lights of the prison-island had disappeared, so rapid had been the progress of the schooner under the steady breeze, and the ocean stretched around, black and desolate.

Gazing upon this gloomy expanse, Rufus Dawes observed a strange phenomenon. Lightning appeared to burst upwards from the sullen bosom of the sea! At intervals, the darkly rolling waves flashed fire, and streaks of dull red flame shot upwards. Transparent films of vapour seemed to stoop from the heavens to receive and quench these fires. The wind increased in violence, and the arch of light was fringed with rain. Cirri, tremulous with flame, advanced over the surface of the sea and appeared to mingle with the water. A dull red glow hung around like the reflection of a conflagration. In the midst of these terrors appeared the reason for Blunt's manoeuvre. Rufus Dawes saw pass under the stern of the trembling vessel a luminous column which a few moments before must have been bearing direct upon her bows. This column was three hundred feet high, luminous in its whole diameter. It moved swiftly over the sea, leaving behind it a train of fire. One might suppose it an *avant-courier* of the tempest; for as it whirled away, a tremendous peal of thunder, accompanied by a terrific downfall of rain, rattled along the sky. The arch of light disappeared, as though some invisible hand had shut the slide of a giant lantern, a

great wall of water rushed, roaring, over the level plain of the
sea, and, with an indescribable medley of sounds, in which
tones of horror, triumph, and torture were blended, the cyclone
swooped upon them.

Rufus Dawes comprehended that the elements had come to
save or destroy him.

In that terrible instant the natural powers of the man rose
equal to the occasion. In a few hours his fate would be decided,
and it was necessary that he should take all precautions. One of
two events seemed inevitable – he would either be drowned
where he lay, or, should the vessel weather the storm, he would
be forced upon deck, and the desperate imposture he had
attempted be discovered.

For a moment despair overwhelmed him, and he contemplated the raging sea as though he would cast himself into it,
and thus end his troubles. A sound dispelled his terror.

The cry of a child.

He remembered that the being he loved best on earth was in
the adjoining cabin, exposed to a like danger with himself.
Cautiously opening the door, he peered out. The cuddy was
lighted by a swinging lamp, which revealed Dora seated at a
table soothing her frightened daughter. As Rufus Dawes looked,
he saw her glance towards the door behind which he lurked
with an air half of hope, half of fear, and he understood that
she expected to see the chaplain appear to comfort her. The
thought gave him an idea. Locking the door, he proceeded
hastily to dress himself in North's clothes. He would wait until
his aid was absolutely required, and then rush out. In the darkness, Dora would mistake him for the priest. He could convey
her to the boat – if recourse to the boats should be rendered
necessary – and then take the hazard of his fortune. While she
was in danger, his place was near her.

He little knew the sort of enemy with whom the *Lady
Franklin* was about to contend.

From the deck of the vessel the scene was appalling. The
clouds had closed in. The arch of light had disappeared, and all
was a dull windy blackness. Gigantic seas seemed to mount in
the horizon and sweep towards and upon them. It was as

though the ship lay in the vortex of a whirlpool, so high on each side of her were piled the rough pyramidal masses of sea. Mighty gusts arose – claps of wind which seemed like strokes of thunder. A sail which had loosened from its tackling was torn away and blown out to sea, disappearing like a shred of white paper to leeward. The mercury in the barometer marked 29.50.

Blunt swore great oaths that no soul on board would see another sun; and when Partridge rebuked him for blasphemy at such a moment, wept spirituous tears. He had been at the rum bottle.

A few minutes after midnight the mainyard broke into three pieces with a crash which was almost trifling amid the roar of the gale. The howling of the wind was terrifying; the very fury of sound enfeebled while it terrified. There was a tone of hideous command in the hoarse voice of the tempest. The wild shrieks and furious bellowings pained and deafened. The sailors, horror-stricken, crawled about the deck, clinging to anything they thought most secure. It was impossible to raise the head to look to windward. The eyelids were driven together, and the face stung by the swift and biting spray. Men breathed this atmosphere of salt and wind and became sickened. Partridge felt that orders were useless. The man at his elbow could not have heard them. The vessel lay almost on her beam-ends, with her helm up, stripped even of the sails which had been furled upon the yards. Mortal hands could do nothing for her.

By five o'clock in the morning, the gale had reached its height. The heavens showered out rain and lightnings; rain which the wind blew away before it reached the sea, lightnings which the ravenous and mountainous sea swallowed before they could pierce the gloom. The ship lay over on her side, held there by the madly rushing wind, which seemed to flatten down the sea, cutting off the tops of the waves, and breaking them into fine white spray, which covered the ocean, like a thick cloud, as high as the topmast heads. Each gust seemed unsurpassable in intensity, but was succeeded, after a pause, that was not a lull but a gasp, by one of more frantic violence. The barometer stood at 27·82. The ship was a complete wreck – a labouring, crazy hull, that might sink at any moment. At half-past five o'clock – when day was softly breaking on land – a terrible darkness reigned. The barometer had fallen to 27·62. Save when lighted by occasional flashes of sheet-lightning, which showed to the cowed wretches their awestricken faces, this tragedy of the elements was performed in a darkness which was almost palpable.

Suddenly the mercury rose to 29·90; and with one awful shriek, the wind dropped to a calm. The *Lady Franklin* had reached the centre of the cyclone.

It is impossible to convey any idea of the disposition of passengers and crew during the progress of the gale. Each soul felt itself alone before God.

When the wind fell, a sailor named Martin Batt called out, 'We've weathered it!' and as he spoke, a huge wave, curling in over the bows, flung him up into its hungry jaws and devoured him.

The fact was, that the sea, released from the pressure of the wind, had risen in tenfold fury. Volumes of water poured in over the vessel, and ran out through her opening seams. It seemed a miracle that she did not sink. Partridge, clinging to the remnants of the helm, now witnessed a hideous sight. The dead body of Batt, all emptied of blood, ghastly white, and with limbs dislocated, was borne back upon the top of a mountain of green water, and passed close to the mate's face. The doomed vessel heeled over. The wind had returned from the opposite side. The hurricane repeated itself from the N.E.

Partridge, glancing to where the great body of drunken Blunt rolled helplessly lashed to the fragment of the mast, felt a strange joy thrill him. If the ship survived, the drunken captain would be dismissed, and he, Partridge the gallant, reign in his stead. In such instants as these Self often intrudes thus impertinently. He cast his eyes around and observed to the N.N.E. a gleam of light. The cyclone was spinning on its axis, as it were. It was passing southward as well as westward. In a short time, if the sore-tried vessel only held together, they might crawl in the sunshine of a calm morning back to port.

At that moment, an immense wave, that glimmered in the darkness, spouted up, rolling its slippery mass like some huge sea monster over the ocean, and towered above them. The wretches that yet clung upon deck could look straight up into its bellying greenness, and an involuntary cry of despair broke from all.

The wave, like a ravening ocean-giant, curling his huge foamfringed lips as though in mockery of their weakness, fell upon them.

The last tremendous effort of the sea, which had swept the deck of the devoted vessel, poured in through the burst hatchway, and tore the door of the cabin from its hinges.

Dora, clasping her child in her arms, found herself surrounded by a wildly-surging torrent, which threatened to overwhelm her. She shrieked aloud for aid, but her voice was inaudible even to herself. The stern cabin was filled with water, and the *Lady Franklin*, buried beneath the weight of the waves, seemed about to be bodily engulphed.

Dora, more dead than alive, clung to the mast, which penetrated the cuddy, and, with her eyes fixed upon the door behind which she imagined was North, whispered a last prayer for succour.

Her prayer was answered.

The door opened, and from out the cabin staggered a figure clad in black.

She looked, and the light of the swaying lamp fell upon a face that was not the face of her lover. She felt the child snatched from her. A pair of dark eyes, that beamed ineffable love and pity, were bent upon her — a pair of dripping arms held the little one aloft above the brine, as she herself had been once held aloft in the misty, mysterious days that were gone.

In that terrible moment, when death — the solver of all riddles, the revealer of all secrets — was close upon her, she felt the cloud that had so long oppressed her brain pass away from it. The action of the strange man before her completed and explained the action of the convict chained to the Port Arthur coal-waggons, of the convict kneeling in the Norfolk Island torture chamber. She remembered the terrible experience of

Macquarie Harbour. She recalled the evening of the boat-building, when, swung into the air by stalwart arms, she had promised the rescuing prisoner to plead for him with her kindred. All the agony and shame of the man's long life of misery became at once apparent to her. She understood how her husband had deceived her, and with what base injustice and falsehood he had bought her young love. No question as to how this doubly-condemned villain had escaped from the terrible isle of punishment she had quitted occurred to her. She asked not — even in her thoughts — how it had been given to him to supplant the chaplain in his place on board the vessel. She only considered, in her sudden awakening, the story of his wrongs, remembered only his marvellous fortitude and love, knew only, in this last instant of her pure, ill-fated life, that as he had saved her once from starvation and death, so had he come again to save her from sin and from despair — to preserve, perhaps, the life of her child, as he had preserved her own.

'Good Mr Dawes!'

The eyes of the man and woman met in one long, wild gaze, she stretched out her white hands and smiled; and then, as the splitting vessel sank under them, and the face of the woman he had loved so long and so hopelessly disappeared in the watery darkness that was death, Rufus Dawes felt that she recognised, thanked, pitied, loved him!

In that awful instant, as the child of Maurice Frere clung about his neck, the convict understood, in his turn, the sad story of the young girl's joyless life, comprehended how he had been sacrificed, knew for the first time the full extent of his wrongs, and saw how Heaven, in depriving him for ever of the fruition of his affection, had placed in his arms, as in those of a saviour, the daughter of his love and of his enemy.

With one last shriek of wrathful triumph, the whistling wind swept onward, and the morning sun — looking down from a suddenly unclouded sky upon the place where the schooner had foundered — saw only two human beings — a man who, insensible himself, clung with the tenacity of death to a spar, and supported in his stiffening arms the inanimate body of a young child.

FREEDOM

'Is he coming to?' asked Captain Staples, of the *Mosquito*, bound from Rio to Sydney, driven out of her course, and forced to put into a strange port by stress of weather and want of water.

'He's better nor yesterday – much the same as the day before.'

'Ay, and as the day before that, and before that, and before that for the last three weeks.'

'A bit cranky, seems to me. The lassie's coming on fine, and cries for her mother less than she did.'

'Poor souls !' says our old friend Will Staples, by the grace of God and Sarah Purfoy's money now a master mariner. 'It will be hard for 'em when they know their "mother" won't see 'em no more. I wonder who the cove is, Tom?'

'Seems like a parson, by his togs, but his 'ands is as 'ard as mine.'

'P'raps a skipper. If he's coming round, I'll have a chat with him.'

But Rufus Dawes did not come round for that day, nor the day after, nor, indeed, until nearly thirty days after the sharp eyes of the ex-whaler had descried him floating insensibly on a mass of wreck some thirteen miles west of the spot where the *Lady Franklin* had suffered shipwreck.

When he did speak, the *Mosquito* had already entered the huge bay of the new settlement, and was bowling along with a fair S.E. breeze, towards the new colony founded by speculative Van Diemen's Land.

'Well,' says Staples, entering the cabin, 'how are you now?'

'Better,' said the shipwrecked man, with a strangely ungrateful abruptness.

'That's right ! You'll be up and about by'n-by. We'll be at anchor in an hour.'

'Where?' asked Rufus Dawes, eagerly.

'Oh,' says Staples, affecting a little mystery by way of cheering his passenger, 'a fine place. Lots o' people, and ships, and houses!'

The convict shuddered. Hobart Town, without doubt. He had been saved to be but doubly lost.

'Get up, lad, and come on deck. The breeze'll revive ye. Ye mustn't lay there all ye're life.'

'I am faint – weak yet. A few moments more –'

'You've had a long bout of it, my chap. We ain't much o' doctors, and we thought you'd slip your cable one time. How did ye get into that pickle, eh? I saw the storm that settled ye rumbling away to leeward of me, but it didn't come my way. Where were ye bound for?'

The convict, shrinking at each question as if a knife had pierced him, made shift to groan,

'By-and-by – I can't tell you now – when I am stronger –'

'I don't want to plague ye,' says good-natured Staples. 'Take a sleep a bit. I'll look in again.'

And so, treading on tiptoe, the captain of the *Mosquito* withdrew, to ponder on the strange man he had rescued.

In truth, the rescued man had not yet decided what to say. Fortune – which had bereft him of all that he had prized in life, at the very moment when it became fully worth the prizing – had so far befriended him as to cast in his path a vessel coming from a place where it was impossible that his true history could be known. But he had not yet formed for himself another history – had not yet forced his bewildered brain to invent a tale which should disarm suspicion. He knew well that the accident of the black clothes had diverted suspicion, and that some weeks would probably elapse before his secret would be discovered. But, dazed as he was, he had yet wit enough left to see that, as soon as the non-arrival of the *Lady Franklin,* having on board an escaped convict and the wife and daughter of the Commandant of Norfolk Island, should be known, all that was strange in his appearance would be at once hideously explained. All unwitting as he was of the former career of Staples, his only chance – he thought, tossing wearily from side to side in his bunk, and pestered with the well-meant questions of the crew – was to evade his rescuers, to slip out of this too narrow ship, and to hide himself far from prying eyes. But where? He would be landed on another prison shore — these cursed Australias were all one vast gaol — and the first man he met would clap him on his scarred back, and hail him as a brother felon. He *might* avoid his fellows; he *might* take to the bush for a while, or even ship for England; but then — the cry of the helpless child in the adjoining bunk went to his heart — what was to be done with *her*. He leant on his elbow and looked at the creature he had preserved. Dotty was sitting up, with one finger in a charming mouth, smiling at him. To what a fate did he propose to doom her! His duty was clear; he must return her to her father. Her father! The wretch who had gloated over his miseries, who had wrecked his hopes! No; he had already enough of self-sacrifice.

'Dotty!'

She frowned; and Rufus Dawes bit his lip, the frown was so like that of his enemy.

'Heaven help me!' he cried, in anguish of hatred and remorse — 'What am I to do?'

The accents of his grief awoke in the baby-girl her gentle mother's nature, and with the inarticulate murmur of infancy, she raised her tiny hand to pull away the brown one of the convict from before his eyes.

Rufus Dawes raised his head, and saw close to him the face of the little maiden — lovely and pure as that of an angel; the bright hair rippled over his great hand, tears of sympathetic childhood trembled in the dark eyes, the sweet moist lips pouted a kiss to him.

His waif and stray, his wonder of the sea, his prize snatched from death, his legacy of confidence and recognition, his dream-child, sanctified by a thousand holy aspirations, a thousand bitter tears, — did she *love* him! Could innocence like this feel no contamination in his most vile presence? Then he would not lose her. He caught her to his breast, weeping over her, as he had wept over her mother long ago.

Unhappy victim of youthful passion. — Heaven, which adjudged to you a punishment that seemed greater than you could bear, could not surely have deemed you all unworthy, or it would not have suffered North to die that he might redeem you from sin, or aided this fair child to live that she might win you to virtue!

The rattling of the anchor-chains roused him from his reverie. They had arrived, then. He opened the port, and looked out fearfully. The *Mosquito* had anchored at the mouth of a shining silver river. To the right lay long sandy reaches, backed by distant hills. As the vessel swung slowly round, the bewildered man could see blue forests rolling to purple mountains, fair plains studded with farms, and behold, stretching away to the left in limitless perspective, a mighty bay, large enough to hold the united navies of the world.

'Hullo!' says Staples, at the door — 'Up? That's right. Bring the lassie, and we'll set ye ashore, my man. Ye'll be glad o' dry land after so much salt-water.'

It seemed in very truth that the shock of near death had dazed the rescued man's brain, for during the passage of the boat between the soft green banks of this unexpected Paradise he said not a word, gazing only with hungry eyes upon the smiling shore.

It was not until they had reached it, and were making for the scattered houses that marked the infant city, that Rufus Dawes spoke.

'What place is this?'

Staples burst into a roar.

'The free settlement of Port Phillip!'

The *free* settlement! Blessed word! And the rescued man — in gratitude, so those around him thought, at his rescue — fell on his knees, there, in the calm sweet morning, and seemed to pray.

When he arose his embarrassment had vanished. He held his head erect and spoke firmly.

'I do not know how to thank you sufficiently,' he said to Staples. 'I may find a way one of these days to do so. I have friends yonder,' pointing to the town. 'I will go to them.'

'You're a rum one,' says Staples, putting out his hand. 'Good-bye, and good luck go with ye. I don't want to pry into no man's secrets.'

But, to the sailor's astonishment, the strange man refused the proffered grasp of friendship.

'No, no; not yet,' he muttered – 'not yet.'

And so, carrying the child, he moved away.

Staples made no effort to detain him, but, fearful lest some mischief might occur to one so erratic in his conduct, made inquiry concerning him that night in the town.

No one had spoken with him, however; only a woman said that she had seen a tall man, with a child in his arms, pass through the settlement along the track that led to the mountains.

BOOK SIX

↤ 2 ↦

THE RETURN OF THE PRODIGAL

On Christmas Eve, 1850, there was a merry party assembled in the old house at Mere.

The four-and-twenty years which had passed over it since we last saw it have effected great changes in it and its inmates.

Mr Francis Devine, millionaire, magistrate, and patron of learning and the fine arts, was a very different person from Frank Devine, the melancholy youth of seventeen, who, with his little sister, had heard read the strange will of his father, in that very room, twenty-four years ago.

The room itself was changed. No longer gloomy, but lighted brilliantly, decorated with holly and mistletoe, and beaming with happy faces. Mr Devine was not a man to have about him aught that spoke of desolation or melancholy. The old house, rejuvenated with new wings, that dwarfed its original proportions, surrounded by gardens that were the pride of the district, and crammed with glowing pictures, rich antiques, and rare books, was a home of elegance and luxury – the chosen residence of the friend of artists, poets, and men of fashion, the celebrated *connoisseur* and man of taste.

Frank Devine had married early; his wife, after bringing him two children, had died at Como, of that English curse – consumption; and Mr Devine, having spent five years among the picture-galleries and art-collections of Europe, had returned to live in refinement and comfort in his own home. He made a point of always spending Christmas at Mere.

The family group is a pleasing one.

Mr Devine, still young, sits in an arm-chair by the fire. An antique lamp throws its mellow light upon his fine face and still elegant figure. Beside him sits his daughter Adelaide, a fair young English girl of sixteen, who, thanks to her early education, combines French vivacity and elegance of motion with English honesty and courage. Though the granddaughter of a ship-builder, she might have been the daughter of an earl, so delicate were her features – so purely graceful her action and carriage.

Opposite to her, knits placidly the lady whom Mr Devine calls 'the best woman in the world' – Miss Lucy Devine – his unmarried sister. Aunt Lucy is known to have had a 'disappointment' in her youth (not so long ago, to judge by her sweet, unwrinkled face), and, faithful to the memory of the soldier who fell in Indian battle, has refused all offers of marriage. Addy vows that her aunt will some day change her condition, and is wont to hint mysteriously at the open admiration expressed for her by several gentlemen of rank and fortune. Aunt Lucy blushes delicately at these insinuations, and says that her duty and hope in life now is but to play the mother to the merry girl, whose chestnut hair she strokes lovingly.

'It is past the time, papa!' cries Adelaide. 'See, nearly five o'clock, and the carriage was sent at three. When does that horrible train come in?'

'At a quarter to four; but then the roads are deep with snow, and Arthur is sure to have enough luggage for a Prince of the Blood.'

'I sent the blankets to Mrs Mills, Frank,' says Aunt Lucy, thinking more of the snow than of Arthur's luggage, 'and the wine to Popjoy. Poor creature, I am afraid that she can't get through the winter.'

'We must have Thornton to see her,' says Mr Devine. 'The poor old soul was tramping after that ungrateful grandson, I suppose.'

'I suppose so,' assented Aunt Lucy, with a gentle sigh; 'but the boy is not ungrateful, Francis, dear, only headstrong and imprudent. Poor Jarvis's money seems to have done but little good.'

'Poor old man. I remember how he used to make faces at me when I was a boy, and frighten me so that I was afraid to go to bed sometimes.'

'Oh, papa! *you* afraid!'

'I was indeed, my dear.'

'That was a strange notion of his, that poor Richard was yet alive and would come back,' said Miss Lucy, 'He persevered in it to his last hour.'

'The haunting fancy of an old man's brain. Poor Dick! I wonder if we shall ever know the mystery of his fate.'

'Uncle Richard who was burn — lost at sea, papa?'

Mr Devine assented by a motion of his head. 'Ah, Addy, you owe all this luxury to your poor uncle. It is his money, not mine; and if he ever comes back I must restore it to him.'

'But he won't take it, papa. He will ask you to share it, and we shall go on living all happily together ever after.'

'Captain Frere wrote that the ship was burnt,' said Aunt Lucy, as though the subject pained her. 'He saw the wreck, you know.'

'I am not satisfied that Richard was on board her, though.'

'My dear Francis! Besides, it is more than twenty years ago.'

— 'Before I was *born* —' cried Addy, as though that event had occurred in some pre-Adamite age. 'Silly Papa! Why, unless poor uncle had been living on a desolate island, like Alexander Selkirk — monarch of all he surveys — *see Cowper*, as Papa's books say — he would have been home long ago. What should have prevented him?'

'What, indeed! Bless me, it's nearly six!' cries Aunt Lucy. 'What can be keeping Arthur? Ah! here's the carriage!'

A crash of wheels upon the gravel, a violent ringing of the bell, and presently Addy, running, with flying hair, to the steps, was caught and embraced by a young man of nineteen.

'Addy! God bless you! Well, father! Merry Christmas! Jane! Mary! Jenny! John! Thomas! how are you all! My dear Auntie! Here, Bob, bring in that bag — no, booby, not *that* one! That's right. Addy, that's for you — Mr Emanuel's last! Aunt Lucy, I've got a cap for you — the most bewitching thing! Where's that portmanteau? Don't drop the hat-box! God bless you all!'

He was a fine stalwart young fellow, with his father's blue eyes, and a merry, hearty, honest way with him, that made for him many friends. At Oxford he was a great favourite. Indeed, the stroke-oar of the University boat could hardly be otherwise. For the rest, he was impetuous and hasty-tempered; a little spoiled by the knowledge that he would be one of the richest commoners in England; liked to exercise his body better than his mind, but was a fair scholar, owing more to quickness of perception than thoroughness of purpose; had an honest contempt for all that was mean, 'snobbish' (which, in his dictionary, meant volumes), or cowardly; preferred the society of unaffected, 'jolly' girls of his own station to that of either Synonyma or Abomyna; was a little afraid of 'clever' women; professed to be a regicidal Democrat, and was, in his own soul, the rankest Tory that ever was heir to twenty thousand a year.

'I don't want my boy to be famous, or clever,' Mr Devine used to say. 'If he grows up a Christian gentleman, that's enough for me.'

Dinner was soon over, amid merry laughter, college stories, mysterious family jesting – unintelligible to all but the initiated – toasts, and little speeches.

'What made you so late, Arthur, dear?' asked his sister, when the family were once more seated round the fire.

'Aunt Lucy's cap!'

'Nonsense!'

'That cap has been a burden to me. It has weighed upon my heart, broken my slumber, disturbed my waking hours. Five times did it go astray. Five times did I, at the peril of my life, rescue it from the hands of strange ladies, who were bearing it away as the prey of their bow and their spear. I should have lost it once altogether had it not been for a fellow passenger, a big fellow, with a beard like one of the kings of Assyria sculptured on the what's his name, at the Exhibition. He plunged after it and flung it over his saddle-bow, crying, "By my halidame, lay but a finger on that damozel and I will crack thee o'er thy knave's costard for thy insolence!"'

'Now, Arthur, he didn't talk like that.'

'No, but he talked a great deal – of battles, sieges, dangers by flood and field, the imminent deadly breach, the cannon's mouth, the bubble reputation, and other matters. By the way, he got out at Harwich, and I heard him asking about a trap. By Jove, if he drives old Bodkin's grey mare, she'll break his entertaining and experienced neck for him, despite his adventures with mules in the Californian mountains.'

'Your friend was a traveller, then?' said Mr Devine.

'Traveller! A man who had put a girdle round the earth in forty minutes, by his own account. But hark — is that noise horse's feet on the gravel?'

It was, and in another instant a ring announced a visitor.

'Who on earth can that be? Old Thornton come over to wish us merry Christmas!' cried mercurial Arthur, rushing to the door. 'Why, by Jove, it *is*! It's Bodkin's pony, and the mysterious stranger! My dear sir, how do you do again? Whatever brings you here? Did I take away one of *your* trunks instead of that blessed bandbox. Why –'

The visitor advanced slowly through the hall, and pausing at the door of the lighted room, looked, somewhat nervously, round upon the assembled party, and then stepping into the full glow of the lamps, said, in a tone that savoured slightly of melodrama.

'Don't you know me, Frank? I am your brother Richard!'

Let us imagine for a moment the effect of such a bombshell.

Addy ran to Arthur as if frightened, Aunt Lucy turned very pale, and Mr Devine held out his hand mechanically.

Mr John Rex spoke again.

'I see you can't quite understand it. It's a long story, but I shall be able to explain it all by-and-by. I only arrived in England yesterday. I suppose I should have gone to your solicitors, but I could not resist coming down to see the old place.' He looked around. 'Why, how you have changed it!'

This carefully-prepared speech had its effect. Arthur seized him by the hand, with youthful impatience of anything like suspicion or discourtesy.

'Sit down, Uncle Dick — if you are Uncle Dick — for I don't know you. I am your nephew, Arthur Devine, and this is my sister Adelaide. Aunt Lucy, don't you recognise uncle?'

Miss Devine arose, nervously playing with her knitting needles, and gazed at the impostor. It was an anxious moment for John Rex; but he had not laboured at this scheme — rehearsed this scene for thirteen years — for nothing.

'I am changed from the days when I used to swing you under the old mulberry-tree, Lucy?'

This speech, also carefully prepared from the memory of the day when, in his character of 'private enquirer,' Mr Lawson had visited Sir Richard Devine, and had seen a little girl swinging in the garden, was not without its effect.

The lady, troubled with a gush of tender memories, fell into his arms; and he, speaking over her shoulder, said – remembering the articles discovered in the trunk of Richard Devine on the day when he lost him at Amsterdam – 'Frank, do you recollect the Elzevir 'Horace' you gave me. I have forgotten how to read it, but I have not forgotten the gift.'

Mr Devine struck his hand on the table with honest delight. 'Yes, yes! Bound in vellum! Of course – of course! With your name in it! Oh! Dick – Dick, where have you been so long?'

'Good gracious,' thought John Rex, with intense relief, as he embraced his relatives, 'How easy these good folks are gulled, to be sure.'

That night there was jubilation. The news spread like wildfire. Arthur rushed downstairs to set beer flowing, and one Jenkins, a groom, excited by unwonted potations, galloped into the town, and set all the bells ringing for joy of the dead that was alive again, the lost which was found.

There was no suspicion of the true character of the man who had come amongst them. Willing to believe his brother alive, Frank Devine was an easy victim, and Rex's artful references, hints, and well-displayed memories – let us remember that he had been preparing for this trial for thirteen years – were sufficiently convincing. The only disappointing thing about him was his manner, which, though guarded and subdued, was not altogether that of a gentleman.

'But,' as he said, 'it's a wonder that one who has knocked about as I have for the last twenty years should have preserved any refinement at all.'

'You must tell us your story, Uncle,' said Addy.

'Yes, dear, of course – and it's a strange one – but not to-night. I am tired. Frank, I suppose you have abolished my old room with the dormer-window and the lattice?'

'You shall have the best room in the house, my dear Richard.'

'And, by the way,' said artful John Rex, drawing him under, as they went up stairs together, 'don't think that I'm coming back to dispossess you. You can do far more good with our poor father's fortune than I can. I only want to live in peace after my wanderings.'

'My dear Richard,' said the honourable gentleman, 'the property is yours – all of it. I have always said that I but held it in trust for you, and that if you ever returned, it should be yours.'

⤙ 2 ⤚

COGITATION

JOHN REX locked his bedroom door and sat down to think. The dream of his life was accomplished. He was a rich man – rich beyond his hopes. He had conducted his iniquitous scheme with consummate ability – so far. He had made, during a period of thirteen years, all imaginable enquiries. He had succeeded – by means of another carefully planned deception – in escaping from the thraldom of his wife; and had visited again those places where he had once tracked the spendthrift son of the shipbuilder. He had proceeded with the utmost caution. He had felt his way step by step, had even lived for weeks together in the towns where Richard Devine might possibly have resided, familiarising himself with streets, making the acquaintance of old inhabitants, drawing into his own hands all loose ends of information which could help to knit the meshes of his net the closer. Such loose ends were not numerous; the prodigal had been too poor, too insignificant, to leave strong memories behind him. Yet Rex knew well by what strange accidents the deceit of an assumed identity is often penetrated. Some old comrade or companion of the lost heir might suddenly appear with keen questions of the memory of trifles which would cut his flimsy web to shreds, as easily as the sword of Saladin divided the floating silk. He could not afford to ignore the most insignificant circumstances. But he hoped that the greater peril had been passed.

The story which he had provided was ingenious. He had been saved from the burning *Hydaspes* by a vessel bound for Rio. Believing that his father had not forgiven him, and prompted by the pride which was known to be a leading feature of his character, he had determined not to return until fortune should have bestowed upon him wealth at least equal to the inheritance from which he had been ousted. In Spanish America he had striven to accumulate that wealth in vain. As *vaquero*, traveller, speculator, sailor, he had toiled for twenty-three years, and had failed. Worn out and penitent, he had returned home to beg a corner of English earth to lay his weary bones. The tale was plausible enough, and in the telling of it he was armed at all points. There was little fear that the navigator of the captured *Osprey*, the man who had lived for five years in Chili, who had suffered shipwreck in China, and had 'cut out' cattle on the Carrum Plains, would prove lacking in knowledge of riding, seamanship, or Spanish customs.

Moreover, he had determined on a course of action which showed his foresight. He had waited for thirteen years to seize this prize, and a year or so more would make but little difference to him. He would not attempt to at once dispossess Francis Devine, and so bring down upon himself a host of sharp-eyed lawyers eager for absolute proof of this and that. Frank and he would divide the estates, and when in the course of nature Frank died, it would be time for the elder brother to assert his full rights. At all events, it was desirable that he should be fully acknowledged before he threw off the mask of friendship. Mr Francis Devine having admitted John Rex as his brother for three or four years, could not in conscience deny him when he claimed what was admittedly his. No; all was done, all won. He had but little now to fear; and as, leaning out of the window, he listened to the joy-bells chiming in the keen wintry air, he smiled at the thought of the fortune his ingenuity had at last won for him. *Honesty the best policy* had been taught at the commercial academy to which his father, the butler, had sent him. Was it so? Surely not, or the bank-clerk, shop-walker, swindler, thief, sailor, squatter, and convict, would not be the acknowledged possessor of more than two hundred thousand pounds!

At the instant he was congratulating himself, a strange thing happened to the man whose heritage he had thus usurped.

⤙ 3 ⤚

WHAT MR LOFTUS'S SHEPHERD FOUND

AT midday on the 26th of December, 1850, Tom Crosbie the shepherd lay on his elbow, on the creek bank, watching his sheep feed in the green plain that lay beneath the distant purple peak of Mount Buninyong.

Tom Crosbie was a trusted servant of Mr Loftus. He had arrived at the station some four years before, carrying a little child, and had begged for work. Work had been given him. He proved useful. Loftus offered him the place of shepherd. Crosbie replied, 'I will take it if you let me be my own hutkeeper.' 'Why?' asked Loftus, astonished. The man pointed to the child. 'I married late in life,' said he, 'my wife died in Melbourne a month ago. This is my only one, and I want her love all to myself.' Mr Loftus – one of those many gentlemen of birth who came to settle in pastoral Port Phillip – comprehended that the wanderer was not of the ordinary type of shepherds, and respected his fancy. 'If you wish it, my man,' said he. So Tom Crosbie lived in the Mountain Hut, and kept Talbot Loftus's sheep for four years, alone. His daughter Dorcas was always with him. When she was too young to toddle far, he carried her. When she was too tired to prattle, he rocked her to sleep in his arms. He was at once her father and her mother. The pair – alone together for weeks – understood each other's nods, sighs, and smiles. As his dog learnt to interpret the glance of his eye, or the motion of his finger, so did Richard Devine learn to interpret each shadow on the brow of the child of the woman he had loved, to understand her childish babble, to comprehend the thoughts which spoke in the dark eyes that never looked aught but love at him. They were perfectly happy. She knew no world but that which blossomed beneath the volcanic hill, thought of no human creature save the man who was to her as a God. He found in her — his dream-child incarnated — compensation for all his torments in the past, realization of all his thoughts of happiness in the future. He asked that kind Heaven which had delivered him from bondage but to let him die there, under the shadow of the lonely hill, and permit the pure hands of this innocent child to plant some humble bush-flower upon his nameless grave.

Yet, at times, thoughts of remorse at what had been done, and terror at what was yet to do, came upon him. The child should be reared in a luxurious home, should have silk dresses to wear, elegant toys to play with; not be the household fairy of a shepherd's hut, wearing but coarse stuff-frocks, and learning to read out of dog's-eared and battered books, her only playmate a dog, her only toys such rude wooden ones as a shepherd's knife could fashion for her. He ought to give her up to her father, Captain Frere, even though that giving up would rend her heart and break his own. It was a hideous selfishness to keep her thus in a barbarous wilderness. So he would argue; now promising himself to teach her all that strange and varied knowledge which his experience of life had achieved for him; now bitterly confessing that he had forgotten much that he should have remembered, and that his scanty earnings were all insufficient to purchase for her the instruction she needed. He promised himself that he would give her up, and then, in agony, prayed the Heaven which had suffered him to save her to work a miracle, and render him rich enough to keep her.

So meditating, this hot summer's afternoon, he strove to think of some plan by which he could achieve fortune. His thoughts ranged back over the past. What wild dreams of boundless wealth had he not — in his hot youth — once cherished! Such dreams are the property of youth; middle age gains in experience what it loses in imagination. Yet old men sometimes clung to such visions, and hoped for such successes. Shuddering, he called to mind how old Mooney in the prison of Norfolk Island, had, with his last breath, urged his friend to believe in his golden dreams. What if Mooney should have been right, and the continent of Australia rich in that dross which the German chemist had so long and vainly sought to wrest from the grasp of baser metals! No; it was impossible. Had not he, the lonely shepherd, searched and searched, in vain, amid the gullies and the rocks for that glittering dust which the old convict believed he had found on the banks of Summerhill Creek, in New South Wales. 'Pick out some narrow gully between the quartz rocks, and when you come to a bit o' good red earth, dig.' How often had not Tom Crosbie dug and found nothing! As he thus meditated, he idly plunged the point of his staff into the soft alluvial soil of the bank. The summer had been unusually dry, and the creek had dwindled to a thread of muddy water, leaving a great portion of its winter bed, on either side, uncovered. A loosened lump of earth rolled down and fell into the stream. As it fell, Richard Devine saw something glitter. So strange a comment upon his thoughts startled him. He leapt to his feet, and hurried down the bank. As is frequently the case in life, accident conferred that which was refused to patience. In an instant he knew his fortune.

Entangled among the roots of the grass tuft was a yellow knob of the bigness of a bean.

Ten minutes after this, the nine-year-old child, who was gravely watching the embers heaped above the camp oven, felt herself clasped in her father's arms, and carried out of the hut into the air, there to be kissed, prayed for, and wept over.

'What *is* the matter, papa?' said the grave little soul, astonished at this outburst from her melancholy father.

'Matter!' cried Richard Devine, 'matter for madness! You shall be a lady, a princess, a queen! Kiss me, and let me go. My darling! Oh, I must think over this, or I shall go mad!'

And he rushed out of the hut again, like a veritable madman.

That evening, Dorcas found her father more silent than ever. He remained sitting with his head between his hands, until long after she was asleep in her little bed, and then rose and walked about under the lustrous Australian sky, as though engaged in battling with some problem difficult to solve. When day dawned, he took his sheep out of the fold without a word, and going down to the creek, spent much pains in erasing all marks of his digging at the bank. That evening, he walked into the station, and asked to see Mr Loftus.

'Well, Tom, what brings *you* here? Rations run out? How's Dotty?'

'If you please, sir, I want to leave.'

'WHAT!'

'I want to leave.'

'What on earth's the matter, Tom?' cries Loftus, who had come to regard the shepherd as a fixture. 'What do you want to leave for?'

'I want to go to Melbourne, sir.'

'Go to Melbourne, eh? Why, you're as white as a sheet! What have you been doing?'

'I saw an advertisement in an old paper which concerns me, sir!' said Richard Devine, forced to lie to keep his secret, 'and I want to see about it at once.'

'Oh, certainly!' returns Loftus, a little nettled. 'I don't want to keep any man against his will. I'll send down Bob in the morning. You want your cheque, I suppose?'

'If you please, sir.'

The cheque was not a despicable one. Thomas Crosbie had been in the service of Talbot Loftus as shepherd and hut-keeper from the 2nd of February, 1847, to the 30th of December, 1850, at a salary of £29 a year and his rations. He had drawn during that period but £15, which represented all his wants for four years. Mr Loftus gave him a cheque for £100.

'Take care you don't knock it down, Tom,' he said. 'I am sorry you are going.'

'You are very kind, sir, but I must go.'

'Do you take the child with you, Tom?' asked Mrs Loftus.

Tom turned a reproachful glance upon her that spoke volumes. 'Of course, madam.'

Good-natured Mrs Loftus, sorry for the utterance of a speech which seemed to have wounded the feelings of the strange shepherd, bustled out and presently returned with a little cape belonging to one of her younger children, and coming upon the man as he was passing the angle of the homestead, on his way back to his hut, gave it to him.

'The nights are cold,' said the good-hearted lady; 'she will want something to keep her warm.'

The shepherd took the gift, and thanked her in terms not free from emotion. It seemed to strike him for the first time that he was acting rather a churlish part in thus abruptly leaving the employer who had treated him so kindly; and, advancing a few steps, he caught the lady by the sleeve.

'I don't want to appear ungrateful,' he said, 'but I *must* go. Tell – tell Mr Loftus to purchase the home station.'

'Purchase the home station! What do you mean?'

'Tell him to *buy* it. It – it is valuable.'

And then, as if fearful of having already said too much, the mysterious Crosbie departed.

When Mrs Loftus told her husband, he laughed.

'Poor Tom! he's getting a little cranky, I suppose, like all shepherds. What should I want to buy the land for?'

About the middle of January, 1851, a bearded man stepped into the shop of a jeweller named Brentano, in Elizabeth-street, and offered for sale seven nuggets of gold, and as much gold dust as would fill a table spoon.

'Where did you get this!' asked the jeweller.

'In California. I landed three days ago from the *San José*.'

'There are 18 ounces here. At £2 10s. an ounce, that will make £45.'

The bearded man pocketed the money without a word, and Brentano, who had made nearly cent. per cent. on his bargain, looked after him suspiciously. If gold wasn't worth more than £2 10s. an ounce in California, Brentano was ill-informed. It was evident that the bearded man had not told the truth. He must have robbed, perhaps murdered, some one. After all – £2 10s. an ounce! – what was it to Brentano?

'It's a pity we can't find a goldfield *here*,' said the jeweller to his assistant, with a sigh. 'One could make some money, then. I think Melbourne's getting slower and slower every day.'

The bearded man laid out his £145 judiciously. He bought, for instance, a team of six bullocks, at £4 each – £24; two tons of flour at £16 per ton – £32; 5 chests of hysonskin tea at £2 9s.

— £12 5s.; a covered waggon, £40; making a total of £108 5s., and £36 15s. left to pay expenses. As his expenses – including those of his daughter – amounted only to £25, he thus had 'in hand,' as clerks say, £11 10s. With this he purchased a pick and shovel, an adze, an axe, a plane, a saw, and some nails. Those who met the team in Collins-street guessed that the bearded man was going up the country to open a small store. So he was.

On the 29th of March, Mr Loftus, riding out upon his run, and coming to the place now called Specimen Hill, saw a bullock dray camped, and beheld two men erecting a hut.

'What's all this?' said he.

His old shepherd, Crosbie, came forward with a smile.

'I am building a store, sir.'

'A store! In the bush! Where do you expect to get customers?'

'Oh, they'll be here soon enough, Mr Loftus.'

'If they go anywhere, they'll go to the township of Buninyong.'

'No, they won't; they'll come here.'

Mr Loftus shook his head, and cantered off, fully convinced that his ex-shepherd was insane.

On the 14th of April the hut was built, and a huge board running its length informed the cockatoos and lorries that the building was called

CROSBIE'S GENERAL STORE.
BEST TEA AND FLOUR SOLD

One or two good folks rode all the way from Buninyong to look at this madman's hut, and even offered to buy some of his tea and sugar, for the fun of the thing.

'No,' said Crosbie, 'but I'll buy all yours, if you will trust me two months; my money's all spent.'

The majority shook their heads; but one fellow, not without a sense of humour, and thinking that if the worst came to the worst he could get his goods back again, sold the lunatic 2000 lbs. of damaged sugar at fivepence a pound, being a considerable advance on Melbourne prices, and thought he had made a commercial hit.

Crosbie stored his purchase, and waited for purchasers. As he was not doing much business, he dug a little, and took secret opportunities to wash the earth he had dug up, in a flat tin dish.

On the 20th of April, marvellous news reached Melbourne. Gold had been found at Bathurst, and the town had been 'rushed' by diggers! The keeper of 'Crosbie's Store' heard the intelligence from a passer-by, and rode over to Loftus.

'I wish you had taken my advice, sir, and bought your home station.'

'Nonsense, Crosbie,' says Loftus, 'why should I?'

'Because of this, sir,' said Crosbie, pulling from his pocket a little bag, and showing its contents.

'Good God, it's Gold!' cries Loftus.

'Yes it is, and you'll have two hundred men camped in your home station paddock before the week's out,' said Crosbie.

'Who knows of this beside yourself?'

'No one.'

'I've been a good master to you. Will you keep the secret until I can get to Melbourne?'

'On one condition I will,' said Crosbie.

'What is that?'

'That you will sell me five hundred of those fat wethers in the Mountain paddock.'

'I'll *give* you a hundred to hold your tongue.'

'No. I am going into business, and I mean to pay my way. There are twenty ounces of gold in this bag. Gold should be worth £3 10s. an ounce; but, as it will soon be found in large quantities, the price will, of necessity, be depreciated. We will say £3. Here, then, is £60. Your wethers are worth six and six-pence in Melbourne. Let us say seven shillings, and that will make £170. Take this bag, and I will owe you £110, which I will pay when I fetch the sheep.'

Loftus, astonished at this mercantile side to his 'cranky' shepherd's character, could only stare at the gold dust in his palm, and consent.

That evening Crosbie added to the legend over his store the words,

PRIME MUTTON EIGHTEENPENCE A POUND

This getting to Buninyong, where a whole sheep was sold for eight shillings, caused another horse-laugh.

In the meantime, Talbot Loftus, attempting to purchase his home station paddock, found that a reward was publicly offered for the discovery of gold, and that Mr La Trobe was not desirous of selling land at present. He posted back again with all speed, in order to be the first on the field, and came to Crosbie's.

'Show me where you found the gold,' said he, 'and I'll make your fortune. There is a reward offered.'

Crosbie laughed in his face.

'Reward! I know what Government rewards are! You hold your tongue, Mr Loftus, and let me sell your sheep for you. We are *standing* on the biggest goldfield in the world!'

'Then why don't you dig?' asked Loftus, not unreasonably.

'I have been digging – quietly, of course. But I want to make money. I've known about this gold for the last four months, but I wanted to get ready for circumstances. Digging is just a lottery; one may dig for weeks and make nothing. Besides, I've got a daughter, and what is to become of her if I'm away digging all day, and she has nothing but a tent to sleep in. No sir; I've thought of a better plan than that. As soon as this goldfield opens, we shall have half the world here. When half the world is mad upon digging, no one thinks of such slow-going trades as those of the butcher and baker. If you get ten ounces of gold a week, and can't buy bread, what's the good of your money? Wouldn't you give five ounces for a loaf?'

'Of course I would,' said Loftus.

'Very good, sir. Then come to CROSBIE'S STORE and we'll sell it to you!'

Poor Loftus, ignorant of the wonderful change which hope and good luck can make in a man, was alarmed at the jaunty language of his once melancholy shepherd, and despite his unanswerable logic, thought him madder than ever.

On the 1st of May, however, gold was found at Clunes; on the 6th of May the discovery was published at Geelong. On the

10th, Crosbie announced his discovery, and called the place Golden Point. In less than a week, Melbourne had run mad.[1]

The story of the rush that followed has been often told. All fell out as Crosbie had predicted. The quiet sheep run swarmed with gold-seekers. Fifty pounds weight of gold was found in two days. In less than a week there were a hundred cradles clacking at Golden Point, and fresh adventurers were arriving at the rate of one hundred daily. The Yarrowee Creek, enlarged by recent rains, ran red with the washings of the tortured earth. The densely-timbered Black Hill echoed with axes, that bid fair to soon render its name no longer applicable. Geelong emptied itself by way of Clunes. Lawyers, doctors, parsons, shopkeepers, shepherds, Jews, thieves, publicans and sinners, arrived hourly. On the 19th September came Mr Commissioner Doveton and Assistant Commissioner Armstrong with troopers, and Loftus took out a licence to mine on his own run, paying 15s. for the privilege, until the end of the month. In the first four days 400 licenses were issued, and, by the 30th of October, 2,246 licenses. On that day were more than 4,000 people on the ground, and 500 yet daily arriving. Eight pounds of gold were washed from two tin dishes of dirt, and some lucky ones made 100 ounces a day. Melbourne would have been deserted had it not been for the crowds constantly arriving. The city became one gigantic hotel, a *caravanserai*, where travellers of all nations halted for a night on their way to Eldorado. The price of provisions trebled itself in a week. Servants were not to be got at any price whatever. The roads leading to Ballarat and Mount Alexander were so cut up by the constant passage of heavy waggons as to be almost impassable. Drays broke down in the mud, and mounted travellers passed whole families sitting disconsolate among the ruins of their household goods. The civil service was likely to come to a dead-lock by reason of the de-

1. I have taken a novelist's liberty in changing names and ante-dating the gold discovery by two months. Esmond was the first gold finder, and he found it at Clunes on the 1st day of July, publishing the news in Geelong on the 9th of the same month. Mr Hiscock found gold in Buninyong early in August, and the Golden Point diggings were not discovered until on or after the 24th August. The merit of this discovery is disputed, but Mr Withers, the careful and accurate historian of Ballarat, seems inclined to assign the merit of priority to a man named Connor. – M.C.

sertion of civil servants. Mr La Trobe – the retiring man of letters, busy with his butterflies and moths – thought the end of the world was come. 'What are we to do when the news reaches England?' he asked, in despair. Members of the nominee council prophesied famine and destruction. The colony would soon be under Lynch law, and the refuge of all the villains in the universe.

In the meantime the living tide poured in, and Crosbie, listening to the ceaseless crashing of 5,000 cradles, and selling his mutton at two shillings a pound, felt like the genie of the fairy tale who raised an army from a pomegranate seed. He had two parties mining under his kitchen, and had already sent down 150 ounces of gold by the escort to his credit at the Union Bank; had three drays on the way up with stores, for which he would receive twice the value in gold dust and nuggets; was honoured by having one of the gold commissioners lodging under his shingle roof, and a consequent guard of troopers outside his wooden door; eat, drank, slept, and bargained with a loaded revolver in his belt; and was the happiest, richest, calmest, most feverish, and most miserable man on the wonderful gold-fields of Ballarat.

❖ 4 ❖

MR RICHARD DEVINE AT HOME

For more than a year, John Rex, or, as he was now called, Mr Richard Devine, remained an inmate of Mere. His ingenuity had saved him from any very searching enquiry into his past life, and there had been as yet no necessity for contact with lawyers – those remorseless exposers of imposture. The story current abroad was simply that the long lost brother had returned, and had been received by his family with open arms. The *Harwich Express* had a leading article on the subject, and a few paragraphs from its pages found their way into other journals.

Mr Richard Devine did not go much into society. 'I was always a rough fellow, Frank,' he would say, 'and my wild life has unfitted me for drawing-rooms. I would rather smoke my pipe at home. You keep your own position, my dear boy.' It thus came about that Mr Richard was regarded as a sort of martyr to affection, a man conscious of his own imperfections, and one whose imperfections were therefore to be lightly dwelt upon.

He had a suite of rooms appropriated to himself, and smoke and drank – a 'little hard', it was whispered – in them. When ladies visited Mere, Mr Richard was usually absent somewhere; but when men about town, visiting in the neighbourhood for sport's sake, met Mr Richard, they found him an agreeable fellow, not the most refined, but thoroughly equal to themselves in all manly accomplishments – that of whist included. They asked him to visit them, and by-and-by there were not a few bachelor dinners – of a card-playing, horse-racing sort – at which Mr Richard Devine was an honoured and frequent guest.

In the first stages of his deception he had been timid and cautious. Then the soothing influence of comfort, respect, and security came upon him and almost refined him. He began to feel almost as he had felt when Mr Leopold Craven was alive. The sensation of being ministered unto by a beautiful girl, who kissed him night and morning, calling him 'Uncle', – of being regarded with admiration by a high-spirited, well-bred boy – of being deferred to in all things by so complete a gentleman as Frank Devine – was novel and pleasing. He felt at times more than half inclined to confess all, and leave his case in the hands of the folk he had injured.

Yet – he thought – such a course would be absurd. It would result in no benefit to anyone, simply in misery to himself. The true Richard Devine was dead, and buried fathoms deep in ocean. All Van Diemen's Land had rung with the suicide – or murder – of the chaplain, the escape of the ruffian convict, and the loss of the vessel in which he had embarked. John Rex flattered himself that he at least usurped the name of no living man, and that, unless one could rise from the dead, Richard Devine would never return to accuse him. So flattering himself, he gradually became bolder, and by slow degrees suffered his true nature to appear. He was violent to the servants, cruel to dogs and horses, often wantonly coarse in speech, and brutally regardless of the feelings of others. He often disgusted his brother, and made his niece blush. Indeed, all sympathy between him and his sister soon vanished. Governed, like most women, solely by her feelings, Miss Devine had at first been more prodigal of her affection to the man she believed to be her favourite brother than any other member of the household. But his rash acts of selfishness, his habits of grossness and self-indulgence disgusted her, and she began to dislike him intensely. For some time she – good creature – fought against this feeling, endeavouring to overcome her instincts of distaste, and arguing with herself that to thus permit a hatred of her brother to arise in her heart was almost criminal; but she was at length forced to succumb.

One day – long after Arthur had returned to college – Mr Richard went out to pass the day with a neighbouring good fellow – a sort of gentleman farmer, only too proud to see at his table so wealthy and wonderful a man. Mr Richard drank a good deal more than was good for him, and came home in a condition of disgusting drunkenness. I say disgusting, because some folk have the art of getting drunk in a humorous method, that robs intoxication of half its grossness. A man of true gentlemanly instincts, when owning a brain not weakened by habitual indulgence, never displays those instincts to better advantage than when overtaken in his cups. With John Rex to be drunk was to be himself – coarse and cruel. Frank was away, and Miss Devine had retired for the night, when the dogcart deposited 'Mr Richard'. The virtuous butler-porter, who opened the door, received a blow in the chest and a demand for 'Brandy!' The groom was cursed, and ordered to instant oblivion. Mr Richard stumbled into the dining-room – veiled in that dim light which the servants considered necessary for a dining-room which was, as it were, 'sitting up' for its master – and ordered 'More candles!' The candles were brought, after some delay, and Mr Richard amused himself by spilling their meltings upon the carpet. 'Let's have 'luminashon!' he cried; and climbing with muddy boots upon the costly chairs, scraping with his feet the polished table, attempted to fix the wax in the silver sconces with which the antiquarian taste of the late owner had adorned the room.

'You'll break the table, sir,' said the servant.

'Damn the table!' said Rex. 'Buy 'nother table. What's table t'you?'

'Oh, certainly, sir,' replied the man.

'Oh cert'nly! Why cert'nly? What do you know about it?'

'Oh, certainly not, sir,' replied the man.

'If I had — stockwhip here — I make you — hic — skip. Whar's brandy?'

'Here, Mr Richard.'

'Have some! Tomkins, you crawler, have some. Tomkins, you'll be lagged some day, Tomkins. You look shif you *had* bin lagged, Tomkins!'

'Ha, ha, Mr Richard!'

'Whar you laugh me for! 'Pertinent schoundrel! Teach you laugh at me!' And the madman threw a book at him, which struck the pier glass and broke it.

'Law, Mr Richard, you've broken the looking-glass.'

'Wars that t'you. My looking-glass, and my broke! If I want break looking-glass, I break looking-glass.'

'Oh, certainly, Mr Richard!'

'Come and drink this brandy! Good brandy! Send for servantsh and have dance. D'you dance, Tomkins?'

'No, Mr Richard.'

'Then you shall dance now, Tomkins. You'll dance upon nothing one day, Tomkins! Here! Halloo! Mary! Susan! Janet! William! Hay! Halloo!' And he began to shout and blaspheme.

'Don't you think it's time for bed, Mr Richard?' one of the men ventured to suggest.

'No!' roared the ex-convict, emphatically, 'I *don't!* I've gone to bed at daylight far too long. We'll have luminashon! I'm master here. Master everything. Richard 'Vine's my name. Isn't it, Tomkins, you villain?'

'Oh-h-h! Ye-yes, Mr Richard.'

'Course it is, and make you know it, too! I'm no d — d painter picture, crockery chap. I'm genelman! Genelman seen the world! Knows what what. There ain't much I ain't fly to. Wait till that long nosed beggar's dead, Tomkins, and you shall see!' More swearing, and awful threats of what the inebriate would do when he was in possession. 'Bring up some brandy!' Crash goes the bottle in the fireplace. 'Light up the droring-rooms; we'll have dance! I'm drunk! what's that? If you'd gone through what I have, you'd be glad to be drunk. I look a fool' — this to his image in another glass. 'I ain't though, or I wouldn't be here. Curse you, you grinning idiot' — crash goes his fist through the mirror — 'don't grin at me. Play up there! Where's old woman? Fetch her out and let's dance!'

'Miss Devine has gone to bed, Mr Richard,' cries Tomkins, aghast, attempting to bar the passage to the upper regions.

'Then let's have her out o' bed,' cries John Rex, plunging to the door.

Tomkins, attempting to restrain him, is instantly hurled into a cabinet of rare china, and the drunken brute essays the stairs. The other servants seize him. He curses and fights like a demon. Doors bang open, lights gleam, maids hover, horrified, asking if it's 'fire?' and begging to be 'put out'. The whole house is in an uproar; in the midst of which Miss Devine appears, and looks down upon the scene. Rex catches sight of her, and bursts into blasphemy. She withdraws, strangely terrified; and the animal, torn, bloody, and blasphemous, is at last got into his own apartments, the groom, whose face has been seriously damaged in the encounter, bestowing a hearty kick on the prostrate carcass at parting.

The next morning, Miss Devine declined to see her brother, though he sent a special apology to her.

'I am afraid I was a little overcome by wine last night,' said he to Tomkins.

'Well, you was, sir,' says Tomkins.

'Ah! A very little wine makes me quite ill, Tomkins. Did I do anything very violent?'

'You *was* rather obstropolous, Mr Richard.'

'Here's a sovereign for you, Tomkins. Did I *say* anything?'

'You cussed a good deal, Mr Richard. Most gents do when they've bin – hum – dining out, Mr Richard.'

'What an infernal ass I am,' thought John Rex, as he dressed. 'I shall spoil everything if I don't take care.' He was right. He was going the right way to spoil everything. However, for this bout he made amends — money soothed the servants' hall, and apologies and time won Miss Devine's forgiveness. Rex, convinced that Frank must sooner or later hear of the broken china, wrote to him, and gave his own version of the story. He was a clever letter writer, and the story lost nothing in the telling.

'I cannot yet conform to English habits, my dear brother,' wrote Rex, 'and feel at times out of place in your quiet home. I think that – if you can spare me a little money – I should like to travel.'

Frank, who had never found in his brother a congenial mind, jumped at the proposition, and begged him to come up to London in order that the 'accounts might be gone into, and the property settled.'

'I must account to you for back rents,' said honest Frank. 'Lucy and I take £5,000 apiece, all the rest is yours.'

This, however, did not suit Rex. He wanted no 'arrangement', for an 'arrangement' would mean a settlement of at least a fourth of the property upon young Arthur and the girls, and he did not wish a settlement to be made. He would let things alone if he could, so that, if he had need, he could insist upon possession at any time.

'I must decline, my dear brother, to intrude upon you in any way. Just let me have enough for my little wants, and manage as you please.'

Upon this, Frank placed £3,000 to Richard Devine's credit at Mastermann's, and wrote to say that he should consider himself as steward of the estate. John Rex grinned, drew the money, and went to Paris.

Fairly started in the world of dissipation and excess, he began to grow reckless. When a young man he had been singularly free from the vice of drunkenness; turning his sobriety – as he did all his virtues – to vicious account. He had learnt to drink deep in the loneliness of the bush, and had frequent opportunities for such regrets as the one which seized him after his debauch at Mere. Master of a large sum of money, he had intended to spend it as he would have spent it in his younger days. He had forgotten that since his death and burial the world had not grown younger. It was possible that Mr Leopold Craven might have discovered some of the old set of fools and knaves with whom he had once mixed. Many of them were alive and flourishing. Mr Lemoine, for instance, was respectably married in his native island of Jersey, and had already threatened to disinherit a nephew who showed a tendency to rake. Blick – the great – had died worth a plum, and Sarah Purfoy's marquis was the guide, philosopher, and friend of Albert the Good, the patron of the Great Exhibition, a pillar of the Low Church, and founder of the notable Crossing Sweepers' Brigade.

But neither the marquis nor Mr Lemoine would care to recognize Mr Leopold Craven, *alias* John Skinner, *alias* John Rex, in his proper person, and it was not expedient that their acquaintance should be made in the person of Richard Devine, lest by some unlucky chance they should recognize the cheat. Thus poor Leopold Craven was compelled to lie still in his grave, and Mr Richard Devine, trusting to a big beard and more burly figure, to keep his secret, was compelled to begin his friendship with Mr Leopold's whilom friends all over again.

But in Paris and London there were plenty of people ready to become hail-fellow-well-met with any gentleman possessing money. Mr Richard Devine's strange history was secretly whispered in many a boudoir and club-room. The history, however, was not always told in the same way. It was generally known that Mr Francis Devine had an elder brother, who, being supposed to be dead, had suddenly returned, to the confusion of his family. But the manner of his return was told in many ways.

In the first place, Mr Francis Devine, millionaire though he was, did not move in that brilliant circle which had lately received his elder brother. There are in England many men of fortune as large as that left by the old shipbuilder, who are positively unknown in that little world which is supposed to contain all the men worth knowing. Francis Devine was a man of mark in his own coterie. Among artists, *bric-à-brac* sellers, and *quasi* men of letters, he was known as a patron and a man of taste. His bankers and his lawyers knew him to be wealthy, but as he neither mixed in politics, 'went into society', betted, or speculated in merchandise, there were tolerably large sections of the community who had never heard his name. Many respectable money-lenders would have required 'further information' before they would discount his bills; and 'club-men' in general – save perhaps those ancient quidnuncs who know everybody from

Adam downwards – had but little acquaintance with him. The advent of Mr Richard Devine – a coarse person of unlimited means – had therefore chief influence upon that sinister circle of male and female rogues who form the 'half-world'. They began to enquire concerning his antecedents, and, failing satisfactory information, to invent lies concerning him. It was generally believed that he was a black sheep, a man whose family 'kept him out of the way,' but who was, in a pecuniary sense, 'good' for a considerable sum.

Thus taken upon trust, Mr Richard Devine mixed in the very best of bad society, and had no lack of agreeable friends to help him to spend his money. So admirably did he spend it, that Frank became at last alarmed at the frequent drafts upon him, and urged his brother to bring his affairs to a final settlement. Richard Devine – in Paris, or Homburg, or London, or elsewhere – could never be got to attack business, and so Frank grew more and more anxious. He had two children, for whom it was necessary that he should provide, and he became ill through the anxiety consequent upon his brother's dissipations. 'I wish, my dear Richard, that you would let me know what to do,' he wrote. 'I wish, my dear Frank, that you would do what you think best,' was his brother's reply. Frank shut up Mere, and lived in a small house in Pimlico.

'I am economizing,' he said.

'I am glad to hear it,' was his brother's answer. '*I* never could economize.'

'Will you let Perkiss and Quaid look into the business,' said Frank.

'I hate lawyers,' said Richard. 'Do what you think best.'

Frank began to repent of his too easy taking of matters in the beginning. Not that he had a suspicion of Rex, but that he remembered that Dick was always a loose fish. Miss Devine, faithfully attending her niece, saw a great change in her brother. He became morose, nervous, excitable. She went privately to the family doctor, who shrugged his shoulders.

'There is no danger,' said he. 'Keep him quiet, and he will live for years, *but* – his father died of heart disease.'

Miss Devine wrote to 'Richard', and begged him to come down for a day or so and settle affairs, 'So as to relieve poor

Frank's mind.' Richard wrote back to say that 'he was compelled to go to Epsom on business of importance, but that he would come down as soon as possible.' He did not come and one morning, Mr Devine not appearing at breakfast, his sister went up and found him asleep – as his father had been. Adelaide and Arthur were orphans.

'Thank God,' said Miss Devine, piously, 'I have enough to live upon. Arthur and Addy shall stay with me.'

'It is most kind of you,' said Mr Richard – attired in a velvet coat, wearing a red necktie, and somewhat stouter than when he had arrived at Mere three years before – 'I regret that my recent losses will prevent me doing anything for them.'

'You are a bad man, Richard Devine,' said Miss Lucy. 'Your brother gave you everything. You might at least provide for his children.'

'I have offered Arthur £500 a year,' said John Rex.

'Which he declines!' cries Arthur. 'I will be no burden upon you or anyone.'

'Oh, all right,' says his uncle. 'That's your affair. Thomas – brandy and soda, in the billiard-room. Major, we will finish our game.'

The dispossessed ones took cheap lodgings in Gloucester-place, Portman-square, from which Arthur – the richest commoner in England no longer – would be often mysteriously absent.

'Thank goodness,' said Aunt Lucy, 'that we are out of that house, defiled by gamblers and blacklegs. Addy, come and kiss me – as long as I have a shilling you shall share it.'

'Who would have thought that Uncle Richard would have been so so cruel?' sighed Addy.

'But what do you intend to do, aunt?'

'My dear Arthur, I have nearly £500 a year. I am going to live abroad – one can well live on that income. You must go to the Bar, and stay with us for your vacations.'

'Dear Aunt Lu,' says Arthur, 'not I. I am going to make my fortune.'

'How?'

'I'm going to the diggings!'

'My darling boy!'

'Oh, Arty!'

'It is no use crying, my dears!' says the young man, with a sob. 'I *won't* be dependent on that man. I have £100 left of my allowance; I took my passage to Melbourne this morning, and I shall come back with a fortune in nuggets – to tell Mr Richard Devine how much I hate him.'

⤛ 5 ⤜

THE LILY OF SPECIMEN HILL

IN the midsummer of the Ballarat diggings – that is to say, about the end of the month of October, 1854 – a girl sat under the shade of Crosbie's bark verandah, reading Oliver Twist.

The verandah was not very large, affording indeed but a narrow strip of shadow; and the space about it was so blocked up with barrels and boxes, that it seemed wonderful how the girl could have squeezed herself and her rocking-chair between them. But this little space behind Crosbie's store was considered a sort of gigantic garden by many an honest digger, wont, for the last three years, to pick his way cautiously between the red lumps of mullock which formed the back of the township of Ballarat. In the front of Crosbie's store – which was likewise the post office – a crowd of men were gathered, waiting for letters, buying tea and flour, or cheapening miners' tools. Crosbie was up to his neck in business, for he sold everything, from the latest invention in cradles to the latest importation in red shirts; and Dorcas – the Lily of Specimen Hill, as she had been christened by some poetic youngster – had retired, to follow the fortunes of Mr Bumble's victim in peace.

Let us look at the creature into which the child of Maurice Frere and Dora Vickers had developed. Tall for her age – she was barely thirteen – she was dressed in the costliest of silks, and adorned with the most expensive jewellery. Indeed, in the days when men hammered nuggets into rings, and one lunatic absolutely shod his horse with gold, jewellery was thought but of little value. The Lily had a deal box full of 'specimens', 'nuggets', brooches, ouches, and earrings of 'colonial gold', presented to her shyly by shamefaced Cornishmen, and honest, hard-handed, soft-hearted fellows in love with her barbaric beauty. For the Lily was beautiful enough to be the princess Golden Point wished to see her. Born under the fierce constellation of the Southern Cross, nurtured in an island whose climate was almost tropical, and growing to girlhood in the free air of the Victorian bush, she was already ripening into womanhood. Her figure, slender as a willow, gave promise of luxuriance of outline; her assured step, confident glance, low-toned and melodious voice, betokened that the woman had awoke within her. A stranger seeing her thus sitting, would have taken her to be a young woman of nineteen or twenty.

Her appearance was peculiar. With the brightest golden hair – hair that rippled and waved rebelliously beneath its bands – she had the darkest eyes in the world, and a complexion like the leaf of a white rose. This last fact – a fact of note in that city of the sun-burned – had doubtless suggested the charming name of affection by which she was known. Her father's vigorous physical nature seemed to have interfused itself with her mother's delicate organisation. The Lily was a paradox in temper as well as in appearance. Now all softness, tenderness, and affection, now wayward, passionate, and cruel, she seemed to be each of her parents by turns. As there were times when Richard Devine – or Crosbie, as we henceforth name him – could have worshipped her for her likeness to her dead mother; so, upon occasions arose in her so fierce a spirit of petulance and contradiction, that, beholding in her her living and still detested father, the victim of Norfolk Island could almost have hated her. Fortunately these outbursts of hereditary evil were becoming more and more rare, and the patience of her saviour, nurse, and teacher, bid fair to be rewarded by the love of a noble, high-souled woman.

He had taught her all he himself knew. His first purchase had been books for her. His earliest leisure had been devoted to her instruction. Many a night when diggers, awakened by a pistol-shot, or a night-cry, had pushed aside the curtain of their tents to gaze affrightedly forth, had they seen the light in 'Crosbie's' steadily burning; and, while congratulating themselves on so wakeful a neighbour, little guessed that the storekeeper was teaching his child. Many a 'poor scholar', seeking on the goldfields the fortune he had failed to find in books, was astonished at the multifarious knowledge which stocked the Lily's golden head, and startled to find that her father had taught her all. To impart such instruction, the lonely man had – sustained by love – schooled himself again in the lessons of his boyhood, had – when Loftus in the bygone times imagined him but sleeping or musing – recalled, with all the strength of a memory still green, the facts of history and science once so little regarded. Dorcas, unaccomplished in the arts of a drawing-room, unwitting of chromatic scales, the long-drawn agonies of crochet, the mysteries of wool-work, the linked inconsequence of Magnall's Questions, had trodden strange paths of science, and was familiar with strange pictures of history. Much that her 'father' taught her was inaccurate, and her learning but ill-digested; but, with her mother's love of books strong in her, she had devoured all, in shape of print, which Crosbie's reckless orders upon the Melbourne booksellers could obtain for her, and thirsted for more. A schoolmaster would have called her uneducated, a scholar would have wondered at her marvellous intelligence. Her mind was as a rough gem, a ruby yet crusted with the diluvium of the mine, but which, to the eye of the lapidary, outvalues a million times the polished and sparkling crystal cut by the thousand to glitter, brilliantly worthless, in the drawing-rooms of ordinary civilisation.

Enough of description, let her character unfold itself in the scenes which follow.

She had been reading for some half-hour, when pausing to turn a leaf, her glance caught something in the prospect before her which seemed to fix her attention.

The prospect was one which was of itself curious. In the flat beneath her, and far away up above and over the opposite hill, stretched lines of white tents, interspersed with wooden buildings. The tents were surrounded on all sides by red heaps, like molehills. From behind these molehills emerged from time to time yellow figures, bare-armed and bearded. Through the midst of these figures ran a stream, and on the banks of this stream ten thousand cradles – sometimes six abreast – whirred, hummed, and sung. An immense clashing, as from a million brazen grass-hoppers, arose up out of this valley of cradles, and a light breeze blowing from the east, lifted clouds of red dust, which powdered the sparse herbage. On the hill floated the flag which marked the Government 'Camp', and here and there flashed the scab-bards of the mounted police, inspecting 'licences'.

The successor of the retiring La Trobe – a naval officer, Sir Charles Hotham, of good intentions and bad advisers – had just issued an order that the police should go two days a week 'dig-ger-hunting'. There were at that time no less than four 'Com-missioners' at Ballarat, and the troopers had their work cut out for them. It being once determined that no man should mine without a licence, it was but reasonable that authority should support itself. The diggers, however, resented this interference with their liberties; and officialdom proceeding, with some ill-judged display of silver-lace and bullion-tags, to the enforcement of the law, it became a humorous point of honour to resist the 'licence business' to the utmost. Both diggers and police must be debited with the commission of many follies. The nature of the digger of that period was not understood by the red-tapists until too late. Dreaming of San Joaquin and San Francisco, the Gov-ernment imagined the population of Ballarat to be composed wholly and solely of adventurers, reckless, extravagant, and given to debauchery. The gold-fever had attracted – as greed of gain will always attract – many ruffians, knaves, and fools. New South Wales and Van Diemen's Land – or Tasmania, as it had been lately rechristened – sent out their quota of emanci-pated and escaped convictism, eager to plunder and defraud.

Among the shiploads that landed daily at Liardet's Beach, it would be strange indeed if some few desperadoes did not mingle. But the majority of the diggers were honest, bold, and law-loving, – as Mr Withers says, 'of the best men of the best towns of Christian Britain, men of invincible spirit, as of moral and law abiding principles.' The mad extravagance which was a characteristic of these digging days, was confined to those be-sotted idiots, who, in more placid times, booze themselves blind with threepenny beer, and squander the earnings of a six-weeks' shearing in the nearest bush grog-shop. The mob of gaudily-dressed men and women who – yet living in Gill's Hogarthian sketches – thronged the streets of Melbourne, and formed the staple of 'English correspondents'' highly-coloured pictures of Australian life, are not to be confounded with the large-hearted, quick-souled men, whose minds, muscular as their bodies, impatient of the bonds of red-tapery, asserted and achieved freedom, – the men who founded and still maintain the intelligent democracy of Australia.

The red-shirted, bearded men, who were summoned to show their permit to toil, had perhaps been, six months before, doctors, collegians, soldiers, men of fortune; independent miners of Cornwall, accustomed to rules, and abiding by recognised authority; intelligent artizans of Edinburgh and Glasgow; sturdy farmers of Kent; enthusiastic Irishmen; impatient Americans, or shrewd, dare-devil cockneys, viciously tenacious of the liberty of Bow Bells. To deal with this body of men, what had the Government provided? A number of 'relations', who demanded to be provided for! Let us say it without offence – for among the officials of that day were many honourable gentlemen, who discharged a difficult duty with temperance and justice – the Government had run riot upon its patrimony of patronage. To be made a Government official was easy, if one was an officer of either service, or owned a second cousin distantly related to the aristocracy. Materials for a police were scarce, and the majority of the constables had seen service – in two capacities – in Van Diemen's Land. The Government, moreover, committed the fatal error of thrusting upon men, inclined by age and circumstance to the freedom of democracy, the tom-foolery of epaulettes and shoulder-knots, which is part of the 'dressing' of that monarchical stage on which ministers suffer kings to display their little pomps and vanities.

The mounted-police, bedizened with silver lace, and officered by young gentlemen not altogether free from that melodramatic weakness for display which characterises the *jeune militaire*, was not by any means in accordance with the temper of the gold-fields. The cadets – smoking their pipes over Grant's novels, or mentally likening themselves to Tom Burke or Harry

Lorrequer – cultivated a proper contempt for the 'diggers' who only worked, and did not always collect the obnoxious tolls with that courtesy which a perusal of the Leverian code of gentility might be expected to create. Combats – not altogether bloodless – took place between these fiery spirits and the men over whom they were placed in brief authority; and in October, 1854, the spectacle of thirty or forty men, handcuffed like criminals, and mounted guard over by a stripling, whose birch-scars yet caused him to sit uneasily in his regulation saddle, was not unfrequent. The cadets were generous boys enough, but as rulers of full-grown men, they were quite out of place.

One of these combats seemed to be now occurring.

Dorcas, attracted by the flash of a steel scabbard, saw down in the valley, a little drama, which, though wordless, was none the less intelligible. Two constables kept watch over a claim, from which, presently, emerged the figure of a man. Some animated conversation – expressed in the pre-Babel language of pantomime – took place between the three. The constables demanded, the digger protested; the constables argued, the digger denied; the constables advanced, the digger bolted! Dodging round the red heaps, stumbling, falling, and recovering himself, headlong through the crowd he came. The advantage of his rapid start was not to be wrested from him. The pursuers fell back, he was almost free, when, from behind a dusty wattle-bush, appeared a cadet of the mounted police, and spurred in pursuit. The hunted man paused, wheeled, and made straight up the hill. The flat instantly bristled with waving arms. 'Run, mate, run! Joe! Joe! Joe!' and at sound of the dreaded watchword, a dozen un-licensed ones abandon tub and cradle, making, like rabbits, for the deeper burrows. The cadet, put on his mettle, forced his horse across all obstacles, and, flushing with indignation, risked his neck gallantly among the broken ground. His hand was almost on the collar of the fugitive, when his nag put his foot into a crab-hole, and man and horse rolled to earth amid a cloud of red dust. A stupendous roar of good-humoured laughter pealed across the flat, and the diggers, regarding the escape of their man as certain, turned to the all-absorbing business in which they were interested.

Occupied in watching the extraction of the cadet's horse, Dorcas did not see that the fugitive digger had already reached the fence, and was preparing to climb it. An unexpected accident, however, prevented him.

⊷ 6 ⊶

UNEXPECTED MEETINGS

Just as the runaway had placed his hands on the top of the fence, and was in the act of pulling himself upwards, a figure rose out of the dry watercourse below and promptly knocked him head over heels.

'You infernal scoundrel,' cried the new-comer, 'I've got you at last!' and pounced forthwith upon his prostrate body.

The Lily of Specimen Hill, excited by the sounds of combat, made her way through the barrels to witness what was to follow.

What she saw was this.

The fugitive digger – a tall, thin man, whose grey hair floated on his shoulders – sprang up, and, drawing a knife, rushed at his assaulter. The other – a youth of three-and-twenty – stood his ground, and clutching by the wrist the murderous hand, twisted his assailant's arm with such happy knack that the weapon flew over the fence and lit at Dorcas' feet.

'Now, you confounded robber, you shall pay for that night at Gisborne,' cried he; and holding his prisoner fast with one hand, loosened his own leathern belt with the other and proceeded to bestow on the writhing digger such a hearty and excellent thrashing, that Dorcas involuntarily uttered a cry for mercy.

The young man turned his head, and beholding close to him the face of a beautiful young girl, gave his prisoner a parting kick and loosed him.

'I beg your pardon,' said he. 'I had no idea there was a lady near me.'

Though dressed in the yellow-stained moleskins of a digger, the accent with which he spoke proclaimed him gentleman; and Dorcas, without knowing why, blushed to the roots of her golden hair.

The fugitive cast one rapid glance around, saw the recovered cadet spurring furiously up the hill, dived through a broken paling in the fence and vanished.

'He's gone!' said Dorcas, not well-knowing what else to say.

'Let him go!' laughed the young man, buckling his belt. 'I owed him a thrashing, and he's got it. Pray forgive me for disturbing you,' and as he turned away he raised his battered hat courteously. The action of turning brought him face to face with the cadet, Mr Frederick Flite, who reined his charger on his haunches (with a tolerable consciousness that the Lily was criticizing his horsemanship), and straightway became as one in authority.

'You confounded ass!' he cried. 'Why didn't you hold the man till I got here? I never saw such — why! — what! — my eyes, is it *you*, Arthur?'

'Don Rinaldo, by Jingo!' exclaimed Arthur Devine, seizing his hand. 'Where on earth did *you* spring from? Get off that gallant steed and tell us your romantic story.'

'I say, Miss Lily,' says Fred, dismounting, 'ask your proud papa to tap the cask, so that we may drink to the Smuggler King, will you. This is my school-fellow — a jovial blade, by the mass — a lad, a boy, a heart of gold — whoa, you brute! — a right bully-blade; and if I crack not a flagon of Rhenish with him to-night, may I be carbonadoed.'

'But what about *him*?' asked Dorcas, nodding her head at the hole through which the digger had crawled.

'Oh, hang *him*!' cried the versatile Fred — whose passion for melodramatic absurdities had obtained him his melodramatic nickname — 'Let him cut his stick, poor beggar. A digger, more or less, won't tarnish the blue and silver? *Sapristi*, but I've had a narrow squeak in that confounded gully. Beastly colony, ain't it, Arty?'

Arthur was about to reply, when the boy caught sight of the knife, and instantly assumed the stern disciplinarian. 'What's that, a knife? May I trouble you, *ma belle*! Thanks! Did he attempt to stab you, old boy?'

'A little,' said Arthur. 'But the shindy was of my own seeking. The fellow tried to stick up the escort at Gisborne two years ago, and I owed him something. He's paid now.'

'Were *you* riding escort?' asked Don Rinaldo, with as much deference as it was possible for him to display. 'I didn't know you were in the service.'

'Dight's Light Horse,'[1] said Arthur.

'Oh!' with a resumption of jauntiness. ''Tis well. You shall tell me your history over an amphora of Massic. Miss Crosbie, suffer me to call you an angel and beg for beer.'

'Still the same Rinaldo Rinaldini,' said Arthur, as they went round the fence. 'Have you fought any more duels, old boy, or run away with any more duchesses?'

'Shut up,' said Don Rinaldo, 'and – um – keep close to me, old boy, for since the rows about these blessed reform leagues, the cheerful digger has not been in the best of odour with our fellows.'

The stroke-oar of the Oxford eight, hardened by two years of the bush, looked at the slight figure of the dandy cadet, and smiled.

'Don't be afraid; I'll keep close to you, Freddy,' said he.

'That's right,' said Freddy, sublimely unconscious of satire. 'The blue and silver may be *hated*; but, by George, it's *feared*, sir, it's feared.'

A word concerning Freddy Flite, not because he is of much importance in our story, but because he may serve as an example of the many burdens laid upon the backs of the diggers of that day. Educated at a public school, he had nursed his imagination on the works of Lever and Dumas, until he imagined that the noblest being on earth was the reckless, devil-may-care *sabreur*, a dead shot with a pistol, a murderous dog with a rapier; Tom Burke, grafted on a cutting from Ducrow, transplanted into that soil where flourished M. D'Artagnan the Captain of the Guard – he with the soul of honour, the voice of velvet, and the hand of iron. Most young men have an ideal, to which they endeavour to make their lives correspond; and Fred had one– the cool, calm, cynical scoundrel of romance – the man who, constantly flying from bailiffs, was yet the soul of

1. The Private Escort.

honour – the man who, everlastingly tormented by a secret grief, was yet the wittiest of the witty – the man in whose veins ran the blood of monarchs – the man who had scorned princesses and humiliated queens – the man for whose existence are responsible Mr Charles Mathews, Mr Charles Lever, and (in the latter days) Mr 'Guy Livingstone' Lawrence.

Arrived in Australia, a commission in the mounted police served to gratify this romantic young man's ambition, and – though barely twenty – he affected a frightful mystery concerning his youth, and hinted dimly at some hideous tale of love and woe, which had compelled him to fly from those fashionable circles which he at once despised and adorned.

In the barracks of the mounted police of that day, such waifs and strays of fortune as Freddy would fain be thought were not unfrequent; and these – silent as to their own histories – complacently listened to Don Rinaldo's romances, and cynically said nothing; but his brother cadets thought him a wonderful fellow, and adored him.

They might have bestowed their affections upon a more unworthy object; for, though Don Rinaldo was imaginative, melodramatic, and vain, yet, despite his sham sentiment, his mock heroics, his 'biting of thumbs', 'flinging of gloves', and the like, he was a thoroughly 'good fellow', with more brains than many of the novelists whom he delighted to honour. Only – and this is somewhat important – a young gentleman of this kind – cursing diggers, damming clodhoppers, consigning working men and plebeian persons to general oblivion – was not the best sort of young gentleman to be entrusted with authority over men like those who were even then organising committees of resistance to military snobbery and official red-tapery.

The pair went into Crosbie's store, and Freddy led the way to a sort of back parlour of weatherboards, with which he seemed to be familiar.

Dorcas was already awaiting them.

'Now, my Pippin,' cries Fred, 'imbibe the cheering bowl!'

Arthur, who had paused on the threshold to reply to a whisper from a little red-haired man in the store, answered to the summons with a somewhat disturbed expression of face.

'I thought sly-grog selling was forbidden,' he said, with a forced laugh, as though to conceal any anxiety he might be suffering.

The Lily flushed crimson.

'We don't *sell* grog,' said she.

'Miss Dorcas offers us hospitality,' says Fred, secretly jamming his spur into Arthur's foot. 'The bottled ale of romance, my boy!'

'I am sure I beg Miss Dorcas' pardon,' said Arthur, unaffectedly. 'But I thought —'

'That my father kept a public-house? Thank you, sir.'

'No — well. The fact is, I have just heard some intelligence which annoyed me, and I was not thinking of what I was saying. I am sure you will forgive me.'

Dorcas blushed again. She was not wont to blush so often, and held out her hand with all her mother's frankness. 'All right. Shake hands.'

Fred bethought him of an introduction.

'Miss Dorcas Crosbie and Mr Arthur —'

'Vern,' says Arthur, quickly, glancing at his schoolfellow; and Fred, who knew that men on the diggings had reasons for changing their names, allowed him to say it unquestioned. His glance, however, fell on the little red-haired man to whom Arthur had been speaking, and as soon as the hand-shaking was complete he said,

'Who's that, Arthur?'

'Paolo Carboni, an Italian.'

'Paolo Carboni,' repeated Fred. 'I've heard his name before. Oh, of course — one of that blessed Reform League. And, by Jove, there's Peter McGrath and Griffiths outside — Why, Arthur, you're not one of that lot?'

Before Arthur could answer, Crosbie entered, and Fred instantly fell upon him.

'I say, Crosbie, why do you let these disaffected beggars muster here? By Jove, you know there'll be a row one of these days, Crosbie. I know these fellows. *Canaille*, sir! *Canaille*! Give me thirty sabres, my dear fellow, and I'll clear the street for you in two twos.'

Crosbie's grim features seemed about to relax into a smile,

when he caught sight of Arthur Devine, who, in the innocence of his soul, was employing the white-handled knife he had captured from the digger to cut up his tobacco. Perhaps there was something in the appearance of the weapon which reminded Richard Devine of the one he had so fatally lost twenty-five years ago; or, perhaps, the appearance of the young man in his rough clothes and his bronzed face was not dissimilar to what his own might have been in those bygone years. He started and turned pale.

'A school-fellow of mine – Mr Vern,' said Fred. 'Arthur, this is our host, Crosbie the Magnificent, the richest man on Ballarat. By George, Crosbie, let us have some champagne to celebrate this auspicious event !'

Crosbie, still staring, took the knife gently out of the young man's hands.

'May I ask where you got this?'

'It is a spoil of war,' laughed Arthur. 'A scoundrel tried to stab me with it just now. Do you know it?'

Crosbie laughed, in his turn, but not so easily.

'No,' said he, 'this knife is a new one, I never saw it before; but there – no matter. Who was the man who attacked you?'

'A rascal who had attempted to rob me once before. I saw him running away from Fred, here, and stopped him. Your daughter cried out and I let him go.'

'Oh, you'll see him again,' said Crosbie. 'Are you going to remain here?'

'Yes. I only arrived yesterday. I have been at Creswick.'

'Oh !' returned Crosbie, with some meaning.

'Well, come up to the Camp, old boy, and let us have a yarn,' cries Fred. 'It's the rummest start, meeting *you* here, that I know.'

'No, I won't go to the Camp. Let us talk here – that is, if we do not disturb Miss Dorcas.'

'Oh, no; I am going out,' returned the girl, pettishly. 'You are neither of you agreeable enough to tempt me to stay.'

'Let me fall upon my sword !' cries Fred. 'Oh, that Fred Flite should be thus skyorned. 'Pon my word, Miss Crosbie, you are too hard.'

Arthur said nothing, but gravely opened the door; and the

poor little Lily, in passing out, felt, somehow or other, that the handsome stranger's sister would not have spoken so flippantly as she had done.

'Now, my noble hero, for the story,' cries Fred, when the pair were alone. 'Are you on the spree, or what? You *can't* be hard up.'

'But I am though,' said Arthur, coolly. 'My uncle, whom we all thought dead, returned, and when my father died, offered me £500 a year. I don't like my uncle, and so I came out here, without anything but my hands and head.'

'By George, you don't say so!' cries the impulsive lad. 'Join us, my boy – wear the blue and silver! I know old Catamaran and old –'

'No,' said Arthur, 'I can't do that, thank you. In fact, my sympathies are all the other way; but light your pipe and I will tell you.'

++ *7* ++

AN IMMIGRANT'S FORTUNES

WE do not propose to give the story of Arthur Devine's progress, from an 'Oxford man' to a gold-digger, in his own words. Such a proceeding would be far too tedious; but a brief description of his fortunes, as gathered from his letters and his conversations, may not be out of place.

He sailed from London on the eighteenth of July, 1852, and reached Melbourne towards the end of September in the same year. The vessel carried a motley crew of passengers, among whom were three men destined to play no unimportant part, not only in Arthur Devine's fortunes, but in the history of the colony. These three were Paolo Carboni, an Italian; Peter McGrath, an Irishman; and Thomas Griffiths, a Welshman. Arthur Devine – or Vern, as he called himself – found that the 'radicalism' which he had cherished at Oxford was welcomed and outdone by these fiery spirits. Paolo, a little, wiry Italian, vivacious, intelligent, and headstrong, had been forced to England on account of his discovered connexion with one of the many secret societies which were rife in his native country. McGrath, something of a politician and much of a Young Ireland patriot, thirsted for the freedom of a Republic. Griffiths, a facile speaker, and a man acutely impatient of all red-tapery and dandyism, was wont to advocate measures of reform, to be carried by the votes of the 'people', and brought about peaceably and without bloodshed. With these three Arthur Devine formed a firm friendship; and his youthful impetuosity, coupled with his superior education, made him a sort of leader in the airy resolutions plotted and carried out – in words – beneath the glory of the tropical midnights.

Arrived in Melbourne, fortune separated the companions. Griffiths, Paolo, and McGrath sought the diggings. What happened to Arthur is best told in one of his early letters to England.

Elizabeth-street, 4th Feb., 1853.

DEAR AUNTIE, I write this in the back room of a little two-roomed hovel, looking out upon a yard filled with rubbish, among which empty gin-cases and broken bottles predominate. I had hoped to get a berth in the *Duke of Bedford* – a big ship moored off Liardet's Beach, and turned into a model lodging-house – but it is too full. I pay £2 a week for this accommodation, and sleep on the floor in my own blankets. In the next room to mine lives a doctor with a large family. He has been very ill with colonial fever, and I verily believe would have died, but for his indomitable pluck. He sits up in bed and prescribes for diggers. His fee is five guineas – or notes, or gold, or nuggets – and, as most of the ailments of the patients who can afford the luxury of medical assistance arise from overdrinking themselves, and everybody drinks, he is doing well.

But to tell you how I got here. I have not been to the diggings yet *as a digger*, but intend to go as soon as this is in the post. In the first place, I only had £25 in my pocket when I landed; and as I was ass enough to put up at the *Criterion Hotel*, which is a little more expensive than Mivarts', *that* sum did not last long. Some friends of mine wished much to lend me money; but, knowing them to be poor, I would not accept their offer, and so they left Melbourne without me.

I did not know what to do; and after acting for two days as Secretary to a rich digger (such fun, my dear aunt!) who paid me liberally, but insisted on making me drink champagne, which I hate, I tried to get a water-cart to drive. Quite a swell thing, I assure you. Young Charley Ebbsworth, the Bishop's nephew, you know, is doing very well with one; but the supply of drivers far exceeds the demand. Luckily, Captain Frere, to whom I sent your letter (Sydney is not close to Melbourne, as we thought), wrote back, sending me an introduction to Major McNab, a military swell, who got my name 'put down' for an appointment by the Governor. This didn't do much good; but McNab, who is a fine fellow, and an old friend of Captain Frere's, introduced me to one of the directors of the Private Escort – they call it *Dight's Light Horse* – and I got appointed as 'a trooper.' A word in parenthesis. I am rather glad that I didn't meet Captain Frere, for I hear that he is one of those most objectionable of people, *a military bully.* The tales that an old (ex-convict) mate of mine tells of him would make your dear old hair stand quite refreshingly on end.

The Directors asked if I could ride, and whether I had ever been in the army. I said 'yes' to the first question, 'no' to the second, adding that I had been stroke-oar of the Oxford boat, if that was any qualification. One of the 'board' – a queer old boy, with a gimlet eye – asked to be allowed to feel my biceps. I complied, and taking up the poker – don't you remember how I astonished Addy with the trick? – bent it as crooked as a ramshorn by a blow across my arm. McNab burst into a roar, and I thought the old gentleman would have injured himself with merriment. Suffice it that I got the appointment. I wish, dear Auntie, that I had space to detail to you the incidents of my first gold journey. A very brief sketch, however, must suffice. We started the next afternoon for Forest Creek and Bendigo. Such an 'Escort' you never saw! The 'carts,' containing empty gold-boxes, blankets, and a few feeds of oats, were drawn each by six horses, and driven by the wildest-looking bandits you can imagine. That gentleman in Addy's scrap-book who wears the beard and pistols, is mild in comparison. Our captain seemed no less wild. He was dressed in an old frock-coat, high mud-boots, and a slouched hat. He wore his hair in long curls, sported a most elegant and curly moustache, which hung down in the most picturesque manner; carried a revolver in his belt, and pistols in his holsters; and rode habitually at full gallop. Who do you think he was? No less a person than the poet and author, Horsa Hengist – You remember Edgar Poe's review of his book?

But to go on. We reached Forest Creek in due course, after being thoroughly wetted by some vigorous showers; and, after a rest, went on to Bendigo. Nothing occurred until we reached Gisborne on the return journey, when an accident happened, which was rather fortunate for me. We got to the Bush Inn in that most melancholy township at about four in the afternoon, when the leading driver – a long-legged Yankee, named Jessop – put the horses in the stable, vowing he would go no further that night. There had been a 'spill' on the road, and Hengist was behind looking for loose nuggets – the roads, dear Auntie, are fearfully and wonderfully made. When he came up he ordered us on, but Jessop pleaded that it was the custom to always bait at this spot. We got something to eat, Hengist walking up and down the verandah in a towering rage, eating bread and cheese, and cursing. By-and-by it came on to rain – a tremendous thunder-storm – and the men jibbed in a body. They would not 'march through Coventry' in weather like this for all the gold in Australia. Hengist came into the bar with his sword drawn, and swore at us most unpoetically. The beggars laughed and asked him to drink. He called them mutineers and pigs, and idiots, and skulkers, vowed that they ought to be hung on the nearest tree, and that it was lucky for them that they were not under army-regulations or he'd blow out their miserable brains – (I believe he would have done so.) Jessop 'chaffed' him, saying that it was 'only his rude way of talking to gentlemen;' and he departed, vowing he would dismiss the whole troop.

The sergeant, Hengist, and I then unloaded the carts, and piled up the gold in a little room on the verandah. The sergeant volunteered to sleep outside the door, and Hengist and I 'coiled' in the room. It was the funniest night I passed for a long time. An awful storm outside. Inside, a pile of gold boxes, on the top of which were placed two revolvers, two pistols, two drawn swords, two lighted candles, with candles in waiting, lucifers, a brandy bottle, and two tumblers. Hengist and I soon made friends. He talked about Elizabethan drama, cursed the publishers – in English, French and Spanish – stood on his head in the corner of the room and clapped his heels in the air, sang a Spanish song about the Moors and the Christians, recounted an adventure with a panther, and gave a minute description of a patent fly-catcher which he had invented. I quoted all the Latin I could think of, as a set-off against his Spanish, and finally fell fast asleep in the middle of a discussion upon the Greek chorus, in which I was getting much the worse of the argument.

I was awoke – now for a 'thrill,' dear aunty – by the report of a pistol, and I saw Hengist furiously lunging with his drawn sword – like Hamlet at Polonius – at a man – an ill-looking villain – who was half out of the window. I seized another pistol, fired, and missed him, I suppose, for the fellow made off in the darkness; and, though the house was roused at once, and the bush searched in all directions, we could find nobody. I shall know the gentleman again though, and if ever I meet him, he may take care!

Of course, this accident frightened the mutineers, and they 'rolled up' in the morning as penitent as might be. Hengist – he had to pay over £50 to the landlord for the liquors and beds! – abused them all soundly, and – in revenge, I suppose, for his broken night's rest – forced on the carts at a hand-gallop. He led the way himself when the ground was more than usually rough, singing his blessed Spanish song all the time! We reached Melbourne in the most frightful plight. One cart had been smashed, and its load divided between the other carts. We only had three swords and two bowie-knives to protect two tons weight of gold (the pistols and carbines were rendered useless by the rain), and three men were left on the road.

In the morning, Hengist reported the affair, and the directors sacked the whole troop, with the exception of the sergeant and myself, who were presented with £50 apiece.

With this £50 I proceeded to Mount Alexander, where I made 130 ounces.

Life in Melbourne I will not attempt to describe. Society is turned upside down, and when beggars are set on horseback, you know the spot to which they proverbially ride. The appearance of the streets is strange. One would think that some frightful earthquake or ship-wreck had just taken place, which compelled the people to rush into the streets for safety or for intelligence. Indeed, it might be fancied that a shipload of pleasure-seekers – dressed in their gayest attire – had been put suddenly ashore. Yellow shawls are the fashion. A digger makes £100 – his first proceeding is to get drunk, his next to get married. The bridal party hire a carriage and pair and proceed to a draper's, where the lady purchases the most expensive *trousseau* obtainable. The party then drive through the streets, drinking cham-pagne. In three days the money is spent, and the newly-married pair separate – he to Bendigo, she to marry someone else probably. Drinking-bars and public-houses abound, and are always full. The most notable thing is the multitude of human beings all intent on revelry with the gold they have got, or hurrying to get more.

A digger's life is a very free one, and one meets some good fellows. But the Government have no more notion about managing the men than I have of making Persian verses. I met a fellow-passenger of mine, one McGrath, at Mount Alexander, and he agrees with me that there will be a serious outbreak soon, unless some change is made. Don't be surprised if you hear of an Australian Republic one of these days! – Arthur Vern – as I am called – President! However, the sub-ject is too serious a one to jest upon. I will treat of it more fully in my next letter to you. I am now off to Ballarat, which has become quite a town already. A fellow, named Grantly – whom I knew at Mount Alexander without a shirt on his back – has got a fine hotel there, I hear, on Specimen Hill, and is hand and glove with the police magistrate and other swells.

I hope that Mr Richard Devine is progressing. I wish him no ill, but, *etc., etc., etc.*

This letter is a pretty good specimen of the sort of life which befell the boy whom John Rex had ousted from his inheritance; and adventures of this nature formed no inconsiderable portion of the story which he related to his old school friend in the parlour of Crosbie's store.

But there was one portion of his history which he did not relate to the young cadet. Galled by the action of the authorities, which I have endeavoured to explain in latter part of the 5th chapter,[1] he had joined the League of which Peter McGrath, Paolo, and Griffiths were active members. It is possible that the disaffection which prevailed would have gradually died out – for Englishmen are law-abiding folk – had it not been for one of these unhappy accidents which, like a casual spark dropped in a powder magazine, produce results as terrible as they are unexpected. As the King of Siam's cannon, captured by a French General, long awaited the hand which was destined to turn them against the towers of the Bastille, so did Mr Jerry Mogford – the scapegrace brother of the landlord of the 'Bell' – unwittingly await for twenty-five years the fatal quarrel which was to result in the Eureka Stockade and the Ballarat Riots.

-◄ 8 ►-

LIFE ON THE DIGGINGS

THE visit which Arthur Devine paid to Crosbie's was not his last. He often found himself there in the evenings chatting to Dorcas, or smoking a pipe with Crosbie. Like most men 'on Ballarat' he often caught himself wondering at the strange store

1. Chapter V. Book VI.

of information which the ex-shepherd possessed, and had often hinted at a desire to be informed as to his past life. But to all such hints Tom Crosbie – or Rufus Dawes – was accustomed to preserve a profound silence. The unfortunate hero of this story admired the young man for his frankness and tenderness of bearing – whatever affinity of blood may exist between uncle and nephew, doubtless existed between them, and assisted their natural liking – but Rufus Dawes – or Richard Devine – his first suspicions aborted by the manner of the cadet, never thought for an instant that the son of his dead brother, ousted from lawful estate by an impostor who had assumed *his* name, was a familiar guest at the household board. The accident of a conversation, a word let slip here or there, would doubtless have revealed all, and brought about a very different ending to his history – but such an accident never happened. As has taken place thousands of times in the history of mankind, and will take place thousands of times more, these three human creatures, not one of whom knew the true history of the other, dined, drank, and conversed together with a full belief that in their mutual relations was nothing but the barest of commonplace.

In their conversations, the all absorbing topic of Diggers' Rights and Government Interference often intruded, and Crosbie strove to inoculate the mind of his young guest with that spirit of caution and submission to authority which was so marked a feature in his own character, and which he had seemed to have learnt in consequence of some of those past experiences he did not choose to reveal.

His reiterated advice appeared to have had some effect. Arthur – though he yet frequented the meetings of the discontented, and stood well affected towards the League – assumed the virtue of conversation though he had it not; and, holding sweet converse with Dorcas, seemed to have forgotten his republican tendencies.

An accident happened, however, which changed all this.

The amusements of the diggings were not of the most refined nature. Drunkenness and gambling, indeed, were the chief entertainments, and, for the exercise of these pleasantries, fitting places were provided. Let not the reader imagine for an instant

that Crosbie's Store was the one wooden building in the golden
city. On the contrary, it had become dwarfed by the regality of
tavern and gambling-house. A modest exterior of weatherboard,
or zinc, often concealed rich furniture, velvet couches, mirrors,
and carpets. When money is plentiful, luxury is rampant; when
money is in excess, luxury becomes extravagance. The population
of the tented and wooden town was not wholly composed of
the honest, hard-working digger. He – honest fellow – lived
with his mates in one of the tents along the hill-side, and surrounded himself with all sorts of devices to obtain and conceal
his treasure. When he desired 'a spell', he would smoke his
pipe at his door, or go down to the 'music hall' and listen to
'Patcher the Inimitable', who (the forerunner of the Great
Vance, the Wondrous Leybourne, or the Marvellous Rickards)
sang songs concerning popular vices, and freely commented on
unpopular authorities. With such entertainment, and a casual
'liquor', the typical digger was satisfied. Being of one sort, it was
possible that he had a wife and children; being of another sort,
it was more than probable that he had occupied in Europe the
position of a gentleman, and scorned vulgar and coarse dissipation. If he desired to gamble, he could gamble with Dicky Jones
of the Blues, Tom Neville of the Foreign Office, or the Honourable Hamilton Hamilton, who 'chummed' together in a tent at
'The Frenchman's'.

The rude ruffian of the lower stratum had more extensive
delectation provided for him. For him blazed the bar of the
'Australian Felix!' for him smiled the blowsy sirens of the
'Salle de San Francisco'; for him were spread the fascinations
of Monte, Faro, and Poker; to him the 'American Restaurant',
with its three hundred plates, forty waiters, card-room, and
drinking bars, poker, bagatelle, and billiards, stood invitingly
open; for him gleamed the tallow candles of 'Coppinger's Californian'; for him rolled the balls in Bobell's Bowling Alley; and
for him was initiated the nightly riot at the 'Eureka'. This last
place was the resort of the lowest ruffians on Ballarat. In the
crowd of Americans, Jews, Germans, Italians, Chinese, English, there were some of the worst ruffians in the colonies. Beneath the surface of respectable diggerdom lay this muddy and
foul substratum of ex-convicts, rascals, swindlers, and thieves.

For such folk the 'Eureka' provided entertainment, and with such ill-gotten gains was Grantly enriching himself. The gentry who stole 'washing' stuff, or washed surreptitiously their neighbours' 'tailings', the sneaking dogs who crawled under tent flaps and abstracted gold-dust by the matchboxful, the merry fellows who 'jumped' the claims of the innocent or the timid, the fraudulent gold buyers, the loafers, the drunkards, and the jail birds, held high jinks at the 'Eureka', and vowed that Grantly was the roaringest of pot-companions. In addition to the character of its patrons, strange tales were whispered concerning the place. Not only – it was hinted – did no honest man go there, but that, did such folk, with well-lined belts, by accident seek supper and a bed, it was more than probable that they would meet with the usual digger's accident, and 'fall down a deserted shaft' – to the intense grief and amazement of Grantly, it need not be added. Let us add to these suspicions the fact that Grantly himself was considered to be a tool of the Government, a spy upon the League, and a secret and influential friend of one Rayner, the most detested of Hotham's magistrates, and we can understand that a very faint puff would be sufficient to cause the smouldering public indignation to blaze into a right fierce flame.

In the meantime, jollity reigned, the faro tables were well patronized, and Patcher the Inimitable gave his nightly entertainments at 'Coppinger's Californian', to the admiration of all beholders.

On the evening of the 10th of October, Arthur Vern – following the example of the typical digger spoken of above – decided to smoke a pipe at Coppinger's. He found there one of his mates, a fat, good-humoured, weak-headed fellow, named Armstrong, and the pair sat down together.

The room was a sort of barn illuminated with tallow-lamps. Seats, with stands for glasses, running along the backs of them – an arrangement borrowed possibly from that in use at old-fashioned churches – filled up all space save that long line down which the waiters flew with the 'nobblers' or the 'spiders'.

A narrow stage, covered with a magnificent carpet, was placed at one end of the room. On this stage appeared a grand piano, a chair, a table, a decanter of water, and a black-board. The 'house' was crowded with men of all nations, sizes, and colours. The audience was motley enough. The only point of resemblance was in age. There were no old men present, and few boys. Of the two hundred diggers, each with pipe and glass, one hundred and ninety were between the ages of twenty-five and thirty years.

As Arthur entered, a whirlwind of applause shook the shingle roof. The Inimitable had just mounted the wooden steps that led to the platform. He was dressed – according to the concert-hall fashion of that day – in black, and blazed with jewellery. There was no reason why he should not so blaze, for his salary was a hundred pounds a week.

When the applause which greeted him subsided, he advanced to the table, took up the piece of chalk which was placed there, and commenced to write upon the black-board. Diggerdom waited breathless.

'A man,' said Mr Patcher, with an affected snuffle, 'spake these words and said, "I am a digger, who wandered from his native home and came to sojourn in a strange land and 'see the elephant!' And behold I saw him; and from the key of his trunk to the end of his tale his whole body passed before me; and I followed until his huge feet stood still before a Clapboard Store: then, with his trunk extended, he pointed to a candle-card tacked upon a shingle, as though he would say, *Read!* And I read,"' continued Mr Patcher, gravely, forming the letters with the chalk,

'"THE DIGGER'S TEN COMMANDMENTS!"'

A roar of delight went up. 'Hurrah! The digger's ten commandments!'

[1] '"First. Thou shalt have none other Claim but one!

'"Second. Thou shalt not make to thyself any false claim, nor any likeness to a mean man by jumping one, whatever thou findest on the top above or on the rock beneath or the crevice under the rock, for I the Australian digger am a jealous digger, and will visit the Commissioner round with my presence to in-

1. For the particulars of the parody put into the mouth of Mr Patcher, see the appendix to Mr Withers' History of Ballarat, p. 215.

vite him on my side; and when he decides against thee, thou shalt take thy pick, and thy pan, and thy shovel, and thy swag, and all that thou hast, and go prospecting both north and south to seek diggings and shalt find none."'

Immense applause followed this exposition of digging morality, and Arthur – though to his simple soul the wit appeared somewhat strongly flavoured – laughed with the rest. The audience was composed of strong thinkers and strong talkers; such a bold parody as this hit their tastes exactly. The Third Commandment was declared to be on the subject of the vice of gambling, and was stated by the Inimitable to address the digger in the following terms: – 'Thou shalt not take thy money, nor thy gold-dust, nor thy good name to the gaming-table in vain; for Monte, Twenty-one, Roulette, Faro, Lansquenet, and Poker will prove to thee that the more thou puttest down the less thou shalt take up; and when thou thinkest of thy wife and children, thou shalt not hold thyself guiltless but insane.'

Much knocking of glasses and laughter followed upon this. Armstrong, indeed, who was getting rapidly the worse for Hennessy's Pale Brandy, declared, with a tremendous oath, that the original Third Commandment 'wasn't a patch upon it', and, despite Arthur's restraining hand, invited the humourist to drink, waving the bottle in the air with exuberant hospitality. Mr Patcher declined, with a graceful wave of the hand, the proffered refreshment, and proceeded.

'The Fourth Commandment. Thou shalt not remember what thy friends do at home on the Sabbath day, lest the remembrance may not compare favourably with what thou doest. Six days mayest thou dig and pick all the body can stand under, but on the seventh day thou shalt wash all thy dirty shirts, darn all thy stockings, top all thy boots, drink all thy nobblers, chop all thy firewood, bake thy bread, and boil thy pork and beans, that thou wait not when thou returnest from thy long task weary. For in six days' labour only thou can'st not work out thy body in two years, but if thou workest hard on Sunday thou canst do it in six months, and thou, and thy son, and thy daughter, and thy male friend, and thy female friend, and thy morals, and thy conscience be none the better for it, shouldest thou justify thyself because the leaders, Jews, and fossickers defy God and civilisation by not keeping the Sabbath day, and wish not for a day's rest such as a true digger's memory, youth and home, make hallowed.'

The room was getting very hot by this time, and Arthur, seeing through a crack in the shingles the broad bright moon shining with cool lustre in the soft purple sky, essayed to move, but Armstrong implored him to listen to but one more, vowing that he would then accompany him.

'I promised to go up to McGrath's by-and-by,' said Arthur.

'Well, there's time enough yet, old man,' pleaded his mate. ' 'Nother drink? Well, if you won't drink, you leave it 'lone, I s'pose.'

'I'll wait for ten minutes more, if you'll come then?'

'Right you are!' says Armstrong, feeling too intoxicated to support an argument.

In the meantime Mr Patcher had got to the Sixth Commandment, which he averred to be concerning the estate of Holy Matrimony; and the duties of bachelors, maids, wives, and widows. 'If,' said Mr Patcher, fixing his black eye upon one American Joe, popularly supposed to be consumed with a secret passion for the Lily of Specimen Hill, 'if thy neighbour has his daughter here, and thou love and covet her lily-white hand in marriage, thou shalt lose no time in seeking her affection, and when thou hast obtained it, thou shalt lose no time in popping the question like a man, lest another more manly than thou art should step in before thee, and thou, disappointed, shall quote the language of the great Republic, and say "Let her rip!" and thy future life be that of a lonely, despised, and comfortless bachelor.'

The room rang with plaudits at this sally, and American Joe buried his face in his tumbler with that abortive attempt to appear careless which characterizes youths in like case under such circumstances.

Arthur sprang up indignantly. Something – he could scarce define the feeling – tugged at his heart and set it beating when he thought of the Lily as the jest of that rude company.

'Come,' he cried, seizing Armstrong by the sleeve, 'we have had enough of this ribaldry. Let us go.'

But even when outside, in the cool night among the long shadows of the tents, and breathing the air aromatic with the sharp odours of the gum-leaves, Armstrong insisted upon further revelry. He wanted to play poker, he demanded brandy, he insisted upon dancing preposterously in dangerous proximity to an open shaft. Arthur, in vain, tried to urge him forward. At last, the young man lost his patience. Armstrong had sat down on a heap of mullock on the top of the hill, and declined to budge.

'You g'on,' he observed. 'I shtop.'

'All right,' said Arthur. 'Stop then, confound you. I'm going home.'

'S'ho'm I,' said Mr Armstrong, with reproachful solemnity. 'Bimeby tho'. Bimeby.'

Arthur left him sitting; but on reaching his tent, turned round and saw, bravely ascending the hill, a figure that might be his. It was going in the direction of the 'Eureka'.

⇥ 9 ⇤

HOW GRANTLY'S HOTEL WAS BURNED

Armstrong did not return that night; and Arthur, going out to work next morning, met an old man running to him, pale and wrathful.

'They've been at it again,' said this man, one Larkin.

'At what?'

'Murder! There's a body up there with its brains in the road.'

Filled with suspicion he scarcely liked to confess, the young man ran up the hill, leaving the bearer of the news to speed onwards to the Camp.

His worst fears were soon realised. On its back in the dust, before the door of the 'Eureka' Hotel, weltering in blood, with unspeculative eyes turned up to the pure morning heaven, lay the corpse of Will Armstrong.

Arthur thundered at the door, which was opened by Grantly himself, stretching his brawny arms and rubbing his naked breast, as one suddenly awakened from sleep.

'What is it?' said he, with an oath.

Arthur pointed to the road.

'Some drunken loafer, I'll go bail,' said Grantly. 'What is the matter with him?'

'He's dead!'

'Dead!' and Grantly turned white. 'Dead! How did he die?'

'Go and see.'

The proprietor of the 'Eureka' took two steps forward, in genuine horror, to examine the body, and as he left the doorway, Arthur's quick eye perceived that the inner room was in violent disorder. The table and floor were covered with broken glass, and across a fractured chair in one corner lay a spade, seemingly flung there by no gentle hand. The young man snatched it up. The handle was splashed with blood, and the blade showed a jagged chip, the edges of which bore the same accusing colour.

'This is how he died,' cried Arthur, rushing out, flourishing the accusing implement. 'This is how he died, and you – you villain – killed him.'

Grantly – he was a big, bull-necked burly ruffian – grew yet paler, and his knees knocked together.

'So help me God – no,' he cried. 'I didn't kill him – on my soul.'

'Someone in your cursed house did, then!' says Arthur. 'He was here last night!'

'N – no,' said Grantly; 'that is, someone came after we had shut up, and made a row to get in. I'd had a drop too much, and as he wouldn't go I came out, and we had a bit of a barney. I didn't know that he was hurt, by Heaven!'

The conversation had attracted others, and there was quite a little crowd gathered.

'Take him up to my place,' said Crosbie. 'Grantly, you shall stand your trial for this.'

'Oh, I'm ready,' said Grantly, recovering himself.

As four men lifted the body, an ominous murmur ran round.

'Lynch him!' cried American Joe.

'Ay, hang him first and try him afterwards!'

Grantly grew pale again, and retreated to his door.

'No, no,' says Arthur. 'We are Englishmen, and under English laws. Let him be tried!'

'To the Camp with him then!'

There were fully a hundred men in front of the building, and from each tent and shanty poured out fresh auditors. Grantly saw that it was useless to protest, and suffered himself to be led behind the corpse of Armstrong to the Camp. He said nothing, but his bloated face flushed faintly when he saw his reputed friend, Mr Rayner, P.M., on the Bench.

Two hours afterwards, Arthur Vern, hot with haste, white with rage, dashed into Crosbie's.

'Grantly's acquitted!'

'No!'

'True, by heaven! He's gone out arm-in-arm with Rayner, the police magistrate. What justice can be expected from these men?'

'They say that he lent Rayner money,' said Crosbie.

'*Gave* it him, you mean. The scoundrel! But we'll not stand this. I've seen McGrath and Carboni. There will be a crowd presently that will astonish these folks.'

'For heaven's sake, be careful!'

'Careful! Hark!'

Crosbie listened. The air was alive with humming, as though a gigantic swarm of bees were approaching. He knew what it meant. It was the hum of indignant voices.

Dorcas ran to the door, and as quickly ran back. An immense crowd was approaching.

'Pray God there'll be no bloodshed!' cried Crosbie.

But Arthur had already run out to meet the advancing tide.

The mob could not be less than 3000 men, and more were pouring up on all sides. Some one had suggested to hold an 'indignation meeting' on the spot where Armstrong had met his death. The stupid fellow had been elevated into a martyr already.

Up the hill the multitude surged, and surrounded the building. At first there was nothing to be distinguished but dust and clamour; then a man in a red shirt was lifted up in the arms of others, and began a speech. This was McGrath. Arthur pushed his way to him, and reached his side. Paolo was there, raving, in his Italian English, of 'cowards,' 'murderers,' and 'assassins.' McGrath rapidly pointed out the injuries the diggers had patiently endured. 'They refuse us leave to toil, and now they allow us to be murdered. Shall we suffer it?' A roar, that bristled with raised fists and threatening picks, was the reply. The crowd increased. The blazing October sun poured down his fiercest rays upon that seething and dusty mass. Twice Arthur nearly stumbled and fell. The second time, he felt himself seized by a strong hand. It was that of Crosbie.

'I have shut *her* up in the store,' he said. 'We must take care, lad, or there'll be more than a "meeting" happen.'

'The police! – the police!' cried a young man to the left of them; and a thousand throats took up the cry, as a party of troopers galloped up and surrounded the ill-omened building.

A little man, named Seacole – able editor of the *Ballarat News* – started a virulent hooting, and a whirlwind of hisses and yells swept over the tossing crowd.

'The spirit of murdered Armstrong looks down upon us,' cries Seacole; and at such a moment his words seemed not laughable, but eloquent.

Mr Frederick Flite – cool enough in his self-conceit – said to the lad next him,

'Fancy old Armstrong hovering above us, Jack!'

But Jack did not laugh.

'Three groans for the traps!' says the boy before mentioned, a lad named Purfoy. 'Ah-h-h!'

'For Heaven's sake, Mr McGrath, speak to them!' says Crosbie. 'To create a riot now would be ruin.'

But McGrath would not, or could not hear.

'He's escaping! – the murderer's escaping!' cries Arthur. 'See yonder!'

And sure enough, under cover of the troopers, some one mounted on a grey horse, and conspicuous by his white shirt-sleeves, dashed out for the Camp. The aspect of the flying horseman roused the men at the Gravel Pits, and fresh streams poured out.

It was now half-past two, and the crowd had increased to 9000.

Cries of 'Down with the place!' 'Down with it!' were heard.

Young Purfoy, flinging a quartz pebble, smashed — more by accident than design — the lamp in front of the building. This was the signal for a general shower of stones, and some of the troopers were hit. The windows disappeared as if they had been blown away. Then arose the ominous cry, '*Burn the house! Burn it!*'

'For God's sake!' cried Crosbie, and dashed in among the foremost, pushing, thrusting, expostulating. In vain.

'The soldiers! The soldiers! Fire the place! Burn it! Burn it!'

'Come on, boys,' cries young Purfoy, running to the windward side of the bowling alley. 'Who's got a match?'

'Here,' said a ragged figure, holding a bundle of rags and paper, and rapidly igniting the mass, he raised it aloft in his lean arm, whirling it to feed the flame, and flung it into the bowling alley.

Arthur had him down on his back in an instant. It was the would-be gold-robber of Gisborne, his assailant of a week back, the London thief, the Sydney horse-stealer, Jerry Mogford!

They grappled, and half a dozen troopers rushed to the spot, but the flames shot up fierce and high.

'Come out of this,' whispered Crosbie to Arthur. 'It is no use staying now, we may be recognised. Let that madman go. You can do no good with him.'

'Hurrah!' shouted Dick Purfoy. 'It burns! it burns!' And just as the summoned soldiers entered Specimen Gully, the flames burst out and upwards, enveloping the roof-ridge with a fiery crest; and as Crosbie dragged Arthur clear of the crowd, the building fell in with a crash, immediately drowned in the cheers of the mob.

⤙ 10 ⤚

ARTHUR MAKES A RASH PROMISE

As the final crash announced the consummation of the deed of violence, a thrill ran through the multitude. Men began to feel that they had accomplished an act which brought those concerned in it within the power of the law. A general movement was made towards the flats, and for some moments the foremost of the rioters were left almost alone in front of the smoking ruins.

This movement acted as a signal for the police. The troopers, in obedience to command, dashed out among the retreating crowd, and striking right and left with the flat of their sabres made to capture such of the diggers as were nearest to them.

The little group of which Crosbie might be considered the centre was surrounded at once. As is not unfrequent, the authorities had missed the actual perpetrator of the offence, and succeeded in seizing only the accessories, some half-dozen persons, among whom the only guilty one was Dick Purfoy.

During the few minutes' scuffling that ensued Arthur felt a hand upon his shoulder, and looking up, saw his schoolfellow bending from his saddle to speak to him.

'Run you, Arty!' said he. 'What on earth brought you here?'

Arthur's reply was an attempt to press forward to where Crosbie was struggling with three constables, but the cadet forced his horse between them.

'It is no use trying to help him *now*, my dear fellow,' he whispered, with his natural jauntiness but slightly impaired. 'And you'd better look after yourself. Our fellows are in the deuce's own taking.'

'Rescue! Rescue!' cried someone from out the crowd, and the mob, recovered from their panic, surged up again around the detested silver lace.

Dick Purfoy, young, agile, and fierce, twice broke from the troopers, and screaming like a woman, bit, scratched, and tore at his assailants. A gigantic constable named O'Donovan seized him by the collar of his woollen shirt. 'Whist, ye little divil, ye'll wake the childer!' said he, roughly dragging the lad by main strength to his horse's shoulder, held him there pinned in a grasp of iron. Seacole, who had been squeaking Homeric threats, was torn away, still gesticulating, by some of his friends, and the returning wave of diggerdom passed over him.

'Down with the traps!' shouted Jerry, borne to the front again. The mob took up the cry, and for an instant it seemed doubtful if the police could retain their prisoners. Two men dashed at the cadet, and Jerry – mindful of his adventure of a few weeks back – got round him with intent to pull him from the saddle. Here Arthur repaid his debt of gratitude with interest, and knocked the enterprising Lurker down for the second time.

Amid a whirlwind of dust and shouting, the bloodless contest raged, when through the dust something was seen to gleam, and through the shouting a measured pulsation made itself heard. The gleam of bayonets and the tramp of soldiers!

'It's up, boys,' cries McGrath. 'They've bested us!'

Riots of this nature are soon begun and soon over. In less than five minutes from the time when the soldiers appeared, the blackened beams and charred boards which marked the scene of the catastrophe were deserted by all save a few idlers.

'It must not end here, Peter,' said Arthur, as they parted.

'End here! No, by heavens! As Bishop somebody said when they burnt him – A fire has been lighted to-day the flame of which shall be seen far and wide. All Australia shall ring with this outrage, lad!'

'What do you think they will do with them?'

'The prisoners? Hang them if they dare. Unless we rescue them.'

'Rescue them! How?'

'By fair means if we can, by force if we can't.'

'We will offer bail for them. If they take it – good. If they decline it – well –'

'Well?'

'I'll take two hundred men and burn the cursed Camp over their heads,' cries Peter McGrath. 'Come up to the Charley Napier to-night, and we'll talk it over.'

'I want to go and see – um – Miss Crosbie,' says Arthur, with a blush; 'but I'll come, of course. Only,' he added – mindful of Crosbie's reiterated pleadings – 'be careful, old man – it is a dangerous game to play you know.'

'Oh, if you're going to turn tail –' said McGrath, with a sneer.

'It is not that, but –'

'But you'd better go and tell Crosbie's daughter that you'll

let her father rot in the hulks in Hobson's Bay!' McGrath
flashed out, 'that's what you'd better do!'

'McGrath, you have no right to speak like that!'

'Haven't I? By the powers, I should like to know who'd
stop me spheakin' when I've a mind to it! Will you come, you
young divil,' says Peter, slipping into his brogue in the excitement of the moment.

'Oh, yes,' says Arthur – 'I'll come!'

⤛ 22 ⤜

TOM CROSBIE IS IN AWKWARD POSITION

ARTHUR went straight to the store. When Dorcas saw him
come in alone, she turned pale.

'Where is he?'

'The police have taken him.'

'The police! And you *let* him be taken? Oh, Mr Vern!'

'It was impossible to prevent it. I think, however, he will
not be retained long in – in the Camp. Others were taken with
him, and there is a meeting directly to consider what is to be
done.'

'And I shall be all alone here – not that I mind that so much
– but – I shall come with you, Mr Vern!'

'My dear girl,' cries Arthur, in alarm, 'you must not
dream of such a thing. You with me, among those men –
impossible!'

'I will go to the Camp, then.'

'No, stay here. I am sure your father would wish it. I will
bring you back word as soon as the meeting is over.'

She looked at him and blushed.

'You promise? Very well, I will stop. I like to do as you
tell me.'

'Do you?' said Arthur. 'Then shut the doors and sit down
and wait for me. There is no danger to your father, or to anyone, I hope. Don't cry now, you little goose, but sit down and
read a book, or sew, or something.'

He had approached her to soothe her but, to his astonishment, she twisted herself away, and burst into tears.

'Sew, or something! That is all I'm fit for, I suppose. Oh – oh – oh, I *wish* I had been born a lady, and—'

'Dorcas!'

'Don't speak to me, don't touch me, don't look at me! Go away! I hate you, with your calmness, and your knowledge, and your fine airs. Go away, I say, will you? You are a gentleman, and I am only a digger's daughter.'

Arthur Devine was not old enough to interpret this outburst. So he stared at the phenomenon in blank amazement.

'What do you mean, Miss Crosbie?'

'What do I mean? Yes, that's just it. You don't know what I mean. You don't care what I mean. Oh, I wish I was dead!'

She had flung herself on the little sofa by this time, and, burying her face in the pillows, sobbed wildly.

Arthur – he had been troubled lately with some qualms of heart as to the absolute fraternity of his affection for her – gently raised her.

'My dear Dorcas, don't talk like that. I don't like it. I am a poor man, far poorer than your father. I assume no superiority to him in any way – or – or to you. I want you to look upon me as your brother.'

The Lily raised a crimson face, blurred with tears.

'I know you do, and that's why I hate you;' but the effort she made to get free was not strong enough, and she sank on his shoulder again.

Arthur's heart gave a great jump, and then began to beat very violently. He turned the face of the sobbing girl to his own.

'Do you *love* me, Dorcas?'

'I suppose I do, you horrid wretch!' said poor Dorcas, with another burst of weeping.

The long-room at the Charley Napier was crowded with wrathful faces. Following the forms of law which they affected to despise, the revolutionists had voted McGrath into the chair, and he sat in state at the head of a table, with Carboni and Griffiths on either hand. A union-jack formed a table-cloth, on which were placed a bible, paper and pens. Arthur made his way to the judgment-seat, and McGrath rose to address the meeting.

His address was short, sharp, and to the purpose. The Government was opposed to the diggers; a series of outrages had culminated in the acquittal of an infamous scoundrel, for the murder of one of their number; in holy revenge, enraged diggerdom had burned the place where the deed of blood had been committed, and for this righteous act of justice these innocent men had been deprived of their liberty. A sort of conversation ensued between the speaker and the audience, as thus:

'You know Tom Crosbie, lads – the honestest man on Ballarat?'

A roar of assent.

'Some of you know his daughter?'

A louder roar.

'You know how he tried his utmost to check the more violent among us?'

'Yes, yes – we do!'

'And they have taken *him*. Shall we suffer it? Shall we let this insult and wrong be put upon us? Which of us will go and tell Tom Crosbie's daughter that her father is to be sent to Melbourne as a felon?'

Arthur, thinking of the Lily alone in the little store, and feeling his lips yet tingling with her parting kiss, joined in the shout of denial which ascended.

'Come to the Camp,' he cried, 'and demand their release!'

McGrath stilled, with rough eloquence, the assenting uproar.

'No violence, mates! Let us act in accordance with the laws. These bloody-minded troopers are outside the laws, and there's where we have 'em. We will demand that they be let out on bail. I suppose we can bail 'em among us?'

Fifty throats swell huge laughter. Fifty hands thrust forward bags of gold-dust on the table. Bail! The humour of the meeting was such it would have bailed Prince Esterhazy, diamonds and all.

'Mates,' said a gentleman who, in the excitement of the times, had become partially intoxicated, 'Look here! What I say is this – Right is Right, and Wrong is *no* bloodyman's Right! We must appoint a Commy*tee*.'

This deference to social custom was received as a happy inspiration, and, amid much applause, a 'Commy*tee*' was formed, consisting of 'Messrs McGrath, Griffiths, Vern, and the mover.'

These four chosen ones, then, followed at a little distance by the crowd, went up to the Camp. The police, seeing so large a body of men approach, drew up in order on the hill, and for the second time in the history of the diggings the two opposing forces confronted each other.

Into the ranks of troopers the four passed – a fanciful person could imagine that the burghers of Calais might have so passed through the serried English archers – and the crowd saw them disappear. There was some difficulty about bail. The action of the mob had thoroughly roused the official mind. The magistrates would not give up the rioters.

Arthur pointed through the open window to the multitude on the flat. 'Look there,' said he, 'those men only want a word to burn these houses about your ears.'

'Silence, sir,' returned Mr Rayner. 'I will commit you.'

An angry roar was borne to them, and the report of a pistol-shot. Carboni, impatient of delay, had fired his revolver in the air, as a sort of note of exclamation.

'For God's sake,' said McGrath to Rayner, solemnly, 'be temperate. The spirit of the men is roused, and they will stop at nothing. If you do not release the prisoners on bail I will not answer for the consequences.'

'You are a rebel, sir,' returned Rayner.

'You will make us all rebels,' was McGrath's bold reply.

When, at last, the bail bonds were signed, another difficulty arose. It had been suggested by some one to chair Crosbie, and the moment he appeared, the crowd made a rush at him. The line of police were thus forced backwards, and a collision seemed imminent. Crosbie, however, by dint of expostulation, kept peace. As the hero of the hour, the mob were inclined to pay attention to him; and singing 'there's a good time coming, boys!' carried him off amid a triumphant volley of revolvers. They broke up at his store door with immense hand-shakings and good wishes.

Crosbie did not respond heartily. It seemed to him that the crowd, having tasted the blood of authority, were eager for more. He began to regret the part he had taken in the matter. It was necessary for him to live quietly, and now he was about to be taken to Melbourne to be tried. No one in Ballarat had recognised in the bearded Tom Crosbie the convict Rufus Dawes; but he might not be so fortunate in Melbourne. Suppose he was recognised and remitted to the hulks, what would become of Dorcas? The events of the day had made him serious. It was probable that the dispute between the opposing parties would end in riots, if not in bloodshed; and to such a risk he must not expose the child of his adoption. Fool that he had been to wait so long. He had already accumulated a moderate fortune. He would strive to accumulate no more, but settle his bail with McGrath and depart. His eyes, sharpened by their sad experience, had observed, moreover, that in the brief greeting between young Vern and Dorcas a significant glance had passed. He had spoken to Dorcas about young Vern, and noticed that she had appeared confused. These facts set him unpleasantly thinking. He had, of course, often contemplated the inevitable marriage of his ward. He knew that one day his dream-child would be taken from him, and become a wife and mother, with others to usurp *his* place in her heart. But he had hoped that that day was far distant; that when it should come, *he* would have chosen the bridegroom, and dowered the bride with wealth and honour. It was most undesirable that this hotheaded, penniless Arthur Vern should carry off his pearl of great price.

That evening Arthur came in, burning to discuss the events of the day.

'I think I shall give up the store and go away,' said Crosbie.

Dorcas turned pale. Arthur laughed.

'You must take your trial first, old fellow,' said he. 'The Majesty of British Justice must be satisfied, you know. The "Commy*tee*" — as poor Carroll calls it — have resolved to do the thing legally.'

'They are right,' Crosbie was compelled to admit. 'Though I had wished they thought otherwise. I had thought of paying my bail money and going, for I hate public talk; but of course it is now out of the question.'

'I dare say we can manage it if you *wish* it,' said Arthur, looking at him a little uneasily. 'But why should you care? You did nothing. Hundreds of men can swear to that.'

'Oh, *that* is not it,' returned poor Crosbie. 'But I am not desirous of being paraded in courts of justice for all the blackguards in the town to grin at.'

'No, it is not pleasant, of course. There are lots of fellows here, I should say, to whom it would be most *un*pleasant. There are a lot of old lags round about these diggings.'

'Indeed!' said Crosbie, puffing hard at his pipe, and enshrouding himself in smoke. 'I suppose there are.'

'That old scoundrel whose neck I nearly twisted yesterday, for example,' pursued Arthur, laughing – 'Long Jerry, as he calls himself. *He* has been an old Vandemonian, I'll swear. Freddy Flite says there is an infallible test by which you can tell an old convict – the way he walks.'

'The wisdom of Mr Flite is as old as Shakespere,' said Crosbie. 'Don't you remember that Falstaff had soldiers who walked wide between the legs, as though they had gyves on?'

And he grinned a ghastly grin.

'But they didn't all wear "gyves," my boy,' returned Arthur, as if he knew all about it. 'There is your young friend and fellow-conspirator, Purfoy, for instance; he doesn't walk wide, but he openly admits having been in the Sydney House of Correction, or whatever the place is called.'

Crosbie knitted his brows. 'So that lad is named Purfoy, is he?' He remembered the strange woman of the convict-ship had borne that name, and albeit the memory of her had faded from his brain, effaced by other and sharper impressions, he felt a sort of uneasiness at thus hearing of her or of hers, as though the web through which he had broken was closing round him again.

The silence following Crosbie's reflection was broken by Dorcas, who, sitting at her father's feet, had not hitherto spoken.

'Poor boy,' said she, 'I am sorry for him.'

'Poor boy!' cried Arthur. 'Young rascal! If ever there was a juvenile gallow's-bird, he is one. He told me that he is the son of a gentleman, and desires to find his father! His father will not be proud of him, I imagine, when he presents himself.'

'I am surprised, Mr Vern, at your talking in that way,' says

Dorcas, warmly. 'It is very heartless, and I did not think that *you* would do it. Because a man is a convict, that is no reason why he should be a bad man.'

'It is a very fair reason why he should be thought so,' said Arthur.

'That is so like a man! You are a Philistine, and you talk bunkum!'

Arthur, amused at the patchwork character of the speech – composed of the Ballarat of her daily life and the *Saturday Review* of her occasional reading – retorted with some platitude about the proverbial sympathy of young ladies for wicked people.

'I am not a young lady, and I pray for all convicts every night on my knees,' Dorcas flashed out.

'Who taught you to do that?' asked the young man, somewhat astonished.

'I did,' said Crosbie, turning away his face.

There was an ominous silence. Dorcas felt that she had, to use her own phraseology, 'put her foot in it.' Crosbie felt angered at being thus compelled to admit a course of action hitherto considered private; and Arthur was oppressed with a strange foreboding. He did not relish this linking of convicts and crime with the person of the young girl whom he loved.

'Of course, a man may be a convict innocently,' he said at last. 'I don't dispute that. But that is his misfortune. He could never come back to society again, you know. He might be proved innocent and all that, but one could not look upon him as the same. The memory of the frightful scenes through which he had passed would taint him.'

Crosbie got up, with a strangely white face.

'You are right, young man,' he said. 'The society of the good and pure would justly refuse to be contaminated by the presence of such a man. He is a leper, from whom all healthy beings shrink with disgust. For him remains no love of sister, wife, or child. He is alone in the world – a being apart and accursed – therefore, Dorcas night and morning prays for him.'

He took up the lamp at his elbow and went out.

The lovers were left staring at each other.

'Do not look so terrified, Arthur dearest,' said Dorcas. 'He used to be often overpowered by these melancholy fits. They have been less frequent of late, but your words have made him sad. Mine did too, when I talked of such things.'

'But,' said Arthur, half repulsing her, 'what does he mean? He teaches you to pray for convicts. He is disturbed at the convict's doom. Oh! – Surely—'

'– Surely he is not a convict? you would ask,' said Dorcas, nestling closer. 'Surely not. He was a sailor, who left his ship in Port Phillip Bay, and took service as a shepherd. My mother was drowned at sea, and *I* lived five years at Loftus's before the diggings broke out at all.'

Arthur gave a sigh of relief and kissed her. She heard the sigh, and interpreting it correctly, made reply after her own untutored fashion.

'You mean sneak! Do you mean to say you would love me less if he had been?'

'Don't use such words, Dotty, dear,' says her lover, fencing with the question.

'Well, but would you?'

'N – No; of course not. But – but it is just as well you are *not*, dear.'

'But why? I am myself, I suppose, if my poor dear dad had been Ali Baba and the Forty Thieves.'

'Yes; but, Dotty, there are certain prejudices, you know. Society –'

'Hang Society! I hate Society! What do I know about Society, or Society about me? I am only a digger's daughter. You are a swell, and have lived among young ladies. Oh dear, I wish I was buried in the shade somewhere.'

'Now, Dotty, be reasonable. You know I dislike to hear you talk like that. You are worth all the "young ladies" *I* have met.'

'Am I? You mean it? You swear it? Well, then, you may kiss me, and we will be friends, Arthur, for I love you very much; and if I thought you didn't love me, I'd break my heart right off.'

Arthur kissed her.

'Did anybody ever kiss you before, Dotty?' said he, when the ceremony had been completed.

'Yes,' said Dotty, simply.

'And who was that?' asked the young man, in profound indignation.

'American Joe,' said Dorcas. 'He pretended to want a pair of moleskins, and when I was reaching up for them, he just took me round the waist and kissed me. My! how I slapped his face!'

There was no gainsaying the honesty of the Lily's chastisement, her cheeks tingled even then with the recollection of it; but Arthur felt strangely annoyed at the thought of American Joe and the moleskins. How strange were the two sides to this girl's character! At one time she would fascinate him with her mother wit, and astonish him with her store of knowledge; at another, he would feel hot and angry at her ignorance of conventionalities, and pained at her liberal use of the slang of the Camp. In good truth the girl, with her natural and inherited talent, and her incongruous and masculine surroundings, was a problem in womankind which more experienced students of human nature than this frank college-bred boy would be at a loss to hurriedly solve. They parted, however, with the usual leave-takings; and when Arthur next day met the man whom he was striving to bring himself to regard as his future father-in-law, he observed no traces of the emotion of the previous evening. Crosbie was grimly quiescent as ever.

One good thing — for Crosbie — came out of the evening's conversation. Seeing how troubled the man was concerning his approaching trial, Arthur interested himself with officialdom, in the person of Fred Flite.

'Don't you think, Freddy,' said he, 'that it is great nonsense sending Crosbie to Melbourne. He is known on the diggings as a man well affected towards the authorities, and plenty of people can give evidence that at the fire he strove to keep back the crowd.'

'Oh, as to that, my dear fellow,' returned Freddy, twisting a youthful moustache, 'I shall be happy to do all I can for him. _I_ saw the way he behaved, you know, and I'll tell Rayner. The fact is that our fellows' blood was up, and they captured anybody they could. I'll see old Rayner about it.'

He was as good as his word, and Rayner, having been 'old fellow'-ed and generally smoothed down, bethought him that it might be a mistake to send for trial a person reputed wealthy and known to be orderly.

'I'll think it over, dear boy,' said he to the cadet. 'We have the others safe enough, and I daresay old Crosbie had nothing to do with it.'

He did think it over, and the result of his thinking was, that Arthur one day informed the storekeeper that the prosecution against him had been withdrawn. The diggers regarded this as a triumph, and came with tin cans and torches to the store to celebrate their favourite's escape. Carboni made a red-hot speech about tyranny and freedom, kissing the tips of his fingers to Dorcas many times in succession; while McGrath vowed that he would never rest until the other victims of oppression were released in like manner from bondage. Crosbie, saturnine, as usual, vouchsafed but brief thanks for the honour done him, only, when the crowd had departed, pistol-firing and tin-pot drubbing, into the Gravel-pits, he took Arthur aside and expressed his gratitude in warm terms.

'I am most grateful to you, Mr Vern,' he said. 'I did not wish to leave my daughter alone here, and I could not have taken her with me. Do you not see how awkward it would have been? I am really most grateful to you. You have taken a weight off my mind.'

Arthur was compelled to be satisfied with this explanation, and affected to make light of the matter. The incident, however, set him reflecting, and his reflection was so far disadvantageous to Crosbie, that he determined to see less of Dorcas.

↢ 12 ↣

SUSPICIONS

THIS determination was not carried into effect without some mental anxiety. The young man was honestly in love with the girl whom he had so strangely met, and all his efforts to forget her were in vain. His new mode of life, his new companion-ships, his consciousness that whatever of fortune he might achieve must be won by his own hands, his contact with human nature in the rough, as it were, all disposed him to make light of those social objections which in his former condition of being would have seemed to render such a match as that which he proposed to himself impossible. If it would have been at best a hazardous and dangerous experiment for Arthur Devine, the millionaire, to marry an unknown and semi-educated girl, who had nothing but her natural beauty and wit to recommend her, there was no reason why Arthur Vern, the gold-digger, should not please himself in such a vital matter. 'I know my aunt and sister will see her good qualities,' he would think, 'and if they are satisfied, I care not for others' opinions.'

The horrible stumbling-block in the way was Crosbie—Crosbie, the storekeeper; Crosbie, the sailor; Crosbie, the man of doubtful antecedents. A dozen times had the boy been on the point of unbosoming himself and demanding the true history of the mysterious father as an interchange for his own con-fession of love for the daughter. A dozen times had his heart failed him at sight of Crosbie's iron visage. If that gloomy, careworn man had a secret to hold, he would hold it despite of fate. Poor Arthur little knew that he himself possessed the 'sesame' which would open the fast-locked doors of that old man's jealous heart – his own name, Devine.

Thus driven hither and thither on the troublous sea of his own emotions, he had formed a thousand wild theories con-cerning the land of certainty and fact that he longed, yet feared to reach. A thousand wild guesses tormented him, some terribly near the truth, some ludicrously far from it. Suppose Crosbie was not her father? Suppose she were the daughter of some rich and evil man who had doomed her to a rank beneath that to which her birth entitled her? Suppose Crosbie had stolen her away? Suppose she was a shipwrecked foundling like Mariana or sweet Perdita? Suppose Crosbie was an escaped felon, and she was his daughter after all? Suppose some terrible crime linked her, unconsciously, to this death's-head? Suppose – but imagination exhausted itself in suppositions. He would give her up – he would not – he could – he could not. He did not love her, he could easily forget. Alas! he loved her too fondly, and coveted ever the sweet agony of remembrance. Whether working, or plotting, listening to the good-humoured jests of his 'mates,' or drinking in the revolutionary eloquence of Carboni and McGrath, the image of the dark-eyed girl haunted him, as the image of her mother had haunted the toiling convict in the days that were dead.

So sped the spring, amid threats of further violence; amid rumours of outbreak and revolution; amid furious speech-makings and popular gatherings; with the 'digger hunts' growing fiercer and fiercer, the 'blue and silver' ramping higher and higher; with all diggerdom waiting for the result of the trial of the incendiaries, as a signal for peace or war; and with the love story of poor Dorcas running through it all – as the silver thread intertwisted through the Persian mourning garments.

One Sunday – towards the end of November – Arthur made his final effort to learn the past history of the pair. He had accustomed himself to visit by fits and starts, striving to make each visit shorter than the last, and affecting a carelessness of demeanour which might deceive Crosbie. To a certain extent his affectation was successful. Crosbie, though he guessed that the young man had an affection for his daughter, did not dream that the pair had as yet got further in their lovemaking than sighing and ogling, and placed no restraint upon the girl in her walks or wanderings.

The bank of the little creek, down which Mr Flite's horse had stumbled on the memorable occasion when the lovers first met, was shaded by a line of gum-trees that had here and there escaped the axe of the digger. Two of these trees formed a natural screen, and of late it had been customary with Dorcas to meet Arthur there. In this primitive shelter, with the tented and wooden-roofed city stretching up and around them, the lovers quarrelled and kissed, wept and laughed, sounded together all the depths and shoals of such sentiment as is common to love's sweet season. Their quarrels were not unfrequent. The necessity for concealment which Arthur, in his hesitation, had impressed upon her, rendered the poor girl miserable. She had never in her life had a secret from her father, and it was a sore burden to bear one now. Against this restriction she had often repined. 'Why not let me tell him?' she had urged again and again. 'By-and-bye,' was Arthur's answer. 'You can surely wait and trust in me?' To such a question there could be but one reply. She waited, yet, in waiting, took every occasion to argue and to rebel. On this particular evening she had come to the place of meeting with a determination to conceal no longer, and on this evening she found Arthur more than usually arbitrary.

'If you love me, you will do as I wish,' said he.

'But if you love *me*, you will not force me to do that which *I don't* wish,' said she. 'What are your reasons, Arthur? I never yet deceived my father, and if he found it out he would be *so* hurt and angry.'

'Would you rather then anger him than me?'

'No, no – but why should *you* be angry? Arthur, it is very hard for me.'

'All will be well soon, dear. We will leave this place and go to England.'

'Why did you come here, Arthur? You should never have left home! You are well educated, and have been living with swells.'

'Don't say "swells," Dotty – with gentlemen.'

'Well, "gentlemen," then. You *are* a swell – I mean a gentleman. What made you come out to the diggings?'

'What made all these people come? A desire to get rich, I suppose. I want to get rich.'

'But you *are* rich, – or you must have been rich to have been able to have learnt so much. You were at college, weren't you?'

'Yes,' said Arthur, with a sigh.

'I have read about college. Pelham was at college. Why did you leave, dear?'

'Misfortune, Dotty. It was thought that I should have had much money, but an accident happened which made me poor.'

'What was that?'

'My uncle, who was thought to be dead, returned, and all the money which I had been taught to look upon as mine was given up to him.'

'And you came out here to make more? Brave boy! What was your uncle's name?'

'I will tell you all about it one of these days, darling,' returned Arthur, avoiding a direct reply; 'but let us talk about yourself. I want to ask you something. You have been questioning me, now I am going to question you a little. Put your head on my shoulder. So. There now, look up.'

'I am ready, dear; question away. I have nothing to tell you that you do not know already.'

'How far back do you remember, Dorcas?'

'How far back? Oh, ages! I remember when Daddy used to go shepherding, and I used to take his tea to him.'

'Not farther than that?'

'Let me see, dear. I remember when our hut was built. I remember a blackfellow who used to throw the boomerang at the posts to amuse me. I remember – oh, I don't remember farther than that – except that I once fell into a waterhole, and Daddy's dog fished me up again. I have the mark of his teeth now. See!'

And in her innocent freedom, she pulled down the top of her frock, exposing a white shoulder dented with three small scars.

Arthur devoured it with his eyes, and she, catching the glance, coloured, and covered it quickly.

'I don't remember any more.'

'But have you no recollection of any person but your father? Don't you remember your mother?'

Dorcas shook her head sorrowfully.

'I have tried hard – oh, so hard – to remember her. Sometimes I have thought I have succeeded, for I have dreamt of a lady in white holding in her arms a child that seemed to be myself, but the face has always faded before I could fix it – faded into coldness and a rushing of waters.'

'Does not your father speak of her?'

'No. He told me once she was drowned, and I think she must have been, for I chiefly think of her when the wind wails at night, or, when lying among the ferns, the tops of the gum trees above me murmur as I fancy the great sea must murmur on the shore.'

'Poor child!'

'I used to cry often, Arthur, when I thought of her, and long to see her. It was ungrateful of me, for Daddy has been my mother as well as my father. He used to rock me to sleep, and sing songs to me, and wash me, and dress me, just like a mother would. He has sat up at nights, after a long day's work, to mend my frocks; and sometimes, Arthur, when he has thought me asleep, I have heard him praying for me; sometimes I have felt his tears warm on my face when he has kissed me. Poor Daddy — Arthur, you should let me tell him.'

But Arthur was firm. There was more in this than Dorcas knew — it was possible that some grave secret lay hid under all this affection.

'I think, Dotty, there is some mystery about you,' said he, 'that demands explanation. It is strange — don't be angry, dear — that a man like your father, a man who has such advanced ideas, and has read so much, and has studied a science so far removed from everyday minds as chemistry, for instance, should pass his life shepherding or gold-digging. Did he ever tell you anything about his early life?'

'No,' said Dora, her eyes blazing with feminine curiosity. 'I never thought about it.'

'Well, I will ask him. I daresay he can easily explain.'

'I *wish* you would let me tell him, dear. I have a presentiment that some grief will befall us if you keep our love a secret longer.'

'Nonsense, goose! Do as I tell you,' says the self-confident young noodle. 'Trust in *me*! Promise, now, that you will not tell him.'

'I promise on one condition, then,' says Dorcas, growing herself again.

'Well?'

'That you will give up these horrid men — McGrath and Carboni, and that lot. They are duffers, I know. They will lead you into mischief.'

'McGrath is away,' said Arthur, with an uneasy laugh.

'Where has he gone?'

'To Melbourne, to demand the release of the men condemned for burning Grantly's. The League sent him.'

'Oh, Arthur, you will get into trouble with that League, I know. What a foolish boy you are, mixing yourself up against the Government! I have heard all about it. I never would have given you all that blue silk if I had known you were going to make a Republican Flag of it.'

'Who told you that?' cries Arthur, with a start.

'Carboni. He came up to the store, kissing his hands, and I had it all out of him in a jiffy.'

'In a what?'

'In a jiffy – in a minute, I mean. Oh, Arthur, *don't* go and make an idiot of yourself. I heard Don Rinaldo talking of it yesterday, and how more soldiers were coming up, and the license business was to be *strictly* enforced.'

'I shan't make an idiot of myself, you little Conservative, but I can't desert my friends.'

'Oh, and if they go attacking the soldiers I suppose you will go too?'

'I cannot desert them, dear.'

'Then I'll tell Father.'

'Tell him what?'

'All about this.'

'Dotty, if you do, I'll – I'll never speak to you again.'

'Then will you promise?'

'I will promise not to attack any one, unless I am myself attacked,' said Arthur, 'if you will keep *your* word.'

'It's a bargain,' said Dotty, sorrowfully. 'You had better kiss me and seal it at once, or I shall change my mind.'

'Until Tuesday then,' said Arthur, and they parted.

That evening when Dorcas got home, she said to Crosbie:

'Father, I want to know who my mother was.'

The unhappy man started as if an adder had stung him. Of late years he had often dreamed of a horror like this, and having awoke in cold sweat, had shaped in the darkness all kinds of unsatisfactory answers.

'Your mother ! Your mother was drowned, child.'

'I know, dear Daddy, but tell me – what was she, what was her name?'

'Her name was the same as your own – what should it have been?' said Crosbie, hoarsely.

'Yes, dear, I know, but her maiden-name – her name before she married you?'

'She was the best of women,' said Crosbie, shuddering.

'But will you not tell me, dear father — what mystery is there, what was her story, her —?'

Rufus Dawes started up and seized her arm.

'What do you mean? Who has set you on to ask this?'

'N — no one.'

'It is untrue! Dorcas, take care! Tell me! You have been prompted to question me. Ah! You blush! Who is it? I will know!'

'Father! You hurt me! Do not frown so! I did not mean! Oh! I will tell you. It was Ar — It was Mr Vern who suggested — Father, do not stare at me so, I meant no harm.'

'Mr Vern! Mr Vern has been prying into my affairs! Ah! What is there between you and him?'

'Nothing, father!'

'You lie! Will you swear it?'

'Yes, yes, I swear it! There is nothing. A word he let drop set me thinking. Oh, father, forgive me, I did not mean to hurt you!'

He flung her off almost roughly, and leant against the wall, pallid with emotion. His sin had found him out at last.

The girl, her rival loves struggling within her, strove to undo the mischief she had unwittingly done.

'I swear there is nothing, father. No one has been questioning me. It was my own thought. Forgive me if I have made you suffer.'

He recovered himself slowly, and turned to her. It was evident to him, despite her words, that the question had not been of her own prompting.

'Dorcas, you must see this young man no more!'

'Father!'

'You hesitate! Do you love him then?'

'Ah, no!'

'Has he spoken to you of love?'

'No, father!'

'I don't believe you, and yet — listen, Dorcas' — his lips were dry and parched, and he could scarcely articulate — 'there *is* a secret concerning your mother. I had promised myself to tell you one of these days — but not yet. Do not start! There is nothing for *you* to blush for. But — I cannot tell you now. You love me do you not?'

'Dear father!'

'Then for my sake seek to know no more.'

'Father, forgive me!'

'One thing I command you. You must not see this boy again!'

She was weeping hysterically.

'Have I your promise?'

'Oh, father, do not ask me that.'

'Then you *do* love him, and you have lied! Viper, you have betrayed and undone me!'

'I don't know what you mean. There, then, I promise. I promise.'

'And you do *not* love him!'

'No, father, no. None but you, but you!'

He carried her in his arms into her little bed-room and laid her down, loosening her dress and chafing her hands, as he did when she was a child. As he stood looking at her, lying there, dishevelled and disordered, he felt a shadow pass between them. For the first time since he had carried her baby figure in his arms, he comprehended his true relation to her. He kissed her forehead, with averted eyes, and stole from the chamber. His empire was over. There was no longer a child beneath his roof, but a woman.

❧ 23 ❧

PROMPTITUDE

CROSBIE did not sleep that night. He understood that a crisis in his life had arrived. It seemed to him that the relentless fate which had pursued him so long had awoke from the slumber of five years, and was again on his track. It was necessary that the enquiries of this intrusive young man be at once baffled. Fool that he had been to suffer him to be so familiar! It was, happily, not too late. Dorcas did not love him. Had she not sworn it? She had but a passing liking for him. She would forget. So comforting himself with arguments he knew in his inmost soul to be false, Rufus Dawes set about contriving a plan to undo the mischief he had suffered to be done. A night's weary thinking showed him but one way – the way he had before proposed to take. Let him but be firm now, fortune opened before him.

In the morning, Dorcas spread the breakfast, and looked for some explanation from her father of his conduct of the previous evening. Crosbie, however, gave none. He kissed her with an air as if nothing had happened, and persistently avoided all allusion to the subject. This course of action chilled her, and she was perforce silent.

When breakfast was over, Crosbie rose.

'I am going into the town,' he said. 'I shall be away until dark. See no one on any pretence. You understand, Dorcas – *no one.*'

She knew what he meant, and her heart sank. He had not forgotten evidently. However, she would see Arthur on Tuesday evening, and bring about an explanation.

Crosbie went to the rival storekeeper. This was a man named Blick, reported to be the son of a noted London 'fence,' and a shrewd fellow.

'Blick,' said he, 'how's business?'

'Oh, very well,' said Blick, as a matter of course.

'I am glad of it. Because I want to sell mine.'

'Sell yours!' says Blick. 'Why?'

'I don't like the way things are shaping,' said Crosbie. 'There'll be a riot here soon.'

'Ah!' says Blick, 'you are right there. They was drilling on Battery Hill last night, I'm told. But it won't be much, bless yer, a flash in the pan. There's military a coming up every day.'

'It's all very well for you; but I have a daughter, and I want to get out of it.'

'Made your pile, eh? Well, I don't say but if I was in your place, I'd do the same.'

'What will you give me for the plant?'

'What, the whole thing? The whole box and dice? Well, I don't know, Mr Crosbie. What do you say to five hundred?'

'You're joking.'

'It isn't worth more, Mr Crosbie.'

'You shall have it for two thousand.'

'It's your turn to joke now.'

'Well, what will you give?'

'Eight hundred cash.'

'No.'

'Well, name your terms.'

'I'll sell it for fifteen hundred pounds cash — goodwill, stock, house, and all.'

After some bargaining, Blick purchased at one thousand pounds cash, and bills for four hundred at one, two, and three months — credit was short on Ballarat in those days.

'When can I have possession?' said he. 'If the soldiers come up, there'll be plenty to do.'

'To-morrow, at mid-day,' said Crosbie, folding up the cheque; 'and you needn't mention I'm going. I don't want to be tin-potted any more.'

As Blick had netted nearly three hundred pounds by his bargain, he was all graciousness.

'Of course not. Let us wet our deal. Will you drink?'

'No; but I want you to do me a favour. Lend me that bay mare of yours for a couple of hours. I want to go to Loftus's.'

'Take her all day if you like,' says generous Blick. 'But you'd better have a nobbler.'

While Blick saddled the mare, Crosbie walked through the red dust, called by courtesy a road, and, entering a wooden-stabled yard, demanded to see Mr Joyce.

Mr Joyce appeared, obedient to the summons.

'Have you sold that mail-waggon I saw here yesterday?'

'The one belonging to them new chums?' says Joyce. 'No, I ain't. The Commissioner he were a looking at her, but he says she's too flash for he. She's a spiff 'un, though, Mr Crosbie; and if you want to tool the young lady out on Sunday arternoons —'

'How much?' says Crosbie, cutting him short.

'One 'undred and fifty pounds to *you*, Mr Crosbie.'

'I'll give a hundred pounds. You needn't argue; it's mine.'

'Well, you *have* such an insinuating way, Mr Crosbie! You'll want a pair of spankers to draw that now. I've got —'

'Thank you. No. Good morning. I'll call on my way back.'

'My, how he dew dew business, he dew,' said Mr Joyce, rubbing his hand over his mouth in meditative admiration. 'Mary, bring us a nobular of P.B., my gal.'

Crosbie set off for Loftus's. Loftus had long since disappeared – swept away in the byewash of gold-digging – but the place, what was left of it, still bore his name.

'Good morning, Mr Prell.'

'Good morning, Mr Crosbie. What brings you here this morning?'

'I've got a commission to buy two smart draught-horses. Have you sold those colts?'

'The very thing, my dear sir,' cries Prell, who, although his father had been a London barber, cultivated a taste for horse-breeding. 'Hitch your mare to the gate, and come and have a nobbler while the boy runs 'em up. Jack! run up the mob that's running in the flat, and look out for those two colts that young Jenkins broke in last spring. Now, Mr Crosbie, which is it to be?'

'Thanks,' said Crosbie, declining the proffered hospitality, 'it's too early for me. You'll be wanting a high price for those horses?'

'Forty pounds apiece,' says Prell, tossing off the brandy, 'and cheap at that. You shall just see 'em – sixteen-and-a-half, sound as roaches, and rising five.'

The horses justified Mr Prell's encomiums. They were a fine pair, a finer pair, indeed, than many a Melbourne gentleman can get now for love or money.

'Can you let the boy bring them in to town?' said Crosbie, pulling out his roll of notes.

'Certainly. Oh, it's all right – any time will do for that.'

'You may as well take it now,' said Crosbie, thrusting the payment into his hand. 'I'm going down to Melbourne, and shan't be back for some time.'

'They'll take you down in a day,' said Prell. 'I had 'em in harness yesterday, and they went like lambs. A nobbler before you start? No. Well here's luck,' and he tossed off another bumper.

When Joyce saw the horses he stared.

'You *have* got a pair, Mr Crosbie,' said he.

'Stable them, and put them in the waggon by daylight in the morning,' says Crosbie. 'I'll try them down the Government-road.'

When he got home it was dusk, and Dorcas was crying.

'Any one been here?'

'No, father.'

'That is well. Now listen. We are going away from here to-morrow morning.'

'Good gracious! Where?'

'To Melbourne. Don't cry dear. It is necessary, or I would not urge it. Some day I will tell you the reason.'

'But, father – the store?'

'Is sold. You will be ready to come with me by twelve o'clock. You need not burden yourself with more baggage than you absolutely want. You need see no one. I want no leave-takings to bring prying eyes into my affairs. Do you understand me?'

'Yes, father.'

'Then you will obey, I know. Do not think me harsh, darling. It *must* be so, for *my* sake.'

She kissed him, with dry eyes, and said nothing. The blow stunned her.

⊷ 14 ⊶

THE BEGINNING OF THE CONFLICT

The next morning a strange rumour ran through the diggings.

'The Government had refused to release the prisoners!'

There was no judging how this report had been put about. As is usual in such cases, everybody had heard it from somebody else. McGrath was to return on the morrow, and then all would be made clear. In the meantime, work was not so brisk. Groups of men, gathered together here and there, spoke hurriedly and rapidly. Picks were left stuck into the soil, while their owners gesticulated at the Charley Napier. It was bruited abroad, by-and-by, that the delegates had been arrested, and the excitement grew fiercer. Mr Tarleton, the American consul, was to be fêted that night, and a troop, with American Joe prominent in their midst, marched up the hill, with the Stars and Stripes flying, and roared 'Hail Columbia.' The Camp bristled with sentries; and Blick was astonished at the number of diggers who came to purchase powder for 'blasting purposes.' Arthur Vern – Secretary to the Committee of the League – could have told what was to become of the powder, had he so chosen. He disbelieved the story of the arrest, and endeavoured to still the tumult that reigned in the committee-room. 'In a few hours McGrath will be here,' said he, 'and explain all. The Government will give way.' His expostulations were vain. He was laughed or shouted down. Every minute reinforcements of rebels arrived. Public feeling was at boiling pitch. The diggings were like a disturbed ant-hill. A monster meeting was called for Wednesday at Bakery Hill. Poor Arthur, longing for McGrath, sat on thorns the whole weary day, burning with impatience. He had made up his mind to see Crosbie, and make a clean breast of it. Away with his unworthy suspicions; now, if ever, he would have the right to defend the girl who loved him.

In the meantime, a detachment of troops, marching along the Ballarat road, met a mail waggon, drawn rapidly by two high-couraged horses. The officer in command of this detachment, staring at the dashing apparition, saw the driver suddenly lean forward to stare at him, and then, turning into a side track, disappear at a gallop into the bush.

'What is the matter, father?' asked the girl, who sat behind the driver. 'Why did you not go straight on?'

'Those soldiers – did you not see?' – gasped Crosbie, checking his horses half-a-mile deep in the forest.

'See what? Why you are deadly pale! What is it?'

'There was one there I never thought to meet again,' said Rufus Dawes, recovering himself and looking at her with an agonised face – 'least of all with you. Dorcas, our departure was fortunate.'

'Why?' asked the girl, in bewilderment.

'Because – because there will be fighting in the Camp to-morrow!'

Dorcas pressed her hands to her bosom to prevent a cry.

At eight o'clock in the evening Arthur hurried to the creek. The trees – haggard and dusty – stood black against the sunset, but beneath them was no white figure. Torn with impatience, he waited an hour. No one came. He went to the store, and saw Crosbie's head man, one McKillop, there. He was pushing his way in when the man stopped him.

'Mr Crosbie's gone, sir.'

'What?'

'He's gone, sir. He's sold the store to Blick.'

Arthur staggered back.

'Where has he gone?'

'To Melbourne. He bought Joyce's mail-waggon yesterday, it seems, and two horses. It's a rum go; but it's right, sir. Our wages are paid to date.'

'And Miss Dorcas?'

'She's gone with him, sir.'

'Did he leave no message for me?'

'No, sir.'

'You are sure?'

'Quite sure.'

Arthur went out again bewildered. What could it mean? Surely Dorcas would never have left him without a word. Why should Crosbie suddenly depart? The mystery about him was increased. In dumb despair Arthur wandered through the town, wondering and fearing. His first impulse was to follow. But the League – the cursed League to which he had pledged himself – held him back. He could not desert his post until his leader returned. Pausing beneath the open windows of the Hotel, where the dinner was proceeding, he heard ominous cheering at ominous American sentiments. Every second man whom he met looked angrily, as if ready for instant fight. Don Rinaldo, mounted on a huge grey charger, was 'on duty' at the hotel door, with half a dozen troopers, and had almost forgotten his jauntiness amid the gravity of the general demeanour. No one had seen or heard of Crosbie. No one had seen or heard of McGrath. Maddened with a consciousness of his helplessness, the young man wandered on until at last he found himself again beneath the trees where he had been accustomed to meet Dorcas.

Was it possible that she had left a note? Was it not most probable?

He felt in the hollow which had served as their post-office, and sure enough his fingers touched a. piece of paper. He ran down the hill and plunged into a tent at the bottom. 'Show us a light, mate,' he cried, with digging freedom, to the occupant. 'You can see it, if you like,' said the owner of the tent, a young man with black hair and a sallow complexion, who was reclining on a rolled blanket, smoking. Arthur untwisted the note.

My Darling,

I am to go away in the morning with father to Melbourne. He says it is necessary. I suppose we shall never meet again. I think it is something to do with the Government. Don't follow me. My heart is broken, dear.

Dorcas.

'Something to do with the Government.' What could she mean? What had Crosbie to do with the Government?

Just then, from out the gully on the left, arose a shouting, followed by the rattle of firearms. He could dimly distinguish plunging horses and overturned waggons. Lights gleamed hither and thither. From the rising ground came the hoarse tones of men in dispute, and then out of the dusky confusion emerged the head of a column of soldiers. Arthur's heart gave a sudden bound.

'Oh, the traitor,' he cried. 'I see now his mystery and his escape. He was a spy.'

'Who was?' asked the sallow young man.

'Crosbie! Tom Crosbie, the storekeeper,' cries Arthur again, dashing his fist against his forehead. 'We are betrayed!' And he rushed out of the tent.

'Melodramatic party,' soliloquised the young man. 'My grandfather used to say that most people under the influence of strong emotion are melodramatic, and he ought to have known.' With which reflection he turned him philosophically to smoke.

Arthur, maddened with rage and despair, made for the Committee-room at the Star. He had no doubt now at all Crosbie was in the pay of the Government, and having betrayed the plans of the League, had stole away, in order to escape the diggers' just vengeance. The first result of this treachery was apparent in the present conflict. But he would baffle him. He would rouse the Camp. He would call the two thousand men that had sworn fidelity to the Southern Cross to arms, he would. He would do everything and nothing. The Star was deserted. The report of the attack on the soldiers had got abroad, and the mounted police were galloping furiously to the rescue. The dinner had broken up in admired disorder, the guests having departed at the report of the attack. It was stated that the diggers had first fired on the troops, and that a drummer boy had been shot. At the top of the hill Arthur felt his arm seized, and turned. It was McGrath.

'Thank God, Peter!' he cried. 'I thought you were arrested.'

'Not I!' said McGrath, with a short laugh. 'They insulted us, but they did not dare to arrest us. What, in Heaven's name, is all this?'

'It is Crosbie's doing,' said Arthur. 'The villain has betrayed us. He left this morning for Melbourne.'

'Stuff!' cries practical McGrath. 'He would not have waited until now. Betray! What is there to betray? We are open enough with our hostility to tyrants.'

Another volley of musketry from the road below them confirmed his words.

McGrath stamped his foot.

'Fools! To provoke their own destruction! By heavens, if any Leaguer began this fray, I'd hang him were he my own brother!'

'The troops fired on the men at the Eureka, they say.'

'They *say*! Who knows what is said at a time like this? Follow me quickly. We must end this madness.'

The two plunged downwards into the road. The troops were slowly advancing, behaving with admirable temper. Conspicuous among them was an officer mounted on a black horse, who sat unmoved among the showers of stones and rattling pistol-shots from the cloud of diggers who hovered on the flank of the detachment.

Young Purfoy, who was among the foremost of the attacking

party, recognised the grim figure, and shook his fist at it with deadly anger.

'Do you know who that is?' he asked the man at his side.

'No,' said Jerry Mogford, stooping for a stone. 'I hain't the honor. Who is he?'

'Captain Frere, of Norfolk Island,' said Dick, with a scowl.

Mr Mogford's affability disappeared. Like every convict, he had heard and shuddered at that hated name; and the stone, flung with the best of bad intent, grazed the ex-commandant's head.

Dick Purfoy laughed.

'*You* won't hit him,' he said. 'It's reserved for me to do that. I've sworn to have that dog's life, and I will. Lend me your revolver, Ned.'

McGrath flung himself into the crowd, cursing and gesticulating. 'The idiots,' he said, 'they will put us all in the wrong with their murderous tomfoolery.' His entreaties and presence had some effect. A cheer was raised for him, and a strong body of mounted police debouching from the Camp, the insurgents fell back.

'Oh, I can wait,' said Dick Purfoy, returning the pistol.

Jerry Mogford, hardened villain as he was, absolutely shuddered at this fierce hatred in one so young. What injury had Captain Frere done to this lad? Sarah Purfoy could have told him.

McGrath, regardless of capture or pistol-shot, sprang upon a stump.

'Go home! go home!' he cried. 'This conduct imperils the cause we fight for. I have returned to you to tell you of the fate of your friends, but I will not deal with madmen. The League knows your wrongs, and will right them. We have not forgotten you. We will not forget you. To-morrow, on yonder hill, we plant the flag of the Republic of Victoria!'

A wild burst of cheering rang through the gullies.

'To-morrow! To-morrow!' roared a thousand throats.

'Ay, to-morrow! We will meet you there.'

'A narrow squeak,' said Griffiths, wiping his brow. 'McGrath, are we not going too far?'

'We may have *gone* too far,' said fiery McGrath. 'It is too late to turn back now. Eh, Arthur?'

'I am with you,' cried Arthur. 'I have been cheated, deceived, and robbed. Do what you will, you can count on me. What do you propose?'

McGrath's eyes sparkled.

'What I have said. A Republic! We will have eight thousand men on Bakery Hill, to-morrow. Creswick will send us three thousand more. We have weapons, ammunition, and food. The rule of red-tape is over. If they refuse to give us what we ask, we will take it.'

'But the men are undisciplined,' said Arthur. 'What can we do against the troops?'

'It is because they are "troops" that I despise them. "Troops" want open ground on which to manœuvre; "troops" want a regular commissariat, and all the appliances of their bloody business under their hands. They cannot move among the mounds. The Eureka is honey-combed with holes – rifle pits ready made.'

'They have three field-pieces in Camp,' said cautious Griffiths.

'I don't care if they had thirty!' cries McGrath, slapping his fist on the table. 'A few slabs on the Eureka hill, and our men will be screened from long-shots. Let them *attack* us, and we will slaughter them like sheep in the gullies. Leonidas at the hot gates of Locris had no better chance than we. By this and by that, boys, but we'll make it a hot gate for some of them!'

'As you wish!' says Arthur, catching the enthusiasm. 'We are in your hands now.'

'Sit down then. You shall be my Minister of War, and draw up our Declaration of Independence!'

'Good Peter,' cries Carboni, in his polyglottic tongue. 'Good Peter, thou von John-Bullied Irishman. Issue thy manifesto, Commander-in-Chief of the Army of Ballarat!'

McGrath seized a pen, and scribbling a few words, flung the paper to the Italian.

It was an 'order of war' for arms and ammunition, signed

PETER McGRATH,
Commander-in-Chief of the Army of the League.

To such a pass had lunacy at last arrived.

The Camp meanwhile was not idle. In the iron-roofed barracks was much loud-talking and military din of preparation. Mr Fred Flite was in a melodramatic simmer of rage at the insult offered to the 'blue and silver' – insults which could only be wiped out in blood, sir, and begged to be led to the field, in order to exterminate, with his single and yet redoubtable arm, all the 'Joes' in the gold-fields. Mr Rayner, P.M., was biting his nails in a fever of anxiety, for he saw an 'enquiry' and dismissal looming hideously in the future. Justly incensed at the unprovoked attack made by the 'rowdies' of the Warrenheip, the soldiers were ripe for reprisals. It was whispered that Colonel McNab himself was on the march, bringing up reinforcements, and that a general attack on the 'rebels' was to be made.

Captain Frere – whose long experience and reputation as a convict disciplinarian had caused him to receive the coveted appointment of Superintendent of Prisons in the new colony – had volunteered to assist in reducing the rioters to reason.

'If I can pick out a few of my lambs,' said he, 'I'll make an example of 'em.'

So, sitting in the Police Barrack with the Gold-field's Commissioner, he held a council of war.

His appearance was but little changed. Time and grief – for, despite what had passed between them, Maurice Frere had believed his wife devoted to him, and the shipwreck which had bereft him at once of wife and child was a sore blow – had lined his face and thinned his hair. But that was all; for the rest, he was as upright, as muscular, as coarse, and vigorous as ever he had been.

'If you take my advice,' he was saying, 'you will just clear the gullies to-morrow morning, and demand the license-fee from every man you catch. If there is any attempt at resistance, proclaim martial law, and call out the troops.'

'You have been accustomed to deal with prisoners, Captain Frere,' said the Commissioner. 'You must remember that these fellows are free men.'

'Yes, and I'd soon make prisoners *of* 'em, if I had my way,' says Frere.

'Upon my word, I don't think they are so much to blame. Of course, my business is to carry out orders, but I think the Government have been too hard.'

Frere was about to reply, when a trooper tapped at the door.

'What is it, O'Donovan?'

'A man wishes to speak with Captain Frayer, ye're honour.'

'With me? What is he?'

'A digger, ye're honour.'

'I'll see him.'

'The system I have always found effectual in preventing things of this sort,' continued Captain Frere, 'is the "private information" system. Whenever you have a large body of men to deal with, you will find some of 'em cowards. You pay these fellows, don't you see, and then you have the crowd!'

'It is a system I should not like to adopt,' said the other. 'Though it may be necessary sometimes.'

'Of course,' said Captain Frere, 'necessary and effectual. There are lots of fellows of that kidney among the virtuous diggers, I have no doubt.'

As if in comment upon his words, O'Donovan introduced Mr Jerry Mogford.

The experienced eye of Maurice Frere saw in an instant the sort of man with whom he had to deal.

'Well, my man, and what do you want?'

The Lurker looked up and down, twisted his ragged old hat between his bony old hands, and, finally, said that he wished to speak in private with his honour.

'We are in private now,' says Frere. 'Go on.'

Still Mr Mogford hesitated.

'Come here,' says Frere, 'and let's look at you.'

Mr Mogford approached with a smirk, and Frere passed the candle across his face, and turned him about, as though he had been a bullock.

'I *don't* know you,' he said, at last. 'You've been on the Sydney side, I suppose?'

Jerry, with a glance at the door, said he had.

'Ah! Then you know Major Deane, and Colonel Culpepper, and Mr Jupp, eh?'

Jerry, more uneasy still, replied that he had heard their names.

'You never heard of Captain Burgess, eh? No, you never did. You never heard of Hyde Park Barracks, eh? Oh, you *have* heard of Hyde Park Barracks. Did you ever hear of a man named Kavanagh?'

Jerry looked up quickly. 'The man your honour took the pistol from? All Sydney knows that story.'

'Oh, then you've heard of *me*?'

'My word!' says the old villain, with a grin.

'Then, if you have, you know I stand no nonsense. What's your name?'

'They calls me Long Jerry, Captain Frere.'

'They call you Long Jerry, do they? I suppose that means that you don't want to be called anything else. Well, Mr Long Jerry, and why do you come here?'

'I've been living – up there,' said Jerry, jerking his thumb towards the east, 'and being a friend of law and order, gentlemen, thought you might perhaps want a little information about matters.'

The Commissioner was about to break out into indignant denial, when Frere checked him.

'What's your price?' he asked, calmly.

'Well, you see, gentlemen,' says Jerry, brightening up at having got so well forward with his scheme, 'I ain't rich, and it's a dangerous caper among those rowdies. I think a pound a day won't be too much.'

'Don't you? I never make bargains. If you bring the Government any information worth having, Government will pay you.'

'But,' says Jerry, going to the door, with a greedy grin, that displayed three or four long white fangs, 'it'll be *right,* you know, gentlemen. You won't bilk a cove, I hope. It's dangerous work, don't yer see, gents, among them rowdies, and I ain't a rich man. I'll rely on your honour, gentlemen; you won't deceive me. I know how many men's 'listed, and how many guns there is, and I can get the names of all the captains.'

'Go and get 'em, then,' said Frere. 'And listen, my bold boy, if you play any tricks, I'll ship you back to Sydney to see if the voyage will improve your memory.'

'A pretty scoundrel,' said the Commissioner, as Jerry shut the door with a fantastic flourish.

'They are *all* scoundrels, my dear sir,' was Maurice Frere's reply. 'I saw that fellow was an old hand at once. Let us go to bed.'

⊷ 15 ⊷

AT THE STOCKADE

THE morrow dawned bright and clear, and the Commander-in-Chief of the Army of the League delivered his report to 12,000 men of all nations and creeds.

A platform had been erected on Bakery Hill, and from a flagstaff fluttered in the gentle breeze the Southern Cross – the insurgent flag. On the platform were the Committee of the League, the delegates, and two Catholic priests, vainly hoping that they could keep peace. The dense crowd cheered at all sentiments of revolution – howled vindictively at all sentiments of temperance.

Griffiths counselled 'moral force,' and was denounced as a 'trimmer.' Allegiance was sworn to the Southern Cross, by ten thousand uplifted hands. Formal resolutions were passed condemning the action of the Government, and all diggers were invited to join the League. 'We will protect no man,' says McGrath, 'who does not join.' Bonfires were made of licenses, salutes were fired, league-tickets of membership were issued, and a monster meeting called for Sunday, at the Adelphi Theatre, at two p.m.

The excitement was tremendous. A sly grog-seller had been plying the black bottle under a burning sun, and whisky and patriotism were conjoined.

'Should any member of the League be dragged to the lock-up,' cries McGrath, 'will a thousand of you volunteer to liberate that man?'

'Yes! yes!'

'Will two thousand of you come forward?'

'Yes! yes! yes!'

'Will four thousand of you march to the Camp to liberate that man?'

'Yes! yes!'

'By God, boys!' shouts McGrath, stretching out his clenched fist, 'are you ready to die?'

'Yes! yes! We are! Hurrah! hurrah!'

And, amid a furious volley of cheers and pistol-shots, the meeting broke up.

'What do you think of that?' says Arthur to Carboni.

'Great works! – great works!' says Carboni, half satirically. 'I wish there wasn't so much blather!'

The next day, Thursday, the 30th November, the diggers were at work as usual, when Captain Maurice Frere succeeded in overcoming the scruples of the Commissioner, and in the afternoon, the police, supported by the whole military force available, with skirmishers in advance, and cavalry on the flanks, formed on the south of the Camp, and advanced upon the Gravel-Pits. The diggers fell back, firing random shots, and a few arrests were made.

The news spread like wild-fire. All the enthusiasm of the previous day was revived.

'To Bakery Hill!' was the cry; and snatching arms from their tents, the diggers hurried to the scene of the previous day's meeting.

McGrath was there, rifle in hand, calling on volunteers to fall in, while Arthur stood at his side taking down the names of the captains of division.

'Let those who have no guns get pikes,' cried McGrath. 'A piece of steel on the end of a pole will suffice to pierce the hearts of tyrants. Forward to the Eureka!'

American Joe ran down the blue and silver flag, and unfurling it, headed the march. McGrath paused opposite the store that had been Crosbie's.

'Plant it here!' he cried.

And the blue silk standard, with its silver cross, floated presently from the top of a pole eighty feet high.

A thousand stalwart men, with breasts aflame at injustice and folly, surrounded it. McGrath, with his left hand grasping the rifle, uncovered his head, and, kneeling down at the foot of the standard, raised his right hand to heaven.

'Let him who fears to join, depart,' he said. 'We want no skulkers!'

The crowd but shifted closer.

'WE SWEAR BY THE SOUTHERN CROSS TO STAND TRULY BY EACH OTHER, AND FIGHT TO DEFEND OUR RIGHTS AND LIBERTIES!'

A firm AMEN burst from every throat.

McGrath, looking down upon those thousand honest hands outstretched in fealty towards him, those earnest faces of so many types of nationalities, those shaggy beards, those brown and muscular arms, and catching the magnetic fire of those up-turned eyes devouring the glorious spectacle of the floating man-ner of their new-born freedom, felt his breast throb with the most terrible of prides – the pride which belongs to the 'kings of men.'

Drilling was instantly begun. The stockade was commenced, by piling together slabs taken from the neighbouring drives. McGrath held his head-quarters in Crosbie's store, and it was proposed to enclose an acre as a fortification. Troops of diggers came pouring in, and the ranks of the pikemen grew stronger and stronger.

Poor Blick began to think he had made a bad bargain, but Arthur gave him receipts for all the goods taken; and McGrath issued an order, that anyone found plundering in the name of the League should be shot. A butcher on the hill sent down fifty carcases, and a German blacksmith was set to work making pikes. All was bustle and earnestness. Fires were lighted, and kettles set on the boil. The insurgents camped by divisions. By six o'clock there were five hundred armed men ready for action.

In the council-room it had been decided – as a last effort to settle matters – that a deputation should wait upon the Com-missioner, explain the case, and demand the release of the pris-oners, and the abolition of licenses. Carboni and Griffiths made part of this deputation.

It returned at nine o'clock to state that the Camp was under arms, the soldiers were ready to attack at any moment, and that all capitulation had been refused.

McGrath adjourned the council meeting until five o'clock in the morning, posted sentries, and waited. Few persons slept in the Camp. Many indeed collected together, relating mutual wrongs. Foremost among these, whenever he could get anyone to listen to him, was the old man known as Long Jerry.

At daylight, the men were at drill; McGrath superintending. It was supposed that an attack would be made; the strength of the stockade was increased. Reinforcements were arriving hourly; and about four in the afternoon the 'Creswick Contingent' marched in, to the tune of 400 men. The moment McGrath saw this addition to his party he became alarmed. The movement had been misrepresented at Creswick. It was stated there that the Ballarat diggers had stores of arms, ammunition, and provisions. The men had marched down without baggage, and were hungry and unarmed.

'For Heaven's sake, Arthur, see to this,' said McGrath. 'There is some treachery here.'

'You must seize all stores,' says Arthur.

'Not yet,' returned the other, 'Not until the last minute. Try what you can do.'

Arthur – heart and soul in the work, for while he worked he could not think – succeeded in collecting provision by sundown; and so the second night of the barricade passed, with some cold, wind, and rain.

The sun standing perpendicularly over the Flagstaff marked twelve o'clock on Saturday, and yet no attack had been made. The stockade began to breathe freely. No man had recollected any 'digger hunt' having taken place on Saturday afternoon, and it was supposed that the authorities had decided to abandon their obnoxious tactics. True to their prudent course, the League had resolved to take no aggressive measures; and, with delight, the majority of men under arms in the stockade departed to their several tents. 'Off to get a bite,' was the word. Between one and two o'clock the fortification was comparatively deserted, and but one hundred men – such as lived far away or had no tent to go to – remained. The talk was all of the meeting on the morrow – the monster meeting at the Adelphi – when it was fondly hoped that a final settlement of all difficulties would be arrived at. Mr Jerry Mogford went out with the rest, and took his way by a circuitous route to the Camp.

But Jerry was not alone.

Young Dick Purfoy, who, armed with a revolver and a pike, had not been behind-hand in the assumption of military service, gave his pike to a friend, pushed his revolver under the breast of his red shirt, and followed his comrade.

He followed him down the hill, and round the mounds, across the creek, and so to the Camp. He saw him speak to the sentry and pass within the hated palisades – now fenced and buttressed with all sorts of makeshift breast-works – firewood, trusses of hay, and corn-bags.

'I thought as much,' said Dick to himself. 'I don't wonder where he got that money from now. He's jumped it.' And he hurried back to tell Arthur.

Mr Mogford made his way to Captain Frere.

'There's no one in the stockade now, your honour,' said he.

'They've gone to dinner, have they?'

'Yes; and now's the time for an assault. They don't suspect nothing, and those slabs ain't no security.'

'The meeting is still for to-morrow?'

'Yes, y'er honour.'

'Are they in the mind to go?'

'Oh yes. Bent on it.'

'What would be the best time?'

'About daylight to-morrow, y'er honour, if I might venture to suggest,' says Jerry, with something of his ancient brilliance. 'Take 'em in the third watch, sir. Men are always sleepier then than at any other time.'

'You are a bright scoundrel,' said Captain Frere.

'I does my dooty and earns my wages,' Jerry made virtuous reply. 'You wouldn't ha' found many coves as would ha' risked their blessed squeeges on this caper, Captain Frere.'

'Well, you must go back again. We shall make no attack before the morning. I want to know the pass-word.'

'My eyes! I don't like risking it no more, sir – upon my sivvy I don't. If Captain McGrath or Mr Vern found me out, sir, they'd scrag me right off the reel.'

'The best thing that could happen to ye,' said the officer who had arrived with the reinforcement. 'Surely, Frere, there is no need to employ this creature.'

'My dear McNab,' says Frere, 'if he saves us trouble, why not employ him? I am sure I don't mind his being scragged. It is only anticipating his fate by a year or so.'

Jerry touched his hat, and grinned.

'Now, sir,' Frere continued, 'no more nonsense. Go back and get the pass-word. Then you can hide your carcase anywhere you choose. Be off, now!'

'If I might ask for a small trifle –' began the wretched spy, but Frere cut him short with a glance.

'Did you not hear me speak, sir? Go! – To-morrow morning – Mac, we'll have all these fellows comfortably in the logs.'

'It's a treacherous business,' says McNab. 'I'd rather storm the place at once.'

'Well,' says Frere, 'if we don't hear from my friend Jerry before midnight, we may conclude either that he has betrayed us or that the Commander-in-Chief has hung him, and you shall have your own way.'

'Are you quite sure of this, boy?' said McGrath to Dick.

'Quite sure. I saw him pass the sentry. There are men under arms in the gully, too; and it is my belief they will attack us at once.'

McGrath looked very grave.

'By heavens!' said Arthur – 'I hear the tramp of men.' They ran out. Joy! It was no enemy, but a reinforcement – the German Rifle Brigade, or 'The Independent Californian Rangers Revolver Brigade,' as they called themselves.

McGrath's fears took flight at once.

'I will change the pass-word, Arthur. And you, boy, take the north gate; if that damned scoundrel can't give a good account of himself, send him about his business. I'll not offend honest men by supposing anyone who has sworn allegiance to yon flag is a spy.'

Some half-dozen about the group raised a faint cheer, and Dick departed, elated at his mission.

The two hundred Californian revolvers having been welcomed and fed, were appointed to the port of honour, the guard of the Council Chamber – that is to say, of Crosbie's store.

It was now getting dusk, and the report of Dick Purfoy had been magnified into nothing less than a general massacre of all concerned. It was stated that the whole of the Melbourne road was swarming with soldiers. Carboni stole out to get information, and saw two hundred red-coats under the foot of the Black Hill. Outside, all the vagabonds in the place – the haunters of grog-shops and dancing-houses – had been plundering stores under pretence of 'pressing for the League.' Blick now congratulated himself that he was *inside* the Stockade, for two of his neighbours outside had been utterly despoiled, the marauders drinking their champagne out of stable buckets, and pouching their tobacco and spare cash. Bearded foragers rode in perpetually – some bringing canisters of gunpowder and bags of shot, others, firearms and boxes of caps. A man with red eyes and a squint was selling grog in the stockade from a keg slung round his neck, and it required McGrath in person to get him kicked outside.[1] Later in the evening a tremendous shouting went up. American Joe, who had been foraging, had returned with the Commissioner's horse. This was looked upon as a profound joke, and a reprisal of excellent character. Arthur, who – raging inwardly – had gone out with a troop to stop any unlawful raids, found posted on a gum-tree, on the debateable ground, the following placard:—

V. R.

NOTICE

No light will be allowed to be kept burning in any tent within musket-shot of the line of sentries after eight o'clock p.m. No discharge of firearms in the neighbourhood of the Camp will be permitted for any purpose whatever.

The sentries have orders to *fire* upon any person offending against these rules.

---

1. *Vide* 'The Eureka Stockade,' by Carboni Raffaello. Melbourne: J. P. Atkinson and Co., 79 Queen-street. 1855.

This was brought in, and caused intense amusement. Carboni would have stuck it up against a tree and fired at it, had not his common sense forbade such a waste of powder and shot. The fear of surprise died away. By ten o'clock all was quiet in the stockade. McGrath lay down in the Council-room to snatch a few hours' sleep. Some of the newly-arrived Californians went 'starring' down the road, in order to intercept reinforcements from Melbourne. The sentries were on the alert, and the pass-word was 'Vinegar Hill.'

Arthur Devine, unable to sleep, leant over a shorter slab which formed a sort of embrasure to the stockade, and looked out over the sleeping diggings. Opposite to him was the Camp with its lights and sentries. All around, the darkness, studded as it were with white specks, which were tents. The moonless heaven bent softly above. Away to the right, he could hear the tramp of a horse-patrol dying into the distance. A hundred paces from him Dick Purfoy walked up and down with his musket shouldered.

Arthur, struck by the military bearing of the lad, and remembering that he had been a convict, began to muse concerning his history. 'What a pity,' he thought, 'that a boy like that should go to ruin. I wonder who is the father of whom he speaks?' He went up to him.

'Sentry.'

The boy saluted, with such intense delight that Arthur smiled.

'All right?'

'All right, sir.'

There was a pause, and then Arthur spoke again.

'They tell me you are looking for your father, Purfoy.'

'Yes,' said Dick, with something like a blush, 'I am.'

'Do you expect to find him here?'

'No, not much. My father is a gentleman,' said Dick. 'I think he's under Government, too. An officer, perhaps.'

'Did you ever see him, then?'

'Not as I know of. But I will. I've made up my mind to find him out.'

'How did you get into trouble, Dick?' said Arthur, after another pause.

'That chap Jerry was partly the cause of it,' said Dick. 'I ran away from home, and he sold me a horse. The horse was stolen. The wretch it belonged to,' – he added, with an oath – 'got me seven years for stealing it. But I'll pay him back one of these days, I know.'

'Who was he?'

'The biggest villain in all the colonies – Maurice Frere!'

Arthur started. His relative did not bear a good name, but he had never heard him so vehemently attacked before.

'He is so very bad then?'

'Bad! Bad ain't no name for him. But he'll get his gruel yet – you mark my words, sir. There's twenty men I knew in Darlinghurst, who vowed to have his life.'

'To have his life! Why?'

'These were old Norfolk Island men,' said Dick, as if that fact would explain everything.

Arthur comprehended that there was something curious about Captain Frere's administration of the government of that convict settlement.

'He's here now,' Dick continued.

'What, Captain Frere? Are you sure?'

'Certain. I saw him that night when we pitched into the troopers at Warrenheip. I don't forget him in a hurry. I hope he comes this way, that's all.'

'Why, boy?'

'Because I'll shoot him,' said Dick, clutching his musket. 'There are two things I am going to do before I die, Mr Vern. Find my father, and kill Captain Frere.'

Arthur shuddered and turned away. She did not know it, but Sarah Purfoy's vengeance was bearing excellent fruit.

As Arthur turned he saw some one at the gate.

'Who goes there?' sang out Dick.

Some reply was given, and the figure began to make motions to seek admittance. Dick went to the gate, and saw the state of affairs in a moment. It was Mr Jerry, somewhat the worse for drink, seeking entrance.

'Advance and give the pass-word,' says Dick, bringing his musket to the present.

'Pass-word be blowed,' says Mr Mogford. 'Let me in, can't

yer? Here have I been rolling up and down these blessed diggings in the sacred cause of freedom all night, and now I can't get in. Blow me, if –'

'Give me the pass-word,' says Dick.

'Well, tell us it then.'

'Look here, Jerry. Your game's up – I saw you go to the Camp.'

'You lie, you young dog,' says Jerry, sobered into ferocity in a moment.

'Oh, no, I don't. I saw you, I say, and you don't come back again. We're honest men here; and, as Captain McGrath says, we don't allow any traitors among us.' He rested the butt of his piece upon the ground, and remained contemplating him satirically. 'You got me lagged once,' said he. 'It's my turn now. You'd better clear out while you have a sound neck.'

On ordinary occasions, it is probable that Jerry would have taken the advice offered in so practical and friendly a spirit, but – under the pretence of patriotism – he had swallowed enough brandy to make him ferocious at being thus baffled. It was now nearly daybreak, and he had promised to return to Frere with the information needed by midnight. It was doubtful even now if he would get any pay, and he knew Frere quite well enough to be certain that, if he did not perform his contract at all, he would be dismissed with ignominy. Now, to lose money on one side, and to be discovered on the other, was too bad.

'Let me in, you young dog,' he growled.

Dick laughed merrily. 'That's likely.'

'Then tell me the pass-word.'

'That's likelier. Go home, old man; go home. You're done this turn.'

He had miscalculated the temper of his man, however. Jerry, placing his foot on a notch in one of the slabs, leapt up, seizing the palisade with his hands, and had flung himself upon the boy almost before the smile had died upon his lips.

'Help! help!' cried Dick, striving to fire his musket; but the old man; mad with rage and liquor, had gripped the piece by the barrel, and before the boy could lower his hands to the trigger, had torn it from him, and swung it back to beat out his brains with the butt.

The manoeuvre was excellent, and would have succeeded, but for one accident. Arthur, who had, of course, overheard the whole colloquy, stepped from out the shadow of the palisade, and caught the murderous arm in mid-air. Jerry turned with a snarl upon his new assailant, and Dick Purfoy, blind with wrath at being thus 'shown up' before his officer, pulled a knife from his boot and drove it into the side of the spy. Jerry let go the musket, and fell with a groan.

'Good God, boy, you've killed him!' said Arthur.

'Have I?' said Dick, with a white face, looking at the bloody knife in Arthur's hand. It had been given him by Arthur some days before, and was the very white-handled one which had so startled Crosbie. 'I did not mean to kill him.'

'Help me to drag him here, then. So. Now, go back to your duty, and be silent. Such a thing as this would alarm the whole Camp for nothing.'

'It was his own fault,' said Dick, sulkily, shouldering his musket. 'What did he jump at me for?'

Arthur went to Carboni.

'Young Purfoy has stabbed that old man,' he said. 'He was right about his being a spy, I think.'

'Is he dead?' asked Carboni.

'Nearly. I am afraid the Camp will be roused. You know what reports there would be. The men would think that the whole Camp was marching on us.'

'Let's bring him in here,' said Carboni. 'He can die here as well as there. Where's Griffiths?'

They went out and brought him in. He was not quite dead, but Griffiths, on seeing him, shook his head.

'Bring me some brandy,' he said, and getting it, poured some down the man's throat. Jerry revived, and opening his eyes, looked about him. The first thing he saw was the white-handled knife which Arthur had brought in with him; and the sight of it lying there, all reddened, seemed to arouse in him a terrible recollection.

'Joe! Joe!' he cried. 'Oh lord, it's Joe!' and fell back again speechless.

The circle stood looking at each other, and presently the old man stretched forth a bony hand, and said in a harsh whisper,

'Money, Joe! Money! I must have money, do you hear?'

'He's wandering,' said Griffiths, again placing the brandy to his lips. 'He won't live long, I'm afraid.'

Jerry seemed to catch the meaning of the sentence, for he roused himself by a great effort.

'What did you say?' he gasped.

'That you'd better make your peace with God Almighty, my man,' said Griffiths. 'You can't live long.'

'Are you sure?' asked Jerry, leaning forward. 'Are you sure of that? I've been told so before, and got well again. Are you sure?'

'Sure? What do you think, you scoundrel?' asked Griffiths, with bitter contempt.

The question would not admit of reply. Indeed, by this hideous test the dying man felt that he was doomed.

'Is there a lawyer here, gentlemen?' said he. 'I want to make a statement.'

A lawyer! It was hardly possible.

'What statement do you want to make?' asked Arthur.

'A confession! Of a crime – a great and horrible crime that – has – haunted me for years, and for which I let an innocent man suffer – Fetch me a lawyer. I want it took down legal – I want –'

'He's gone again,' cries Griffiths. 'More brandy. Run out, Vern, and see if you can't catch a lawyer. Perhaps some poor devil is still suffering for this "ruffian's" crime. There was a man enrolled to-day, a young fellow who said he was a lawyer, I think.'

'I know him,' said Carboni, 'he has the next tent to mine' – and hurrying out he presently returned with the sallow-faced young man, into whose tent Arthur had so unceremoniously burst five nights before. This young man had been an attorney, but being dissipated and of evil repute, had ran away to the diggings.

'Are you a lawyer?' said Jerry.

'Yes.'

'What is your name?' asked Arthur.

'Silas Quaid,' said the young man. 'If the gentleman on the floor has belonged to the thieving profession, which, from his appearance, I should say was not impossible, he may have heard the name before. It belonged to my grandfather, an Old Bailey practitioner of considerable eminence.'

The name, indeed, had produced such an effect upon Jerry that he almost fainted again.

'The man is dying, sir,' said Griffiths, with some sternness. 'This is no time for jesting.'

'Well, then, let us come to business,' said the young Mr Quaid, carelessly. 'Give me a pen, and paper and ink. This is the 30th, isn't it? Good – and your names? I have them. Now, my friend, what is your name?'

'Jeremiah Mogford.'

Young Mr Quaid gave a start, and looked fixedly at his client.

'I have heard my grandfather speak of a man of your name,' said he. 'He kept the Bell in Holborn.'

'That was my brother,' said Jerry, with a groan.

There was no carelessness about Mr Quaid now. He wrote carefully and eagerly, and asked only such questions as were absolutely needful. Amid a silence only broken by the scratching of the lawyer's pen, Jerry told the true story of the murder that had been committed twenty-six years before.

'I had meant to do it,' he said, 'for his jewellery, and climbed up the water-pipe to get in at the window. But when I got up and looked in, he was lying in his blood, with the case of jewels open. The murderer, who had been before me, was bending over him, and fearful lest he should see me, I slid down.'

'Well?' said Mr Quaid, pausing, with his remorseless pen suspended over the paper. 'Go on.'

'I hid myself in a house where I was known until I heard that the trial was over, and that an innocent man was condemned in my place.'

'Monster!' cries Arthur, impelled by some sudden impulse to speak. 'Who was the wretch who suffered in your stead?'

'A man called Rufus Dawes, a sailor,' said the dying man, feebly. 'He was the companion of the German who was murdered. The evidence, it seemed, was not sufficient to hang him, and they sentenced him to transportation for life.'

The scraping of Mr Quaid's pen reiterated 'transportation for life.'

'But who was the murderer?' asked Arthur.

'Ay, who? I have carried the secret long enough. Come closer. I will tell you. It was –'

The candle flickered palely blue against the shadows of the newly-born day. All bent forward to hear the end to this strange confession.

The dying wretch made a last effort, and gripping the pillow with both hands, raised himself nearly erect.

'It was –'

At that moment a sharp sound broke the silence. A musket-shot! And, winding far above them in the pure morning air, rang the notes of a bugle. All started to their feet.

An Alarm! To arms! The attack on the stockade had begun! and amid the crackle of musketry and the shouting of the surprised camp, the three insurgents rushed out of the tent.

There was left only the dying penitent and the lawyer.

'Well?' said the latter, unmoved. 'Go on. It was – ?'

The other whispered a name, and fell back.

Silas Quaid entered the name gravely on his papers, and turning to question his strange client further, found that he was alone.

Jerry Mogford was dead.

The rattle of musketry grew louder and louder, and putting his documents together, the lawyer left the corpse staring at the newly-risen day.

⚁ 16 ⚁

DORCAS MEETS A FRIEND

At six o'clock on the evening of the 18th of December, a well-appointed mail-waggon drove into the stable-yard of the Criterion Hotel, in Collins-street. The stables were full of horses, and the hotel was full of people.

'Private rooms!' said the landlord. 'We don't let private rooms.'

'I will pay,' said Crosbie.

'How many do you want?'

'Two bedrooms and a sitting-room, with attendance and board, for a week.'

'There's a lady here,' said the landlord, persuasively, 'who is going home by the mail, and *she* only has one room.'

'How much?' was Crosbie's only question.

'Fifty pounds for the week – all drinks extra.'

'Very well.'

The landlord looked disgusted. 'Made his pile, I suppose. I wish I'd asked more now.'

The rooms, if dear, were comfortable; and Crosbie, sitting down to an excellent dinner, began to feel easier in his mind.

'Come, Dotty, we have got out of our troubles at last.'

Poor Dotty, torn with terrors about her lover, did not make immediate reply.

'You look tired, my dear. No wonder. You must go early to bed, and get a good night's rest.'

'Where are we going, father? You do not mean to stop here?'

'I am going to buy a house and garden, Dot, somewhere in the country, and we will do nothing all day but strive to make each other happy.'

There was such an accent of tenderness in his voice that the girl's heart smote her.

'No more work, or trouble, Dot,' Crosbie continued. 'I have made enough money to keep us both comfortably during the rest of our days. We will live together quietly, dear, and love each other as we used to do. Ah, God has been good to suffer me to realise at last this dream of my life.'

He drew her to him and kissed her on the forehead.

The loving touch of his lips gave her courage.

'Oh, Daddy dear, I am a wicked girl,' she cried, falling on her knees at his feet. 'I am not worthy your love for me. I have deceived you.'

'Dorcas! What do you mean?'

'About Arthur Vern. I said I did not love him. I said what was not true. I do love him, and I have told him so.'

Rufus Dawes turned pale. Had not ill-fortune done with him yet? In the very hour of his self-gratulation, when the peaceful ambition he had so long cherished seemed about to be gratified, must he learn that the child of his adoption had given her heart to another? It was hard.

'Oh, forgive me, dear! I should have told you, but he made me promise; he —'

'*He* made you promise!' Rufus Dawes burst out. 'Who is he to make you promise such a thing? To take advantage of your youth and tenderness to make you deceive your father. He is not worthy of your love, no, nor of the love of any honest woman. Let me hear no more of this.'

'But, father,' she sobbed, 'he is so unhappy. He should have been rich and a man of mark in England, and accident drove him here.'

'Let him bear it,' said Crosbie, sternly. 'Other men have borne burdens as heavy, and not complained.'

'But he loves me. He does, father, and I love him. Oh, my dear daddy, I cannot help it. How can we help our lives! My mother could not help loving you, I suppose?'

The stab so unconsciously given struck the unhappy man to the heart. After all, by what authority did *he* presume to question her right to love when she chose. He unfastened her clinging hands, and paced the room.

'You should have told me this before, Dorcas. It is too late now.'

'Too late! Why?'

'Because your lover has become a rebel and a criminal. Did you not hear at Bacchus Marsh about the attack on the troops? If he had loved you, he would not have uselessly perilled his life with rioters.'

'You are unjust, father,' cries she, with flashing eyes. 'They are not rioters, you know it. They are men fighting for their liberties, and Arthur did *right* to join them.'

Compare this with her adjurations to Arthur *not* to join, and wonder at feminine consistency.

'Then let him stay with them, and share the punishment of

their folly,' retorted Rufus Dawes, his natural violence of temper getting the better of his judgment. 'When you hear that he has been shot through the head by some booby of a trooper, you will regret these heroics.'

The picture thus presented to her instantly changed the current of her thoughts. The spectacle of Arthur, wounded and bloody, swam in a mist of tears before her eyes. She advanced and caught her father's hands.

'Oh, father, save him! You can! Let us go back.'

'Go back!'

'Yes, back to Ballarat. I will persuade him. You shall order him. We will get him out of that place, and –'

'And then? Then you will leave me for him.'

She disregarded this selfish speech. It seemed to her so strange that men cannot understand what different sort of love a woman bears to her husband and to her father. Arthur had upbraided her for loving her father to his own detriment, and here was her father angry lest she should love him less than Arthur.

'You will save him, Daddy dear? Go at once. I will wait here, if you wish; but bring him back with you.'

The proposition was certainly alarming. After having fled from Ballarat, like a thief in the night, because of impending trouble, to be asked to go back again without delay. After having escaped by a miracle the sharp eyes of Maurice Frere – the man who boasted that he 'never forgot a face' – to be called upon to deliberately place himself within his grasp. After having succeeded in avoiding inquisition into his past life, to be requested to place himself in a position which would probably necessitate an appearance at the Supreme Court, and a cross-examination by a Crown prosecutor.

'It is quite out of the question, Dorcas. I cannot go to Ballarat. Mr Vern must take his chance with other men. There, go to bed and sleep, child. We will talk this over to-morrow.'

It was useless to argue further with him then, and Dorcas felt it to be so. She turned her face upwards for the nightly kiss without a word, and went to her own room.

Rufus Dawes rang the bell for brandy – as a rule he never drank spirits – and, lighting his pipe, set to work to puzzle out a satisfactory end to this new complication. The landlord, who slept in the next room, wondered what manner of man a customer could be, who, paying £2 for a bed, chose to spend the night walking up and down the sitting-room.

Dorcas, on her part, had thrown herself on the bed in tears. She was not used to weeping; but the fatigues of the journey, her fears concerning her lover, and the interview with her father, had unstrung her nerves. What was to be done? What would Arthur think of her? He might never get her note. He might be killed. Perhaps even now he was lying dead beneath the mocking folds of the Southern Cross banner, which her own fingers had embroidered. How could she help him? Her reverie was broken by a knock, followed by the rustle of a silk dress.

'I beg your pardon,' said a soft voice, 'but I occupy the next room to this, and I heard you sobbing.'

Dorcas sat up and looked at the speaker — evidently the notable lady who was going home by the mail — a tall well-preserved woman of about forty-five years of age, dressed richly in black, and bearing her candle in a white shapely hand which twinkled with rings of price.

'My name is Mrs Carr. Can I help you?'

At the prospect of comfort and converse with one of her own sex, Dorcas's tears burst out afresh.

Mrs Carr softly advanced, caressing her.

'What is it, my dear? There, don't cry. Who is he?'

'How do you know there is a "he" at all?' asked Dotty indignantly, through her tears.

'Somebody used to say to every tale of misfortune, "Who is she?" meaning that a woman must be at the bottom of the mischief. Somebody was a man, of course. Now, I being a woman, whenever I see a woman crying, ask, "Who is he?" because I think that a *man* must be at the bottom of it.'

Dotty smiled.

'He is Arthur Vern, and my lover,' she said simply.

A change came over Mrs Carr's comely face, and her black eyes sparkled.

'Come into my room and talk it over,' she said.

And almost before Dorcas realised the fact, she was sitting

at a little table, covered with letters and papers, listening to her neighbour.

'The room is a little in disorder, Miss? – Crosbie, thanks, – Miss Crosbie, because I am going to England to-morrow by the mail, and have been packing my things. But you can find a chair somewhere. Now, tell me, how old is this Arthur Vern of yours?'

'He is about twenty-two, I think.'

'With fair hair, and beard, blue eyes, rather muscular.'

'You know him then?'

'No; I've heard of him from a friend of mine.'

She glanced, as she spoke, towards the papers which loaded the table, and her eye seemed to indicate a letter signed 'Kenneth McNab,' which was lying on the top of the bundle.

'Did Mr Vern ever tell you anything about his early life, Miss Crosbie?'

'No,' says Dorcas, getting a little frightened. 'He only said that he had been always told that he was to be a rich man, and that an uncle, thought to be dead, suddenly returned to England and took all the money. That is all he told me.'

Mrs Carr smiled with apparent satisfaction.

'Did he tell you his uncle's name?'

'No.'

'Nor describe him in any way?'

'No.'

'You don't know whether he is tall or short, fair or dark, eh?'

'No, madam.'

'Don't be frightened, dear child. I am only asking out of kindness sake. I mistrust all men, from my own experience of them.'

Dorcas looked at the black dress.

'You are a widow?' she asked, softly.

'No, a deserted wife. I am going to England to find my husband.'

Dorcas felt uneasy at the tone with which the word 'find' was uttered. If Mrs Carr had said 'kill,' she could not have pronounced it more vindictively.

'A deserted wife. Ah, then, you have reason to mistrust men.'

'Ay, but the circumstances of my desertion are curious. What should you say to a man who, when a woman has saved him from death — and a fate worse than death — has endowed him with fortune and studied nothing her life through but to please him, basely deserts her, not for another love, but for money?'

'Such a wretch is not a man,' said Dorcas.

'Such a wretch is my husband. Five years ago he put in execution a plan he must have carried in his black heart for years before — robbed me and left me. Under a changed name he gained — by robbing others — wealth and station in England. He thought, perhaps, that I should forget him. *Forget!* I am rich. I prosecuted enquiries everywhere. In America, England, and the Continent my agents were at work. I vowed I would spend my last shilling in feeing a detective but I would hunt this man down and be revenged upon him. Now I have found him. This is he!'

She snatched from among the papers an illustrated journal — some Sunday organ of sporting opinion — and pointed to a portrait engraved on the centre page. It represented a broad-shouldered, bushy-whiskered man, dressed in the fashion affected by turfites and lovers of horseflesh, standing beside a pedestal on which were piled a variety of racing cups and trophies. Dorcas read underneath this work of art the name

MR RICHARD DEVINE,

The Leviathan of the Turf

and the

Richest Commoner in England

Little guessing upon what a discovery she had stumbled, Dorcas handed back the paper with the brief remark,

'And that is your husband?'

'That is my husband. I had reason to cry for men, you see. Now tell me what wrong Mr Vern has done to you.'

'No wrong,' said Dorcas. 'I was crying because he is in danger and I am not with him.'

'In danger. Where?'

'He is one of the rioters at Ballarat, and I am afraid he will get into trouble.'

'But why did you not bring him down with you? You came down to-day, did you not?'

'My father does not like him.'

'Indeed, and pray why not?'

'Do not ask me. I – I cannot tell. I think it is because he loves me so well that he cannot bear to think another person should share my affection.'

'How like a man,' said Mrs Carr, leaning back in her chair to laugh a little laugh. 'Selfishness is their ruling passion.'

Dorcas rose with a faint flush in her cheeks. 'My father is not selfish, madam. You do not know him. I think I will go. I fear I have said too much, perhaps.'

Mrs Carr laid a hand upon her arm. 'I did not mean to offend you, my dear. How quick-tempered you are.'

The crimson in the girl's cheeks grew deeper, and all her father's evil spirit arose within her. 'I will go myself to Ballarat and save him.'

'What, alone! Nonsense, child!'

'I have thought of it coming down. Arthur loves me, and my duty is to save him. My father will forgive me when I return.'

'But how will you go?'

'I will ride,' said the bush-bred girl, calmly. 'Those horses go in saddle, I know. I can make the journey in two days.'

'But you will not start to-night?'

'This instant.'

Mrs Carr felt her heart – such as it was – thrill with pity for the high-spirited child, and going to her she put her arms about her. 'I will help you, my dear. But you must not go to-night. It would be folly. To ride alone in the darkness, with a tired horse and the roads in the state they are. You goose, you would never get half way. Listen, and I will tell you what to do.'

'Well,' said Dorcas, twisting her hands together, 'tell me. Go I must, and will.'

'Lie down until day-light. Then go down to the stable and get your horses. Here is money, see – tush, I have plenty – the groom will lend you a saddle if you pay him. I will give you a riding-skirt. You leave a note for your father telling him what you have done, and when he gets it you will be thirty miles on the road. You can reach the Camp at Ballarat by noon on Saturday.'

'I think I can.'

'Well, then, go and lie down.' She wrote a few lines at the table and sealed the envelope. 'Here is a present — shall I say a wedding present? — for you. Don't open it until you meet Mr Vern, and then ask him to read it to you.'

Dorcas took the paper, and, moved by sudden impulse, kissed her strange friend. 'I don't know who you are, madam, but you are a good woman.'

Honest tears started to Sarah Purfoy's eyes.

'There, never mind my goodness, we shan't see each other any more, I daresay. Good night, and good luck.'

There is no need to detail the process by which Rufus Dawes solved the problem he was working. It was broad daylight when he flung himself on his bed, a conqueror in the struggle with his selfishness. 'Her mother called me "Good Mr Dawes," ' he thought; 'she gave her into my arms, and I will not abuse the trust. She loves this young man. It is natural for young folks to love each other. What am I that I should seek to engage the whole heart of a girl? North, my friend, my saviour, by whose death I have lived again, help me! I will save him for her.'

Calm in his self-sacrifice, prepared to see the flush of pleasure with which she would greet him, he knocked at Dorcas's door.

No reply.

He knocked again.

No reply.

A cold hand seized his heart. He flung wide the door. The room was empty. On the table lay a note.

Dear Father — I have gone to save Arthur. You need not follow me.
Your loving child,

DOTTY.

For a moment he stood speechless. The blow was too cruel. He felt the keen ridicule of his position. He had been all night making up his mind to grant a favour, and, lo! it had been taken without his permission. It was as though he had gone with his heart in his hand to offer it up as a sacrifice, and was met by a slap in the face. He felt his ears tingle at the insult. Crushing the note in his hand, he turned angrily to leave the chamber. How much greater was her love for this boy, whom she saw but yesterday, than for him who had nursed her from childhood! Then the thought of the poor child's loneliness and misery, the desperation of her love, the madness of her journey came upon him, and melted all his anger into pity.

'Poor Dotty,' said he, smoothing out the letter. 'And did you think that I would *not* follow you?'

In another instant he was in the stables.

'My horses!'

'The young lady took 'em,' said the groom with a grin. 'She said it was all right.'

'True,' said Rufus Dawes, unmoved. 'I had forgotten. Get me others.'

The man stared — much as Ball Hughes' groom might have stared when his master cried, 'More phaetons!'

'Where from, sir?'

'Anywhere. Have you none on hire?'

'No.'

'Then I must buy a pair, I suppose,' and he strode into the hotel.

The groom, looking after him, remarked only, 'Another — nugget, I suppose!'

Rufus Dawes pushed his way down the 'long room', filled with lucky diggers, speculators, and new arrivals, drinking, smoking, and talking. He caught the landlord by the sleeve, and distracted him from a 'nobbler.'

'See here. I want a pair of horses at once. Cash, of course. I may be away a few days. I'll keep the rooms and pay in advance, if you like.'

'You're the sort,' said the landlord, briefly. 'Bottomed a jeweller's shop, eh?'

'Can I have the horses?'

'Of course. Fifty, if you like to pay for 'em. You can have the Bank of Australasia, if you like to buy it, I suppose.'

'What terms?'

'Deposit £50, and you can have a pair of horses for five pound a-day. Will that suit you?'

'Give me a receipt and some breakfast.'

'Tom, give the gentleman a receipt for fifty notes, and tell them to put the brown cobs into his trap. As for breakfast, sir,' he continued, with some respect, 'you must get that yourself. It's first come first served here, you see. Nobblers for ten! — Right you are!'

As Mr Crosbie drove out of the yard with the brown cobs, he saw at one of the windows a face which caused him a moment's pang of hesitant recollection.

'That can't be the woman of the *Malabar*,' he thought. 'Yet it is quite likely. All the world is here. I must get out of this town. I should as soon have thought to see that villain Rex rise again from the dead. Oh, Dotty, let me find you safe, and we will put away these memories.'

If the remorseless fate that had pursued him so long had but relented now, and suffered him to discover that the woman he saw would, in an hour, be on her way to England to claim as husband, the man who, unknown to him, was occupying his name and heritage!

↞ 17 ↠

THE ATTACK ON THE STOCKADE

THE non-appearance of the spy had confirmed Captain Frere's desire to hurry on the attack.

'The fellows are warned,' said he to McNab. 'If we wait much longer, they will have entrenched themselves. As it is, one determined rush will carry the place, and restore order.'

'I am afraid of the excited feeling of the men,' said McNab. 'They are most incensed against the diggers.'

'My dear fellow,' says Frere, 'they will be more incensed to-morrow and next day. Take my advice, and let's have it over.'

So, in the calm Sabbath dawn, two hundred men advanced upon the Stockade. Out of this two hundred, ninety were troopers, and the rest infantry. McNab himself commanded a detachment of eighty-seven men. The attack was made in this wise. The mounted police, among whom was Fred Flite, advanced upon the right. McNab held a reserve of the 12th and 40th at the Free Trade Hotel, from which advanced the storming party under Captain Frere. A mounted detachment of the 40th occupied the high ground on the left of the palisades. The Stockade was thus attacked on three sides simultaneously.

The attack was so sudden and decisive that it took all the insurgents by surprise. The forces within did not muster above a hundred men, but at the first note of alarm they stood manfully to their arms. The shepherds' holes inside the lower part of the stockade were occupied by the Revolver Brigade, some thirty men in all, and they opened fire at once on the head of the column. American Joe, under cover of the slabs, picked off three men before McGrath checked him.

'Hold your fire, for heaven's sake,' he cried, 'until they are close to us. Now then! Now!'

Arthur and the others, rushing from the tent where self-possessed Quaid was still alone with the corpse of the spy, saw at once that resistance was hopeless.

'Steady!' cried McGrath, in despair. 'Steady! and we'll drive them back, though they are ten to one.'

The rifles rang again, and were answered by a volley of musketry. The troopers from the north, and the mounted soldiers from the south, broke into a trot. 'Forward!' cried Frere, waving his sword; and as he spoke a bullet from Dick Purfoy shattered it to the hilt.

'Well aimed, youngster,' roared McGrath, leaping on the slabs. 'Don't show yourselves, men. Down among the holes, and fire low!' As he spoke, his left arm fell useless to his side, and Arthur caught him in his arms. 'Never mind me, boy. Put me down, anywhere. That will do. Now slap at them!'

A tearing volley staggered the advancing column. But only for an instant. A little boy-bugler on the left of the gully jumped gallantly upon a stump and tootle-tooed the 'advance.' The line belched with flame, and a shower of ball-cartridge, poured in at pistol-shot, mowed down all who showed their heads above the barricade. Griffiths fell, shot in the mouth; American Joe, wounded in the thigh, hopped about, shrieking Yankee defiance, and firing incessantly.

'Pikes there! Pikes!' cried poor McGrath, raising himself on his right arm. 'Arthur, keep them steady, for God's sake.'

The red-coats were now within twenty yards of the stockade.

'Charge!' they heard Frere cry; and the next instant a mass of troopers and soldiers came tumbling in over the barricade, shouting and yelling, with fixed bayonets.

There passed an heroic five minutes. The insurgents fought like wild cats. McGrath, prostrate, plunged his pike upwards, as did Eliezer when he fought the elephant. Griffiths, spitting his grinders on the ground, twice drove back the pressing troops from the point he defended. Carboni, pierced by a bayonet, grasped the musket barrel with his hands, and wriggling himself along the weapon that pierced him, placed his revolver to his assailant's ear, and, with a choice Italian curse, blew out his brains, falling dead with him. Dick Purfoy grasped Frere by the knees, and plunging a pistol muzzle into his face, pulled the trigger. The weapon missed fire, and Frere, savagely striking the lad with his clenched fist, flung him to a trooper to hold.

'You'll work on the roads for that, you young whelp,' said he. 'Down with the flag, men! Down with it!'

But the standard was not so easily taken. Out-numbered, out-generalled, devoid of ammunition, and with their leaders dead about them, the diggers made one desperate rally round the emblem of their brief freedom. Arthur was the centre of this group, and resolving to sell his life dearly, set his back against the pole. For three seconds all was smoke and flame. Then, from out the livid and hideous *mêlée*, a slight figure, with fair hair back blown, and blue eyes laughing at danger, leapt, sword in hand. Two slashes at the cord, and the gay ensign was flapping down upon and embarassing its defenders. Fred Flite, as eager as though he were at football, caught it as it descended, and tore it from the pole. As he bent forwards, the grog-seller of the day before plunged his pike into his back, and he fell, rolling the silk about his body. Arthur, with a curse, shot the pikeman in the breast.

'Thanks, old boy,' gasped Freddy. 'These cads always take — take — advantage of a gentleman!'

So, wrapped in the blue and silver folds of the insurgent standard, gallant Don Rinaldo died.

The sinking of the standard was the signal for flight. To struggle longer was clearly hopeless, and flinging down their arms, the diggers fled in all directions. In a few seconds more, the little mound at the foot of the flagstaff was crimson with shouting soldiers, who dragged the 'Southern Cross' through the dust, as though it was a prize torn from a May-pole.

So far so good. The authorities had conquered in fair fight, and the sympathy of honest folk must of necessity go with them. Had they paused content with their victory, the most disaffected among the insurgents could not have complained. But to the angry hearts and smarting wounds of the long-suffering troopers, a corrosive unguent was not wanting. Captain Maurice Frere, bleeding from a sabre-cut across the face, was in no mood for generosity.

'Take those dogs to the lock-up,' he roared, pointing with his broken sword to the group of vanquished, into which Dick Purfoy had been roughly thrust, 'and let us give Joe a lesson!'

A shout of acclamation went up; and Frere, seizing a brand from the large fire which had been burning in the centre of the stockade, fired the nearest tent. His example was speedily followed. In a few moments, the wooden huts and tents within the stockade were blazing ten yards high. The howling and yelling that ensued upon the perpetration of this devil's work was terrible. The wounded who had crawled into the shelter of the tents were burned to death. A frightful odour of roast-meat caused Arthur, crouching, with a shattered wrist, in the gully beyond Crosbie's Store, to turn deadly sick. The madness of slaughter seemed to have seized upon the victors. The prisoners, enclosed in a hollow square, were marched through the ruins of their homes. As they walked, the blood dropped from many. Now and then one fell. The troopers shouted to each other, 'We've waked up Joe!' 'Ay, and sent Joe to sleep again!'[1] The 'Southern Cross,' reeling through the air, was pitched from one to the other, and trampled upon until its blue brightness was extinguished in blood and mire. Carts were brought for the bodies. On the slope in front of the barricade lay fifteen corpses, with their wounds in front. Where he fell, Griffiths lay, with his pike in his hand. He yet breathed, and at every heave of his

1. *Geelong Advertiser*, December 5, 1854.

chest the blood bubbled. His mouth was full of bullets. Carboni
lay stretched upon the soldier he killed. The bayonet, snapped
at the hilt, protruded from between his shoulders. The body of
American Joe was further to the right. A little terrier that he
owned sat upon the breast of it, howling. When they flung the
carcase with the others into the cart, the dog jumped in, and
licking the dead man's face, sat shivering and crying. The
diggings were cowed into horror-stricken submission. From
adjoining tents they brought rags, handkerchiefs, and bed
furniture, to cover the faces of the dead.

McGrath, lying on a rug behind the slabs of a sort of cellar
at Crosbie's, had intelligence brought him of this massacre, and,
groaning, tore his bandages, praying that he might not survive
the followers he had deluded. Young Quaid, with an air of
raven-like complacency on his sallow face, sat beside him, con-
ning over the deposition of Jerry Mogford.

'You'd have been President to the Australian Republic if
you'd been successful,' said he, by way of consolation. 'It's all
accident, my dear sir. Man, as my grandfather used to say, is
the creature of circumstances. He might have meant,' he continued, below his breath, glancing at the papers in his hands,
'the creature of circumstantial evidence.'

⁘ 18 ⁘

PER HOSTES

MEANWHILE poor Arthur, lurking dismally in his gully, had
leisure to reflect upon Radicalism. It was nearly noon. He
had tasted nothing since the previous evening. He was exhausted from loss of blood, and the pain of his wound was
intense. Added to these evils, was the terror of his position, the
uncertainty as to the fate of his comrades, and the mental torture
of losing his love. As he lay beneath the boughs that sheltered
the watercourse, he renewed his reflections upon the conduct of
Crosbie, and came more decidedly than ever to the conclusion
that Crosbie was a traitor. Gnashing his teeth in futile rage, he
vowed that, did he escape, he would make it his business to

hunt down Crosbie and exact from him a bitter reckoning. Escape! Why should he escape? He was a wanderer and an alien. He had been deprived of fortune, and forced to quit his country. Here, having foregone his claims to consideration, and set himself to manual labour, if haply by it he might win from the golden ground a second birthright and return to succour the dear ones left behind, he had been despited and trodden down. He rose against tyrants, and tyrants conquered him. He loved, and his love had been torn from him. He was twenty-two, and had fasted seventeen hours. Life had clearly no more charms for him. Honour, love-sickness, and an empty stomach demanded that he should die.

He got stiffly out of his hiding place, and clambered up the crumbling red clay of the little gorge. A young man sitting on the top, philosophically smoking, saluted him.

'Hallo, mate. Another Joseph coming out of the pit?'

Arthur recognised the self-possessed 'lawyer,' who had taken the deposition of the spy on the previous night.

'What has happened? Where is McGrath?'

'Why, it's the Secretary of State!' cries young Mr Quaid, 'and wounded, too. Here, have a sup of this.'

Arthur took a pull at the flask, and then stood upright.

'Dead, I suppose,' he said, interpreting Quaid's silence concerning McGrath in the gloomiest manner, 'like the rest. I only have escaped – to skulk into a hole like a poisoned rat.'

'If you are going to air your conscience, my dear Mr Secretary, I can't help you. The sovereignest thing on earth, a high authority informs us, is parmaceti for an *inward* bruise; but as I haven't any of that unguent by me, allow me to recommend brandy.'

'Is he dead, man? – can't you speak out?'

'No, my dear sir; he is not dead. I've just come from his temporary residence of slabs, where, wrapped in his martial cloak, the Commander in Chief of the Army of the League has been hiding from the "traps." A worthy young surgeon, who came out to these colonies with me – which his name, as Mrs Gamp would say, is Pine – is at present attending him. The President is likely to recover; but the young surgeon, with that laudable desire to improve in the practice of his profession which should characterise all young surgeons, strongly advises amputation of the left arm.'

Having delivered this apparently heartless speech, Mr Quaid again tendered the flask.

'This is no time for tomfoolery, sir!' cries Arthur, with heat. 'McGrath is safe?'

'Of course, you very sensible young Solon, or *I* should not be here. Dr Pine, F.R.C.S., X.Y.Z., Student of Guy's, and myself carried him to the hut of a worthy friend of ours, and eluded the pursuit of the myrmidons of justice with some difficulty in consequence.'

Arthur began to comprehend that the good-hearted young man was affecting to be a bad-hearted old one, and held out his hand with frank apology. 'Forgive me; but —'

'But you had better "make tracks," as poor Joe used to say. Have another nip, and then steady your nerves to read something. Come here my Mucius Scævola, and tell me if I shall make a little pocket-money.'

He led him to a big gum-tree that overhung the Melbourne Road, and there, nailed on its gnarled trunk, was a canvas placard, on which was painted the following: —

V.  **R.**

£500 REWARD

FOR THE APPREHENSION OF
ARTHUR VERN.

———

WHEREAS

A man known by the name of VERN has unlawfully, rebelliously, and traitorously levied and arrayed Armed Men at Ballarat, in the Colony of Victoria, with the view of making war against Our Sovereign Lady the QUEEN:

NOTICE IS HEREBY GIVEN

That whoever will give such information as may lead to the apprehension of the said VERN, shall receive

A REWARD OF £500.

Arthur stopped short at the description of his person which followed, and turned a blank look upon Quaid.

However bold a man may be, he is not likely to read such a statement unmoved.

Quaid watched his eye.

'They say that there is a wonderful charm in seeing one's name in print for the first time,' said he. 'You don't seem to experience any extraordinary delight, at any rate.'

Arthur, crimson with rage, made a step as though to tear down the obnoxious placard, but the other caught his arm.

'Don't be an ass,' he remarked. 'What is the good of pulling it down? There are plenty more about. McGrath figures in one a foot bigger than this. They say that Frere has seized upon the news office, arrested poor little Seacole for "sedition," and is printing these things with the biggest wood-blocks in stock. That is what is called Military Promptitude. However, you needn't alarm yourself for half an hour. Heroes must eat as well as common men, and the Army is at dinner just now.'

Arthur, despite all the misery past, present, and future, could not but smile at this young philosopher.

'That's right, my boy. Laugh and grow fat. I used to laugh once, but a too enthusiastic attention to the study of the law has afflicted me with a pernicious gravity. Come to my tent – if it isn't burnt, by the way – and have some cold mutton, if the Lord Chancellor hasn't broken loose and eaten it.'

On their way to the tent – in front of which the Lord Chancellor, a most ferocious-looking mongrel, was yapping and yowing, tearing at his collar the while – Arthur's notice was attracted by two clouds of dust which appeared to be approaching them from the Melbourne road. The first cloud moved slowly, and dissipated itself, as it were, in little low, curling vapours. The second cloud, denser in volume, ascended more rapidly and hung high in air. The first appearance was caused by some horseman easily cantering a horse; the second, by some heavy vehicle driven at a furious speed. As he shaded his eyes with his hand in order to distinguish the persons of those approaching, Quaid clutched his arm.

'Look the other way, man!' he cried.

Arthur turned and saw, galloping up the rise to the breach in the Stockade, a small party of mounted men. The flashing of steel accoutrements proclaimed their errand.

'The troopers!'

Quaid whipped out his consolatory flask, and pressed it to the young man's lips.

'Run, my boy, run,' he whispered. 'Down the hill with you, and across the road – it's your only chance!'

He spoke truly, and the pair, dodging among the red mullock heaps, so as to place the sheltering hill between themselves and the rebel-hunters, made for the road as hard as their legs could carry them. As they gained it, Arthur uttered a cry, and bounded past Quaid like a tennis ball. The rider of the cantering horse was a woman, and that woman was Dorcas!

In another instant she was in his arms.

'Dotty! You here! In Heaven's name –'

'Hush! Not a word. Thank God I have found you in time. Mount. He is fresh; I rode the other most of the way. See! they come. Quick, Arthur, quick. My father would have stopped me, but I have beaten him. Quick; mount, I say! What is this? Your arm! Oh, Heaven, you are wounded! Am I too late? Arthur! dear Arthur!'

Red with dust, white with fatigue and terror, the Lily clung to his neck. From the one side approached Crosbie, his horses galloping as the horses of an enraged father might reasonably be presumed to gallop. From the other broke the jangling of the troopers, and the voice of some one yet concealed by the hill shouted, 'By twos! Trot!'

Arthur, in blank amazement, kissed the upturned face of his recovered love, and glanced from the one side to the other, irresolute.

'Mount!' she cried, passionately, untwisting his arms. 'Mount, for dear love's sake!'

'I cannot leave you like this,' says Arthur, still holding her.

Mr Prell's bay horse, scenting the approach of his kind, neighed and plucked the bridle. The hoof-strokes of the coming troop seemed to shake the ground.

Young Mr Quaid arrived breathless, like Horace's *deus ex machinâ*, a little late for his part.

'Mount! You confounded idiot, mount!' he gasped. 'There's

time enough for kissing when you're safe. The traps'll be here
in five seconds, and I swear I'll get the five hundred, and give
you up.'

Thus adjured by common sense, Arthur pressed the girl in
his arms, swung himself to saddle, and dashed into the timber.

Crosbie, furiously lashing his horses, passed within hands-
breadth of him.

'Ride, boy, ride!' he shouted. 'You carry her heart with you.
Save it, if you are a man!'

Dorcas, with outstretched arms, and eyes glazing with
weariness, staggered to the side of the suddenly-checked waggon. 'You are too late, father. He is safe!'

Rufus Dawes, stopping, caught her to his heart with one
powerful arm, as if she were still the child he fain would have
her. 'I am too late, indeed, my darling, for it was *I* who would
have saved him.'

'Father!'

The troopers topped the hill.

Mr Quaid had dived into a convenient hole, and Captain
Maurice Frere saw only a mail-waggon, containing a well-
dressed man of middle age and a young girl.

'It is Mr Crosbie, the storekeeper, your honour,' said
O'Donovan.

'He did well to sell his store, I'm thinking,' said another.

And Frere, with a harsh 'Silence!' clattered up the road,
regardless.

Dorcas watched his retreating figure with terror in her eyes.

'Father, have I ever seen that man before? He frightens me!'

'Hush, my dear!' says Rufus Dawes, drawing a long breath.
'Let us hope all frightenings are over now. There – sit still –
we will have your story another time. I was harsh to you last
night, but we are friends yet, dear, are we not?'

'Oh, daddy!' and she hid her face on his heart.

When the road was clear, Mr Quaid emerged, still smoking,
from his hole.

'I don't like these sort of games,' soliloquised the young
philosopher; 'they are too romantic for a member of the honor-

able association of attorneys. 'Gad! how she hung round his neck, though! I'll cut digging, and go into practice. The old bird seems a rum sort. I wonder what *her* name is? Young Vern is an ass. We're all asses, more or less — creatures of circumstances. I'll certainly cut digging. *Effodiuntur opes, irritamenta malorum.* Glad I've not forgotten my Eton Latin Grammar. Quite a chance I learnt Latin. Circumstance again! Hullo! what's this?'

It was Sarah Purfoy's note, which had fallen unheeded from Dorcas's dress.

'A billy dux, as showed as how, by poison, she died with her tooral-lol, tooral-lol. No address upon it. Let us discover:

Mr ARTHUR VERN, If your name, as I am assured it is, is Arthur Devine, communicate in three months' time with S.P., care of Messrs. Purkiss and Quaid, 2 Thavies Inn, London, and you will hear of something much to your advantage.

A woman's writing; worded like the second column of the *Times*, and addressed to my uncle's firm. As the friend of Arthur Vern, and the Australian representative of the noted firm of Purkiss and Quaid, I consider myself justified, dear S. P., in taking charge of your mysterious message.'

And, leisurely strolling homewards, the grandson of the man who had defended Rufus Dawes placed the letter, which had for its purpose the restoring of Richard Devine to his fortune, side by side with the confession which, made in Crosbie's store, told the true story of the murder at the Bell.

The elder Mr Quaid had truly some grounds for observing that men are the creatures of circumstance.

BOOK SEVEN

MR RICHARD DEVINE AT HOME

ON the evening of the 26th May, 1855 – that memorable day when Mr Richard Devine's 'Pretender' won the Derby – Miss Lucy Devine and her niece sat alone in the drawing-room of their lodgings in Gloucester-place, Portman-square.

'I am sure, my dear girl, that it would be the best thing to do,' said Miss Lucy. 'He could not refuse.'

'I would not ask him for a penny!' cried Adelaide, with flashing eyes. 'I'd serve in a shop first.'

'But, my dear, you are growing up, and you ought to be brought "out", you know,' sighed poor Miss Lucy. 'I am afraid that, with my small income –'

'He is a wretch,' says Addy. 'I hate him. The great, gross, horseracing monster! No, auntie; I'd rather go and join poor Arthur, wherever *he* is. Fancy the poor boy hiding from the police for two months!'

'Well, everybody was pardoned at last, you know – he told us so in the letter – so it will only be a lesson to him. *Your* future, my dear child, is of far more importance. If your uncle now would only make some allowance –'

'I hope to goodness he won't, and then we'll go to Germany, auntie – won't we?'

'I hope he will, my dear,' said Aunt Lucy. 'If he does not, the Continent will be the best place for us. Living is cheaper there, and –'

'And I may marry a Count, like Annie Sartoris. She is the Gräfinn von Himmelshaüsen. Not that I want to be married; I am content to live with you all my life, auntie.'

Miss Lucy shook her head.

'I shall call upon your uncle tomorrow, and if he does not consent, we will write to Madame Blinzler.'

'Why not go and stay with *her*, auntie?'

'My dear, I have no claim upon her, save that she was my governess. I have not written to her for ten years; besides, she lives in Holland.'

'Delightful! Canals, and black tulips, and windmills, and – and beer, and – well, I don't think I should like to live in Holland. Why doesn't she go to her friends at Esslingen?'

'She lives with an invalid sister who has a house there,' said Miss Lucy. 'They are not rich people, and probably cannot afford to change their residence.'

'Well,' returned Addy, looking round upon the sordid little chamber – the ragged horse-hair sofa, the comfortless chairs, the ricketty card-table, the tasteless chimney ornaments, the threadbare carpet – taking in with one comprehensive look of disgust all the meanness of the abode to which her reverse of fortune had doomed her, 'I don't much care where we go, so that it be away from these horrid lodging-houses. Go and see that dreadful uncle and have it settled, dear, one way or the other.'

The town house of the 'Leviathan of the Turf' was in Clarges-street. Not that the very modest mansion there situated was the only establishment which owned Richard Devine as master. Mr John Rex, upon whose shoulders the fleshy mantle of Richard Devine had fallen, had – as we know – expensive tastes. He neither 'shot' nor 'hunted', so he had no capital invested in Scotch moors or Leicestershire hunting-boxes. But his tables were the wonder of London, he owned almost a racing village near Doncaster, kept a yacht at Cowes, and in addition to a house in Paris, paid the rent of a villa at Brompton. He was member of several clubs of the faster sort, and might have lived like a prince at any one of them had he been so minded, but the constant and haunting fear of discovery – a fear which five years of unquestioned ease and unbridled riot had not dispelled – led him to prefer the privacy of his own house, where he could choose his own society. He rarely visited Mere, and when he did so, he mixed but with such of the surrounding gentry as shared his coarser tastes. The library and picture-gallery – upon which Mr Francis Devine had expended £15,000 – were deserted in favour of the billiard-room upon which Mr Richard had expended only £1,500.

The house in Clarges-street was decorated in conformity with the tastes of its owner. The pictures were pictures of horses, the books were records of races, or novels purporting to describe sporting life. Miss Lucy, waiting for the advent of her rich brother on the morning following the conversation, sighed as she thought of the cultured glories of Mere.

Mr Richard appeared in that monkey-jacketted condition in which men of fashion in 1855 were accustomed to 'go of a morning'. Five years of good living and hard drinking had deprived his figure of its athletic beauty. He was fifty-two years of age – a period of life when all healthy men become conscious of a paunch. The sudden cessation from the severe bodily toil to which his active life as convict and squatter had accustomed him, caused Mr Richard's natural proneness to the honours of a belly to increase, and instead of being portly he had become gross. His cheeks were inflamed with frequent application of hot and rebellious liquors to his blood. His hands were swollen, and not as steady as of yore. His whiskers were streaked with unhealthy grey. His eyes, bright and black as ever, lurked in a thicket of crow's feet. He had become prematurely bald – a sure sign of mental or bodily excess. He spoke with affected heartiness, and in that boisterous tone which betrays its own assumption of ease.

'My dear Lucy! Sit down. What brings *you* to bachelor's quarters?'

'I want to speak with you, Richard, about Adelaide.'

'About Adelaide? Delighted! Have you breakfasted? Of course you have. *I* was up rather late last night – my horse won the race yesterday, and we had a little supper. Quite sure you won't have anything? A glass of wine? No. Then sit down and tell me about my niece.'

'I want to know, Richard, if you intend to make any provision for her?'

'Provision? Why of course; and for Arthur, too. I would have helped him before, only the young gentleman chose to ride the high horse. She is provided for all right.'

'Yes. When you die, I have no doubt,' said Miss Lucy, calmly. 'We know that you can leave the property to anybody you choose; but I did not imagine for a moment that you would forget your brother's son. But it is *now* that I mean. I want money for Addy now. She ought to come out into society.'

'Look here, my dear sister,' said Mr Richard, with a somewhat ugly look on his face. 'It is all very well coming to me with these stories, but when I offered Arthur £500 a year, he wouldn't take it. *You* volunteered to be responsible for the children, and it is hardly fair to come upon me now.'

'You are a hard-hearted man, Richard.'

'So you have said before; but I can stand hard words. The fact is, Lucy – and you may as well know it at once – I am much pushed for money. Winning a Derby is an expensive matter.'

'Pushed for money!' cried Miss Devine, in horror. 'Why Frank said the estates were worth twenty thousand a year.'

'So they were – five years ago – but my horse-racing, and betting, and other amusements, concerning which you need not too curiously enquire, have reduced their value considerably.'

He spoke recklessly and roughly. It was evident that success had but developed his ruffianism. His 'dandyism' was but comparative. The impulse of poverty and scheming which led him to affect the 'gentleman' having been removed, the natural brutality of his nature showed itself in all its native deformity.

Miss Devine gathered her modest silks together with a motion of distaste.

'I do not want to hear of your debaucheries,' she said. 'Our name has been already sufficiently disgraced in my hearing.'

'What is got over the devil's back, goes under his belly,' replied Mr Richard, coarsely. 'My old father got his money by dirtier ways than those in which I spend it. As villainous an old scoundrel and skinflint as ever poisoned a seaman, I'll go bail.'

The lady rose.

'You need not revile your father, Richard – he left you all.'

'Ay, but by pure accident. He didn't mean it. If he hadn't died in the nick of time, that unhung murderous villain, Maurice Frere, would have come in for it. By the way, Lucy,' he added, with a change of tone, 'do you ever hear anything of Maurice?'

'Only from Arthur,' said Miss Devine. 'Maurice himself has not written since he lost his wife. He is head of the Convict Department in Melbourne, I believe.'

'Is he?' said Mr Richard, with something like a shiver. 'Hope he'll stop there. Well, but about Addy. I am sorry I can't do anything for her, but the fact is, that – that I am thinking of selling everything.'

'Selling everything!'

'Yes, 'pon my soul I will. Mere and all.'

'Sell Mere!' repeated poor Miss Lucy, in bewilderment. 'Why, Fonthill Abbey is the only place like it in England.'

'I can't help that,' laughed Mr Richard, ringing the bell. 'I want cash, and cash I must have. Breakfast, Smithers. I'm going to travel.'

Poor Miss Devine was breathless with astonishment. Educated and reared as she had been, she would as soon have thought of proposing to sell St Paul's Cathedral, as to sell Mere.

'Surely, Richard, you are not in earnest,' she gasped.

'I am, indeed.'

'But – but who will buy it?'

'Plenty of people. I shall cut it up into building allotments. Besides, they are talking of a branch line from Harwich to Colchester, which will just cut the new wing in half. You are quite sure you've breakfasted? Then pardon *me*.'

'Richard, you are jesting with me? You will never let them do such a thing!'

'I'm thinking of a trip to America,' says Mr Richard, cracking an egg. 'I am sick of Europe. After all, what is the good of people like us pretending to be "old families", with "seats" and all that humbug? Money is the thing now, Lucy, my dear. Hard cash! That's the ticket for soup, you may depend.'

'But what is to become of Arthur?'

'He'll get what's left when I go off the hooks,' said Mr Richard, pleasantly; 'and in the meantime let him work for his living. I had plenty of knocking about when I was a young man. Why shouldn't he have the same?'

'Then you positively decline to do anything for Addy?'

'No, I don't – I wish you will have a cup of tea or something – but you must wait, my dear Lucy. I'm dipped, I tell you – most infernally dipped, and at the present moment I really can't make any arrangement. If a cheque for fifty –'

'Thank you. We are not beggars. If you decline to make your

brother's child a provision suitable to your fortune and her position, she shall share my income.'

'That's just what she's been doing all along, ain't it?' remarked Mr Richard, helping himself to potted grouse.

'I shall take her abroad,' continued Miss Devine, ignoring the sneer. 'I wrote to my old governess last night, but I thought I would not post the letter until I saw you. You will regret this, Richard.'

'Well, if you must go, you must. I am sorry you won't listen to reason, Lucy; but, as I said before, if a fifty —'

'Good morning, sir.' And drawing her shawl about her, the gentlewoman went out.

'I should be a flat to make provision, as she calls it,' soliloquised Rex, as he resumed his breakfast. 'No, let 'em go abroad, best place for 'em, to Germany or Jerusalem, if they like, the farther the better for me. I'll sell off the property and make myself scarce. A trip to America will benefit my health.'

A knock at the door made him start.

'Come in! Curse it, how nervous I'm getting. What's that? Letters. Give them to me; and why the devil don't you put the brandy on the table, Smithers?'

He drank some of the spirit greedily, and began to open his correspondence.

'Cussed brute,' said Mr Smithers, outside the door. 'He couldn't use wuss langwidge if he was a dook, dam 'im! — Yessir,' he added, suddenly, as a roar from his master recalled him.

'When did *this* come?' asked Mr Richard, holding out a letter that seemed more than usually disfigured with stampings.

'Lar's night, sir. It's bin to Mere, sir, and come down directed with the h'others.' The angry glare of the black eyes induced him to subjoin, 'I 'ope there's nothink wrong, sir.'

'Nothing, you infernal ass and idiot,' burst out Mr Richard, apparently white with rage, 'except that I should have had this instantly. Can't you see it's marked *urgent*? Can you read? Can you spell? There, that will do. No lies. Get out!'

Left to himself again, Mr Richard walked hurriedly up and down the chamber, wiped his forehead, drank a stiff jorum of brandy, and finally sat down and re-read the letter. It was short, but terribly to the purpose.

My Dear Jack,

I found you out, you see. Never mind how just at present. I know all about your proceedings, and unless Mr Richard Devine receives his *wife* with due propriety, he'll find himself in the custody of the police. Telegraph, dear, to Mrs Richard Devine at above address.

Yours as ever, Jack
SARAH.

To Richard Devine, Esq.,
  The Mere,
    Nr. Harwich,
      Essex.

Mr Richard swore a great oath. The blow was so unexpected and so severe. In the very high tide and flush of assured success to be thus plucked backwards into the old bondage. Despite the affectionate tone of the letter, he knew the woman with whom he had to deal. For some furious minutes he sat motionless, gazing at the letter. He did not speak – men seldom do under such circumstances – but his thoughts ran in this fashion. 'Here is this cursed woman again! Just as I was congratulating myself on my freedom. How did she discover me? Small use asking that. What shall I do? I can do nothing. It is absurd to run away, for I shall be caught. Besides, I've no money. My account at Mastermann's is overdrawn £1,800. If I bolt at all, I must bolt at once – within twenty-four hours. Rich as I am, I don't suppose I could raise more than £1,000 in twenty-four hours. These things take a day or two, say forty-eight hours. In forty-eight hours I could raise £10,000, but forty-eight hours is too long. Curse the woman! I wonder if I could pretend to fall in with her wishes and give her the slip. No; too dangerous. I know her. How in the fiend's name did she discover me? It's a bad job. – However she's not inclined to be gratuitously disagreeable. How lucky I never married again! I had better make terms and trust to fortune. After all she's been a good friend to me. – Poor Sally! – I might have rotted on that infernal Eagle Hawk Neck, if it hadn't been for her. She is not a bad sort. Handsome woman, too, and will not disgrace me. I may make it up with her. I shall have to sell off and go away after all. – It might be worse. – I dare say the property's worth £100,000. Not bad for a start in America. And I may get rid of her yet.

Yes. I must give in. – Oh, curse her! – [*ringing the bell*] Smithers!'

Smithers appears.

'A telegraph form and a cab! Stay. Pack me a dressing-bag, I shall have to go away for a day or so. [*Sotto voce*] I'd better see her myself. – [*Aloud*] – Bring me a Bradshaw! [*Sotto voce*] – Damn the woman!'

As John Rex wrote the telegram which conveyed to Sarah Purfoy the intelligence that he would sup with her that night at Plymouth, Miss Lucy posted her letter to her old governess. The letter was directed

à Madame
> Madame Clara Blinzler,
> Der Lievens Straat,
> bij de Singel,
> Amsterdam.

❖ 2 ❖

AT AMSTERDAM

THERE is probably no city in the world which can rival Amsterdam in the cleanliness of its larger streets and the filth of its smaller ones. The houses which abut upon the small canals reek with perpetual moisture, and Dutch cleanliness is taxed to the uttermost to preserve by constant friction that brilliancy of the brass and iron ware which is so dear to the Dutch heart. The sluggish movement of the heavily laden barges along these turbid streams causes in the hot weather sickening effluvia to arise. The water is then said to 'grow'. It is to these by-streets that the dredging-vessels chiefly resort, and between these green and water-stained quays that they most eagerly ply their mud-scraping trade. It is on account of the existence of these water-lanes that the sluices of the sea-city are closed by regulation each day for a short period at high water, in order that the numerous lanes may be flooded. It is on account of the natural nastiness engendered by these slimy thoroughfares that the Dutch housewives have become celebrated throughout the world for their detestation of dirt. They *must* be clean to live, and scrubbing-brush, water-bucket, and paint-pot are called into requisition to combat and defeat the universal and omnipresent enemy.

Yet within the picturesque and ancient houses which rub noses with each other across the green stagnation of the minor canals, passes a life of the utmost purity and peace. Beneath those tiled and antique roofs, behind those peaked and beam-supported gables, in a dimness cross-lighted by rays that enter the diamonded panes of heavily-leaded lattices, is transacted that homely and comfortable existence rendered familiar to us by the paintings of Ostade, Jan Steen, de Hooghe or Gerard Douw. From those vast rooms, those winding staircases, those huge chimneys and gloomy furniture, come the firelight gleam-ings of Rembrandt, the candle-shadow mimickings of Brouwer and Vanderhelst. The grotesque and repellant beauties of the Muiderstraat – the Monmouth-street or Judengaase of Amster-dam – beauties abounding in broad and flickering shadows, sud-den and brilliant colours, deep and fantastic flame-glows – had an unholy attraction for the realistic painters of the age. The glories of motley raggedness, the generous richness of furs and jewels, the gleam of sallow waters and cool reflection of lapping tides, all the spirit of mingled splendour and squalor of mercan-tile success which animates the works of the artists of Holland, has been absorbed from the floating home-lights of these narrow by-ways. To comprehend a Mieris or a Rachel Ruisch – in which blooms, perhaps, a tulip, whose every petal invites the micro-scope – we must have lived in those gloomy and gigantic wood-piles, contemplated the sluggish and melancholy tide, analyzed the smoke-wreaths of a Dutch-pipe; watched the fire-light glow long nights together upon Dutch tiles; meditated, amid the gloom of a Dutch winter, upon the red sun glowering through his silver fogs; huddled round the stove in a corner of the great chamber; or clambered up the black and ghostly staircases amid the misty aureole of our solitary candle. The atmosphere, heavy and dispiriting, invites to melancholy ease. Surrounded by sad-coloured flats, grey sands, and dismal sea, we shrink within our houses and, shutting close the flapping shutter, let the chill world speed on as it may. The home life is the best life. Within our four walls we elect to dwell for ever. The 'house' becomes more than a dwelling – it is part of ourselves, it partakes of our phlegm, it defies the cold blasts comfortably with us, it shares our warm days until its gilt vane burns again, it holds deep in its ruddy winter-memories whatever secrets we have given to the grotesque keeping of the firelight and the shadows. In such houses, generations, with their thousand aspirations, hopes, loves, fears, crimes, and secrets, have been born, lived, and died one after the other, without wishing to pass beyond the door lintel. In such houses, in such a country, there are folks who vegetate for a life-time, without hope or wish of change. They are born, cry, play, fall in love, marry, have children, grow rich, and die; they play out their whole life-drama without a change of scene. Have they ambitions, loves, hatreds, secrets? The old house has room, and to spare, for them all.

In one of these small and sordid streets called Lievens-straat – probably so named after the second-rate painter of that name – stood an old house of this nature. It was inhabited by two sisters named Blinzler, who had occupied it for nearly thirty years. The sisters were women of middle age. The elder, Clara, who had been a governess in the house of the dead Sir Richard Devine, was indeed nearly sixty, but of healthy and upright carriage. The younger, Dorothea, was forty-seven, but she looked older. She suffered from an affection of the spine, which caused her to stoop. It was perhaps because the morbid sensitiveness which is the portion of invalids, led her to dread the comments of the public on her deformity, that she seldom went out of doors. Indeed, there were few of the neighbours who could remember having seen the deformed little sister of Madame Blinzler.

The Dutch are not a curious people, and the neighbours of the two ladies did not speculate much upon their strange mode of life. If two women, who appeared to possess an independent income, chose to live in solitude, what was it to any one? And then they had lived undisturbed for twenty years! In point of fact, the residence of the two old maids, instead of exciting attention by reason of its length, was really but beginning to lose the charm of novelty. Families who had vegetated in their house-pots for two centuries, had at first looked with suspicion upon the Belgian interlopers. They had reported – in the year 1823, when the great flood nearly swept away the town – that the father of little flaxen-haired Dorothea was a wizard, and vowed that he had been seen nightly in communion with Satan by the glare of a red-hot furnace. They had called their neighbours together to witness the monstrous shadow of the interloper – visible through the open window of a garret – bobbing upon the damp wall of the opposite house, and had begged their neighbours to declare if they did not observe horns projecting from that bald head. When one night an explosion occurred, which shattered the window-glass and injured the experimentalists' assitant, they were inclined to believe that the Evil One had claimed his bond. They had hinted of alchemy, of necromancy, of unholy commerce, and of German diabolism. They had said the weird flaxen-haired child was an imp, and that in the good days of a century back she and her father would have been burnt in due course as magicians, heretics, and dealers in devilish devices. But all that nonsense was forgotten now. The huge window, barred and screened, had long been dark. The interloping German, returning to his own devilish country, had died there in the most ordinary manner. The sister of the flaxen-haired orphan had come from England to protect her, and the two had lived a hum-drum lifetime ever since in the most orthodox Dutch manner.

It had been reported that the pair had money – it was evident that they were independent – and about the years 1832 and 1833 one or two worthy Dutchmen endeavoured to gain entrance into the house with a view of marriage. But they did not succeed. Fraulein Blinzler always answered them that her sister was too sick to receive visitors, and that, for her own part, she had resolved never to marry. This was thought a foolish resolution, as the Fraulein Blinzler was comely, and of good manners. But she rigorously adhered to it, and the honest Dutchmen dropped off by-and-bye, and in due time married somebody else. Thus it came to pass that, for the last ten years, the sisters Blinzler had lived as completely alone in their huge house as if they had been imprisoned in the Château d'If or the fortress of Spandau.

Perhaps this unnatural and gloomy life had become in reality a sort of imprisonment for one of the women. Madame Clara Blinzler, when she had tendered her resignation to Mrs Gibb, twelve months after the death of Sir Richard Devine, in order that she might 'return to Germany to her sister, who had been suddenly left without a protector,' had surrendered herself, body and mind, to a thraldom she was now powerless to break. Arrived at the house in the gloomy spring of 1828, she found her sister alone, and enfeebled by recent illness. With an affection which the difference of their ages rendered rather maternal than sisterly, she steadily nursed her to a recovery, and her reward was to find the girl transformed into a lifelong invalid, petulant, self-willed, and low-spirited, regarding herself as specially accursed of God, specially set apart and marked out for suffering, specially reserved as the instrument of some strange and terrible manifestation of the power and providence of the Almighty. The mystery – if mystery there could be said to be – which the old house held in its dark and many-chambered penetralia, was this mystery of a dominant Idea. Though in all the practical affairs of life the elder sister controlled the younger, still, in the matter of the inner life of the two – of that existence of dreams and portents, whispers, omens, signs, recollections and forebodings, which was the spirit of the ancient mansion – the younger sister was omnipotent. Her flaxen hair silvered, her blue eyes steeled, her red lips paled, and her once white hands withered by the presence of her haunting thought, Dorothea Blinzler had waited for twenty-eight years in that old house expecting the call of God.

It has been related that women, whose husbands have been lost at sea, or from whom some unexplained and horrible crime has snatched father or friend, have so sat waiting – waiting with frightful calmness during a lifetime for the dead who never could return. Before the abstraction of her sister, Clara was powerless. She was fascinated, awed, and silent before the Idea which was thus incarnated, as it were, by the deformed, pain-racked body, which has sustained itself from youth to age, by virtue of this awful Patience.

'I will wait,' said Dorothea Blinzler, when her sister raised her from her fever-bed, and she had waited well. For twenty-eight years she hoped against hope, wearying God with prayers and supplications. The old house had absorbed this agony of a life-time, until it had become saturated with it; the atmosphere seemed electrical with expectation; the air was charged with that bodeful silence which precedes a thunder-clap. Yet when, on this bright May morning, the intelligence, hoped for for half a lifetime, fell from Clara Blinzler's lips, Dorothea uttered no cry of surprise.

She was on the way to her bedroom when the elder woman, breathless, stopped her with the letter of Miss Lucy's which told of the cruel conduct of Mr Richard Devine, open in her hand.

'You were right, Dorothea. He was not drowned. He has returned! He is in England!'

Dorothea was silent for an instant, and then said, pressing her pale hands together.

'Good. I will go to him!'

The old maid was so astonished by this extraordinary and unlooked-for determination, that she stood staring, unable to reply.

Her sister looked at her with triumph in her eyes.

'Give me this,' she cried, snatching the letter. 'I will read it myself, alone,' and so passed up the garret stairs.

The door of the dead chemist's laboratory — where the devil had appeared by the light of the furnace fire to frighten the boors — was locked with bolts that had not turned in their sockets for twenty-eight years. She paused at the desolate door, speaking as though there was something behind that solid oak which could hear and understand. 'At last, father! At last!' she said, softly.

3

A MEETING

JOHN REX found the George disagreeably prepared for his august arrival. Obsequious waiters flew to rescue his dressing-bag and over-coat, the landlord himself welcomed him at the door. Two naval gentlemen came out of the coffee-room to stare at the owner of the Derby winner. 'Have you any more luggage, Mr Devine?' asked the landlord, as he flung open the door of the best drawing-room. It was awkwardly evident that his wife had no notion of suffering him to hide his borrowed light under a bushel.

A supper-table laid for two people gleamed bright from the cheeriest corner. A fire crackled beneath the marble mantel-shelf. The latest evening paper lay upon a chair; and, brushing it carelessly with her costly silks, the woman he had so basely deserted came smiling to meet him.

'Well, Mr Richard Devine,' said she, 'you did not expect to see me again, did you?'

Although, on his journey down, he had composed an elaborate speech wherewith to greet her, this unnatural civility dumbfounded him.

'Sarah ! I never meant to –'

'Hush, my dear Richard – it must be Richard now, I suppose – This is not the time for explanations. Besides, the waiter might hear you. Let us have some supper now, you must be hungry I am sure.'

He advanced to the table mechanically.

'How fat you have got !' she continued. 'Too good living I suppose. You were not so fat at Port Ar – Oh, I forgot, my dear ! Come and sit down. That's right. I have told them all that I am your wife, for whom you have specially sent. They regard me with some interest and respect in consequence. Don't spoil their good opinion of me.'

He was about to utter some imprecation, but she stopped him by a glance.

'No bad language, John, or I shall ring for a constable. Let us understand one another, my dear. You are my runaway husband – an escaped convict. If you don't eat your supper civilly, I shall certainly send for the police.'

'Sarah!' he burst out, 'I never meant to desert you. Upon my word. It is all a mistake. Let me explain.'

'There is no need for explanations yet, Jack – I mean Richard. Have your supper. Ah! I know what you want.'

She poured out half-a-tumbler of brandy, and gave it to him. He took the glass from her hand, drank the contents, and then, as though warmed by the spirit, laughed.

'What a woman you are, Sarah. I have been a great brute, I confess.'

'You have been an ungrateful villain,' said she, with sudden passion, 'a hardened, selfish villain.'

'But, Sarah –'

'Don't touch me!'

''Pon my word, you are a fine creature, and I was a fool to leave you.'

The compliment seemed to soothe her, for her tone changed somewhat.

'It was a wicked, cruel act, Jack. You whom I saved from death – whom I nursed – whom I enriched. It was the act of a coward.'

'I admit it. It was.'

'You admit it. Have you no shame then? Have you no pity for me for what I have suffered all these years?'

'I don't suppose you cared much.'

'Don't you? You never thought about me at all. I have cared this much, John Rex – bah! the door is shut close enough – that I have spent a fortune in hunting you down; and now I have found you, I will make you suffer in your turn.'

He laughed again, but uneasily.

'You have been clever in finding me out at all events. I give you credit for that.'

'There is not a single act of your life, John Rex, that I do not know. I have traced you from the day you stole out of my house until now. I know your continental trips, your journeyings here and there in search of a lost clue. I pieced together the puzzle, as you have done, and I know that, by some foul fortune, you have stolen the secret of a dead man to ruin an innocent and virtuous family.'

'Hullo! hullo,' says John Rex. 'Since when have *you* learnt to talk of virtue? And how did I learn this secret, pray? Did you find that out too?'

'That was of small importance – some comrade of the poor fellow who was drowned at sea, some old servant of the family, some hint of one of your fellow convicts who had known and seen him. How are such deceptions contrived, I neither know nor care.'

John Rex gave vent to a sigh of relief. She did not know *everything*, then. Her next sentence sank him to the depths again.

'But you have got to the end of your tether now, Jack. I have communicated with the boy whose fortune you have stolen. I expect to hear from Arthur Devine in a day or so.'

'Well – and when you hear?'

'I shall give him back his fortune at the price of his silence!'

'Ho! ho! Will you?'

'Yes; and if my husband does not come back and live with me quietly, I shall call in the police.'

John Rex sprang up.

'Who will believe you, you idiot?' he cried. 'I'll have you sent to gaol as an impostor.'

'You forget, my dear,' she returned, playing coquettishly with her rings, and glancing sideways as she spoke, 'that you have already acknowledged me as your wife before the landlord and people. Oh, my dear Jack, you think you are very clever, but I am as clever as you.'

Smothering a curse, he sat down beside her.

'Listen, Sarah. What is the use of fighting like a couple of children? I am rich –'

'So am I. There is a township where my station was. You forget the diggings, John.'

'Well, so much the better. We will join our riches together. I admit that I was a fool and a cur to leave you; but I played for a great stake. The name of Richard Devine was worth a million and a half of money. It is mine. I won it. Share it with me. Sarah, you and I defied the world years ago. Don't let us quarrel. I was ungrateful. Forget it. We know by this time that we are not either of us angels. We started in life together – Do you remember, Sally, when I met you first? – determined to make money. We have succeeded. Why then set to work to destroy each other? You are handsome as ever, I have not lost my wits. Is there any need for you to tell the world that I am a runaway convict, and that you are – well, no, of course, there is no need. Kiss, and be friends, Sarah. I would have escaped you if I could, I admit. You have found me out. I accept the position. You claim me as Mrs Richard Devine. Come down to Mere, then, and possess that name with me. You have all your life wanted to be a great lady. Now is your chance!'

Much as she had cause to hate him, well as she knew his treacherous and ungrateful character, little as she had reason to trust him, the old glamour of her strange and distempered affection for the scoundrel came upon her again with gathering strength. As she sat beside him, listening to the soft tones of the voice she had learned to love so well, greedily drinking in the promise of a future fidelity which she was well aware was made but to be broken, her memory recalled the past days of trust and happiness, and her woman's fancy once more invested the selfish villain she had reclaimed with those attributes which had once enchained her wilful and wayward affections. The unselfish devotion which had marked her conduct to the swindler and convict was, indeed, her redeeming virtue; and perhaps she felt dimly – poor woman – that it were better for her to cling to that, if she lost all the world beside. Her wish for vengeance melted under the influence of these thoughts. The bitterness of despised love, the shame and anger of desertion, ingratitude, and betrayal, all vanished. The tears of a sweet forgiveness trembled in her eyes, the unreasoning love of her sex – faithful to nought but love, and faithful to love in death – shook in her voice. She took his coward hand and kissed it, pardoning all his baseness with the sole reproach, 'Oh, John, John, you might have trusted me after all?'

John Rex felt that he had conquered, and smiled as he embraced her.

'I wish I had,' said he; 'it would have saved me many regrets; but never mind. Sit down; *now* we will have supper.'

So he resumed his empire with scarce a struggle.

'Your preference has one drawback, Sarah,' he said, when the meal was concluded, and the two sat down to consider their immediate course of action, 'it doubles the chance of detection.'

'How so?'

'People have accepted me without inquiry, but I am not without dislike. Lucy Devine and young Arthur are both unfriendly. When they find I have a mysterious wife their dislike will become suspicion. Is it likely that I should have been married all these years and not have informed them?'

'Very unlikely,' returned Sarah calmly, 'and that is just the reason why you have *not* been married all these years. Really,' she added, with a laugh, 'the male intellect is very coarse. You have already told some ten thousand lies about this affair, and yet you don't see your way to tell one more.'

'What do you mean?'

'Why, my dear Richard, you surely cannot have forgotten that you married me last year on the Continent? By the way, it *was* last year that you were there, was it not? I am the daughter of a poor clergyman of the Church of England; name – anything you please – and you met me – Where shall we say? Baden, Aix, Brussels? Cross the Alps if you like, dear, and say Rome.'

John Rex put his hand to his head.

'Of course – I am stupid,' said he. 'I have not been well lately. Too much brandy and racket, I suppose.'

'Well, we will alter all that,' she returned, with a laugh, which her anxious glance at him belied. 'You are going to be domestic now, Jack – I mean Dick.'

'Go on,' said he, impatiently. 'What then?'

'Then, having settled these little preliminaries, you take me up to London and introduce me to your relatives and friends.'

He started.

'A bold game.'

'Bold! Nonsense! The only safe one. People don't, as a rule, suspect, unless one is mysterious. You *must* do it; I have arranged for your doing it. The waiters here all know me as your wife. There is not the least danger – unless, indeed, you are married already,' she added, with a quick and angry suspicion.

'You need not be alarmed. I was not such an ass as to marry another woman while *you* were alive – had I even seen one I would have cared to marry. But what of the boy? Young Arthur. You say you have told him.'

'I have told him to communicate with Purkiss and Quaid, in order to hear something to his advantage. But he has not availed himself of the invitation. If you had been rebellious, John, the "something" would have been a letter from me telling him who you really are. Now you have proved obedient, the "something" will be £500 a year, paid quarterly, on condition that he does not return to England. What do you think of that, Mr Richard Devine?'

'You deserve success, Sarah,' said the old schemer, in genuine admiration. 'By Jove, this is something like the old days, when we were Mr and Mrs Craven!'

'Or Mr and Mrs Skinner, eh, John?' she said, with as much tenderness in her voice as though she had been a virtuous matron recalling her honeymoon. 'That was an unlucky name, wasn't it dear? You should have taken my advice there.'

And, immersed in grateful recollection of their past rogueries, the worthy pair rested an instant, pensively smiling.

Rex was the first to awake. 'I will be guided by you then. What next?'

'Next – for, as you say, my presence doubles the danger – we will contrive to withdraw quietly from England. The introduction to Miss Lucy over, and Arthur disposed of, we will go down to Mere, and live there for a while. During that time you must turn into cash as much property as you dare. We will then go abroad for the "season" – and stop there. After a year or so on the Continent, you can write to our agent to sell more property; and finally, when we are regarded as permanent absentees – and three or four years will bring that about – we will get rid of everything, and slip over to America, then you can endow a charity if you like, or build a church to the memory of the man you have displaced.'

John Rex burst into a laugh.

'You are wonderful! An excellent plan. I like the idea of the Charity – the Devine Hospital, eh?'

'By the way, how did you find out the particulars of this man's life? He was burned in the *Hydaspes*, wasn't he?'

John Rex saw the necessity for an immediate lie. He would not tell his wife *everything*, at all events.

'From a shipmate of his,' said he, 'who was with me in South America. It is a long story. The particulars weren't numerous, and if the fools had been half sharp they would have bowled me out. But the fact was they *wanted* to find the fellow alive, and were willing to take a good deal on trust. I'll tell you all about it another time. I think I'll go to bed now; I'm tired, and my head aches as though it would split.'

'Then it is decided that you follow my directions?'

'Yes.'

She rose and placed her hand on the bell.

'What are you going to do?' he asked uneasily.

'*I* am going to do nothing. *You* are going to telegraph to your servants to have the house in London prepared for your wife, who will return with you the day after tomorrow.'

John Rex stayed her hand with an angry gesture. 'This is all devilish fine,' he said; 'but suppose it fails?'

'That is your affair, John. You need not go on with this business at all, unless you like. I had rather you didn't.'

'What the deuce am I to do, then?'

'I am not as rich as you are; but, with my station and so on, I am worth twelve thousand a year. Come back to Australia with me, and let these poor people enjoy their own again. Ah, John, it is the best thing to do, believe me. We can afford to be honest now.'

'A fine scheme!' cried he. 'Give up half a million of money, and go back to Australia! You must be mad!'

'Then telegraph.'

'But, my dear –'

'Hush, here's the waiter.'

As he wrote, John Rex felt gloomily that, though he had succeeded in recalling her affection, that affection was as imperious as of yore.

4

MRS RICHARD DEVINE MAKES
HER APPEARANCE

THE house in Clarges-street having been duly placed at the disposal of Mrs Richard Devine, who was installed in it, to the profound astonishment and disgust of Mr Smithers and his fellow-servants, it only remained that the lady should be formally recognized by Miss Lucy. The rest of the ingenious programme would follow as a matter of course. To say the truth, Mr Richard had rather hoped that Miss Lucy would decline to have anything to do with him, and that the ordeal of presenting his wife would not be necessary. Much to his disgust, however, Miss Lucy replied to the letter which he had sent to her at Sarah's dictation, and accepted his invitation. For the rest – the world of servants, waiters; those to whom servants and waiters could babble; and such turfites and men-about-town as had reason to enquire concerning Mr Richard's domestic affairs – no opinion was expressed, save that 'Devine's married somebody, I hear,' and variations to the same effect. As we know the great world, the Society, whose scandal would have been really injurious, had long ceased to trouble itself with Mr Richard's doings in any particular. If it had been reported that the Leviathan of the Turf had married his washerwoman, Society would only have intimated that 'it was just what might have been expected of him.'

Nevertheless, Mr Richard, sitting with his wife in the drawing-room, about a week after he had so suddenly found her, awaited the advent of his sister with some uneasiness.

'I feel deuced shaky, Sarah,' he said; 'let's have a nip of something.'

'You have been "nipping" too much for the last five years, Dick' (she had quite schooled her tongue to the new name). 'Your shakiness is the result of "nipping", I am afraid.'

'Oh, don't preach; I'm not in the humour for it.'

'Help yourself, then. You are quite sure you are ready with your story.'

The brandy revived him.

'Oh, yes,' he laughed. 'I'm not forgetting my profession. I'm like the gentleman who wanted to be a doorkeeper in the house of Israel, or something. "May my right hand forget her cunning," don't you know? Here they are. Now for it.'

The stopping of a vehicle and the rapping at the door announced, in fact, the arrival of the ladies. The two adventurers composed themselves, and Smithers, flinging open the door, ushered in Miss Devine and Adelaide.

John Rex uprose with affected heartiness.

'My dear Lucy, allow me to –'

He paused, for behind Miss Lucy came another lady – a little fair woman, clad in black, who walked lame.

The smile of welcome died on Sarah's lips as Miss Devine advanced towards her.

'Madam,' said Miss Devine, 'either you or I have been terribly deceived. Am I to understand that my brother is about to present you to me as his wife?'

'Certainly,' cried John Rex.

Sarah did not answer, but measured this unexpected adversary with pale face and fearless eyes. What was the unknown and uncontemplated danger?

'Richard Devine,' said the lady in black, speaking painfully, and with a foreign accent, 'do you not know me?' and she lifted her veil.

John Rex, looking astonished into the cold, careworn face of Dorothea Blinzler, felt a cold hand clutch his heart.

'No, madam,' he stammered, 'I have never seen you before to my knowledge.'

'You have had time to forget me, and I have had time to change.' She took a little packet from her bosom and gave it to Miss Lucy. 'But *these* do not change. Though you deserted me twenty-eight years ago, and I have mourned you as dead – you villain and coward – I have not forgotten you. I have prayed God night and day that I might meet you, and know you when we met. I have not forgotten you.'

John Rex stood speechless. He knew that, among the secrets of his old comrade, Rufus Dawes, there was one he had never penetrated – that, in the life of Richard Devine, as he had traced it, there was one link missing. Here, in the person of this unknown woman, was the Witness he had dreaded ready to complete the puzzle with one missing piece. What was the revelation that was about to crush him? He stood dumbfounded, his hands clutching his neckcloth, trembling.

Sarah Purfoy, trembling also – but more with rage than terror – swept with one stride towards Miss Lucy.

'What is the meaning of this? Who is this woman?'

The cripple pointed with her withered hand to the packet.

'There are the proofs which will show you who I am,' she said, in an even voice. 'I am the sister of that lady's governess – the daughter of a chemist in Amsterdam – the deserted wife of twenty-eight years – the wife of Richard Devine!'

All looked at the man to whom she pointed. He stood, still speechless, in the same attitude, his features worked convulsively, his cheeks were purple with suffused blood, upon his lips a slight foam seemed gathering.

The wife of Richard Devine! Who could imagine that Richard Devine had a wife?

The unhappy lady, her keen eyes glittering with the morbid excitement which had sustained her, touched him on the arm.

'Richard,' she said, 'my love has long since faded; I have long despised you for your treachery; have long learnt that you have never loved me. Do not fear that I am come to drag you back to the home you deserted. No, no. But' – and her voice fell to a whisper, whilst she glanced round with the swift stealthy glance that ever accompanies mischief in the brain – 'tell me, Richard! What have you done with my father?'

The explanation came upon him at last with blinding brilliance. Her father was the German pedlar! He had changed identities with a Murderer, and this woman – who was at once the daughter of the victim and the wife of the assassin – had come to demand justice! The frightful truth stunned him. He was as one who, wandering in a strange land in the darkness of a tempest, sees suddenly the whole terrific horizon illuminated by the lightning flash which strikes him instantaneously to earth. His brain, already enfeebled by excessive anxiety, was unable to sustain this last shock. He gasped for breath; his straining hands, tugging at his collar, rent away the linen that covered his breast, and wagging his head from side to side, as a beast who has received a mortal stroke, he staggered, and, but for a cabinet against which he lent, would have fallen.

Dorothea advanced and stood before him, her eyes bent upon him, as though she would read his soul. All, breathless, waited for his reply.

Suddenly, across the face of the cripple passed a swift change of expression. Expectation gave place to wonder, wonder to terror; and, uttering a shrill cry, she pointed to the uncovered neck of the man she had just claimed as her husband.

'My husband had the scar of a furnace fire across his breast. THIS MAN IS NOT RICHARD DEVINE!'

The sentence, flung at him as it were, seemed to rouse him. Fear drove the blood back to his heart. His face grew paler; the momentary vertigo passed. He drew a long breath, and, steadying himself, looked round defiantly.

Sarah Purfoy, seeing at once the advantage which the statement of her rival gave her, made one last gallant effort.

'This is very wild talk,' she said, distorting her white lips with a ghastly attempt at a smile. 'This lady first claims Mr Devine as her husband, and then says that he is not Mr Devine. Pray, if he is not Mr Devine, will you tell us who he is?'

But Dorothea was mute. The reaction had begun. She stood staring with stony eyes, stunned by the discovery which she had made. Miss Lucy and Adelaide even looked at her with suspicion and alarm, and did not frown when Sarah tapped her forehead significantly. It was just possible that the game might have been saved, had it not been for the principal player. John Rex, seemingly forgetful of all save anger against the woman who had unexpectedly betrayed him, strode towards her, and seized her by the wrist.

'Listen, here!' he cried fiercely. 'I am *not* Richard Devine. You are right there. Richard Devine is dead.'

Dorothea pressed her hand to her forehead. 'Yes, yes. He is dead. He was drowned at sea.'

John Rex burst into a harsh laugh. 'Yes, he was drowned at sea.'

'In the *Hydaspes*,' fell from Miss Devine's pale lips.

John Rex seized Dorothea by the wrist. 'He died escaping

from Norfolk Island. *Your husband was a convict, transported for life for killing your father.* Now you know the truth, and I wish you joy of it !'

Mr Smithers, reading *Bell's Life* in the lower region of the house, was startled by hearing a series of violent screams which issued from the drawing-room; and the screams being followed by a furious peal of the bell, he hurried up-stairs.

✦ *5* ✦

FLIGHT

SOME strange scene had evidently taken place. Mr and Mrs Devine were standing apart by the window, Adelaide was crying, and Miss Lucy was bending over the prostrate figure of the German lady, striving in vain to raise her.

The servant looked to his master for orders, but his master appeared strangely agitated, and incapable of speech. It was Mrs Devine who – a little pale, perhaps, with the natural weakness of a woman at sight of sickness – spoke to him.

'This lady is unwell. Send for the servants, and have a room prepared for her.'

As the man closed the door, Miss Devine made a motion of refusal, but Sarah declined to consider it.

'However matters may be settled,' said she, loftily, 'at present I am in the position of mistress of this house, and you must suffer me to assist you.'

'You are very good,' said poor Miss Devine. 'I – I don't know what to do.'

'See that this poor lady is disposed safely upstairs,' said Sarah, softly. 'I will follow you when I have seen what becomes of *him*,' and she glanced at Rex, with a glance in which her infernal genius contrived to blend the grief of an injured love and the indignation of a wounded pride. 'I will ask your advice, if you will let me.'

Miss Lucy – bewildered at her position, for her worst suspicion had been that her brother had deserted the wife of his youth — was fain to be glad of the opportunity of sympathy. She pitied the betrayed 'daughter of a poor clergyman,' and vowed to help her. 'Very well, my dear,' she said. 'Come quickly.'

The instant, however, that the door had closed upon the group, Sarah flew to Rex.

'Rouse yourself, John,' she cried, 'for Heaven's sake. Think what is to be done. We have not a moment.'

John Rex passed his hand over his forehead, wearily.

'I cannot think. I am broken down. I am ill, my brain seems dead.'

She caught her own head in both her hands.

'There must be a way. If one could but gain time to think. All is not lost yet.'

Rex moved to the door. 'It's all up,' said he. 'Let us go. They will send for the police.'

She caught him by the arm.

'Go! Where? You have no money. You have no plans. You would be arrested before night. No. Our only hope is to keep this rash confession of yours a secret for a few hours longer. No one knows it yet but ourselves.'

'It can't be kept long.'

'If it is kept until night it will be something. I have it. Go to your room and lie down. I will devise a plan. Go and wait till I come to you.'

He turned his dull eyes upon her.

'You won't give me up?'

'Give you up! Go and do as I say, and trust me.'

In emergencies of this sort a man would drink brandy. Sarah went to her bed-room, bathed her face in cold water, washed her hands, and drank half a tumbler of sal volatile and water. Then — composed and cool — she forced herself to sit still and think. She went down stairs in five minutes with her plan of action matured.

'May I come in?'

'Certainly!' Miss Devine opened the door herself. They had put the woman who claimed to be the wife of Richard Devine into bed, and she lay speechless. Sarah saw at once that there was little danger there.

'We must send for a doctor,' said she. 'Poor woman, the shock has unnerved her. Is she not a little mad?'

'She certainly has behaved most strangely. She came to us three days ago, alone. She said she had travelled from Amsterdam by herself.'

As if in sudden memory of the frightful catastrophe in which her coming had resulted, Sarah burst into tears.

'Oh! what am I to do, Miss Devine? Is this terrible thing true? Who is my husband?'

Miss Devine was honestly affected.

'He has admitted that he is not my brother. But I cannot understand it. He says my brother was – was a convict.'

'It is very dreadful; and I am so helpless, too. How could a man pretend to be somebody else all this time and not be discovered?'

'We had no suspicions latterly,' said Miss Lucy. 'Poor Frank used at first to hint at things to me, but – but he is very like Richard.'

Sarah gave a little scream.

'Oh! can it be that *his* mind is affected by the accusation of this poor creature! Perhaps it is. He is lying down now quite overcome. I cannot think him such a villain.'

'I do not know what to think,' said Miss Lucy.

'The servants, too. What a frightful scandal!'

'They do not know,' said Miss Lucy; 'at least I have said nothing.'

'If we could only get advice,' says Sarah. 'This terrible mystery ought to be cleared up at once. Could you not get a lawyer to come?'

'I know no one,' said poor Miss Lucy, terrified at the prospect of seeking such a person.

A sudden and heroic resolution appeared to seize Sarah.

'*I* will go,' she said. 'I know a lawyer – a friend of poor papa's; he will tell us what to do, and I will send a doctor for this lady.'

'But the – the man upstairs?' hesitated Miss Lucy. 'He will not be violent?'

'Oh, no! He is lying down. You can get Smithers to be outside the door. We cannot leave this poor lady alone.'

'Certainly not,' said Miss Lucy. 'I will remain, then. You will not be longer than you can help.'

'I will take the brougham. I suppose the coachman can be trusted not to talk?'

'You had better take a cab, I think,' said Miss Devine. 'There is no need for more scandal than we can help.'

'If you think it is best,' said the artful Sarah, who had intended to do so from the first. 'Wait for me then. I will be as quick as I can.'

Hurrying on a dark cloak and veil, she proceeded to the nearest cabstand, and told the driver of the vehicle she selected to go to 'The Bank of Australasia, No. 4 Threadneedle-street.'

She was not many minutes there, but the mention of her name secured her an interview with the manager at once.

'That's a rich woman,' said one of the clerks to his friend. 'A widow, too!'

'Chance for you, Tom,' returned the other; and presently from out the sacred presence came another clerk with a request for 'a draft on the Melbourne branch for three thousand, less premium,' and bearing a cheque, signed 'Sarah Carr', for £200, which he 'took' in notes, and so returned again.

'Fine woman,' remarked Mr Tom, respectfully, as she came out. 'A de-eucéd fine woman.'

From the bank she was taken to 'Green's Shipping Office.'

'I want to take a cabin in the first ship for Melbourne, please.'

The shipping clerk looked at a board.

'The *Highflyer* goes in twelve days, madam, and there is one cabin vacant.'

'I want to go at once – tomorrow, or next day.'

He smiled.

'I am afraid that is impossible,' said he. 'You will not find a ship with a vacant cabin; we are usually filled up a month in advance.'

She bit her lips with vexation. Fortune was going against her.

One of the partners came out of his private room with a telegram in his hand and beckoned the shipping clerk.

Sarah was about to depart for another office, when the clerk came hastily back.

'Just the thing for you, ma'am,' said he. 'We have got a telegram from a gentleman who has a first cabin in the *Wellesley* to say that his wife has been taken ill, and he must give up his berth.'

'When does the *Wellesley* sail?'

'Tomorrow morning. She is at Plymouth, waiting for the mails. If you go down tonight by the mail-train which leaves at 12.20 you will be in plenty of time, and we will telegraph.'

'I will take the cabin.'

'Two berths?'

'Yes. How much?'

'One hundred and thirty pounds, madam,' said he.

She produced her notes. 'Pray count it yourself. We have been delayed in the same manner ourselves. My husband is a great invalid, but I was not so fortunate as to get someone to refund *us* our passage-money.'

'Not in our firm that?' asked the clerk, counting. 'No? Money Wigram's line. Quite so. They are *rather* sharp, ma'am. What name did you say? Mr and Mrs Carr. Thank you,' and he handed her the slip of paper.

'Thank *you*,' said Sarah, with a bewitching smile, and swept down to her cab again. 'To Silver's, Cornhill.'

'You will have them at the Great Western Station by half-past eleven, please, and let the man wait until he sees me. Carr is the name – Mrs Carr. Thank you. Good morning.'

'*Now* you may go back. Turn out of Oxford-street, and stop at the first doctor's brass-plate, will you?'

In half an hour more, she had requested a surgeon to call at Clarges-street in an hour, and had dismissed the cabman with a sovereign at the corner. 'If you will be here at eleven o'clock,' said she, 'I will give you a job.'

'Thanky, mum,' says cabby. 'I'll be here.'

'I have seen my lawyer,' said she to Miss Devine. 'He will be here tomorrow. I had *such* trouble to find a doctor, but I succeeded at last.'

'You look quite worn out,' said Miss Devine. 'Have a cup of tea, my dear.'

'I must go and see how *he* is getting on,' said Sarah, with a sigh. 'Bad as he may be, he is my husband.',

And the devoted creature ran upstairs.

John Rex was pacing the room.

'Well, what news?'

She displayed the passage-ticket.

'You are saved! By the time Miss Devine gets her wits together, and that German creature recovers her speech, we shall be past the Needles.'

'To Melbourne!' cries Rex, angrily, looking at the warrant. 'Why there of all places in God's earth?'

Sarah tapped her foot on the floor angrily.

'Ungrateful, eh! Then stop behind.'

'But why to Australia, Sarah? Surely any other place would do as well.'

'No – not for my purpose. *Your* scheme has failed. Now this is mine. You have deserted me once, you will do so again in any other country. I save you, but I mean to keep you. I will bring you to Australia, where the first trooper will arrest you at my bidding as an escaped convict. If you don't like to come, stay behind. I don't care, I am rich, I have done no wrong. The law cannot touch me.'

John Rex saw the force of her reasoning, and was silent.

'You must stop here until I come up for you at eleven tonight; I will say you are ill. I have ordered a cab and we can catch the night train. Do you agree or not?'

'Oh, of course, my dear.'

That evening was long remembered by Miss Devine and her niece. The doctor came and pronounced the sick lady in the greatest danger.

'Effusion of blood on the brain. Must be kept *absolutely* quiet. No noise. No disturbing influence. Nothing to eat yet. Ice on the head,' and so forth.

Mrs Richard Devine partook of a melancholy tea, during which she recounted how the man upstairs – 'who I am horrified to say is quite *stupid* with drink' – wooed and won her, seeking the blessing of that shadowy being, the poor clergyman of the Church of England.

'I do not know what to do,' she said. 'We are poor at home, but my father is well connected, and this frightful blow –'

'I pity you from the bottom of my heart,' said Aunt Lucy, 'yet this story may be the result of madness. All may be cleared up; however, you have a friend in *me*.'

So they parted for the night tenderly, Sarah volunteering to install the nurse in the sick-chamber. 'This has been a wearing day, and I shall go to bed,' said Sarah, at ten o'clock.

By half-past ten the household had retired; and, at eleven, the appointed cab received two persons – a lady and gentleman.

'To the Great Western Railway Station, quick!'

'You had better pay the boatmen,' said Mrs Carr to her husband, as they ranged alongside the *Wellesley*, gaunt and grim, in the early dawn of a bleak May morning.

Mr Carr put his hand to his pocket, and uttered a melancholy laugh.

'I have come away without a shilling!'

His wife, woman-like, could not forbear the merited sneer.

'You haven't gained much, then, by your desertion of me, after all.'

BOOK EIGHT

MR QUAID, JUNIOR, HAS A NEW CLIENT

THE announcement made in the *Argus* of the 14th September 1855, to the effect that that evening would witness

The first appearance of the world-renowned
Artiste,
LOLA MONTES,
Assisted by Mr. Folland,
The American Comedian.

attracted a large audience to the newly-built Theatre Royal, and among the visitors to the boxes was Mr Silas Quaid, junior.

The civilization which followed upon the first settlement of the gold-fields' disturbances had brought fortune to our philosophical attorney. Eliminating from his outward man all tokens of the red-shirted digger who had taken the deposition of Mr Mogford on the night of the storming of the Eureka Stockade, the careful Silas had swum with the stream, established an office near Kirk's Horse Bazaar, dressed himself in professional black, and sought acquaintance with the wealthy and the well bred. His sarcasms found an outlet in the columns of newly-born *Melbourne Punch*, he visited in the aristocratic circles of Jolimont, and was received at Government House. On this particular evening, the attraction of 'the novel and peculiar drama, *Lola Montes in Bavaria,*' had drawn him to the theatre, and he went to be amused in the most respectable manner.

The fashion of theatres had kept pace with the times. The days of the 'Old Tin Pot', to gain which diggers carried bundles of rumpled satin through knee-deep mud to the dress-circle entrance had departed. The ancient days (three years ago!) when the boxes were crammed with drunken revellers habited in shirt-sleeves, and ornamented with short pipes; when 'Hamlet' had been 'made a target for an empty bottle'; when the Gravedigger was chaffed about the depth of the sinking and return to the dish; when nuggets – not bouquets – were flung upon the stage; and when diggerdom, impressed with the good-fellowship of the King, sent him down a bottle of brandy by the thong of a stockwhip, had vanished for ever. The new Theatre Royal was a building larger than the London Haymarket, and was frequented by an orderly and numerous audience. Now and then, a waif and stray of the old days would appear in the gallery, or some enriched publican would astonish his patrons in the pit by the gorgeous advent of his wife and daughters to the boxes, but this was only sufficiently rare to be laughable. The over-boilage of the ancient riot-pot still seethed and bubbled in the infamous 'Vestibule', as the drinking-bars in front of the house were called; and on occasions of peculiar attraction, the hall into which these places opened was crowded with an obscene and filthy crew, but it was patent that order and decency were fast prevailing. Victoria, from a 'diggings', had become a 'country'; and barristers, merchants, journalists, and physicians came, not to 'dig' and depart, but to settle their families and practise their professions.

There will be no occasion to criticise the performance of the dashing Lola. The *Argus* did not speak of it with much respect the next morning, but the pit and gallery cheered the 'ex-Queen of Bavaria' until the house rang again. The 'novel and peculiar drama', moreover, was very well put upon the stage, and the acting of a Mr G. H. Rogers, as the 'King', was highly thought of; indeed, the manager of 'Coppin's Olympic', despite the attractions of G. V. Brooke in *Love's Sacrifice*, and Mr Pablo Fanque on the tight rope, was heard that night to lament his ill luck in having failed to secure a star of such magnitude.

Amid uproarious expressions of delight, the play proceeded. Mr Silas Quaid, in the glory of immaculate necktie and decorous black, surveyed the house and the stage from the front row of a seat as near to the Governor's box as he could achieve. The performance pleased him, and he applauded with fervour. Indeed when Lola was called before the curtain, he leant respectably forward and flung a bouquet which he had brought with him for that purpose. A young man in the stalls, who, leaning against the wall in a listless way, was occupied in scanning the faces of the audience in the dress circle, found his vision momentarily impeded by the flying bouquet, and instinctively turned his gaze to the quarter from whence it came. The curtain having fallen, Mr Quaid had risen to his feet, and blandly staring into vacancy awaited the time when the pressure of the out-going audience would enable him to quit the box. The young man in the stalls, thus having a full view of his features, uttered an exclamation of joyful surprise, and hastily plunged into the crowd that blocked the door of egress.

In a few moments more Mr Quaid escaped from the noisy mob surrounding the vestibule gates, strolled leisurely up Bourke-street, and humming the butt end of the orchestral *finale*, debated within himself as to whether he should conclude his evening's amusement by the eating of a dozen Sydney oysters, or by the smoking of a solitary pipe in his own quarters. He was awakened from his soliloquy by the touch of a hand upon his sleeve, and turning, beheld a young man dressed in a pea-jacket, and wearing the breeches and boots common at that epoch to sojourners up country.

'You don't remember me?' said the young man.

'I have not the pleasure,' returned Mr Quaid, somewhat annoyed that his respectability should be thus intruded upon.

'You have not forgotten the Eureka stockade?' urged his interrogator. 'My name is Arthur Vern.'

The sallow face of Quaid flushed with pleasurable recognition instantly.

'Arthur Vern! The very man of all others I have had most in my thoughts. Of course, I remember you. Where have you been all this while?'

'On Bendigo,' said Arthur, with a laugh. 'I am so glad for to have met you. I have been here two days seeking information, which I think you can give me.'

'Information,' returned Quaid, 'that is what I want from you. Have you heard any more of your mysterious correspondent?'

'What mysterious correspondent?'

'Why the "S.P." who desired you to communicate with Purkiss and Quaid.'

'I don't know what you mean. Who are Purkiss and Quaid?'

'My grandfather's firm in London. But you have not heard. Good. My dear Mr Vern, or Devine, to speak more correctly, then, I have news for you.'

'You know my name!' cried Arthur starting back. 'How did you learn it?'

'Come up and smoke a pipe,' said Quaid. 'This way. I have rooms over my office, here. We must have a talk over this.'

Arthur bewilderedly followed his conductor up the uncarpeted stairs of the 'office', and said nothing until Mr Quaid had lit a lamp in a comfortably furnished sitting-room, and produced a bottle of brandy and cigars.

'Now my dear Mr Devine, make yourself happy and tell me where you have been hiding for the last twelve months. Our parting was most romantic. Help yourself to brandy.'

'But how did you learn my name,' persisted Arthur. 'Let me know that first, please?'

Mr Quaid unlocked a safe, and taking from it a bundle of papers, selected one. It was the note which Sarah Purfoy had given to Dorcas the night before the latter started for Ballarat.

'Read this, and be informed,' said he. 'The young lady should have given it to you, but in the haste of the romantic meeting she forgot it I suppose.'

Arthur read it with further astonishment.

'S. P.', he repeated, 'S. P., I don't know any S. P.'

'There is the mystery. Neither do I, nor Miss Crosbie, nor anybody else.'

'You know Miss Crosbie?' cries Arthur, starting up. 'I am in search of her.'

'So I supposed. She is equally anxious to meet you. It's all right, my dear fellow. "Two souls with but a single thought, two hearts that beat as one." I know the symptoms. Pass the brandy.'

'Does *she* know the contents of this letter?'

'Not a syllable. She never opened it, and seeing that there was some mystery afloat, *I* have followed the example of my worthy grandfather, who made it a boast that he never told a woman a secret in his life, and contented myself with ascertaining how she obtained it.'

'How was that?'

'In talking over that miraculous escape of yours, she informed me that a Mrs Carr, whom she met at the Criterion Hotel, and under whose advice she arranged your rescue, gave it to her sealed. Do you know a Mrs Carr?'

'No.'

'All Miss Crosbie knows of her is that she is a handsome lady, whose husband has deserted her — I don't like those sort of ladies myself — that the husband has called himself by some other name, which Miss Crosbie doesn't remember, and that Mrs Carr was to start the next morning for England, to catch him.'

'And you didn't tell her that you had read the note?'

'Not I. The "Quaid" of the firm referred to was my grandfather, and I wanted to get the information myself. I wrote home privately and asked the old man to tell me what he knew, but he's a queer old file, and we hadn't parted on good terms, so he didn't reply. It's quite possible he won't, for he knows a great many queer things, does my grandfather, and a great many queer people. It would never do for him to tell all he knows, even to me.'

'He can know nothing about *me* that he need be afraid to tell, at any rate,' said Arthur, haughtily.

'Why did you change your name, my dear sir?' asked the composed Quaid.

Arthur flushed.

'Because — because I came out second class, and I —'

'— You were afraid of disgracing the honourable name of Devine, eh? My dear fellow, your worthy uncle has done that for you already.'

'What do you mean, Mr Quaid?'

'My dear sir, seeing the name "Devine" in our friend S. P.'s letter, I naturally made inquiries about him, and my correspondent says that he is — well, a man of large fortune and low tastes, to put it mildly.'

'He is an unmitigated blackguard!' suddenly cries Arthur.

'If you prefer to put it that way, I have no objection. I am afraid he is.'

'Look here,' said the young man, suddenly. 'My uncle has

been thought to be dead for many years. He came home five years ago. He was my father's elder brother, and he took possession of everything.' Quaid nodded. 'He had passed his life, it seems, as a sailor, and his manners were brutal and violent. I hated him, and, when my poor father died, I came out here. That is the reason why I changed my name.'

Mr Quaid took a thoughtful sip of his brandy and water.

'For how many years was this excellent uncle of yours thought to be dead?' he asked.

'Oh! a lifetime. He sailed from London for India in – in 1827, I think, and the ship was lost. He, it seems, was saved, and wandered about in South America, and other places, until the fit took him to come home.'

'And was there any particular reason *why* he should have wandered about for so long?'

'Not that I am aware of.'

'No, I thought not,' says Quaid, with a smile.

'What do you mean? What reason should there be, save that of a love of low company and liquor? Many men have done things as foolish.'

'I wish I could find this S. P.,' mused Quaid.

'Why?'

'Because I expect that there is some disgraceful story connected with your uncle's absence, and that S. P. knows it. It is possible that S. P. is Mrs Carr. Was your uncle married?'

'No.'

'He may have married S. P. under the name of Carr, and deserted her. Yet she wouldn't write to *you* if he had. It is a queer case. I've often had a mind to ask Miss Crosbie if the name she heard was "Devine", but knowing that it was your name, and that you were in love with her and, not knowing why you changed it, I didn't like to risk opening an ugly subject.'

'I am very glad you didn't say anything,' said Arthur, earnestly. 'Very glad. I want to tell her myself. I have come down to ask her to marry me.'

'I thought you didn't know where she lived.'

'Neither do I,' said Arthur. 'But you do.'

Quaid smiled with that affectation of philosophy which was a feature in his demeanour.

'Ho! ho! I am to be your *Leporello*, eh. Well, Miss Dorcas is a charming girl, and will have money. *You* ought to have some by and by, if we can discover your uncle's weak point. What will you pay me now, for the secret of Miss Crosbie's "bower".'

'It is surely no secret,' said Arthur, for there was something more than banter in the tone in which Quaid spoke. 'I suppose Crosbie doesn't lock her up.'

'No, but he locks himself up. He has bought a fine house standing in a garden just out of the city. He lives in very good style, keeps a carriage and servants, and so on, but he never goes out anywhere.'

'Perhaps he doesn't care about it?'

'Perhaps not. He dabbles in science, it appears, and spends the best part of his time pottering about in a laboratory he has had fitted up. He was asked to dinner once or twice by the neighbours, but he made some excuse, and didn't go.'

'Indeed.'

'Yes. We never see him in Society,' added Quaid, with calm self-complacency.

'But Dorcas – she is not compelled to stop at home?'

'Well, no. But, you see – excuse me, my dear fellow, but the fact of Old Crosbie keeping a shanty, don't you know, is rather against her. There are houses, however, to which she goes, but I don't think the old man cares about it, for he always comes himself to fetch her in the carriage.'

'Why doesn't he take her to England, if the people here won't receive her?' cries Arthur, with some heat.

'*That* fortune, my dear sir, is reserved for you. I don't think the old man cares about England. There is a skeleton in *his* closet too, or I am mistaken.'

'I once thought that he had been a spy for the Government at Ballarat,' said Arthur.

'Oh no. I think not. He is a high-minded, honourable man, so far as I know him. I don't think that he would be a spy upon any one. No; I am rather inclined to fancy, though perhaps my professional training, aided by a natural taste for finding out that which other people wish to keep secret, may bias my judgement, that there is a "story" about the young lady's mother.'

'I have suspected it.'

'Well, I would advise you to know the truth, whatever it may be. As my grandfather used to say, "One family secret will employ a dozen lawyers." '

'And how did *you* become so intimate with this man?'

'In the most ordinary way in the world,' said Mr Quaid. 'I am his lawyer. The property which he purchased belonged to a publican of bibulous tendencies, who did me the honour to become my first client. In the course of business, it became necessary that I should see Mr Crosbie. He seemed struck by my — hem — abilities, and hinting in a delicate way that he had heard my name before — it is somewhat a professionally celebrated one — made me his legal adviser. He is a very acute man of business, and a large buyer of land (he is the ground landlord of the Royal, by the way) and my services are in frequent request. I have become a privileged visitor at his house.'

Arthur got up and paced the room. 'My acquaintance with you has not been a lengthy one,' said he, 'but you saved my life in all probability. I wish you would help me in this matter, Quaid.'

'On one condition, certainly,' returned the philosophic Quaid.

'What is it?'

'That *you* make me your legal adviser, and allow me to ferret out this Uncle business. It seems that your mysterious relative has deprived you of about a quarter of a million of money. Now a quarter of a million cannot easily pass through a lawyer's hands, without some of it sticking. If you make me your lawyer, it may pass through *my* hands. Do you see, my dear sir, — a very business-like and selfish proposition, but to be business-like and selfish is my aim in life.'

'If *that* is your only condition, I accept at once,' says Arthur, 'for as my uncle can leave his money to whom he pleases, I am not likely to see much of it.'

'I will take my chance on that,' said the old-young man. 'I have a sort of instinct that there is some devilish curious "case" to be got out of all this.'

'It is easy to imagine a romance,' said Arthur laughing, 'but I am afraid that you will find our family story to be a very common place one. At the worst, my uncle will prove to be only a drunken scoundrel, who deserts his wife and squanders his money. There is not much of a "case" in that. But you will help me?'

'Mr Quaid took down a small ledger, and, with an air of semi-burlesque, commenced to write in it.

'This must be a professional matter,' said he. 'I shall open an account — "To drinking three glasses of brandy, and hearing your love-story, six-and-eightpence." Am I to say Devine or Vern?'

'Vern at present,' said Arthur, shortly.

'Very good. Now then. Consult.'

'Well,' says Arthur, smiling in spite of himself at the whimsical turn the conversation was taking, 'what would you advise me to do?'

'How much money have you got?'

'Two hundred pounds.'

'And where are you living?'

'At the Bull and Mouth Hotel.'

'Oh! And you propose to go to Mr Thomas Crosbie, and say, "I am the Arthur Vern for whom the reward was offered. I have been working on Bendigo, until I have made two hundred pounds. I have come to town, put up at the most expensive hotel I can find, and I want to marry your daughter." I don't think that is the best course to pursue.'

'What do you advise, then?' says Arthur, somewhat piqued.

'*I* should advise that you go to Crosbie and say, "My name is Arthur Devine, my uncle is worth a quarter of a million, I am his heir, he has no children, and I want to marry your daughter. For a reference to respectability, see my solicitor, Mr Silas Quaid." That seems to me to be a better way of putting it.'

'Does it?' said Arthur.

'Certainly. You are an ass — speaking professionally — to conceal your name. Arthur Vern is a rioter, and a suspected person, without an influential friend. Arthur Devine is, at all events, the cousin of Captain Maurice Frere, and Captain Maurice Frere, Inspector-General of Penal Establishments in Victoria, has many good official billets at his command. I should spend some of the two hundred pounds in the purchase of civilized costume, and make my suit as Arthur Devine without hesitation.'

'I have not spoken to Captain Frere since I landed,' said Arthur. 'From what I have heard of him, I took a dislike to him.'

'He is not an amiable being, I believe,' Quaid returned, 'but he has the reputation of being a thorough disciplinarian. By Jove, those gentlemen at the Hulks stand in awe of him, I can tell you. However, it is growing late for a respectable fellow like me. Finish your brandy-and-water and retire. I shall go to bed. Think over my advice – six-and eightpence remember – and write to Crosbie in the morning.'

'I will go and see him.'

'Better write. The chances are that he won't see you. Oh! – I forgot – you want to ask the young lady to forgive you for galloping away so unceremoniously! – Well, it is but natural. Let me know the result of your interview, and I will charge your account with six-and-eightpence more. Here's the address. Good night.'

'Good night,' said Arthur, laughing. 'You are a queer fellow. But you have taken a load off my heart. I'll follow your advice and –'

'I'll charge you another six-and-eightpence if you don't go down stairs,' returned the respectable young attorney. 'It is nearly one o'clock!'

⁓ 2 ⊷

WHAT CAME OF MR QUAID'S ADVICE

THE Bull and Mouth Hotel in 1855 did considerably more business than it does now. It was the great 'coaching house', and King Cobb held his court there. The advent and departure of coaches kept the house constantly awake, and late arrivals were sure of finding there some makeship for a bed after every other hostelry in the city had closed its doors. It was this noted wakefulness which had caused it to be honoured by the presence of Mr and Mrs John Carr, newly landed from the *Wellesley*, late on the evening of Madame Lola's *debût*. The worthy couple were seated awaiting breakfast in a comfortable private room, on the morning after their arrival; and, Sarah, looking into busy Bourke-street, had admiringly observed, 'This is a great city, John.'

'Is it?' returned John, wearily. 'I wish they'd bring breakfast.'

He had changed very considerably since the discovery which had bereft him of the fruits of his well-planned villainy. The shock which the revelation of the German wife of the man whom he had impersonated had given him seemed to have left its marks in his swollen features and uncertain eye. His memory was failing – his sight impaired. He complained at times of a dull pain in his head. He slept much. He was nervous, and impatient of control. The fact that he was utterly dependent on the woman whom he had deserted seemed to prey upon him, and during the voyage they had frequent quarrels, in which she had been invariably victorious. After these quarrels, he drank brandy, and brandy made him worse. Sarah – rather frightened about him – determined to consult a doctor. It seemed to her not improbable that the intellectual power, in which the scoundrel had taken such an evil pride, weakened by excess, and rudely attacked by anxiety and regret, would one day fail him altogether.

'Your breakfast will be here directly, John,' she said, with an effort to rouse him. 'You are quite safe – no one saw you last night. For goodness' sake, don't look as if you were going to be hanged.'

'Don't talk of hanging. I don't like it,' said he, peevishly. 'I dreamt that I *was* hanged the other night, and awoke choking.'

She glanced at him anxiously.

'You had been at the brandy again, I suppose.'

'I had nothing except a nip with the skipper. Why are you always bullying me about what I drink?'

'It is for your own good. You'll die in a drunken fit one of these days.'

'I'd just as soon die as live to be bullied. How long are we going to stop here? You are in command now, I suppose. I'm nobody.'

'Only long enough for me to pay Captain Frere the debt I owe him.'

'It's an infernal scheme,' said he, rolling himself about uneasily. 'I don't like the notion of it. How revengeful you women are. Why, I've forgiven him long ago.'

'He never injured you, as he did me, John. You cannot realise – though I have told you often – what that man made me suffer.'

'If you had been in poor Dawes's shoes, I could have understood you. And what a hell upon earth that man's life was to him. Well you'll pay it back with interest. I wonder what became of the boy?'

'I don't know, but I expect that Captain Frere, Inspector-General of the Penal Establishments of Victoria, will have a search made for him when he learns who he is.'

'I wish you'd tell him quickly, then, and get it over,' said Rex, rousing himself and walking to the window. 'I don't like to live in the same colony with Frere, somehow or other.'

At that moment a figure crossed the road, the sight of which caused Mr John Carr to hurriedly screen himself behind the window curtain. It was the figure of Arthur Vern, who, having taken Quaid's advice, and expended a portion of his money in the purchase of the most civilised garments he could select, looked sufficiently like the Arthur Devine of two years back, to account for Mr Carr's emotion.

'What is the matter?' asked Sarah.

'Why, the boy – young Arthur Devine – did you not see him – there, crossing now. – He is coming in! If he should see me.'

Sarah laughed contemptuously.

'So that is the poor boy, is it. Where is your courage, man! Are you afraid of a lad like that. The chances are that he would not know you if he saw you. I will find out about him. He is probably stopping here for a day or two only. If he *lives* here we can easily go somewhere else. In the meantime you can easily avoid him by not going out. Here's the breakfast see, eat and put some heart into you.'

'Bring me a nip of brandy,' says Rex to the waiter, and then piteously to the devoted woman who had saved him, 'I can't help it, Sarah, I am as nervous as a cat since that affair. I'm afraid of my own shadow sometimes.'

Unconscious of the consternation he excited, Arthur pressed his way up Bourke-street, towards the address which Quaid had given him. He had not very far to go. In what is now termed Victoria Parade, and facing the Waterworks reserve, stands at this moment the house which Crosbie had purchased – a two storied white house, having a verandah round the lower part of it and standing in about a quarter of an acre of garden, surrounded on three sides by a low, red-brick wall, thickly bristling with broken bottles. It is now somewhat in need of repair, its garden is cheerless, and its gates rusty. In 1855, however, it was a different sort of place. It then was almost the only private house of its size in the suburbs. It stood alone. It owned not a quarter of an acre, but nearly three acres of garden. It was regarded as a palace by the residents in the little, iron-roofed huts in which gentility was forced to hide, and – a consideration which, perhaps, outweighed all others with its purchaser – it was surrounded, not by a low wall, but by a high and substantial wooden-paling, which effectually shut out all view of its internal economy from the passers-by. To this old house – for houses built in the fashion customary twenty years back, have become 'old' in 1872 – Arthur betook himself. The September morning was sweet and fair, the heats of summer had not yet whitened the leaves of the English trees, with which the bibulous publican had planted his garden. Their waving branches, just high enough to top the palisades, seemed to give promise of a hidden oasis in strong contrast to the dusty road that led to infant Collingwood.

With beating heart and many misgivings, Arthur pulled the wooden bell handle which hung by the side of the jealous door. A few minutes passed, and then the trap in the wide centre-panel was drawn back, and the face of a servant appeared.

'Is Mr Crosbie at home?'

'No,' said the man surlily.

'Is Miss Crosbie at home?'

A still more surly negative.

Arthur produced a sovereign.

'I want to see Mr Crosbie particularly. He knows me. I will wait until he returns.'

The man opened the heavy door at this, and interposing his body in the opening, stretched out a greedy hand.

'My orders is strict, not to admit anybody, but of course if you are on particular business' – and he eyed Arthur's pocket significantly.

It is possible that the boy would have produced another sovereign, and had the gate shut in his face for his pains, had not the very accident he had hoped for happened. A voice behind the greedy janitor, suddenly exclaimed.

'Who is that at the gate, Bartlett? My father has told you over and over again not to gossip at the gate. Come away at once.'

The man hastily withdrew his hand, but before he could close the wicket, Arthur flung him aside, and found himself face to face with Dorcas.

She uttered a faint cry, and blushed crimson. Then instantly jumping with a woman's quick wit at the conclusion, held out her hand, and said,

'I am so glad to see you. Come in. Papa will be back shortly. Shut the gate, Bartlett.'

Bartlett, murmuring mentally at the loss of his second sovereign, obeyed and withdrew.

Then began that sort of dialogue in which both interlocutors ask questions and neither answers.

'How can I ever thank you, Dorcas?'

'Arthur ! Where have you been all this time?'

'How came you to follow me?'

'Is your arm well again?'

'Have you ever thought of me, darling?'

'Why did you not write to me?'

'How came you to live here?'

And so on.

By and by they drew breath, and he told her of his past history, and his present residence.

'I have never ceased to love you, Dorcas !'

'Nor I to dream of you, Arthur !'

'My darling!'

'My love!'

And the trees waved, and the birds twittered, and the sun cast their young shadows on the grass.

There was a garden seat under some trees at a little distance, and Arthur led her to it.

'I have come to ask you to marry me.'

'What need is there to ask again,' said Dorcas, simply. 'I have waited for you.'

'But your father?'

'He has consented already,' said Dorcas. 'He consented when – when he found I loved you.' And the blush which a lady-like young person would have bestowed upon her consent to marry, this untutored girl found to arrive more readily at the memory of her confession to her father. It is possible that she reasoned thus: 'I love Arthur, and therefore why should I be ashamed to marry him, whom else *could* I marry? But to tell my love to a third person – ah – that *is* something to blush at.'

'Where is your father?' asked Arthur.

'It is his day for the chaplain.'

'His day for the chaplain! What do you mean? What chaplain?'

'The chaplain of the jail. Father goes every week to one of the chaplains at Pentridge, or the jail, and gives him money for the convicts.'

'Gives him money for the convicts. That is generous.'

'Papa is very generous, though no one knows it. He never gets out of the carriage even, but sends the money in, and the clergyman sends out a sort of account of what has been done with the former gift. He has made some sort of stipulation that the clergyman shall not see him or thank him.'

'It is very generous,' repeated Arthur, thinking also that it was rather mysterious. 'Your father is very rich.'

'I believe so,' says Dorcas. 'He has worked hard. And all for me.'

'You must live dull here, darling.'

'Well, yes. I was thinking too much of you, naughty boy, and that made me feel dull. But I had plenty to do.'

'Indeed.'

'Oh, yes. Dancing masters, and singing masters, and music masters. I am getting quite accomplished. But I would not learn too fast because of you.'

'Because of me! Why should I prevent you from being accomplished? I have a sister, and I want you to be like her.'

'I was afraid of leaving Australia without hearing of you. Papa has hoped – I have sometimes thought – that you might not return. He does not care to talk of you, nor of the old days at Ballarat. Papa wants me to be a "lady." He wants to take me home.'

'To England?'

'No, he doesn't like England. To Italy, or to France. He says that his memories of England are bitter.'

Arthur was silent for a moment, and said at last,

'Dorcas, before we marry, there are two secrets to be told.'

'Two secrets! My goodness, Arthur, what do you mean?'

'The first is one I have to tell you. My name is not Arthur Vern.'

She moved a little further from him, with a gesture of alarm.

'What is it, then?'

'Arthur Devine. Don't start, my darling, there is no shame in it, only misfortune. I should be the wealthiest man in England, if my uncle, whom we supposed to be dead, had not returned and dispossessed me.'

'So you told me,' said Dorcas, 'So your name is Devine.' She pouted and tossed her head. 'I hate people who go under false names.'

'It was foolish,' he was beginning to explain, when a twinkle in her eyes stopped him.

'I have written *Dorcas Vern* a hundred times,' said she, 'and now all my trouble is thrown away!'

He kissed her, of course.

'There, that will do. Now about the other secret.'

'That is more important, dear. It is about your early life. I want to know who and what your father is. He must have some history and antecedents, and it is right that I should know them.'

'You must ask him yourself, Arthur. I do not know.'

'Do you know nothing?'

'Nothing but what I have already told you. I never saw my mother.'

'You do not know her maiden name?'

'No. There is some secret about her, for my father told me so. What it is I do not know.'

'And you have heard nothing of your father's friends?'

'No, dear Arthur. But for him, I am alone in the world.'

'Not as my wife, dear one,' he cried, embracing her. 'My fortunes are linked with yours. When I tell your father the story of my love for you, I shall expect him to tell the secret of your birth to me. – Ah!'

Something came suddenly between them and the sun, and they started apart. Arthur leapt to his feet, to confront the lowering brows and wrathful glance of Crosbie.

'You will do what?' cried the old man, in a voice that shook with passion. 'You will demand secrets from me! You will come into my house, prying and inquiring! You! you! Is it not enough that my girl risked her good name once to save your worthless life, but you must imperil it again. How came you here? I see, by bribery.' He turned furiously to the trembling Bartlett. '*You* leave to-morrow. And now, Mr Vern, what have you to say before I have you turned out "like a dog" at the gate?'

The aspect of the gaunt, grim figure of the man, as, with eyes blazing with indignation at the words his unexpected return had enabled him to hear, he made as though he would spurn the intruder from his presence, was calculated to impress.

'Come, sir, answer! You can find words enough to befool silly girls with, I make no doubt. What business had you in my garden?'

'Pray go, Arthur,' whispered Dorcas. '*I* will speak with him.'

Arthur, conscious that if strict right were in question, he should not have forced an entrance, stammered something about waiting to see Miss Crosbie.

'To make inquiries about her father, I presume,' said Crosbie, between his teeth. 'Go, sir; there is the gate.'

The three were now alone together, and Arthur, driven to bay, burst out with his errand.

'I do not know how much you have overheard – in England

we do not consider it the part of a gentleman to listen – but I had a right to inquire concerning the mystery in which you have chosen to enshroud yourself. This young lady is to be my wife. I shall take her home to my sister – to my family. What *you* have been, I do not wish to know! I knew you in an honest trade, and that suffices. But I *must* and will know who *she* is; for, as there is a Heaven above me, I believe her no child of yours!'

Crosbie's face blanched with passion.

'No child of mine! Impudent scoundrel! She is to be your wife – to be honoured by being made the wife of Arthur Vern, the proscribed rebel, the cowardly dog who led his comrades into bloodshed, and then ran – with a girl's help – to shelter! Get ye gone! Out, I say! –'

'Father!' screamed Dorcas, covering her eyes; but it was too late. The furious man, galled in the sorest spot of his much-tortured breast, had struck the boy to the earth by one terrible blow.

There was a silence of a few moments – a silence that to Dorcas seemed hours – and then she became conscious that her father had raised her, that she had fainted, that the garden door was open, and that her lover had gone.

'My bird!' said Crosbie. 'You are not hurt! Look up! Speak to me!'

'Oh, father, how could you strike him! Cruel! – cruel!'

'Did you not hear him, Dorcas?' said he. 'It was beyond endurance, and my fierce temper conquered me. Forgive me, birdie!'

'Oh, father! You struck him! Shamed him! – and I love him. You have shamed *me* !'

'You must not think of him, Dorcas. No, no. I have brighter hopes for you than to make you the wife of Arthur Vern, the proscribed rebel.'

'His name is not Arthur Vern!'

'Oh, well. What then?'

'Arthur Devine. He would be the richest man in England, had not his uncle returned and seized upon his fortune. Heavens! father – what ails you!'

'What name?' gasped Rufus Dawes. '*Devine*, did you say! Oh God, it is not possible! No! Devine!'

'Father! What is this? What have I said? Devine was the name –'

He rose and put her from him hurriedly.

'Go in, my child, go in. I must think over this. It is' – he laughed piteously – 'possible that I have misjudged this young man. Go in, dear. I would be alone.'

She went in bewildered, and from an upper window watched him, walking up and down the grass, saw him gesticulate, as if conversing or striving to recall the arguments of past conversations. He would raise his hands to his head, as if in despair – would stamp his foot as if in wrath. By and by the paroxysm passed, he appeared to grow calmer, and presently came in and sought her.

'Can you tell me Mr Devine's address, my dear?'

She told him, and then fearing lest evil should come of it, inquired,

'Why do you want to know, father?'

'Because I am going to apologise to him for the insults I have inflicted on him.'

'My dear old daddy! There is no need of that – he will forgive you.'

She had made a motion as though she would have flung herself upon his neck, but something in his troubled air and pale face awed her, and she paused midway.

He put her from him with a gesture in which pain and tenderness were strangely mingled.

'There may be great need,' he said, and went out without another word.

3

CROSBIE LEARNS WHO ARTHUR VERN IS

ARTHUR made his way back as one in a dream. This was the result of Quaid's advice. This the outcome of his hopes and dreams! He had been thrust like a cur from the gate. He had been struck – struck in *her* presence by *her* father. All was over now. Even when he had arisen from the ground, and for his love's sake forced himself to restrain the impulse which prompted him to avenge the insult he had received in the only method in which it could be avenged, the furious old man had refused to listen to the explanation he would then have given. What should he do. How wipe out the memory of this indignity, how regain his self-respect, how revenge himself upon his avenger? He could not think calmly of it! Should he force his way into the house from which he had been thrust, and claim, regardless of all obstacles, the love which was his. No, *she* had beheld his degradation, had seen the blow, and watched him – him whom she should respect – grovelling in the dust at her father's feet. He reached his room, and locking the door, flung himself on the bed in agony of shame and wounded pride. Let it stand recorded that as he writhed in his self-torture, tears – hot tears which were no stain upon his youthful manhood – wetted the pillow. What need to further paint the bitter shame of a high spirit groaning under the first insult it finds itself powerless to avenge.

It was about three o'clock in the afternoon, when a knock came at his door.

'Who's there?'

It was a waiter. 'A gentleman below to see you, Mr Vern.'

'I cannot see him. Who is he?'

'Mr Crosbie,' said the man, not without respect. 'He says that he wished to see you particularly.'

'I will not see him.'

'Sir?'

'I will *not* see him, I tell you.'

Presently the man returned, 'He says that he will not keep you a moment, sir. He has a message for you.'

This was the last argument that could be used. Perhaps it was a message from *her*.

'I will come down then.'

The waiter led him to a private room, which looked upon the street, where Crosbie's heavy carriage – the carriages imported in 1855 were not of the newest fashion – was waiting for its master. Crosbie was sitting in the shadow of the curtain, and rose as he approached.

'I have come to ask your pardon,' he said.

'I thought you had a message,' was Arthur's retort.

'That is it. I come as from *her*, to ask if you would forget my violence.'

'It was so cruel a wrong, and in her presence, too! But that you were her father –'

'Stop,' said Crosbie, in a cold voice. 'You must accept the regrets I offer. Tush! we cannot fight a duel over it. If you love this young lady' – Arthur wondered why he did not say *my daughter* – 'you can consent to overlook the violence of a man twice your age, who has been instrumental in saving your life. Accept or refuse – it is little to me, save that, by accepting, we can talk on equal terms of a subject bearing on your own happiness.'

Arthur was disarmed by the sorrowful sternness of the tone, and held out his hand.

'You mean my love for your daughter, Mr Crosbie? I accept. I was as much to blame as yourself. I had no right to enter your house unknown to you.'

Crosbie did not take the proffered hand, but, bowing his head in acquiescence, went to the door and locked it.

'It is not about your marriage to the young lady whom you said this morning was not my daughter that I wish to speak. It is about yourself.'

'Myself!' *It is the money*, was the ill-considered thought that passed through Arthur's mind for an instant. 'What about myself?'

'Your name is not Vern.'

'I came this morning to tell you that it was not. It is Devine.'

Crosbie, still hiding as it were in the window curtains, continued.

'Would you mind telling me from what county you come, Mr Devine?'

'I was born in London, but my father's principal estate was in Essex.'

'Whereabouts?' asks Crosbie, after a pause.

'Near Harwich.'

'Your grandfather was a shipbuilder then?' says Crosbie, in a voice from which the last tone of hope seemed to have departed.

'I believe he was. Did you know him?' asks Arthur, striving to catch a glimpse of the face which is persistently kept in shadow.

'I have heard of him. But – but, let us continue, if you please. You said something about an uncle having returned and dispossessed you. Pray explain. Was there a dispute then?'

'No,' said Arthur, strangely moved. 'But my father's fortune belonged to my Uncle Richard, who was thought to be drowned in the *Hydaspes*. He returned five years ago and claimed the property that had been willed to him.'

'What!' cries Crosbie, suddenly coming out of his shadow, and thrusting forward a shaking hand wherewith to clasp the boy's wrist.

'He came back again,' said Arthur. 'He was not dead, as we thought.'

An expression of bewilderment passed over Crosbie's white wet face.

'I do not understand you, boy. Your Uncle Richard returned alive?'

'Yes. He had not been drowned after all. He had passed his life abroad in South America, in the Indies, on the Continent. What is the matter, sir? Are you ill?'

'No, no. I am tired – a spasm – go on, pray. This is a romance.'

'He presented himself at our house one Christmas eve. His tale was so strange that at first we doubted. But when he told my father stories of their youth, when he reminded my aunt of their childish play together, he was recognised and welcomed

– welcomed the more readily, for that we had always held the memory of "poor uncle Richard" as a household sorrow – Mr Crosbie!'

Crosbie, with a deep groan, had allowed his head to fall upon the table. At the touch of the young man's hand he starts up, and dashes a hand across his eyes.

'It is nothing – I – I knew a wanderer like him of whom you speak – who – ah me! – never came back to the loving hearts that waited for him.' Arthur imagines that he is speaking of his own early history, and is about to proceed, when the other checks him.

'What sort of man was this uncle of yours?' he asks, drawing back into the shadow.

'Tall, robust, black-haired, and bearded. A strong man. One of about your own height and bearing.'

There is a silence of some seconds. At last Crosbie speaks again in a low voice.

'It is a strange story. And he repaid the affection shown him by tenderness and consideration?'

Arthur laughs bitterly.

'No, by insolence, extravagance, and cruelty, by brutality, by intemperance, and by greed. Having once securely grasped our property, he squandered it in gambling and vice. Our house became a scene of riot and debauchery, he broke my father's heart, turned my sister from his door, refused us a pittance of the wealth we had resigned to him, and forced me to seek my fortune here under a changed name, a beggar and an outcast!'

Carried away by the memory of his wrongs, he has almost forgotten the presence of the man before him. Crosbie suddenly leaps up, and seizing him by the shoulders, drags him to the window, gazing into his face there with agonized eyes, as though to read in his soul the truth or falsehood of his story. A moment suffices for such examination. It is true, true without a doubt, and Crosbie, loosing his hold, flings up his hands as though about to wildly call on Heaven, but stifling the cry when upon his very lips, presently forces himself to sit, trembling.

'What is it?' cries Arthur. 'What has moved you? Did you know my uncle?'

Crosbie, silent and shaking, makes effort to reply, but finally nods only.

'I have seen Quaid about it. You know Quaid; and he is under the impression that there is some mystery about him. Do you think so?'

Crosbie rose, and it was evident that the thick stick which he carried, more it would seem for whim rather than necessity, had become essential to him.

'Come to me to-morrow — to-morrow at noon — I shall have something to say to you,' he says with averted face.

Arthur held out his hand.

'I do not comprehend this, Mr Crosbie, but I will do as you wish. Let us part friends.'

Crosbie moved to the door.

'I may see your daughter?'

'Can you not wait until to-morrow?' cries Crosbie with a piteous accent. 'It is not long to wait.'

And pushing aside the arm offered him, he hurried down the stairs.

As he stepped into his carriage, Mr John Rex, lurking at his window, caught sight of him, and uttered a cry of surprise.

'What is it?' said Sarah. 'Another of the Devine family?'

He said that it was 'only a woman nearly run over,' and began to talk at a furious rate on indifferent subjects. By-and-bye she went out of the room, and he hurriedly summoned the waiter.

'There was a gentleman here with a carriage and pair just now. Who is he?'

'Mr Crosbie, sir.'

'Crosbie, eh? Where does he live?'

'In a large house atop o' Bourke-street, sir. You can't well miss it; it's all alone.'

'Thank you. I think I know him. A rich man, ain't he?'

'Oh, very, sir.'

' 'Tis Rufus Dawes, or his ghost,' he said to himself when the waiter had gone. 'My luck's in. He's a rich man, is he? If I don't get enough out of him to take me clean away from *you*,' he added, shaking his fist at the door which led to his room,

'I'll consent to be tied to your devilish apron-string for the rest of my life.'

⇥ 4 ⇤

A SOUL'S TRAGEDY

WHEN Crosbie reached home Dorcas ran to meet him, and hanging to him, whispered,

'Well, father, what does he say?'

'You will see him to-morrow,' said Crosbie; and then, with his eyes fixed as though he looked upon something beyond her which she saw not, he essayed to pass on.

'Why, how cold your hands are, father! Come into the dining room. I will have a fire lighted.'

'No, no!' said he, still gazing into vacancy, 'I have work to do.'

He was half-way down the passage which led to the laboratory door, when she called him reproachfully back.

'You never kissed me!'

He turned, and caught her suddenly to his breast.

'Dorcas! Tell me! Do you indeed love this boy?'

'I have already told you father,' she replied, looking up through her blushes with steadfast eyes.

'Better than all the world besides?'

'I love him.'

'Better than you love me?'

'No – Yes – Oh! father!' she said, hiding her face, 'it is so different!'

'True,' he murmured, the far-gazing look returning, 'It is different,' and so, without kissing, turned and left her.

The laboratory had been specially constructed on a portion of the grounds where the bibulous publican had intended to build a 'smoking divan.' It was a two-storied brick building with a stone floor. On the lower story Crosbie had placed his furnaces and apparatus. In the upper he had contrived for himself a sort of study and bed-chamber. A writing table and chair made the study; an iron camp-bed with the simplest furniture, the bed-chamber. Though rich, Crosbie was not luxurious. Locking the door of the lower room behind him as he entered, he lit a lamp placed for him on a wooden table, and without bestowing a glance upon the various implements which lay scattered around as though some experiment of moment had been but recently interrupted, he tried the iron shutters to the windows, and finding them fast, ascended to the upper story, locking the doors as he went. Safe in his retreat the restraint he had put upon himself gave way, and burying his face in his hands he abandoned himself to the torrent of his thoughts.

A worse evil than he had ever dreamt of had come upon him. Imagining that he had safely escaped from out the awful ocean of his fate, a recurring wave, mightier than all the rest, had rushed upwards and overwhelmed him. Richard Devine was dead, had doubly died, as Rufus Dawes the convict, and as Tom Crosbie the shepherd. Yet here was Richard Devine's nephew, armed with a story that Richard Devine yet lived. Who was the imposter who had claimed, and held an heritage so fraught with evil, so weighted with sin and woe? There was no comrade of Crosbie's who could have guessed the secret. In the wild life of the diggings and the camp, Crosbie had ever taught his tongue the grimmest silence. The usurper must have arisen out of some darker and more dismal depth. He was a companion of Dawes, some fellow-sufferer of the chain and lash, some loosened tiger of Port Arthur, some escaped monster of Norfolk Island, some one of those doomed wretches among whom Rufus Dawes had learnt to curse God and live.

Pressing his hands upon his eyes, he sought within the dismal chambers of his memory for a clue to the recollection of the man who had achieved so monstrous a victory over fortune. In vain! In vain he summoned before him those hideous phantoms whose foul faces he had prayed long nights together might be banished from his dreams. In vain he called out about him in the dusk of the dimly-lighted chamber, the terrible ghosts of his former comrades. In vain among the villanous heads, which uprose one after another in the mirror of his memory, did he strive to find one upon whom he could fix suspicion. All types of the man-beast were reflected in that sinister looking-glass – the fox, the wolf, the tiger, and ape, grinned, snarled, yawned, and mowed by turns — but the face he sought for had not yet appeared. Ah! It comes! A dim twilight reigns in the foul barracoon of Norfolk Island prison. A boy sits adjusting the handkerchief, which he wears woman-wise upon his head, and behind the boy lounges a tall figure, black-browed, muscular, and broad-chested. The talk is of escape, of crimes undiscovered, of innocence unproved. The tall man relates how he traversed Europe to find a shipbuilder's son, and lost him. The marvellous machinery of the brain repeated the scene again, look for look, word for word, and to the lips of Crosbie rose again the question that had risen seventeen years before to the lips of Rufus Dawes. 'Should you know him again?' Yes, he *had* known him. It was Rex. Rex, who by some miracle of Satan's working, had been snatched from death. Rex, the greatest villain of them all!

He sprang up and paced the room with hurried steps, pacing up and down as paces a wild beast, seeking an outlet for escape and finding none. What should he do? How foil this villain, how assert his rights, and free his kindred from the incubus that oppressed their fortunes? The way was plain — to England and oust the imposter! Ay, and be denounced as an escaped convict! The same difficulty which had deterred him when, camped at the deserted settlement, he learned from the lips of Maurice Frere the story of his wealth, deterred him now. He could not speak without revealing that which would condemn him. Should he meet lie with lie? Rex had invented a story, so could he. True, — and be met by the demand to *prove* his tale, a demand which never had been made on the first claimant to Sir Richard's treasure. Rex had been acknowledged by the dead Frank Devine, Rex had influence and aid of circumstance, Rex was in possession. To charge the false Richard Devine with his imposture would be to call from him the simple sentence, 'This man is an escaped convict. True he says that I am one, but let public opinion judge between us.' Then the awful scandal, the ruin to his nephew, the misery to his child. *His* child! Ah, there again the shadow of his doom falls upon him, blighting his warm hopes with its cold shadow. She was not his child. An enquiry made into *his* antecedants would of necessity embrace *hers*. She would learn the story of her birth. Her father, the detested Frere, would claim her. She would be taught to hate the hypocrite who had stolen her from comfort to share the poverty that accident alone had softened and relieved. Then the old story of his crime and sentence to be again upon men's lips. The frightful evidence that had condemned him to be again discussed. The world – enriched by *her*, his only dream of Heaven in it – to again brand him with the name of 'Murderer.' No, no. He dare not face this cunning devil who had dispossessed him.

Cunning devil! Ay, but cannot cunning be matched with cunning? Cannot this mysterious Richard Devine who had driven the true heir from his house and hearth, be tempted into a departure as mysterious as his advent? Cannot acutely worded threats and hints of impending discovery artfully conveyed to him, force him to quit for safety's sake his hold upon his booty? Money can accomplish much – can purchase the service of brains unscrupulous to plan, and hands daring to execute. Might not that fortune which – ere it was won from the mine – he had thought to devote to the proving of his own innocence, be justly applied to the restoration of another's rights? What need for him to return at all? What need for any revelation of his past, any humiliation in his future life. Arthur Devine knew him but as Crosbie the digger, and did not love Dorcas the less because he met her first beneath the bark-roof of a country store. He would say nothing, and let them marry. Yet stay – Arthur had demanded to know the story of the girl's birth. Well – a lie could be found to fit. All would go well. Let Rex keep the money of the ship-builder. Let him squander it in riot and excess. It was fitting that a fortune gained by parsimony and greed should be expended in profligacy and vice. Let Rex be still Devine; Crosbie would be Crosbie still, and live beloved and blessed by the two young hearts who would know him but as their benefactor and their friend. Why struggle against his destiny? He had surely had enough of sacrifice. Once before, upon the barren beach of Hell's Gates, the means of escape had been ready to his hand, and he had sacrificed himself for a sentiment. A sentiment! Oh, pitiful thought! 'Twas a sentiment of honour and affection, a sentiment born of manliness and love. A sacrifice, did he say? – miserable selfishness! The rising night wind stirred around the house and moaned as moaned the sea on that eventful morning. The sea! – Ay, yonder it stretches sparkling and fair, and here at his feet the sweet sentence shapes itself again.

'GOOD MR DAWES!'

Bathed in sweat, and his whole frame trembling with the violence of that passion-storm which in man cannot break in tears, he flung himself on his knees by the table, and prayed for strength to aid in his resolve. There was but one course for him – the terrible course from which he had persistently turned while shuddering mindful of it. To reach this villain who had emerged from the abyss, it would be necessary for him to descend himself again into it. The happiness of Arthur and Dorcas could be only secured by complete confession. The only man who could place Arthur in possession of his fortune was the true Richard Devine. The only man who could remove the stain which seemed to rest upon Dorcas' birth was Rufus Dawes the convict; but the true Richard Devine, cannot live again but by means of Rufus Dawes, the convict. Rufus Dawes cannot live but through Crosbie the respectable and honoured. The frightful problem admitted but of one solution. To prove that he is Richard Devine, Thomas Crosbie must confess that he is Rufus Dawes! *Now Rufus Dawes is an escaped convict, and the punishment for escaped convicts is hanging.*

In the human soul are depths which the intellect fails to fathom. In the great crisis of our life, when brought face to face with annihilation, we are suspended gasping over the great emptiness of death – we become conscious that the 'self' which we think we know so well has strange and terrible capabilities. The mists that encompass our self-knowledge become transparent. Deep calls to deep within us. We look down into the profundity of our own souls and are appalled. In those undreamed-of voids our consciousness cannot fly. An infinity of sensations is beneath us; to look is to swoon, to lose grasp of ourselves, to fall headlong. The terrible Duality which is Man is alone with itself in that horrible solitude of consciousness, and our soul at once judges and defends, condemns and pleads, asserts the majesty of our good, and dismally confesses the power of our evil. Become at once God and Satan, our soul contends with itself for the Heaven of its own approval.

To describe a tempest of the elements is not easy, but to describe a tempest of the soul is impossible. How can one set down in cold blood – laboriously drawing characters upon paper – the multitudinous and varied sensations that go to make up the myriad ideas sweeping like storm-birds over that waste and awful ocean whose shores no man hath touched, nor will touch while time rolls. Amid the fury of such a tempest, a thousand memories – each bearing in its breast the corpse of some dead deed whose influence haunts us yet – are driven like feathers before the blast, as unsubstantial and as unregarded. Our lonely, helpless egotism is afloat rudderless in the storm. We lose our individuality, and by and by, when the bright sun shines and the clouds pass, the poor 'I' that was so taut and trim in the morning, lies shattered and water-logged, scarce able to crawl to port. This much we can feel and tell, but who, escaping thus, can coldly describe the hurricane which has overwhelmed him? As well ask the rescued sailor to tell you of the marvels of mid-sea, when the great deeps swallowed him, and the darkness of death encompassed him round about.

How is it possible to paint the visions which enfolded the soul of Richard Devine. He lay motionless in ecstasy of self-communion. Before him, vast and terrible, swept the array of phantoms which he knew to be his past deeds. Again he played a boy upon the beach, again the hammers tinkled in the sheds, and the sweet smell of new-mown hay floated from the fields of Mere. Once more the ribald song was sung, once more he heard the hard shrill laugh and caught the echoes of unholy mirth. The lights in foreign billiard rooms burn bright, hark how the balls click-click together! To gamble is to live, excitement is a need more absolute than bread. How ludicrous the shifts of poverty, the pawned shirt, the buttoned coat, the meanness which stoops to borrow from those we despise, the extravagance which compels to repay such lenders a hundred fold. High foams the flood in the old Dutch town, our profligate has met his fate at last. Yet no, yon fair-haired girl has saved him. Poor waif and stray, one could almost pity so great a dandy blowing bellows for the alchemist who dreams of precious stones and life-elixirs. A diamond mine! One for the law to light upon. It might have been guessed moreover, that the miser-knight would not have pardoned a poor marriage, but who could have foretold an end to the fateful journey, so bloody and so sudden? For life! The convict ship, the fever, and the wreck. Why not confess the secret? No, he did right, though life was bitter on that barren shore. Sweet Dora, but for thee — for thee. For thee, embodiment of all my dreams of confidence and love, for thee, sweet minister of pity. What matter hunger, thirst, and toil. The sharp brine stings, the gloomy sea is cold as death, but I will save her. What is my life to me that I should pause to risk it. Life! To live has been my curse. Despised by all, death even spurns me — gentle-handed death, the tender soother of all sorrows. The desert casts me out of her, the roaring sea, insatiable of lives, scorns mine. Abandoned by fortune, mine the doom to live while luckier men win at the murder-lottery of the straws. Now I have conquered. I am an escaped convict, and for such the gibbet creaks. They cannot choose but hang me. It is best. I could not live that life again. I am too old. I learned to live, to be respected, to be human. It is not death I fear. I could die now and happily. It is the awful method of the death, the violent and brutal wrenching out of life. The jeers, the noose, the — Oh! it revolts, it shames me. But one step — one little step from all this present comfort and I tread a gallows floor, the lawful chattel of the hangman with his rope, the surgeon with his knife. And this for honor! Honor that will never be accorded to me. Honor, barren honor, that monumental stone colder than the corpse it covers. God! I must go lonely to my death — for by that death I earn the horror of all those who loved me. In hot impulsive youth I dared the sacrifice — but now! — now when my blood is cold, my hair is grey, when life swift-drawing to its natural close claims comfort and regard, now when aweary and wayworn, I linger yet a little with my broken hopes a lonely man with but one soul to love him — *now* to be summoned for a public shame! O it is too cruel! Is there no other way? No other way my friend my brother?

Thou who did'st deign to clasp my bloodstained hand in thine – thou who did'st weep and pray with me – thou who did'st draw my soul alive out of the pit. North! North! my prison-Christ, who died that I might live for her, hear me and help me!

If what some say be true, and, from the great Unknown, spirits of friends love-linked to us, return to cheer and guide us in our trouble, then might this convict claim to be comforted by spirit-words, and soothed by loving touch of spirit fingers. Dora and North – the Woman and the Priest – those twin sweet influences that, balm-like, fell into his bruised and passion-wasted heart, to heal it by the power of Love and Mercy – surely they might aid him in this crisis of his fate, and save his struggling soul. The lamp burned low and faded as the night melted in morning. The pure dawn blew from the bay, and as the opal light stole into being timidly, he heard, or thought he heard, North's voice. 'Be of good cheer! My brother!' And with that, raising his head, if haply he might catch one glimpse of the bright spirit he made sure had glorified that gloom he thought to find about him, the sweet wind lifted his hair, and on his heated brow laid its cool breath. 'A woman's hand!' he cried. 'Dora!' and starting suddenly to life – the room was empty, and the Day had come.

His duty lay before him.

⇤ 5 ⇥

ARTHUR IS THE BEARER OF A MESSAGE

THE next morning Mrs Carr observed in her husband a change for the better. He had become almost cheerful, and ate his breakfast with apparent relish.

'Sarah,' said he, during the progress of that meal, 'I have been ill-tempered of late, but I hope we shall have no more tiffs. I am going to turn over a new leaf and make the best of things. I wish we were back in New South Wales again.'

The poor woman, with all her suspicions of him, was wonderfully touched by this expression of regret.

'Ah! John, if you would only use me kindly, how happy we might be! I do speak sharply sometimes, I know, but it is for your good.'

'I wish with all my heart we were back,' repeats John. 'I am afraid to move because of this boy. I am not at all sure that he didn't see me yesterday.'

'I have only to see Frere, and then we can go at once,' said she, her heart fluttering with an almost youthful affection. 'Indeed, I won't see him if you so particularly object.'

John Rex frowned.

'Oh, you may as well do *that*, after all your waiting. After all, I shall not be sorry to hear of his setting down. He deserves more than you can say to him, I'm sure; only I wish you'd get it over.'

'I'll go this afternoon,' she said, willing to fall in with his humour.

He smiled this time.

'Very well. You'll find your hate revive when you see him, I'll be bound. By George, I'm curious to know what he'll say, though. It will be a surprise for him, eh? I shall be on thorns till you return.'

'Why not get a buggy from these people, and go for a drive?' she said, patting his head as one who soothes a fretful child. 'You must be moped to death here.'

'No, no,' said he. 'No drives for me in this town. I'm afraid to show, and that's a fact. I shan't be comfortable until we get back to Nine Creeks!'

'As you wish, dear,' returned his wife, kissing him tenderly. 'I will go out to the Stockade this afternoon. That done, you will be free to go home, John!'

'Ay,' says John. 'I hope so.'

Arthur Devine, in the public room below, did not eat much breakfast. The memory of his strange interview with Crosbie had caused him to pass a sleepless night. Why had the man exhibited such emotion? What would be the news he was now to hear from his lips? He could not swallow a mouthful, and having forced himself, with the utmost difficulty, to wait until the elaborately-ornamented coffee-room clock pointed to the hour of nine, interpreted the word 'morning' in his own fashion, and dashed off to the appointment.

His ring at the bell was this time answered with alacrity, and Bartlett preceded him humbly to the house. It was evident that he was expected. He looked about him for some sign of Dorcas, but saw none.

'Miss Crosbie down yet?' he asked with that assumption of carelessness which lovers fondly think deceives.

'Mr Crosbie said that I was to take you straight to *him*, sir,' replied the man. 'He's in his lab'try.'

The heavy door was open, but the servant did not venture beyond the threshold.

'Mr Crosbie's upstairs. Straight on, sir.'

Arthur looked about him for an instant, and noticed that the laboratory was in perfect order. All bottles, jars, and apparatus were carefully put in their places, and even the crucibles were emptied and put away. 'Quaid said he was always pottering about here,' said Arthur. 'The place looks as if it had not been touched for a month.' The reflection was not unnatural, for how could he guess that Crosbie had spent two hours in thus putting his affairs in order?

He mounted the stairs. The door of the upper-room was also open, and the man he sought sat at the writing table.

He was sitting composedly in the arm-chair, with his hands folded in the attitude of a man who, having accomplished a task satisfactorily, is wearily, yet gratefully, waiting for the reward of his labours. A little sealed packet, which from its size would seem to contain a quire of note-paper, lay at his right hand, a letter on his left.

'Good morning, Mr Devine,' said he. 'I have been waiting for you.'

Arthur bowed. It was evident, from the calm and gentle tones in which the old man addressed him, that he had not only made up his mind firmly upon his course of action, but that that course of action was a kindly one. He hastened to assure himself.

'Have I your consent, sir?'

'It is unnecessary,' said Crosbie. 'Dorcas loves you. I trust you are equally sure that you love her?'

'I *do* love her, indeed, sir,' returned Arthur, with simple earnestness.

Crosbie sighed softly, and laid his hand upon the letter.

'I hope you do. – Will you please take this to its address.'

Arthur stared, and took the letter. The address was

> *Captain Maurice Frere,*
> > *Inspector-General of Penal Establishments,*
> > > *The Stockade,*
> > > > *Pentridge.*

The young man flushed.

'Captain Frere is a distant relation of mine. A sort of second cousin, but he knows nothing of me, if that is what you mean, sir.'

'You mistake me,' said Crosbie, quietly. 'You were speaking yesterday of some mystery about your uncle. I can explain it, and to do so it will be necessary for me to see Captain Frere.'

'If it is anything disgraceful,' said Arthur, 'I do not want it explained. I bear him no malice.'

A faint red tinge overspread Crosbie's face. 'You are generous,' said he sadly but firmly, 'I am glad of it, but this mystery not only concerns your own happiness, but that of the young lady you propose to marry. You must hear it explained.'

'May I see her?' asked Arthur.

'When you return. I then relinquish all control over her. Now go. Take that letter to Captain Frere, and he will return with you. He will doubtless tell you its contents, and you will be in some measure prepared for the rest.'

'But –'

'Oblige me by going at once. There is a horse saddled for you in the stables. It is urgent, I assure you – most urgent, or I would not ask it.'

'One would think it was a matter of life and death, to hear you talk, sir,' said Arthur, with a smile. 'Well, I'll go; though, since you have given your consent, it's rather hard I shouldn't see her first.'

Crosbie motioned impatiently with his hand.

'*Pray* do as I ask you,' he said. 'I have told you that my

consent to your marriage has been rendered quite unnecessary. When you return, you will understand everything that now seems inexplicable. The sooner you see Captain Frere, the sooner will your mind be at ease. Go, if you please. I will wait for you.'

There was an air of authority in the tone so calm and assured, that Arthur felt constrained to obey.

As he made his way out he heard Crosbie's bell ring, and the servant accompanied him to the stables.

'I told the young lady, sir,' said he, with a grin.

True enough, by the side of the saddled horse stood Dorcas, rosily expectant.

'What news?' she asked, as Arthur caught the bridle, and with a nod dismissed the grooms. 'I could learn nothing from him last night.'

'All well, I hope, darling. Have you seen him?'

'No. He has forbidden me to approach him until your return. Where are you going to, Arthur? and what does this mean?'

He showed her the letter.

'There is some mystery to be solved, it seems, by the aid of this cousin of mine, Captain Frere. I suppose I shall know when I see him.'

'There is something in all this that frightens me, Arthur,' said she. 'By what right are secrets built up between us? Hasten, darling, hasten, and put an end to these mysteries.' So, pressing a kiss upon her lips, he rode away.

⊷ 6 ⊶

THE CONVICTS' PROTEST

DURING the night which had witnessed Richard Devine's struggle with himself, one of those frantic protests against the murderously-foolish system of convict discipline favoured by Captain Maurice Frere, had been resolved upon by certain prisoners in Pentridge Stockade.

The fine old practices of knocking men down and jumping

on them, of striking them with 'neddies,' of 'searching' them violently and unnecessarily, of savagely taunting them when under punishment, were in full swing. The hulks – the *Success* and the *President* – bore indeed a worse reputation. The doubly-dyed scoundrels who were there confined had been tormented into beings near akin to fiends, and the utmost severity was necessary. Yet needful severity exercised capriciously, accompanied by jeers, and supplemented by acts of personal violence, was apt to become tyranny. After enduring the life in these 'floating hells' for a little, one might not impossibly have arrived at the same conclusion as did a notable prisoner, who was there confined until death released him – 'By God, sir, I would as soon commit a murder as kiss a maid!'[1] In Pentridge, therefore, prisoners had the consolation of knowing that there was still a worse place to which they might be sent. Captain Frere, whose duties took him to each place in turn, however, contrived to keep them very enjoyably employed by many ingenious devices. Sometimes, however, he met with a spirit as fierce as his own, and then horrible contests of sullenness and tyranny would take place, to the great amusement and edification of the other prisoners.

A spirit of this nature dwelt in the breast of Purfoy – a young man who, captured at the Eureka, had been recognised by the hawk-eyed Frere, as a 'Sydney-sider.' Young Purfoy avowed with many oaths and protestations that he had 'done his time,' but Frere was not to be so gainsaid. 'Then you'll do a little more, my boy,' said he. 'No lies. They won't do here.' 'It is you that lie!' cries Purfoy, and so the battle began between them. The report of his daring speech, and the fact that though so young, he was once a 'Sydney-sider' and a rebel, combined to make Purfoy somewhat distinguished in the prison. He broached a theory also about his birth, which made him doubly interesting. 'My father's a swell,' he would say, 'and when I get out I'll find him.' It appeared that some hint of this boast reached the ears of Captain Frere, for one day that funny fellow stopped Purfoy at his shovelling (the gang were occupied with some improvements) and said,

1. The prisoner known as Melville. Vict. P.P. 1856-7. 'Penal Establishments,' 720.

'Well, Mr Purfoy, have you heard of your father yet?' Purfoy grew crimson with rage, but said nothing. The gang guffawed as in duty bound.

'Come, Purfoy, haven't you got a tongue?'

'What's my father got to do with *you*,' said Purfoy, at last; 'my father's a gentleman, that's more than what you are.'

'Insolent, eh!' laughed Captain Frere. 'I tell you what it is, my lad, I never had the honour of knowing your gentlemanly father, but I knew a woman of your name, and if she's your mother, you're the son of as great a –'

He did not finish the sentence, for the lad struck him, and was the next instant felled himself to earth.

The sympathising gang prophesied a flogging, and the hulks, but one or two old hands knew their tyrant's temper better. 'He'll never bring you up, lad, for the blow was of his own provoking, d'ye see, and he don't want the magistrate to know that just now. But he'll make your life a hell to ye here, make no mistake about that.'

The old hands were right. Maurice Frere said nothing, but Purfoy was, from that moment, marked for destruction. It became a struggle between the two fierce spirits. When Purfoy was treated to the Stone – a punishment which consisted simply in making a prisoner sit chained and handcuffed, on a big stone, doing nothing, and eating nothing until he gave in – he would affect intense enjoyment, and when his aching back-bones, and empty belly, compelled him to surrender, he would assume that he had thus sat and starved for his own pleasure. Even Captain Frere's little jests on such occasions – such as 'Well my man, you look comfortable. Would you like a holiday this afternoon to write to your friends? – ' or, 'Ha Jack, wouldn't you like a nice beefsteak now? a brown juicy fellow, hey? with onions, hey?' did not move him. When put into the 'cells' he begged to be allowed to stop there, and would openly state that he preferred to live in the Crystal Palace. The 'Crystal Palace' was an acre or so of ground fenced in recently with heavy slabs. Inside this fence were huts about twelve feet long, ten feet wide, and nine feet high, which, being supplied with wheels, could be moved about. In each of these huts, nineteen, and sometimes twenty men slept, their hammocks being slung to an iron bar which ran along the centre of the hut. Such refractory prisoners as Purfoy were locked up in this place.

A gentleman of sporting tastes, who lived some years in the colonies, was struck when visiting a well-appointed kennel in the shires, at the similarity between the provision for the comfort of hounds and for the comfort of convicts. The chief difference lay in the unreasoning obedience of the hounds, who sat whimpering upon their several tails until their names were called. 'If we could only have got our fellows to *do that!*' remarked regretfully the worthy gentleman.

In the gloom of this Crystal Palace, Purfoy said one night, 'I stand this no longer. Better be dead than lead this life,' and by and by it was gradually understood that a 'protest' against Captain Frere's method of treating his fellow creatures should take place on the first opportunity.

Arthur reached the prison at mid-day, and gave his name as 'Mr Arthur Devine, with an urgent message for Captain Frere.'

He was asked into the room where the visiting justice and such great people were accustomed to leave their hats, and after due delay Captain Frere appeared.

'Mr Arthur Devine, – surely not –'

'A relation of yours? – Yes. I am a cousin I believe.'

'A son of Frank, eh! 'Pon my soul now, I shouldn't have thought it. I heard you had come out here from Colonel McNab. Pray, young man, how was it you never called on me before?'

'I didn't care about it,' said Arthur boldly. 'You see I had just experienced a great reverse of fortune. I had been digging, and, – I was in the Eureka affair.'

'Indeed,' said Frere with a laugh. 'Stupid absurdity. I am glad you didn't get into a mess though. Well, how is your Uncle? I ask after him because I feel a sort of interest in his welfare peculiar to myself. You are aware I suppose that I was nearly getting the family fortune.'

'I have heard of it,' said Arthur, 'but never mind that now. I have brought a letter with me for you, which I want you to read at once,' and he gave him Crosbie's note.

Maurice Frere opened it leisurely, read it eagerly, and then sprang up with an astonished oath. 'Who gave you this?'

'A man who knows Uncle Richard — why? — what is the matter?'

'Read this,' said Frere, and gave it to him.

To Captain Maurice Frere

SIR, The bearer of this, Mr Arthur Devine, will bring you to a house where you will find an escaped convict, Rufus Dawes, living under the name of Thomas Crosbie. Be kind enough to come yourself, as Dawes can relate particulars of the wreck of the Lady Franklin, which are fit for your ears only.

'What do you think of that?' asked Frere.

'Think,' cried Arthur, 'I do not know what to think. Why, it's the man himself.'

'What do you mean?'

'It is the writer, who is Thomas Crosbie, or Rufus Dawes. Great heavens, I expected a mystery, but not such a dreadful one as this.'

'And pray,' added Frere, laughing his evil laugh, 'how did you come across this escaped convict?'

'I met him at the diggings,' said Arthur.

'Oh — and how came you to be the bearer of his messages to me?'

'I — I am engaged to be married to his daughter,' said Arthur, feeling that he was blushing despite himself.

'Ho, ho!' says Frere. That is it, is it. Cute dog. I see his game. He's tired of the concealment which puts him in fear of his life, and he is in hopes that as *you* want to marry his daughter, *I* will let him off. But he's mistaken for once.'

'Captain Frere,' cries Arthur, in great alarm, 'I had not thought of this, believe me. I understood that this letter contained some information about my uncle Richard. You will not surely —'

'Uncle Richard be damned,' Frere interrupted in great heat. 'It's all a dodge of the scoundrel's, don't you see,' and he snatched the letter. 'But I'll show him that I am not to be trifled with in this fashion. Here, Hailey! Bisset!' he called, stepping to the door. 'My dog cart! Come on, young man,' he added, striding down the yard toward the prison. 'We will go and look up this future father-in-law of yours!'

'Captain Frere,' cries Arthur, 'Do not do this! I beg you, I implore you! It is a mistake, it must be a mistake. The man is rich, well-known, and respected. This is some madness, some joke, Captain Frere! Even if it be true, what good can it do to anyone to arrest him. Think of his daughter. Think –'

They had already passed through two doors, and had well nigh penetrated to the innermost yard. Frere turned angrily back at the last door.

'Confound his daughter!' he cried, 'What is his daughter to me? I've got my duty to do. This scoundrel has defied me often enough in days gone by. Impudent villain! I'll make him smart for it!'

The warder held the door open, and as Frere passed through, Arthur caught his arm.

'For God's sake, sir! Have mercy. You may need it yourself one day. What good can it do you to plunge again into misery a man who had escaped and lived honourably. Turn back. Let us reconsider this, I implore you!'

They had reached an angle of the wall, by the side of which the Crystal Palace gang were working. Arthur held Frere by the arm, and strove with all his might to draw him back.

'It is not yet too late,' he cried. 'Be merciful!'

'Curse the boy!' cries Frere, savagely. 'Why should I be merciful. Let me go!' and he turned the angle.

There was a scream, a scuffle, the sound of dull blows, and then Arthur, pressing on, saw the Inspector prone upon the ground, bleeding in the head, while some twenty or thirty convicts struck at his prostrate body with shovels, battered it with stones, and jumped savagely upon it with iron heels.

The 'protest' had been made at last, in the only form in which, to convict minds, it was likely to be successful.

Calling loudly for help, Arthur dashed at the body and dragged it away. Half a dozen men, whooping, rushed at him, but a young man who seemed the ringleader of the attack drove them back with a whirl of his bloody spade.

'That's enough, mates!' he cried. 'I swore I'd kill the devil, and I've done it. We don't want anyone else.'

The men retreated in a mob, as though terrified at their own act; and a rush of warders and constables to the spot drove them within the palisading.

Frere, lying helpless in Arthur's arms, groaned only.

'Let us carry him out of this,' said Arthur, horrified at the sudden change in their relative positions. 'Get the doctor quick. He's dying.'

'Yes,' says Hailey. 'They've threatened him a long time, but they've done it now for certain.'

The stockade was humming like a disturbed hive. If the other prisoners got news of the murder, there was every probability of a general riot.

'Let us take him out of the prison,' said Hailey, 'if we can. Through the little door, and turn to the right. There's an empty yard there, and we can get him to his own quarters without anyone seeing him.'

The frightened bearers obeyed, running with the body. At each jolt of their uneven pace, the unhappy man groaned. As they entered the little yard, they were met by Mr Pine, the newly-appointed surgeon.

'Bring him this way,' said he. 'Steady! there is no danger. The guards are doubled, and the Superintendent has sent for the troops. Gently now! This way with him. Into the chaplain's room.'

The young man spoke calmly and firmly. His father had been for many years surgeon to convict ships, and it was possible that firmness and calmness were family virtues.

The chaplain – a portly and comfortable gentleman, by name Meekin – received the ghastly burden, with many expressions of horror-stricken regret.

'Good Heaven! The villains! The Inspector, too! How awful, Mr Pine! In the midst of life – dear me! Pray bring him in. – Mind his poor head! – And all in a moment! Carefully, my dear young sir! And a lady waiting to see him!'

'There, that will do,' said Pine to the bearers. 'You may go. I don't know your name, sir, but as you were with him, you had better stop. Raise his head. Hand me the scissors. Set the window open.'

He rapidly cut away the coat and shirt, and then, snipping the hair from the temples, proceeded to examine the nature and the extent of his injuries. It appeared that the skull had been cut by some sharp instrument – probably a spade – but the brain had not been injured. Two ribs were fractured, and the chest much bruised and cut.

'There's some vinegar – bathe his temples,' said Pine; and then, feeling him all over, pursed up his lips with an expression of alarm.

'Dear me; is it fatal?' asked Meekin.

Pine shook his head ominously.

'We had best get the villains identified at once,' said he. 'He won't last long.'

As he spoke, Frere opened his eyes.

'I've got it this time,' he said, and then relapsed again. Pine mixed some brandy and water.

'Give him that,' said he to Arthur, 'when he revives. We must get these men brought up here at all risks.'

'There is a lady in the next room,' says Meekin, 'whom I met enquiring for him. She says she has urgent business. I had better ask her to go.'

'Of course, ask her,' said Pine, going. 'He is not in a fit state to see anyone – *now*, at all events.'

Meekin quitted the room, and Arthur was left alone with the wounded man. The sudden and fearful fate which had overtaken this trifler with men's lives seemed to be in a manner retributive for his hardness of heart. 'If he had only turned back with me this would not have happened,' he thought.

Frere opened his eyes, and presently sat up.

'Where am I? Oh, I rememeber.' He made a movement to get off the bed, but failed. 'Send Hailey to me. That young villain shall swing for this!'

'Lie down, sir! – lie down! They will be here in a moment.'

There came from the next room the sound of Meekin's gentle tones expostulating, and then a woman's voice said,

'I say I must see him, sir! It is important.'

Frere started.

'Whose voice is that? I know that voice. Come in! Let her come in there!'

Arthur, hearing on the gravelled walk that swept around the cottage the tramp of feet, strove to quiet him.

'Hush! sir! hush! here comes the doctor with the prisoners. One moment!'

'Confound it, who are you?' cried Frere, his violence of temper conquering his weakness, 'Am I to be obeyed or not! Come in there, I say!' and he fell back exhausted on his pillow, just as Mrs Carr entered by one door, and the prisoner, Purfoy, handcuffed, ironed, and guarded, was pushed forward through the other.

Frere raised his head and the clanking of the irons attracting his attention, he looked first at the prisoner.

'That is my murderer,' said he, slowly and vindictively. 'He struck me with his spade. I recognized you, Richard Purfoy, sharp as you think yourself, and you shall hang for this!'

'I don't deny it,' said Purfoy, doggedly, 'I have hated you all my life, and if I've killed you I'll die happy.'

The woman at the door uttered a piercing scream and started forward.

'God forgive me,' she cried, 'I never thought it would come to this. Maurice, he is *your son*!'

The wounded man twisted himself round upon his pillow, and caught her savagely by the wrist.

'So it is you – she-devil, is it? But you lie.'

Purfoy turned ghastly pale – the paler for the red splash upon his young face – 'Mother!' he said, and stood with chattering teeth.

'I am not your mother, poor lad,' said Sarah, trembling also. 'Your mother is dead. This villain let her die in the streets of Hobart Town, and I took you from her arms that I might be revenged upon him. Have you forgotten Lucy Barnes, Maurice?'

Frere groaned, and loosed his grasp of her wrist. Many things that he had once wondered at were plain to him now. The memory of the departure from Hobart Town. The child he had seen in the garden at Sydney. He understood the plot which the woman he had degraded had formed against him. Firm to the last, however, in his indomitable courage, he flung the torture back upon her.

'Son or no son. He shall hang for this. Take him away. He is my murderer!'

Arthur sickened, made from the room.

The warders, horror-stricken, pulled the unhappy boy by the arms, but he remained with open mouth and hanging jaw, over-powered by the appalling fact, that in the man whom he hated most, he had murdered the 'father' whom he had all his life yearned to honour.

'For Heaven's sake take him out,' cried Pine. 'Madam, what does this all mean.'

But Sarah stood silent, rigid, terrible, her hair bristling with horror, her eyes dilated.

Suddenly the gaze of the boy, previously fixed upon the implacable face of the wounded man, turned as if fascinated to her own. Raising his hand with a frightful curse, he made as though to sprinkle her with the blood in which it had been imbrued, and then shriek after shriek bursting from his lips, they dragged him away.

Sarah fell on her knees by the bed side. 'Maurice! Unsay those words! Do not let them hang your own son. He is your son, I swear it. I meant but you should find him a convict – a convict like those you have tormented.'

Frere pushed her away, and beckoned Pine. 'There is a letter in my pocket, give it to me.' Pine found it, it was soaked with his blood. 'I am dying,' said he, 'but I'm not beaten. That boy shall hang were he ten times my son. And here,' he continued, shaking the letter with a violence that nothing but his passion could have inspired in him, 'here is another villain who shall hang too. A villain who has baffled me often, but I have him now. Rufus Dawes!'

Sarah rose to her feet, absolutely calmed by this new cause of excitement.

'Rufus Dawes alive! God help you! Alive! He is your cousin – the man whom my husband personated – he is Richard Devine!'

Frere gasped – 'Richard Devine! He! And he has a daughter! A daughter! O God!' The awful clearness of vision which comes with approaching death illuminated all the dismal story. 'A daughter! Quick! Where's that boy who was here? Pine! Fetch him! Do you hear me?'

Arthur was already hurrying from the place, when a running

warder stopped him. 'You're wanted, sir. The Captain has sent for you. He is dying.'

Arthur, mastering his disinclination, turned back.

Frere was nearly gone. He lay in Pine's arms, breathing hard. When they told him that the person for whom he asked had returned, he roused himself and drank some brandy. 'Clear the room!' he said. 'Leave me alone with this gentleman.' He was obeyed, and then drawing the young man to him, with one hand, – the other still clutching the fatal letter – he whispered, 'You spoke of a daughter to this man! What is her name?'

'Dorcas!'

'What is she like? Quick, boy, quick!' His face was changing, softening, and as Arthur looked he found there a strange likeness.

'Dark – with brown eyes – Oh, heaven, she is like – like –'

'Like *me*!' said the dying man, with a smile. 'You are right; she is my daughter. He saved her. I understand it now – now, when it is too late. Here,' he thrust the letter into Arthur's shaking hand. 'Take it to him – Tell him – poor fellow, he need not be afraid of me – of me – any more!' with a groan he fell back, dead.

✦ 7 ✦

JOHN REX PLAYS HIS LAST CARD

TERRIFIED at the strange revelation, no less than at the unexpected and dreadful death of the unhappy man, Arthur, having summoned assistance, made from the room. He rode Melbourne-wards at a hand-gallop, eager to consult with Quaid as to the best course to be adopted in the complicated circumstances in which he found himself, and on the road he passed the carriage of Sarah Purfoy. In order to arrive at a right comprehension of the course events afterwards followed, we must endeavour to simultaneously bear in mind the action of each of these two persons. It so fell out that, pulled by different strings, each was drawn to the same spot – the house of Crosbie.

Arthur, full of perturbation, sought Quaid. 'Here is a frightful thing,' he cried, and narrated the circumstances of the murder. 'It seems that Crosbie is a convict! A convict, transported for murder!'

'A convict, eh?'

'Yes. He had written to poor Frere to give himself up. Dorcas is Frere's daughter!'

'Frere's daughter! There is some extraordinary mystery about *that*! I can understand the other item of news. Crosbie is a convict, is he?'

'Yes – his real name is Rufus Dawes – he –'

'Rufus Dawes!' cries Quaid, jumping up and running to his brand-new safe. 'Rufus Dawes, did you say? Splendid! Come with me! Oh, this is wonderful!'

'What do you mean?' asked Arthur, amazed. 'I do not understand –'

'Never you mind,' cries Quaid, slapping his papers. 'Oh, this is glorious! Crosbie Rufus Dawes! That my worthy grandfather had lived to see this day! Come with me! Let us go and see him! He is a noble fellow! – or a most astute villain! Let us go!'

In the meantime Sarah Purfoy, her nerves unstrung by the scene through which she had passed, reached the Bull and Mouth, eager to tell Rex the dreadful end to her hideous plotting.

'Mr Carr was out.'

She shuddered with presentiment of evil.

'Where?'

The waiter – bribed with a sovereign – did not know. Mr Carr had gone out shortly after Mrs Carr had left. The waiter did not know where.

Sarah stifled her terrors, and knowing Rex's customs of bribery, mentally calculated his resources, and then produced *five* pounds.

'I want to know where he is gone. I will give you this if you will tell me.'

The waiter, who saw in Sarah nothing more alarming than a jealous woman, took the money and at once opened his heart.

'He didn't exactly know where the gentleman had gone, but

he could guess. Mr Crosbie was here to see a young man who was stopping in the house. Mr Carr asked Mr Crosbie's address, last night, and asked it again before he went out.'

'What was the name of the young man?'

'His name was Vern!'

A light flashed upon Sarah, who saw, with woman's keenness, a great portion of the truth. She knew that the young man, Vern, was none other than Arthur Devine – the dispossessed. Vern was in love with the rich Crosbie's niece; what more likely but that Rex had gone to the rich Crosbie with a proposal to sell him the secret of Arthur's fortune (a secret which then was, and would be for at least a month longer, known only to himself) for the means of escape from *her*. Her lips tightened at the thought, and she regained her courage.

'That will do – thank you. I understand. Go and have the horse put in again.'

She would go at once to Crosbie's, and if Rex had deceived her, he should pay the penalty with his life. She would give him up.

What Rex, however, had really gone to do was this. The last glimmer of his old audacity had led him to the contrivance of a bold and desperate scheme, to the rapid execution of which he was urged by certain ominous symptoms of rebellion in his hitherto obedient brain. His dissipated life in Europe, and the shock he had received in the house in Clarges-street, had combined to injure that 'intellect' on which the scoundrel prided himself. He was conscious that he was not the man he had been, and had primed himself for a last daring exploit. He had gone to Rufus Dawes to say, – 'You are my comrade, an escaped convict; you are rich, I have been personating you. I have been detected. There is a vast fortune at your feet – *give me half, or I give you up to justice!*'

According to the notion he held of human hearts, this threat should be all powerful.

Richard Devine was still seated before the table, in the attitude in which he had parted from Arthur, when the servant announced a 'gentleman on urgent private business, who would not give his name.' At any other time, perhaps, Richard Devine would have refused to see a visitor who intruded himself so vaguely and abruptly, but now – having put away from himself all worldly ties and human associates, being (in his own mind) a creature devoted to death – he was prepared to receive this visitor with the same indifference with which the martyr views a staring bystander. His absence or his presence made but small difference. The torture must proceed whether he came or went.

'I will see him.'

John Rex entered, and carefully closed the door.

'You do not know me!'

'I do not, sir.'

'I know you though. Your name is Rufus Dawes.'

John Rex had intended the utterance of that name to be a thunderbolt, which should strike the escaped convict to earth. The escaped convict however said merely, 'I am ready to go with you, sir.'

He imagined him, in fact, to be an officer of justice, sent by Maurice Frere.

'I don't want to take you,' said Rex, with some astonishment. 'I want you to remain here and enjoy your property, only I want to share it. Give me ten thousand pounds, and I will keep your secret.'

'It is too late,' said Richard Devine.

'Not it. No one knows it but myself – and I –'

'No one but yourself? Then – Villain, who are you?'

'I am your old mate of Port Arthur, John Rex.'

Richard Devine sprang up and almost struck the other in his rage.

'Wretch, why come *here*? Were you not content in England? You had my fortune –'

'And lost it. The game was up. Your German wife returned, and knew that I was not her husband.'

Richard Devine sat down trembling. He saw at once that his great sacrifice had been again needless. The villany of Rex had been already defeated; perhaps even now a letter was on its way to Arthur to tell him of his fortune. Yet a strange pleasure arose in him, in thinking that, by the very means he had taken to secure his own condemnation, that of the impostor who had counterfeited him was equally certain. The men who came to arrest Rufus Dawes would find John Rex also. Captain Frere would kill two gaol birds with one stone.

'Look here,' says Rex, his beating brain urging him to rapid speech, 'I know all your story. You murdered your wife's father, and were lagged for it. I thought you were dead – drowned in that vessel coming from Norfolk Island; all the papers said so. There was a fortune waiting for a bold man. I claimed it. I was found out. Well – I escaped. Go you home and take it.'

'No,' said Richard Devine, 'I will not.'

'Will you help me?'

'I will not.'

'Come, then, if you won't take your father's fortune, what will you give me to hold my tongue and let you keep the money you have made for yourself?'

'Nothing.'

'You defy me, eh? You think, I suppose, that I haven't calculated my chances. You think, I suppose, that you can betray *me*, if I betray *you*. I have not schemed all my life for nothing, my good Mr Crosbie. An anonymous letter to the police office – posted on the day I sail for Sydney – describing the marks on your body, and asking the authorities to see if Mr Crosbie hasn't the tattooings of the cat on his back, would arouse a suspicion which would lodge you in gaol very soon.'

Richard Devine smiled.

'Oh,' said Rex, misinterpreting the sad meaning of that smile, 'you needn't grin. I can do it. I know all the marks upon you. I made it my business to learn all those long ago. I did learn 'em all, too, except that cursed burn that your wife wanted to see – I forgot that.'

At the mention of the word 'wife', the smile passed away from Richard Devine's face.

'What did she say?' he asked, in softened tones.

'She!' rejoined Rex, brutally – 'she said you had basely deserted her – that is what she said. Come, let us to business; I have no time to lose. What will you give me to hold my tongue?'

An expression of pain twitched the lips of the unhappy man as he comprehended that which he had not hitherto dared to confess to himself – that he had been again misjudged by the very creature for whom he had sacrificed his life. The effect of this wringing of his soul was to make it tender.

'Listen, John Rex,' he said, 'and judge if I am likely to give you money for your silence. I yesterday made acquaintance with my nephew – the boy whom you dispossessed. He told me that his "uncle" had returned. I determined to oust the impostor by the only way in my power, by proving who and what I was. To that end I –'

'Well?' says Rex, looking round anxiously; 'you what?'

'I sent to Captain Frere to give myself up.'

'No!' cries Rex, growing purple, 'you were never such a fool!'

'Ask the boy himself. I expect the officers here every moment – the door is open, sir; you had better go.'

'I don't believe you,' says Rex, furiously; 'you are lying. No man would be such an idiot.'

Richard Devine shrugged his shoulders with a gesture so convincing that Rex, grown desperate at this failure to all his hopes, felt his head to swim, and his temples to throb, as they had done on the occasion of that terrible surprise when the little German cripple had dashed his fortunes to earth with her withered white hand.

'Look here, Dawes,' said he, with all his dandyism departing, and the coarseness of mind which was natural to him coming out of him and covering him, as it might be, with a garment of ruffianism and greed. 'Don't say that. That's foolish! – d — d foolish! What is the good of that? If you give yourself up, the Crown takes all the money! Why should it? There is time even now. Let us go together – you and I. I won't betray you, Dawes!' and in his eagerness he laid his hand upon that of Richard Devine.

Richard Devine clasped it – not roughly – and with the other hand pointed to the door.

'What I have done, I have done. It is my own sacrifice. You need not share it. Go, go and repent – if indeed such a man as I am may dare to urge you to repentance. In a few moments the officers will be here, and you know best whether you can face them. Go!'

John Rex, overawed by the exhibition of that unselfishness

which he had all his life denied, and oppressed by that vertigo which had before threatened to prostrate him, made staggering for the door. He reached it, only to be confronted by another figure – his wife!

Sarah had given her card to the servant, with woman's wit had rapidly followed him to the door of the laboratory, and then guessing that the man she sought was there, had made her entrance alone.

'Where are you going, John?' said she with an evil smile.

John Rex uttered an inarticulate cry of rage, tore at his collar, raised one coward arm to strike the woman who was at once his good and evil genius, and then his overwrought brain giving way, fell foaming at her feet.

Footsteps were heard on the stairs, and Richard Devine guessed that the crisis of his fate had come. He stepped between the prostrate body and the staircase.

'It is the police,' he whispered to the woman, 'Take him away, hide him! They seek only me. They will not search for him. Ah, too late, they are here!'

But it was only Arthur and Quaid.

'Did you not give my letter, boy?' cries Richard Devine, astonished.

'Yes.'

'Well, where is Captain Frere?'

'Captain Frere is dead – murdered,' said Arthur, holding out the blood-stained letter, 'he bid me give you this and say *"he need fear me no more."*'

'Then you know who I am?' asked Richard Devine, bewilderedly taking the letter.

'You are Rufus Dawes, an escaped convict,' said Arthur coldly. 'That is little to me. I do not wish to give you to justice. It is of importance, however, that you are not the father of the young lady whom I wish to marry. She is the daughter of Captain Frere. Oh, Mr Crosbie – Rufus Dawes – whatever you choose to call yourself, tell me what is this terrible mystery of murder, of villainy, which surrounds you. Who are you?'

'I am your uncle! I am Richard Devine!'

Arthur, in his alarmed unbelief, strode into the room, looked hurriedly round, and saw John Rex supported on the knees of Sarah Purfoy. It was his turn to be astonished.

'Why! – This! – *This* man is my uncle! This man is Richard Devine! How comes he here, with you?' He turned to Sarah Purfoy. 'Who are you, madam, and who is this man?'

She turned upon them all with a snarl, like a wild beast over its cub.

'This man is my husband. He deceived you. All is known in England. He is not Richard Devine. You see him. – Stand up, John, lean on me. – He is not Richard Devine, I say. That man is right. *He* is your uncle. – John, it is I. – Let us go, gentlemen; we shall not trouble you more. – Steady, John. There, there; no one will harm you. – My God, his brain is gone; he does not know me; let us go. – The step there; lift your foot. John, you are safe with me!'

'Let them go,' said Richard Devine, 'Let them go....
DORCAS! you here!'

'I heard a fall,' said Dorcas, 'a noise of people entering. What does this mean? Arthur! Father!'

As Rex was led from the room by the woman whose office it was henceforth to nurse him till he died – died, ignorant of her tenderness, a mere animal, lacking the human intellect he had in his pride abused, Dorcas flung herself on Richard Devine's breast. 'Father, what does this mean?'

He looked at her lovingly.

'Dorcas, I am going to leave you. You will not see me again. It is necessary that we should part. Do not cry, my darling – see here is your husband waiting for you.' He took the packet which was on the table, and placed it in her hands. 'That will explain all,' he said, 'I only ask that you will first read it together at the place I have named – Good-bye. Mr Devine, take her away please.'

He kissed her on the forehead, and then turned abruptly away.

Dorcas, terrified and bewildered, clung to him, but Quaid spoke for the first time.

'Go,' he whispered; 'do as he bids. Leave the rest to me. You sought my advice,' he added, as Arthur seemed to hesitate; 'follow it. Take her into the garden, and wait until I come.'

Arthur obeyed, and the young man, closing the door behind the pair, went up to where Richard Devine was sitting, and touched him on the shoulder.

'Rufus Dawes,' he said, 'my grandfather, nearly thirty years ago, defended you because he thought you guilty; I offer to defend you because I know you are innocent.'

Richard Devine lifted his pale face.

'No, no; let us have no more trials. I am exhausted; I am tired of all this. I am innocent of the crime for which I suffered, but you can have no proof of that.'

'I have moral proof. I hope legal proof,' said the excited young man, tapping his papers. 'I have here the name of the murderer.'

'WHAT?' cried the other, flushing with new hope.

Quaid opened the paper, and read the dying declaration made by Jerry Mogford at the Ballarat Stockade, on the night of the 2nd December, 1854.

'I meant to do it for his jewellery, and climbed up the water-pipe to get in at the window. But when I got up and looked in, he was lying in his blood, with the case of jewels open. The murderer who had been before me was bending over him, and, fearful lest I should be seen, I slid down. I hid myself in a house where I was known until I heard that the trial was over, and an innocent man had been condemned in my place. A man called Rufus Dawes, a sailor. He was the companion of the man who was murdered. The murderer was my own brother, Joseph.'

'Great heavens!' cried Richard Devine, 'the landlord! I never suspected *him?* But now – I remember. He saw the jewels. I met him in the passage going to the very room. He arrested me. He –'

'It is a curious instance of the dovetailing of circumstances,' said Quaid, regaining his legal composure. 'The landlord wanted to cast suspicion upon you, and had you arrested. The landlord's brother had climbed up the water-pipe to do the very deed his brother had done – witnessed the murder, and, horror-stricken, fled. My father, stopping at the house, saw the brother climb the pipe, saw him descend, heard afterwards of the murder, and imagined, of course, that *you* were the man seen by the pipe-climber. His strange love for the winning of apparently hopeless cases urged him to undertake your defence. His plan – the story became a stock one with him before he died – was to so work upon the fears of the landlord as to get the brother out of the way, and – being assured that he was safe – to divert the suspicion of the crime from you to him. He fully believed you guilty, and has often said that he nearly threw up the case when you urged him in the prison to "hunt down" the missing man and bring him to justice.'

'So that is the simple end of the mystery I have so long tried to solve. And the landlord – what became of him?'

'It seemed that he gambled, and had mortgaged the house to a money-lender named Blick. Hence – as I have since read it – his motive for the crime. He paid off the mortgage – I suppose now, with the stolen money – but he never prospered. He took to drinking. The business went to the deuce, and my grandfather would terminate his story with a moral reflection on the fact, that, of the two brothers who figured in the plot he laid for your escape from the gallows, one had been transported for pocket-picking, the other! – "once a wealthy man, sir!" – was picked up in the gutter in a fit of drunken delirium, was carried to the nearest hospital, and died there, raving. By Jove! if the old gentleman was only alive now to hear the conclusion to his story!'

Richard Devine wiped his brows. 'It is quite clear and simple now.'

'Not quite,' said Quaid, leaning over him. 'Not quite. There was one thing my grandfather could never understand – why did you not give your history of your relations with the German?'

'I had reason.'

'Why, at all events, then, did you not say you were Richard Devine, the son of the wealthiest man in London?'

'Because my father had urged me to do a base action, and I had resolved to separate myself from him altogether.'

'At the very day of your trial as Rufus Dawes, you were worth a fortune.'

'I did not know that. It might not have altered my determination if I had known it. However, it is useless to talk of that now. This morning, when I had resolved to give myself back to justice, I wrote an account of whatever mystery there was in my past life, in order that when I was dead the truth might be told to those whom I loved. Arthur has the packet. He will read it — for I am dead to all friends now.'

'Why?' asked Quaid.

'They will hear that I have been a convict. I cannot face them. There is no need for me to see them. Arthur can at once take the property which will be his when I die. I wish to be considered as dead.'

'And pray what do you mean to do?' asked Quaid again.

'To go away somewhere. This house is mine. I have property which I can sell. I shall go away and live somewhere else.'

'That is cowardly.'

'What?'

'Cowardly! it is a moral suicide. You have acted nobly hitherto. Why propose such a feeble end to all your struggles and sacrifices. Listen to my proposal. I am a man of the world, and my advice is practically good. Come home with me and claim your fortune. No one will prevent you. Arthur and Dorcas can be married, and if you then wish to resign your property to them, do so. To your own relatives you can tell, if you wish, the story of your long life of torment — they will but pity you. Should the law again attempt to seize you, armed with this confession, and a fortune to back it, you can establish your innocence. Moreover, I understand you have a wife. Is it just to her to live as you propose?'

Richard Devine was silent for a few moments, and then he raised his face with new light in it.

'You have shown me my duty. You are right. I will go to England. I will place my sister and my relatives in firm possession of what is theirs, and then I will go to my wife.'

Quaid flung open the window, and pointed to the pair in the garden.

'Let us join them.'

'No,' said the old man; 'I will not see them until they have both judged of the history of my life. I have·written it, but it must not be read here. We will meet them in England. Tell them so.'

Quaid, radiant, ran to the garden and found Arthur and Dorcas together.

'You must get married and go to England,' he said. 'I have arranged it all with your uncle. Miss Crosbie – your father's name is not Crosbie, but Devine (Hush! Arthur: let her think so), and Master Arthur is his nephew. He is a good man – a man who has been severely tried by fortune. We must humour him. He wishes you to be married. You must not see him until you meet in England. No words now. I am the legal adviser of both of you. Expecting something would happen to prevent him speaking with you, he wrote an explanation. It is here!'

The packet was twofold. Underneath the silk which bound it was a second packet, labelled 'FOR DORCAS.' This contained one hundred bank-notes, each for £100 – as much of Crosbie's fortune as he could realise in twenty-four hours. The other was sealed, and was marked, 'THE STORY OF MY LIFE. TO BE READ IN THE LABORATORY OF HANS BLINZLER, IN THE LIEVEN'S STRAAT, AT AMSTERDAM.'

'I do not understand this,' said Arthur.

'Your course is plain,' cried Quaid. 'You have a fortune. Get married. Here is the story of the secret. Go to Amsterdam and read it!'

BOOK NINE

++ *1* ++

IN ENGLAND

WHEN the strange story of Richard Devine's life became in after years a theme for after-dinner chat, Quaid, rolling in his luxurious chair, was wont to dwell tenderly upon one part of that eventful relation.

'I was not much given in those days to veneration,' he would say. 'Indeed, I had less then than I have now, but if ever I learned to reverence unselfishness and charity in a man, I learned it when travelling home with Richard Devine. He kept his promise of not seeing Mr Arthur. Dorcas and he were married a few days after the funeral of Maurice Frere, and even when the letter arrived from Miss Devine, announcing the flight of Rex, and begging Arthur to return, Devine would not admit the boy to his room. "No," he said, "I have made up my mind. I see no one until I see them in England."

'When the vessel sailed, I saw the pair on board and urged them to go straight to Amsterdam. "It is there where that confession, upon which he lays so much stress, is to be read. It is there Miss Devine and your sister have found an asylum. The money has been placed in the hands of trustees. That can wait until *we* get home. *You* first unravel this tangled skein." I told Devine what I had done, and he was gratified, counting the days which should bring them to their journey's end. Two days after they had sailed, we took passage, and when the Heads of Port Phillip faded finally from sight, a load seemed to drop from him. He regained his spirits and became cheerful. All loved him. His dignity and tenderness won all hearts. For myself, I was amazed at the prodigious range of his reading, the power of his memory, and the boldness of his philosophical speculation. "I am a born chemist," he said, one day, "Had I received a scientific instruction, I might have done something great. I may have helped to do something curious as it is." I asked him what he meant, and he replied that I should hear from Arthur. His thoughts all turned to the future. The past he banished. "Thirty years ago, I wished to begin a new life. Now, grown old before my time, I shall begin a third – one of usefulness and humility, I hope." That was all the allusion he made to his transportation. His expressed thought was always in the future, "When will they arrive?"

'When we reached London, he went first to the Bell, and we examined (with much the same feeling I should think as that with which one opens a grave) the bedroom in which the murder had been done. The water-pipe was still there, and on looking out I could see the iron supporting bands on which Jerry's feet must have rested as he climbed. The bedstead was a new one. He seemed relieved when he found this to be the case. The interview with the lawyers was a trying one, but he bore it bravely. I assure you, gentlemen, it was a ticklish situation once or twice, but I flatter myself that I – but no matter. It was decided that the best course to take would be to allow Arthur to come into possession, and not disturb the public mind by any further complication. In the meantime interest was brought to bear upon the Home Secretary, and the facts of the case were privately explained, with what happy results you know.

'At Harwich the scene was very touching. He took up his abode in the portion of the house which had been left untouched by the improvements effected by his brother. He showed me the little room he had slept in when a boy, and pointed out his initials "R. D.", cut on a beam in the roof. A striking proof of his identity, if proof was needed, occurred during our short stay there. He told me that when ten years old he had locked into the pantry an old servant named Jarvis, and to prevent the possibility of the man getting out had thrown the key into a great cistern on the top of the house. We had the cistern drained and found the key! I wonder what thoughts passed through the poor fellow's mind as he looked at it.

'We had ordered the yacht round from Cowes, and would take short cruises. Nothing afforded him greater delight than to handle the ropes and manage the craft. But through all these pursuits one thought was ever uppermost – "When will they arrive?"

'At last I got a letter from Arthur, dated Genoa, stating that the vessel had touched at the Azores, and he had taken passage thence in a vessel bound for Lisbon with oranges, and intended to come on overland. I showed this letter to Richard Devine, and told him that in a few days at farthest all would be known. He evinced much impatience and restlessness, and at last I proposed, what I knew he was ashamed to propose himself, and that was to run the yacht over to Helvoet and then make for Amsterdam. He jumped at the proposal, and the rest fell out as I have told you.'

‹‹ 2 ››

THE SECRET OF HANS BLINZLER

On the morning of the 3rd of May, 1856, the inhabitants of the Lieven's straat were startled to see a carriage drive up the narrow street and stop at the door of the two sisters. Some curiosity had been already excited in the neighbourhood by the fact that two English ladies — as fabulously rich as all English people are — arrived one afternoon with the invalid sister (who had mysteriously departed some two months before), and had remained in the house ever since. The carriage, then, probably belonged to the great nobleman who was the husband of the elder lady, and the Lieven's straat craned its short neck to see the distinguished visitor alight. What they saw, however, was not what they expected. A young man got out of the carriage and assisted a very beautiful young woman. The young man knocked, the door opened — (an old lady of quick ears vowed she heard a scream) — and the mysterious pair entered.

It was Aunt Lucy who had uttered the scream. She had seen the carriage, had recognized Arthur, and ran down to throw herself in his arms.

For a few moments there was nothing but congratulations. 'How you are grown! A beard, too! How brown you are! And this is Dorcas; kiss me, my dear. This is your sister Adelaide. This is Madame Clara Blinzler, and this — this is Mrs Richard Devine!'

Dorothea had recovered from her attack, with difficulty. She did not remember persons' faces as well as she had formerly done. She slept more and seldom spoke. The poor woman, in fact, was wasting under a new torment — the torment of believing that her husband, whom she had only credited with cowardice and desertion, was a thief and a murderer. In vain had Miss Devine repeated her belief in the innocence of Richard; in vain did she read to her Arthur's letter containing an account of the statement made by Quaid as to the confession of the real criminal. Dorothea would not believe. 'If he were to return and tell me with his own lips, I might believe him,' she said, 'but nothing short of that.' When she saw Arthur she coloured. 'You are like *him*,' she remarked.

Arthur thought it best to delay no longer.

'Mrs Devine,' he said, drawing out the sealed packet, 'this was placed in my hands by your husband, my uncle. It contains a statement of the reasons which induced him to conceal his name, and to suffer wrongful condemnation. Will you allow me to read it to you?'

She bowed her head.

'Then, let us go to the room he indicates,' and he pointed to the superscription.

Clara Blinzler started. 'That room has not been opened for thirty years. That was my father's laboratory.'

'It shall be opened now,' said Dorothea. 'Come.'

They followed her up the broad stairs until they reached the massive doors. Though Arthur strove, the bolts, rusted into the staples, would not move. The key would not turn in the lock. It was as though the old room guarded its secret jealously. At last the door opened with a great crash and cloud of dust, and they saw into the chamber. It was lighted by three windows looking out upon the canal, the panes thick with dust and grime. A furnace was at one end of it, and rusted tongs and crucibles piled in corners attested that the owner had put his house in order, as in anticipation of a long absence. The atmosphere was stifling, but the latticed windows, opening forty feet above the canal, had been left unsecured, and Arthur pushed one open. The sudden burst of unwonted light frightened into congenial darkness a colony of bloated spiders, and caused the motes to dance in the brilliant beam, as though the heavy air of the chamber was impregnated with gold dust.

'It is the chamber of an Alchemist!' cried Arthur; 'enter, and let us read.'

In the centre of the room stood a shell of iron composed of two flanged hemispheres very strongly bolted together, the whole resting in a rough wooden cup fastened to the floor. Standing, with one hand upon this strange contrivance, Arthur cut the silk which bound the packet, and began to read: —

'Melbourne,
'4 a.m., 16th September, 1855.

'Having resolved to accomplish the sacrifice or the duty which is necessary to oust from my father's house an impostor and a villain, I have also resolved to put into words that which I have long kept secret.

'When you read this, I shall be dead, and the world will know me only as a profligate son, who, under the name of Rufus Dawes, committed a murder, and, being transported for life, escaped, and so rendered himself liable to the punishment he has just undergone. It does not matter much now, but I wish in the first place to declare here solemnly before God, that I am innocent of that charge of murder. I have been a great villain, a blasphemous sullen villain, but I did not do that murder. I think if I had not been sent to herd with convicts, I should have been a better man. If you will not think it wrong of me to ask that your wife may not be taught to hate me, I would ask you to let her think that, had I not been sent to herd with convicts, I should be a better man.

'I ran away from my father's house before I was twenty years of age, and plunged into all dissipation. If you should have a son, Mr. Devine, do not be too strict or parsimonious in your treatment of him. It is not good to be so. In those years of wanderings in the public-houses of the continent, of serving before the mast in foreign vessels, of low brawls and unwholesome pleasure, I was reduced to the condition of a homeless, hopeless vagabond, wishing only for one thing to happen – the death of my father and my consequent accession to his wealth. I had heard that he had determined, with that strange perversity which was a part of his warped nature, to leave his fortune altogether away from his family, to leave it to a nephew, my cousin Maurice Frere, a person whom, as a boy, I cordially disliked. Inspired by these feelings of animosity and dread, I roamed about Paris or Brussels, regardless of aught save the satisfaction of the moment. One day I was starving. I had walked from Brussels to Antwerp, thinking that I might get work at the dockyard there, but was too late. I walked to the edge of the quay, and was going to drown myself. I felt a hand on my shoulder and turning, saw a little man smoking. We fell into talk, I went home with him. His name was Hans Cornelius Drebell Blinzler, he was a chemist, and he engaged me as his assistant. That was the man whom I was accused of murdering.

'Blinzler fed and clothed me. We became friends. He was descended from a family of inventors, and he had inventive dreams. His grand uncle was the Cornelius Drebell who made for James the First a ship which would sail under water, and his grandfather had married the grand-daughter of Caspar Kaltoph – the man of whom it is said that he invented the steam-engine, in 1628, for the Marquis of Worcester. Blinzler's genius ran in the way of chemistry. He imagined it possible to transmute metals. I am not sure that it is not possible. After some time he confided to me his ambition. It was to make a diamond. "The diamond," said he, "is merely crystallized carbon. Carbon will not crystallize by any process of which we are aware, because it has so great an affinity for oxygen. Let us succeed in getting rid of the oxygen, and we can crystallize what is left." We tried many methods to effect this, of which one, which resulted in an explosion, burnt me severely, I can give as a sample. We forced through a blast-furnace a current of chlorine, by which we thought the iron when in fusion would be converted into protochloride of iron, which could be volatilized, leaving the carbon intact. At last he informed me that he had contrived a method which must result in success, but was more costly than he had at first imagined. We proceeded to carry out his idea, and between us constructed with considerable labour, the machine which he had planned, placed in it the needful materials, and then – found we had expended our last ryder. The process which Blinzler hoped to bring about was a slow one, and in this plight he suggested that we should leave this experiment to complete itself in its own slow way, and attempt another and more rapid method. Now during the diamond-making, Blinzler had hit upon a discovery – which anticipated by thirty years the chemists of our own day. He invented a method of making artificial sapphires, rubies, and zircons, which we found were not to be distinguished from real stones, save by the most experienced lapidaries of Amsterdam, and he proposed me to sell the false stones to raise the needful money. A few weeks before I should have readily consented, but a circumstance had happened which caused me to refuse. Blinzler had two daughters, one of whom was in England as a governess, and the other, Dorothea, lived with him. Charmed by the peaceful and calm life of that Dutch home

(we had gone to Amsterdam), I was soothed by the presence of Dorothea, and, willing to spend my days in that peaceful haven, I asked
her to marry me. She consented, we were married, and I found that
she had but two thoughts in her life – her father and myself. After
six months of wedded life, I found out another thing – I did not love
her.'

Mrs Devine uttered a sigh.

'But it seemed to me, grateful as I was for the love and kindness
which snatched me from death, that being unable to return to her the
great love she lavished upon me, I ought to jealously guard against
any violence being done to that honour and esteem which she had for
her father. To his proposal to sell the artificial stones I at once gave a
blank denial. He represented that his money was all spent, that we
should starve, that the gems were to all intents and purposes as good
as those made in the laboratory of nature; in short, blinded by his
fervour for his diamond making project, he urged the scheme upon
me by every means in his power. To quiet his importunities I resolved
to sacrifice my pride and to write to my father.

'I wrote, telling of my marriage, and my determination to lead an
honest life. He replied in the coarsest terms, abusing with all the bitter
skill of an old worldling my wife and my father-in-law, swore that
two such swindlers and fortune-hunters should not have a shilling of
his money, and ended by stating that the only condition on which he
would help me or see me was, that I deserted my wife and denied
my marriage; if I did not do that, I had better leave Europe. When
that letter came, we had but two guilders in the house. With rage and
despair, I rushed out on the quays, meditating what to say to my
father. I determined to break with him for good and all, and to suffer
him to think that I had left Europe. I went back to Blinzler and told
him that I was ready to do as he proposed. He sold ninety pounds
worth of the false gems that night, to a diamond-cutting house, and
the next day we started for London. He told my wife that we were
going to Antwerp and should not return for six weeks, desiring me
to lock the laboratory door, give her the key, and desired her not to
open the chamber on any pretence, until she received word from one
of us.

'We reached Harwich in safety, and there sleeping with the old
familiar places and names about me, I took a resolution that I would
not proceed with the journey, but return. Blinzler and I argued the
question fiercely, and it ended by my going by coach to London with
him. All the journey we still argued, and at last he consented. I would
only take enough money for my passage, and resolved to walk to

Harwich. We slept that night at the Bell, Holborn; Blinzler, I think rather incautiously, displaying the leather case in which he insisted on carrying the stones. There was nothing remarkable that evening save that he and I had a slight quarrel, because – angry at my penniless condition (I had slunk through Harwich like a dog) I had suggested that the proceeds of the gem-selling might be devoted to our private ends, and not to that great scheme of the diamonds concerning which he was always talking. But when I went into his room – I had myself slept in it on the night when I ran away from home – he had grown composed, and freely forgave me. I never saw him again alive: he was murdered that night for the gems, but not by me – before God, Arthur, not by me.

'In the morning I went out along the North Road, and posted the letter to my father informing him that I had gone to Calcutta. I chose the name *Hydaspes* because I had heard somebody on the coach mention that vessel as being the one in which his brother was to sail, and that he was coming to London to see him off. When I reached Highgate I was arrested. The rest you can learn from the newspapers.

'Now for the reason of my silence. At this lapse of time, and having due regard to the condition of mind in which I was during that terrible period between my arrest and condemnation, I can only say that I acted from an overwhelming sense of the duty I owed my wife. If I stated, as I was pressed to state, all particulars concerning the murdered man, I should betray the secret of the gems; and, by causing inquiry to be made at the house in Amsterdam, nullify whatever hope of success there was in the experiment so laboriously made. The grief that would be caused to the murdered man's daughter by his disappearance would be excessive, and that grief would but be increased by the information that her father was little better than a common swindler, and that her husband had been accused, possibly convicted, of his murder. Nor did it occur to me to give my real name, and claim my father's interest. To put this alternative on plain grounds – I doubted if he would have acknowledged me – and if he did, it could only be the more clearly visible that I was a broken adventurer, abandoned by my kindred, and prepared for any desperate villany. Moreover, the story of the gems would have to be told, for I could not have invented any defence which would account for my possession of them.

'If I had felt by any means certain that, by a full confession, I might have escaped out of the toils which had encompassed me, I might – in my selfishness – have confessed, and so saved a life which I had even then learned to despise; but sitting – maddened with thinking – in my cell at Newgate, I saw no chance. It was more than probable that, do what I might, prove myself to be whom I might, the weight of circumstantial evidence would be too strong for me, and I should die on the scaffold a death which would disgrace all connected with me. This being granted – and the remorseless logic of experience forced me to grant it – I had two duties to consider: one to my father and his kindred, one to my wife and her kindred. My father had cast me off, and I had written to him to say that I had already left the country. (Bear in mind, Arthur, I did not know that he had died.) I had given at Bow-street the name Rufus Dawes, chiefly because the initials of that name were the same as my own. I would sink my identity in that name, and let my father imagine that I had sailed for India. So, if I died, my family would not be disgraced by my death; and, if I lived, I still preserved that independence which my father had forced upon me.

'My wife! Ah! there was the pang. She must ever think me a base and cruel man, who deserted her in her hour of need. But if I confessed, she would have her heart torn by hearing of her father's duplicity; be dragged, perhaps, to witness as to his mode of life, and, having had her name made a byword through England, see, perhaps, after all this, her husband die upon the scaffold. I determined, therefore, to keep silence. If I lived, I might by-and-bye, after the lapse of years, return and tell the story. If I died, she would, at least, be spared the pang of knowing her father an impostor, and her husband a suspected murderer. She would live with the respect for the memory of that father who had so mysteriously disappeared, and only hating – if one so gentle could be capable of hate – the husband who had deserted her. I felt that I owed her this in return for a loveless marriage, and I was ready to die. *God help me, I was doomed to live! –*'

So eager were they all listening to this revelation of so strange a secret, that no one heeded the knocking at, or opening of, the house-door – no one heard a footfall on the stairs.

'Oh, my husband!' cried Dorothea, with streaming eyes, and face radiant with forgiving love and sorrow, 'I have held you in abhorrence as a criminal, when I should have worshipped you as a martyr! Reichart! Reichart! –'

'– Ist hier!' cried Richard Devine, his tongue falling again into the once familiar speech; and, followed by Quaid, he burst into the room, and caught her in his arms.

'There is no need to read further,' said Richard Devine; 'the rest is but a record of my despair. Yet no – not all despair. To you – wife, I will one day tell how in that gulf a Woman's tenderness kept hope alive; how, from that man-made Hell, a Brother's sympathy redeemed and saved me. Read no more now. This is a meeting that should make us glad. Read no more, Arthur,' he repeated, gently withdrawing the paper from the young man's hands. 'I would not that the memory of such a tale as mine should blur the happy future which I see in store for us. – Wife, let us go!'

'But the diamond!' cried Dorothea. 'What of my father's work? What of the diamond, Richard?'

The old man shook his head with a smile, and advanced to the strange machine which occupied the centre of the floor.

'Before the halves of this globe were united, as you now see them,' said he, 'your father deposited in the lower half the materials for generating as much carbonic acid gas as would – at common pressure – fill this room. Great care was taken to prevent the possibility of leakage, in order that the gas might be compressed and liquefied. Some water, also, was previously poured into the vessel, for his opinion was that diamonds are formed by Nature from gas absorbed by water, under enormous pressure, it being known that water does absorb many times its volume of carbonic acid gas. The vessel contained, in addition to the water and the gas-generating materials, another substance with which his studies had made him acquainted, and the function of which was to separate the oxygen from the carbon of the gas and condense it. On the surface of that absorbent of oxygen he placed a small natural diamond, to form, according to expectation, the nucleus of a magnificent gem. Now, if the looked-for condensation has really occurred, and no leakage has taken place, this valve, which opens inwards, may easily be pushed down, if we can get the nut off. Let us try.'

He looked round, and from the dust-covered implements essayed to raise a heavy hammer. The handle had rotted in the rusty eye. So taking up in both hands the heavy head, he struck with it a blow straight down upon the end of the valve-stem, which projected beyond the nut. The thread stripped; the bridge flew off; the valve fell in, and amid the clatter and the clang, not a hiss gave token of escaping gas.

All pressed forward to examine.

'Hold – the spanner will never move these rusty nuts. Stay, Arthur. Help me to turn over the shell, and anything weighty and free will drop through the valve-hole.'

Between them they inverted the vessel, and Richard Devine, holding his hand beneath the aperture, felt a small hard body drop into it.

'Well,' asked Quaid eagerly, 'What is it?'

The old man opened his hand, and there lay the result of the chemist's labours – a lump of charcoal!

'See!' he said sadly, crushing on his palm as he spoke the lustreless mass. 'A black and useless atom, fit emblem of my dark and wasted life.'

'An emblem, indeed!' cried Dorcas, as leaning on her husband's arm she pointed to the original gem which, thus revealed, flashed in the sunlight. 'But not as you would view it. That which was Pure remains – for see, undimmed by thirty years of darkness and neglect, the Diamond sparkles still!'

(p. 32) *a newly-raised regiment*: The 39th (Dorsetshire) regiment of foot arrived in Australia in 1827, though it was not raised for the occasion.

(p. 32) *the funeral of Queen Caroline*: Queen Caroline was excluded from her husband George IV's coronation in 1820. Shortly after she died, and the passing of her body through the City of London was marked by riots in which two men were killed.

(p. 32) *Torres Vedras*: At this Portuguese site Wellington built his famous defensive lines of 1810.

(p. 32) *Burmah*: The British invaded Burma in 1824 (Treaty of Yandabo, 1826).

(p. 33) *cornet*: A junior officer.

(p. 33) *young Mr Kean*: Charles John, son of the celebrated Edmund Kean, appeared in 1827 as Young Norval in J. Home's romantic tragedy *Douglas* (1756). He was about fifteen years old at the time.

(p. 33) *James Wallack as* Rolla: James Wallack (1791–1864) was a member of a family of actors well-known in both England and the U.S.A. He made his early appearance in Drury Lane, but from 1818 spent much time on New York stages, and in 1837 took over the management of the National Theatre in New York. Rolla is a character in R. B. Sheridan's play *Pizarro* (1799), an adaptation of a popular drama, *Die Spanier in Peru*, written by the German dramatist A. F. F. Kotzebue.

(p. 33) *Botany Bay*: This large shallow inlet some miles south of Sydney was discovered by Captain James Cook in 1770, and was the original destination of the First Fleet (1788) which settled Australia. On arrival Botany Bay was immediately abandoned for Port Jackson, on the shores of which Sydney was built. 'Botany Bay' continued to be used for many decades as a general term for the British settlement in New South Wales, although the usage was geographically absurd.

(p. 42) *the Turkish fleet ... the new Alliance*: At this time attention was concentrated on the 'Eastern Question', with Britain, France and Russia (Treaty of London, 1827) massing their fleets in the Mediterranean with a view to humbling Turkey and securing the independence of Greece. In October 1827 the Turkish and Egyptian fleets were destroyed in Navarino Bay.

(p. 47) *Jupiter gone Io-courting*: Io was the daughter of the King of

Argos with whom Zeus (Jupiter) fell in love. He turned her into a
heifer to conceal her!

(p. 49) *'horses on'*: The practice of changing horse-teams at the end
of a stage and continuing one's journey immediately which is
implied in the term 'post-chaise'. An expensive means of transport,
but a rapid one, it has given rise to the term 'post haste'.

(p. 50) *wrapped in roquelaure*: This refers to a knee-length cloak
named after the Duke of Roquelaure (1716).

(p. 52) *the First Gentleman of Europe*: The Prince Regent, subsequently George IV.

(p. 54) *eskytor*: Escritoire, writing desk.

(p. 56) *for a poney*: Pony, a wager of £25.

(p. 65) *'Mussoo'*: A corruption of *monsieur*, often used derogatively
for a Frenchman.

(p. 67) *a hackney coach*: A four-wheeled, two-horse coach for six,
kept for hire.

(p. 68) *jarvey*: A hackney coachman.

(p. 67) *Fox and Crown*: This tavern stood in West Hill, Highgate,
until 1898. Clarke's statement is an anachronism. The incident referred to occurred in 1837, when the landlord stopped the bolting
horses of Queen Victoria's carriage. He was presented with the
royal arms, which the inn displayed.

(p. 72) *Doll Tearsheet*: A character in Shakespeare's *Henry IV*,
Part II.

(p 73) *buys a 'dying speech'*: Last speeches from the gallows, genuine
or otherwise, were a popular form of broadside literature of the
streets.

(p. 73) *Tom Thumb*: 'General Tom Thumb' (Charles S. Stratton),
the famous dwarf, toured Europe under the aegis of P. T. Barnum
between 1841 and 1865.

(p. 73) *Ching-Chang*: Clarke presumably refers here to the original
Siamese twins, Eng-in and Chang-chun (1811–74), naturalized in
the U.S.A. under the name of Bunker. They were widely exhibited
from 1829 until their deaths.

(p 73) *winking pictures*: Presumably the booklets of near-identical
photographs which, on being flicked through, gave the illusion of
animation.

(p. 79) *weasand*: Throat.

(p. 92) *padding-ken*: A meeting-place of thieves.

(p. 92) *Holy Land*: The underworld area around Seven Dials, so-
called possibly because of its strong Irish population.

(p. 92) *Pattering Jemmy*: 'Pattering' because fluent in the cant jargon
or 'patter' of thieves.

(p. 92) *a 'warm man'*: Comfortably off.

(p. 95) *lubby'ud*: Lovely one.

(p. 97) *S'eph be*: So help me.

(p. 100) *pudding-snammer*: A cook-shop thief.

(p. 101) *Acres' courage*: Bob Acres is a character in Sheridan's *The Rivals*.

(p. 138) *only breeched the other day*: Boys were often kept in dresses until about five years old.

(p. 148) *pomp and circumstance of glorious war*: A quotation from *Othello*.

(p. 154) *the night-house ruffian*: A night-house was a low-class tavern serving as a doss.

(p. 154) *barracoon*: An enclosure for slaves.

(p. 154) *You won't hang you gib for them*: Probably related to the phrase 'As melancholy as a gib cat', i.e. as a tom cat frustrated in his amorous intentions.

(p. 155) *Their morning fake in the prigging lay!*: Their morning's chancy stint of thieving.

(p. 155) *You didn't get seven penn'orth for tops singing!*: You aren't entitled to make gallows speeches for a mere seven years' sentence.

(p. 155) *culver head*: Pigeon-head.

(p. 159) *cock-boat*: A small ship's boat.

(p. 174) *'the Moocher'*: One who hangs about for thieving purposes.

(p. 175) *a bit of a 'brim'*: A bit of a trollop.

(p. 175) *some screeving fakement*: Some piece of forgery.

(p. 175) *charley*: A watchman.

(p. 175) *my kinchen*: My lad.

(p. 176) *ken cracker*: House burglar.

(p. 178) *blowen*: Moll.

(p. 182) *rampsman*: One who perpetrates robbery with violence.

(p. 194) *Argus eyes . . . Briarean hands*: Argus, a mythological herdsman with eyes all over his body. Briareos, one of the hundred-handed giants, sons of Uranus and Ge.

(p. 194) *'neddied' constables*: To neddy was to attack with bludgeons.

(p. 200) *'I don't see no wipe'*: A wipe was a handkerchief.

(p. 203) *'a freak of my girl Sarah!'*: A whim.

(p. 209) Solus cum sola non orabunt Pater Noster: 'A man and a woman together will not recite the Pater Noster'—an ungrammatical Latin tag, probably of medieval origin.

(p. 213) *thaumatoscope*: Clarke apparently means a 'thaumatrope', a toy in which different figures on each side of a card merge into each other when the card is rotated rapidly.

(p. 228) *They came to Break-o'-Day Plains*: An attack by Aboriginals on a settler's house at Break-of-Day Plains is recorded in the *Hobart Town Courier* of 8 December 1827.

(p. 229) *The topography of Van Diemen's Land*: Mr Michael Saclier, Principal Archivist of Tasmania, has suggested that there is 'more poetry than science' in this account, the major cavil being some of the geographical details in Clarke's description of the approach to Hobart by sea.

(p. 230) *the Iron Pot*: A lighthouse in the Derwent River.

(p. 230) *two thousand years ago*: Clarke would have been more nearly correct had he written 'ten thousand years ago'.

(p. 230) *Hobson's Bay*: Clarke means Port Phillip Bay, of which Hobson's Bay is merely the north-west corner, around which Melbourne is built. Port Phillip Bay was not excavated by the sea but by the river Yarra.

(p. 231) *Hell's Gates*: Macquarie Harbour is an inlet on the west coast of Tasmania some twenty miles deep. A penal establishment was commenced here in 1822, and was regarded as a place of 'secondary' punishment for serious and repeated offenders; it was abandoned in 1834. Sarah or Settlement Island is now a historic reserve.

(p. 232) *Heemskirk and Zeehan*: The names (slightly anglicized) of the mountains on the west coast of Tasmania, named after the ships of Abel Tasman, discovered of Tasmania (1642).

(p. 232) *Hobart Town in 1830*: Much of this chapter consists of almost verbatim quotes from Ross's *Hobart Town Almanac* for 1830. The following corrections to Clarke's account may be noted: the St David's organ was built in 1824, not 1832; Governor Arthur may have been parsimonious, but he was never 'penurious'; and the government journal referred to, the *Hobart Town Gazette*, was in fact pirated not from 'Mr Melville' but from Andrew Bent.

(p. 234) *Colonel Sorell*: Clarke's dismissial of Sorell, Lieutenant-Governor of Van Diemen's Lane 1816–24, is unjust. Sorell was an excellent administrator; his 'profligacy' consisted of living with a woman not his wife. This eventually brought about his recall.

(p. 235) *Ultima Thule*: Thule was the ancient Greek and Latin name for a land north of Britain, the limit of the known world. Hence the figurative use of the phrase to mean 'the utmost limit'.

(p. 239) *the Black War*: With the increasing European occupation of Aboriginal lands the later 1820s in Van Diemen's Land saw a series of attacks and atrocities levelled by settlers against the Aboriginals and vice versa. In November 1828 Governor Arthur proclaimed martial law, and roving parties of soldiers, police and convicts were used to hunt down the Aboriginals and to kill or capture them. Finally came the Line – an attempt in 1830 to drive all Aboriginals in Van Diemen's Land into the south-east corner of the island. The results were negligible, but in the early 1830s a Hobart master builder, G. A. Robinson, established friendly relations with the Aboriginals in a series of remarkable journeys and persuaded them to accept deportation to Flinders Island in Bass Strait. Here, within ten or twelve years, most of the survivors of the Tasmanian people died, though a few individuals lingered for some decades. See Clive Turnbull: Black War (Melbourne, 1965) and N. J. B. Plomley (ed.): *Friendly Mission* (Tasmanian Historical Research Association (1966).

(p. 240) *Dr Ross*: James Ross (1786–1838), schoolmaster and editor of the *Hobart Town Almanac* from 1829. Clarke's use of Ross and other sources for his book is discussed in L. L. Robson: 'The Historical Basis of *For the Term of His Natural Life*' in Australian *Literary Studies*, Vol. 1, No. 2, December 1963.

(p. 241) *Backhouse, the Quaker missionary*: James Backhouse (1794–1869), author of *A Narrative of a Visit to the Australian Colonies* (London, 1843). As a confirmed Temperance man Backhouse was not, perhaps, an impartial witness! ·

(p. 241) *from the Bishop of Tasmania a pamphlet*: Francis Nixon, the Bishop of Tasmania, gave evidence in 1847 before a House of Lords committee on the evils of the transportation system, and the pamphlet *Transportation*, his communication to the committee, was published in London and subsequently in Launceston.

(p. 246) *ticket-of-leave*: Good conduct prisoners were allowed to work for wages and to choose their own masters, under certain conditions. The ticket of leave was an important element in convict discipline throughout the transportation period in the Australian colonies.

(p. 247) *Maria Island*: An island off the east coast of Tasmania used as a penal settlement 1825–32.

(p. 251) *The* Cyprus *affair has sickened 'em*: The brig *Cyprus* was seized by convicts between Hobart and Macquarie Harbour in 1829 and was sailed to Japan. Subsequently a number of the convicts concerned were arrested in England. Two were hanged and three others returned to Van Diemen's Land, where another of the pirates, captured on Tahiti, was also hanged.

(p. 259) *like Festus*: Clarke is in error. He means Gallio, who 'cared for none of those things'. Acts XVIII, 17.

(p. 261) *Amadis of Gaul*: A famous mediaeval romance of chivalry,

Iberian in origin. Cervantes praised it highly and the epic clearly influenced *Don Quixote*.

(p. 273) *the Banshee*: These and the following are, of course, Irish folklore stories.

(p. 278) *'swag'*. An Australian term for personal effects carried by a person travelling on foot.

(p. 279) *Gabbett's cannibalism*: This is based on the true story of Alexander Pearce (or Pierce), hanged in Hobart in 1824. Pearce was one of the first to escape from Macquarie Harbour.

(p. 283) *The seizure of the brig*: This account follows closely the incidents in the real-life cutting-out of the *Cyprus*, referred to above, and in the capture of the *Frederick* in Macquarie Harbour in 1834, on the occasion of the abandonment of the settlement (as here). The *Frederick* was sailed to Chile, where four of the absconders were arrested, returned to Hobart, and hanged. Here Clarke follows an account in the *Hobart Town Almanack for 1838* very closely. As with the *Osprey*, the leader of the *Cyprus* affair evaded full responsibility for his role. A coracle was built, on the same lines as Dawes's coracle, by prisoners marooned from the *Cyprus*, and an engraving in the *Hobart Town Courier* of 12 December 1829 shows two convicts building the coracle, with a woman holding her baby standing by, and Lieutenant Carew sitting in despair with his face in his hands. See Frank Clune and P. R. Stephensen: *The Pirates of the Brig Cyprus* (London, 1962). The parallel with Clarke's account is, of course, the closest.

(p. 285) *Pheayton*: Phaeton.

(p. 293) *armed cap-a-pie*: Armed from head to foot.

(p. 295) *lay-figure*: A jointed wooden figure used by artists; a nonentity.

(p. 300) *damper*: A unleavened loaf baked in the ashes of a camp-fire.

(p. 305) *fribble*: A person of no consequence.

(p. 317) *springes*: Snares.

(p. 344) *Belteshazzar*: Belshazzar. See Daniel V.

(p. 352) *Sir John Franklin*: Governor of Van Diemen's Land 1837–43, and famous as an Arctic explorer. Franklin died on a North-West Passage expedition in 1847.

(p. 362) *Poisoning his niece*: The allusion is to Thomas Wainewright (1794–1847), artist, litterateur, forger and suspected murderer, who is said to have admitted to poisoning his sister-in-law because 'her ankles were too thick'.

(p. 368) *glorious John*: John Dryden wrote these words in *Alexander's Feast*.

(p. 370) *The 'assignment system'*: Under this system some convicts were 'assigned' to settlers and other masters as servants and labourers.

(p. 371) *their father's station*: A 'station' is a country property given over to grazing.

(p. 371) *the pass-holders*: Convicts-at-large, ticket-of-leave men and emancipists were supposed to carry at all times a pass or similar document testifying to their right to be abroad.

(p. 372) *The Factory Laundry*: The Female Factory was a prison for female convicts.

(p. 376) *All gone to Port Phillip*: The Port Phillip area of southern Australia, later to become the colony of Victoria, was settled largely from Van Diemen's Land, from the year 1835.

(p. 378) *a deserted Ariadne – a suppliant Medea*: In Greek mythology Ariadne, daughter of Minos of Crete, fell in love with Theseus and helped him kill the monster of the Labyrinth, but was subsequently deserted by Theseus on the island of Naxos. Medea, daughter of the King of Colchis, fell in love with Jason of the *Argo* and fled to Corinth with him. In Euripides' play she was placed under sentence of banishment when Jason arranged to marry another princess, but by dissimulation obtained a respite which she used to exact her vengeance.

(p. 413) *nipper . . . chaney*. 'Nipper' – a smart one. 'Chaney' – a piece of china.

(p. 413) *not a signal station*: Means of communication was by mechanical semaphore.

(p. 444) *Port Arthur*: This penal settlement was situated on the Tasman Peninsula in south-eastern Tasmania, about sixty miles from Hobart. Founded in 1830, it served as Tasmania's main penal station until its abandonment in 1877. Its impressive public buildings are now, as ruins, a considerable tourist attraction. The Isle of the Dead was the cemetery for Port Arthur. For an account of Marcus Clarke's own visit to Port Arthur, in the dying days of the settlement, see 'Port Arthur Visited, 1870' in Bill Wannan (ed.): *A Marcus Clarke Reader* (Melbourne, 1963). Marcus Clarke's copy of *Rules and Regulations for the Penal Settlement on Tasman's Peninsula* (Hobart Town, 1868) is in the Parliamentary Library, Melbourne. It was acquired by him in 1869.

(p. 449) *Brighton or Schnapper Point*: Popular watering places near Melbourne. Schnapper Point is now called Mornington.

(p. 490) *Forrester's Peninsula*: Properly Forestier Peninsula.

(p. 503) *an Emancipist*: A former convict. By the 1830s the emancipists in New South Wales, and their descendants, were winning considerable political and social ground.

(p. 506) *the 'Rum Hospital'*: The contractors who built the Sydney hospital between 1811 and 1816 received a monopoly of the colony's far from inconsiderable rum traffic for three years, in return for their labours. Part of the original Rum Hospital is the central portion of the present Parliament House of New South Wales.

(p. 508 note) *Bêche-de-la-mer*: *Bêche-de-mer*, trepang, or sea cucumbers are sausage-shaped marine animals of the class Holothuroidea, found in tropical waters and valued in the Far East as an ingredient for soups.

(p. 519) *a southerly burster*: Usually a 'southerly buster': a gale, often sudden and violent, from the south.

(p. 549) *Mount Erebus*: An active volcano in Antarctica, discovered in 1841.

(p. 553) *frequent cooeys*: 'Coo-ee,' the high-pitched call of the Aboriginals, used frequently for communication in the Australian bush.

(p. 562) *my* socius: My companion.

(p. 563) *The Stagyrite says*: Aristotle, born in Stagira, a city of Macedonia.

(p. 563) *Alcaics*: Alcaeus was a lyric poet of Mytilene, about 600 B.C. 'Alcaics' refers to the metre in which he wrote.

(p. 564) *she has known the Factory*: The female penitentiary.

(p. 564) O matre pulchra . . .: 'O daughter more beautiful than a beautiful mother' – Horace, *Odes* I. xvi. 1.

(p. 568) fons Bandusiae . . .: 'Spring of Bandusia, brighter than glass' Horace, *Odes* III. xiii. 1.

(p. 568) *Massic*: A wine from Campania, Italy, often mentioned in classical literature.

(p. 568) *when Manlius was consul*: Horace writes of his 'gentle wine-jar' born at the same time as he himself, when Manlius was consul. *Odes* III. xxi. 1.

(p. 570) *'For this sort cometh not out . . .'*: Matthew XVII, 21; Mark IX, 29.

(p. 570) *on the eve of a vacant garter*: When a Knighthood of the Garter has fallen vacant.

(p. 571) *the Pythoness*: A woman possessed of a familiar spirit, a soothsayer; especially the priestess of the god Apollo, presiding over his shrine at Delphi.

(p. 577) *any 'currency flash'*: Any native-born Australian.

(p. 577) *'crackers'*: The silken slip at the end of the stock-whip which produces the crack.

(p. 577) *puffterlooner*: Pufftaloons are made by frying cakes of dough in fat, and may be eaten with jam.

(p. 578) *Norfolk Island*. Norfolk Island lies 930 miles north-east of Sydney, and is about thirteen square miles in extent. It was a penal settlement from 1788–1813 and again from 1825–55. In this latter period it was used as a prison for English long-term convicts as well as a place of secondary punishment for those already in Australia, and acquired a notoriety only slightly mitigated by the humanity of Alexander Maconochie, a prison reformer of note who was Commandant 1840–44, but was removed because of criticisms of his liberal regime. A great deal of what Clarke writes on Norfolk Island is taken from official sources. On Maconochie, see J. V. Barry: *Alexander Maconochie of Norfolk Island* (Melbourne, 1958). Maconochie is clearly to be identified with the Major Pratt of Clarke's narrative. In 1856 descendants of the *Bounty* mutineers were settled on Norfolk Island from Pitcairn Island. Today Norfolk Island is a popular tourist resort, with some notable old prison buildings still surviving.

(p. 582) *Alsatia*: The Whitefriars district of London – until 1697 the possessor of certain privileges which made it a haunt of debtors and criminals.

(p. 582) *the 'ring'*: 'Of the reality of the Ring as an association of the toughest convicts in the settlement there can be no doubt." (J. V. Barry, p. 97.)

(p. 583) *Bedlam*: A madhouse, from 'Bethlehem' in London, England's first lunatic asylum (1403).

(p. 583) *Caffres*: Kaffirs, from southern Africa.

(p. 591) *Asmodeus, I write no more*: Asmodeus is an 'evil demon' appearing in the Apocryphal book of Tobit. His role was to plot against the newly-wedded.

(p. 592) *The riot of the 1st July, 1846*: Clarke's account follows in the closest detail the actual riot of this date, which actually took place however not under the 'weak' Commandant (as here) but under his brutal successor. See J. V. Barry, op. cit., p. 157 ff.

(p. 595) Book V, Chapter V: In her article on this novel in *All About Books* (Vol. II, No. 9, 15 September 1930) the distinguished librarian Miss Ida Leeson claimed that the very brief Chapter V to Book V, only three lines long, was a lapse 'doubtless' due to a printer's error, and that these lines properly belonged with Chapter VI. Failing any evidence to support this I have retained the original. The attenuated chapter comes at the end of an episode in the original serial and appears to be an effective device for heightening suspense.

(p. 598) *he'll get served the same one of these days*! The character of

Frere is modelled in part on that of the notorious John Price (1807–57), who took over as Commandant of Norfolk Island in 1846, and was later, while head of the penal department in Melbourne, murdered by his own convicts. The Reverend James North's experiences, on Norfolk Island at least, are modelled on those of the Reverend Thomas Rogers, also an Anglican clergyman, whom Price had removed from the island and on whose published *Correspondence* ... (1849) Clarke drew heavily for detail. Rogers lived until 1903. See J. V. Barry: *The Life and Death of John Price* (Melbourne, 1964), especially Chapter Six.

(p. 605) *'Le grand ecueil est le ridicule.'* : Ridicule is the great danger.

(p. 606) *this marriage of the Minotaur* : The minotaur of Crete, in Greek mythology, lived in the Labyrinth and consumed youths and maidens sent by Athens as a tribute.

(p. 612 note) *Subaudite – 'dog'*. That is, it is to be understood that 'kangaroo' in this context means 'kangaroo dog'.

(p. 613) *the laughing jackasses* : Native birds, now called kookaburras, of the kingfisher family, and with a distinctive cackling call.

(p. 613) *a foraging opossum* : The correct name of these arboreal, nocturnal marsupials is 'possum'.

(p. 614) *the assembled 'huts'* : The station workmen who lived in huts near the main homestead.

(p. 615) *the Honeysuckle scrub* : 'Honeysuckle' was the early term for Banksia.

(p. 616) *my Infant Roscius ... my young Ducrow* : The young Roscius was charged with the murder of his father by some ruthless conspirators seeking his property, and was successfully defended by Cicero in 80 B.C. (The classically-educated bullock-driver is a familiar figure in nineteenth-century Australian writing.) Andrew Ducrow (1793–1842) was a celebrated equestrian circus performer.

(p. 617) *a camping 'poler'* : 'Polers' are those bullocks in a team which support the weight of the pole attached to the wagon.

(p. 618) *'With a bird's-eye fogle about his squeeze.'* : With a spotted handkerchief aroud his neck.

(p. 620) *at the feet of Christian* : In Bunyan's *Pilgrim's Progress*.

(p. 623) *Mooney was one of the 'First Fleeters'* : One of the convicts who arrived at Sydney Cove under Australia's founding Governor, Arthur Phillip, in 1788 (not 1789). In view of his reference to existing buildings in Sydney when Mooney arrived, Clarke however probably means that Mooney was a member of the Second Fleet, which arrived in 1790.

(p. 623 note) *to Mrs Chisholm* : Caroline Chisholm (1808–77), one of

Australia's great women, Catholic, philanthropist, and notable especially for her humanizing of emigration to Australia, especially as it applied to women and children.

(p. 624) Mooney's statement: Vicious and sadistic though convict discipline often was in early Australia in today's terms, not all of Mooney's (or Glasshouse's) statement can be accepted. Labour was too scarce to be needlessly sacrificed, nor are there any records of anything approaching the mass slaughter of convicts. At the Toongabbie rising of 1804 (which may be being referred to here), fifteen rebels were killed and nine executed, of some four hundred taking part.

(p 627) 'You're not such a pebble . . .': A 'pebble' was a person or animal-refractory, difficult to handle, tough.

(p. 639) go to Summerhill Creek: Gold was found at Summer Hill Creek, near Bathurst, New South Wales, in 1851.

(p. 641) to Helen, to Juliet, to Rosalind: Helen of Troy; Juliet of Romeo and Juliet; Rosalind, of Spenser's 'Shepheard's Calender'.

(p. 641) Circe's cup. In the Odyssey Circe, the beautiful enchantress of the island of Aeaea, drugs Odysseus' men with a poisoned dish and turns them into swine.

(p. 646) a George Sand or a Mary Montague. George Sand (1804–76), pseudonym of Armadine Dupin, French novelist. Lady Mary Wortley Montague (1689–1762) is remembered for her letters, her poems, and her quarrels with the poet Alexander Pope.

(p. 694) at the Exhibition. The famous Exhibition of 1851, at the Crystal Palace. Clarke has erred here. In the original serial the date of the Christmas party is given as 1851, hence the reference to the Exhibition. However, for historical reasons related to the Australian gold discoveries, an editorial note in the subsequent instalment altered this date to 1850. The reference to the Exhibition is thus anachronistic.

(p. 696) the Elzevir 'Horace': The Elzeviers were a family of famous Dutch printers (1592–1680). Their editions of the classics are prized by collectors.

(p. 697) the sword of Saladin. Saladin (1137–93) was the adversary in the Crusades of Richard Coeur-de-Lion; his magnaminity was popularized by Scott in The Talisman. Saladin, in the well-known story, was said to have displayed the keenness of his blade by slicing in two a cushion thrown into the air.

(p 698) vaquero: Cowboy.

(p. 701) Crosbie's gold discovery: Mount Buninyong lies hard by Ballarat, Victoria, and the Ballarat goldfield has been one of the world's richest. Hutkeepers of Crosbie's type (old 'lags' from Van Diemen's Land, some of them) were certainly involved in the initial discovery and working of gold on the Ballarat and Bendigo fields.

(p. 703) *a jeweller named Brentano*: Early in 1849 a young shepherd named Thomas Chapman called at Charles Brentani's jeweller's shop in Collins Street, Melbourne, and sold a nugget. This appears to have set off the Victorian gold-fever, but the story is obscure. See 'Garryowen's' (Edmund Finn's) *The Chronicles of Early Melbourne* ... (Melbourne, 1888), Vol. II, Chapter LVII.

(p. 703) *hysonskin tea*: A kind of green tea from China.

(p. 704) *the cockatoos and lorries*: Australian birds.

(p. 706) *Mr La Trobe*: C. J. La Trobe (1801–75), appointed Superintendent of the Port Phillip District in 1839, becoming Lieutenant-Governor of the colony of Victoria after 'Separation' (from New South Wales) in 1851.

(p. 719) *Magnall's Questions*: Richard Magnall's *Historical and Miscellaneous Questions* appeared in 1800, and was being reprinted at least until 1869.

(p. 720) *Dreaming of San Joaquin and San Francisco*: The Californian gold-diggings of 1849 and later.

(p 720) *Liardet's Beach*: Now Port Melbourne.

(p. 721) *Gill's Hogarthian sketches*: Samual Thomas Gill (1818–80) was the characteristic artist of the Victorian gold-diggings. His sketches and prints now command high prices.

(p. 721) *Grant's novels*: James Grant (1822–1887), a popular mid-century novelist.

(p. 722) *Tom Burke or Harry Lorrequer*: Tom Burke is the hero of Charles Lever's historical romance *Tom Burke of Ours* (1844), and Harry Lorrequer of Lever's *The Confessions of Harry Lorrequer* (1837).

(p. 722) *the Leverian code of gentility*: Charles Lever (1806–72), popular novelist.

(p. 722) *'Joe! Joe! Joe'*: A term of opprobrium on the diggings, from Charles Joseph La Trobe, the Lieutenant-Governor. Specially applied to troopers conducting licence-hunts, it was also used as a general insult.

(p. 724) *Don Rinaldo, by Jingo*: Rinaldo, one of the greatest of Charlemagne's paladins, and a famous character in medieval romances.

(p. 724) *may I be carbonadoed*: Broiled on the coals.

(p. 725) *sabreur*: A cavalryman.

(p. 726) *Mr Charles Mathews ... Mr 'Guy Livingstone' Lawrence*:

Charles James Mathews (1803–78), actor and dramatist. George Alfred Lawrence (1827–76), author of the swashbuckling novel *Guy Livingstone* (1857).

(p. 727) *Mr Arthur Vern*: The Eureka Stockade, Australia's only armed clash, took place on the Eureka lead near Ballarat on 3 December 1854. About three hundred soldiers and police attacked and routed about one hundred diggers, of whom about twenty were killed. Though the grievances (effectively pointed up by Clarke) over which the diggers took to arms were in the process of being rectified at the time of the clash, the Stockade has always held a forward place in the Australian democratic myth, and the Southern Cross flag of the diggers is mirrored in the Australian flag today. Clarke writes, however, of the personalities and events of Eureka with extreme licence. In particular his close and misleading adoption of actual names, for instance Arthur Vern (Frederick Vern), Peter McGrath (Peter Lalor) and Paolo Carboni (Raffaello Carboni), is open to criticism. On Eureka, Geoffrey Serle: *The Golden Age* (Melbourne, 1963).

(p. 730) *more expensive than Mivarts'*: Mivart's Hotel stood in Brook Street, London, on the present site of Claridge's.

(p. 731) *Horsa Hengist*: Richard Hengist ('Orion') Horne (1802–84), poet and colourful litterateur, who spent seventeen years on the Victorian goldfields, and at one time commanded a gold escort. See Ann Blainey: *The Farthing Poet* (London, 1968). The incident described is from Horne's *Australian Facts and Prospects* (London, 1859).

(p. 736) *Patcher the Inimitable*: The 'Inimitable' Charles Robert Thatcher, goldfields entertainer (died 1878). See Hugh Anderson: *The Colonial Minstrel* (Melbourne, 1960).

(p. 736) *the Great Vance, the Wondrous Leybourne, or the Marvellous Rickards*: The Great Vance was Alfred Peck Stevens (1839–88), a music-hall comic noted for his Cockney acts, and a friend and rival of George Leybourne (Joe Saunders, 1842–84) who, as 'Champagne Charlie', has been called the original 'lion comique'. Harry Rickards was an English music-hall singer who first visited Australia in 1872, and in later years built up in that country an extensive theatrical empire based on variety. He died in 1911.

(p. 737) Grantley's Eureka Hotel: In reality, Bentley's Eureka Hotel.

(p. 737) *'washing' stuff*: Gold-bearing alluvium.

(p. 737) *tailings*: The washed alluvium, often capable of being re-washed for a further dividend.

(p. 747) *Bishop somebody*: Bishop Latimer, 1555.

(p. 750) *would have hailed Prince Esterhazy*: The Esterhazys were a noble and wealthy Hungarian family.

(p 758) *like Mariana or sweet Perdita*: Mariana in *Measure for Measure*, Perdita in *The Winter's Tale*.

(p. 760) *Pelham was at college*: In Bulwer Lytton's *Pelham, or The Adventures of a Gentleman* (1828).

(p. 775) *Leonidas at the hot gates of Locris*: Leonidas, King of Sparta, at Thermopylae, 48 B.C.

(p. 783) *their blessed squeeges*: Their 'squeezers' – their necks.

(p. 783) *upon my sivvy*: On my word of honour!

(p. 783) *they'd scrag me right off the reel*: I'd be hanged.

(p 786) *went 'starring' down the road*: 'Starring', in the game of pool, is to buy additional lives. Here, presumably, to recruit.

(p. 786) *'Vinegar Hill'*: This was in fact Peter Lalor's password for the night before Eureka. It refers to the battle of 1798 in Co. Wexford, Ireland, when a body of Irish rebels was defeated; and to a rising of convicts near Sydney in 1804. The password was taken to be a bad omen by some and there were desertions from the Stockade.

(p. 804) *as did Eliezer when he fought the elephant*: Eleazar, brother of Judas Maccabee, fought his way to the largest elephant in the Syrian army, killed it and died under it. I Maccabees VI, 43–6.

(p. 807) *another Joseph coming out of the pit*: Genesis XXXVII, 28.

(p. 807) *parmaceti for an inward bruise*: *King Henry IV*, Part I, Act I, Scene iiii.

(p. 807) *The President is likely to recover*: Peter Lalor did lose an arm at the Stockade. He later became Speaker of the Victorian Legislative Assembly.

(p. 808) *My Mucius Scaevola*: Gaius Mucius Scaevola, a legendary Roman who, when threatened with death as a prisoner, thrust his right hand into a fire to show his indifference. Released, he was known as Scaevola, 'left-handed'.

(p. 810) *deus et machina*: Presumably a misprint for *deus ex machina*, a reference to the ancient stage convention of having gods descend on to the stage from above. Originally a phrase of Lucian's, it is referred to obliquely by Horace, *Ars Poetica* I. 191.

(p. 812) *Effodiuntur opes, irritamenta malorum*: Referring to the metals iron and gold, Ovid writes 'The earth yields up her stores, of every ill, the instigators . . .'. *Metamorphoses* I, 140.

(p. 812) *billy dux*: *Billet-doux*, a love-letter. Quaid is echoing the old music-hall song 'Villikens and his Dinah'.

(p. 813) *the Gräfinn von Himmelshaüsen*: Clarke's German is a bit shaky. This should be spelt 'the Gräfin von Himmelshäuser'.

(p. 818) *I should be a flat*: A simpleton.

(p. 820) *Bring me a Bradshaw*: A railway guide.

(p. 821) *the Muiderstraat* ...: Clarke is referring to the Jewish quarters of Amsterdam, London and (possibly) Vienna. Clarke unfortunately possessed a strong anti-semitic streak. 'Judengaase' should read 'Judengasse'.

(p. 823) *Chateau d'If*: In Victor Hugo's *Les Miserables*.

(p. 823) *the fortress of Spandau*: In Berlin.

(p. 834) *a doorkeeper in the house of Israel* ... *May my right hand forget her cunning*: Psalms LXXXIV, 10; CXXXVII. 5.

(p. 844) *Lola Montes*: Lola Montez was the stage name of Marie Dolores Eliza Rosanna Gilbert (1818–61), of Irish origin, an international dancer, courtesan and adventuress who spent nearly four years in Victoria during the gold rushes. She had previously been mistress of Ludwig I of Bavaria, and the virtual ruler of that country before her expulsion.

(p. 844) *the 'Old Tin Pot'*: The 'Iron Pot' was the nickname of a prefabricated theatre imported from Manchester and opened by George Coppin in Melbourne in 1855 as the Olympic Theatre. (Clarke's reference is therefore – no doubt deliberately – anachronistic.) It was an immediate success, and favoured actors and actresses there were frequently pelted with gold. The new Theatre Royal also opened in 1855 but, despite Lola Montez, was soon in financial difficulties.

(p. 850) *your Leporello*: Don Giovanni's servant in Mozart's opera.

(p. 853) *King Cobb*: Cobb & Co. was a famous coaching company, founded in 1853, which served the inland areas of Australia for over seventy years.

(p. 870) *the demand to* prove *his tale*: Clarke undoubtedly has in mind the famous Tichborne case in which Arthur Orton, the 'butcher of Wagga', claimed the fortune of the missing Roger Tichborne, heir to a baronetcy, and was 'recognized' by Roger Tichborne's mother as her son. The action concluded in March 1872, and in 1874 Orton was sentenced to fourteen years' gaol.

(p. 880) *a 'Sydney-sider'*: Used generally in Victoria as meaning a person from the New South Wales side of the Murray River, but here meaning a transport or ex-transportee. Victoria was a 'free' colony in the sense that transportees were not accepted there.